MW00476176

"A great book. Sommers has written an enthra[...] Leone, focusing on the young fighters and h[...] culture to make sense of the world and their e[...] lows us to make sense of the carnival of violence unleashed as a resistance script of modernity and challenges politicians and development practitioners to take young people seriously."

> —**Alex de Waal**, Executive Director, World Peace Foundation, Research Professor, The Fletcher School, Tufts University, and author of *The Real Politics of the Horn of Africa: Money, War, and the Business of Power*

"A palpable reminder of how the restless youth of Sierra Leone and many other parts of Africa can refashion global popular culture to challenge state repression. The call for a meaningful and transformative response to this governance challenge remains urgent and relevant."

> —**Ismail Rashid**, professor at Vassar College and coeditor of *The Paradoxes of History and Memory in Post-Colonial Sierra Leone*

"Sierra Leone's civil war has often generated more heat than light, with shock at reports of gang rape, amputation, and drug-fueled viciousness drowning out analysis. In this remarkable account, Sommers resists sensationalism and skirts stereotype, retaining compassion for those swept up in the horror. By focusing on three Western icons who served as inspirational role models for the youngsters who perpetrated the worst of the violence—Rambo, Marley, and Tupac—he gets under the skin of Sierra Leone's dysfunctional society and conflict dynamics in a way few have equaled."

> —**Michela Wrong**, author of *Do Not Disturb: The Story of a Political Murder and an African Regime Gone Bad*

"Strongly informed by many interviews, this rich and interesting book shines a light on musical and cinematic influences in Sierra Leone's war. It shows, for example, how Tupac Shakur's music was important to a variety of rebel and rogue soldier groups and how his music—in songs such as 'Only God Can Judge Me'—were used by abusive groups to motivate and legitimize their attacks."

> —**David Keen**, Professor of Conflict Studies, London School of Economics and Political Science, and author of *Conflict and Collusion in Sierra Leone*

"*We the Young Fighters* is a compelling story of what drove violent conflict in Sierra Leone, weaving in how drugs and pop culture helped sustain terror practices during the war. The book focuses on the significance of national governance and how states can alienate their expanding youth populations and increase prospects for violence and conflict. It illuminates the lessons we still need to learn from Sierra Leone's conflict, including the critical need to broaden diplomacy and security reforms. Most important, this book highlights how to harness the energy of youth for building sustainable peace."

> —**Elizabeth (Liz) Hume**, Executive Director, Alliance for Peacebuilding

"Marc Sommers's insightful book takes young Sierra Leoneans' perspectives, frustrations, and desires for dignity seriously. In doing so, this work not only deepens our understanding of Sierra Leone's devastating civil war but also points the way toward a greater appreciation for the powerful intersection of pop culture and political action that is only growing more complex and important in the digital age."

—**Michelle Gavin**, Ralph Bunche Senior Fellow for Africa Policy Studies, Council on Foreign Relations, and Former U.S. Ambassador to Botswana

"Recognizing the importance of music and cinema in young people's lives, this riveting book illuminates the world of Sierra Leonean youth during Sierra Leone's civil war. Sommers deftly shows how youth were moved by popular culture and appropriated it in seeking justice and social transformation. The lyrics of Marley and Tupac, together with the images of Rambo, inspired marginalized youth to become child soldiers who dreamt of social equity yet were also capable of horrific atrocities. I hugely enjoyed reading *We the Young Fighters*. It's a gem."

—**Michael Wessells**, Professor, Program on Forced Migration and Health, Columbia University, and author of *Child Soldiers: From Violence to Protection*

"In *We the Young Fighters: Pop Culture, Terror, and War in Sierra Leone*, Marc Sommers offers an important intervention on the influence of cultural production across contexts, particularly in war-affected zones where narratives of resistance and freedom are all too easily understood in binaries. Sommers's carefully woven stories of how international pop culture became an instrument of youth resistance, violence, and postwar adaptation in Sierra Leone are compelling. *We the Young Fighters* is a must-read for those seeking to understand the complex dynamics of youth involvement in armed conflict."

—**'Funmi Olonisakin**, Vice President (International, Engagement, and Service) and Professor of Security, Leadership, and Development, King's College London, and author of *Peacekeeping in Sierra Leone: The Story of UNAMSIL*

"*We the Young Fighters* is published just over twenty years after the end of the vicious Sierra Leone civil war. Marc Sommers eloquently re-examines the drivers of the conflict, focusing on alienated female and male youth and pop culture. Sommers employs an instructive perspective, treating states as adversaries and charting how some youth are radicalized, recruited, and mobilized into armed groups. This book seeks to provide learning for mitigating contemporary African conflicts. A must-read for scholars, policy makers, and humanitarian workers."

—**Dr. Alex Vines OBE**, Director, Africa Programme, Chatham House, and Assistant Professor, Faculty of Arts and Humanities, Coventry University

We the Young Fighters

Also by Marc Sommers

PUBLISHED BY THE UNIVERSITY OF GEORGIA PRESS

The Outcast Majority: War, Development, and Youth in Africa

Stuck: Rwandan Youth and the Struggle for Adulthood

OTHER BOOKS

*Trust-Based, Qualitative Field Methods:
A Manual for Researchers of Violent Extremism*

*Islands of Education: Schooling, Civil War, and
the Southern Sudanese (1983–2004)*

*Co-ordinating Education during Emergencies and
Reconstruction: Challenges and Responsibilities*

*Parallel Worlds: Rebuilding the Education System in Kosovo:
A Case Study*
(Peter Buckland, coauthor)

Fear in Bongoland: Burundi Refugees in Urban Tanzania

The Dynamics of Coordination

NATO and Humanitarian Action in the Kosovo Crisis
(Larry Minear and Ted Van Baarda, coauthors)

Mural of Bob Marley, Sierra Leone

Mural of Tupac Shakur, Sierra Leone

We the Young Fighters

POP CULTURE, TERROR, AND WAR IN SIERRA LEONE

Marc Sommers

The University of Georgia Press
ATHENS

TITLE PAGE IMAGE: Young fighters, Sierra Leone, 1998

Pubished by the University of Georgia Press
Athens, Georgia 30602
www.ugapress.org
© 2023 by Marc Sommers
Photographs © 2023 by Marc Sommers
All rights reserved
Designed by Kaelin Chappell Broaddus
Set in 10/13 Warnock Pro Regular by Kaelin Chappell Broaddus
Printed and bound by Sheridan Books, Inc.
The paper in this book meets the guidelines for permanence
and durability of the Committee on Production Guidelines for
Book Longevity of the Council on Library Resources.

Most University of Georgia Press titles are
available from popular e-book vendors.

Printed in the United States of America
27 26 25 24 23 P 5 4 3 2 1

Library of Congress Cataloging-in-Publication Data

Names: Sommers, Marc, author.
Title: We the young fighters : pop culture, terror, and war in Sierra Leone / Marc Sommers.
Description: Athens : The University of Georgia Press, 2023. | Includes bibliographical
    references and index.
Identifiers: LCCN 2023012990 | ISBN 9780820364735 (hardback) | ISBN 9780820364742
    (paperback) | ISBN 9780820364759 (epub) | ISBN 9780820364766 (pdf)
Subjects: LCSH: Marley, Bob—Influence. | Rambo, John J. (Fictitious character)—
    Influence. | Shakur, Tupac, 1971–1996—Influence. | Youth and war—Sierra Leone. |
    Popular culture—Sierra Leone—Influence. | Drug abuse—Sierra Leone. | Domestic
    terrorism—Sierra Leone. | Sierra Leone—History—Civil War, 1991–2002.
Classification: LCC HQ799.2.W37 S666 2023 | DDC 303.66083509664—dc23/eng/20230316
LC record available at https://lccn.loc.gov/2023012990

To the four fellas in my life:
Arthur, Fergus, Isaiah, and Henry

CONTENTS

ILLUSTRATIONS

ABBREVIATIONS

AFRC	Armed Forces Revolutionary Council
APC	All People's Congress
CDF	Civil Defense Force
CSW	commercial sex worker
CVE	countering violent extremism
DDR	disarmament, demobilization and reintegration
ECOMOG	Economic Community of West African States Monitoring Group
EO	Executive Outcomes
FGM	female genital mutilation
FFU	Food Finding Unit
Frelimo	Frente de Libertação de Moçambique, or Front for the Liberation of Mozambique
FSU	Family Support Unit
FSW	female sex worker
GSG	Gurkha Security Guard
HRW	Human Rights Watch
ICRC	International Committee of the Red Cross
IDP	internally displaced person
IMF	International Monetary Fund
ISU	Internal Security Unit
MDG	Millennium Development Goal
MNRRR	Ministry of National Reconstruction, Resettlement, and Rehabilitation
NCRRR	National Commission for Reconstruction, Resettlement, and Rehabilitation
NGO	nongovernmental organization
NPFL	National Patriotic Front of Liberia
NPRC	National Provisional Ruling Council
PHR	Physicians for Human Rights
PVE	preventing violent extremism
Renamo	Resistência Nacional Moçambicano, or Mozambican National Resistance
RPG	rocket-propelled grenade

RUF	Revolutionary United Front
RUFP	Revolutionary United Front Party
SBU	Small Boys Unit
SDG	Sustainable Development Goal
SGU	Small Girls Unit
SLA	Sierra Leone Army
SLPP	Sierra Leone People's Party
SLST	Sierra Leone Selection Trust
SRSG	Special Representative to the Secretary-General (United Nations)
SSD	Special Security Division
TRC	Sierra Leone Truth and Reconciliation Commission
UNAMSIL	United Nations Mission in Sierra Leone
UNDP	United Nations Development Programme
UNHCR	United Nations High Commissioner for Refugees
UNOMSIL	United Nations Observer Mission in Sierra Leone
WSB	West Side Boys
YEP	Youth Employment Program

PREFACE

This book is at once a history of a nation, the story of a war, and the saga of downtrodden young people and three pop culture superstars. It grew from a surprising and unexpected field interview with refugees from Sierra Leone many years ago. It took shape over time, as I learned ever more about Sierra Leone's complex war, where it came from, and how in the world two musicians and one movie character could have influenced a conflict and a country's youth so significantly.

The unforeseen inspiration took place in October 2000 when I arranged to meet four Sierra Leonean refugee men the next morning. I was in the upcountry town of Basse, in the tiny finger-shaped West African nation of Gambia, researching the refugees' work lives. Places with small numbers of refugees, I have learned, are backwaters. Few people ever visit, services for refugees are generally poor, and corruption—in this case, widespread reports of spots on the lists for resettlement to America being up for sale—can thrive. So when an opportunity arrived to gain access to a foreign researcher (me), interest in the small Sierra Leonean community ran high. After arriving the next afternoon, I found more than fifty refugees waiting for me.

The refugees were agitated. They milled closely around me and pressed their right hands forward, creating an electric, almost carnival atmosphere. I shook hands and greeted everyone. Meanwhile, the four refugee men whom I originally had asked to interview gradually took control. Although it was scorching hot, no one seemed to mind. Some sat in the sun, others in the shade. The interview began.

In my experience, it is useful and appropriate to invite refugees to tell their stories of flight at the outset of an interview. This time, several men and women instantly spoke at once. Some jumped up and gestured passionately. The memories were raw and recent: all had fled Sierra Leone's capital city, Freetown, in the wake of what Sierra Leoneans still call "January 6." On that date in 1999, one of the most horrific attacks in modern wartime history began. "Operation No Living Thing" was the code name the rebels used for their punishing sweep across northern and western Sierra Leone, culminating in the capital, where they really let loose.

Junger's (2006) assertion that "war does not get worse" than January 6 proved an understatement. Highly drugged children and male youth, and some female youth, charged out of trucks and vans to conduct a style of frenzied terror that the contemporary world has rarely seen. They killed people of all kinds, from infants to old people, from simple civilians to nuns. They dragged entire families out of their houses to kill them together. They burned people alive in houses and apartment buildings and tossed children into the flames. They forced lines of women to lie down in streets and gang raped them all. They tortured people, including hospital patients, for real or invented reasons. Among the many whose limbs they amputated was an infant boy of twenty months (Keen 2005: 228). They stole whatever they liked and killed people who didn't have what they sought.[1]

What did the refugees in Basse recall? What did they most want to tell me? More than anything else, they mentioned pop culture icons and drugs. Later, I learned that they had been in the part of Freetown where rebel soldiers devoted to Tupac Shakur and what they considered "Tupac Tactics" had invaded. In that area, one refugee explained that "Tupac T-shirts were their uniforms. They also tied American flags around their heads." The references were to two of the most influential pop culture icons in Sierra Leone and very far beyond. The black T-shirt "uniform" featured the face of the American hip-hop star Tupac Shakur and the words "All Eyez on Me" (a youth alienation anthem) on the front. The T-shirt had become ubiquitous in African cities and towns, and during Sierra Leone's civil war, civilians could be attacked or killed for wearing it: military forces might consider them rebels, and rebels might demand the T-shirt or shoot or abduct the person. Or they might take the "uniform" and then fire. The "American flag" was actually printed on a bandanna and worn "Rambo-style," a reference to Sylvester Stallone's world-famous movie character.

The uniform and bandannas were only the beginning. The rebels entered their neighborhoods in vehicles (mostly white vans and pickup trucks) that had some of Tupac's words painted on the side. "Which words?" I asked. Several refugees called out the words at once. Among those they mentioned were "Me against the World," "Hit 'Em Up," "California Love," "Only God Can Judge Me," and "All Eyez on Me." All of these are the names of songs by Tupac. Small wonder that, as one refugee man commented, "Elders see Tupac as destroying our culture."

I struggled to keep up. What were Tupac Shakur's songs doing on soldiers' shirts and military vehicles? Why dress like Rambo? Later, the refugees mentioned Joe Hill, a Jamaican reggae star who "sang antirebel songs, but some of his words seemed too antigovernment," so when he performed in Freetown, "they turned the lights out on him." Nonetheless, "he inspired the youth," one man explained.

Still another man mentioned what turned out to be the most important popular culture figure to Sierra Leonean youth and to virtually all other Sierra

Leonean combatant groups during the civil war: the most renowned reggae musician of them all, Bob Marley. One mentioned Marley's "Get Up, Stand Up" as an important rebel fight song. The refugees also spoke of the rebels' extensive drug abuse. "Most rebels cut their arms or head, put some drugs in a Band-Aid, and stick it into their skin." "Which drugs do they use?" I asked. "Marijuana is the most popular," one told me. "They need it to keep them tranquilized," another said. "They control marijuana" in the country, said a third.

The refugees' collective story of war in Sierra Leone was surprising and strange to me, even though I had already been there in times of conflict and tenuous peace. My first visit took place early in 1997 in the tentative aftermath of the Abidjan Peace Accord involving the Revolutionary United Front (RUF) rebels and Sierra Leone's newly elected president. I had read as much as I could about Sierra Leone's civil war before entering the country. But nothing prepared me for what I would learn from war survivors and ex-combatants in Sierra Leone, not even my time in Rwanda right after the 1994 genocide. Sierra Leone was different. Perverse and extremely brutal atrocities committed by very young children were widespread. It seemed as if most female youth and women had been raped extensively. Girls were hard to find. People who had escaped rebel attacks by running to a "hiding place" (*soquoihun* in Mende)[2] in the rain forest returned severely traumatized, especially children (Sommers 1997: 8).

The refugees' stories of popular culture and war in Basse captivated me, and afterward I began to ask people in warring and postwar countries (as a sideline fieldwork activity I came to call "tracking Tupac") about international popular culture stars like Bob Marley, Tupac Shakur, and John Rambo. While I never found a place where such figures influenced warriors and the practice of war to the degree I found in Sierra Leone, the renown of Bob Marley and Tupac Shakur in particular was widespread. Both, in their way, were global phenomena who continue to hold a magnetic influence over many young people.

In Sierra Leone, mention of Bob Marley, Tupac Shakur, Rambo, and even Joseph Hill in published writing about the war mostly is anecdotal: a colorful detail from a terrifying and seemingly bizarre war. Eventually I received funding to return to Sierra Leone in late 2005 to research whether the stories the refugees in Basse had related signaled a deeper impact of popular culture's influence in the war. The research not only confirmed the expansive impact of what I came to consider "the Big Three" (Bob Marley, Tupac Shakur, and John Rambo), it also introduced a degree of influence that I hadn't yet appreciated: that these icons, and especially Bob Marley, were not only influential prior to and during the war. Their impact on youth (male youth in particular) remained after the war had ended. Across these contexts, young people regularly looked to Marley for inspiration, Tupac for friendship, and Rambo for instruction. My return to Sierra Leone in 2010 expanded my understanding of popular culture, war, and youth.

The singular significance of Sierra Leone's experience of war and peace led me to write this book, the heart of which explores how worldwide icons of popular culture came to influence Sierra Leonean youth and the war that convulsed them. This story of terror-based warfare, young people, and popular culture might seem exotic, strange, and entirely foreign. It's not. *We the Young Fighters* underscores the extraordinarily strong influence that instantly recognizable pop culture superstars can have—and in ways that no one can predict. Marley, Tupac, and Rambo entered the world of Sierra Leone through the lens of culture and context. Moving through that lens to attain meaning, local-level interpretations transformed them, making them exceptionally accessible and significant to many Sierra Leoneans, youth most especially.

Over the years, I have found that challenges to cherished ideas about venerated pop heroes often stir immense passion. Three instances of surprise and pushback illustrate this. A huge fan of Bob Marley was a work colleague at the U.S. Department of State. When I explained that Marley's music and his direct connection to marijuana use were both exploited to drive extreme warfare, he refused to believe it. Marley only stood for peace, he insisted. What I said could not be true. His take is not uncommon: a recollection of Marley (on the seventy-fifth anniversary of his birth) declared that he had been "adopted across the globe as a figurehead of peace and love" (McIndoe 2020). When I added that many people in other parts of the world (including Sierra Leoneans) listen carefully to Marley's lyrics about resistance (including, sometimes, violent resistance) in addition to his songs about peace, my colleague confessed that he had never heard the resistance side in Marley's music. As if it wasn't there.

Ardent fans of Tupac seem well aware that some of Tupac's music connects to entrapment, resistance, and sometimes even the pull toward violence. That side of the artist can cause uneasiness. When I taught a course on conflict in Africa at the Fletcher School (Tufts University), my discussion of Tupac's presence and use in Sierra Leone's war inspired one of my students to visit me during office hours. Tupac was one of his favorite musicians. He was concerned with the emphasis on the negative side of Tupac's work in class. When I explained how the presentation had drawn from field research about Tupac's wartime influence, the student steadfastly insisted that the positive side of Tupac was being overlooked. I reminded him that youth in Sierra Leone were quite familiar with Tupac's more peaceful, positive side, as I also had noted in class. Yet the student remained concerned. A few days later, he provided me with a CD he titled "Positive Tupac," featuring some of Tupac's most empathic, upbeat songs.

A third example arose during an event in which I presented about movies featuring Sylvester Stallone's John Rambo film character and how youth in Sierra Leone viewed the films as having deep inner significance. I noted that female as well as male youth admired Rambo and were inspired by him. One panelist found that difficult to accept: Rambo only represented masculine violence, the panelist insisted. The idea of female youth admiring him seemed to disturb her. It could not be true.

Of course it could be true. Across the globe, pop culture heroes inspire intimate, personal connection. They are important. However, interpretations of them and their work cannot be controlled. Sierra Leone shows us how pop culture icons are rare metals that users on the ground shape to suit their changing needs. Global luminaries filled a void for young Sierra Leoneans feeling the weight of repression and the absence of voice. Their messages resonated deeply, local translations gave them extra-special power, and the undertow of events leading to warfare awarded them epic significance—and easy opportunities for exploitation. The fact that one was a fictional movie character (Rambo), one had died long before the war had started (Marley), and one died midway through the war (Tupac) seemed to facilitate local analysis and manipulation.

The drama of Sierra Leone's international pop culture experience emerges from the extremity of war, the punishing conditions that led to it, and the unsteady peace that followed. It reminds us that once an idol is snatched from the global ether, no one really knows what it will mean, or for what purposes the idol will be used, once it lands in a particular locality. One such story emerged in Sierra Leone, and it is remarkable.

To readers of this book with strong feelings about Marley, Tupac, and/or Rambo, I have a request: please give the takes featured here a chance. Sierra Leone's youth developed sophisticated, nuanced interpretations of Marley, Tupac, and Rambo. The manipulations of wartime leaders also are revealing. Expect to be surprised about many things. Here are three possible examples:

- Bob Marley was the most dominant international pop culture figure before, during, and after the civil war in Sierra Leone.
- Tupac's bravura fearlessness and celebration of a thug identity inspired young male listeners.
- Rambo stood as a model warrior with whom all youth could identify.

Three works delineate the trio's collective influence. Marley's stirring "Get Up, Stand Up" encourages listeners to personally drive change and demand respect. Tupac's propulsive "Only God Can Judge Me" validates bold action.

The first Rambo film (*First Blood*) provides a playbook for resourceful forest combat. In essence, Marley ignited Sierra Leone's despised, down-and-out youth to fight back, Tupac allowed them to do whatever they needed to do, and Rambo demonstrated how to get it done. The three heroes combined to provide a motive, a rationale, and a method for aggressive resistance. They helped military commanders goad the cornered young people under their control.

Commanders also juiced children and youth with virtually nonstop quantities of marijuana. By itself, the locally grown marijuana was more than powerful enough to inspire the violence that followed. Even so, commanders added many other drugs to the mix. As a result, the young warriors became highly effective terror warriors (while being highly ineffective in battle). After the war, two of the pop superstars (Marley and Tupac) helped former combatants endure as misunderstood outsiders.

This book serves as a companion volume to an earlier one, *The Outcast Majority: War, Development, and Youth in Africa* (2015). *The Outcast Majority* spotlights the vast gap that separates the perspectives and priorities of war-affected African youth with those that inform the practice of international development in today's youth-dominated world. After detailing how international development aid is generally ineffective at reaching and addressing youth priorities (and sometimes unintentionally makes matters worse for young people), that book concludes with a framework for reforming the approach and work of development by agencies and governments.

The story of Sierra Leone and its youth in *We the Young Fighters* focuses more on security and governance than development concerns. The book probes how international pop culture icons and drugs played critical roles in prewar resistance and the practice of terror during the civil war yet counterintuitively also served as aids for helping youth adapt to postwar existence. Black Bob Marley and Tupac T-shirts, and Rambo bandannas, it turns out, are not peculiar details in a macabre and distant conflict. Instead, they broadcast two carefully considered messages: rebellion against predatory states and resistance to condemnation. These messages emanate from a profoundly dysfunctional yet all-too-common contemporary circumstance: nations with immense populations of disempowered, excluded female and male youth. In such places, states and elite society often perceive the masses of marginalized young people in their midst as the problem. Many of these young people, in turn, struggle with states that routinely target them while having limited (or no) options for improving their lot in life.

We the Young Fighters allows readers to grasp how entrapped young people, in a country weakened by state predation and upended by disturbing, terror-infused warfare, searched for a way to endure and move their lives forward. In Sierra Leone, ostracized youth looked to Rambo's righteous fight against a perversely structured society and interpreted songs like "Crazy Baldhead" and "All Eyez on Me" as siren calls to resist and reinvent themselves. This book ends by extracting lessons learned from Sierra Leone that can be applied elsewhere. All eyes on me indeed.

ACKNOWLEDGMENTS

No book I've written has taken the amount of time that *We the Young Fighters* has required to germinate, research, and write. Across many years, support from five institutions helped me complete it.

The first arose in 2005. I received funding for field research from the Mellon-MIT Inter-University Program on Non-Governmental Organizations (NGOs) and Forced Migration. Without Sharon Stanton Russell and the support of other members of the Mellon-MIT program, *We the Young Fighters* may never have gotten off the ground.

The second source of support arose during my tenure at the Fletcher School at Tufts University. My faculty position came with a small research budget. Standing in line to get my all-important university ID card, on my very first day at work in 2005, I started a conversation with the person in front of me. He was an incoming student at the Fletcher School named Marcus Holknekt. I told him a bit about my own work (including on Sierra Leone). I learned that he was very interested in conflict issues; he also sidelined as a rapper and knew an enormous amount about Tupac Shakur's music and life. He became one of my first research assistant hires for this project. During my years at Fletcher, I hired fourteen student research assistants to work on various dimensions of the Sierra Leone research project (the title came later). It was an inquisitive, spirited, energetic, dedicated, and talented group. I thank all of my former research assistants for their contributions: Marcus Holknekt and Christof Kurz (2007); Raul Chavez, Angie Nguyen, Claire Putzeys, and Sujatha Sebastian (2008); Regina Wilson, Kate Cummings, Lisa Inks, Ndeye-Fatu Sesay, Leigh Stefanik, and Regina Wilson (2009); and Rebekah Mierau, Justin Shilad, and Michele Wehle (2010).

The third source of support was the game changer. I received a Jennings Randolph Senior Fellowship at the United States Institute of Peace. After beginning my term in 2009, the director of the fellowship program at USIP, Dr. Chantal de Jonge Oudraat, informed the fellows that research funds for travel were available. I thus returned to Sierra Leone early in 2010 to conduct additional field research before returning to USIP to write the initial book chapters. I extend deep thanks and gratitude to Chantal, as well as Dr. Elizabeth A. "Lili" Cole and Shari Lowenstein, and to many other wonderful colleagues at

USIP. I also thank my team of research interns, who contributed essential research work for the project. Dr. Julie Guyot led the team with flair and excellence. It also featured Katie Gresham, Gerard McCarthy, Sarah Soroui, and Jason Starr.

Fourth, I received an academic writing residency at the Rockefeller Foundation's Bellagio Center in 2019. There, I tightened up some chapter drafts and began writing the concluding chapters. It is an inspirational place to think and write. I offer my thanks especially to Pilar Palacià, the managing director of the Bellagio Center, and to Alice Luperto, the residents' coordinator in Italy; Bethany Martin-Breen at the Rockefeller Foundation in New York; and all of my fellow fellows, and their partners, who joined my wife and me at the Bellagio Center.

The final institutional support source is the African Studies Center of Boston University, with which I have been affiliated since 1995. Since that time, it has been a vital source of support and exchange. Many colleagues have contributed ideas and assistance concerning my extended work on this book, including Timothy Longman, James McCann, Fallou Ngom, the late James Pritchett, Peter Quella, Eric Schmidt, Parker Shipton, and Mark Storella. In the African Studies Library and over many years, Beth Restrick, David Westley, and the late Gretchen Walsh provided me with always helpful and friendly assistance. I extend my thanks to all of you.

None of the fieldwork for this book could have been done without the guidance and support of many people in Sierra Leone. More than anyone else, Rev. Moses Khanu provided high-quality collaboration and contributions across many years. His talents as a field researcher, translator, and field colleague were exceptional, and his friendship is deeply appreciated. Thanks also to Theophilus Saar Gbenda, Daniel Kaindaneh, and James Vincent.

Many others have shared their wisdom and insights about Sierra Leone and this book. My editor at the University of Georgia Press, Mick Gusinde-Duffy, has been a wonderful source of support and friendship. Thank you for believing in me and this book. I extend my gratitude to the entire University of Georgia Press team that helped me get this book to the finish line, including Elizabeth Adams, Jason Bennett, Christina Cotter, and the managing editor, Jon Davies, in addition to my copyeditor, Lori Rider. I also wish to thank Malual Bol Kiir, Peter Buckland, Magnus Conteh, Derek Langford, Elizabeth McClintock, Paul Richards, Rosalind Shaw, Cecily Sommers, Mats Utas, Peter Uvin, and Michael Wessells, as well as my son, Isaiah Sommers, for our many enlightening exchanges about pop culture over many years. Thanks also to my brother, Christopher, for sharing so many insights on Tupac and rap music. To each of you and many more, thanks for absorbing and sharing so many great ideas about this book with me.

Finally, thank you to my amazing wife, Lesley-Anne Long, for your unstinting support for me and this book. I thank you deeply for believing in both. Your many contributions included weathering countless exchanges about the book and contributing invaluable ideas and edits. Without you, this book still wouldn't be done.

We the Young Fighters

PART 1

Upside Down

CHAPTER 1

The Innovator

Lord of War

Sierra Leone's civil war is best known for grisly details. Journalists and the *Blood Diamond* movie highlighted boys committing unspeakable atrocities without, it appeared, a conscience. This inspired many to probe how such a war could surface. Yet while the roots of rebellion lie in Sierra Leone's history, the spark of war lies elsewhere. The terror tactics featured in Sierra Leone's civil war cannot be grasped without understanding the devious ways of the igniter of that spark. This book thus begins with Charles Taylor, from neighboring Liberia.

"Just wait: one day I'm going to be president of my country!" The recollection of this outwardly outrageous statement came from a former student who had regularly attended meetings of African and Africanist students at Boston University in the 1970s.[1] She was talking about Charles Taylor, then a graduate student at nearby Bentley College (where he received an economics degree; Smillie 2010: 83). At the meetings, she remembered, other African students viewed Taylor as pompous and boastful. They didn't take his prediction of becoming Liberia's president seriously. The claim seemed preposterous. So did he.

A bookend to this memory of Charles Taylor is one of my own. Traveling in 2005 on "snake patrol" (a term coined for having to constantly drive "like a snake" around enormous potholes) on the devastated national roadway linking Liberia's capital, Monrovia, to the nation's second-largest city (tiny Buchanan), my Liberian colleague and I passed a parade of tall electric towers along one side of the road. The towers had been part of the nation's electric grid, my colleague explained. The electricity used to flow through thick wiring made of rubber-coated copper. The towers had held them up. All of the wiring was long gone.

Who took it all down? I asked. President Taylor's soldiers, he explained. Even after Taylor had achieved his all-consuming ambition of becoming Liberia's president in 1997, his fighters—who had become the nation's army—continued to enact his long-standing policy of "Pay Yourself" by climbing up the towers, cutting down the wires, and selling the copper for personal profit.

A stop at a village near the main highway revealed a sampling of Taylor's legendary cunning. The village had been wired for small amounts of electricity, powered by solar panels that stood at the town's entrance. Taylor was hugely popular there: he had brought them the panels. They were impossible to miss, situated on a raised wooden platform at the roadside, like altars in homage to their famous donor. Taylor had again managed to have it both ways: he could allow, perhaps encourage, national soldiers to plunder the country's infrastructure (even while serving as head of state) because then it generated new ways to increase his influence and popularity. Once again, destruction had created opportunity.

It has always been a mistake to underestimate Charles Taylor, West Africa's chief catalyst for war and predation from 1989 until his arrest in 2003. He was ahead of his time in so many unfortunate ways, pushing the outermost edges of Machiavellian assaults on power and profit, during both the war he started and the peace he bequeathed by agreeing to run for president and winning in an overwhelming landslide in 1997. His subsequent forced ouster from power in August 2003, his exile in Nigeria, his 2006 arrest and trial by Sierra Leone's Special Court, and his fifty-year sentence in 2013 should not overshadow his extraordinary influence over recent West African history. Reflecting back on Charles Taylor's multifaceted influence on West Africa—after having been arrested by Taylor's forces in Liberia in 1990, forced to join what became the primary rebel group during Sierra Leone's civil war (the RUF) and climbing to the rank of general—the ex-officer stated simply, "Taylor was an innovative man."

He most certainly was. Taylor's 1989 attack on a government outpost in Nimba County drove Liberia to become "the first sovereign entity to degenerate into a newly conceived category: the failed state" (Cain 1999: 267). The audacious raid he led from neighboring Côte d'Ivoire with perhaps a hundred men (Ellis 2006: 75) introduced the world to two of his remarkably effective military tactics: spreading rumors in advance of an assault and attacking on the eve of a major holiday. Liberia's civil war began on Christmas Eve. "With alarming alacrity," Taylor's offensive fluoresced into a conflict "characterized by total state collapse and a relentless campaign of sadistic, wanton violence unimaginable to those unfamiliar with the details of man's capacity to visit the abyss" (Cain 1999: 268). The result was sweeping ruin: the civil war that Taylor kicked off eventually left 85 percent of the Liberian population either dead or living as refugees or internally displaced persons (IDPs). Cain characterized Taylor's ascendance to the Liberian presidency as "Evil Triumphant" (269).

Such bombastic condemnations of Dahkpannah Dr. Charles Ghankay Taylor,[2] so commonplace in literature about Liberia's civil war and the Tay-

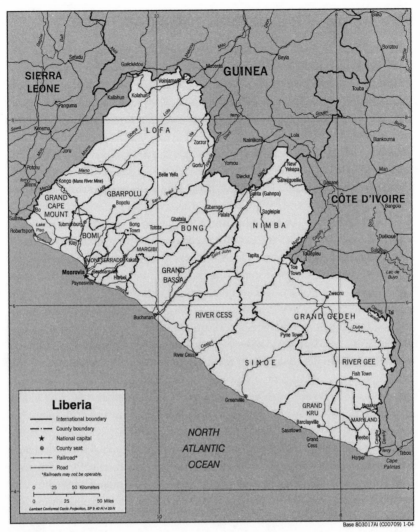

Map of Liberia (Political)
Source: U.S. Central Intelligence Agency, 2004.

lor presidency, miss the point. Moralistic labeling of Taylor as bad or evil obscures a much more important endeavor: learning from him. Taylor was a wartime innovator par excellence. He seemed to wear the "warlord" moniker like a mantle, and why not? If ever there was a lord of war in the modern era, it was he. For many years, Taylor's mastery of terror tactics, his entrepreneurial genius, and his ability to control people and economic sectors in the midst of wartime instability collectively rewarded him with fearsome power, astounding wealth, and both fame and infamy.

Life in Taylorland

Charles Taylor seemed to have a sublime understanding of ambiguity and psychology. In one of the poorest regions in the world, an area justly renowned for weak state institutions and opportunistic power grabs, this proved to be an extraordinary advantage. Borders in the West African Forest Frontier—the forest area linking Liberia to its three neighbors, Sierra Leone, Guinea, and Côte d'Ivoire—are regularly ignored. The forests themselves are "crisscrossed with tracks along which local people move easily on foot" (Richards 2006a: 197). In the middle of this area, in the war zone he birthed, Taylor hatched an entity he called Greater Liberia, which eventually stretched across almost all of Liberia and into parts of Guinea and Sierra Leone (Harris 1999: 434). Reno called it "Taylor's Shadow State," which demonstrated that "in at least some parts of Africa the near future does not point to centralized states" but to the 1860s, "when some chiefs built their authority on competition for coastal trade with foreign firms" (Reno 1993: 178). Liberians simply and aptly called the area "Taylorland" (Reno 1998: 92).

Taylorland was a world where its overlord could act rapaciously, maintain tight control over people and resources, and negotiate deals with foreign firms to help him exploit the region's diamonds, timber, rubber, and iron ore—Reno estimated that "the total yields of Taylor's warlord economy approached $200–250 million a year" over a five-year period (1990–94) (1998: 99)—and do it all with pure, absolute impunity.[3] More than that, Taylor, and rival Liberian warlords who followed in his wake, demonstrated "a new logic of organization" wherein "warlords assert their authority without the benefit of globally recognized sovereignty" (79, 80). On the contrary, Taylor would "ideally incorporate as many commercial networks as possible into his warlord league." Reno compares Taylor's setup with Colombia's Medellín drug cartel: both cared far more about controlling commercial transactions than specific territory (93). Reportedly, Taylor's vision of regional dominance even featured the creation of a series of interlinked states that bore his brand of economic exploitation and dictatorial rule: "It seems Taylor and his key ally, Burkina Faso's President Blaise Compaoré, envisage a string of military-style states from Niger through to Guinea, Guinea Bissau and Gambia. They would be led by younger, authoritarian leaders, happy to build a network of informal (often criminal) business operations, and grateful to Monrovia and Ouagadougou" (Africa Confidential 1999: 2). Though he did not entirely achieve that vision, for nearly fourteen years, as warlord and as president (1990–2003), Charles Taylor thrived.

Taylor's innovations hardly stopped there. He took children, many of them war orphans, and created Small Boys Units (SBUs). These child soldiers "were to prove not only intrepid fighters but also exceptionally loyal to the man they called their father or 'papay,' Charles Taylor" (Ellis 2006: 79). Taylor never worried about compensating his fighters because of his infamous "Pay Yourself" policy, wherein victorious soldiers took whatever they liked: goods, food, women. Yet another Taylor innovation was to regularly telephone BBC Radio after taking a new town. The BBC's reporters, in turn, unintentionally helped promote Taylor's legitimacy and notoriety by granting him a widely respected international platform for shaping his image and the war to his liking (something that subsequent rebel leaders copied with BBC Radio reporters, such as Laurent Kabila in the former Zaire and Foday Sankoh in Sierra Leone). These were hardly idle chats: a BBC reporter noted that "throughout the 1990s Mr. Taylor conducted a series of dramatic telephone interviews with the BBC's Focus on Africa [radio] programme. The first, from the then–relatively unknown warlord, announced his invasion of Liberia" (Doyle 2009: 1). Taylor, indeed, had begun using Focus on Africa—"West Africa's favourite news programme" (Ellis 2006: 75)—to serve his ends a mere eight days into the war: on New Year's Day, 1990.[4]

Taylorland, in addition, naturally awarded its ruler the opportunity to dominate communication within and beyond his area of control. Taylor did so with his trademark combination of ingenuity, brutality, and a craving for power and attention. A key military tactic of Taylor's was to "eliminate enemy broadcasting capabilities while supplementing or expanding" his own (Innes 2003: 8). One can only imagine what it might have been like to try to gather useful information in Liberia when Taylor proved so effective at dominating the airwaves. During the 1997 presidential election campaign, Taylor's two stations (KISS FM and Radio Liberia International) were among the most readily available radio frequencies across Liberia (Harris 1999: 438). It was an advantage that former American president Jimmy Carter, in Liberia as an election monitor, conceded to Taylor as well (Innes 2003: 14). Taylor seemed to be everywhere during the 1997 presidential elections, and radio presence only enhanced the impact of his terror tactics. Small wonder that he garnered three-quarters of the vote. Two popular phrases in Liberia from that period help explain why Taylor won, and so convincingly. One was "He who spoil it, let him fix it" (Harris 1999: 451). A second was much more famous. It was contained in a campaign song:

> He killed my pa,
> He killed my ma,
> I'll vote for him. (Quoted in International Crisis Group 2002: 13)

Given Taylor's power and propensity for predation and control, the implicit message suggests that perhaps Charles Taylor would ease off ordinary Liberians if he gained the presidency. Let him become president, if he wants it so much. After he won, Taylor became one of the main investors in Liberia's only mobile phone service provider from 2000 to 2004, Lone Star Communications (New Democrat 2009: 1). His thirst for influence and power only increased.

Taylor, in short, made himself into the Liberian Colossus, a virtually omnipresent force in the lives of Liberia's citizenry. President Taylor's relentless style also made a strong impression on the diplomatic community. Swaying Taylor was difficult to do. A veteran diplomat from the West shared this reflection: "Every talk I ever had with Taylor wandered all over the lot. He digressed from his digressions. The only way to get him to listen was to let him talk and allow him to wear down. He couldn't stay on one subject for more than five minutes. I've met many heads of state. But this was my only experience of talking with a leader of a country or faction who was totally incoherent."[5]

We are now hopefully in the denouement of Charles Taylor's spectacular story. Taylor was forced from power in 2003 (Simmons 2003) and charged in 2007 with planning, executing, ordering, committing, and otherwise aiding and abetting a succession of serious crimes in Sierra Leone (Taylor never has been tried and convicted for his crimes on Liberian soil). The charges include terrorizing the civilian population, unlawful killings, sexual violence, child soldiering, abductions, and forced labor (Special Court for Sierra Leone 2007). He pleaded his innocence to all charges. In 2010, while on trial before the International Criminal Court in The Hague, Mr. Taylor fathered a child (the result of subsidized conjugal visits) during his detention in twin private cells. He also boycotted his own trial for a day because he considered sitting handcuffed in a vehicle for several minutes to be, in his words, "disrespectful" (Carvajal 2010: 3). On September 26, 2013, Taylor "lost his appeal against a war-crimes conviction . . . as judges confirmed a 50-year jail term against the Liberian ex-president for encouraging rebels in Sierra Leone to mutilate, rape and murder victims in its civil war" (Escritt 2013). In 2020, Taylor tried again. This time, the Residual Special Court for Sierra Leone (RSCSL) judge "vehemently denied" his appeal to be sent to a "safe third country" due to the "massive outbreak" of COVID-19 in the United Kingdom (Johnson 2020).

Charles Taylor remains a political presence in Liberia even in prison. In 2017, during Liberia's presidential election season, he phoned Liberia from the high-security Frankland Prison in Durham, England, to encourage supporters for the incumbent, George Weah, and his new deputy. Weah had chosen Taylor's former wife, the aptly named Jewel Taylor, to run as his vice president. Part of the deal was to align Charles Taylor's former party (and Jewel's current one), the National Patriotic Party (NPP), with Weah's Congress for Democratic Change (CDC). On Charles Taylor's call, he is reported to have said that "this revolution" was the focus of his life. Weah and Jewel Taylor won the election. Charles Taylor retains many supporters in Liberia (though the proportion is unclear). "Even with the sound of the gun, life was better" in Liberia under Charles Taylor, a "frustrated young man" reminisced, lamenting "the lack of basic necessities in the country" (Attwood 2017).

A core theme of this book is that one must understand ruthless, opportunistic wartime innovators to begin to address their legacy and future impact. Charles Taylor created a blueprint for terror warfare that his Sierra Leonean colleagues adopted and enhanced. Sierra Leone's civil war and its aftermath thus provide an unusually instructive case for exploring this theme and for grasping the global significance of one of its signature dimensions: the use of pop culture icons to fuel war.

Charles Taylor nourished the birth and growth of Foday Sankoh's RUF and kept his fingers in its diamond-studded till right across Sierra Leone's war years (1991–2002). The RUF's military advances in Sierra Leone simultaneously advanced Taylor's economic empire. The similarities between the two main rebel groups—Taylor's National Patriotic Front of Liberia (NPFL) and Sankoh's RUF—are not at all coincidental. Taylor and Sankoh met in Libya as West African revolutionaries who were trained and spurred toward rebellion by Libya's ruler, Mu'ammar Gaddhafi. Taylor had much closer ties to Gaddhafi, and at the outset of their relationship Sankoh was, in many ways, Taylor's protégé. Back in Taylorland, Sankoh and his tiny band of upstarts received more training and support from Taylor and his NPFL minions. In March 1991, and under direct guidance from Taylor, Sankoh led an invading force about the same size as Taylor's original outfit (a hundred people) into the peninsula-shaped district of Kailahun.

Sankoh's tiny force uncorked a rebellion that was waiting to happen and soon would engulf Sierra Leone in a complex war of terror. The RUF's methods featured terror against civilians while largely shunning engagements with other combat forces. They had an unusually young fighting force, even by the awful standards of child soldiering. Drug use was a near constant with the RUF and virtually every other Sierra Leonean force involved in the war. Rape, too, became thoroughly commonplace across military outfits. Cannibalism surfaced during the war. Amputating civilians' limbs became the worldwide trademark for Sierra Leone's brand of terror warfare.

Then there was the use of pop culture icons. Out of remote rain forests and towns in Sierra Leone, and in urban neighborhoods, rebel leaders transformed Bob Marley into a kind of patron saint to inspire their efforts. Marley's diction was excellent, and the messages that young Sierra Leoneans received from his songs were clear: resist and remember that you are right. Recognize that there's a struggle going on, chase those crazy baldheads, and push for your rights. When war finally broke out, commanders began to exploit and deploy Marley's music strategically to inspire their fighters and help justify their actions. Sankoh himself regularly quoted Bob Marley's song lyrics in speeches to his troops. The music, philosophy, and style of the American hip-hop star Tupac Shakur entered the scene during the war years as well, directly and heavily influencing the West Side Boys militia and the RUF's "Tupac groups." The RUF also used movies featuring John Rambo, the renegade American Green Beret, as training videos for their soldiers.

What follows is a story of war and peace in Sierra Leone that, while it may have been spawned in Taylorland, evolved into a signature brand of terror and an approach to postwar life. The through lines for this story are how terror and certain pop culture icons, particularly Bob Marley, saturated Sierra Leone's theater of war. Then, with Marley again leading the way, some of the same global pop culture heroes retained a potent hold over marginalized youth in peacetime.

CHAPTER 2

The Perverse Universe

An Upside-Down World

Picture, if you can, boys and girls of ten or twelve running at you, dazed by drugs and carrying machine guns. They are hostile and so high that you cannot possibly reason with them. For adult refugees from Sierra Leone whom I interviewed in 1997, such scenes froze them in their tracks and unseated their lives in an instant. "They are harvesting our children," a refugee father remarked about the rebel leaders. He said it in a way that expressed ongoing disbelief. The atrocities these children committed—rape, amputation, burning people alive—scalded the memories of the refugee parents. Children, the men and women explained, are supposed to be protected and nourished. But using them to commit unspeakable atrocities obliterated the everyday and turned the normal world upside down.

That was the point. Forcing an extremely brutal, "perverse universe" (Keen 2005: 76) onto civilians created a brand of terror that powerfully shaped war and peace in Sierra Leone. Some rebels considered their horrific mayhem to be heroic because they believed that their cause was mighty and just. As a result, they led a movement that operated in isolation and tortured potential followers.

Perverting the everyday and raging against everyday perversions are themes coursing through Sierra Leone's prewar resistance, wartime rebellion, and postwar adaptation. The resistance that took place prior to the outbreak of civil war in 1991 pushed against realities of repression that outlawed political critique, including in music, and forced people to accept their ruler's exploitation of citizens and resources as normal. The wartime rebels pushed against such government abuse, but in a way that exploited and punished civilians, *not* government exploiters, using tactics that made the abnormal normal and the unjust just. Years after the civil war subsided, many Sierra Leonean youth still viewed their world as perverse, still put down by a world ruled by corruption, nepotism, and inequality.

In all of this, certain popular culture icons from other parts of the world had a formative impact on the practice of war and peace in Sierra Leone. The messages that Sierra Leoneans drew from these icons were used to support rationales for resistance and rebellion. Military leaders exploited them to inform and inspire the practice of terror during the civil war. The central message that many Sierra Leonean youth extracted from the work of Jamaican reggae legend Bob Marley and other pop culture icons—that societies are unfairly and perversely structured—maintained its power in the postwar era. Even after a ruinous war, their world remained mostly unfair and upside down.

This book finds that influential pop culture icons in youth-dominated societies, and especially for excluded male youth, are drivers of a particular kind of resistance in theaters of war and peace. As youth increasingly venerate pop culture icons and dominate today's war and postwar worlds, securing stability in fragile states cannot be attained until the condemnation of excluded youth is recognized and social perversions are addressed. This chapter and the next one set terror warfare and popular culture into context.

Terror Warfare and Child Soldiering

Terror was the crux of war in Sierra Leone. Warriors practiced warfare mainly by committing terror tactics against unarmed civilians. The combatants made very sure that nothing was sacred in their pursuit of terror: acts that were bestial, gruesome, obscene—it was all fair game. New ways to undermine and control ordinary people seemed to proliferate as soon as they emerged: disemboweling pregnant women, raping prolifically, amputating some people's arms and legs while castrating or beheading others, practicing cannibalism, enslaving people to produce food, dig for diamonds, or provide sex.

One reason that Sierra Leone's civil war potentially is so instructive is because the practice of terror there seemed to have no limit. One only needs to reflect on Operation No Living Thing to gather a sense of Sierra Leone's brand of organized and thoroughly extreme mayhem. The use of children and youth to create an environment of absolute horror reached a kind of modern-day zenith in Sierra Leone. You can take young people and create an uprising, Sierra Leone's mode of waging war seems to suggest, if you push the outermost limits of depraved violence.

A central argument of this book is that we must learn from this way of practicing warfare: how it worked, where it came from, why it was used, and whether it was successful. In so doing, we can begin to anticipate and prepare for a future where such practices may be employed—in contexts of both insurgency and terrorism. The war and its aftermath also are instructive for understanding and addressing a related modern phenomenon: the exclusion of large youth populations. Two of the central practices of Sierra Leone's war—the featured roles of popular culture and drugs—will be prominent themes in this exploration of extreme wartime practices and their rationales and impacts.

There is debate over whether a civil war insurgent group that conducts terror tactics, such as the RUF, also can be considered a terrorist group. This is not a small concern, since "the vast majority—75 to 85 percent by most estimates—of all terrorism is domestic." Insurgent groups start or enter civil wars because their grievance against the state is deemed "serious enough" to take up arms in rebellion and seek to overthrow the government. Some "use terrorism as part of their repertoire of tactics whereas others do not" (Fortna 2015: 521). However, it is not entirely clear how such groups should be categorized. For example, in Ünal's view, terrorist groups "exploit the high impact of sensational attacks on symbolic targets to trigger an aggressive [state] reaction." On the other hand, insurgencies "need large populations to support their cause, as well as their politico-military campaign" (Ünal 2016: 29). Although most of their terror tactics focused on ordinary civilians in remote villages and small towns, the RUF certainly were part of sensational, attention-grabbing terror attacks as well, particularly the January 1999 assault on Freetown (together with their rebel colleagues, the Armed Forces Revolutionary Council [AFRC] and the West Side Boys). But they also never had large numbers of supporters. Virtually everything the rebel groups did was by force. In Ünal's conception, the RUF thus stands as a kind of tweener: neither a pure terrorist group nor a traditional insurgency.

Fortna's estimation leads to a more definitive conclusion. She considered the common definition of terrorist rebel groups as those who intentionally attack civilians (instead of military targets) insubstantial. That is because "civilian targeting is ubiquitous" in civil wars, and by both sides ("almost all" of rebel and state forces do this). Accordingly, a terrorist rebel group is one that conducts "a systematic campaign of indiscriminate violence against public civilian targets to influence a wider audience." This sort of terror is random and outrageous, and the assaults aim "not to influence the [civilian] victims but to send a political message to a wider audience." Plenty of rebel groups in civil wars rely on tactics to terrify civilian populations, such as conducting massacres and burning homes and crops. Yet these are not the sort of sensational, random acts of horrifying violence that can be tied to political messaging. They generally contain a military purpose. As a result, Fortna concluded that the RUF used terror tactics but was not a terrorist rebel group (2015: 522, 523).

Her take makes sense. As will be described, the RUF conducted a modicum of political messaging with a small selection of their atrocities (amputating hands during one wartime phase to announce their opposition to voting for the mainstream presidential candidate). But that was about it. Across the entire war, the RUF unquestionably focused on terrifying civilians while killing relatively few, abducting significant numbers and forcing mass displacement. Their approach allowed them to achieve a number of military purposes, such as control over diamond mines, keeping their field units stocked with members and cultivating calamity for the opposition via the hordes of refugees and IDPs they created. This focus allowed them to demonstrate influence while avoiding too many encounters with military forces. That was a critical concern, since the RUF were poor fighters and usually lost or withdrew from combat with armed adversaries. With the RUF in the lead, virtually every military group involved in Sierra Leone's civil war employed terror tactics against unarmed civilians, including those who were viewed as either spies or collaborators with the enemy. However, this did not transform these armed outfits into terrorists. Terror tactics were just the way they all made war.

Carolyn Nordstrom's theory of terror warfare thus becomes an apt and useful fit for understanding the RUF's approach to war in Sierra Leone.[1] It provides a powerful framework for analyzing why some armed groups use terror tactics and whether they are effective. Creating terror, she asserted, was based not on killing people but on terrifying them. "If political will is a dynamic attribute of one's self and identity," Nordstrom argued, "killing a 'body' will not necessarily kill the dynamic font of political will." As a result, terror warfare "focuses less on killing the physical body than on terrifying the population as a whole into, the military strategists hope, cowed acquiescence." While terror warfare includes "strategic murder," the "prime weapons in the arsenal of terror warfare" don't involve killing: "torture, community destruction, sexual abuse, and starvation" (Nordstrom 1998: 105). Terror warfare assumes that "if all the supports that make people's lives meaningful are taken from them, they will be incapacitated by the ensuing disorder" (Nordstrom 1997: 14). It is directed "against all sense of a reasonable and humane world." You control people not "through fear of force, but through the horror of it" (Nordstrom 1998: 107–108). The theory appears to apply equally to peacetime contexts where acts of terrorism take place.

Attacking "core definitions of humanity" (Nordstrom 1998: 109) includes attacking people in their homes. Transforming the home into a battle zone further aids the process of dehumanization, since "to have no home is not to be human" (166). Crucially, Nordstrom asserts that children are regular targets of terror warfare tactics since "nowhere is the fundamental security of daily life undermined more than in attacks on children." The goal of terror warfare is to separate people from their own humanity and "undermine the fundamental ontological security of an entire society" (Nordstrom 1998: 108). Once dehumanization through terror is accomplished, "the population can then be domesticated like any other animal" (Nordstrom 1997: 167).

The inspiration for Nordstrom's terror warfare theory is the former Mozambican rebel group (and current political party) Renamo (Resistência Nacional Moçambicano, or Mozambican National Resistance).[2] It is a fitting selection. Rosen's review of child soldiering, for example, includes the statement that "some recent wars are primarily terrorist in nature." He then names two groups whose activities highlight this point: Sierra Leone's primary rebel group, the RUF, which aimed for "the devastation of the civilian population," and Renamo, which employed "a particularly horrifying form of terrorism" (Rosen 2005: 11). Rosen has not been the only expert to link the practices of the RUF and Renamo. Abdullah, for example, argues that the two organizations were "strikingly similar" and that "what connects the two is the wanton violence on women and children, the systematic destruction of the economy, and the general terror in the countryside" (1998: 222). It seems entirely possible that the connection between the two is not coincidental but intentional. Effective terror warfare techniques, however shocking and depraved they seem to most people, strike a few as inventive and useful. The RUF may have intentionally adapted terror techniques for war in Sierra Leone that Renamo had deployed earlier in Mozambique. What follows in this section is an examination of Renamo's hell-bent style of terror warfare and the high degree of similarity between the war conduct of Renamo and the RUF.

Renamo was first hatched by the White-majority government in neighboring Rhodesia in 1977 (Honwana 2006: 7) to punish the assistance that Mozambique's new government, the Marxist-Leninist, Black-majority Frelimo (Frente de Libertação de Moçambique, or Front for the Liberation of Mozambique), was supplying to Black Rhodesian rebel forces. When Rhodesia became Zimbabwe in 1980, Renamo's main benefactor became apartheid South Africa's Defense Forces (Frelimo also was supporting anti-apartheid groups in South Africa). Renamo's central purpose never wavered: to destabilize Frelimo. As Nordstrom states, "Renamo's war developed as a destructive one" (1997: 39). While Renamo certainly aimed to undercut Mozambique's national infrastructure (blowing up bridges, roads, railway and power lines, oil storage depots), its métier was terrorizing civilians in rural areas. In this, it was ferociously effective.

Renamo, in fact, displayed several prominent characteristics for which Sierra Leone's RUF were later known. First, both groups were remarkably low-technology military outfits. Renamo, for example, appeared to have "virtually no mechanized transport anywhere in Mozambique" (Gersony 1988: 17). Second, both received worldwide notoriety for the ferocity and expanse of their violence. Renamo's human rights practices, for instance, "earned it the baneful reputation as the 'Khmer Rouge' of Africa" (Hume 1994: 14).

Third, like the RUF, Renamo mainly operated in rural areas and had an intriguing ideology and philosophy that it rarely shared with civilians. Gersony is clear on this issue: Mozambican refugees who had lived in Renamo-controlled areas reported that there was "virtually no effort by Renamo to explain to the civilians the purpose of the insurgency, its proposed program or its aspirations" (1988: 40). A handful of exceptions to this tendency existed, and Renamo's stated government model made traditional leaders particularly prominent. Nordstrom, for example, reports that despite the fact that "terror tactics more than nation-building were infused into [Renamo's] military strategy and tactics" (1998: 105), in some cases (largely, it appears, in especially remote areas of Mozambique), "equanimity had been achieved between Renamo and its subjects" (1997: 100). In addition, some ex-Renamo combatants "recalled being instructed by Afonso Dhlakama, president of Renamo, to respect local elders and traditions. Strong emphasis was put on the return of former chiefs and holders of traditional titles to the posts from which they had been removed by Frelimo" (Schafer 2004: 92).

Yet overwhelmingly, reports of Renamo's interactions with civilians detail extreme terror and control. Honwana, for example, states that any of Renamo's gains in popularity with citizens came "in spite of its massive cruelty against the civilian population" (2006: 8). Gersony relates that there were "virtually no reports of attempts [by Renamo] to win the loyalty—or even the neutrality—of the villagers." The primary offering that either Renamo or the RUF made to most civilians was, as Gersony remarked about Renamo's former captives whom he interviewed, "the possibility of remaining alive" (Gersony 1988: 40). Indeed, reports of Renamo and the RUF enslaving civilians were commonplace.

Two other important similarities exist between Renamo and the RUF. They both proved crucially important to the style of terror warfare and the nature of military success. The first commonality was the featured use of boy and girl soldiers. Renamo and the RUF both retained sizable numbers of girl child soldiers among their troops. It was estimated, for example, that 40 percent of Renamo's child soldiers were girls (Singer 2005: 185). Second, both groups relied on an astounding number of perpetrated atrocities against civilians: Gersony's litany of systematic abuses by Renamo featured "forced portering, beatings, rape, looting, burning of villages, abductions and mutilations" (1988: 39). The last-mentioned abuse—mutilation—gained Renamo worldwide notoriety, as it became known as the military group that cut off people's lips and ears. The RUF later developed international renown of its own for horrifying amputations.[3]

Are the similarities between Renamo and the RUF coincidental? To be sure, some of what Renamo practiced may well be derived from Mozambique's own history. "Renamo did not come from Hell," Finnegan memorably stated. "Renamo came from Mozambique" (1992: 26). Citing evidence from precolonial and Portuguese colonial periods in Mozambique, Nordstrom notes that "resistance, and the creativities that shape resistance, have been in place as long as have the cycles of political and military terror" (1997: 68). Similarly, scholars such as Shaw (2002) and Rosen (2005) argue that Sierra Leone's traditions and history—particularly its direct and extensive involvement in the Atlantic slave trade—have directly impacted the terror-focused nature and the pronounced child exploitation in Sierra Leone's recent civil war.

Despite the influence of local history on both Renamo and the RUF, it seems unlikely that the mode of warfare practiced by the RUF was not influenced by Renamo's terror war practices. The similarities appear too strong to be coincidental. Certainly Charles Taylor's Liberia-based NPFL, which prefigures the RUF and directly supported its takeoff, is part of the mix as well. Like Renamo and the RUF, the NPFL and the myriad other military groups of Liberia's civil war practiced terror war tactics. What resonates more profoundly, however, is that the similarities between Renamo and the RUF are so pronounced. These two military outfits both had explicit, rural-based political philosophies[4]—albeit neither well detailed nor much practiced—as well as strong reliance on child soldiers and the very same trademark atrocity: amputation. Such conspicuous similarities between rebel outfits on opposite sides of the African continent suggest that terror warfare is an international phenomenon, perhaps even a movement, where trademark terror tactics developed in one war theater eventually surface in others.

It is of course conceivable that the RUF, and later in the civil war, their rebel brethren, the AFRC and the West Side Boys rebel militia came up with the idea of amputation themselves (or, as some contend, were influenced by Liberian commanders in their midst). Denials by former RUF commanders during interviews over the influence of Renamo's practices in Sierra Leone do not undermine suggestive indications to the contrary: it would be unusual to admit to such activities.

Moreover, there is a wealth of evidence to plausibly suggest that the RUF may have sought inspiration from rebel military groups in other countries. Keen, for example, asserts that the RUF "adopted tactics reminiscent of both the NPFL in Liberia and the Renamo rebels in Mozambique" (2005: 41), while Richards refers to RUF military tactics and modes of organization that were "favoured by the Shining Path in Peru" (1996: 6; see also 27–28). Honwana contends that soldiers, military advisers, and mercenaries actively transmit information about war tactics and technologies from one war zone to another. Information also moves via media reports and war films as well as in a diversity of forms on the Internet. Over time, practices such as child soldiering become "acceptable war practices" (Honwana 2006: 45). Bassey's research on rebel groups in contemporary civil wars, moreover, observes that "analysts have found similarities in values, organization and levels of accountability between [Renamo's] violence in Mozambique and that of the RUF in Sierra Leone and the NPLF in Liberia." Rebel groups such as these "have been motivated less by ideological considerations and more by material considerations in their gladiatorial contest for power" (Bassey 2003: 45).[5] Another researcher with extensive experience in wartime and postwar Sierra Leone reported seeing books by a host of revolutionary thinkers and leaders in the library of one of the RUF's former leaders. There were several books by North Korea's Kim Il Sung, among others. The leader had highlighted sections that addressed how to organize guerrilla groups in forests.[6]

Taken together, given the widespread infamy and notoriety of Renamo's amputations in the international media (Gersony's report, for example, attracted considerable international attention following its 1988 release) and the broad similarities in war practices, it is possible if not probable that Charles Taylor, Foday Sankoh, and other military leaders in the circle of military rebel leaders who were active in the 1980s and 1990s in West Africa learned about and directly drew from Renamo's sensational terror war tactics. While most people recoil in horror and disbelief while listening to a radio news story or reading a human rights report about atrocities by Renamo or some other terror war group, some seem to pay very close attention, noting the "innovative" nature and apparent effectiveness of particular practices and preparing to apply them in their own wars. What are horrific human rights abuses to most, in short, are highly useful wartime innovations to a few.

Using small numbers of children to carry out the indiscriminate brutalization of ordinary civilians (usually in rural areas) creates an array of useful military results. Civilians can provide military groups with food, loot, sex, slaves, and new troops. Forcing civilians to vacate areas promotes the power of small child-based outfits by spreading fear across wide areas: when civilians in nearby areas learn about and see the results of the brutality, they frequently become terrified themselves and flee. When this occurs, the military groups double their returns: they both enhance the impression of their power in the outside world (which, of course, can greatly enhance their bargaining power should peace negotiations become an option) while forcing captured civilians to grow food or dig in mines for them in the vacated areas. The child soldiers, in turn, are easy to train and manage. Singer, for example, notes that children require minimal training to become soldiers and, because they are "weakened psychologically and fearful of their commanders," they "can become obedient killers, willing to carry out the most dangerous and horrifying assignments" (2005: 80). In addition, as today's human population features a large and expanding percentage of young people (Freemantle 2011; Elliott Green 2012; United Nations Department of Economic and Social Affairs 2020), the sheer abundance of readily available children for capture makes them exceptionally easy to replace.

The result is a recipe for war that features small, agile troop units requiring minimal capital or capacity investment and promising potentially huge payoffs (at least as long as the war holds out). While it is adaptable to a variety of contexts, it apparently requires a particular set of conditions to succeed: huge populations of young people, a weak state and national military, expanses of mostly ungoverned territory, and an entrepreneurial leader (like Charles Taylor) or set of reliable benefactors (like the support that Rhodesia and then apartheid South Africa gave to Renamo) to help direct the diabolical way forward. The recipe differs from the one described by Hugo Slim. He describes three kinds of explicitly overlapping reasons for civilian killing: "Power-dominance and subjugation"; "Because it works—utility"; and "Because it pays—profit" (2008: 137, 151, 161). He also devotes considerable time to the rationales and processes of genocide. The terror warfare concept, in contrast, emphasizes a preference for torturing and exploiting civilians over killing them.

Nordstrom argues that, ultimately, terror warfare fails. Half of Mozambique's population of sixteen million "were directly affected by" the country's civil war (1997: 12), mostly because of almost unthinkable atrocity and brutality (mainly by Renamo). Yet the civilians there nonetheless responded with what she calls "creative resistance to violence" (220). Nordstrom found that most civilians acted in war zones with "a strong code of humane ethics," and many refused to run away. In such cases, ordinary people "defy danger, and defying equates to a sense of control" (13, 14). Through such acts, "Average civilians unmade the possibility and the power of violence, and in doing so they set the stage for peace. They, in fact, created the conditions of peace. They made war an impossibility. And it was on this work that the peace accords were built" (220). Notwithstanding this conclusion, Nordstrom noted (over two decades ago) that terror warfare was spreading. In her view, despite evidence that terror war tactics "do not prove successful in the long run, and in fact appear to undermine a military's ultimate objectives," it "has not deterred the continuation of such tactics" (68).

What may explain the growing popularity and spread of terror war practices is that its practitioners discount her assessment. Civilians may recover, as Nordstrom details, but terror war tactics also can yield somewhat viable postwar political parties (in Renamo's case), amnesty-laden peace treaties (such as for the RUF), and the presidency of a nation (for Charles Taylor). None of these outcomes provided substantial long-term impact for the trio discussed here (Renamo, the RUF, and Taylor). Beyond these examples lies a simple calculus: that the sort of person who seeks to create a terror war outfit is looking for a quick bang for their buck and by any means necessary. It is fairly impossible to deny that the model of warfare that Liberia's NPFL and Sierra Leone's RUF deployed made a small number of people extremely wealthy and, for many years, exceptionally influential. And for such people, the RUF and the array of other fighting forces in Sierra Leone certainly appeared to constitute a kind of cutting edge of the terror war model.

The use of terror tactics is expanding. Almost always, the setting is conflict countries ("over 97 per cent of terrorist attacks in 2021" took place "in countries in conflict" [Institute for Economics and Peace 2022: 2]). Acts of terror have led to the founding of entirely new states (such as the declared caliphate of the Islamic State in Iraq and Syria [ISIS]).[7] Following Fortna's definition of terrorist groups (reviewed earlier in this chapter), the intentionally arbitrary, attention-grabbing, and outrage-inducing violence of ISIS (such as videos of beheadings shared online) has its differences from terror tactics employed by insurgent groups like the RUF. One is that ISIS "is fighting a war of attrition or exhaustion," where the intent is to "drain the resources of the opponent powers such that they no longer have the will to continue the struggle" (Steed 2016: 35–36). The RUF, in contrast, used terror tactics to secure territory and control civilians, among other purposes.

Nonetheless, ISIS has important similarities with the RUF. Both groups have enslaved large numbers of women (in the case of ISIS, they are "nonbelieving women" who "are considered as chattel and can be bought and sold and traded as any other property" [Steed 2016: 40]). ISIS operatives also are among those who use drugs to "fuel their members" (as well as to drive a hugely profitable illicit business). Both the RUF and ISIS appear to have used amphetamines because it promises to increase "aggression, violent behaviour, psychosis, and impulsiveness" in their fighting forces. Another such drug— tramadol—"is reportedly used by terrorists and fighters in order to reduce pain, to increase endurance strength, and to alter the senses" (Santacroce et al. 2018: 67). Similarly, drugging fighters was standard practice for the RUF and many other military outfits during Sierra Leone's war.

The RUF led the way with their early and persistent reliance on terror tactics during Sierra Leone's civil war. For them, the gist of terror warfare appeared to be this: Avoid clashes with military adversaries. Target civilians. Don't kill too many of them, but don't try too hard to win their hearts and minds, either. Terrorize them, by whatever means you prefer. Force them to fear you deeply. Never let up.

CHAPTER 3

Popular Culture in War and Peace

Three Models for Resistance

Perhaps no modern war has been more heavily influenced by popular culture figures than Sierra Leone's civil war. During my field research work in twenty-two war-affected countries, Sierra Leonean youth seemed much more captivated by pop culture icons than their counterparts in other countries. Across years if not decades, many youth and adults viewed Bob Marley as a prophet and the Rambo movie character as a model warrior. Tupac Shakur, in contrast, developed a much more complicated reputation. He signified a degree of wartime defiance and aggression that made him as reviled (and feared) by adults as he was popular with male youth.

Three passages from Ishmael Beah's memoir of being a child soldier for Sierra Leonean government forces illustrate the magnetic attraction and multitude of ways that these three popular culture figures played central roles in Sierra Leone's war. After one ambush, Beah searches the dead bodies of the rebel RUF soldiers who had fallen. He finds one boy, "whose uncombed hair was now soaked with blood," wearing "a Tupac Shakur T-shirt that said: 'All eyes on me'" (2007: 119). Later, back at his base camp, Beah says that he had become addicted to drugs (marijuana, amphetamines, and brown-brown, a mixture of cocaine and gunpowder). While high on such drugs, he and other child soldiers watched movies at night: "*Rambo: First Blood, Rambo II, Commando* [starring Arnold Schwarzenegger]," and other war films, using a generator or car battery for electricity. Then he comments, "We all wanted to be like Rambo; we couldn't wait to implement his techniques" (121). Later, while recovering from bullet wounds during a hospital stay, Beah found solace by listening to Bob Marley songs and memorizing the lyrics. Listening to Marley's "Exodus" on cassette, he recalls that he "grew up on reggae music" and loved hearing about Rastafarianism and the history of Ethiopia (162, 163). These three recollections provide an overview of popular culture's influence in Sierra Leone: the application of Tupac Shakur's music and messages in times of combat, the use of Rambo and other war movies to inform military tactics, and the popularity of Bob Marley dating back to before the civil war.

While the meaning and influence of Bob Marley, Tupac Shakur, and Rambo may be outsized in Sierra Leone, the ability of international popular culture icons to influence young people's ideas and become subjects of local interpretation is a worldwide phenomenon. In Adjumani, Uganda, in 2003, for example, a group of adolescent boys asked me to settle their argument over whether Tupac was alive or not. One group was convinced that he was still living (mainly because there had been a steady stream of new Tupac music since his shooting in 1996) while the other group was not sure whether or not he really had died. In Zanzibar, Tanzania, in 1989, several male youth approached me on a beach to ask me to resolve a pressing dispute: did Rambo also play the movie character, Rocky, or did Rocky also act as Rambo? Their debate was over which of the two characters was real and which one was not. The youth met my answer—that the same American actor, Sylvester Stallone, played both characters—with dumbfounded silence. In their minds, they *knew* that my explanation couldn't be true.[1] So they ignored my contribution and returned to their debate. Over time, I have learned that children and youth in many countries interpret movies about Rambo, among others, as being completely authentic—like real-time documentaries, perhaps. Rambo became, to many young people, a genuine American soldier. Similarly, the vast importance and enduring popularity of Tupac Shakur and Bob Marley to youth across the globe is in itself remarkable, as well as a testament to the power of their artistry and ideas.

Bob Marley, Tupac Shakur, and John Rambo have achieved lasting fame and influence across the planet. Marley died in 1981 and Shakur in 1996. Both were in the top thirteen highest-earning "dead celebrities" of 2007, all of whom were considered "lynchpins of enormously profitable—and growing—merchandising empires." Tupac Shakur ("a hot commercial property" [Goldman and Paine 2007a]) ranked eighth (Goldman and Ewalt 2007), generating $9 million in royalties from sales of his music and other goods in a single year. Bob Marley came in at number twelve ($4 million; Goldman and Paine 2007b). Marley then continued to climb up the ladder, ranking between numbers four and six across eight years (2012–2019) in the *Forbes* magazine dead celebrity annual standings, and earning a yearly average of $20,375,000.[2] These numbers only begin to account for the enduring global presence of Bob Marley and Tupac Shakur. One measure of Rambo's international popularity is suggested by the fact that, collectively, the five Rambo movies have grossed well over three-quarters of a billion U.S. dollars ($817,962,398 worldwide; The Numbers, n.d.).[3]

For Jeremy Prestholdt, the reason why Rambo, Marley, and Tupac (the latter two in particular) have had such spectacular global appeal is because they are "icons of dissent." He defines icons as "products of the popular imagination." International audiences use these products to draw and project meaning (2019: 6). Certain icons, however, break away from the rest, gaining special prominence as mighty resisters to the status quo. The icons of dissent heroically stand "against systemic forms of domination and inequality" (4). Their renown and influence are gendered: nearly all are men who "perform, confirm and amplify conventional male traits, including aggression." Moreover, "their resistance to structures of power entails redemptive violence" (13).

The global renown of two musicians who died decades ago and an action movie character represent confections that only lightly draw from actual details about all three. This is because the touchstone for their "iconic imagery" is "individual and collective interpretations of them" by people and societies around the globe. As a result, their international reputations really are simply "popular myths based on the lives of individuals" (5). During Sierra Leone's war, Prestholdt found that Marley, Tupac, and Rambo all addressed "young people's desires for myth-like heroes" (112). How young Sierra Leoneans fashioned these three icons to suit their needs, and how military operators manipulated the meanings of all three, is a prominent theme in this book. The remainder of this chapter sets the stage for this discussion.

Bob Marley

Robert Nesta (Bob) Marley sang poetically about freedom, love, rebellion, resistance, pride, inequality, injustice, righteousness, and Africa. His music "explored, celebrated, and translated the experiences of the marginalized, giving a resolute and spirited voice to the global underclass" (Prestholdt 2019: 75). Throughout the 1980s and 1990s in sub-Saharan Africa, his songs were ubiquitous. So was, in cities, the sight of African Rastas: usually young men with long dreadlocks tucked underneath knit hats bearing the colors of Ethiopia's flag (red, yellow, and green). Over time, Marley's music came to represent the struggle against state segregation in South Africa and freedom for Zimbabwe. His songs were heard regularly on the radio and in cafés, clubs, bars, and restaurants; his image was on T-shirts and in painted murals; and his cassettes were widely available. Bob Marley was probably the most popular musician in sub-Saharan Africa during that time. As Prestholdt observed, "So strong was the affinity for Marley's music on the African continent that many fans claimed him as one of their own" (89). Toynbee further asserted that "Bob Marley stands alone as a third world superstar. So far, no other music maker coming from a third world country has become a global celebrity. No other artist from anywhere has attracted such a following in the poorer periphery of the capitalist world system" (2007: 10).

Gilroy provided additional detail to explain Marley's pervasive and lasting influence across the globe. Writing in 2005, he observed,

> More than two decades after his premature death, Bob Marley's many recordings are still selling all over the world. He has become an immortal, uncanny presence. Across the planet, his serious, pained and permanently youthful expression looks out from T-shirts, hats, badges, walls and posters. His digitally remastered voice talks back to power, exploitation and indifference with all the insolent style and complex rhetoric of a rebel captured in the process of becoming a revolutionary. That unchanging face now represents an iconic, godly embodiment of the universal struggle for justice, peace and human rights. (Gilroy 2005: 226)

Hagerman spotlights an elemental tension between the "two prevalent representations of Bob Marley in popular culture" that Gilroy identifies. The conception of "Marley as an icon of peace" rests uneasily with "Marley as a revolutionary." A common response has been to focus on the former while overlooking the latter. "It has become increasingly fashionable among scholars, popular writers, and fans," Hagerman observes, "to represent Bob Marley as a peacenik with a streamlined message of peace, love, and unity for the world" (2012: 380, 381). This imaging fits snugly with "postmodern consumer culture," which "cleansed" Marley's image "of any embarrassing political residues that might make him into a threatening or frightening figure" (Gilroy 2005: 227).

Supporting the effort to homogenize Marley is the sound of his music, which combines lilting beats with bright accents. It is dance music, and it seduces some listeners "to smile and nod when listening to the musical statements in [Marley's] songs and to be caught up in the sheer 'listenability' of the music" (Smith 2005: 11). Indeed, many people with whom I've discussed the key themes in this book are surprised to learn that Bob Marley's music had been adapted (or manipulated) to fuel warfare. Even as he is adored by multitudes, these conversations suggest that some of Marley's fans misunderstand his work. As Smith observed, if one listens carefully to Marley's songs, "one is struck by the militancy, the calls to action, and the consistent call for justice one finds in those same seemingly benign songs. This is not happy-go-lucky, pot-induced, 'safe' music; it is transformative ideology, intended to engage the people to take action against all forms of oppression and injustice" (2005: 11). More precisely, the call to action embodied in Marley's song lyrics "often refer[s] to acts of violence as a necessary part of the revolutionary struggle" (Hagerman 2012: 381).

Resistance and revolution took hold early in Marley's life. He emerged as an artist in 1960s Kingston, Jamaica, when "marginalized young men" residing in the city's "poorest urban spaces had already begun to openly reject the dominant social order." The young male outcasts called themselves "rude boys." Bob Marley and the Wailers' music from this period "expressed dissatisfaction with social and political systems through their empathy with youthful rebelliousness." By the following decade, Jamaican politicians started to conscript "rude boys and gunmen" to carry out "turf wars" on their behalf. Bob Marley and the Wailers responded by lamenting "the inescapable traumas of the ghetto" in songs such as "Burnin' and Lootin'"—a song that expresses a mix of active resistance and despair (Reynolds 2010: 238, 239).[4] Unsurprisingly, Marley's work has had a special resonance with poor male youth. Moyer has observed, "The worldwide popularity of [Bob Marley's] image and music is undeniable, especially among young men living at the margins of global capitalism" (2005: 35). Marley's formative years took place in an environment—where excluded male youth challenged the status quo and some were corralled and exploited by devious politicians—that bore striking similarities to the milieu in Sierra Leone.

Part of Marley's appeal draws from the fact that his music is religious. Marley was a devout worshipper of Jah, the Rastafarian name for God. The messianic quality in some of Marley's work was intentional. Jacobs notes that Marley "believed that God was the source of his music, and that its purpose was to act as a vehicle delivering God's messages" (2009: 27). He backs this up with a quotation from Marley himself: "if God hadn't given me a song to sing, I wouldn't have a song to sing" (Sheridan 1999: 80, quoted in Jacobs 2009: 27). As Rastafarians are taught, Marley read the Bible daily, and with a critical eye.

The founding event for Rastafarians took place in 1930, when Ras Tafari was coronated as Haile Selassie I, emperor of Ethiopia. The nation stood out as independent on a continent engulfed by the colonies of European powers. Rastafarians view Selassie as their living God and maintain that "the Bible predicts and validates the rise of Jah [or Lord] Rastafari at the head of African people everywhere, with the concomitant defeat of Babylon" (Toynbee 2007: 62, 63). For Rastas, Ethiopia became Zion, the coming Exodus became the repatriation of descendants of former African slaves back to Africa (Smith 2005: 9), and Babylon became "identified with whiteness." Rastafari religion, in fact, reverses "the European doctrine of white superiority on which African slavery was premised" (Toynbee 2007: 64). Rastafarians contend that Africans "are the superior race" (Smith 2005: 64). The religion is also fundamentally patriarchal. Toynbee asserts that "subordination of women is an article of [Rastafari] faith," which derives its justification from the Bible (2007: 65).

In addition, the Rastafarian religion draws on "African traditions of spirit possession and herbal remedies" through their "sacramental" use of marijuana (known as ganja, cannabis sativa, or, in Sierra Leone, *djamba*). Rastafarians believe that ganja was the source of Solomon's wisdom. It helps Rastas "see the truth" and "increase their understanding of Jah" (Smith 2005: 8). In their view, the rulers of "Babylon System" make smoking marijuana illegal because it has the power to open people's minds to truth (Edmonds 2003: 61). Rastas wore their hair in "dreadlocks" to "shock middle-class and upper-class Jamaicans" whom they believed were trying to pass as White people (Smith 2005: 8). Baldheads, in contrast, never wore dreads. Instead, they styled their hair or had it cut short (9).

Marley's engagement with Babylon was profound. He employed the term "Babylon System" (also the title of one of his songs) to characterize "the institutional violence" carried out against "the sufferahs"—the same term that many male youth in Sierra Leone often use to describe themselves. Prominent examples of Babylon's violence could be found in institutions such as the police, the military, established Christian churches—Marley and other Rastas targeted Catholicism in particular, as they "firmly believed the Vatican to be part of Babylon"—and governments. The world indeed was at war, in Marley's view, and it pitted Rastafarians against Babylon. Zion was good and Babylon was evil. Fighting Babylon thus was necessary not just to secure equal rights. It also was "a holy war" (Hagerman 2012: 383, 384).

Marley employed a variety of techniques to propel his rebel identity and message. Together with other followers of the Rastafari religion, he drew from a created blend of "English, African dialects, Creole, French patois and other linguistic influences" to accentuate his "intentional resistance" to Babylon (Smith 2005: 8). Rastafarians also invented a new set of pronouns, which Marley also deployed in his songs. He routinely used "me" instead of "I" to underscore his opposition to the status quo, and also because "I" alone typically was reserved for Jah. Marley and other Rastafarians used "I and I" to signify "the two of us" or "I and Jah" (8–9). In addition, Marley's impeccable diction as a singer helped make his music remarkably accessible. It certainly facilitated Marley's dramatic impact across Sierra Leone, where Krio, the local English Creole language, is widely spoken.

Krio began as the language of freed slaves (known as Creoles or Krios). They were "usually literate, and dominant in the colonial civil service." During the British colonial period, many Freetown Creoles "felt closer ties with the West than with the rest of the country" of Sierra Leone (Keen 2005: 14). Indeed, "they scorned non-Creoles," whom "they perceived as uneducated and ill-exposed to Western culture and traditions" (Joseph Bangura 2009: 585). As up-country Sierra Leoneans began to migrate to Freetown during the colonial era, the Krios eventually lost "a numerical majority, and eventually their political and economic dominance in the capital" (Tucker 2013: 20). However, their language remained influential: "The prevalence of Creole language, Krio, is the most expressive testament to the enduring, and expanding, hegemony of Creole culture. Though there are two large indigenous languages spoken in the country, Temne and Mende, it was Krio that, in the course of the 20th century, evolved into a lingua franca for daily speech, trade, national discourse on radio and television, in election speeches, and popular arts in the whole of Sierra Leone" (Stasik 2012: 61–62). Nuxoll speculates that the ability of Sierra Leoneans to grasp Marley was because "Jamaican Patois" and Krio "bear linguistic and structural similarities" (2015: 8). With simplified grammar, Marley sang slowly and with extraordinary clarity. It was not difficult for Sierra Leoneans, even those with a limited knowledge of English, to grasp what Marley said in his songs.

All of these qualities facilitated the ascent of Marley's music across Sierra Leone. Marley was easily understood and his messages resonated deeply. The explicit Rastafarian connection between listening to reggae music and smoking marijuana propelled local adherents to analyze their plight within Sierra Leone's version of the Babylon System. A simple truth for Bob Marley, Tupac Shakur, and so many other artists, as well as for popular culture products (such as the Rambo movies), is that the meaning of a work of expression ultimately is controlled by those who receive and interpret it. Marley's music helped inspire local interpretations of his songs' meanings, and how to apply their precepts in life. For some in Sierra Leone, government officials transformed into baldhead oppressors of the Babylon state.

Tupac Shakur

"Tupac [Shakur] was like a God to me," the Palestinian hip-hop artist Abeer (her stage name is Sabreena da Witch) announced in a public presentation in Washington, D.C., in 2008.[5] Referring to Tupac Amaru (2Pac) Shakur, she explained that Palestinian youth "were actually introduced to hip hop by Tupac. He is literally our God. No matter if people can say he's a killer or not, he would still be our God." Abeer considered Tupac a revolutionary leader and highlighted the controversy that continues to surround him long after his mysterious murder in 1996. "Some people might be called revolutionaries for fighting for rights, [while] some others might consider them criminals for doing some actions that [have] to lead to it." Her statement of Tupac Shakur's profound influence with Palestinian youth is supported by LeVine's assessment. It also could characterize the artist's influence over youth enduring similar conditions across the globe: "Tupac's powerful intersection of political and gangsta rap has served as the perfect model for young Palestinians whose neighborhoods are similarly drug- and crime-ridden, whose schools are underfunded and subpar, and who are surrounded by a hyperconsumerist culture that is out of reach for most. His tragic and meaningless death resonates strongly with young people who have little hope for the future, however talented they might be" (LeVine 2008: 120).

For Abeer and so many other youth across the globe, Tupac is a no-nonsense truth teller. Before hearing his music, Abeer, a Palestinian living inside Israel, thought that the streets in America "looked very beautiful: beautiful flowers, beautiful White people, great malls, great schools." But Tupac, a Black American—who, like her, was a member of a minority population living in a violent environment—revealed an entirely new American world in his songs. The tone of her description is personalized, as if the artist was actually her close confidant: "Tupac came and told me, "'Oh no, there are ghettos that you don't know of [in America].' Drugs? Killing? Gangsters? This is not Tupac, this is the system. This is the government. Tupac just talked about it." Abeer's identification with Tupac is strikingly strong. Palestinian youth "took Tupac's songs and replaced each 'Black' word with 'Palestinian,'" she explained. "Because we were the 'Black' for the Israelis, [just] as Tupac was the 'Black' for the Americans."[6]

Abeer's analysis cuts to the core of Tupac's popularity and influence with poor youth the world over, particularly those living in circumstances of violence and conflict. Tupac speaks passionately, sometimes violently, about living in a violent world:

> What [Palestinians living inside of Israel] write about is violence. We were told many times that we're violent. I was told that I, as a Palestinian, I represent violence. Well, you tell me: imagine your life without water, without electricity, having tanks going around every day, from morning till dawn, depending on when the Israelis want to pass you . . . You tell me how I cannot be called violent when I talk about it.
>
> Violence is coming from you, from the government, from the people who are standing on the checkpoints . . . I don't believe hip hop is violent. I believe that the people who try to avoid it, and what it contains, and what it's trying to tell us, just want to call it violent so people will stop hearing [hip-hop].

For Abeer, the hip-hop music genre inspires young Palestinians to resist and rebel. "With hip-hop, we reached a point where we are able to fight for our rights." Then she mentions the two primary influences on their fight. "Bob Marley talked about it, Tupac talked about it," she explained. "We took it from them."

Tupac's particular influence over male youth and military commanders in Sierra Leone, often as an example of heroic resistance more radical than Marley, surfaced in many locations. In the South Pacific, on the island of Guadalcanal, "Tupac lives again as the patron saint" of a gang of teenage boys. They were attracted to Tupac—his music and his approach to life—for many of the same reasons as their counterparts in Sierra Leone. Tupac was "a man of action" and "wasn't afraid of dying," one gang member stated. He and his comrades "copy Tupac's strut, hand gestures and tattoos." They wear Tupac T-shirts, after graduating from Bob Marley to Tupac. As one gang member explained, "We used to be into Bob Marley, who sings 'Get up, stand up, fight for your rights.' . . . But when we stood up, the police shot at us. Then we became outlaws, like Tupac" (Wehrfritz 1999). The idea that Tupac exemplified outlaw-level resistance also found its way to Sierra Leone and other locations in Africa. A Libyan rebel who fought against the regime of Mu'ammar Gaddhafi explained, "I only listen to 2Pac before going to shoot Gaddhafi boys" (Rogers 2011), an application of Tupac's music that Sierra Leonean rebels also employed. A second use (also found in Sierra Leone's war) was reported in Libya: playing Tupac as a soundtrack for actual battle. Moreover, wearing Tupac T-shirts as military uniforms proved as common in Côte d'Ivoire (Rogers 2011) and eastern Democratic Republic of the Congo (Prestholdt 2019: 110) as it was in Sierra Leone. Five years after Tupac's death, he was found to be influential with youth in West Africa, South Africa, Uganda, and Zimbabwe. A journalist summed up his sway over male youth because they identify with him ("He's everyman") and because "he's full of contradictions, and that's where his power comes from" (Phillips 2001).

On the surface, the songs of Marley and Tupac seem entirely different. Marley's songs mostly feature gentle, rocking rhythms while much of Tupac's music is revved up and burning. Marley tends to sing slowly while Tupac raps in quick cadences. Yet the messages of Marley and Tupac are complementary: Marley describes structural injustice while Tupac details what it's like to live within it. Marley's influence on Sierra Leoneans was mainly ideological while Tupac's influence was more concrete. The interrelated nature of the messages of Marley and Tupac is telling. In his song "Them Belly Full (but We Hungry)," Marley poetically says that hunger is inescapable for impoverished people, and it can lead to frustration and anger.[7] Tupac, in a sense, provides the voice of one of the young underclass sufferahs that Marley describes in his songs. Forever urgent and direct, he is the man without options. In "Me against the World," Tupac contemplates how long he'll manage to stay alive. Then he supplies his answer. He raps that he lives in a perilous world where he's unloved, distrustful of everyone he doesn't know, and has no choice but to arm himself. Unapologetic about his use of violence, he adds that youth like him only attract attention when they're in firefights. His life is pure alienation and he knows it.[8] Speaking of Tupac's "nihilistic double bind," Toop describes how the success Tupac rapped about was bound to be short-lived: "money, women, expensive cars, champagne, fame and California love led to the same conclusion: penitentiary, violent death, no place in our society. Something to die for" (2000: xviii).

Tupac was born into revolutionary politics. His mother was a Black Panther. She named her son after an Incan chief, Tupac Amaru, who was brutally murdered by Spanish conquistadores in the eighteenth century. Over time, Tupac became feverishly defiant: being Black in a world of punishing discrimination against Blacks is a central element of Tupac's worldwide appeal. He regularly suggested that he was trapped in a violent, unjust society. Some Sierra Leonean youth considered Tupac a fighter in "the American war." Tupac had style, he was truthful, he was defiant, he was emotional, he was an incisive political analyst, and he was exceptionally proud. He also regularly predicted that he would die young. Tupac, in short, had a compelling story to tell about his life and his world, and eventually it radiated across the globe. Tupac was someone with whom dispossessed, disempowered, aggrieved young people everywhere could identify. He was real.

Tupac wrote over four hundred songs (and acted in six films) in his short career (Dyson 2020: 165). Reeves divides his vast output into two discrete phases. The first spans his first three albums. His second phase arrived with his fourth album, the groundbreaking *All Eyez on Me*, released in the year of his fatal shooting, 1996. It set Tupac's music on a different course. "Gone were the messages of resistance and painful urban blues," says Reeves. On *All Eyez on Me*, they were "replaced by a postprison hedonism, materialism (thanks to the bundle of money provided by his [recording] label), and an egotistical drive to commercially crush his rap competition. No longer the urban desperado, Tupac remade himself into the flashy rap icon totally representing the West Coast" (2008: 174). Tupac's outsized emotions and dramatic lifestyle proved more difficult to homogenize than Marley. He nonetheless has been heroized as well as deified. Hodge asserts that Tupac was a prophet who connected "God to a people who could never imagine gracing the pristine hallways of a church" (2017: 96–97). "Unexpected and imperfect," Grimes intones, "Tupac operates as theologian for the crucified people" (2014: 329). For Dyson, Tupac was "looking for a black Jesus that understands the internal dynamics of [his] suffering." Long after his passing, "his spirit continues to exist in a beautiful way" (2020: 165).

Tupac attacked life. He was "full of passion, rage, anger, love, thoughtfulness, and even carelessness" (Hodge 2017: 96). His legions of fans study his songs irrespective of those contrasts. It is something that Dimitriadis drew from his interviews with poor, disenfranchised African American youth in a small American town about the importance of Tupac Shakur to them. It is also a finding from my research with war-affected youth in many countries. Youth absorb and interpret Tupac's conflicting messages, and many are able to identify with him. The youth in Dimitriadis's research put together a picture of Tupac that combined three characteristics: his "superhuman invulnerability"; his challenge to "the stereotyping of African Americans as violent and pathological"; and his ability to detail personal feelings "in profoundly moving ways." For the youth who Dimitriadis worked with, and for youth in so many other corners of the globe, "Tupac—without question—represented a validated kind of self" (2001: 118).

One loaded word that Tupac regularly used was "thug," together with his "thug life" philosophy. Tupac famously tattooed the words across his belly, mixing a pistol into the "h" and using a bullet for the "i." They proved unusually powerful for male youth in Sierra Leone, many of whom were regularly condemned as thugs prior to the arrival of Tupac's music and image. Dyson shares Tupac's definition of thug life in the artist's own words, and it is revealing:

> It's not thugging like I'm robbing people, 'cause that's not what I'm doing . . . I mean like I'm not scared to say how I feel. Part of being [a thug] is to stand up for your responsibilities and say this is what I do even though I know people are going to hate me and say, "It's so politically un-correct," and "How could you make black people look like that? Do you know how buffoonish you all look with money and girls and all that?" That's what I want to do. I want to be real with myself. (Dyson 2001: 113)

As Tupac knew, common understandings of being a thug are negative. His take was different, and his intentions inspired strong and varied reactions. On the international stage, Tupac's trademark determination to be edgy, controversial, and confrontational through his music opened the door to varieties of local interpretation. One might see Tupac as reacting to being trapped in a violent world and doing what he has to do, as Abeer intimated. On the other hand, some former combatants in Sierra Leone venerated Tupac for his fearlessness and frank talk about violence. They clearly stated during interviews that they wanted to be a thug like Tupac and live the thug life like Tupac. In war zones, doing this often meant becoming ferocious and, for some, profoundly vicious.

If Tupac Shakur remains a mammoth presence in rap music, the genre itself, by its very nature, invites local readings. Magubane contends it is an art form that contains inherently conflicting tendencies. On one hand, he says, "rap music celebrates individualism, racial chauvinism, consumerism, capitalism, and sexual dominance—core values that have shaped the trajectory of modernity and its bitter fruits." At the same time, it critiques and protests against Western modernity's tendency toward structural inequality. Magubane asserts that rap music, as a "complicated mix" of these two conflicting themes, is subject to "interpretation and incorporation" when it becomes "indigenized" by artists in a particular locale. In South Africa, he says that local rap artists "have seized upon both traditions" (2006: 210). In Sierra Leone, the attraction did not seem quite so binary. There, Tupac's aura of fearlessness and cool drove his popularity.

John Rambo

In 2005, I arrived at Roberts International Airport, located just outside Liberia's capital, Monrovia, after midnight. A driver was there to pick me up and take me to my hotel. When we got to the appointed hotel—a spacious, family-run enterprise in a protected part of town—my reservation somehow had evaporated. So my driver took me downtown, to Broad Street, where there was a tiny room still available in a hotel above a bar and restaurant. Tired yet wired from my long flight, I went down to the bar for a beer before bed. There I found two waitresses sitting and watching a television perched over the bar. I sat nearby so I also could watch TV. *Rambo III* was on. The two waitresses, who had clearly each seen the movie many times, talked animatedly about the film as they watched. Eventually I asked the waitress sitting nearest me about the movie and what she thought of Rambo. "I love him," she replied. When I asked why, she said, succinctly, "Because he act. He does action."

He does indeed. The extraordinary global influence of the three heroic John Rambo movies of the 1980s (referred to here as the Rambo Trilogy)[9] had virtually nothing to do with the controversy that the films spun in the United States, caught as they were within the prism of domestic politics. There, references to Vietnam were meaningful (in Sierra Leone and many other parts of the world, they were not). In the concluding scene of the first Rambo film (*First Blood*, 1982), Colonel Samuel Trautman, Rambo's former American commander in Vietnam, states that Rambo is cornered and commands him to surrender. Then, for the first and only time in the film, Rambo speaks with vigor, explaining how he was forced to fight a war that was not his own, and then was not allowed to win it. The same theme reappears in the opening scene of the next film, *Rambo: First Blood Part II* (1985), when Rambo and Colonel Trautman discuss the prospect of Rambo's return to Vietnam. Rambo asks whether they'll be allowed to win the war this time around. Colonel Trautman replies that Rambo won't be held back. The two scenes communicate the same revisionist idea: the United States would have won its war with Vietnamese communists had politicians not shackled the military.[10]

As a decorated yet forgotten American veteran of a war that the United States lost, Rambo inspired fierce emotional responses. Fiedler's take is illustrative. He castigated Sylvester Stallone, the actor of the Rambo character, as "a shameless purveyor of schlock, with no artistic pretensions, whom hightone critics therefore condemned sight unseen even before his first Vietnam movie had appeared." Fiedler considered the Rambo films to be "incredibly ill constructed and poorly acted, as well as melodramatic, sentimental, gratuitously violent—and, of course, politically reactionary" (1990: 397). In the American context, a second observer noted, "Rambo is [about] getting even, for himself, for his comrades killed in Vietnam, and for feelings of betrayal by the entire U.S. army, government, and public" (Fellman 1998: 109). Yet only betrayal had anything to do with Rambo's incredible international appeal. Well beyond the United States and the West, the first three Rambo movies arose within entirely different contexts, ignited different kinds of interpretations, and were put to somewhat unexpected uses. Illustrative of this is Fiedler's surprise. After blasting the Rambo character and the Rambo films, he confessed that he was "a little astonished" by a report of "a band of Maoist guerrillas in the Philippines watching *Rambo* on their Betamax" (1990: 397–398). It was as if Fiedler and the Filipino guerrillas were watching different movies.

But they weren't. A careful examination of the Rambo Trilogy films, shorn of their American frame of reference, reveals a series of dramatic adventures featuring an extraordinarily heroic, ingenious lone warrior named John Rambo. The filmmakers went out of their way to enhance the image of Rambo as an undeniably magnetic model fighter. Kellner identified one method: "Camera positioning and lighting help frame Sylvester Stallone as a mythic hero in *Rambo*; an abundance of lower camera angles present Rambo as a mythic warrior, and frequent close-ups present him as a larger-than-life human being" (1995: 67). Unquestionably brave, determined, cast aside, and thoroughly suspicious of superiors (except for Colonel Trautman, the only one who knows, understands, and is forever loyal to him), a victim of horrific wartime torture, Rambo could be vicious and violent—but only if he had no other options. Government institutions from his own country—the police and military in the first Rambo movie, politicians in the second—unjustifiably transform Rambo into an outlaw, deliberately attacking him or impeding his actions. In *Rambo III*, Soviet invaders of Afghanistan replace the American turncoats as evil adversaries, taking Colonel Trautman hostage and attacking Rambo's newfound friends (the Afghan Mujahideen).

Against all of these foes, Rambo is singularly resourceful. No institution or military force can defeat him. He is a far cry from a James Bond figure working loyally for a government that mostly believes in him and has technological wizardry at his disposal. Instead, Rambo usually works alone, singlehandedly taking on armies and institutions that wrongly seek to undermine or destroy him. His suffering is immense and his "victimization is made quite obvious through the use of Christ imagery" (Rambo is tortured in crucifix-like poses) (Sweeney 1999: 66). This invites compassion for Rambo, transforming him "from an uncomplicated threat to a locus of sympathy and pity, making his savagery . . . less dangerous" (McClancy 2014: 504). And he always wins.

As an old-style fighter swept up in modern-day conflicts, Rambo awakens familiar themes. Zur, for example, found that John Rambo's approach to warfare harkens back to Homer's *Iliad*. For Achilles as well as Rambo, "War becomes a rite that tests human ability, bravery and endurance," where the practice of warfare "becomes a rite of passage for boys from childhood to adulthood" (Zur 1987: 129). Zur further argued that even though the Rambo movies are exceptionally violent, they are not mainly about violence. Instead, they tell dramatic stories in which wars are "more about ecstasy, prestige and romance" and less about violence and killing (130). Yoder considered the "Rambo theory" of war as one that "mobilizes men collectively in enterprises of killing and dying which they consider imperative, sometimes heroic, sometimes risky for themselves." Warriors who follow it are rewarded with a good conscience and pride in what they do. The pervasiveness of this way of justifying warfare, he noted, "is allegedly used in the training and motivating of elite fighting corps" (Yoder 1995: 90).

Yet Rambo's movies are not only relevant for training elite soldiers. Nair found that many child soldiers in Africa were enamored with John Rambo. The influence is deep and troubling. Evidence of "the legend of Rambo" presented itself to her in graffiti in South Africa in the early 1990s, when violent, politically inspired clashes engulfed many youth there. The graffiti read: "We are soldiers we kill and rape. Rambo is our hero fuck the world." Nair said that some of the boy soldiers who got caught up in conflict searched for ways "to make sense of their new roles as violent participants." The Rambo movie character proved an available and useful resource. But boys adopted "the hero Rambo as father," an event that "parallels the isolation of young people in poverty stricken conflict situations where fathers and adult men are powerless to provide protection" (Nair 1999: 1, 2). Accordingly, following Rambo's example promises to help the boys combat the threat of emasculation in their own lives. Nair further argued that "a boy becoming a Rambo soldier assumes an aggressive masculine identity" (3) and inserts rape as a component of that. This underscores how Rambo, as a pop culture icon on the global stage, can assume meanings that are not present in the works that made the icon famous. Excepting a brief romantic interlude in the second film, Rambo is practically asexual, a kind of principled, gallant, ascetic warrior. What appears to resonate, in South Africa as well as Sierra Leone, is Rambo's indomitable spirit and his relentless drive toward military victory. From there, local interpretations of violent masculinity take over: toward rape, murder, and manhood in South Africa and (as will be detailed) toward boundless military aggression in Sierra Leone.

Unlike Marley and Tupac, Rambo is White (though not entirely: it surfaces in the second Rambo film that he has some Native American ancestry as well). Sierra Leonean male youth frequently mentioned that they identified closely with Bob Marley and Tupac Shakur in part because they too were Black. Rambo is also a loner who relies on tradition, discipline, courage, and ingenuity. He fights modern armies with a knife, a bow and arrow (even if some of the arrows explode on contact), and some novel homemade devices. The ever-resourceful Rambo uses what Sierra Leonean former soldiers called "Rambo Tactics" to bring down modern, mechanized forces all by himself. He is, in short, "the perfect soldier" (Fellman 1998: 112). Colonel Trautman himself drives this point home early in *Rambo: First Blood Part II* (1985). Rambo, he states, is the best fighter he's seen in his entire career, fearless and prepared to die for the cause of victory. In *Rambo III* (1988), Colonel Trautman expands on Rambo's perfect soldier ethos. You can't hide from Rambo, he tells his torturer and the leader of the Soviet military forces in the area, Colonel Zaysen. Zaysen is incredulous at the idea of one man succeeding against the many fighters in his armed fortress. He's not God, Zaysen reminds Trautman. Trautman agrees, adding that God would have mercy. Rambo, in contrast, is merciless.

The idea of Rambo as a solitary, underestimated, and despised underdog is one that Richards investigated in his research about war and Sierra Leonean youth. Youth there identify with Rambo in part because, like them, he is socially excluded. "Young Sierra Leoneans," he suggested, take away an existential point from the first Rambo film: "The need to draw upon inner resources in a world of social exclusion." The Rambo example, he further asserted, provided an inspirational example for young RUF soldiers during the civil war: "Rambo overcomes social rejection through his tricky resourcefulness, just as the young cadres of the [RUF] rejoice in their cleverness at beating a numerically superior and better armed 'adult' opponent" (Richards 1999: 7).[11] Sierra Leonean youth drew an array of vital lessons from the Rambo and other action/war films. In a survey from the early 1990s (while the war was underway), male youth reported that the films helped them learn how to "manoeuvre in times of trouble" and "know skills for fighting." Female youth related that the violent videos helped them know how to "run away from (the rebels)," "use techniques to defend oneself," and "tell us to be aware and ready at any time" (Richards 1994: 93). A displaced female youth illustrated Rambo's powerful influence on young Sierra Leoneans: "it was the thought of John Rambo coping in the forest without a friend in sight that had given her the courage to flee alone 'through the forest' to escape an RUF attack on her village in Kono" (Richards 1996: 111).

Connecting Rambo to survival and combat tactics in Sierra Leone was an easy leap, since the Rambo films vividly portrayed valiant acts of warfare. Like Marley and Tupac, Rambo also had a powerful religious dimension (largely derived from the torture scenes). In addition, the underlying messages about alienation, morality, and action radiating from the Rambo movies are remarkably similar to those emanating from the works of Bob Marley and Tupac Shakur.

All three pop culture icons inspire others to advocate for themselves—especially when they are seen as a menace to those who dominate society. Being misunderstood and castigated by the system is part of the package, all three convey. So anticipate injustice and respond to it. The works of Marley and Tupac and the Rambo action movies combined to provide young people in Sierra Leone with a philosophy, an analytical framework, a rationale for resistance, and a way to fight back. It was a powerful blend. As will unfold in this book, their impact in Sierra Leone stretched from the prewar days across more than a decade of warfare, and then onward into the postwar period.

CHAPTER 4

Trust and Understatement

Sources of Research

Morality limits insights about war. Applying binary ideas (like good and evil) to wartime situations blocks one's ability to comprehend what goes on in a war zone, and why. While conducting research analysis for this book, initially I set aside moral judgments of war zone accounts. Through that process, I sought to gauge the underlying motives for terror war tactics during Sierra Leone's civil war, as well as the life decisions that commanders, fighters, rebel "wives," and others made during and after the war. I also used Nordstrom's theory of terror warfare to enhance my appreciation for and analysis of the terror tactics that characterized Sierra Leone's civil war.

My definition of youth drew from prior analysis of youth concerns. Before detailing this, two especially common youth definitions require mention. The first is at once explicit and confusing. For governments and international agencies, youth are people circumscribed by an age range. This ultimately is disorienting. Sierra Leone's government uses the same age range for youth (15–35) as the African Union (Chipika 2012: 1; United Nations Department of Economic and Social Affairs (UNDESA), n.d.: 2). However, the U.S. Agency for International Development (USAID) defines youth as those aged 10–29 (USAID 2012: 4) while most United Nations agencies employ a 15–24 age range. Meanwhile, UNICEF, the World Health Organization (WHO), and the UN Population Fund (UNFPA) confusingly apply overlapping age ranges for three categories: 15–24 for youth, 10–19 for adolescents, and 10–24 for young people. This turns people aged 15–19 simultaneously into youth, adolescents, and young people (UNDESA, n.d.: 2).

The second common youth definition is implicit: "youth" mainly (often exclusively) refers to male youth. This has been found to be commonplace not only across Africa (Shepler 2010b: 100) but also among practitioners of international development (Sommers 2015: 15) and those working in the field known either as countering violent extremism (CVE) or preventing violent extremism (PVE) (Sommers 2019a: 17). Male youth as the implicit frame for "youth" also is a near constant in literature on Sierra Leone. An exception is Shepler, who notes that the period of being a youth in Sierra Leone "is over when one marries. Boys usually marry later than girls because they need time to acquire the money and status required to marry. The effect of this is that boys are youths much longer than girls" (2014: 26). For this book, I will use the following definition: "a young person with a tenuous social status and a hoped-for social transformation into adulthood" (Sommers 2015: 14).

I collected information for this book from five main sources. Following my startling interview with Sierra Leonean refugees about pop culture and war in 2000 (detailed at the outset of the preface), I headed out to Sierra Leone to explore this issue (and others) in 2005. I conducted interviews in Freetown neighborhoods, restaurants, coffee shops, and offices, in Makeni and nearby villages around the city, and in some of the diamond mines in Kono District. I interviewed former civil war commanders and ex-combatants and many other male and female youth (including many diamond miners). I also interviewed officials working for the Sierra Leonean government, the Truth and Reconciliation Commission (TRC), Sierra Leonean nongovernment organizations (NGOs), and members of international organizations operating in Sierra Leone (donor, UN, NGO), including members of the Special Court for Sierra Leone.

The interviews featured open-ended, qualitative questions about life experiences during and since the war, terror war practices and rationales, and whether and how the works of popular culture icons may have influenced war practices and adaptations to postwar life. The research confirmed prior indications from my 2000 research in Gambia of the centrality of Bob Marley, Tupac Shakur, and John Rambo in Sierra Leone's war and the lives of its youth. It also buttressed findings on the significance of Rambo movies (Richards 1994, 1996) and expanded evidence of Bob Marley's influence over prewar resistance and wartime rebellion in Sierra Leone (e.g., Abdullah 2004; Nuxoll 2015; Prestholdt 2019) as well as Tupac Shakur's impact on terror tactics (Fofanah 1998a; Sommers 2003a, 2003b; Prestholdt 2009, 2019; Tucker 2013).

Early in 2010, I returned to Sierra Leone. I spent nearly all of my time either in or near Kenema, the main town of eastern Sierra Leone, or in Freetown. The research further detailed the dominant influence of Bob Marley's music and ideas on virtually all Sierra Leonean military groups, as well as the secondary and more specific application of the Rambo Trilogy movies and

Tupac Shakur's music and ideas in war zones. It also highlighted the pervasive use of drugs across the Sierra Leonean war era and their ongoing influence in postwar society. I gained this information by again interviewing former civil war commanders, ex-combatants, and other male and female youth, as well as officials working for the Sierra Leonean government, members of national and international organizations active in Sierra Leone, and experts on Sierra Leone's war years. I also interviewed (male) village elders and adult women.[1]

An additional focus for interviews were youth from two cultural categories: those known as Rarray Boys and Rarray Girls, and those who were not. The distinction is meaningful. To some youth, a Rarray Girl refers to girls who are "modern" in their mores and style of dress. They are also thought to be sexually assertive, even promiscuous. However, to most Sierra Leoneans, a Rarray Girl is nothing more than a prostitute. Indeed, female prostitutes (or commercial sex workers) were the only group of female youth about whom everyone seemed to agree were authentic Rarray Girls. I interviewed some of them. Almost all had been rebel captives. I also approached male youth who were widely thought to be Rarray Boys, such as those washing cars in a stream or "harvesting sand" from a river. In addition, I interviewed male and female youth working in a rock quarry, female youth plaiting hair in markets, and other out-of-school youth who either held down various kinds of jobs or farmed. Most were parents (although not married).

A third source of research data came from field interviews conducted by my research associate, an experienced researcher in Sierra Leone. He carried out interviews in the area around the town of Makeni in 2009 and 2010, interviewing former rebel combatants, elders, officials of Sierra Leonean nongovernment agencies, and various local leaders.

A fourth source was field interviews from earlier trips to Sierra Leone, as well as to Guinea and Gambia, where at the time many thousands of Sierra Leonean refugees resided. These trips predated my research on terror and pop culture in 2005 and 2010 and provided rich, vivid detail about the nature of Sierra Leone's war from the viewpoint of firsthand witnesses and survivors, both civilian and military. I first went to Sierra Leone and refugee camps in Guinea in 1997, during the short period between the signing of the first peace accord in November 1996 and the resumption of war in May 1997. I returned to Sierra Leone late in 1998, carrying out field research mainly in Freetown but also Masingbi (a town occupied by peacekeeper forces and surrounded by rebel fighters). The third research trip took place in Gambia in 2000, with Sierra Leonean refugees living in or near the capital of Banjul and the sweltering upriver town of Basse. Additionally, I conducted interviews on my return to Sierra Leone in 2013. The fifth and final information source is the wealth of published works about Sierra Leone's prewar, wartime, and postwar periods.

Two Observations

I will conclude this chapter with two sets of observations. The first is that many of those interviewed understated the profound hardship they suffered during the war. Often, they relayed what had taken place with concise, matter-of-fact statements that subtly communicated personal wartime horrors. For example, one woman summed up her experience of flight with the following unadorned observation: "Wherever I went, the rebels followed." A second woman detailed the outcome of an RUF attack with precision: "The rebels captured my family," she told me. After managing to escape from the RUF (together with three of her children and three of her grandchildren), she added, "I don't know where [my other relatives] are or if they're alive." She also explained, "The rebels captured and burnt my daughter." A male youth of twenty-eight, who had fled Freetown during the famously ferocious No Living Thing assault in January 1999, modestly summed up his dramatic decision to become a refugee: "I left the country because the situation was not too favorable." No, it most certainly was not.

I did not find, however, that people relied on understatement to sidestep discussions about major personal wartime experiences. On the contrary, interviews routinely extended far beyond an hour, and often two. All of them were voluntary: I always read a script before every interview to make it clear that participating in interviews was voluntary (as did my research associate, in separate interviews). Very few Sierra Leoneans declined interview opportunities. In general, Sierra Leoneans whom I interviewed wanted to tell their stories and share their analysis of the war and the actors involved in it. The style of expression regularly was declarative. It appeared to be a practiced means for cutting emotion away from intellectual analysis. Sierra Leoneans sensibly tended to select this approach as they relayed bitter memories. A downside was that understatement made it more challenging to appreciate the depth of suffering they had lived through.

The second observation concerns the challenge of determining the proportion of people whom I interviewed who were associated with or served in a military group during the war. On a few occasions, it was not entirely clear. The reason was that a small proportion of youth did not want to announce their wartime identity. It was an understandable self-protection strategy. The identification might threaten their social or legal situation. During the war, they may have been associated with the RUF or the AFRC, perhaps as a combatant, porter, wife, concubine, spy (recce; pronounced reh-KEY), some other role, or a mixture of several roles. Sometimes their experience in military outfits surfaced in bird's-eye descriptions of what they saw or experienced, or in their analysis of figures or events. But not always: there were a handful of times where I never found out, with absolute certainty, whether a particular person whom I had interviewed was a former "rebel." Accordingly, a limited number of those I interviewed contain a particular kind of asterisk: youth who likely were former combatants (or served other roles for military groups) but refrained from declaring it outright.

Most had no such concerns. Extended interviews with ninety-five former members of military outfits—all of whom clearly stated that they had been members either of the RUF, AFRC, West Side Boys, Kamajor units, or the national army—form the analytical core of this book. In 2005 and 2010, I interviewed seventy-five of them: six top commanders and organization officials, nine field-level officers, thirty-one male youth foot soldier/members and twenty-nine female foot soldier/members. In 2009 and 2010, my research associate interviewed another twenty (eleven male youth, nine female youth), in addition to noncombatant civilians.

For the commanders and officials, as well as the field officers, it was easy for them to identify their affiliation.[2] However, some of the foot soldiers, and other young people who swelled the ranks of rebel combatant groups, were unsure of their groups' ultimate affiliation (RUF or AFRC). It often wasn't clear to them. This especially was the case for female youth. Appreciating the identity, ideology, or purpose of a particular fighting force was hardly their priority: the apparent "occupation" of many of the abducted female youth could best be described as sex slave.

Among the noncombatants whom I interviewed (and including a small number by my research associate) were paramount and town chiefs, district and town councilors, high court judges, a member of the Truth and Reconciliation Commission, a high-ranking former police official, officials of the Special Court for Sierra Leone, officials of Sierra Leonean and international NGOs, security and intelligence experts for the United Nations, veteran researchers of Sierra Leone, professional rap musicians, nightclub DJs, a pharmacist, a longtime supporter (a kind of supervisor and sponsor) of miners, local civilian leaders who negotiated either with the RUF or the AFRC, village elders and village women's groups, associations created to assist ex-combatant female youth, dozens of Sierra Leonean civilians with firsthand experiences of the war, including noncombatant youth in and around Freetown, Kenema, Koidu, and Makeni.[3] Field interviews were written by hand, with an effort to record, as much as possible, the precise words of every person we interviewed. For this book, I analyzed findings from more than three thousand pages of handwritten field interview notes.[4]

For all interviews, my research associate and I employed trust-based, qualitative research methods (I trained my colleague in these techniques). The interview data collected for *We the Young Fighters* ended years before the publication of my book on field research methods (Sommers 2019b). Yet they align with those detailed there. That is because, over the years, my methods haven't changed all that much. Across my research career, I have used simple, declarative questions that generally translate well, aim to empower those I interview, and position the interviewee as expert. I also strongly favor peer over focus groups, and I employ snowball sampling methods. Entering into an interview is always voluntary.

These methods facilitate deep discussions about challenging subject matter. At the same time, if someone wishes to sidestep a particular topic, or perhaps shed unbalanced light on it, the methods cannot stop that. While I employ many techniques to corroborate findings, each interviewee has the final decision on what he or she will share during the interview. For example, for the research for this book, most former male military commanders and combatants declined to discuss sexual violence. In one case, when I raised the topic with an ex-commander, the man looked at me and issued a low, deep chuckle. He would not discuss the subject. However, I received a great deal of firsthand information about this topic from interviews with female civilians and former female members of military outfits.

Taken together, the trust-based techniques my research associate and I employed in all of our field interviews, infused with rich detail drawn from published research, ultimately provided the landscape for what follows in this book.

PART 2

Thugs and the Government Façade

CHAPTER 5

The Trampled Land

A Misunderstood War

Sierra Leone's civil war may be Africa's most misunderstood. An apparently disparate band of mostly child soldiers brought a country the size of Ireland to its knees and kept it there for more than a decade. At the helm, it appeared to many, were sadistic, greedy predators who simultaneously raped the country's women and its mineral resources, lopped off the arms of its citizenry, stole and exploited children before discarding them like spent lottery tickets, and ultimately seemed to revel in their reputation as being among the most evil people on earth—together, of course, with Liberia's notorious former president, Charles Taylor. Meanwhile, Ukrainian mercenaries, Nepalese Gurkhas, secret societies for men and women, and traditional hunters sporting bullet-preventing charms and a reputation for cannibalism contributed to the ghoulish exotica that still distorts understandings of Sierra Leone's civil war.

The mythology about this war is tied to actual facts. Starting with the onset of conflict in March 1991, the RUF rebels, joined later in the war by the AFRC and the West Side Boys, established a wartime pattern of terror featuring horrifying and seemingly endless acts of atrocity, the killing of some men, the raping of many women, and the abduction of children. Their exploitation of children and women was extreme and extensive, the horror they left in their wake was appalling, they stole large portions of the country's diamonds, and outsiders like Taylor and Gaddhafi influenced the war theater. Noted much less often were the child exploitation, atrocities, and diamond smuggling carried out by various forces fighting on the Sierra Leonean government side (it is important to say "fighting on the government side" because in the latter war years no national army existed). Yet across the arc of war, the main media story was the RUF's apparent lunacy. Indeed, nothing seemed to keep alive stereotypical depictions of Africa as violent, hopeless, and mystifying as much as the rebels who appeared to spearhead Sierra Leone's macabre and mad conflict.

Many of the West's misunderstandings of Sierra Leone's war can be found in Robert D. Kaplan's "The Coming Anarchy" (1994). Kaplan's thesis about Africa is a touchstone not only for Paul Richards's attack on "The New Barbarianism" ethic (1996) but also for its powerful use of war-torn Sierra Leone to describe Kaplan's chilling and influential view of the African future. In the process of developing his thesis, however, Kaplan did not speak to those he considered the wick of Africa's explosive fate: young men. Kaplan's depiction of urban youth as "loose molecules in a very unstable social fluid, a fluid that was clearly on the verge of igniting" (1994: 54), and his view that rural dwellers were "draining into dense slums by the coast" (49) like sewage flowing into an ocean, collectively gave the impression that Africa is primordial, dangerous, and sinking fast into a muck of cultural disintegration. It was as if Henry Morton Stanley's *In Darkest Africa* (1890) and Joseph Conrad's *Heart of Darkness* (1902) were contemporary bestsellers, describing the same bleak world as Kaplan. But that was not the case—not even close. The vibrant reality of Sierra Leone's war was regularly horrific, but not because of any elemental cultural dysfunction, as Kaplan's work suggests. On the contrary, Sierra Leone's civil war was, in its essence, entirely modern, drawing as it did on the latest terror war techniques and spawning innovations as well.

The rise of new kinds of warfare has unnerved many, and inspired political analysts to perceive changes in the world of conflict. Kaldor created an influential dichotomy for examining the kinds of conflicts that erupted following the fall of the Soviet Union in January 1992 and the close of the Cold War era. She characterized post–Cold War conflicts as "new wars." These new sorts of conflicts are "post-modern" in that they differ fundamentally "from the wars that could be said to be characteristic of classical modernity" (Kaldor 1999: 2)—that is, war "as we have known it for the last two centuries" (152). One central difference is that "the goals of the new wars are about identity politics in contrast to the geo-political or ideological goals of earlier wars" (6). "In all the new wars," she continued, "there are local people and places who struggle against the politics of exclusivism" that arose in weak or corrupt states (10). If the military units of new wars are irregular and "highly decentralized" instead of the "vertically organized hierarchical units that were typical of 'old wars,'" Kaldor also depicted the "new globalized war economy" as similarly "decentralized" and "almost exactly the opposite of the war economies of the two world wars" (8, 9). "The key to any long-term solution," she asserted, "is the restoration of legitimacy, the reconstitution of the control of organized violence by public authorities, whether local, national or global" (10).

As with Kaplan, Samuel Huntington (1996), and many other Western political analysts, one senses in Kaldor's work nostalgia for the past and dread for the future. Via their shared view, the apparent wildness and uncertainty of post–Cold War conflicts compares most unfavorably with prior eras. Collectively, their take is that this is not just a new era but a worse one. It is a selective conception. Kalyvas aptly observes that "our understanding of violence is culturally defined" (2001: 115). While Western observers may see a more acceptable form of warfare in earlier times, the use of mustard gas in the First World War, nuclear bombs in the Second, napalm and cluster bombs in Southeast Asia, and so on suggest that so-called old wars were just as appalling and more deadly than anything arising in contemporary times.

That said, the terror warfare that emerged in Sierra Leone proved to be a highly effective means of conducting war in that country. While the form of military engagement that emerged there may have been innovative and adapted to local context, it is difficult to see how it represented something entirely new. With regard to civil wars in "old" and "new" eras, Kalyvas asserts that "both the perception that violence in old civil wars is limited, disciplined, or understandable and the view that violence in new civil wars is senseless, gratuitous and uncontrolled [fail] to find support in available evidence" (2001: 116). De Waal proposes a related argument. For him, Kaldor's idea of new wars merely "describes conflicts in less governed countries, rather than truly new forms of conflict" (2009: 101). Research for this book supports these conclusions.

Understanding the nature of Sierra Leone's war requires a look at its causes. There are many possible sources. Some argue that the war mainly came from outside Sierra Leone. This perspective lays much of the blame on Charles Taylor for creating the RUF and inspiring their tactics of terror and atrocity. Koroma, for example, notes that "the fire of rebel conflict which enveloped Liberia was lit in Sierra Leone in 1991 in a nightmarish glow of death and destruction" (1996: 138). Prior to this event, during the presidencies of Stevens and Momoh, which extended into a third decade and up to the beginning of civil war, Koroma contends that "the Sierra Leonean was treated with a respectable measure of decency" and "remained a respected individual with equality before the law." Despite economic difficulties, "the citizen indulged in merriment at the least opportunity." He summed up life in Sierra Leone as "easy and casual with few molestations" (251). Following the RUF's incursion into Kailahun, "Traumatic events unknown in the annals of [Sierra Leonean] existence became the daily experience of many a citizen." To Koroma, Sierra Leone's civil war "transformed a once gentle, hospitable people into remorseless killers" (252).

Koroma's view of life under Presidents Stevens and Momoh is unquestionably the minority perspective among those who write about Sierra Leone. Indeed, one issue that most commentators seem to agree on is that life for most Sierra Leoneans at the dawn of war was difficult and conspicuously unfair. This is suggested in Alie's history of Sierra Leone. Near the book's close, he declares that "Sierra Leone's economic situation is in a deplorable state." Published in 1990, a year before civil war began, the book ends with a warning: "Until serious efforts are made to radically restructure the economy and control mismanagement, smuggling and corruption, the living standards of the people will continue to deteriorate" (Alie 1990: 273). Keen rightly points out that "although the 1991 [RUF] rebellion in the country was ignited by civil war in Liberia, it was the underlying resentments inside the country that fuelled the rebellion" (2005: 9).

The nature of Sierra Leonean governance has long been central to the nation's problems. Christensen, for example, has remarked that "if we accept the idea that the state can be approached as a sovereign, unitary power centre our fantasy will, indeed, collapse when looking at the state of Sierra Leone" (2012: 62). Add to this the fact that, as Abdullah and Muana observe, the role of alienated youth is central to understanding Sierra Leone's civil war (1998: 172). Taken together, if the ragtag band of RUF commandos had not entered Sierra Leone in March 1991, it appears likely that another rebellion—one perhaps not as vicious as the RUF but a violent rebellion nonetheless—eventually would have surfaced in Sierra Leone. At the same time, while it may be fashionable to declare that Sierra Leone's reputation for governmental weakness and inequality could have emerged only following the nation's independence in 1961, that was not the case. The seeds of disparity, fertilized with violence, were first planted centuries, not decades, before civil war took place.

Slaves, Chiefs, and Stevens

"Sierra Leone" evolved from the Portuguese Serra Lyoa, a name allegedly given by mid-fifteenth-century voyagers to the lionlike mountains on the peninsula jutting into the Atlantic (Fyfe 1962: 1). Shaw provides a second take on the story: the term means "lion uplands," which a specific Portuguese explorer, Pedro da Sintra, chose in 1462 "because the sound of the waves crashing on the rocks reminded him of the roaring of lions" (2002: 27). The peninsula is where the nation's capital, Freetown, is perched. From the start, the Portuguese traded manufactured European goods for many local commodities, including the "most lucrative of all—slaves" (28). English traders "replaced Portuguese traders in the domination of the slave trade" in the eighteenth century (29) and effectively allowed slave trading to continue until 1929 (38).[1]

Mbembe asserts that "any historical account of the rise of modern terror needs to address slavery" (2019: 74). This examination of the roots of Sierra Leone's civil war thus begins with three aspects of the international slave trade, as they have direct relevance to this study. Collectively, they have left profound impacts on the landscapes of gender norms, family life, and society, and deep imprints on Sierra Leone's terror-based warfare.

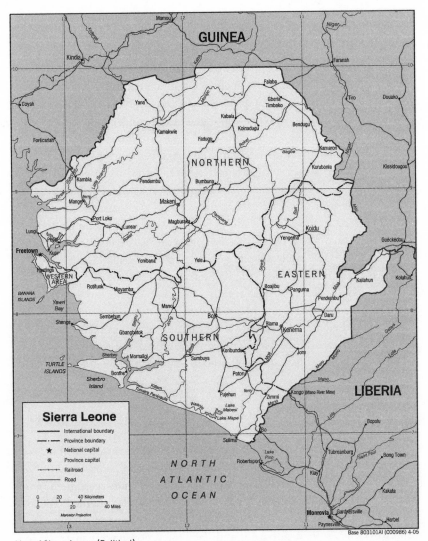

Map of Sierra Leone (Political)
Source: U.S. Central Intelligence Agency, 2005.

The first arises from how the slaves were secured. "Unlike the large slave-trading states" in other parts of West Africa, "this region had no major political or geographical boundary separating those who raided and those who were taken as slaves: the small chiefdoms into which Sierra Leone was organized included both those who raided for slaves and those who could be captured by raiders." European trading agents fueled the conflict fires by regularly supplying arms "to both sides in a dispute" (Shaw 2002: 31). Over time, the sharp uptick in violent conflicts increasingly involved male youth as fighters. Shepler, for example, notes the rise of two kinds of "war boys": mercenaries from nearby areas who terrorized people in locations they controlled (Shepler 2014: 47–48, referencing Siddle 1968: 50), and those who worked as bodyguards and members of private armies for Mende chiefs (Little 1967: 29, discussed in Shepler 2014: 48). In the British colonial era, elders opposed to the colonial creation of paramount chiefs (more on that shortly) mobilized male youth in active opposition. Shepler adds that the "pattern of recruitment of young men for political violence continued into the independence era" (Shepler 2014: 48), including using male youth "to rig elections and threaten voters" (49, referencing Nunley 1987: 59). She concludes that "there is a continuity in the practice of recruiting disaffected youth into violent political protest, and a tradition of youth violence as an expression of wider political discontent" (Shepler 2014: 48, 49). In short, the slave trade era and the local wars it incited created an unsettling trend in Sierra Leone: using male youth to intimidate and terrorize according to the wishes and agendas of powerful men.

Second, the slave trade shaped gender relations in significant ways. The slaving era commenced following da Sintra's arrival into what is now Freetown in 1462. By the eighteenth century, British traders had overtaken their Portuguese counterparts and began to dominate the slave trade. Shaw considers the mid-eighteenth century "a time of unprecedented slaving and warfare" and cites an estimate that four to six thousand slaves exited Sierra Leone every year (Rodney 1970: 250–251, cited in Shaw 2002: 29). Speaking of that century as well, Fyfe observes that "the slave trade gave a livelihood" to British manufacturers, middlemen, shippers, and investors while awarding "Africans a market where they could easily obtain European goods at the price of one another's bodies" (1962: 12).

Crucially, the bodies traded in international and domestic slave markets were gender specific. Starting in the seventeenth century across most of West Africa, "most slaves exported through the Atlantic trade were men, while most slaves retained for the internal African market were women." The lowered ratio of men to women in the region "often increased women's agricultural workloads" (Shaw 2002: 32) and "facilitated polygynous marriage, enabling rulers and wealthy merchants in particular to marry large numbers of wives" (Patrick Manning 1990: 131–132, quoted in Shaw 2002: 33).

The "expanding presence of female slaves in polygynous marriages" attracted Shaw's attention because it appears to have opened the door to "the supernatural dangers of wives within their husband's household" (Shaw 2002: 33). Ferme's study of ethnic Mende culture and society in Sierra Leone broadly supports Shaw's finding. She notes that the idea of unbridled femininity, which emerged as a legacy of slaving, posed an intimate threat to household stability. Ferme reports that in Mende society (though it appears to have been believed by other Sierra Leonean ethnic groups as well) "women must be controlled and remarried if husbandless, lest they pose a threat to the social order" (2001: 110). Women are "reminders of both the existence of an order of concealment and the social instability of power" (111). The theme of femininity as both mysterious and threatening to male power surfaces again later in this book as a key motivator of widespread sexual violence during the war.

The third major theme is slavery's sculpting influence over patron-client relations. Social relationships are always vertical and hierarchical, starting in households, where husbands are dominant patrons and wives are dominated, restricted, and dependent clients. Ferme observes that "the links between marriage and slavery help place in context the degrees of dependence that underpin the Mende notion that everybody is under someone's patronage" (84). Notions of "individual autonomy and independence" are considered threatening, and "those who are on their own are liable to be suspected of antisocial behavior, such as witchcraft" (110). As I will detail, patronage, particularly that of the patrimonial "Big Man" kind, is a fundamental component of Sierra Leonean society. Slave economies appear to have increased the perceived stature of rulers. "Some rulers were called kings," Fyfe observed, "and had ascendancy over others." During this period, however, "their powers were limited." In fact, local Sierra Leonean rulers merely "lived by trade" (1962: 10). Their prosperity was transitory, since "their riches, European manufactures, were unproductive consumer goods, soon worn out, drunk, or given away to their subjects, who looked to them for maintenance" (11). Shaw notes how, during the slave trade era, chiefs had "obligations toward those in their chiefdoms [which] kept their wealth circulating among their dependents" (2002: 36).

The situation changed dramatically once Sierra Leone became a British protectorate in 1896 (effectively, it was a colony), after it had first become "a settlement for freed slaves in 1787" (Keen 2005: 8). Almost from the beginning, governance of the British protectorate was informed by the weakness of its foreign rulers and their increasing reliance on Sierra Leonean chiefs. In an interview, a paramount chief shared his take on the history and social standing of his position. "Chiefs were called kings before the colonial masters came," the paramount chief stated. However, "Because the British had a king in the UK, they called us paramount chiefs. Since the British considered themselves superior to us, they didn't want us to take names like king and queen." The chief also explained his role as an intensely powerful patriarch: "The paramount chief is the be-all and end-all of the chiefdom. For everything, people look to the paramount chief for solutions: he's their president, their magistrate, he's their everything. The paramount chief is always seen as a father who should be able to solve all types of problems. Everything depends on me. My authority is vested in the will of God."

Asking for directions to the paramount chief's house prior to my interview with him underscored his profound authority and stature in the postwar era. One town resident called it "the powerful house." Another simply described it as "the finest house," making it impossible to miss. He was correct. Mention of precise markings was indeed unnecessary, given its opulence compared to all other town structures. The house was in fact a compound composed of a series of dwellings, with a courtyard inside the walls and a wide verandah near the courtyard's entrance. There sat perhaps twenty elders and a couple of elite male youth.

While a form of Sierra Leonean aristocracy had existed long before the arrival of British colonials, the British dramatically boosted the power and authority of some chiefs while effectively squashing the rest. The British integrated them into their governance and economic structure and, ultimately, became dependent on them. This ironic alignment drew from one particular precept of governance. Keen notes, "In accordance with the British colonial tradition of indirect rule, the powers of the most important chiefs, known as Paramount Chiefs, were increased" (2005: 10). One purpose of indirect rule was to keep political action localized and limit prospects for colony-wide resistance. Yet the means for doing this—awarding paramount chiefs with unrestricted, absolute local authority—permanently and indelibly changed Sierra Leone.

It was quite a deal. Those fortunate enough to become paramount chiefs assumed lifetime positions that only their descendants could inherit. The British helped suppress their rivals. Among other benefits, the new local overlords "received generous salaries" and "kept large numbers of slaves well into the twentieth century." Breaking with tradition, these new chiefs "were in many ways less reliant on their supporters." Instead, the British-anointed paramount chiefs did the reverse: they increased the reliance of supporters on *them*, such as by seeking to control the new development programs that held patronage potential (Keen 2005: 10). In the end, Reno observed that "chiefs built their authority with British aid but in a manner that denied colonial rulers direct control" (1995: 35). Although "the British taught the new [Paramount] chiefs to expect direct economic gain for their political loyalty," they also relied on paramount chiefs to govern their locality themselves; to personally become the local authority for health, education and the law; and to control all settlement, immigration, and land issues in their territories (46). This brand-new set of powers and privileges transformed handpicked local chiefs into unassailable royals, each in command of their very own chiefdom. Indirect colonial rule ended up creating these power centers—each controlled by one man—that transformed Sierra Leone into a quilt of chiefdoms.

Two major outcomes from this curious colonial setup require mention. First, the virtually untethered powers of paramount chiefs naturally invited overreach and exploitation. As Keen noted, "Discontent over chiefs' abuses was common in Sierra Leone, often centering on excessive cash levies, unpopular land allocations, forced labour, and the punishment of dissenters." Ominously, he adds, "All of this helped store up anger which erupted later" (2005: 10). In fact, it began to spill over during the colonial era. Keen relates that in ethnic Mende areas in southern and eastern Sierra Leone, for example, "the 'youngmen'—that is, those males with little power in chiefdom affairs—were frequently involved in violence against chiefs" (11). Male youth drawn or dragged into thuggish service for the powerful is a theme that has surfaced regularly in Sierra Leone's history.

The second outcome concerns the rise and pervasive power of patrimonial governance. It is a simple concept. Patrimonialism, Richards explains, "involves redistributing national resources as marks of *personal* favour to followers" (1996: 34, emphasis in original). Followers, in turn, "respond with loyalty to the leader rather than the institution the leader represents." Murphy notes that "in prewar Liberia and Sierra Leone, the president and senior officials in the government were 'big men' who provided, through personal ties, what a moribund national infrastructure failed to provide." In a patrimonial state, "rulers treat the territory and subjects as one large household controlled for their use and benefit." The system is fundamentally and emphatically undemocratic, unequal, and extractive, given that "the nation itself is viewed as the patrimony of the elite" (Murphy 2003: 67). Patrimonial systems deliver extensive and unchecked power, authority, and wealth to Big Men—everything a state or system has to offer, essentially—while infantilizing and controlling their followers, with threatened or actual violence if necessary. Obey the commands of your patron and you can access food, land, work, and so on. That is the deal: *the Big Man commands, the follower submits.* Resist and you invite ruin.

De Waal asserts that patrimonial systems are organized according to "the marketplace of loyalties," which is guided by some "basic rules of political bargaining." According to de Waal, "Provincial elite members seek to maximize the price they can obtain for their loyalty from metropolitan elites (mostly governments). They do this using the tools at their disposal, which include votes, extending or withdrawing economic cooperation, and the use of violence" (2009: 103–104). What is striking about Sierra Leone's case is how the British colonialists established a patrimonial system and made it hum by assuming the role of second-level players. The terms of trade that de Waal describes between the periphery and the center regularly played into the hands of paramount chiefs, not the British. This new arrangement set the stage for what followed: the "Shadow State," which Reno defines as "the emergence of rulers drawing authority from their ability to control markets and their material rewards" (1995: 3).

The economic market that increasingly shaped this new shadow state, and the patrimonial system that underlay it, was diamonds. When diamonds were discovered in Sierra Leone in 1927, the British colonial administration responded by signing a concessionary agreement with the Sierra Leone Selection Trust (SLST), a subsidiary of the De Beers diamond enterprise, in 1932 (Reno 1995: 47). However, three challenges to controlling the diamond trade in Sierra Leone presented themselves. One is their size: diamonds can be hugely valuable yet small, making them easy to conceal. A second is the fact that many diamonds in Sierra Leone are alluvial, available to anyone sifting through sand, sediment, topsoil, and gravel in the right place. The third is their widespread distribution. Sierra Leone's diamond mining fields eventually covered over a quarter (28.5 percent) of the entire country (Gberie 2005: 22). These three facts set the stage for a booming illicit mining economy that emerged in the colonial era, helped fuel predatory governments and civil war following independence, and persists as a governmental challenge (though perhaps to a lesser degree than in earlier eras) since the war's end.

British government officials evidently believed that they would address this trio of challenges via the new SLST, which would "provide the legal means to control illicit indigenous mining." But that was never going to work: paramount chiefs with diamonds in their chiefdoms had other ideas.[2] The chiefs "increasingly identified their informal involvement in the area's economic development as an additional 'customary' right" (Reno 1995: 48). In diamond areas, this meant that so-called strangers (that is, tenants) paid chiefs rent to mine for diamonds "in exchange for protection" (49). Over time, these strangers included "wealthier African and Lebanese strangers already involved in illicit mining." Chiefs in diamond-rich Kono "approved licenses, assigned lands for mining and collected a 'surface rent'" (63). The colonial government, in turn, tried to purchase the loyalty of local chiefs, giving them salaries and "loans for cars, home construction and education for [their] sons" (53).

The British unwittingly had created and let loose an entire corps of powerful overlords. The paramount chiefs were being enriched formally with salaries and benefits from the colonial administration and informally via rents and licenses paid by strangers that allowed them to mine illicitly. No one could control them, though the British administration certainly tried. Unfortunately for them, they relied on men—holding positions *they* had invented— to maintain stability and control in their colony. Yet their efforts only ended up furthering the chiefs' wealth and power, often at British expense (Reno 1995: 62). Chiefs with diamond mines in their chiefdoms became especially powerful and wealthy. To this day, Sierra Leone's paramount chiefs lie at the core of how Sierra Leone really operates.

One outcome of the emerging system, which the chiefs dominated, was how it laid waste to formal government structures. Smillie describes the result:

> In minimizing direct control over most of the country, the British colonial authorities had, by the time of independence, created the appearance of a national infrastructure without investing huge sums. As a result, the writ of the central government was only wafer-thin. Police, courts, army and civil servants were a veneer on the surface of colonial life, more prominent in Freetown than elsewhere, and weaker with every mile away from the capital. It was essentially a system of tributors: of chiefs, Lebanese entrepreneurs and a handful of foreign companies willing to collect or pay taxes to the centre as long as they were given a significant measure of freedom in the periphery. (Smillie 2010: 97)

The system Smillie calls one of tributors is the same one Reno calls a shadow state, and what many others consider patrimonialism. However it is labeled, it signaled how government structures and systems mainly supported a parallel system of power and influence. Starting in the colonial era, the national center was exceptionally weak while local overlords held sway.

It is useful to set two outcomes of colonial rule—the weak central government and the rise of the paramount chiefs—into context. Ever since I first entered the Sierra Leone scene in 1997, I have read about and heard Sierra Leoneans and foreigners alike complain about weak governance and endemic corruption. Certainly I have found both generally to be present. To be sure, feeble public service, fraud and bribery, and so on have the power to frustrate and appall, particularly in a country as poor and unequal as Sierra Leone.

Yet the collective stigma these characteristics promote also serve up an ahistoric distortion. In Sierra Leone, the central government was not constructed to lead, much less stand on its own, given the unprecedented power of the paramount chiefs. Meanwhile, handfuls of empowered strangers (amid a breathtaking expanse of disempowered residents) upheld this new structure. The official government remains feeble because it is not really the point. British colonial officials in Sierra Leone ended up as mere cogs in a system of power and wealth accumulation largely orchestrated by their most lasting local creation: the paramount chiefs. Though bumped from their perch during the war period, the chiefs returned to prominence right after the war, and they remain powerful today.

Fortunately for the chiefs and others benefiting from the colonial system, Sierra Leone's first prime minister embraced it. The new era of independence was not accompanied by any significant governmental alterations. On the contrary, a telling trait of Sir Milton Margai, who became the nation's first prime minister on July 9, 1960, was his disdain for reform generally and youth in particular. As Alie notes, "Sir Milton was a conservative ruler who was opposed to change. He had great respect for traditional authority and attached much importance to age, maturity and experience. Thus, he refused to be pressurized into elevating young Sierra Leoneans to positions of supreme authority." The prime minister supported the patrimonial status quo. His political party "worked mainly through chiefs and other influential people." Sir Milton also "detested mass participation in politics, for he felt this would lead to dictatorship" (Alie 1990: 226). After Sir Milton's brother, Sir Albert Margai, succeeded him as prime minister in 1964 (during which time "corruption was rife" and "the civil service was unreliable" [236]), Siaka Stevens became the nation's third and by far its most impactful national leader in 1967.

Stevens lorded over a purely neocolonial state, with a system for control and resource extraction that built on the handiwork of British colonials. The primary difference from the colonial era was that most of Sierra Leone's wealth and power stayed in the hands of individuals: Stevens and his colleagues in collusion—paramount chiefs and Lebanese diamond traders, among others. This allowed Stevens to run the country of Sierra Leone like a private company. Although Stevens has had his supporters (Koroma, for example, speaks of him as a "great man" [1996: ix]), the following fact underscores the effectiveness of Stevens's efforts to use the state to enrich himself and his associates. Before Stevens came to power, diamonds had created about USD $200 million in formal economy profits in Sierra Leone. By 1987, two years after he had retired from office, "the diamonds that passed through formal taxable channels were valued at only $100,000" (Reno 1998: 116) or .005 percent of the earlier total.

Stevens balanced profiteering on a colossal scale with a general neglect of the country's expanding poverty. As Keen notes, "Whilst Stevens built up his personal fortune and power-base through the clever use of patronage and intimidation, his mineral-rich and fertile country remained one of the poorest in the world" (2005: 16). He and his associates also "destroyed the effectiveness of most state institutions, starving them of formal sources of revenue and turning them into extensions of their private patronage networks" (Reno 1998: 116). In Sierra Leone, "informal markets become instruments of the 'big men's' power," which caused "the formal economy as well as government services to atrophy" (Murphy 2003: 68).

Even though the rapacious style of rule of Stevens (1967–1985) and his doomed, handpicked successor, Joseph Momoh (1985–1992), left many Sierra Leoneans destitute, the government nonetheless attracted "resources from many patrons by virtue of [Sierra Leone's] poverty" (Reno 1998: 114). In other words, intentionally undermining much of their government and economy (largely by siphoning off rivers of revenue) opened the door to direct outside support that fueled Stevens's patrimonial system. Keen notes how international food aid during Stevens's tenure (most of it coming from the United States) "was used as an instrument of patronage" (2005: 24). In Stevens's Sierra Leone, aid from the outside was merely another resource to control and exploit. War only increased international development aid, which rose from 123.3 percent of internal revenue in prewar 1988 to 178.2 percent in wartime 1993 (Reno 1998: 115). In 1996, long after Stevens had left the scene and the civil war had begun, Richards declared that those international donor agencies seeking to support government reform were "leaning not on a real set of institutions, but on a façade" (1996: 60). It is the same metaphor that Reno employed to describe how shadow states (such as in Sierra Leone) "rely upon the willingness of outsiders to recognize the façade of formal sovereignty" (2000: 437). He also noted that independent Sierra Leone "developed behind the façade of statehood" (2003: 45–46). These depictions are similar to Smillie's evocation of Sierra Leone's "wafer-thin" central government in colonial times.

Despite this long-standing reality, many outsiders persistently have failed to realize that Sierra Leone's state of public service is weak by design. The oversight is reflected in the following recollection. In an interview, a veteran international agency official described her capacity-building work with the Sierra Leonean government prior to the start of the civil war. After two years of effort, the official concluded (with considerable exasperation) that there was "no way" to enhance the capabilities of Sierra Leonean government officials; corruption had made reliable public service, in her view, a complete and absolute impossibility. As with so many of her colleagues, the official saw Sierra Leone as it should exist, not as it did.

The Stevens era is often referred to as the time when Sierra Leonean society became unglued and fell into decline. Take, for example, the following description of merely one outcome of the Siaka Stevens era: "Under Stevens's rule, most societal institutions were completely corrupted. . . . Institutions, both public and private, were successfully emasculated through a combination of co-optation, bribery, intimidation, repression, and blackmail. . . . The consequence of this official culture of corruption and mismanagement was the internalization in Sierra Leone society of corruption as 'a way of life'" (Bøås 2007: 43–44). Siaka Stevens used his control over Sierra Leone's government to devour it. Beyond those enriching themselves inside his patronage system, little improved and much collapsed. In this context, Stevens's choice of a successor proved, in the short term at least, shrewd and cynical. Like a good patron, he chose a loyal client: Maj. Gen. Joseph Saidu Momoh, who certainly knew who his sponsor was. Stevens and his enormous wealth were safe. Yet Momoh proved largely incapable. Assessments of his abilities have not stood the test of time particularly well. Gberie, for example, describes him as "a benign figure, if a thoroughly incompetent one" (2005: 37). Kandeh considered Momoh a leader who "clearly lacked the stature and political acumen of Stevens" (1999: 352). Peters states, "Foolishly, President Momoh openly advertised the extent to which political or state patronage was now unavailable to the younger generation." His comment in a speech that education was "a privilege and not a right" was subsequently employed by the RUF "as one of its justifications to go to war" (2011a: 46).

Momoh's era, in addition, was a time when poverty and desperation accelerated. Under pressure from the International Monetary Fund (IMF), the government cut most state subsidies. As a result, in 1989–1990, the price of gasoline rose 300 percent and rice by 180 percent (Reno 1995: 171). Shaw notes that the leone had dropped from Le2 against the British pound in 1977 to Le1,000 by 1992, the year Momoh was ousted (2002: 195). In the 1980s, at the end of Stevens's administration and the beginning of Momoh's, "civil servants received only sporadic salary payments." Television broadcasts ended in 1987 when the minister of information simply sold the TV transmitter to an investor from Kuwait. Radio transmissions beyond Freetown ended in 1989 when the radio tower tipped over and wasn't repaired (Reno 2003: 48). In short, Momoh took over a state "on the verge of collapse" (Kandeh 1999: 352) and ran it into the ground. By the end of Momoh's tenure as head of state, when Sierra Leone's economy was in freefall (helped in large part by the government's economic austerity measures), the government allegedly became even more predatory than under Stevens (353), and government services and capacity, despite some efforts to counteract Momoh's influence, remained poor and corrupted.

One final dimension of Sierra Leone's quarter century under Stevens and Momoh requires consideration. As background, it is important to note that Stevens encountered military and civilian resistance to his rule. It began the day after he was appointed prime minister on March 21, 1967 (he had just won national elections), when a military coup swept him out of office (Alie 1990: 233). Just over a month later (April 26), Stevens returned from Guinea, where he had fled, to become prime minister a second time (239). There was an alleged coup attempt against Stevens in 1970 and an actual one in March 1971. The following month, a new constitution awarded Stevens "enormous powers" as executive president of a new republic (242).

President Stevens subsequently created his Special Security Division (SSD, popularly known as Siaka Stevens's Dogs) in 1973 to intimidate opponents but also, unsurprisingly given his experience with coup attempts, "as a counter to the regular army." Their members, together with "informally recruited" thugs loyal to his political party, were known to intimidate voters, opposing politicians, and protesting students, sometimes with violence (Keen 2005: 17). A Cuban-trained police force, the Internal Security Unit (ISU, popularly known as I Shoot You) were among those who joined Stevens's efforts to "suppress civil and political rights and instil fear in the population" (Denov 2010: 55). Although Stevens reportedly was known to declare that "force is the only language the ordinary man understands" (Kandeh 1999: 359), there was another dimension to his motivations: he mistrusted the national army. It was another trend that Stevens created: undermining the nation's military and hiring others to fill the gap.

CHAPTER 6

Rebellion Rising

No Way Out

Sierra Leone has worn hegemonic masculinity effortlessly. The theory fuses gender to power relations, making its influence comprehensive. Hegemonic masculinity explains how the predominant masculine model legitimates "unequal gender relations between men and women, between masculinity and femininity, and among masculinities" (Messerschmidt 2019: 86). In Sierra Leone, Big Man hegemons have ruled the heavily gendered landscape as masters of the patrimony. They maintain age-old demands for male and female youth to follow through and meet the expectations that tradition has marked out for them. The pressures on both are tinged with submission: to chiefs, male elders, and other power brokers for male youth, and nearly all men (husbands especially) for female youth.

By the time of the Siaka Stevens era, Sierra Leone had a colossal youth underclass, virtually all of whom had struggled to move ahead under the collective thumbs of their male hegemons. Since the days of the international slave trade, female youth (and adult women) were viewed as threats to male power who must be subjugated and controlled. This powerful theme surfaces regularly in this book (and is highlighted in chapter 19). Male youth in this fix inspire many names to describe their inescapably difficult and emasculating circumstances, such as being "sufferers" who are "disgruntled." They proved to be exceptionally unpopular. Indeed, it is striking just how many names have been used to describe all or some of the male component of this massive cohort (the critiques are gender specific). Kandeh, for example, considers Sierra Leone's "lumpens" as "an inchoate mass of thugs, hoodlums, pickpockets, transients, vagabonds, panhandlers, and discharged jailbirds" (1999: 356–357). Yusuf Bangura asserts that such youth are members of "a stratum of Sierra Leonean society that is hooked on drugs, alcohol and street gambling," have "very limited education" and are "prone to gangster type activities" (2004: 20–21). Abdullah adds a cultural dimension to this social stratum. "Lumpen" male youth have an "anti-social" culture that leaves them "prone to criminal behaviour, petty theft, drugs, drunkenness and gross indiscipline," are "largely unemployed and unemployable," and "live by their wits or . . . have one foot in what is generally referred to as the informal or underground economy" (2004: 45). Former president Joseph Momoh chimed in while in exile in Guinea (he fled Sierra Leone in 1992). Describing new Sierra Leone Army (SLA) conscripts, he warned that many of them probably were "undesirables, waifs, strays, layabouts and bandits" (quoted in Stevens 1996: 1676).

How did so many young male Sierra Leoneans become demonized pariahs? The general implication arising from the vigorous name-calling is that these boys are to blame for their problems. They are not like the rest of us, the collective thinking suggests. Somehow, a large number of the nation's male youth went bad, transforming themselves into threats to mainstream society. Something is wrong with them. They deserve to be despised.

Perhaps not. A persistent trend in Sierra Leonean history, and a central theme in this book, has been the repeated use of male youth to serve the purposes of powerful men. Exploiting or enticing desperate young males to perform violence and intimidation on the behalf of Big Men is an unfortunate tradition dating back centuries. Beginning with war boys in the slave era, chiefs, Stevens, and a host of other politicians and military leaders all have used male youth to terrify and maim. And they all exploited an easy target: those pitched by society toward public failure.

Drawing from literature on Sierra Leone, here are two theories for how this happened. Both focus on the patriarchs that dominate Sierra Leone, and how they have mistreated young people. Shepler's field research highlighted the following finding: "Probably the number one reason given by Sierra Leoneans for the war is *we no lehk wisehf* (we don't like/love ourselves)" (2014: 44, emphasis in original). After admitting that such an explanation "may sound unbelievable," she interprets the Krio phrase not as self-hatred but as a "a critique of the breakdown of a patrimonial political and economic system." Then she explains her point: "What Sierra Leoneans are really saying when they say 'we no lehk wisehf' is that people in power do not do enough to help people without power. In particular, elders do not help the youth, with jobs, education, or even access to corrupt political systems" (44, 45, emphasis in original). In this take, the refusal of elders to assist youth ultimately led young people to rise up.

Richards and Peters have highlighted the "crisis of youth" as the main cause of war. Just as in Shepler's analysis, it focuses on those with power (elders) and those who do not have it (youth). Richards argues that the patron-client social system that arose after the slave era was based on the following: dependents got protection via their "attachment to an owner" (Richards 2006a: 202). The marriage system locked these patron-client relations into place by trapping male youth. The ruse drew from the fact that, in general, older men had the resources to pay bridewealth and marry women while male youth did not. The females that older men married usually were much younger, often child brides. Wealthy older men could afford to accumulate many young wives.

Having many young females all married to the same old man opened the door for wives to have affairs with unmarried male youth. These affairs—real or alleged—awarded wealthy husbands with two enticing options. They could drag an alleged male lover into a customary court to "extract substantial damages" from the male youth, often in the form of farm labor. Or they could take him to a formal court, where a male youth found guilty could be charged with "women damage" (that is, adultery) and then "face fines they cannot pay" (Richards 2006a: 203, 204). Either way, the male youth entered into slave-like relations with the rich, older man who took him to court.

The plight of female youth, who essentially are consigned to being overlooked and maybe married off to old men, is discounted (or overlooked) in these analyses. Their situation has been just as subordinate and even more confined than the circumstances male youth faced. The difference seems to lie in the very public failure and humiliation that male youth routinely and historically have endured. The punishments that their female youth counterparts have sustained mostly have been private. In many wartime cases, girls and female youth were little more than property, snatched to become sex slaves, concubine wives, and household laborers. Female youth in Sierra Leonean society, as well as in most analyses of Sierra Leone and its war, are distinguished by their frightening invisibility.

The focus on male youth nonetheless is vital, partly due to their unintended role as dynamic drivers of Sierra Leone's recent history. Richards asserts that the inability for many male youth in rural areas to marry led some to migrate. It is again worth noting what such youth are called: in this case, "outlaws and vagrants" who "run away" from fines and punishments and end up in diamond mines or forest reserves (Richards 2006a: 204). If they go to the mines, they generally work under "gang masters" (commonly called supporters) who serve as "protectors and patrons to young men" in circumstances that tend to be exceptionally exploitative of miners (205). Peters states that male youth who become miners end up "in the pay of one or another of the stop-at-nothing lords of the diamond fields" (2011a: 53). For Richards, the mines constitute another system "held together by the patriarchal values and patrimonial social institutions associated with post-slavery societies" (2006a: 205). It is an indication of just how difficult it was to escape patrimonial control and how slave-like the options were. Whether male youth remained in villages or escaped, the impediments that many have faced in securing a traditional marriage "[keep] poor men as youths, with limited family (and thus social) responsibilities well into their middle age." Richards asserts that, during the civil war, some male youth became fighters "to accumulate bride wealth, while others use[d] sexual violence to express rage and frustration at a system that denies them the chance to form recognized families" (204). This explanation for the obsessive sexual violence that surfaced during Sierra Leone's civil war will be considered later in this book.

One possible way to escape the patrimonial screws was to gain a good education. Yet Peters states that "the economic crisis of the 1980s" transformed this potential avenue for success into "a false hope." Primary and secondary education collapsed during this period, he notes, leaving "even the lowest rungs on the [education] ladder inaccessible" to many youth. Indeed, "children and youth in the rural areas were among the first to drop out of school." This left rural youth with three options. They could "remain in the village and involve [themselves] in (semi-subsistence) agriculture and (for a boy) labour indebtedness, or (for a girl) early, and often near-obligatory marriage." They could migrate to the mines temporarily or forever, "to try one's luck in the alluvial mining areas, where the boys laboured and the girls would provide sexual or domestic services." Or they could migrate to Freetown or another city and "hope for some kind of unskilled work in the urban informal sector" (Peters 2011a: 53).

Despite the urban dimension, Peters, like Richards, focuses on the "socioeconomic crisis among rural youth" in prewar Sierra Leone. Peters also shares his take on why there was civil war in Sierra Leone. He suggests that two factors—the simultaneous collapse of the patrimonial system under Stevens and Momoh and the marginalization of rural youth—"are particularly pernicious where they interact." The result is "a highly explosive mix" in which "rebellion of an extremely destructive nature is a possible outcome." This is precisely what took place in Sierra Leone, Peters concludes, as patrimonial collapse and youth marginalization "resulted in a decade-long war" (2011a: 61).

Did this combination really lead to war? If a patrimonial state begins to fail, Big Men would have difficulty controlling male youth. Since this did not seem to occur, it would appear that patrimonialism retained considerable strength, even in the face of economic difficulty. In addition, most Sierra Leonean male youth never enlisted in any military unit. As Barker and Ricardo observe, "only a minority of young men participate in conflicts." We know much less about youth majorities who resist engagement in war than the relatively few who join. "The vast majority of young men" in Liberia and Sierra Leone did not participate in either civil war, "even those unemployed and out of school," who might seem to have had a reason do to so (Barker and Ricardo 2006: 181). This begs the following question: *why did so few male youth join in*? The answer remains elusive because, as will be explained, the rebels abducted most of their members, terrorized potential supporters, and undercut the possibility of leading a popular rebellion.

The focus on the state of rural youth by Richards and Peters is complemented by Abdullah's description of male youth outliers who thronged prewar Freetown. Abdullah paints a picture of a particularly surly crowd. Again, one gets the sense that poor, excluded, and indignant male youth in Sierra Leone are undeserving of compassion or empathy. Shepler posits a reason why: "Undisciplined youth has always been a dangerous social class and always controlled for political reasons" (2014: 47). Abdullah's description of unruly male youth in prewar Freetown presents them unquestionably as volatile and, much like their impoverished and trapped counterparts in diamond mines and villages, cut off from the rest of society. What differs, it appears, is that urban youth were much less prone to taking social condemnation sitting down. As "products of a rebellious youth culture" (Abdullah 1998: 204), Freetown's members were defiant and sometimes aggressive.

Abdullah cites the origins of unruly urban youth in the "militant Youth League" founded in 1939. The Youth League tactic of "continuous agitation" influenced Sierra Leone's emerging labor movement in the 1950s. Siaka Stevens was a labor leader (of a sort) prior to becoming president. Once that occurred, he reversed course and moved strongly against outside agitators. For Abdullah, this pushed "students and youth" (it is not clear why these two groups are separate categories) to become "the informal opposition to the corrupt and decadent" ruling party, the All People's Congress (APC) (205, 207). While the APC and its political adversary, the Sierra Leone People's Party (SLPP), engaged urban youth in their youth wings, the youth themselves had no influence or power. Abdullah also characterizes the rise of "the so-called rarray boy culture" in dark terms: it is "male-specific" and "oppositional," and it "easily lends itself to violence" (208). Rarray Boys congregated in what were known as *potes* (Abdullah has defined a pote as "a meeting point, a place to hang out, a rendezvous, where youths congregate to smoke weed, gamble, and just talk" [2013: 216]). He states that youth who frequented potes loved *odelays*, which were outdoor carnivals known for the sort of "revelry and riotous behaviour" that "alienated them from the city inhabitants" (Abdullah 1998: 208). Over time, the Rarray Boys attracted middle-class male youth—some with education, some not, but nearly all of them unemployed—to their ranks. Potes no longer only featured groups of poor and undereducated male youth. Significantly, the expansion of pote members "coincided with the coming of reggae music and a decided turn to the political" (209). Abdullah and Muana also note that "the popularity of marijuana—the drug of choice—brought many participants to the *pote*" (1998: 174). As will be noted later in the book, marijuana grown in Sierra Leone was a relatively new arrival and, by itself, was potent enough to capture the minds and drive the actions of young people caught up in the war.

A turning point for youth in "this rebellious culture" came in 1977 (Abdullah 1998: 210), when students at Fourah Bay College (the national university) demonstrated for political reform and the ISU and "local unemployed youth" attacked them violently (Reno 2006: 48). Nonetheless, at least on the surface, the student demonstrators got results: government reforms and a general election. However, Gberie notes that, prior to the subsequent elections and referendum on a one-party state, the state intimidated voters and rigged the results (2005: 44). Referring to a trademark phrase from Bob Marley's music (one love), Abdullah says that during this tumultuous period "one love and brotherhood was the slogan" of the new pote membership, which combined, essentially, university students and other middle-class youth with the underclass youth who had originated pote traditions (1998: 210).

Over time, the declining economy and rising unemployment under Stevens and Momoh gathered these disparate "lumpenproletariat" together. The new mixing of youth across social and economic classes effectively created "an army of unemployed secondary school leavers, drop outs and university graduates" in the growing informal economic sector. "The talk about revolution" among "rebellious youths" in potes was one result, Abdullah states, as well as a merging of the two classes of young people into one (211). Changing terms that pote youth called themselves reflected this social integration: from "service man" individuals to "man dem" community members (210) to more revolutionary concepts like "comrade" and "brothers and sisters" (211). Abdullah ultimately argues that "the centrality and dynamics of [the] rebellious youth culture" in Freetown potes shaped "the process leading to the rebellion and war." "A lumpen social movement bred a lumpen social revolution," he concludes (223). Eventually, the RUF were at the head of the prewar resistance (and then the war itself). Abdullah acidly labels them "the ruffians" (222).

As the RUF "ruffians" allegedly germinated from underclass lumpens, it is revealing to note another of Abdullah's shorthand characterizations: that lumpens are "thugs" (207). It turns out that "thug" is a common way that Sierra Leone experts describe underclass youth, particularly those working for political parties (especially the APC ruling party). Abdullah twice calls youth who "do the dirty work" for politicians "thugs" (207, 208, 209). Kandeh notes that the APC politicians under Stevens used "urban thugs and rural drifters" to commit "violence and thuggery" on their behalf (1999: 359). The TRC spotted "an especially ominous development": "the emergence of 'drugging' as a means of preparing thugs to participate in electoral violence" (TRC 2004a: 57). Drugging young combatants prior to attacks later became a common pre-attack procedure during the war. Keen also refers to "APC 'thugs'" who were frequently recruited from potes (2005: 17).

The point is once again clear: the so-called thugs constituted a problem population, even if there was no way for most to succeed or gain acceptance in either mainstream rural or urban society. Some indeed became intimidators and worse for party hacks. More broadly, however, the following circumstance persisted: a great many rural and urban male youth were locked into a seemingly inescapable future of public failure and denigration. For many in society, they were dangerous losers.

Enter the Internationals

Into this dispiriting void entered the work of a number of captivating figures who collectively communicated that young outcast Sierra Leoneans were not alone. State controls on local expression by the governments of Stevens and Momoh helped create this. A senior Sierra Leonean NGO official recalled that during their presidencies "it was almost impossible for [local] artists to criticize the government in their songs." Most either were "praise singers" or those who "taught moral lessons for society or those in love," the official recalled. A senior official in a religious NGO explained that prior to the civil war, Sierra Leonean musicians "all sang praise for the government. They dared not criticize for fear of being jailed or killed." Politicians also were influencing musicians directly. As Stasik notes, "collaboration between popular [Sierra Leonean] musicians and the political elite came to the fore" in 1980s Sierra Leone. The declining economy also meant that most local bands "could not generate enough revenue to continue to be viable" (2012: 77).

Censoring youth is a persistent theme in Sierra Leone's history. As will be described, paramount chiefs were at least as tough on dissent as the national government. It was not allowed. The absence of local musicians who could speak out about mounting challenges in prewar Sierra Leone helps explain, at least in part, why so many Sierra Leonean youth developed a particular thirst for foreign artists and the messages their work communicated. It has long seemed to me that the fascination with foreign artists among Sierra Leonean youth and ideas is even stronger than among their counterparts in other countries where I have conducted youth research. A West Africa music expert concurred. "The orientation of popular culture in Freetown is almost exclusively oriented towards Black music in the West, from the Americas and from England." He added that "maybe five percent" of foreign artists revered in Freetown "aren't Black." He considered it an orientation toward "the Black Atlantic" or "the Black West" and noted that, in his experience, "the interest in the West is stronger in Sierra Leone than anywhere else I've been in West Africa."

One musician from the Black Atlantic single-handedly turned the tables on condemnation for being a thug. On the other side of the world, an African

American male youth in Los Angeles proudly tattooed "Thug Life" across the front of his torso, performed with his shirt off, and defiantly rapped about being a thug. An ardent fan in Sierra Leone explained why so many young Sierra Leoneans were drawn to Tupac Shakur and his music:

> Tupac, he knew his destiny. He was singing like he knew what would happen to him, like he could see his destiny in everything. He saw everything. He knew he wouldn't last long. He wasn't afraid. He preached the way of the truth and the way of the gangster and the way of his own destiny. In his music, he's talking too much reality. He's like the legendary Bob Marley, but he's a rapper. Both were talking about reality things. Tupac was doing songs about things you'd end up seeing in Sierra Leone. The other rappers in the [United] States didn't like him because he was so much better than them.

Several themes arising in this quotation resonated in interviews with other youth and adults in Sierra Leone. Tupac seemed to know that he would live a short life; he was honest and fearless, and for many Sierra Leonean male youth, he made being an outlaw—"the way of the gangster"—honorable. More than that, he rapped about issues that resonated in Sierra Leone. It was as if Tupac was one of them and knew how they suffered. His perceived ability to predict the future was a quality he shared with Bob Marley. For outlier male youth in Sierra Leone, Tupac and Marley were seers.

Tupac's music, videos, T-shirts, and antihero persona arrived in Sierra Leone following the release of his first album late in 1991, the year the war began. Bob Marley had arrived two decades before him. Over time, the enduring appeal of Marley and Tupac on boys and male youth proved powerful. Across these decades, a former military commander explained, "Most youth were interested in music. So they started to imitate musicians." The imitation and reverence extended far beyond simply listening to the artist's songs. "Some young boys saw that there was a system to follow: they can join [the] Bob Marley System, the Tupac System." Using Tupac as an example, he explained what "system" meant: "If you look at his clips [videos], he's more of a gangster. But if you have no job, you begin to walk like Tupac, dress like Tupac. Most [followers] are out of school, living in the ghettos and elsewhere. Those who watched those Tupac Shakur clips had admiration [for him]. That's what got them to behave like outcasts." What emerged, starting in the 1970s, is that some followers of particular popular culture figures identified with them deeply and carefully modeled their behavior and lifestyle after them. In this case, "Tupac System" or "Bob Marley System" equates with using them as role models.

John Rambo and "Rambo System" arrived in Sierra Leone after *First Blood*, the initial Rambo movie, was released in 1982. Richards details one way that he entered the scene: via stationary video parlors and traveling video businesses. Drawing from a September 1993 interview in a diamond mining area of Sierra Leone, Richards reports the views of two brothers in their mid-thirties who ran a video operation. The two men "scrape a living touring the remote mining localities of the border zone [inside Sierra Leone, near Liberia], showing films on a borrowed video machine powered by a portable generator" (1996: 102). Working the diamond mining areas, the brothers described how their primary customers—male diamond miners—preferred "Action Films," which Richards defined as "essentially a genre comprising Kung Fu and American war movies, but also embracing violent science fiction epics such as *Terminator*" (103, emphasis in original). One of the brothers explained why: "'People like Action Films because they teach skills and attitudes needed to survive on your own in a hostile world.'" The brothers related that "Rambo is especially admired" by their customers. Referring to the first Rambo film in particular, one of the brothers explained that such films "help bring home quickly the skills you need to survive in a tricky world." The brothers, Richards asserts, read *First Blood* as an "educational drama" instead of a "documentary" (103).

The pedagogical, "educative" (109) dimension of music videos and full-length movies helped fuel the deep impact that Rambo had on young Sierra Leoneans. A veteran NGO official from Sierra Leone, with experience working with former combatants after the war, commented, "Rambo was a figure of cunning, strength. He could tolerate pain. Yet he was a great fighter, a man-like figure. For years, they played Rambo One, Two, and Three all over Sierra Leone. All the boys wanted to be like Rambo." A Sierra Leonean father shared a similar recollection. "Before the war, they were showing war films in villages at night," he said. "They were part of regular video shows." He added, "Of course, Rambo One, Two, and Three, they were the most popular films."

It is significant to note what came next. After watching the films, probably over and over again, the father related that "children started to imitate the same fighter skills, boxing how to fight back, how to do ambushes. In the street and in schools, they were acting like Rambo." The descriptions highlight how young viewers used Rambo films to enhance their skills as fighters. It thus appears to have been a small step from children imitating Rambo before the war to rebel armies using Rambo films to train newcomers during it. The rebels merely exploited a practice that already had existed, turning Rambo imitations into what became known either as "Rambo Tactics" or a component of "Rambo System." That a generation of young Sierra Leoneans seemed to have memorized the Rambo films provided an added boost. Rebel military trainers didn't need to show any of the Rambo films: the trainees already knew them by heart.

Modeling the behavior and practices of Rambo in his films and Tupac in his songs and videos helped set the stage for the important roles they both would play during the civil war years. The two were among the international popular culture figures whom youth viewed as authentic role models for wartime living. As one male youth in Kenema related following the war, "I like Tupac because he's a gangster and I like the gangster lifestyle. I like the way he dresses. Tupac has killed! He was always in jail. He was in the American war, so he knows war." Such sentiments appeared to resonate deeply with male youth across Sierra Leone before and during the civil war.

Research for this book reveals that Bob Marley's impact was more encompassing, in terms of the breadth of his appeal and influence in Sierra Leone, than any other international popular culture figure. From virtually every segment of society, people expressed familiarity with and were prepared to discuss Marley's music and messages during interviews. For example, a retired police inspector related how youth in Sierra Leone "are only supposed to obey the chiefs and their elders. But Bob Marley tells you to stand up for your rights." In a nutshell, the inspector identifies perhaps the most compelling and enduring dimension of Marley's influence in Sierra Leone: his call to advocate for your rights and challenge the powers that seek to control you (in Sierra Leone's case, the patrimonial overlords and their minions). A second indispensable component of "Marley System" was smoking marijuana (djamba). For many Sierra Leoneans, the two were inseparable: followers of Marley listened to his music and smoked djamba. As a former male RUF fighter related, "Bob Marley is shaping our life. He is helping us to be conscious of our rights. The djamba is also helping us to meditate on our rights. We the youth, we are people of no nonsense."

Many Sierra Leonean followers of Marley reported that his music and ideas made a person "conscious." It is a critically important concept. A sampling of comments from interviews with ex-combatants and adult survivors of the war shed light on its significance. An elderly man explained, "When youth listen to Marley's songs they become conscious of their rights." He followed this statement with a lament: "The unfortunate thing is that they took up arms to fight for them." A town councilor from Makeni reflected on Marley's influence in Sierra Leone by emphasizing his appeal for adults as well as youth. A critical difference, she observed, was that younger Sierra Leoneans also paid attention to the significance of djamba for Marley: "Marley started influencing people even before his death. In the eighties, Bob was the greatest musician in Sierra Leone. Everybody desired to listen to his songs, which he described as 'these songs of freedom.' While adults were deeply interested in the message of the songs, youth were particularly interested in Marley's attitude toward djamba, and they promoted its smoking. Youth believed that Marley's source of inspiration for his music was the marijuana he smoked." An ex-combatant who was abducted by the RUF shed additional light on Marley's prewar influence in Sierra Leone: "In the 1980s, when Marley's songs became popular, young people admired him not only for the message of his songs but for the way he appeared, wearing dreadlocks, and the marijuana he smoked. Young people started behaving like Bob Marley, calling themselves Ghetto Boys or Rastamen. They began to wear their hair like Marley and dress with faded jeans [like him]. Youth became conscious of the issues of social injustice."

A veteran Sierra Leonean journalist defined "conscious music" as "music that will make people learn new things and prepare for the challenges ahead, especially 'Get Up, Stand Up.'"[1] Making direct reference to one particular Bob Marley song was no coincidence. In compelling, clear language, Marley urged everyone to make a move and advocate for their rights. Droves of young Sierra Leoneans took notice and began to follow his "system." In the context of the Stevens era in Sierra Leone, this could be dangerous. Reflecting on Marley's influence during this period, the head of an NGO in Sierra Leone explained the danger: "Before the war, Bob Marley was big here. His words inspired you to speak out. For a very long time, it was all Bob Marley. He opens your eyes and inspires you to speak your mind. There was a time in the 1980s [under Stevens] when even [government] ministers and famous people were afraid to talk [due to government intimidation]. So the adults wouldn't talk. It's youth who spoke out because they were unafraid." Interviews with youth and adults alike signaled that, just as the Rambo films were the most important movies for young Sierra Leoneans before and during the war, Marley's "Get Up, Stand Up" became the most significant song for youth across both eras as well.

The ferment that combined new music from abroad with resistant lifestyles and expression naturally spilled into Sierra Leone's prewar political arena. Nearly all of the focus in published literature is on Freetown. "Reggae music in the *potes* reinforced the message of student radicals that the political system was decadent and in need of radical change," Kandeh observed (1999: 359). Another observation of prewar potes was that the lyrics of reggae songs by Bob Marley, Peter Tosh, and Bunny Wailer "depicted realities of the day—hardship, degradation and oppression—in a style of social commentary known as 'system dread'" (TRC 2004b: 348). Abdullah stated that "*pote* discourse" was influenced by Bob Marley, fellow reggae musicians Peter Tosh and Bunny Wailer, and the outspoken Nigerian musician Fela Kuti. He also observed that during the 1970s and 1980s "the drug culture was silently gaining grudging acceptance from officialdom and parents alike." This drug culture "extolled the imagined virtues of the weed [that is, marijuana]" and received explicit influence from "Rastafarians in Jamaica and elsewhere" (Abdullah 2002: 31).

Additionally, Abdullah noted that middle-class youth "appropriated the 'rock 'n roll' culture from the west" and founded the Gardener's Club at Fourah Bay College, which became "a forum for radical non-conformist students in the 70s and 80s" (30). Others highlighted the significance of the Gardener's Club as well. A police official and a veteran Sierra Leonean scholar I interviewed both related that, in the scholar's words, initiation into the club "featured djamba and Bob Marley." He added, "A lot of the revolutionaries came from the Gardener's Club." Such members read from *The Green Book*, authored by former Libyan ruler Mu'ammar Gaddhafi. The scholar continued, "The core of the RUF ideology and the rebellion came from the Gardener's Club." The connection between smoking marijuana, Bob Marley's music, and revolution was explicit and will be examined in chapter 8.

A somewhat parallel trend was arising among youth in rural Sierra Leone as well. While heavy drug use may not have been part of the mix, the disquiet emerging from Freetown neighborhoods corresponded to sentiments surfacing among youth in the hinterland. For example, the hunting societies based in rural areas reportedly had much in common with youth activities in Freetown potes. As Hoffman details about the traditional hunting societies (which evolved into formidable fighting forces during the war years, particularly the ethnic Mende Kamajors): "What is significant about the hunting societies and ode-lay troupes for understanding the kamajors is the tradition of giving political weight to an overlapping iconography of the rural hunter—with his volatility, his violence, and his extraordinary power—and the popular culture of the global black underclass. Tupac Shakur, Rambo, and Bob Marley were rallying figures for the kamajors just as they had been for other youth mobilizations since the 1970s" (Hoffman 2011: 67).

A second example of rural youth engagement with the global Black underclass (and global youth culture more broadly) is found in Ishmael Beah's upbringing near Mattru Jong in southern Sierra Leone. His early life featured a fascination with rap music that he shared with other boys his age: at age eight, with two friends and his older brother, they had formed "a rap and dance group." By the time he first was "touched by war" in January 1993, he was twelve. Before the war arrived on his doorstep, he recalls, "The only wars I knew of were those I had read about in books or seen in movies such as *Rambo: First Blood*, and the one in neighboring Liberia that I had heard about on the BBC news" (Beah 2007: 5–6, emphasis in original). Beah's example is not one of explicit political resistance, as in the Freetown neighborhoods. But his frame of reference, and connection to the larger youth world, was similar. The language of popular culture featuring rebellious youth was the same.

The most salient theme about youth in prewar Sierra Leone is this: large numbers of young Sierra Leoneans had no escape from poverty or degradation. Regardless of location, most were shut out from access to marriage, educa-

tion, adulthood, and hope for a life of reasonable stability and social acceptance. Their entrapment took place while their exploiters—powerful men ruling encompassing patrimonial systems—blatantly enriched themselves and
controlled a social, cultural, and state system based on ruthless exploitation
and rule by threat and force.

In such a punishingly unequal and emasculating context, it is hardly surprising that male youth (and some female youth) sought and found meaning
and direction in faraway sources. Largely bereft of formal education, youth
studied and interpreted the works and images of Tupac, Rambo, and other
popular culture figures intensely, but none more than Bob Marley, the towering Rastafarian reggae musician-oracle. As a male former combatant succinctly stated, "Bob Marley is the king of youth." These faraway figures lent
validation and meaning to young lives, helping Sierra Leonean youth interpret their context and advocate for their rights. They also inspired admiration. "Bob Marley is like a messiah for us," an ex-combatant male youth related. "He talks to us, he talks for us: about our rights, our freedom." "I love
Tupac because he had the same [Black] skin and the same life," said another.
"Tupac makes us bold because he's a Black man talking the truth," a third declared. "Saying, 'Me against the world.' That makes us love him. That message
means a lot to sufferers like us."

Sierra Leone's production of huge numbers of young male sufferers set
the stage for things to blow. Sierra Leone at the dawn of war featured a state
run like an illegitimate (and violent) business and young people disparaged
for acting as cornered people without rights—precisely what they were. The
situation was fundamentally perverse, and it is in this environment where
Tupac Shakur, John Rambo, and Bob Marley all arose as "iconic young men
whose exploits upset the existing order, who achieve[d] an ambiguous great-
ness not only because of their political platforms but through rebellion and
often through violence" (Hoffman 2011: 67). What followed was a complex,
intentionally and intensely terrifying yet in many ways instructive civil war,
where the compelling works and images of Tupac, Rambo, Marley, and others helped influence the practice of war and the perspectives of young Sierra
Leoneans.

PART 3

The Arc of War

CHAPTER 7

Terror and Purpose

The Sudden Shift

Why on earth would Foday Sankoh and his Revolutionary United Front turn so quickly and dramatically to terror war tactics at the earliest stages of Sierra Leone's civil war? After decades of predation, state violence, the promotion of colossal inequality under the administrations of Stevens and Momoh and a puny national army,[1] the nation was entirely ripe for a popular uprising. Certainly a great many civilians of Kailahun—the nation's underdeveloped, easternmost district surrounded on three sides by Guinea and Liberia and the place where the civil war began—were ready to support and fight for the RUF. Instead, and within a few short weeks of the March 23, 1991, attacks on two towns along the Sierra Leone–Liberia border that launched the RUF's entrance into Sierra Leone (Gberie 2005: 59), Sankoh and his followers transformed their miniscule rebel movement into a terror outfit. They mainly attacked the very civilians who were, particularly at first, eager to support them. From the dawn of the war, the RUF practiced violent perversion by preying on potential supporters.

The firsthand recollections of a Kailahun town resident (who then became a longtime refugee in neighboring Guinea) provide a glimpse into the origins of Sankoh's peculiar start to civil war. The RUF, he recalled, was strict and disciplined at first. Highlighting inequality, an early speech from RUF leaders to Kailahun town residents revealed the potential for a popular rebellion: "The RUF leaders told us, 'Nobody should run away. You should not be afraid of us. We have come to liberate you from the long suffering we have had. We have a lot of diamonds, a lot of gold.' They named all the minerals. 'We have all the coffee and cocoa and other cash crops. But none of it is benefiting you. There are no drugs in the hospital, school fees are high, and the roads are bad.' People were cheering, saying 'Yes, that is true!'" The former refugee made a distinction between the initial group of RUF fighters who entered Kailahun town—"who were just like pioneers to build the people's interest in supporting them"—and the "other group of rebels" who joined them shortly afterward. This second set of rebels, he said, "were very aggressive." Commanders (many of whom were Liberian, from Taylor's NPFL) eventually lost control over their fighters because of two factors: the propensity of the fighters to be on drugs—a tendency that would play a predominant role in the war— and the rebels' need to, eventually, secure the dwindling food that town residents had on hand. The rebels' push-pull between brutality against civilians and their need to have some civilians provide them with food—another pattern that soon became a rebel trademark—evidently started then too. When this second rebel group sought food, "Everybody was tied up and flogged if you resisted."[2]

Naturally, people realized that the rebels' brutality was bound to increase as family food stocks dwindled. So Kailahun town residents began to escape at night, heading northward into the forests, toward the Makona River and Guinea on the other side. Foreshadowing what would become a widespread survival tactic that civilians practiced across the civil war years—escaping to rain forest "hiding places" (*soquoihun* in Mende) in small survival groups— the fleeing civilians gradually divided into smaller and smaller groups. "While heading for Guinea, we would walk together until it got noisy," the former refugee recalled. "Then we would break into smaller groups again."

As Kailahun town began to empty, an RUF contingent went to the riverside and invited some of the civilians located just inside Guinea to come back and "Talk to Papay" Foday Sankoh himself (Papay means "father" or "Papa" in Liberia [Gberie 2005: 62]). The former refugee was among the delegation who crossed back into Sierra Leone. Sankoh urged the return of all the townspeople who had fled. "All the refugees should come back," he told the delegation. "I have warned my soldiers not to wrong any civilian." He also publicly flogged two commanders, presumably for their brutality against civilians. This greatly impressed the delegation. Sankoh also explained how some civilian youth had perished during the RUF's advance into Kailahun town. "I'm very sorry," the former refugee recalled Sankoh saying. "They were caught in the crossfire." Many in the delegation did not know what "crossfire" meant; they had never heard the word before. Sankoh explained: "When people shoot from one angle to another, and the others return fire, and you want to run in and between them, you'll be caught by bullets from either side. So anytime you hear guns firing, lie flat on the ground and take cover, because you won't know from which direction the bullets are coming." This explanation of unintended civilian deaths encouraged many refugees to return to Kailahun on that day. Not all: the former refugee who related this account was unconvinced by Sankoh and returned to the Guinea side afterward. But others who had fled to Guinea with him decided to cross back to the Sierra Leone side of the river.

The RUF immediately seized all of them. "We need more manpower," the rebels explained. Interviews with refugees from Kailahun in Guinea in 1997 corroborated the general framework of this account: of Kailahun residents seeking to support the RUF and being abducted instead. "I think that this was the time when atrocities and terror started," the former refugee explained. "The RUF rebels would take middle-aged men and boys to be trained. The women would be taken to another place to be sexed [raped] by the rebels at any time. Adult men and women became 'taygo' ['take-go'; in other words, porters]."

There are other versions of the beginning of civil war in Kailahun. A colonel in the Sierra Leone Army (SLA) claimed that the RUF didn't start to turn against civilians until they lost an early battle for Daru in the early weeks of the RUF's entrance into Kailahun. An SLA battalion was based at Daru. The RUF's "failure to capture Daru resulted in a massacre," the colonel recalled (Peters 2011a: 64). Peters does not dwell on this early sharp turn to RUF brutality against civilians. Gberie's account, in contrast, most certainly does. He describes a videotape the RUF made of Sankoh following their capture of the town of Koidu,[3] soon after the RUF's incursion into Kailahun from Liberia. The video, Gberie notes, captured Sankoh's right-hand man, Sam Bockarie, the notorious Mosquito, pointing his gun "menacingly" at a crowd of townspeople. Sankoh, in turn, speaks to the civilians in a "hectoring and threatening" tone. He says that he has come to Koidu "to liberate 'you people'" as part of "a fight everyone has been asking for." The ruling APC, he says, is "rotten and oppressive, and it is time to oust them and institute 'people's power.'" A woman bravely asks Sankoh whether he knows who the looters were since the RUF's entrance into Koidu, and whether civilians will be protected. Sankoh, Gberie says, shoots her a cold glance and states that "everything will be all right now that he is in town." After this, his teenage soldiers—many, Gberie notes, with "distinctly Liberian accents"—sing a song featuring the line "Anyone who does not support Sankoh will be killed like a dog." Thus concluded an early firsthand example of Sankoh's way of generating popular support for his struggle. Gberie called it "the performance of the conqueror" (2005: 60, 61).

What matters here is marking a profound turning point in the practice of warfare in Sierra Leone soon after it began. Within weeks, Sankoh and his minions would turn away from winning hearts and minds and instead focus on terror. Those in the RUF who disagreed were summarily dismissed or eliminated. Gberie details the recollection of an abducted ex-RUF fighter regarding his entrance into the RUF. After being captured by Bockarie's men and forced to witness the rebel soldiers' execution of both his parents, he describes being taken before Sankoh with the other new captives. After Sankoh urged the captives to join him in "purging the system," one captive asked why Sankoh's men were killing, maiming, and looting civilians. Sankoh immediately ordered the questioner shot (Gberie 2005: 61–62). Sankoh also had nearly all of the RUF's so-called radical intellectual supporters eliminated in the first year of the war. Keen cites a series of sources that collectively relate how "the 1992 purge" left perhaps three hundred university student radicals dead. They had committed the crime of condemning the RUF's human rights abuses (Keen 2005: 47). That left Sankoh, Bockarie, and a host of mostly undereducated adults leading the RUF. Keen observed that they had a poorly developed sense of rights and justice but a well-cultivated feeling of anger, together with a strong "anti-intellectual stance" (46). As he aptly noted, "What most militates against interpreting the RUF as a coherent political movement . . . is its persistent abuses, including extreme atrocities, against the very civilians it claimed to represent" (41). Smillie came to the same conclusion: "Whatever ideology the RUF may have had when [the RUF war] began, it vanished as Sankoh put his 'revolution' into practice" (2010: 103).

Thus, soon after the war began, the die was cast. Eventually shedding the Liberian and Burkinabé fighters (Charles Taylor had sent "the wildest and most violent fighters to join the RUF" [Smillie 2010: 37]) who had entered Sierra Leone with Sankoh (Marks 2013: 361, 362), and eliminating anyone questioning their purpose and methods, Sankoh and Bockarie led an RUF that saw itself as a people's rebellion by maintaining the sort of depraved purity that Pol Pot no doubt would have admired. What remained was to keep the uprising moving forward and the hope of government takeover by whatever means necessary: the more terrifying the means, quite evidently, the better.

An Enduring Debate

Sankoh's confounding decision at the dawn of civil war to turn on the welter of potential supporters and undermine prospects for a popular rebellion forms the touchstone for heated debates that eventually surfaced over the RUF's intent and rationale. To be sure, the RUF had some published documentation (though almost no one in Sierra Leone appeared to have read it), some degree of military discipline, and a semblance of organization, albeit one that was decentralized. It also had a perverse way of putting its professed ideas into practice.

One way to analyze the extreme violence and terror of the RUF is from a detached, intellectual perspective. Stepping back from the intense awfulness of RUF tactics (and, as will be explained, those of other military groups involved in the civil war), some authors have argued that RUF horrors were informed by a set of political purposes. Hoffman, for example, proposes that "we consider the war in Sierra Leone as a violent, and ongoing, post–Cold War political project." In his view, warfare itself is "a form of discourse" while wartime violence becomes "a quest for [combatants'] recognition as political speakers" (2006: 3). Using amputations of civilian limbs by RUF soldiers

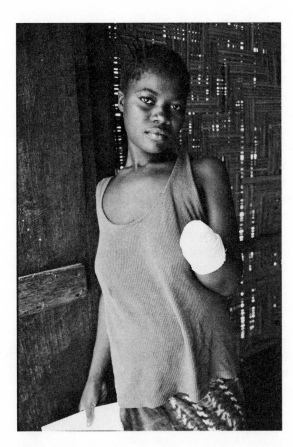

A girl amputee, in early 1997. She was given the so-called long sleeve amputation: a cut between the elbow and wrist. The girl and her sister were both left amputated in late 1996. She was too young to vote.

as an example, he asserts that "combatants in West African conflicts . . . have used increasingly dramatic displays of violence to achieve recognition as serious forces deserving of attention and respect" (13). While it seems likely that such acts garner far more attention than respect from others, some amputations had a degree of political intent. In the lengthy decision against Charles Taylor, for example, the Special Court for Sierra Leone provided testimony about how a rebel commander named Staff Alhaji amputated the hands of six civilian men and then told them that "'now they would never be able to vote for [Sierra Leone's] President Kabbah again and that they should keep their hands out of politics.'" Reportedly, four of the six new amputees subsequently died (Special Court for Sierra Leone 2012: 264). Other RUF amputations lacked reference to voting, since they were carried out on children not old enough to vote (Yusuf Bangura 2004: 18).

A commander who had fought against the RUF assigned more general significance to such acts. First, RUF atrocities against civilians "served to convince villagers that the government was powerless to protect them." Second, the atrocities were, in his words, "'the best way to be taken seriously' by the

United Nations and other (wealthy) international agencies willing to contribute resources to ending such practices" (Ferme and Hoffman 2004: 88, 89).

Identifying vague political meanings in extreme wartime atrocity is one thing. Recognizing a coherent rationale for rebellion via the perpetration of such acts is quite another. These are among the intriguing and provocative intentions of Paul Richards. Before reviewing some of his assertions, it is useful to reflect on one issue that informs his work. With few exceptions, Richards provides limited information about his research methods and information sources for his analyses of the RUF. In his book published in the midst of the civil war (1996), and for his subsequent examinations of the RUF, the evidence base often is not clear.[4] One reason for this arises from the simple fact that direct information about the RUF during the civil war was challenging to obtain. Richards observes that it was difficult for RUF members to escape: "Child captives of the RUF found that even if they escaped the movement they faced death at the hands of soldiers, or even (on occasion) village lynch mobs. The RUF made this a more certain fate by its practice of branding or tattooing new recruits. Lacking realistic exit options the young captives had little choice but to try and survive as members of the movement" (2003: 14). In addition, the RUF was unusually hostile to outsiders. Crossing into RUF-held areas was potentially perilous. During the war, the RUF took foreigners as hostages and "in some instances RUF rebels also ambushed and killed foreign nationals as part of the terror campaign" (Dumbuya 2008: 174). In one interview, an ex-RUF commander recalled the limitations of this effort. "It was difficult to catch a White man during that war," he mused.

A strategy Richards employed to unearth meaning was via the application of academic theories. One was anthropologist Mary Douglas's theory about "the irresponsible world of the excluded intellectual." Richards notes that it is difficult to decipher "why the RUF insurgents connive at the destruction of forest communities whose predicament they share and whose interests they claim to want to protect." Drawing from Douglas, he presents his interpretation: "The rural mayhem is intended to teach a lesson to those who sit pretty in the capital. The suffering of the masses is an idea in which they have come to believe. They are blind to its reality all around them, except as proof that they were right all along. This is academic talk—the world view of the lonely and disregarded intellectual—not the practical wisdom of those who know that forest beliefs must work for the community, or there will be no one left to inherit the vision" (Richards 1996: 84). In another passage, he states, "The irresponsible destructiveness of excluded intellectual elites can be very great" (27). However, the ferocity and expanse of RUF terror and destruction, and the fact that the intellectuals' anger (that is, the leaders of the RUF) is not directed at those with whom they are angry, makes it a challenging theoretical interpretation. So does the fact that the RUF's leader, Foday Sankoh, as well as his second-in-command for most of the war, Sam Bockarie, do not come across as particularly intellectual. For Bockarie in particular, such an assessment seems beyond dispute. As for Sankoh, apparently he could not read.[5] The early slaughter of three hundred or so student radicals supports the impression that RUF leaders were opposed to intellectuals and housed limited numbers of individuals who could be branded as one.

Richards also used Emile Durkheim's theory of the purpose of religion to comprehend RUF practices. "At the heart of the Durkheimian account of religion," Richards explained, "is a notion of group improvisatory performance—the group believes because it acts together" (2006b: 652). He argues that "the RUF sodality was rich in worship" and asserts that the Executive Outcomes mercenaries from South Africa (hired by Sierra Leone's government to lead an attack on the RUF) "failed to understand (or dangerously underestimated) the RUF and its sectarian dynamic" (658). Characterizing the RUF as "despairing practitioners" who were "threatened with the loss of all sense of society," Richards delivers a startling conclusion: Executive Outcomes and others "who chose to seek a total military solution" are largely responsible for the RUF's "sociological implosion" that fostered "rites of lacerating violence" (659). In short, Richards viewed the RUF as not especially culpable for the extreme violence they perpetrated on, for the most part, ordinary civilians.

For Richards, the RUF was a peculiar concoction: "a populist movement without popular support" (2005a: 120). He argued that the excluded intellectuals leading the RUF and their emergence (via his interpretations) as a religious sect help make their actions comprehensible. He further viewed RUF methods as unexceptional. "There is little if any analytical value," he declared, "in distinguishing between cheap war based on killing with knives and cutlasses [the RUF case], and expensive wars in which civilians are maimed or destroyed with sophisticated laser-guided weapons" (1996: xx).

Yet in at least one way, the difference between the two kinds of warfare is notable. Costly wars featuring bombs from the sky are impersonal: no one knows exactly who dropped them on a village, military outpost, or city. Sierra Leone's civil war was just the opposite: it was intentionally personal. As will be detailed later in the book, some young RUF rebel fighters were sent to attack their former village homes, and sometimes to rape or kill family members. Furthermore, the terror warfare the RUF (and others) practiced featured tactics bent on the promotion of fear among survivors.

Richards's take on the RUF's immoderate violence incited a strong reaction from many other scholars and journalists. Gberie, for example, launched the following volley: "Richards' spirited defence of a group that was already notorious for apparently gratuitous attacks on the rural peasantry, wanton arson and rape, and which had favoured no one with a coherent explanation of its activities, made many Sierra Leoneans livid" (2005: 145). Gberie char-

acterized the RUF as having a "violent pathology" and an "essentially mercenary character" (151). He concludes that the RUF was "largely conceived as a
mercenary enterprise, and never evolved beyond banditism: it never became
a political, still less a revolutionary organization" (153). For his part, Abdullah asserts that "there were no radical or excluded intellectuals in the RUF,
nor did the movement establish any meaningful relationship with the peasantry based on the acceptance of a common programme produced within
the context of a revolutionary dialogue. The RUF had a chronic lack of cadres
imbued with any revolutionary ideology" (1998: 223). A third Sierra Leonean
scholar, Yusuf Bangura, presents a host of critiques of Richards's analysis of
the RUF, including the assertion that Richards's "treating all behaviour as rational" makes it "difficult to say when a seemingly rational action is in fact irrational" (2004: 18). He adds that "RUF violence does not have only one logic,
but several: there is obviously the logic of political violence, aspects of which
are covered in Richards's analysis; but this competes, coexists and interacts
with the logics of banditry, hedonism and brutality" (24).

These assessments of RUF motivations and logic align well with those of
the RUF's chief ally and benefactor: Liberia's Charles Taylor (in addition to
his main supporting actor, Burkina Faso's former president Blaise Compaoré).
Taylor in particular appeared to have no particular underlying ideology of significance beyond a virtually unquenchable personal need to dominate, control, and extract wealth. Reflecting on this issue, a seasoned diplomat who had
engaged regularly with Taylor remarked, "The RUF certainly did not get ideology from Taylor. If they had any ideology, it most certainly came from somewhere else."[6] Employing violence to serve Taylor's ends was just fine, as were
efforts to destabilize nearby regions and nations: Charles Taylor was mainly
interested in Charles Taylor. If Foday Sankoh and the RUF did construct an
ideology or philosophy along the lines that Richards and others describe, it
is unlikely that Taylor and Compaoré were their models. In addition, RUF
leaders (including Sankoh) demonstrated no particular ideological bent when
they did get close to power. During such times, and as will be explained, Sankoh's main focus—like so many others during the war—was diamonds, together with a passion for patrimonial-style dominance.

The vibrancy and spirited nature of this debate has continued. Nearly a decade after the civil war had ended, Krijn Peters produced an extended treatment of the RUF that largely aligned with Richards's analysis. Like Richards,
he uses the works of Durkheim and Douglas (in his words, "neo-Durkheimian
cultural theory as developed by Mary Douglas and others" [2011a: 229]) to
help him analyze the RUF. His emphasis on the rationality of RUF actions, regardless of their extremity or the profile of their victims, also is similar. Take,
for example, his contention that "if the RUF was largely made up of young
people only weakly incorporated in rural society, the violence can be read

as the most marginalised group increasingly turning against the very society which had first excluded them" (235). In contrast, Mitton concludes that "the rational political and military aims of the RUF were shaped by powerful emotions, and these led to violence that was often far from rational" (2015: 269).

Curiously, this corrosive debate centers only on what took place during the first half of the war. Peters and Richards explain that "when the RUF joined the military AFRC junta in Freetown from April 1997 onwards, it no longer had any effective ideological direction" (2011: 385). Implied is that the early war years were the RUF's ideological heyday. That, of course, is disputed. But following those early war years, the context for caustic exchanges about RUF purposes and intentions evaporate. No ideology surfaced when the RUF reached the pinnacle of power following the April 1997 coup (alongside its AFRC allies, with whom the RUF's relations were forever testy). The absence of any articulated rebel ideology (much less a plan) following the Freetown takeover was obvious to all. When the RUF finally had a chance to broadcast what they were really about, they had nothing to say.

Research for this book suggests that the opposing takes on the RUF coexisted during the war. During interviews, some former RUF conscripts described a creed existing within the confines of their respective field units. It centered around a simplistic promise: since you youth have been exploited, you will run the country after we win. That wasn't much, but it was far more than the RUF's rebel compatriots, the Armed Forces Revolutionary Council (AFRC), had in mind. Together with their West Side Boys allies, the AFRC mainly promised revenge. Some have maintained that the RUF had a relative degree of self-control regarding violence against civilians during the war. As Peters noted, "It is highly unlikely that all RUF fighters were involved in frequent atrocities and killings" (2011a: 162). However, that proportion appears to have been quite small and only existed during the early war years. The bigger picture was that virtually all military groups in the war practiced terror focused intensely on civilians, as this book will examine.

The RUF's training and internal discipline was intended to limit terror practices. However, few appeared to have received it. After the war had ended, a former top RUF commander confessed that the reach of the RUF's organizational teachings and ideas (including those concerning troop discipline and restraint) was exceptionally limited. After first estimating that the entire "RUF army was forty-seven thousand" (which included "fighters, small soldiers, wives, Big Men, porters, and recces" [spies for the RUF]), the former general stated, "Maybe only three thousand of the forty-seven thousand [6.38 percent] really believed in the RUF ideology." In addition, marauding Liberian commanders and fighters were with the RUF from the outset (such as the infamous Superman, who surfaces later in the story). Their motives are widely agreed to have been mercenary throughout, together with the Burkinabé fighters (that is, those from Burkina Faso) who also took part. Add to this the extreme violence of other military actors—the AFRC, the West Side Boys, nonrebels such as the Sierra Leonean soldiers committing atrocities (the so-called sobels), and many of the Civil Defense Forces (especially the Kama-jors)—and the following picture emerges: only a narrow slice of the rebel pie featured members with even a modicum of the sort of political ideology debated in this chapter. The evidence strongly suggests that the overwhelming majority of those thought to be rebels, including nearly all RUF members, did not.

Instead, inside rebel units on the ground (and some civil defense force units) arose a manipulated and distorted interpretation of messages from Bob Marley's music, fueled by very heavy marijuana use. Many reggae musicians, and sometimes Tupac, also were part of the idea mix that commanders discussed, primarily with their male troops. But Marley's ideas held sway. There were very good reasons for this. The war had arrived in Sierra Leone in 1991 when the economy was in freefall and inequality, corruption, repression, and poverty were just about everywhere. Over nearly two decades preceding the war, Marley's ideas had circulated across Sierra Leone. Studying his songs (coaxed by marijuana use) revealed insightful political and social analysis.

Many Sierra Leoneans considered Marley's philosophy to be custom-made for their country. Some of his songs also instructed listeners how to respond to their plight. Foday Sankoh took it from there.

CHAPTER 8

Bob Marley and Foday Sankoh

The Rebel Leader

There is no way that Bob Marley could have foreseen how his ideas would be distorted and exploited by Foday Sankoh and the RUF. The same most certainly must be said for Tupac Shakur, the makers of the Rambo films, and other popular culture figures from whom military leaders, commanders, and fighters drew during Sierra Leone's civil war.

Yet Marley in particular was a mainstay for many Freetown youth and a formidable up-country influence in many young Sierra Leonean lives. Marley and marijuana were directly tied to revolutionary thinking and acting, embodied in system dread and other forms of discourse in Freetown potes in the 1970s and 1980s, the Gardener's Club at Fourah Bay College, and so much more. Indeed, it would have been hard for the RUF *not* to draw from Bob Marley and marijuana practice in Sierra Leone, given their centrality in prewar resistance. A great many young people had set the Rambo films to memory in the 1980s. And as the war unfolded early in the 1990s, Tupac's music and messages entered the youth air as well.

The pronounced presence of Marley, Rambo, Tupac, and still other popular culture figures in youth imaginations and culture made them available resources to manipulate and misuse, particularly given the youthfulness of the RUF's combat groups, as well as virtually all the other Sierra Leonean fighting forces. It is thus essential to see Marley, Tupac, and Rambo through the lens of Sierra Leone's desperate situation at the dawn of war, where most youth faced dead-end futures, repression and social control were strongly present at local and national levels, and the broader population was well aware that the lords of their land were exploiting them.

Before turning to RUF thinking and Bob Marley's featured role in it (the usage of Tupac and Rambo will come later), it is important to get a sense of the RUF's founder and leader, Foday Sankoh. Beginning early in his life, Foday Saybana Sankoh was an outsider. Born into poverty in the northern dis-

trict of Tonkolili in the early 1930s, he considered himself "stubborn and troublesome." As a child, he loved fighting with other children and "was known
as a bully" (Gberie 2005: 39). Although his education only extended to primary school, he was a trained military man. In 1956, he joined the colonial
army, which was "seen largely as an instrument of colonial repression, and
a particularly brutal one at that" (40). He remained in the army until 1971,
never getting beyond the rank of colonel, but learning about radio and television operations. Sankoh was thought to know about the coup attempt against
Siaka Stevens in 1971 and subsequently was tried and sent to Freetown's notorious Pademba Road prison for seven years (42). Many sources mention that
Sankoh exited prison a bitter man, furious at Stevens and his APC one-party
state. Shifting to Bo, he became a photographer. A neighbor of his in Bo described him as reclusive: strange, funny, and jovial yet secretive, unmarried,
and having few associates (46–47). Gberie describes an incident during this
period illuminating two personality characteristics lying just below the surface: an "adolescent sense of entitlement" and "blind rage" at the APC government (48). A third comes up as well: the threat of vengeance. During his
time in Bo, Sankoh joined a radical student group and subsequently founded
the RUF in 1982 (Dumbuya 2008: 139). His association with political radicals
eventually opened the door for him to go to Libya "for military and ideological training" in 1987–1988 (Abdullah and Muana 1998: 177).

Whether former Libyan ruler Mu'ammar Gaddhafi's *Green Book* actually
influenced the RUF is disputed: Richards (1996) is among those who insist
that it did, while Abdullah (1998) opposes the idea altogether. Nonetheless,
it is worth briefly dipping into some of the text (in this case, part 1, which
lays out the author's political philosophy), since Sankoh was among the Sierra Leoneans who were introduced to the book and its author. Gaddhafi,
whose name is spelled in many ways (including Qaddafi, Gaddafi, Gadhafi,
and Kadafi; Alexiou 2011), critiqued many established institutions of modern
democracy: he hammered parliaments, political parties, constitutions, and
plebiscites. For some reason plebiscites received particular condemnation:
the idea that people should choose between two options seemed to enrage
the author. Gaddhafi called plebiscites both "a fraud against democracy" and
"sham democracy" (1976: 23, 34). He also condemned the ways in which class,
political party, tribe, and sect, when represented as minorities in a nation,
come to dominate the national scene. All of these approaches to democracy
instead lead toward undemocratic societies and even dictatorship, in his view.

For Gaddhafi, there is but one way to achieve democracy. In his words,
"The people's authority has only one face and it can be realized only by one
method, namely, popular congresses and people's committees" (28). The legal landscape also cannot be deliberated: some mix of traditional and religious law is best, since they both affirm "natural law" (34). In other words,

democratic ideas and principles do not arise through a democratic process. *The Green Book* is, in a sense, a recipe book for building democracy that contains a single recipe. Surprisingly, a book about a "happy" democratic discovery ends on a foreboding note. "Realistically," Gaddhafi concludes, "the strong always rule" (41). One might argue that this is precisely what happened in Libya under the author's very long period in power. One observer stated that "Qaddafi and his cronies maintained an iron grip" over Libya. "The popular congresses were called into session a few times a year—at Qaddafi's whim—and they simply reaffirmed the leader's wishes" (Bazzi 2011). When Gaddhafi operationalized his notion of direct democracy, it appears to have become an exceptionally directive one, sprinkled with a bit of controlled socialism.

If the imprint of *The Green Book* on Sankoh and the RUF is hard to determine, the influence of its author is not. Gaddhafi directly influenced Foday Sankoh's trajectory, and thus that of the RUF. In the years between exiting prison and leading the RUF to war, Sankoh's disposition was described in the following way: "Sankoh was not interested in reading, he was an action-oriented man who was impatient with the slow process of acquiring knowledge and understanding of the situation which a revolutionary project entails. Put in another way, Sankoh was a militarist" (Abdullah 1998: 218). Sankoh's invitation to visit Gaddhafi's World Revolutionary Headquarters fueled Sankoh's military aspirations. Established by the Libyan secret services, the purpose of the institute "was to train volunteers in revolutionary warfare from all over the world." Gaddhafi's "vast revolutionary ambitions" reached across all of the Middle East and Africa—he personally sought to "rid Africa of European imperialism"—as well as "from Northern Ireland to Colombia and the Philippines" (Ellis 2006: 69). Sankoh returned to Sierra Leone determined to stir up a revolution. Together with two other trainees, he toured parts of Sierra Leone (including diamond mining areas) and failed. He returned to Freetown "destitute and dejected" (Gberie 2005: 51).

Events leading up to Sierra Leone's civil war turned Charles Taylor into its catalyst. Together with Sankoh, Taylor also was among those who went to Gaddhafi's World Revolutionary Headquarters, which Ellis later described as "the Harvard and Yale of a whole generation of African revolutionaries" (2006: 71–72). Gaddhafi subsequently urged Taylor "to create a pan-African revolutionary force" (70). Based in Burkina Faso with his newfound friend, Blaise Compaoré, Taylor went on a recruiting tour to several neighboring countries, including Sierra Leone, in 1988. Sankoh was among the Sierra Leoneans who joined Taylor in Burkina Faso. By mid-1989, Taylor "had managed to seal an alliance with a group of Libyan-trained Sierra Leoneans." Their leader was Sankoh, and they called themselves the Revolutionary United Front/Sierra Leone (71). Beginning on Christmas Eve of that year, Sankoh and his RUF colleagues, as members of Taylor's National Patriotic Front of Liberia

(NPFL), entered Liberia and initiated civil war (Gberie 2005: 54). In 1990, Sankoh spent his time in the NPFL war theater preparing the RUF to invade Sierra Leone, using NPFL bases and logistics "to train Sierra Leoneans from diverse backgrounds who had been caught up in the turmoil in Liberia." These trainees became known as "RUF vanguards" (TRC 2004b: 351). Then, at one of Taylor's military bases in March 1991, Sankoh borrowed Taylor's technique of speaking about military attacks on BBC Radio to announce that he was leading "his 'people's struggle' against [President Joseph] Momoh's venal regime." He added that the RUF would be "spearheading that 'struggle'" (Gberie 2005: 59). The Truth and Reconciliation Commission neatly sums up which sorts of Sierra Leonean youth were involved with the RUF over time: "Educated youths were involved in the formulation of ideas for revolution and regime change, instigating the training in Libya. Marginalised urban youths were involved in the bulk of the military training [in Liberia] and launch of the insurgency. Thereafter the bulk of the growing manpower of the RUF [once inside Sierra Leone] consisted of marginalised rural youths" (TRC 2004b: 351).

As the leader of a military outfit that brutalized both its members and innocent civilians, drawing a bead on Foday Sankoh is not easy to do. Commentary from those who have studied Sierra Leone's civil war illuminate a broad array of personality traits. Sankoh was messianic. "I am a man of God," he declared in 1999. "God chose me to lead the revolution that will save Sierra Leone" (Ninja 1999, quoted in Gberie 2005: 59–60). He promoted a culture of violence in his organization (Denov 2010: 119). He had "delusions of grandeur" (Gberie 2005: 163). He was paranoid about "plots to undermine and ultimately assassinate him" (TRC 2004a: 186). He was a "charismatic sociopath" (Smillie 2010: 96). He "consciously modelled himself on warlord leaders of the past" (Peters 2011a: 158). Fear of his own fighters caused him to leave his military base every week or two during the war (reported in Keen 2005: 43). He was ruthless, apparently using RUF leader Sam Bockarie (known both as Mosquito and Maskita) as a personal henchman to carry out his "'dirty work'" (TRC 2004a: 187). He was consumed by "a self-defeating need to keep his hatred [of Joseph Momoh and the ruling APC] alive" (Jackson 2004: 142). He was pathological, systematically raping Agnes Deen-Jalloh for several years and inflicting "prolonged psychological torture on the victim's husband, Ibrahim Deen-Jalloh" as well (TRC 2004a: 208).

Yet ensconced in his secluded, sheltered wartime world, Foday Sankoh was popular. Several former RUF members who were interviewed referred to the RUF leader as alluring and empathic. Some believed that he had magical powers. The admiration that Sankoh generally inspired among his followers is reflected in the following comment from a former RUF leader: "He had special powers: if he stood before two thousand people, he could impress them all.

He was a gifted man." During the decade of civil war, Foday Sankoh was in his sixties. A short, rather rotund man with a graying beard, he was mainly surrounded by children. Even though "almost half" of the 18,354 RUF soldiers were children by the end of the war and many were orphans (Gberie 2005: 149), Gberie relayed an important point about the RUF: "it was overwhelmingly dominated by very young people, a large number of them teenagers or in some cases pre-teenagers—a whole generation of whom literally grew up within the group" (148).

The RUF most probably was among the youngest military outfits in modern history; it would be difficult for troops to get much younger. The youngest soldier I learned about, from a Sierra Leonean working with former child soldiers for a humanitarian agency in 1997, was age five. Reportedly, the child's ability to hold a gun allowed him to become a rebel fighter. Accordingly, labeling RUF fighters exclusively as "youth" is inaccurate, given that a sizable proportion were children. Some former combatants in Sierra Leone supplied what appeared to be a common strategy for addressing this unusual situation. A child who entered the RUF, or any other military unit during the war, was a *pikin* (Krio for "child"). But a child soldier could no longer be called a child. Instead, they were called "small boy" or "small girl." They also could be given the label *smɔl smɔl yut* (very small youth). Once the small boy, small girl, or *smɔl smɔl yut* got older, he or she became the more familiar *yut* (youth). This also was reflected in military organization; the RUF in particular deployed Small Boys Units (SBUs) and Small Girls Units (SGUs) containing the youngest child soldiers. The other soldiers generally were in their teens and early twenties. The RUF's uncommon youthfulness made it natural for its adult leaders to collectively become "some kind of surrogate parenthood" (Gberie 2005: 149). Sankoh stood above them all as the grandfatherly Papei or Pa Foday (Abdullah 1998: 218), a charismatic figure known for displays of generosity (Gberie 2005: 195).

Marijuana and Marley's Messages

Sankoh generally maintained a distanced connection to RUF warfare. He is believed to have developed the "operational plan for guerrilla warfare" and "assumed the sole prerogative for strategic thinking" for the RUF (TRC 2004a: 186). He also has been depicted as a "master strategist" and the RUF's "head of ideology" (Abdullah 1998: 220, 223).

One way in which he demonstrated the latter two roles was to regularly give speeches either in person or on radio calls to combatant groups on other bases. In both cases, Sankoh has been described as highlighting Bob Marley in his speeches and integrating lyrics from Marley's songs into them. "Get Up,

Stand Up" was the primary song from which Sankoh quoted. A male former commander, for example, shared the following recollection: "Foday said, 'Let us look at the music of Bob Marley to get up and stand up for our rights. You cannot stand up to the government because you'll be manhandled. But you can remember Bob Marley and stand up for your rights and stimulate your soul.'" "Get Up, Stand Up" was the Marley song that Sierra Leonean youth—fighters and nonfighters—mentioned most during interviews.

In the Sierra Leonean context, this particular Bob Marley song had two important meanings. The first is that it constituted, essentially, a clarion call for young people to push back against the infantilizing and emasculating effects of patrimonial control. No one interviewed for this book mentioned the song's critique of Christian leadership and messaging. Their focus was on Marley's urging for personal responsibility and direct action. From the start, the song is confrontational and electric. Christian preachers have deceived ordinary folk, Marley expounds. Life is not as it seems. God (Jah) calls on people never to accept the status quo but instead to fight for something better. Once downtrodden people realize that they've been conned, Marley predicts, then advocating to gain authentic justice becomes imperative. The song is an unswerving, intimate, and urgent call for radical, personal activism.[1]

Youth who push hard for their rights are typically construed as exhibiting *fityai*: disrespectfulness/resistance. In discussions with elders in Sierra Leone, it became clear that when young people disagree or disregard elders who control the system, being called a "*fityai* boy" or "*fityai* girl" is almost expected. As Shepler notes, "youth are notoriously *fityai*" in Sierra Leone (2010a: 632). It is a subject about which government officials and community elders seem particularly sensitive. As a paramount chief passionately stated: "You must talk to elders in a respectful manner. If you don't present your problem in a respectful manner, that's where *fityai* comes from. It is a disrespectful way of talking to elders, taking into account our traditions and customs." In effect, assuming the *fityai* approach that the paramount chief condemned is precisely what Marley's "Get Up, Stand Up" is calling on youth to do: to advocate for their rights after realizing systemic injustice. In the context of Sierra Leone, it is an inherently revolutionary song. In Sankoh's hands, the song had additional utility. "Standing up for your right" can be manipulated to endorse individual resistance to patrimonial oppression as well as armed insurrection, in this case by the RUF.

The extraordinary significance of "Get Up, Stand Up" during the war is reflected in commentary by two elders who lived through RUF occupations of their villages. A town chief recalled learning from rebel soldiers that "Bob Marley's song, 'Get Up, Stand Up,' was so inspiring that rebels fought the war with zeal and hope of winning one day in the future." A female pastor recalled how the song was connected to armed rebellion and smoking marijuana:

> To rebels, the song "Stand Up for Your Right" [that is, "Get Up, Stand Up"] means to take up guns and fight against the government. This song was so inspiring that the rebels were not ready to lay down their arms and talk peace. They were determined to fight and eventually take Freetown. They were convinced that this was the time youth should be liberated from their deprived conditions. The worst of all was the smoking of marijuana. When the rebels smoke marijuana they can do anything they wanted to do without any regret.

It is not surprising that both elders mentioned that the song was "so inspiring." It appears that rebels consistently played and replayed "Get Up, Stand Up" in their base camps and in the villages they occupied as a kind of RUF hymn. The connection between Marley's music and marijuana, mentioned by the female pastor, dates back to the prewar era. The issue will be revisited later, as marijuana was a crucial instrument of indoctrination into rebel culture and absolutely vital to terror warfare.

One former RUF commander mentioned two other Bob Marley songs that were important to the RUF's war effort. Both underscored and extended the messages contained in "Get Up, Stand Up": "Baldheads were our enemies. While Baldheads run away, we chase them. 'Get Up, Stand Up,' 'Chase Those Crazy Baldheads,' and 'Could You Be Loved'—these three songs have a good message. When we listened to them in the jungle, it gave you more zeal to fight. Foday Sankoh only spoke of Bob Marley because only the songs of Bob Marley had the message of struggle." Singing slowly, Marley opens "Crazy Baldhead" by repeating an alarming, eerie cry—a cry of resistance, perhaps. Then he delivers a very clear prediction: we're going to drive "crazy Baldheads" away. Marley then turns to reasons why driving out remorseless exploiters—the Baldheads—is justified. He asks whether his people were slaves in this land (the answer is yes). Yet even after their enslavement has passed, Baldheads still look down on him and continue to abuse him. Marley implies that Baldheads, as former slave owners and current exploiters, are deserving of personalized, righteous vengeance. In fact, they provide the rationale for what comes next: forced exile. Just like in "Get Up, Stand Up," Marley warns against being seduced by the powerful. Don't let Baldheads trick or bribe you. Instead, you must expel them from your town.[2] Marley's description of an environment involving deception, bribery, and the struggle for survival, plus earlier references to being enslaved, all resonate powerfully in the Sierra Leonean context. The song ends with Marley reminding listeners what must be done to address the situation: drive away Baldhead exploiters.

Like "Get Up, Stand Up," "Crazy Baldhead" is a call to action. The difference is that "Crazy Baldhead" delineates the target of revenge and justifies action against the oppressors. In the hands of the RUF, the song became an explicit justification for war. Interestingly, many Sierra Leoneans seemed to know who the local Baldheads were. As a retired police inspector explained, "People like me are called Baldheads. They are straight people with a tie—conservative." In fact, a Baldhead can be construed much more explicitly: as a ruling party official or a government bureaucrat. Baldheads, in short, ran the government, and what the RUF sought to do was chase them out (perhaps by killing them) and take over.

The commander's mention of "Could You Be Loved" also is significant, as it radiates a recurrent theme in Marley's music: those in power deceive, manipulate, exploit, and even try to brainwash ordinary folk. In response, forceful pushback is necessary. It is another of Marley's songs that warns listeners against treachery while encouraging self-belief. The song's refrain—asking whether a person could be loved—might be considered a call to pull back from self-hatred and realize that the problem lies elsewhere. Over and over again, Marley preaches grassroots, revolutionary activism.[3]

A second former RUF commander related that "the music of Bob Marley was the RUF music." He stated that Marley's "Natural Mystic" also was important to the RUF. The commander recited from memory his version of some of the song's lyrics. In the commander's version, and in Marley's original song, the message is clear: for unknown reasons, a lot more suffering and death is inescapable and will take place. "Natural Mystic" emphasizes mystery: changes in the world have erased the old ways, yet mystical powers nonetheless sculpt human lives.[4] In RUF hands, the song urges wartime perseverance. The fighting must continue and suffering must be endured, even though the end result is unclear.

Nuxoll relates that RUF soldiers took "the lyrics of reggae songs that were popular within the cadres" and "sometimes transformed [them] to fit the RUF context." She uses a portion of the lyrics of Marley's song "War" as an example. In a key passage in the song, Marley predicts that Africans will have to battle against the forces of evil, a conflict in which they know they will be victorious.[5] Nuxoll states that RUF members altered the lyrics "in an attempt not only to appropriate the song for motivational purposes but also to claim more personal ownership over it." She reports that "rebel song versions were sung during moments of rest on the military base, but they also accompanied looting operations." Two RUF versions of "War" went as follows:

War, war, no matter war	War, war, no matter war
And until that day	And until that day
RUF will be in [at] peace	RUF will be in [at] peace

We RUF fighters will fight	We should fight in this country
We find it necessary	We shouldn't fight another country
And we know we shall win	We should fight for our own purpose
And we have confidence	And we have confidence
In the victory	In the victory (Nuxoll 2015: 9)

What resonates most in all of this is the simplicity of Marley's messages. The themes that Sankoh and other RUF leaders drew from Bob Marley were elemental. Listen to Bob, smoke djamba, and become conscious of systemic oppression. Don't let the powerful deceive you, believe in yourself, advocate for your rights, chase the Baldhead enemy, and keep fighting. Sankoh also used the widespread connection between Marley's music and resisting apartheid in South Africa to support the RUF war effort.

The RUF's interpretations of Marley's music ably served their cause, and in the process it magnified Sankoh's mystique as the RUF leader. The end result is reflected in the following comment from a former RUF child soldier:

> During the war, Foday Sankoh was treating us right. We loved and respected him. Most of the time, he addressed us nicely and encouraged us to continue with the struggle and not give up. He said to us, "Let us fight for our rights." Foday said things were out of hand in the country. We should fight to bring normalcy. He told us to fight for our country so no one would trample on our rights. We believed him—whatever he told us during the war, we were on his side. Foday Sankoh loved Bob Marley music.

Marley's influence on RUF thinking is not reflected in most analyses of the RUF and Sierra Leone's war. The search for an RUF belief system generally led in other directions. For example, Peters is among those who contend that the RUF drew from *The Green Book* to help them champion "a simple populist revolutionary agenda, principally focused on land, education, health, and an end to corruption" (2011a: 126). However, the extent of *The Green Book*'s impact on the RUF became difficult to detect after nearly all of Sankoh's more intellectual counterparts, many of whom reportedly were influenced by *Green Book* precepts, were either run out or executed very early in the war era. Once that took place, a Sierra Leonean scholar remarked, "Foday took total control. He changed his tactics again. After chasing the academics, he replaced them with small boys. They were playing the Bob Marley music. Marley was a revolutionary, he and Peter Tosh [another popular reggae musician]. The youth used Marley's music to help them. They also took a lot of marijuana." The comment suggests that the young RUF fighters, on their own, were listening to Marley (and other reggae musicians) and smoking marijuana. Sankoh's use of Marley supported an existing interest in Marley among his young troops. As for *The Green Book*, while it may have been used (to some degree),

Sankoh appears to have drawn less from Gaddhafi's ideas than the gist of what both were after: authoritarian command, where the leader ran the show from above.

A similar result appears to have arisen from a second alleged ideological influence on the RUF. In an interview, one of Sankoh's former RUF associates mentioned his particular fondness for Kim Il Sung: "I read a book by Kim Il Sung about the Korean revolution. I was so fired up by it. You have stages of a revolution. The youth must take over and move the revolution forward. Then you had the people's army—that was the name the RUF used." Kim Il Sung was the leader of North Korea (also known as the Democratic People's Republic of Korea) from its founding in 1948 until Kim's death in 1994. His philosophy of *juche* featured elements that easily could be seen in the RUF. In Kim's own words, *juche* meant "being the master of revolution and reconstruction in one's own country," "holding fast to an independent position," "rejecting dependence on others," and "displaying the revolutionary spirit of self-reliance" (quoted in Lee 2003: 105). Key elements to operationalizing *juche* included directing a large proportion of the national budget toward the military, even in the face of widespread famine (Lee 2003: 111), indoctrinating North Koreans in *juche* ideology (110), unilaterally declaring "*juche* to be the governing principle of all aspects of North Korean life" while Kim himself assumed "godlike status" (111) and transformed North Korea into "a hermit kingdom because of the huge stigma *juche* places upon cooperation with outside powers" (106).

Some basic elements of *juche* and how it was operationalized were present in RUF beliefs and activities. The RUF had a simplistic idea of revolution, and Sankoh was the revered "godlike" leader at the top. Its approach to expenditures for security and food also were similar to that of Kim Il Sung. Starting in 1995, when "the RUF were in firm control of the diamond fields of Kono District and Tongo Field" (Smillie 2010: 104), the RUF almost certainly had more than enough funds to support its troops capably. Yet it chose not to: as will be described, hunger was an enduring problem for the RUF's "people's army" while the availability of arms was not. Also like Kim's North Korea, the RUF indoctrinated its members and cut itself off from the rest of the world, rigorously maintaining an enforced isolation for its membership and civilians under its control (Peters 2011a: 89; Gberie 2005: 65). Like Kim and Gaddhafi, Sankoh demanded the sort of loyalty that comes from threat. A high-ranking RUF officer who worked closely with Foday Sankoh for years shed light on this. "I had no objection to the RUF," he explained. "If you objected, you would be killed. As soon as you refuse to do anything, you are dead."

In the end, there appear to have been two outcomes. First, as Peters and the Truth and Reconciliation Commission detail, the RUF was a structured military organization. Internally, it had an ideology of sorts, with messages from Bob Marley's music prominent within it. Over time, however, spotting an ideology much beyond an amalgam of messages from Bob Marley's music became difficult to do, particularly within active RUF units on the ground. The boiling down of purpose and intent to a highly selective interpretation of Marley coincided with an increase in RUF violence. Peters provides one reason for how this came to pass: "By promoting [officers] on the basis of military success—perhaps because of the movement's belief in meritocracy—the RUF ended up promoting some commanders with pathological leanings prepared to undertake killing without compunction" (2011a: 127).

Two top former RUF officials supplied an alternative perspective. They argued that extreme RUF violence was unintentional. The RUF's structure and ideas did not allow it. An extended interview with them recorded flat denials that the RUF carried out amputations, raped women, or took drugs. One explained that although "we weren't amputating people, sometimes, during heavy artillery, people's arms or hands were hurt." Both also insisted that "Charles Taylor took no diamonds from Sierra Leone." These assertions are disingenuous, fatuous, self-serving, and almost certainly false. The evidence against them is overwhelming. Similarly, their assertion that only a portion of commanders undertook "killing without compunction" does not align with the historical record. As will be described, the RUF carried out extensive atrocities almost everywhere they went. Restraint did exist, and Peters describes the isolated RUF-controlled areas well. But evidence from a multitude of sources points to a pronounced and sustained trend toward terror warfare. As Peters aptly observed, "Sierra Leone needed major reform of its institutions and values, but the armed revolution of the RUF mainly brought an end to the suffering of the people by killing them" (2011a: 125).

Standing above the fray, significantly, was the RUF's leader, Foday Sankoh. Reviled by the outside world, Sankoh successfully became a leader adored by many RUF members despite the atrocities carried out under his command and the violence infused into RUF camp life. It was a nifty trick. "When Foday stands before you, he will be happy," a former RUF officer said. "I have pictures of him in my room." The connection between Sankoh and Marley also was explicit in the memories of many RUF members. A former rebel wife, for example, recalled that "Marley to the RUF was like their grandfather and Foday Sankoh their father. This was the reason why Marley was highly respected among the RUF. They smoke marijuana and celebrate with his songs in honor of his name."

Castells defines revolution as "the complete change of social rules" (2021: 260). Surrounded by thousands of exceptionally young and undereducated followers, Sankoh's vision for the Revolutionary United Front was not revolutionary. Gberie and Peters both assert that all Sankoh really wanted was to replace the existing patrimonial system with one that he controlled. The

RUF did not seek "egalitarian social revolution," Peters insists, but "a better, more functional, fairer, patrimonialism" (2011a: 93). "Lacking the imagination and political maturity to articulate new ideas and doctrine," Gberie concludes, Sankoh "simply settled on the belief that he was better equipped to engage in a more down-to-earth—and therefore more effective—form of patrimonialism, having attracted mainly underdogs to his movement" (2005: 196).

Bob Marley's exacting revolutionary fervor demanded significantly more from Foday Sankoh than he had planned to deliver. Foday merely sought control over Sierra Leone's patrimonial system. Marley, in essence, called for its overthrow.

CHAPTER 9

Both Sides Now

Run-up to War

By the time of his retirement in 1985, Siaka Stevens successfully had gamed the system he created. For starters, he left office with an estimated USD $500 million (equal to nearly $1.3 billion in 2021)[1] in his pocket, explaining that "he wanted to enjoy his wealth in Sierra Leone" (Reno 1998: 116). But Stevens was fabulously shortsighted too. His personalized systems for extracting diamonds and violently repressing dissent ultimately upended the national government he had led. While General Joseph Momoh, who had been "the commander of the largely unarmed army" of Sierra Leone (Reno 2003: 56), clearly was not up to the task of succeeding Stevens, the system also stacked the cards against his successor. As Momoh struggled with minimal success to keep Sierra Leone's government on its feet, other forces and factors conspired to weaken him. It thus is useful to start this overview of the initial years of warfare in Sierra Leone (up to the end of 1996) by briefly revisiting what took place after Stevens finally left the political scene.

Sierra Leone in the run-up to civil war (1985–1991) did not embody present-day notions of a state. Most scholars consider the Treaty of Westphalia in 1648 as the point when "feudal principalities" transitioned into "sovereign states" (Farr 2005: 156). Yet Stevens's style of rule resembled lording over a principality much more than presiding over a modern nation. He transformed Sierra Leone into a kind of personal fiefdom. Government institutions were weak and impotent by specific intention. The national army, for example, although judged to be "virtually the only state institution that retained any significant organizational identity" (Reno 1998: 115–116), nonetheless was puny, poorly trained, and paid only on occasion. The nation's borders were porous, as subsequently underscored by foreign fighters' easy entrance into the country as the war began. More to the point, Stevens and his cronies in collusion "appropriated much of" the country's diamond bounty, as well as the "profits and assets from other state enterprises, most notably from oil and rice marketing." As a result, "they destroyed the effectiveness of most state institutions, starving them of formal sources of revenue and turning them into extensions of their private patronage networks." Writing in 1998, Reno argued that "each succeeding president" sought to elevate his own patronage networks over those of "his predecessor's" (116).

Not a whiff of public responsibility or sense of public service enters the picture in Momoh's Sierra Leone. Here, for example, is a recounting from a former high-level member of the national police on his role in elections during Momoh's time: "Under Momoh, I'd collect the voting ballot boxes and return them to Freetown with arms. I was told to take votes cast from the ballot boxes and put them on the APC candidates' side. My job was connected to the victory of the APC men. The ballots are publicly sealed. Sealed: but who are the police to open [them]? They're under the APC. It was all a sham. It was so ridiculous. Sometimes they'd announce the winner without counting the ballots." Unquenchable avarice and loyal (that is, well-paid) followers drove politicians. Sierra Leone was a world of patriarchy and patronage. In such an environment, corruption was not quite what it seemed. Beyond simple greed and personal accumulation, state graft under Momoh probably also reflected his "presidential concern with building a personal power base against the freewheeling strongmen who increasingly diverted the state's traditional sources of revenue under the patronage of previous rulers"—that is, Stevens and *his* cronies (Reno 1998: 116). Alas, since Momoh sought to compete within the system that Siaka Stevens had established for himself (and his supporters), he was almost doomed to fail.

He did. Sierra Leone, at the dawn of war, featured a "crisis of youth," as Peters and Richards explained (Peters 2011a; Richards 1995). It also featured a profound crisis of the state. By the time the war began in 1991, the state was so weak that it scarcely existed: it couldn't pay its debts or its civil servants, and it provided close to no public services. Ultimately, it was another military man who took over Sierra Leone's government. His motivation is indicative of the world in which he lived. Captain Valentine Strasser did not act out of patriotism or power. It was diamonds: he "reportedly made his move after a rebel attack had disrupted his unit's illicit mining operation" (Reno 1998: 123).

This chapter focuses on key issues and incidents in the first half of Sierra Leone's complex civil war, which extends from Momoh's demise as the war began in March 1991 until the signing of the first peace accord, the Abidjan Peace Agreement, on November 30, 1996.[2] The next chapter considers indications of influence from popular culture figures (particularly Bob Marley and Tupac Shakur) on the war. Chapter 11 then features a firsthand investigation in Sierra Leone and nearby Guinea during the spooky half-year intermezzo between the accord in Abidjan and the successful coup undertaken by the Armed Forces Revolutionary Council (AFRC) on May 25, 1997. The AFRC coup emphatically marked the resumption of civil war. This is where chapter 12 begins. It also considers two key themes that directly informed the nature of Sierra Leone's war years: diamond mining and a sharp divide between humanitarian and development actors on the ground. Chapters 13 and 14 review the war's concluding years, when wartime violence engulfed the nation, terror warfare reached its peak, and then the rebel effort gradually receded. The war did not formally end until January 18, 2002, nearly eleven years after it had begun. Indications of influence from Marley, Tupac, Rambo, and other international popular culture figures will be noted throughout.

Before turning to the fall of Momoh, the rise of Strasser and his National Provisional Ruling Council (NPRC)—led by "a group of young, largely inexperienced army officers, whose average age was only twenty-six years" (Conteh-Morgan and Dixon-Fyle 1999: 130)—and other wartime concerns, a brief look at the analysis of Jimmy Kandeh is useful, as it connects trends arising before the war to the civil war era. Kandeh's take is passionate, provocative, and complex. His outcry against the trail of ruin that politicians and those considered lumpens have left in Sierra Leone is emphatic. His analysis provides insightful context for terror warfare in Sierra Leone. He asserts that Sierra Leone's predatory government system—which turned "state offices and public resources into sources of private wealth" (1999: 351)—began just as soon as Sierra Leone became independent in 1961. Still, it was Stevens who mixed a strong dose of state predation with an equal amount of state violence. It is this particular mixture that, in Kandeh's view, eventually gave rise to terror-based warfare.

Under Stevens, economic heavyweights like Jamil Sahid Mohammed (to whom Stevens "turned over the entire diamond and fishing industry") had easy access to and heavy influence in government. Meanwhile, Stevens's secretary, Abdul Karim, "patrimonialised the civil service" with "an elaborate tribute system of appointments and promotions based on bribes" (Kandeh 1999: 351). As state revenues went down, the "the private resource base of political patrons" went up (354). Momoh, who made the state "more predatory but less repressive" than under Stevens, sucked the state dry by the time of his overthrow in 1992. By the end, his government lacked the ability to function, even for corrupt ends. It was spent (353). The next set of rulers, the NPRC, eventually went on their own massive spending spree, creating "an elaborate diamond laundry scheme" as one way to secure their wealth (and then use it to purchase property overseas). And so on: Kandeh rails about subsequent regimes as well. State venality and corruption was as long-standing as it was comprehensive. Leaders forgiving rogues from prior regimes for their wretched deeds was commonplace (355).

Alongside nepotism and colossal, systemic corruption, the state promoted violence. Starting in the 1970s, the Stevens regime created a "massive intrusion of thuggery and violence" that focused on helping his associates hold on to power. Two important events during the Stevens regime shed light, respectively, on the conduct and the consequence of the state violence. The first was what became known as "All Thugs Day." In late January 1977, students at Fourah Bay College protested against the policies of their president, Siaka Stevens (who also was the school's chancellor). On January 31, Stevens fought back (Gordon 2006). Members of his Internal Security Unit, together with armed youth who backed the APC ruling party, did not merely attack demonstrators. In a style "resembling future RUF operations," the state-backed ruffians harassed nearby traders, broke into shops, and at least attempted to assault women (Reno 2003: 55).

The second event was Sierra Leone's hosting of the 1980 annual meeting of the Organization of African Unity (OAU). Incredibly, spending for the event ultimately amounted to more than half of the nation's annual budget (Conteh-Morgan and Dixon-Fyle 1999: 113). Outwardly, Sierra Leoneans reportedly had no problem with this use of state resources. However, Conteh-Morgan and Dixon-Fyle explain that "the widespread support of the masses for hosting the OAU conference was not based on any rational economic calculations of long-term payoffs, but on fear of punishment" (114). Field interviews with Sierra Leoneans recalling the Stevens era regularly communicated an ingrained fear of the president himself, who had a knack for climbing into the minds of his citizens and haunting them.

Who were the violent male youth who carried out wild violence on behalf of their patrons? Kandeh says that Stevens and his associates "relied almost exclusively on the recruitment of urban thugs and rural drifters" (1999: 359). He adds that the APC eventually preferred the rural lumpens, who "were expected to be more subservient to the interests of their patrons," over the urban lumpens, "whose loyalties were inherently suspect" (360). All such lumpens "are products of a culture that is steeped in violence, thuggery, hooliganism and banditry" (362). In a perspective shared with a number of commentators on Sierra Leone, there is the intimation that certain marginalized male youth had somehow become very bad people, and quite different from the rest: those deserving of derision and active disgust. Unsurprisingly, field interviews indicate that some of those regarded as thugs in Sierra Leone identified with Tupac's "Thug Life" tattoo and his celebration of being viewed as "bad."

Disregard for disregarded male youth, together with their exploitation, are themes that keep surfacing in the story of Sierra Leone. It is widely accepted that youth in Sierra Leone have long been discounted by their government. Stevens and Momoh displayed a particular mastery for alienating ordinary citizens. As noted in chapter 5, Momoh "was on record as saying that education was a privilege rather than a right for citizens" (357). Yet the accent on privilege started with Stevens. Between 1980 and 1987, the government's spending on health and education fell by 60 percent (Reno 1998: 116). Moreover, patronage and ethnicity determined who received government scholarships, not qualifications. This practice "expressed precisely the sort of injustices that alienated the vast majority of Sierra Leonean youth" (Kandeh 1999: 357).

Kandeh divides Sierra Leone's regimes into two categories: (1) the "predatory lumpen dictatorships" of the NPRC and the AFRC (together with the RUF), and (2) the "predatory elite dictatorships" of the APC (that is, Stevens and Momoh) and the nation's other dominant political party, the Sierra Leone People's Party (SLPP, the party of the pre-Stevens regimes). The main difference between the two is revealing: "whereas public resources were the main targets of APC plunder, the 'equal opportunity' pillage of the AFRC/RUF made no distinction between public and private property." Moreover, while elite leaders used violence to maintain their positions and dominance, the "subaltern usurpers" and their leaders used violence to extract and extort from anyone they pleased (Kandeh 1999: 356).[3] For Kandeh, RUF/AFRC rebels, and the NPRC government took "the pillage ethos of the political class" and made it comprehensive (365). However, he also contended that the elite and lumpen dictators were essentially the same. They were bandits, and they had no limits: "What elites do, especially how they exercise state power and how they engage political opponents, condition what subalterns consider permissible. The violent elimination of political opponents by the AFRC/RUF is reminiscent of what they were mobilised by elites to do in the past. The main difference today is that the thugs who elites once relied on to intimidate and eliminate their opponents *have come home to roost*" (361, emphasis in original).

Two consequences of the decades-long tradition of leaders being "more interested in holding on to power than legitimating their dominance" (359) are worth noting here. The first was immediate: a disloyal national army. Kandeh details what he calls "the transformation of army regulars into brigands and armed robbers" (362). During the civil war, the phenomenon of the *sobel*, a blend of "soldier" and "rebel," referred to "soldiers by day, rebels by night" (Ferme 2001: 223). Kandeh states, "While 'sobels' were disproportionately soldiers with lumpen backgrounds, senior officers in the army also colluded on a routine basis" with sobels and rebels alike. This unsightly combination of rogues wreaked havoc on the ground and havoc in the national military. Acceptance and active support for sobels undermined the army by shattering "rank discipline and contradict[ing] the very *raison d'être* of the military as a state institution" (Kandeh 1999: 362, emphasis in original). On the other hand, if the sobels themselves were opportunists, they were desperate ones. Some had been plucked from rural families too poor to support them. Others had been forced to join the army. Kandeh contends that the army surely could have defeated the RUF rebels early on, were it not for the dominance of sobels in their ranks. This seems like a stretch: the army was not, in any way, a unified national force. They were freelancers. In the end, it was Sierra Leonean civilians who "bore the brunt of the mayhem unleashed by 'sobelised' soldiers and their rebel allies" (364).

A second consequence of the example that Sierra Leone's self-serving leaders had set arose from the wildly unprofessional nature of Sierra Leone's military. It was the privatization of security needs. As will be described, successive Sierra Leonean governments engulfed by the war relied on mercenaries and foreign troops instead of their own national army because, in essence, they did not have one.

When the RUF started the civil war, the national army (often called the Sierra Leone Army, or SLA) consisted of a mere three thousand soldiers. Momoh's response presaged much that was to come. Most of the eleven thousand recruits he subsequently ordered into service were of the kind that so many routinely condemned: excluded male youth living along Sierra Leone's edges with no shot at improving their lives. In other words: the hated lumpens and subalterns, or, perhaps, "marginals—'raray man dem', 'dregman dem' or Kaplan's 'loose molecules'" (Kandeh 1999: 363). Momoh's move may appear cynical. It probably was. At the same time, decades of government leaders had undermined a shared sense of public service or national purpose. It would have been difficult to secure any volunteers, particularly when the army historically was so weak and overlooked. Stevens had ensured that this would be the case, as his "suspicion of a strong army had tended to leave the army with a largely ceremonial role" (Keen 2005: 83).

Sierra Leone's national army, suddenly 367 percent bigger and much more uncontrollable, was thrust into combat. It had little ammunition and outdated equipment, and soldiers still received little or no pay (83). There also is no indication that the newcomers received any kind of serious training or preparation to become fighters. Even when government funds were earmarked for the war effort, graft by top military leaders was so substantial that troops in the field had "shortages of fuel, food, medication, spare parts and salaries" (Koroma 1996: 148–149, cited in Keen 2005: 83). In addition, the sobel categorization carried with it an interesting twist. In the early part of the war, Keen notes that SLA soldiers were fearful in part because they had difficulty "telling who was a civilian and who was a rebel" (Keen 2005: 84); sobels confronting "civbels," perhaps. With the entire corps of national soldiers so untrained, scarcely compensated, and generally disregarded, and with no apparent cultivation of national honor, duty, or esprit de corps in their ranks, the eventual rise of the sobel phenomenon is entirely unremarkable.

Meanwhile, Momoh was in increasing trouble. As political pressures grew,

Momoh lifted a ban on establishing new political parties, something inconceivable under Stevens (Keen 2005: 86). The main source of government revenue—the diamond trade—had virtually evaporated. Reno relates that official diamond exports fell to a mere USD $22,000 in 1988 while "Momoh's rivals [that is, allies of Stevens] were exporting diamonds estimated to be worth $250 million" (Reno 1998: 120). Momoh was having difficulty attracting investors while the IMF and other creditors pressed for reform.

To change the dynamic, Momoh promised to provide security for diamond mining firms interested in doing business with his government. He instituted two military operations, Operation Clear All and Operation Clean Sweep. For a man seeking to bolster government credibility and his personal patronage system simultaneously (this was Sierra Leone, after all), the results were disastrous. Just as the names suggest, the operations forced twenty-five thousand miners to flee. Even worse, in the words of one army officer, "These operations were the best recruiting tool the rebels had" (Reno 1998: 121). The army's soldiers also were demonstrating aggression at civilians generally, regularly distrusting and turning on people, particularly young men suspected of having rebel sympathies (Keen 2005: 88, 89). Alienated soldiers were battling alienated civilians.

With nothing working, Momoh's overthrow mercifully arrived. The so-called Tigers (a unit within the army's Fourth Battalion) entered Freetown from their Kenema base on April 29, 1992. Resistance was slight. Captain Valentine Strasser, a "very young-looking 26-year-old" who was "a one-time competitive disco dancer," became the nation's new leader. Given all that ordinary Sierra Leoneans had gone through, Keen notes, "Some saw the youthfulness of Strasser . . . as a particular source of hope, a much-needed injection of innocence into a corrupt polity." He certainly was inexperienced: "Strasser read his speeches like a nervous schoolboy reading an essay" (2005: 94). The new regime, led by a cadre of very young and very poorly educated military officers, began with much popular support.

Rastafarians on the Loose

Thirty-one years and two days before the NPRC coup took place, Sierra Leone became an independent nation (April 27, 1961). In many newly self-governing African countries, musicians wrote songs that celebrated their national leaders. Many of the brand-new governments also sought to support local musicians as a way to "strengthen national identity and social coherence."

The Sierra Leonean government attempted this as well. However, it didn't work because the leaders "did not find much support from the side of the musicians" (Stasik 2012: 71). As one musician who was active in the 1960s in Freetown recalled, "We never had political music." In fact, "nationalist or patriotic sentiments were marginal to non-existent in Freetown's popular music scene" during that period (71). Siaka Stevens shared the musicians' disinterest in patriotism. One of the curious dimensions of his brand of governance, following his rise to the top in 1967, was his disinterest in cultivating a national ethos. Opala notes that the official national symbols of Sierra Leone (the flag, the coat of arms framed by lions, the national anthem, and so on) "received surprisingly little emphasis under the APC" (the party of Stevens). This was perhaps not entirely unexpected, since Stevens in particular "was more concerned with projecting the emblems of the APC party—its red banner, song, and rising sun emblem" (Opala 1994: 207). Emphasizing the ruling party over the state evidently made much sense to a dictator who had survived three coup attempts and was a self-interested partisan.

The coup that overthrew Momoh stimulated not only jubilation but an astonishing awakening for many citizens—particularly male youth in Freetown, evidently including a good number of the infamous so-called lumpens. Writing in 1994, Opala noted that the population of Freetown had doubled over the previous decade. The main cause was rural-urban migration, particularly by young men (or male youth) "with little education and few prospects for full-time employment" (197). He then details the sort of work they found: petty trade, work in government security (army, SSD, police), work on the docks, as watchmen, or as house servants, and for some, street crime or petty theft.

At the outset, the young NPRC soldiers who had driven out Momoh were a hit. They promised to "end the war swiftly and return the country to political pluralism." In addition, the new leaders made it clear that they were, at first blush, stunningly different from all prior regimes. The radio broadcast that announced their successful coup "was accompanied by continuous reggae and rap music." To youthful listeners, after two decades of encountering trouble from the state due to their love of such music, the tunes played on state radio must have been a revelation. Young citizens very quickly realized that "Sierra Leonean youth and the junta leaders had similar backgrounds and referred to the same youth culture and music." After decades of self-centered governance, the coup inspired "a new wave of patriotism and support for the military leadership swept through the country."

Citizen connections to the young new leaders had a definite reggae flavor, as "Young Sierra Leoneans demonstrated their allegiance to their peers in power by exchanging Rastafarian salutes with the junta soldiers" (Nuxoll 2015: 7). It started on the first day of the coup, when "crowds of young people stood on the road-sides, hailing the soldiers, and saluting them with the thumbs-up gesture and the phrase 'One Love!' (or 'unity'), that they knew from reggae music and Rastafarianism. After the coup the gesture and the phrase became the unofficial symbols of the NPRC. Now, when young people meet, they say either 'One Love' or 'Respect', and they extend their fists, thumbs up, or press their fists together, in a gesture called *bayn* (from English 'bind') denoting solidarity" (Opala 1994: 205–206).

In his uplifting "One Love," Marley famously urges togetherness and shared joy.[4] The NPRC had brought a lightness to governance, and an immediate connection between officials and the many down-and-out young people that thronged towns and cities (as well as diamond mines). The "conscious" music and Rastafarian ideas, which had "contributed to the development of a more revolutionary and radical political stance among disaffected youth" under Stevens and Momoh, were now out in the open (Nuxoll 2015: 7).

Overnight, Bob Marley, reggae music, and Rastafarianism were not just allowed; they directly influenced government leaders and their views. Like Sankoh, "Strasser regularly quoted Bob Marley in his speeches," a veteran Sierra Leonean journalist recalled. The NPRC leaders "were all ganga [marijuana] smokers. They made Marley even more popular. They loved Rastafarian ideology" as well. A former RUF member shared the following recollection of these early days. "When the NPRC took over power, they were hailed as liberators and saviors. They saw themselves as freedom fighters who have come to free people from the hands of the oppressive rule of the APC." From the very beginning of their rule, he explained, the NPRC leaders used Marley to inform important actions and decisions. He shared two examples:

> Like in Marley's song, "Chase those crazy Baldheads out of town," the NPRC started targeting APC leaders like the then-inspector general of police, Barbay Kamara, Col. Kahota Dumbuya [a senior military officer], and many others who were considered as crazy Baldheads who must be eliminated.
>
> During this period, marijuana also was almost legalized. Smoking was rampant among the soldiers. Bob Marley Night—that is, May 11—was like a national event. Soldiers celebrated this day with smoking marijuana and singing of Marley's songs of liberation.

Bob Marley died of cancer on May 11, 1981. Marley fans then initiated an annual Bob Marley Day (or Bob Marley Night) every May 11 by playing his music and smoking lots of marijuana. A Sierra Leonean religious leader recalled, "By the end of the 1980s, celebration of Marley's death became so popular that marijuana smoking was permitted on that day" every year. By 1992, Sierra Leone's NPRC government commemorated the day and led the celebrations. The following year, at a concert in Freetown by the Jamaican reggae band Culture (featuring Joseph Hill), Sierra Leone's new era was underscored by the following reported scene: the nation's head of state (Strasser), as well as "most of the main figures in government," sitting together "in the front row, smoking spleefs of marijuana."[5] Djamba was the smoke (or drug) of choice, and "One Love" effectively had become the government brand and, perhaps for a time, a political philosophy. A Freetown resident (and a youth during the time of Strasser) recalled that "the slogan was, 'One love to the revo'" (that is, to Strasser's revolution). As Opala observed, "The bond between the soldiers and the urban youth was apparent from the very beginning" (1994: 197).

The NPRC marked their early days in power with a decision that accelerated the completely newfound national fervor: an order to make the last Saturday of every month a day for cleaning up the nation's rubbish. This may sound like an unusual way for a government to gain popularity. But the public areas of cities had been ignored under Momoh and were filthy. There were heaps of uncollected trash, silt, and debris clotting street gutters, as well as related refuse problems. In response, and on the appointed Saturdays, "young soldiers patrolled the streets in the morning," calling citizens to clean areas in front of their homes. Opala reported that "the new government's clean-up campaign was extremely popular, and Captain Strasser, the NPRC Chairman, and other high officials were photographed helping to shovel rubbish from the gutters" (1994: 195, 196). The government worked with citizens to clean up Sierra Leone and in the process cultivate national pride.

The civil war brought a swift reality check. Until the day before the coup, the young national leaders were military officers in the war zone. Adjusting to directing the war effort and governing a nation at the same time proved a challenge. By October 1992, the "euphoria generated by the 29 April coup and the popular clean-up campaign that followed" dissipated when the RUF took over Koidu, the capital town of diamond-rich Kono District. But the regime's popularity had bounced back by December. In short order, the NPRC leadership announced that they had put down an attempted "counter-coup" and executed the alleged plotters. The executions led Sierra Leone's former colonizers, the British government, to suspend a portion of their aid assistance. Then NPRC forces recaptured Koidu. "Enthusiasm for the NPRC rose to new heights" after the failed coup and executions. It grew even stronger after the military victory in Koidu (Opala 1994: 196).

Then, in January 1993, the popular response from "working class [male] youths in Freetown" in support of the NPRC created a unique moment in time. A wave of patriotism and national pride burst free, led by normally downtrodden and denigrated urban male youth who "formed themselves into neighbourhood 'youth organizations', and set about patching streets, cleaning gutters, and painting curbs and median strips on a massive scale throughout the city" of Freetown. This was a male youth–led endeavor: while young women were "allowed to join" the youth organizations, they were "expected to take supporting roles" (Opala 1994: 197, 198). As was so often the case in Sierra Leone, the focus and reference point for "youth" was male youth. Female youth (or young women) remained in the background.

The fact that unsung and routinely derided male youth claimed a leading role in exuberant expressions of national pride and support for the government is, by itself, both extraordinary and exceptional in Sierra Leone's history. After many years of being viewed as pernicious threats to mainstream society, here were male youth converting themselves into movement leaders. In a country "with almost no tradition for patriotic imagery," urban youth suddenly created "a type of art almost unprecedented in Sierra Leone—patriotic art as glorifying the nation's history and culture, and extolling the [NPRC] revolution" (Opala 1994: 198). Entirely on their own, they created "symbols of national consciousness" where none had existed. The absence of state control (and threat) was equally remarkable, given well over two decades of throttling governance.

The ferment on the streets was revolution, and the young artists "enjoyed almost total creative freedom" (199). Opala asserted that the destruction of "a once prosperous and harmonious community" was APC-specific: he reckoned that Sierra Leoneans in 1993 looked back fondly on the time of the nation's first prime minister (Milton Margai) as well as (somewhat surprisingly) the British colonial period, "when national leaders acted according to the dictates of morality and religious faith." Given the political undercurrents of this spontaneous activity, the mayor of Freetown's response was predictable. He "objected strongly to the uncoordinated actions of thousands of youths." However, "the soldiers"—now connected directly to those running the nation—"came down decisively on the side of the young people" (204, 215).

The male youth artists are reported to have been particularly impressed by three currents of ideas and actors: (1) "the exploits of pre-colonial chiefs and warriors, such as Bai Bureh, Madam Yoko, and Sengbe Pieh";[6] (2) the "NPRC's style of revolutionary militancy"; and (3) "Rastafarianism with its emphasis on African unity, brotherhood, and peace." Opala proudly reported that the artists "see all of these things as providing the inspiration that Sierra Leoneans will need to overcome decades of political corruption and moral decay" (204, 205). He was hardly a dispassionate observer of this remarkable outburst of creative national euphoria, having taught a course called Art, Anthropology, and National Consciousness at the nation's main university, Fourah Bay College. In his course, Opala urged the young artists in his class "to use their talents to promote popular awareness of Sierra Leone's history and culture" (201).

Opala must have been overwhelmed with delight in seeing the outpouring of portraits and murals that sprang up across Freetown. The subjects included NPRC leaders, famous heroes of Sierra Leone's past, slogans connecting reggae Rastafarianism to the government (including "One Love"), Pan-Africanism, Christian scenes mixing Jesus, Mary, and Moses with well-known Sierra Leonean religious leaders, and murals that "all seek, in one way or another, to associate Rastafarianism with the NPRC Revolution" (209–210).

Some of the associations were explicit, such as a complicated scene featuring "a 'Rasta Man' with his dreadlocks flying and his arms raised high, holding a map of Africa above him" with the slogan: "'29 April Revolution—Lead us to Freedom—Jah Bless.'" Still other murals featured young Rastas painted "in dreadlocks and beads, [who are] supporting the revolution." Finally, there also were murals of the war. One featured NPRC soldiers capturing a certain Nasty Rambo, known to be "a notorious rebel whose *ronko* [traditional war vest] was said to be bullet-proof." In it, Nasty Rambo's face is a skull, and he wears "a war shirt covered in animal horns and fetishes" (210, emphasis in original).

"Sierra Leone's spontaneous festival of art" lasted all of three months. By April 1993, the enthusiasm had waned, citizens no longer were contributing funds to support the young artists and their paintings, and normalcy returned. Rain eventually eroded or washed away some of the street art. Opala also noted that "all the young people suffered from excessive expectations" (215). His recollections on all that took place are poignant and hopeful, and no doubt also reflect a teacher's pride in the work of his students:

> The young soldiers of the NPRC made a revolution on 29 April 1992, but Freetown's working class youth made another eight months later. The first was a revolution in political leadership; the second, in consciousness. These young people are the first generation since independence whose loyalty to "tribe" has faded. Most of them left the rural areas when they were very young. Some grew up entirely in the city and have never known their parents' homes upcountry. Many speak only Krio, the nation's lingua franca, and not their parents' languages. They represent all of Sierra Leone's ethnic groups Mende, Temne, Limba, Loko, Susu, etc., but they owe allegiance more to one another than to "tribe," and they have learned to depend upon one another in the hardest of circumstances. The 29 April coup, by young men their own age, gave these disadvantaged young people a new sense of importance, and from January through March 1993 they set out to define themselves. Their grandparents cobbled together a new nation thirty years ago, but they are the first generation to take "Sierra Leonean" as their primary identity. They are Sierra Leoneans first and foremost, and in twelve weeks they forged powerful new symbols to give that identity a new pride and a new reality. It is only a beginning, but there is no turning back. (218)

The dramatic events of early 1993, spurred by the military coup and the NPRC's super-young leaders from ordinary backgrounds, stirred in young Sierra Leoneans a sense of national pride and a newfound expectation that their national government could be inspirational, supportive, and worthy of their admiration. It also appeared to have brought urban male youth together. Cities, it turns out, have a way of cultivating a cosmopolitan urban identity that absorbs new young people, underemphasizes ethnic difference, and promotes stability (Urdal and Hoelscher 2009: 17). What took place in Freetown early in 1993 illustrated this trend.

There were two important additional outcomes from this uplifting wartime period. First, it marked a time when Sierra Leone's government and the RUF rebel group *both* hailed Bob Marley and Rastafarianism as ideological guides (with other reggae musicians playing key supporting roles). As Nuxoll observed of this period, "For a short while, youth culture, music, popular music figures, and politics were consolidated in novel ways, putting commonly marginalized and disaffected youth and their lifestyles on the political map, propelling subcultural music into the cultural and political mainstream for the first time." All of this took place while "behind rebel lines, reggae music also was popular with RUF combatants" (Nuxoll 2015: 7, 8).

This unusual confluence of events, where the works of Bob Marley and other reggae musicians, seasoned with Rastafarian religious and Pan-Africanist ideas, were guiding lights not just over youth but the leaders running both Sierra Leone's government and their rebel adversary, did not last. After the explosion of youth culture and art centered in Freetown, "the momentum had waned and made way to general disappointment among youths who did not see their expectations met by the NPRC they had so fervently promoted, not least because the military junta came to resemble the very regime it had ousted" (7). NPRC leaders did not live up to the revolutionary expectations the youth had set for them during the early months of their government. They were locked in a war with the RUF. Many of those in the military had never stopped demonstrating sobel behavior in war zones. Sadly, it also turned out that the NPRC leaders were not all that different from their predecessors. Although the thumbs-up sign of "One Love" remained (and, as will be noted, flashed its significance in disturbing ways on the war front), Sierra Leone's young new leaders were as grasping as Stevens and Momoh. They most certainly were not revolutionaries. After a brief burst of promise and joy, many urban male youth once again assumed their discouraging status as debased lumpens.

The second notable outcome from the initially joyous period of NPRC rule proved to have remarkable staying power: the widespread and heavy use of djamba. The tradition of smoking marijuana (while listening to reggae) arose in the 1970s. Smoking marijuana technically was illegal, but its use was widespread. By 1992, Sierra Leone's new head of state openly smoked djamba and celebrated Bob Marley. So did government ministers, military officers, and soldiers, and so did their RUF adversaries. Over time, marijuana and warfare seemed to merge. All reports for this book clearly indicate that the drug grown in the country was unusually potent. As it became central to what abducted rebel boys and girls ate and drank, it thus gained the power to facilitate and fuel terror warfare. Members of all of Sierra Leone's wartime actors—RUF and AFRC rebels, as well as civil defense units and the national military—recalled smoking heavily and regularly during the war, often while listening to Bob Marley's music. Everyone practiced marijuana-infused warfare. Strasser and his NPRC government's active endorsement of djamba, together with reggae music generally and Bob Marley specifically, marked a kind of turning point in Sierra Leonean history. From that point onward, marijuana and Marley were out in the open.

Return to War

There has been a succession of books that feature Sierra Leone's Revolutionary United Front. It is easy to appreciate why. The RUF started the civil war, had a consistent leader, and even had a kind of ideology (even if most Sierra Leoneans never knew what it was). It was a coherent and capable military organization. Sierra Leone's own national army (the SLA) was not. Virtually everything it did was haphazard or undistinguished: recruitment, training (excepting a few officers), organization, logistics. What it seemingly provided to its members was a uniform, some arms, and a decentralized brand of organization. To say that a shared ethos or admirable collective purpose disintegrated during the war years would imply that it once had existed.

The foot soldiers of the SLA and the RUF had much in common. Most were young, poor, and male, with limited (or no) prospects for advancement. Many came from suspect backgrounds. For example, when Strasser and the NPRC expanded the ranks of the military to fourteen thousand, he "recruited from the unemployed youth, some of whom had earlier joined armed gangs or earned a living through crime" (Reno 2004: 56). Both sides had child soldiers. By 1993 the NPRC had child orphans from RUF attacks in their ranks, amounting to "over 1,000 boys under fifteen years of age, some as young as seven" (Gberie 2005: 77). Reno observed that "Sankoh and the NPRC soldiers shared a similar political analysis of the country's problem—it was potentially rich, but politicians had stolen about anything worth stealing." He also observes that the NPRC's leaders "hailed from among the marginalized segments of the population who in other circumstances sought the patronage of strongmen in return for acting as political muscle" (Reno 2004: 57).

Another shared trait was the use of terror war tactics. Both RUF fighters and SLA soldiers did not just steal to get even or get ahead. They practiced extreme violence. Their shared trademark was committing public acts that brutalized and terrified ordinary people. As Keen observed, "as with the rebels, a sense of powerlessness and material deprivation seems to have fuelled the desire [of soldiers in the SLA] to assert power through violence—often against civilians." It is during this early stage of the war that government soldiers and RUF rebel fighters both "were increasingly adopting Rambo-style headbands." Keen does not find this surprising, given that "the Rambo films feature a Vietnam vet betrayed by his own politicians" (2005: 109).

A thumbnail of what took place in the early war years will be provided here (mainly drawn from Gberie 2005). After the NPRC coup had become a reality, RUF spokesmen (via the BBC) let it be known that they had initiated a unilateral ceasefire and sought to negotiate a peace settlement. Not for the last time, the RUF was underestimated. Strasser referred to them as mere bandits in the employ of Charles Taylor, who were in Sierra Leone merely to create chaos. Both sides misread their adversary: the NPRC apparently thought that the RUF "could be hunted down and crushed" while the RUF believed that "their participation in the NPRC junta was imperative" (Gberie 2005: 74). War resumed, particularly in the diamond mining areas.

To get a sense of what was taking place, it is illuminating to reflect on the various battles for Koidu. When the RUF first seized the town in October 1992, the national soldiers "appear to have been busy mining diamonds when the rebels struck there." A response known as Operation Genesis ensued, and the military recaptured Koidu. But once again, in 1993, "NPRC soldiers were busy mining diamonds when the rebels struck at the town and took it" again (Gberie 2005: 77, 79). Gradually the NPRC gained the upper hand, driving into rebel-held territory with its "brutal troops" that considered "anyone in 'rebel territory'" a rebel (indiscriminate violence is inferred). By December 1993, Strasser announced a ceasefire, calling on the RUF to give up (80). The NPRC seemed to be in command. Even the RUF knew this. In their *Footpaths to Democracy* treatise,[7] they state:

> By late 1993 we had been forced to beat a hasty retreat as successful infiltration almost destroyed our ranks. We were pushed to the border with Liberia. Frankly, we were beaten and were on the run but our pride and deep sense of calling would not let us face the disgrace of crossing into Liberia as refugees or prisoners of war. We dispersed into smaller units, whatever remained of our fighting force. The civilians were advised to abandon the towns and cities, which they did. We destroyed all our vehicles and heavy weapons that would retard our progress as well as expose our locations. We now relied on light weapons and on our feet, brains and knowledge of the countryside. We moved deeper into the comforting bosom of our mother earth—the forest.
>
> The forest welcomed us and gave us succour and sustenance. The forest continues to be our main sources of survival and defense to date. (Revolutionary United Front, n.d.)

Six comments help unpack this passage:

- The document suggests that army soldiers had infiltrated the RUF and nearly destroyed them. While this sometimes may have been the case, most reports underscore the sobel phenomenon, in which soldiers did not enter the rebel group but merely *acted* like the RUF (mainly by committing acts of terror against civilians).

- The passage claims that only their shared "pride and deep sense of calling" prevented fleeing into Liberia. Perhaps, but they also may have been fearful of what might have awaited them upon arrival in Liberia.

- The passage also does not detail how Sankoh initiated the RUF's tactical shift with what appeared to be a second purge. After the RUF's "stinging military losses" in 1993 eventually "led to infighting," Sankoh responded dramatically and violently. He had "dozens of accused traitors" within the RUF "tortured and killed," including his "much-admired, militarily skilled second-in-command, Rashid Mansaray," who ultimately was replaced by the super-violent "hardliner," Sam "Mosquito" Bockarie (Marks 2013: 362, 365). Sankoh enacted other stunning acts of violence, including the "public torture, including sexual torture" of one of his wives. Almost predictably, Sankoh's response to crisis highlighted "heavy-handed violence." It helped him affirm his control over the RUF, reset the RUF's military command, and reinforce "the value of the unapologetic use of force in an increasingly mercurial organization" (362).

- The idea of civilians being "advised" to leave their homes has to be taken with many grains of salt. It is difficult to imagine an ordinary person refusing an RUF soldier's intimation that it would be best for them to flee. Remaining at home almost certainly meant death.

- Praise for the forest. This part of the passage is accurate. The 1993 retreat of the RUF (into the Gola Forest, near Sierra Leone's border with Liberia) marked a significant change in military tactics. Starting in 1994, "the RUF became a forest-based guerrilla force, with jungle bases in inaccessible terrain and using hit-and-run attacks or ambushes as its main fighting tactics. In the jungle camps the RUF was beyond the reach of the government soldiers, mainly operating with heavy, and thus road-bound, equipment" (Peters 2011a: 147). While this assessment is imprecise (the RUF often left the jungle to take and occupy villages, towns, and mines), a general shift in tactics was apparent.

- The reference to reliance on light weapons (such as AK-47 guns) and "our feet, brains and knowledge of the countryside," followed by praise

for "the forest," underscore the primacy and utility of what many former rebels whom I interviewed called "Rambo Tactics." These tactics
feature simple technologies and draw from a person's wits, knowledge
of the forest, and the element of surprise. (Rambo Tactics will be discussed in detail in chapter 15.)

Instead of retreat leading to surrender, the RUF began to hit back hard
early in 1994, retaking Koidu yet again and recapturing the diamond-rich
Kono District, and then threatening Bo, the country's second-largest city.
Where were the NPRC soldiers? Once more, their inattention to the duties of
soldiering erased their gains. This time, instead of mining for diamonds, soldiers had vacated their positions to watch soccer. Many had gone to Freetown to attend a "hugely popular" regional football tournament. They were
"convinced that the war was over" and so had "abandoned their positions at
the front to watch the matches, and thus provided an opportunity for the rebels to regroup and launch deadly offensives" (Gberie 2005: 80). Those left behind on the war front (including "irregulars" receiving no pay) naturally "felt
betrayed by their superiors." Gberie suspects that these soldiers turned to
banditry or joined the rebels. After this, the terror war expanded. The now-
emboldened RUF began to ambush vehicles on highways, burn down villages
and towns, and take hostages (taking foreigners as hostages proved particularly effective, as it always attracted considerable attention and embarrassed
the NPRC). Their efforts "created the impression of great power which was
vastly disproportionate to their actual strength" (81). In April 1994, they attacked the Northern Province for the first time (87).

The NPRC leaders seemed to have no learning curve. They repeatedly un-
derrated and misjudged their rebel adversary. Worse, the war was growing
more complex. Acts of complicity involving soldiers and rebels became common, including a dramatic rebel attack on bauxite and titanium mines in January 1995, when Major (and future coup leader) Johnny Paul Koroma and soldiers under his command allegedly joined in looting and destroying the mines
(Gberie 2005: 88). Civil Defense Forces (CDF; considered traditional hunting
societies adapted for warfare) were composed of ethnic-based and locally organized forces. One of these, the Kamajors of the south and east, also joined
the fray, often attacking the RUF with great success and eventually becoming
a major player in the war.[8] The war also had become deadlier and more intense. Indicative of this was the reaction of the RUF to women activists who
entered Kailahun District (which the RUF held for the entire civil war period)
to plead for a ceasefire. The RUF executed them (89). Late in 1994, the government admitted that "at least twenty percent of its soldiers were disloyal"
(Gberie 2005: 91). That undoubtedly was an exceptionally low estimate. As

Hoffman observed, "There were those in the state military for whom a continued war and a continued relationship with the rebels was simply more profitable than peace" (Hoffman 2011: 38).

In 1994 the government was also becoming unbound, entering 1995 facing "incipient anarchy and dissolution" (Gberie 2005: 91). That is when the NPRC again turned the tables on the RUF. This time, the force in the lead were mercenaries: the unscrupulous national army had made "surrogate forces . . . the order of the day" (Hoffman 2011: 39). The first mercenary unit were the Gurkha Security Guards (GSGs), the Nepalese fighters in the British army. The famous Gurkhas didn't last a month. Their commander, Robert Mackenzie, relied on a part of the national army that he evidently had not screened and did not know. Sierra Leonean soldiers ambushed and killed him in late February 1995. The following month, the NPRC hired helicopter gunships flown by Ukrainian mercenaries to back their troops and an ECOMOG (Economic Community of West African States Monitoring Group) contingent of Nigerian soldiers (the army also had a military unit from Guinea operating elsewhere in the country). The force attacked a highway position called Mile 38, which the RUF held. The troops flattened it. The rebels returned to the forest (Gberie 2005: 91, 92). As with other apparent victories during the war, Mile 38 looked like a government victory. But the rebels merely had vacated a known location. They had made the forest their home and sought to avoid direct confrontations with rival forces.

Strasser finally turned to the South African mercenary outfit, Executive Outcomes (EO), in May 1995. For a while, the decision was decisive. The 150 EO soldiers trained some army and Kamajor units in counterinsurgency. Backed by substantial military hardware, they attacked the RUF in the east and south, while the Nigerians and Guineans struck the RUF in the north. The collective effort made big gains (Gberie 2005: 92–93, 94). The RUF again was backpedaling, under pressure, and in retreat. Some RUF members surrendered (Richards 1996: 17). Meanwhile, in Freetown there were plans afoot to have national elections and shift from the NPRC junta government to civilian rule. Major Strasser suddenly wanted to be seen as a civilian. But by this time, the NPRC had become as violent and rapacious as the RUF. Both were "profoundly unpopular" in Sierra Leone (Keen 2005: 154). Strasser's own deputy, Julius Maada Bio, who recently had jumped from captain all the way to brigadier general, made his move and overthrew Strasser in January 1996 (155).

The skies over Sierra Leone appeared to clear in 1996. It started badly: the rebels (and some soldiers) amputated the limbs of at least fifty-two civilians in the early months of 1996 to terrorize people and stop them from voting. But the elections proceeded in March. Ahmed Tejan Kabbah, a longtime veteran of the United Nations and the leader of one of Sierra Leone's oldest political parties, the SLPP, became president (Gberie 2005: 94, 95). Peace talks

A taxicab interior in March 1997, a few short months after the first peace agreement had been signed in Abidjan. The dashboard photo appears to have been taken during the February 1996 meeting in Abidjan. It features a sheepish Brig. Gen. Julius Maada Bio in the dark uniform on the left. Bio was briefly head of state in Sierra Leone early in 1996, as the leader of an internal NPRC coup. In the center is a tired Foday Sankoh, the RUF's leader. The taxi driver points to the confident military man on the right, Tom Nyuma, a second well-known military commander, as well as a onetime NPRC official. In 2018, long after the war had ended, Bio again became Sierra Leone's head of state, this time as an elected civilian president.

with the RUF ensued. They were peculiar. Bio and Foday Sankoh were downright friendly and cordial with each other during a February meeting in Abidjan. It made some wonder about collusion and deals over diamonds. That Bio's sister, Agnes Deen-Jalloh, was a top RUF official (after having been abducted three years previously) helped cultivate the impression of collusion. Kabbah promised the RUF amnesty in June.

But the war simultaneously continued. The Kamajors pressed both "rogue soldiers" of the national army and the RUF successfully. Kabbah's fondness and preference for the Kamajors over his army began to shine through. He "threatened an all-out kamajor offensive if the RUF did not sign a peace accord by the beginning of December 1996." Meanwhile, donors promised major rehabilitation funds if a deal could be done. The RUF and the government signed the Abidjan peace agreement on November 30 (Keen 2005: 155, 158).

Fatefully, the RUF successfully negotiated to have Executive Outcomes leave Sierra Leone as part of the peace deal. This returned responsibility for the country's security to the national army—a terrible idea. The arrangement stayed in place (more or less) for six months. As Gberie noted, "The experiment in democracy lasted until May 1997" (2005: 95). Authentic peace remained very far away too.

CHAPTER 10

Groups and T-Shirts

Weaving Pop Culture into Warfare

Across Sierra Leone's war, popular culture wove itself into wartime practice. To appreciate what took place, it is helpful to reflect briefly on the dearth of role models for youth in prewar Sierra Leone. In the time of Stevens and Momoh, public expression was circumscribed and dissent was dangerous. From this unfortunate starting point arose admiration, sometimes adulation, and, to a degree, imitation of international popular culture stars. The strong sentiments, particularly among male youth, for iconic heroes such as Bob Marley and John Rambo (with still others in the background, such as reggae stars Joseph Hill and Peter Tosh, and action movie personalities Arnold Schwarzenegger [in *Commando*] and Chuck Norris) entered the scene in many ways. Over time, the imitation intensified. Reggae followers smoked marijuana and sometimes wore faded jeans. One mark of an authentic follower was dreadlock-style hair and being seen as a "Rasta."

Tupac Shakur's arrival in Sierra Leone reportedly followed the release of his initial music album (*2Pacalypse Now*) in late 1991, the year the war began. After that, an array of outward styles denoting "Tupac System" arose. They could include tattoos, usually on a person's shoulder. For some, any tattoo—with words or pictures—could signify that a person was both a follower of Tupac and a rebel fighter.[1] A Tupac follower also may wear a "turn-up," where one trouser leg is rolled up high, or don a vest. As with dreadlocks for Rastas, one true mark of a Tupac devotee was a shaved head. During the war, followers of Rambo wore particular bandannas (also called bonarias, bandarias, or bandas), such as one featuring an American flag (known as the "American Banda"), which connected the wearer to Rambo (and secondarily to Tupac, who regularly wore a bandanna, and sometimes even to Marley, who did not). A second bandanna was black with many dollar signs on it. That connected mainly to Tupac. A third "bandaria" was red. It evidently connected the wearer to both Rambo and Tupac. Rebel units reportedly wore them, at different times and in various places, across the entire war period.

But the T-shirts, particularly black ones depicting Marley or Tupac on the front, were the big deal. During Sierra Leone's war, the military organization of the rebels (and the CDF) was decentralized. Field units were small and mobile. The frame of reference of nearly every ex-combatant who was interviewed was the specific fighting unit to which they had belonged. While rebel field units appeared to be adept at maintaining radio contact with their superiors, the power of a field commander over his unit was encompassing. As the war wore on, the number of field units increased dramatically. Some interviewees reported that it could be difficult to tell units apart. As a veteran former RUF soldier commented, T-shirts helped field units "identify themselves from other factions. There were so many [rebel] factions. That's why they called it a senseless war."

Thus entered the rise of visual signatures for wartime groups.[2] A few examples demonstrate the considerable diversity: In one group, every male wore dreadlocks, from the field commander down to the smallest and youngest male fighter. The Rambo Group that circulated around Makeni in the latter war years wore the telltale red bandanna. Undoubtedly the most "Tupac" of the Tupac-follower groups was the West Side Boys, a militia with many field units. Many members reportedly sported shaved heads, tattoos (Tupac on the right shoulder, a panther on the left), vests, the turn-up style of trousers, bandannas, and "Tupac T-shirts" (more about them shortly).

There also were subdivisions of field units that each wore different T-shirts. A former RUF combatant explained that "sometimes you'd have Tupac and Bob Marley Groups" within the same unit. During military encounters "the two groups would attack at the same time. We were able to identify each other by the T-shirt we wore." A second ex-RUF combatant described how some RUF field units divided their fighters into those wearing either the Bob Marley or Tupac T-shirts. In this combatant's field unit, "The Tupac squadron was braver than the Bob Marley squad." Bob Marley and Tupac T-shirts that were black reportedly helped field units attack at night. They also did not show dirt as fast. Not least, the T-shirts were exceedingly popular with youth, underscoring the youth orientation of rebel and CDF ideas.

Journalist Lansana Fofana led the way in noting the significance of T-shirts to the rebel cause. In 1995, he reported that approximately fifty RUF rebels attacked a northern village, with all of them wearing Bob Marley T-shirts (1995). Three years later, he recorded a second attack, where "young men and women in their hundreds, clad in rap T-shirts" all bearing the image of Tupac Shakur, attacked the town of Kukuna. The attack left some civilians killed, others amputated, many houses burned, and food stolen. Fofana notes that Kukuna survivors subsequently outlawed the Tupac T-shirt from the town. Then he put the significance of rebels and T-shirts into context: "In the early days of the war, people wearing T-shirts, bearing the late Jamaican reggae idol Bob Marley's portrait, which were popular with the rebels, were detained or lynched in combat zones" (1998a).[3]

The Tupac T-Shirts

Interviews with former combatants indicated that black Bob Marley T-shirts had long-standing popularity with rebel (and Kamajor) fighters. They were around before the war, and they were present and popular with fighters during the conflict. But the Tupac T-shirts had a special cachet with boy and male youth fighters. One can appreciate why. In a way, Tupac was "their" hero. Marley was the movement godfather, known as the "King of Reggae" and a special favorite of Foday Sankoh and his commanders. He also was popular with many Sierra Leonean adults. T-shirts featuring Marley were familiar. Tupac, in contrast, was new: he arrived in Sierra Leone just as the war took off. His strongest appeal, by far, was with boys and male youth, and the genre of his music (rap or hip-hop) was emphatically a youth style.[4] As will be discussed in part 5 of this book, Tupac's influence with rebel units also connected him to hard drugs (cocaine in particular) and extreme violence.

The initial reports of Tupac T-shirts in the war theater arrived from a veteran former RUF fighter. He was an early abductee: "They captured me in 1991" in Kailahun (where the war began), he said. Soon afterward,[5] "We ambushed a vehicle containing that [Tupac] T-shirt. From there, [the rebels] loved it." He added, "We [had] learned about Tupac beforehand. We used Tupac to fight because he was aggressive. He gave you morale. We took cocaine before we [would] fight." By the following year, the RUF's use of Tupac T-shirts appears to have expanded. Field interviews included reports of RUF soldiers in Tupac T-shirts during the RUF's initial (and briefly successful) assault on Kono District in 1992 (Smith, Gambette, and Longley 2004: 331). A civilian survivor of this assault recalled that "in 1992, the rebels were wearing Tupac T-shirts and red headbands in Kono, with Tupac tattoos. Some had shaved heads too. The tattoos were words and also scorpions, spiders. Eighty percent of the rebels in the 1992 Kono attack were wearing Tupac T-shirts." A former diamond miner near the city of Bo recalled "Tupac attacks" on his mine in 1992 and 1993. Noting both his admiration for Tupac and what became the RUF's penchant for traveling via rain forest, he described the scene when RUF rebels, adorned in Tupac T-shirts, entered his world: "You know, Tupac is a tough man and this is a tough life. [The RUF rebels] walked through the bush, not on the road. When they came to a town, they captured others. They [would] say, 'We are Tupac Thug Life. We live by ourselves; no one can control us. We do what we want to do. And no one can stop us.' That is Tupac. That is Thug Life." Once this rebel unit took a town, the former miner continued, the rebels wrote "'2Pac' on walls. They had '2Pac' tattoos on their

A Sierra Leonean male youth proudly sports one Tupac T-shirt version, featuring Tupac Shakur and his "All eyez on me" signature, in 1998.

arms. They used stones to write 2Pac; 2Pac on the walls, on the ground: 2Pac everywhere."

Another large cache of Tupac T-shirts reportedly was uncovered in Makeni in February 1998, after the RUF (and their new rebel allies, the AFRC) had sacked the town (Smith, Gambette, and Longley 2004: 127). The rebels appeared to have uncovered a Tupac T-shirt mother lode. One former RUF combatant on the scene recalled that, before the Makeni attack, "the elderly soldiers" in his unit (evidently including his commander) "only gave us a red tie—red on your head"—that is, a red bandanna. But Makeni, he said, was where "the Tupac" started. "This is where they found lots of Tupac T-shirts. Lots and lots of fighters were wearing the Tupac [T-shirt]" from this point onward.

Across the course of the civil war, thirst for pop culture items informed the goal of many rebel attacks. Rebels routinely identified the things they wanted as "government property"—that is, theirs. Rice and other foodstuffs were government property. Marijuana always was. In addition, a male civilian could be forced to hand over the T-shirt he wore at rebel gunpoint. However, shops in villages, towns, and cities were a particular priority. There was interest in carrying off new T-shirts of Bob Marley and Tupac, as well as new bandannas. Nuxoll also relates how rebels sought batteries, solar panels, and music cassettes (2015: 12). Solar panels were used to play videos and films in rebel camps (noisy generators attracted unwanted attention) while batteries were needed for portable music players. There were reports of rebels playing music as they attacked and rebels celebrating, dancing to Marley or Tupac music, after they took a town or village. The overwhelming interest in T-shirts had a corollary: there also were many reports of civilians being attacked or arrested for wearing Bob Marley or Tupac T-shirts. In the minds of many, on both sides of the war, they had morphed into rebel uniforms.

Many Kamajor fighters loved Marley and Tupac T-shirts too. As with their rebel counterparts, one reason for this was practical. The traditional Kamajor uniform was made of natural fibers drawn from the forest. A former Kamajor commander related that "we used Bob Marley and Tupac T-shirts. It was because the Kamajor uniform smelled so bad. We never washed our uniforms: if you washed them, they [would] fall apart." Accordingly, "If you have a Tupac or Bob Marley T-shirt, you put the charms on the T-shirt." Affixing the charms to all uniforms was necessary because "they protect you" during fights. A second former Kamajor commander detailed what must have been an absolutely bewildering scene for ordinary civilians to witness. "There were times when we were wearing Bob Marley and Tupac T-shirts," he recalled, "and the P.A. [the People's Army, a name the RUF and the AFRC gave to themselves] attacked us, all wearing Tupac T-shirts"—two adversaries in a firefight, with members on both sides wearing the treasured T-shirts.

A final point must be made about specialty groups. These were warrior units known and feared for particular terror practices. Here is a small handful of examples from field interviews. On the rebel side, there reportedly was a "Rambo Group of girls" whose signature was raping men. The Adama Cut Hand Group (led by Adama Cut Hand herself) was known for amputating hands and arms.[6] On the Kamajor side, a former commander recalled two specialty groups in particular. One was the Yarmotor Group, who practiced cannibalism. If there was "something delicious to eat when they'd capture an enemy, they'd butcher it like a cow, roast the person, and eat him."[7] He also mentioned the Black December Group, which, judging from the responses of other former fighters and civilians, seems to have cultivated an even more substantial reputation.[8] He explained their activities and style of dress in the following way: "These were the wicked ones. They liked to do ambushes on the highway. They wore charms, but they always wore black T-Shirts: Bob Marley, Tupac, Joe Hill. Whatever: the T-shirt had to be black. They also wore black trousers, shoes, and bandannas. They'd kill and cook and eat people.

And they'd make a lot of war. They'd listen to Bob Marley, Tupac, and all the Rasta music. They just behaved like Rastas."

There will be much more discussion of terror practices, including cannibalism, in parts 4 and 5. But first, the arc of Sierra Leone's war must be completed. The next chapter examines the period between the November 1996 peace agreement and the explosive return to war in May 1997. Chapters 12 through 14 detail what took place next, right up to the war's end.

CHAPTER 11

When the War Came to Us

Entering Sierra Leone

Before preparing to enter Sierra Leone for my first time in 1997, I gathered up documents to study. The pickings were slim: for a war that had lasted more than five years, little was available about it. There also was no agreement on what the fight was about. Up to that point, I had studied many African conflict environments in the center, east, and south of the continent, conducting field research in Ethiopia, Rwanda, and Somalia, and with refugees from Burundi, Rwanda, Mozambique, and Somalia. Researching genocide in Rwanda and Burundi was a part of the mix. But there was no genocide in Sierra Leone, and there seemed to be no underlying ethnic conflict. There were amputations—lots of them, reportedly, although the rationale for these acts was unclear. Sierra Leone's war was disturbing and mysterious.

Perhaps appropriately, entering Sierra Leone also was disorienting. For reasons that are not easily apparent, the airport is positioned a good distance from the capital, on the other side of a broad bay (or estuary, as it is the mouth of the Sierra Leone River) from Freetown. Getting into the capital city is not straightforward. Each option seemed to have a downside. Traveling by road was difficult, slow, and potentially quite dangerous (cars were known to be vulnerable to bandit attack). Ferry rides were irregular and could take a long time. Hiring a small private boat, in the middle of the night and my first time in the country, seemed dicey. A private company ran a helicopter service. I had been instructed in advance to take this option: the swiftest, perhaps the most reliable, and definitely the most expensive means.

I arrived into Lungi International Airport at night. The area beyond the airport was pitch black. The air was steamy. Making my way through immigration and the baggage and (entirely informal) customs areas, politely sidestepping hustling porters along the way, I asked for the location of the helicopter. I was pushed ahead with other arriving passengers (and a great many porters) into a narrow area just outside the airport. Pressed by the crowd around me, I made my way along the metal bars that separated me from a second crowd that pressed in from the other side of the barrier. Someone pointed to a darkened, narrow corridor between two cement buildings as the route to the helicopter. I hesitated; it seemed an odd location for the next leg of my trip. But as it was clear that I had no choice, I hoisted my suitcase, carried it along the path between the two buildings, and found a creaky Soviet helicopter on the other side. Buckling up on a bench before the ride took off, I realized that my sweater, which I been carrying since leaving the plane, was gone. Someone had lifted it away as I moved along the metal bars. No matter; I was tired and unsettled, and looking forward to resting in a bed.

My journey over the water ended by entering a local taxi on the other side of the bay. For quite a few dollars, the driver took me a very short way to the Mammy Yoko Hotel, nearly next door to the landing site. At that point (mid-March 1997) the Mammy Yoko was merely a well-known international hotel. It became famous on June 2, when the rebels burned it to the ground in a desperate clash mainly with Nigerian soldiers. Between the successful military coup on May 25 and the second of June, the Mammy Yoko was the site for many hundreds of Sierra Leoneans and internationals seeking evacuation.[1] Their escape was dangerous, the Mammy Yoko was left a smoldering ruin, and the civil war had restarted. The worst was yet to come.

All that was in the future. Less than four months earlier, on November 30, 1996, the government of Sierra Leone and the RUF had signed the Abidjan Peace Accord. Yusuf Bangura wrote about it soon afterward. In his view, the accord marked "the official ending of Sierra Leone's five and a half years of war, which has ravaged much of its country side, killed more than 10,000 civilians, left hundreds of innocent bystanders maimed and traumatised, displaced almost a million and a half people from their homes and livelihoods, orphaned thousands of young children, and imposed financial and social burdens on much of the relatively stable population." Bangura highlighted an important change that the war had caused: "the transformation of the country from a predominantly rural society of small, sparsely populated and widely dispersed villages into pockets of dense urban settlements." He depicted the conflict as an "anti-rural war" and labeled the accord "a potent indicator of the basic unity of the country." He also cited "the long-standing determination of most people to put an end to what they have all along rightly regarded as a senseless war" (Yusuf Bangura 1997: 57).

Bangura's description mixes hope with utter disregard and disdain for the RUF. He noted, for example, that the RUF "is hated by the vast majority of villagers and urban dwellers for its employment of a savage methodology of exterminating or maiming the very people it seeks to liberate." He also spotlighted the impact of the Kamajors, who had caused the RUF to suffer "very serious set-backs in the battle field." In an assessment shared by many Sierra Leoneans whom I would interview, Bangura viewed the Kamajors as patriotic heroes. These "modern-day traditional hunters and fighters . . . were determined to defend and reclaim their villages and root out all traces of RUF activities from their localities" (62). Bangura also cited "a new hypothesis" that at the time was "making the rounds in Sierra Leone." The shared contention was that "some of the Kamajors are 'super rebels,'" former RUF members who left to join the Kamajors. Bangura claimed that "this explains why the Kamajors have been more effective than the army," since the Kamajors "know all the hideouts, strategies and tricks of the RUF." Bangura further asserted that the Kamajors' "role in the war has been decisive in changing the balance of power on the ground" (64).

Most of the assertions in Bangura's analysis resonated with what I heard from many of the international officials and Sierra Leonean leaders whom I interviewed during my trip: the war is over, it had been pointless, the Kamajors are gallant patriots, the RUF are on the verge of collapse, and the army is insignificant. All of these themes, it turned out, were either false or entirely debatable. To begin with, as Smith, Gambette, and Longley (2004) detail, the war most certainly was not over. In fact, it had never really subsided. An important provision of the Abidjan Peace Accord was the stipulation that all foreign forces, as well as Executive Outcomes mercenaries, would leave Sierra Leone (Executive Outcomes had exited the country by early 1997; the foreign forces remained). In its place was a three-way, low intensity war. In some places, the army and the Kamajors attacked the RUF in tandem, such as at the RUF's "Camp Libya" in the south. In others, the Kamajors attacked the RUF on their own, such as in the Kangari Hills, located in Sierra Leone's center. Yet the RUF also made gains, taking Kamakwie in the country's northwest. Still more confrontations, during this period of so-called peace, took place between Civil Defense Forces (CDF, mainly composed of Kamajors) and the army. It also was the case that "civilian populations fared badly throughout areas controlled by both CDF and SLA [Sierra Leonean army] forces." For example, in two districts "civilians suspected of being 'RUF collaborators' or who were considered to be insufficiently supportive or respectful of the CDF, were subjected to gruesome punishments" (Smith, Gambette, and Longley 2004: 30). In short, the war carried on, all the armed groups were brutal, the Kamajors were hardly heroic, and the SLA continued to be a major actor in the war.

Denial of reality was a major theme of the field research in March and April 1997. It is difficult to envision a capital city, overflowing with throngs of citizens displaced by warfare—Yusuf Bangura attests that the city's population more than doubled due to the civil war, from about a half million to over one million (1997: 57)—as a place where the war's impact consistently was understated. But it was: during interviews, national leaders and international actors mostly spoke about the war as a faraway concern, not something affecting everyday lives in their world. Sure, the conflict was terrible and its impact had to be addressed. However, it had taken place in the bush, not Freetown. As Alie observed, "For a long time the rebel war [in Sierra Leone] was viewed largely as a provincial affair which had little to do with the capital city" (2006: 20). By the end of my trip to Sierra Leone and the refugee camps in nearby Guinea, when I returned to Freetown to debrief officials of the Sierra Leonean government and nongovernment agencies, my impression was that most decision makers and elites in Freetown had sequestered themselves from devastating realities practically on their doorstep. The findings I shared did more than shock most of them; they depicted a reality about which most expressed little or no awareness. The near-complete absence of detailed knowledge about up-country horrors was stunning.

Following my arrival, I conducted initial meetings in Freetown before flying to Bo, the capital of the Southern Province. From there, I hitched rides with international NGO cars to Senehun, in Moyamba District, and Sahn Malen, in Pujehun District (the capital town of the chiefdom, where the paramount chief resided), and to a nearby diamond mine. Next, I flew to Kenema, the capital city of the Eastern Province. It was a puddle jump of a flight, since it is merely 38 miles (61 kilometers) from Bo. However, travel on Sierra Leone's main highways was absolutely off limits, as it might attract attacks by armed groups (for some reason, driving out of Bo on small roads was thought to be reasonably safe). Not so in Kenema, which (at that time) was small and eerily quiet. Kenema is perched on the doorstep of Kailahun District, the fingerlike part of Sierra Leone that the RUF dominated across the entire civil war period. Fear of the RUF rebels was strong in Kenema. It also was real: there was a nighttime curfew, and international agencies had deemed road travel outside the town much too dangerous to attempt. Some of the officials I met also warned of many RUF *recces* (spies) operating inside Kenema.

I stayed put in Kenema, before flying back to Freetown. From there, I flew into U-shaped Guinea: first to Conakry (northwest of Sierra Leone), and then to the Forest Region (southeast of Sierra Leone). My travels ultimately took me into an area known as the Parrot's Beak of Guinea (Onishi 2001). Extending southwest of the town of Guéckédou, it borders Kailahun, located just across the Makona and Meli Rivers, and is surrounded by Sierra Leone on three sides. Many tens of thousands of Sierra Leoneans fled into that area, a dense forest thinly populated with Guineans and bereft of decent roadways. After visiting the largest camps for Sierra Leonean refugees (known as Koulomba and Fangamadou; tens of thousands of Liberian refugees were in the area too), I flew back to Conakry and onward to Freetown, where my fieldwork came to an end.

Sierra Leone in early 1997, together with the refugee camps hosting Sierra Leonean and Liberian refugees in Guinea, featured floundering bureaucracies. Inside Sierra Leone, international actors seemed unaware of the fact that government institutions were weak by design. That was what Siaka Stevens had created during his period in power, and that is how they had remained. Yet intentional weakness was not the only reason for the government's general ineffectiveness. International humanitarian actors, fortified with donor funds and urgency, regularly sidestepped government officials and agencies to deliver goods and services on the ground. The general sense was that the government, led by its Ministry of National Reconstruction, Resettlement, and Rehabilitation (MNRRR), was not prepared to address the needs of masses truly desperate, war-affected Sierra Leoneans. Effectively, foreign entities were filling the governance void.

Tensions and frustrations ran high on both sides. An exasperated MNRRR official stated, "The government can't control the [international] NGOs." International donors "prefer to go through the NGOs, creating a parallel system that bypasses the government." As influential donors funnel money to international agencies (and not the Sierra Leonean government), the available funds for the government "are so small. How do you monitor NGOs in the field if you have no transport and they have vehicles with AC [air-conditioning]? Can you control their work? Can you? Realistically, no; you only can hope the NGOs come in with their conditionalities and their money."

The bureaucratic power in the country appeared to have settled onto international agencies. In one of my first interviews, a UN official summed up the standoff. "The MNRRR tries to control NGOs, but the NGOs balked. The NGOs come to Sierra Leone to do their work. They don't go through the government, and the government is bitter." The country director of an international NGO was dismissive of the Sierra Leonean government. In the director's view, "The Sierra Leonean government has never been outside Freetown during the war. The officials are reluctant to go out." In addition, "government ministries compete with each other for resources and legitimacy. They all lack systems, procedures, and guidelines. There also is a lack of competency." As a result, "the government complains that NGOs have taken over their role." A second UN agency official stated that there was "a great deal of suspicion between foreign agencies and the government" of Sierra Leone. Not noted by any of these officials was one crucial fact: if government institutions were mostly hapless, the powerful donor agencies were exacerbating their historic weaknesses.

Over and again, international agency officials mentioned one—and only one—Sierra Leonean government official whom they respected. He was a high-ranking official in the MNRRR. Reflecting the general attitude of international actors, a foreign official explained, "There's a reliance on the credibility of one man in Freetown." Another official considered this man "the

MNRRR entry point. He's the most able at the Ministry, a very good individual." It was apparent that international agency officials routinely overlooked formal government procedures and policies—the same procedures and policies that some international officials had criticized as weak—and instead headed to the office of the lone government official who, in their collective view, was credible and deserving of their respect. This way of getting things done undermined governmental capacity still further.

Just before leaving Sierra Leone, I succeeded in meeting the singular government official worthy of high international regard. He was distracted and busy. One could see why: our meeting was delayed because a clutch of international agency officials had jumped the appointment line and entered the government official's office ahead of me. He said that this happened with regularity. I shared some of my main findings, nearly all of which were new to him. The meeting ended abruptly, as yet another group of foreign officials required his urgent attention.

The administrative situation in the refugee camps for Sierra Leonean and Liberian refugees in Guinea was similarly abysmal. The context of the bureaucratic challenges, however, was entirely different. The power broker lording over the refugees, and even the international NGOs that implemented various programs for refugees, was a single agency: the United Nations High Commissioner for Refugees (UNHCR). Implementing agencies (another term for the international NGOs, since the presence and influence of national NGOs was minimal) blasted UNHCR's ability to protect and administer support to refugees. Their officials variously described UNHCR as corrupt, disorganized, incoherent, negligent, detached, incompetent, disinterested, and simply incapable of managing refugee-related affairs. UNHCR was attacked for reportedly not investigating cases where refugee girls allegedly had been raped or abused by teachers, planning the repatriation of refugees inadequately, selling food that had been earmarked for refugees for a profit, and not keeping track of refugee children.

UNHCR officials, in turn, were remarkably impassive to the plight of refugees. One remarked that, nearly six years after refugees had entered Guinea, "no specific program for [refugee] children has been done until now." "We know the refugees do not have enough food," the official continued. "But we just give them what we can." A second UNHCR official described their agency's opposition to orphanages. In the official's view, such institutions "are not part of the African tradition." Instead, "in Africa, normal people take care of children. African context is key—children are accepted." The result was a potentially perilous situation in which unaccompanied children (who may not have known if their parents were dead or alive) simply were placed with ordinary refugee families. In other cases (particularly inside Sierra Leone), it appeared that some adults seized children—girls in particular—who were available for the taking.

Refugee populations expressed their frustration about UNHCR carefully: they clearly were afraid of negative repercussions from UNHCR if officials uncovered the source of refugee complaints. Among the refugee leaders (all of whom were men), one suggested that they had been infantilized. Evidently, the pattern was for leaders to make requests to UNHCR officials and then hope for a response. "We are just like babies," the leader explained. "We are only here to wait." UNHCR officials, in turn, "only say that we can ask Geneva," the site of UNHCR's headquarters. Like refugees, UNHCR officials in Guinea reportedly expressed powerlessness to respond to refugee concerns. As with international NGOs and their donor benefactors inside Sierra Leone, institutional power seemed to emanate from the West, not from within Sierra Leone or Guinea.

Children, Gender, and War

In the vacuum of viable and dependable institutional authority inside Sierra Leone and within the refugee camps, Sierra Leone's complicated war zone world endured. There was not peace, just eerie ambiguity. At every turn during my field trip, I found ordinary Sierra Leoneans unprotected and grappling with a general sense of insecurity. There were rumors of RUF *recces* in their midst (particularly in Kenema), reports of vengeful government officials, and deep fear of military groups of all kinds: government soldiers, RUF rebels, and Kamajor warriors. Emerging from this period of uncertainty were three particularly significant sets of field research findings.

The first concerned gender. War had upended the order of things, but not always in ways that might have been anticipated. One surprising issue surfaced from the availability of education in camps and settlements for refugees in Guinea and internally displaced persons (IDPs) inside Sierra Leone. In these settings, education was accessible to significant numbers of girls as well as boys. This alarmed many adults. In the town of Sahn Malen, for example, several teachers explained that many girls were encouraged not to attend school. Reportedly, there was a widespread belief that education makes girls "wayward," inspiring them to migrate to cities, wear short trousers, drink soft drinks (perhaps with alcohol), and have boyfriends. The belief that schooling for girls led them down a road to social disaster (and, by extension, social humiliation for their families) was expressed elsewhere too. A leading women's civil society official in Bo reported, "Many believe that if girls learn English, they likely will become prostitutes." Knowledge of English would enable girls to converse with foreigners, such as international humanitarian officials and military personnel. Such people had money. This inevitably would lead young Sierra Leonean girls toward commercial sex. A woman official for a women's health NGO in Sierra Leone noted that "the percentage of illiterate girls as compared to boys is very high." She summed up the pervasive view as follows: "Education is bad for women."

The perception of education as perilous for daughters effectively reinvented education as a road to prostitution. It also transformed keeping girls out of school into a child protection strategy. The same beliefs were present in Guinea's refugee camps as well, where primary education for boys as well as girls was readily available and actively encouraged (some secondary schools also existed). A leading refugee education administrator explained the "common belief" held by many Sierra Leonean adults that "if a girl gets schooling, she won't obey her parents." Disrespect for her parents meant that "her father will be unable to find a husband for her." Just as in Sierra Leone, many contended that educated girls would "probably become prostitutes." The principal of a primary school for refugees stated, "All [refugee] parents have the opportunity to send their daughters to school. But they believe that school is not meaningful and a waste of time [for their daughters] because the girls won't finish. They believe that if the girls go to school, they will become pregnant. They are afraid that when girls are without supervision, they will become pregnant. Boys will ruin their lives. The parents also believe that educated girls won't get jobs." The fear of prostitution also resonated in comments from a male refugee leader. The man explained that a girl or woman who became a prostitute would be viewed as "spoiled"—that is, no longer virginal and pure. He continued, "Men can't marry them. We are afraid of STDs [sexually transmitted diseases]." The collective indication from these comments was that females who ended up in prostitution (also known as commercial sex work) faced permanent social marginalization.

Refugee education professionals had devised three arguments to persuade refugee parents and guardians—most of whom had little to no formal education—to send their girls to school. The first argument of the "community awareness campaign" was that only those with education "can work for expatriates" (that is, international agencies) in Guinea and Sierra Leone. Second, "even if you go back" to Sierra Leone, "only the educated will benefit from reconstruction projects," which probably would be funded and run by the very same expatriates referenced above. The third argument was immediately practical: since "you will have to read notices of entitlements" in order to receive them, families will need literate children to gain access to packages of assistance. Taken together, the arguments highlighted the need to adjust to and accept permanent change, which included yielding to powerful nongov-

ernment institutions from the West. Since all three arguments implied a reduction in adult control over girls, it was not surprising to learn that the three
arguments were not gaining traction among refugee parents.

While Sierra Leone's civil war unquestionably had eroded parental control
over their daughters (as well as their sons), the most devastating outcomes for
girls emerged from something much more elemental: the absence of many
parents. Civil war exploded Sierra Leonean families. Parents were killed or
separated from their children. Girls were vulnerable to exploitation, including
sexual abuse. Indeed, their capacity to provide domestic labor and sex converted them into unusually valuable commodities.

Whether in Sierra Leone or as a refugee in Guinea, unaccompanied girls
did not seem to stay unaccompanied for long. Readily available and desperate,
many reportedly were enticed or snatched up by various households. "You
can call it slave labor or foster family care," stated the director of a major international NGO in Sierra Leone during this period. "Girls are just more economically useful to a family than boys." A Sierra Leonean official working for
an international NGO remarked, "The men who take in young women often
impregnate them." If the girls are in school, "they will leave to support their
child. Now, this girl [an unmarried mother] is largely unwanted. The father
[of the child] may be married already." The manager of an IDP camp (in Graf-
ton, near Freetown) stated that "girls ages twelve to eighteen are taken into relationships by men of all ages." Girls taken into families, on the other hand,
"may stay at home [to do housework] so the daughter of her guardian can go
to school," said a refugee education official in Guinea. Older, "mature" girls
who are orphans are not absorbed into families. Instead, the official said they
must "get married to manage life. It may not be their choice, but they have
to." While it was not clear how often forced marriages took place, the official
added that "a large portion of young women are unmarried with children or
are widows."

The exceptional value and utility of adolescent girls and female youth was
underscored by reports about rebel military encampments. In mid-April
1997, an international official tracking the war related that "the Kamajors in
Magburaka [the capital of Tonkolili District, in the north of Sierra Leone]
have brought out thirty-eight [RUF] rebels." He also reported that there were
far more women than men in the [RUF] camps. And yet "no women have
come out." Field research for this book revealed a trend that supported this
assessment. For the RUF, as well as their eventual colleagues from the military
(the Armed Forces Revolutionary Council), the number of women (including
wives) in rebel camps fluctuated. As securing enough food to eat was a near-
constant preoccupation of rebel groups, a pattern appeared to emerge. When
food was regularly available, the population of girls and female youth in the
camps expanded, sometimes exponentially.

Sierra Leonean employees of international organizations often worked in or along the edges of conflict zones, and often with those who somehow had escaped from RUF-controlled areas. An interview with five men fitting this profile found broad agreement that the ratio of males to females in RUF camps fluctuated. In the view of one, "The percentage of young women among rebel captives is far higher than the boys. Maybe each rebel [fighter] has six wives in one camp." But he added that "Kamajors and government soldiers also have young women at their service." Other reports suggested that high female-to-male ratios only applied when rebel groups had food. When food ran low, girls and female youth reportedly were the first to be forced out of rebel camps (or executed). A field researcher I met in Bo provided one indication of life as a rebel girl. She estimated that "over ninety percent of girls and young women who are former rebel captives are infected with STDs." Subsequent reporting supported the suggestion of sexual abuse: "Girls associated with fighting forces are at a high risk for sexually transmitted diseases (STDs) and reproductive services are seldom available to them" (McKay and Mazurana 2004: 62).

What about the boys? If girls were deemed "more economically useful to a family than boys," the opposite was the case in the mines. In eastern and southern Sierra Leone, a remarkable component of the research was regular comments about adolescent boys and male youth heading to work in alluvial diamond mines (often at the urging of their families). Relatively few were in the refugee camps, nor were many present in the towns and villages I visited in the east and south. Either parents had sent sons into the mines (hopefully to send money back home) or the boys had decided to go there. While diamond mines seemed to be a logical destination for orphan boys and male youth, some of them reportedly mined because they had no choice. A government field officer for disarmament, demobilization, and reintegration (DDR) related that "Sierra Leoneans with capital or power put boys into the mines. I fear that orphans and unaccompanied minors are forced to mine for others." The issue of slavery in the diamond mines surfaces again in the next chapter.

A trip into one diamond mine in Pujehun shed light on mine dynamics at that time. During a visit to Sahn Malen, ten male youth miners offered to show me their claim in a nearby mine. Eight of them were between ages twenty and twenty-eight. Another was thirty-five, and the tenth was fifteen. In a theme that was almost ever-present in recollections of wartime experiences, one of the youth stated their main motivation for mining: "There's no other way to get food besides mining," he explained. "I have food now. I have to learn to live on my own." A Lebanese diamond trader had provided food and supplies ("rice, sugar, petrol, supplies, and tools") to the ten male youth in return for, one presumes, a very significant cut of any diamonds the boys dis-

A surly mine leader and some of the miners under his control, following the war. The leader awarded me permission to visit the mine and interview some of the miners.

covered. Like all gamblers, the youth miners all lived on hope. One explained how "one head miner—thirty-five years old—found [a] one-hundred-percent pure one-carat diamond." Even for such a small discovery, "he got three hundred thousand leones [USD $305.53], and he found it after looking for only one month."[2] Hopefully, similar luck would come their way soon.

We walked down a hill away from town, surrounded by dense forest. In a clearing near the bottom of the hill, a large tract of land came into view. Boys of all sizes and ages stopped their digging to gape at me. A loud pump sucked water out of the bottom of a long, narrow pit and deposited it into the forest. The youngest and smallest of the boys seemed to be operating in the water. Rimmed by tall trees, the mine contained only dirt and mud.

A minute or two after entering the area, a burly middle-aged man carrying an AK came toward me. Evidently the leader of the entire mining area, he was furious with the ten boys for bringing me there. He also was angry that I had been allowed to leave the path that wound its way across the hard dirt above the pit. The man barked at me, demanding that I stay on the narrow path. The reason, the boys explained, was that anywhere away from that path—even a few inches to one or the other side—constituted trespassing onto a plot of land claimed by someone and reserved for mining. Even small bits of dirt that stuck to my shoe might have tiny diamonds in them, they explained. Looking around, the mine seemed to consist mainly of men with machine guns, a couple of male youth manning the pump on the other side of the pit, and boys and youth collecting or looking through mud. I drank in the scene and was allowed to take some photos. Then, while vigilantly keeping on the path, I was escorted out of the mine and back into the forest by some of the boys who had taken me there. Behind me, I heard the leader giving a tongue-lashing to those in the group who had remained behind. I did not turn around to look.

In Sierra Leone in early 1997, it certainly appeared that the abduction of children and youth was both common and widespread. While unaccompanied and orphaned girls were vulnerable to forced labor for families (and sex for men), some of their male counterparts evidently were forced to mine. Forced abductions into military groups already had become well established, starting right after the civil war had begun. During my early 1997 field trip, a field officer of a DDR program for former combatants reported that, of the sixty-six former rebel fighters in his program in 1997 (all of whom were boys), only one said he had volunteered to join the rebels. However, the field officer contended that "even he was actually abducted."

Hiding Places

The easy availability of children was a consequence of war and flight. The second prominent field research finding arising from the 1997 field research concerned a highly common, yet commonly overlooked, destination: the rain forest, which Sierra Leoneans (among many others) routinely call "the bush." Before turning to that, the dynamics of the attacks, by RUF fighters or others, is useful to consider. A common phrase that many Sierra Leoneans employed during interviews about the war was "When the war came to us." The impact of the war in their lives often began when some military force attacked their village. Many Sierra Leoneans evidently fled their homes only when a direct military attack took place. Regardless of rumors or stories or evidence of nearby attacks, many seemed to stay put until attackers entered their village. The gathered evidence from interviews highlighted a number of different responses. Quite often, the attackers sought to trap villagers. Various atrocities ensued: burning people alive in their homes, shooting others, cutting open pregnant women (and sometimes cutting up the fetus), amputating the arms, legs, or heads of still other victims, and, quite often, raping many of the girls and women. Sometimes parents would be tied up and forced to watch male attackers rape their daughters. Or they would force husbands to watch fighters rape their wives. Or they would do both. The militias also often sought to abduct some residents, usually children. In other cases, it appears that sometimes the fighters wanted to force residents to flee so that they could take their food and not have to share it.

War is a penetrating revealer of character. In an instant, a person's world is upended. Stories of flight shared by refugees in Guinea revealed that some Sierra Leoneans panicked and ran when rebels or soldiers entered their village, leaving family members of all kinds behind. Across interviews in many countries with people who have lived through awful wartime events, it has become clear that such a response is not uncommon. The snap reaction can leave a person with feelings of guilt and shame afterward: they saved their own lives while abandoning others. Those unable to escape, such as elderly people, infants, and the physically handicapped, were among those who were trapped. Sometimes people fled together, and sometimes they tried to sneak back into their villages to attempt to rescue relatives and friends. While these are acts of extraordinary bravery and heroism, we mainly hear of those who succeed.

For those who fled, there appeared to be three destinations: cities inside Sierra Leone that were not held by rebel forces, across Sierra Leone's border and into another country (mainly Guinea), or straight into the nearby forest. Those who entered and remained inside Sierra Leone's forested areas informally became known as "bush people," with the children sometimes called "bush kids" or "bush children." There appear to have been truly large numbers of them, perhaps numbering tens or even hundreds of thousands of people. Officials from one international NGO, for example, stated that the current "caseload" of IDPs early in 1997 was 708,000. Yet the estimate of all IDPs in Sierra Leone was 1.2 million. The officials related that international agencies "were aware of another half million" of IDPs. There was no accounting of the missing half million Sierra Leoneans who were displaced somewhere inside the country. Many aid agency officials on the ground in Bo and Kenema knew that some proportion of the uncounted IDP population were "bush people." My interviews strongly suggested that many if not most of the uncounted IDPs were hiding in forests. However, at the time of my initial entry into Sierra Leone, early in 1997, national government and international agency officials in Freetown were scarcely aware of the bush people and their experiences. There also was no agreed estimate about their numbers. As they were unrecognized, unregistered, and uncounted, no humanitarian aid for them existed. A new class of Sierra Leoneans had arisen whose social position lay at the very bottom.

Flying over Sierra Leone for the first time, en route from Freetown to Bo, my window seat allowed me to scan the countryside. There were roadways and rivers and, occasionally, a clearing of farmland and houses, signifying a village. But for most of the trip, I looked down at a dense, dark green canopy. I remember the following phrase entering my thoughts: the country is "a carpet of forest." The image is instructive, not only because rain forests extend across much of Sierra Leone, but also because the forests were a prime location for the civil war.

Up to this point in the war, nearly all theaters of conflict took place in rural areas. Most Sierra Leonean farms, villages, and towns are close to or surrounded by the bush. As a result, "when the war came" to them, the immediate destination for most civilians was the rain forest. Usually, there were no other options. Rural Sierra Leoneans are skilled at farming for foods (and some medicines) in the forest. It is not an unfamiliar place. But for people who fled there during the war, bush yams and wild cabbage did not merely supplement everyday diets. If bush people did not find enough food, they starved. The bush people were among the unluckiest and most overlooked of all Sierra Leoneans. Most never made it to cities like Bo, where they could enter an IDP camp, or managed to cross a border. If they entered Guinea (and not war-torn Liberia), they might get to a refugee camp. Neither location was optimal: both were loaded with problems and hardship. But there also were food, shelter, and services in the settlements and camps. In the rain forest, people were fortunate just to stay alive.

The recollection of one man who emerged from the bush early in 1997 provided a window into the extreme suffering that took place there. He was a leader of one group that had fled the town of Sahn Malen. The man's recollection is chilling. He first provided context. Many people from his town fled to the bush twice. The first time came soon after the rebels had entered Sahn Malen on April 20, 1991, mere weeks after the war had begun in Kailahun. The man estimated that perhaps seven hundred RUF soldiers entered the town, gathering about a thousand residents together. The rebels, he recalled, handcuffed their paramount chief. Then they told the residents that they had "come to redeem [them], and didn't like Momoh's government." People from the town were suspicious. "If somebody says he comes here to redeem you, to help you, I would not recognize him as a good person," he related. The rebels looted the town for four hours (they mostly sought food) and then released the paramount chief. The chief subsequently left his chiefdom and its people. "He went to Freetown," the man said, while "we fled to the bush"—but not before the rebels "took about twenty women and about a hundred men, from age fifteen and up." On this first trip into the bush, people stayed over three months (until July 25). They returned to Sahn Malen after hearing that the government soldiers had regained control over Pujehun District.

Two years later, the rebels returned to Sahn Malen. As usual, it was difficult for residents to know who these rebels were: "At times, the rebels dressed like soldiers, so you can't tell who is a rebel and who is a soldier. At other times, the rebels dressed like Kamajors." Whoever they were, the invaders again sought food: "rice, cassava, vegetables, and grains." And this time, those who fled into the bush stayed there, apparently, for years. At this point, it is useful to reflect on where Sahn Malen is located. It is a mere 40 kilometers from Bo, the capital of Sierra Leone's Southern Province. A Sierra Leonean working for an international humanitarian agency surmised that those who never got to Bo and instead ended up in the bush "had the misfortune to run the wrong way." But the man had another version of events: "those who had money went by car to Bo." The rest (those without money) ran into the nearby rain forest. Although the man related that his group had tried to reach Bo, "the rebels stopped [their] way." They were trapped inside the forest. That is where they remained.

The man recounted what took place next in a matter-of-fact way. Members of thirty different families fled into the bush together. Only twenty were children, and "most of them died: a two-year-old, a four-year-old, a five-year-old, a three-year-old." In addition, "The head wife, mother of five [children], died" (reference to a head wife indicated that the husband had had more than one). The survivors "lived on bush yams and cabbage." During their time in the forest, the group from Sahn Malen "met other families along the way. Sometimes there were five hundred people together at a time." The man recalled that they had to "steal from farms just to survive. So many children died because of hunger," he said.

The division of labor in bush camps was gender specific. The man from Sahn Malen related that men "were lookouts for rebels" while "women searched for food." But the terror of being discovered by rebel soldiers dominated the lives of the bush people. To try to avoid their discovery by rebels, bush camp members were forced to follow harsh rules. One boy detailed them. He had lived in a bush camp before the RUF abducted him. After escaping their clutches and making it to Bo, he described the environment in what ethnic Mende (the dominant ethnic group in southern and eastern Sierra Leone) called a *soquoihun*, meaning "hiding place." A female youth who experienced life in a soquoihun much later in the war defined the term in the following way: "Soquoihun means 'special hideout,' so nobody takes notice of you in the bush. It could be between rocks, in a cave, by waterfalls, in a deep valley, or on an island: anywhere where no one can notice you." All cooking in the soquoihun took place at night. Cooking fires themselves were hidden. Women dug holes in the ground, started a fire, and lay whatever food they had—yams, potatoes, cassava, cabbage, and so on—onto the fire. The fire then was covered for two reasons: to douse any light from the fire and to create a lot of ash (straining water through ash produced salt).

Children had to be terrified into silence. As the ex-combatant boy explained, "Children are told: 'If you talk, the people [that is, rebels] will come and kill you. So stay quiet.'" When food was short, nursing mothers ran out of milk. This, of course, caused babies to cry, which could lead rebel soldiers straight to them. As a result, "Often, the crying child had to be left behind. You have to cover the child and leave the child behind." Sometimes, the boy explained that "mothers would have to be alone with the crying baby." In such cases, bush camp members would have to abandon the mother and child. Mothers in mourning had to be left behind as well, apparently because their crying was dangerously loud.

Children often were on the front lines of bush camps. Girls were among those who went out searching for bush yams and cabbage while boys joined men as lookouts for any rebel movements in the forest. An ex-combatant recalled what one rebel group did when they came across "a girl looking for yams." Evidently in exchange for her life, she informed the rebels where her bush camp was. After the rebels entered the bush camp, the boy explained what took place next. "Since the rebels couldn't use the elders," he recalled, "they killed them. Then they threatened to kill us [boys and girls in the camp] if we did not join them. So we did."

After the December 1996 peace accord, people living in IDP camps (mainly in Bo) began to return to their villages. They traveled there with their ration cards—the cards they had received in the camps that would continue to entitle them to humanitarian handouts in their home villages. The challenge that awaited international aid agency officials was that many of those present were returning from the forest, not the IDP camps. As the "bush people" did not have ration cards, they were not entitled to receive the humanitarian aid that the agencies provided. An aid agency official related, "When we go back to the villages, there are so many people who don't have ration cards." As a result, "we are facing a problem: there are more and more people coming out of the bush." Interviews with residents of Sahn Malen, as well as aid officials providing food there, indicated that a new, bifurcated social system was arising in rural Sierra Leone. Those who had ration cards received food and could concentrate on rebuilding their homes and lives. Those returning from the bush were hungry. There were reports of former bush people working for those with ration cards in exchange for food.

I did not visit an IDP camp while in Bo in early 1997. They recently had been closed. While they may have been miserable, the camps also provided residents with a modicum of stability and normality, such as primary schooling and humanitarian handouts. Their counterparts in the bush, of course, had no such support. Survival was the primary aim. In addition, vulnerability to rebel attacks and abductions appeared to be an ever-present dimension of forest life. As one former rebel soldier explained, "The [rebel] captives came from bush camps. Not IDP camps." While bush camps were not the only source of rebel abductions (the rebels also preyed on diamond miners and abducted people during their attacks on villages and towns), it was evident that life inside the forests also traumatized those whom the rebels did not abduct. Research suggested that the trauma caused by life in the bush was particularly excruciating for child survivors.

This photograph is from Sahn Malen in 1997. The men in this photo proudly display their ration cards, which allow them to secure food rations. The cards signified that they had returned home from camps for the internally displaced in Bo. Their contemporaries, fellow citizens of Sahn Malen who had hidden in the bush, had no ration cards. This separation appeared to have created a new social division in the chiefdom, with those emerging from the "bush" residing beneath those arriving from the camps.

During my visit to Sahn Malen, I carried out an experiment. I brought small boxes of colored crayons and markers, along with a stack of blank photocopy paper. While interviewing teachers and parents, I invited children to draw whatever they wanted. This method allowed me to find out what the children were thinking about. It also allowed me to invite them to describe their pictures to me.

The results were shocking. The bush kids immediately revealed themselves. Many of those who had recently emerged from hiding in the forest expressed their trauma and fear by drawing themselves without mouths or arms. Some struggled to draw anything, and many found it hard to speak; teachers and parents related how "bush kids" in school often remained quiet. They seemed to be in shock, and they probably were malnourished. In stark contrast, the "Bo camp" children (they had made it to IDP camps there) drew with confidence. They depicted their faces and bodies in considerable detail (and with mouths and arms), and they deployed many more colors in their images. The experience shed powerful light on the extreme conditions that people surviving in Sierra Leone's forests endured, the youngest in particular.

The third main theme arising from my 1997 field research was hunger. In Sierra Leone, food scarcity was a near-constant through line in discussions about military groups and noncombatants. The need to secure food regularly drove the decisions and actions of people in Sierra Leone's war theater. As Shepler noted, "The first—and most obvious—effect of the war on Sierra Leoneans' experience of food was scarcity. People went hungry much of the time" (2011: 47). Yet hunger caused by war was not a military strategy as much as a result of the chaos that conflict and displacement created. The war made farming dangerous. Tending fields exposed farmers to hungry fighters of all kinds. Indeed, crop harvests served as magnets for military forces. Soldiers did not protect farmers; they raided their stocks.

By the time I had arrived in Sierra Leone, an already dire food supply situation in the war-affected areas had gotten much worse. In most interviews, there were references to hunger and a lack of food. An international humanitarian official stated that "food is guiding the instability in Sierra Leone," explaining that "with approaching starvation, young men with guns are robbing for food." In an interview on April 1, a government official related that "April is the hungry season." He expressed his fear that farmers "will eat their rice and potato seedlings," which meant that "there can't be enough to harvest." Many others also expressed this concern. Since the RUF stole or traded for food to survive, they were suffering too. One analyst stated early in April that "the RUF haven't eaten anything but yams and bananas for two months." His assessment suggested that they were starving. In a sequence of recollections of rebel attacks, survivors related how the rebels went straight for the food. "They ate the food they found," one recalled. "They came back and took our vegetables and rice seedlings," said another. In the areas of Guinea where refugees lived, just across the Makona River from the RUF base in Kailahun, a high-ranking refugee education official from Sierra Leone reported that Guinean soldiers and smugglers were trading "salt, cigarettes, weapons, ammunition, and food" in exchange for items the RUF had on hand: "palm oil, cocoa, coffee, and diamonds."

Peace is much better than war (for most people). But was Sierra Leone really at peace? Though it may be fashionable to envision postwar lands as sites for reconciliation or revenge, quite often the main motivator is survival. Sierra Leone was like that. Many lives and livelihoods had been devastated or wiped out. Three enduring memories from this period of shaky security and grave dread underscore the desperate nature of life for so many Sierra Leoneans.

The first was a visit to the amputee camp in Bo (run by international agencies). Nearly all of the amputees were children and youth. They were accustomed to talking with foreigners about how they had lost their limbs. I played that role. There were dozens of victims in the camp; I spoke to perhaps ten. Most reported that they were orphans, or they did not know if their parents and siblings were alive or dead. The amputees shared harrowing stories in a matter-of-fact way, maybe because they had told their tales of physical and psychic loss so many times. A girl of sixteen and her cousin of the same age had had their hands amputated. "The rebels said they had enough women [in their camps]. So they amputated their arms instead." This is the same rebel rationale that a girl of fifteen related. The rebels first lay her down alongside two older women on a metal sheet then cut all their hands off. "The rebels said they already had enough women to help them, so they only came to cut us up," she recalled. She added, "When the rebels attack, they tell us that God was at their side. They say, 'We are the Gods for today.' So we do what they say." A young boy in the camp said that the rebels shot his father and killed his mother. Then "they just amputated my leg. They left me there and went away. My grandmother brought me to Bo."

A second lasting memory was an interview with members of the Women's Society of Fangamadou Refugee Camp in Guinea. Approximately one hundred women met with me, sitting on benches under a huge tree. It was a story of hardship arising from war, demographics, and Sierra Leone's pronounced patriarchal order. "Even before the war began in Sierra Leone," a young woman explained, "there was a man shortage and a woman surplus." This imbalance also existed during the Atlantic slave trade era, when the traders mainly abducted boys and men from Sierra Leone. The same outcome again was underway. "Because of the war," one woman explained, "most men were killed or forced to join the army" (later in the meeting, it became clear that many also had joined or were abducted by the RUF). Some of the relatively few men who had arrived in Guinea had returned to Sierra Leone to fight or mine or search for food and supplies and then never came back. As a result, the refugee camp was estimated to be 75 percent female (Sommers 1997: 18). Most of the girls and women in the camp lived without a husband or partner. This created two kinds of problems. One was transactional sex: a despairing woman might trade sex for help getting firewood from the forest. Men could be choosy: a pregnant or older woman reportedly had little chance of attracting a man. The woman explained that those who managed to trade sex for male labor eventually became pregnant. In such cases, "You are left with belly and no man."

Another set of problems concerned the traditional role of women. All members of the Refugee Committee for Fangamadou Camp were men. As one woman explained, "The culture is disturbing the women. It does not allow a woman to confront men and tell them about our problems. If a woman is found speaking out about problems, the men will say, 'She does not respect our culture.'" In addition, "We didn't know we had the right to present our problems directly to UNHCR." Lacking a reliable means to communicate their struggles, the women asked me to take their problems to the Refugee Committee. When I did, it immediately became clear that the men were having a hard time interacting with and representing women. They lacked experience and were thoroughly befuddled by the masses of needy women seeking their assistance.

A senior member of the Women's Society of Fangamadou Refugee Camp ended our meeting with analysis about the war. For her, it clearly was not over: few of the husbands, brothers, and sons who had exited the camp for Sierra Leone had ever returned. But like so many still inside Sierra Leone, there was hope that the Kamajors could deliver peace. However, her analysis echoed a theme that arose in interviews with Sierra Leoneans across many years, that those who gain power in their land abuse it: "We believe the Kamajors can bring the war to an end. As typical Sierra Leoneans, we believe God has used his mystery to give the Kamajors power. But now, we believe that the Kamajors are starting to misuse it. Corruption and the misuse of power will cause them to lose God's mystery. If they do not misuse it, we believe the war can end."

An interview with the "supreme commander" of a local Kamajor unit, in a village in Moyamba District (on a day trip out of Bo), sketched a picture of how the Kamajors evidently had gained an advantage in the war. The local commander was an intense, imperious man adorned with traditional charms and armed with a large knife and the kind of vintage rifle Kamajors were known to carry (and from which the "Single Barrel" nickname for Kamajors was derived). Supervising a Kamajor checkpoint manned by members of his detail, the commander outlined an unadorned fighting philosophy. He "blamed all trouble on the rebels." He provided an easy definition of a rebel: "Anyone who stole our food or who raided our homes are rebels. Anyone who occupied a village when we arrived are rebels." Then he added, "We don't wait to find out who they are. If they are there [when we arrive], we kill them." That included women discovered during raids of rebel camps. "We kill them. They are rebels," he simply stated. The chilling encounter with the intimidating supreme commander, lording over the village of frightened civilians while his boys manned the highway checkpoint, is a third prominent memory from my first trip to Sierra Leone.

By the end of my 1997 journey to Sierra Leone and Guinea, it had become clear that something was missing from commonplace depictions of Kamajors as heroes and RUF rebels as dastardly enemies. It was Sierra Leone's national army, the SLA. The soldiers' behavior may have been uncomfortable for government sources to discuss and beside the point for international agencies focused on humanitarian relief and demobilizing rebels. A veteran foreign researcher was convinced of this. "Nobody wants to talk officially about the problem of wild army soldiers doing much of the damage," the researcher related. That, and so much else, was about to change.

CHAPTER 12

Diamonds, Humanitarians, and the Rebel Takeover

Lumpen Revenge

A new phase of Sierra Leone's civil war started on May 25, 1997. With the entrance of the Armed Forces Revolutionary Council (AFRC), the conflict shifted to urban warfare, with Freetown as its focus and Sierra Leone's forests, diamond mines, and smaller towns suddenly in the background (if only for a while). This was the second major military coup of the war, but it was different than the first. For one thing, many of the RUF's fighters and commanders left the bush and joined the new regime. For another, while the NPRC confronted next to no resistance on reaching Freetown and starting a new government, this new set of leaders had to wrest power from the government. It wasn't all that difficult, but the response sure was.

For a time, the NPRC had been seen as heroes by many if not most civilians in Freetown. The AFRC, in direct contrast, was distinctly unpopular from the start with Freetownians. In addition, the international condemnation that blanketed the AFRC throughout differed quite significantly from the response of foreign institutions to the NPRC. Most foreign governments and major international institutions like the IMF negotiated and did business with the NPRC. The same could not be said for the AFRC and their RUF colleagues, who were thought to be "people who had no conception of governance" (Gberie 2005: 98). To be sure, they had their international supporters. But they were an entirely separate ilk, such as Presidents Charles Taylor of Liberia and Blaise Compaoré of Burkina Faso, two leaders in the locality with records of success (in some ways) but also with unenviable and notorious reputations in the larger international community.

One reason for the stark difference in response to the AFRC was the nature of the government they overthrew. While the NPRC deposed disastrous Joseph Momoh, the AFRC toppled democratically elected president Ahmed Tejan Kabbah. It turns out that Kabbah had something promising to show for his few months in power. The economy had reversed course from negative to positive growth (Gberie 2005: 100).[1] At the same time, Kabbah had swiftly moved to set up his very own patronage system, something of a tradition among Sierra Leonean rulers (Keen 2005: 219). Kabbah also unintentionally forced the hand of the military by adopting a tradition that Stevens had started: undermining and weakening the national army. The difference was that Kabbah would be doing it while a formidable military adversary still operated inside the country.

Kabbah's move to cut the size of his military may have precipitated the coup. A great many SLA members were unnerved by the prospect of losing their status as soldiers, as they had been operating with near-complete impunity. Gberie highlights a survey of the national military from early in 1997 indicating that most military members were secondary school dropouts, nearly 30 percent were "totally illiterate," and less than 3 percent sought to be demobilized (2005: 104). He concludes that there was "little doubt that fear of demobilization was a strong factor leading to the coup." In addition, President Kabbah publicly announced cuts in subsidized rice for the army, which Gberie considered "an incredibly impolitic move" (105).

Keen provides several additional reasons for a military coup. The army was concerned about "fear of recrimination, including prosecution" after cuts in the size of the military. Kabbah, in fact, was seeking to reduce the size of the military by two-thirds: from ten to twelve thousand down to three to four thousand (Keen 2005: 197). After their conduct in the war, soldiers were unpopular; many were about to be out of a job and would be vulnerable to arrest. There were still other issues as well. One was a peculiar concern about corruption within the military: it didn't reach down far enough. Senior officers weren't sharing proceeds with junior officers (201). Finally and perhaps most significantly, members of the army had "anger and anxiety" over the rise of the Kamajors, which they found "both alarming and humiliating." By the time of the coup, there were more Kamajors than soldiers: fifteen to twenty thousand and still growing. Increasingly, the Kamajors were replacing their antique muskets with AK47s and rocket-propelled grenades (RPGs). Naturally enough, tensions between the Kamajors and soldiers were highest in the diamond-mining areas, particularly in Mende-dominated diamond areas like Tongo and Zimmi. Mende elites were using the new diamond wealth to boost support for Kabbah's SLPP and the Kamajors (198, 199). It did not help matters that Kabbah had made the leader of the Kamajors, Sam Hinga Norman, his deputy defense minister (as Kabbah himself was the minister of defense, Norman had considerable power). Once in that position, "Norman made no secret of his efforts to mobilize and train kamajoisia [Kamajors] for every chiefdom in the south and east" (that is, across all Mende-dominated areas; Hoffman 2011: 42). From the point of view of the army, the game was up: the Kamajors were ascendant, and they may be headed to prison.

While it may have seemed like a good time for a coup, the result was an

A group of Kamajors near the battle front in 1998. While three hold single-barrel muskets, a male youth wearing a T-shirt featuring the image of a stuffed teddy bear holds an Automat Kalashnikova 1947 (AK-47) machine gun.

absurd and very violent fiasco. The boys were back, and they were wild. On May 25, 1997, in Freetown, a group of soldiers arrested some of their senior officers. They then used grenades to free six hundred prisoners in Pademba Road prison, a mix of soldiers and professional criminals. Next, the newly ex-convicts and soldiers moved to State House, where they overwhelmed a Nigerian military contingent. Kabbah and many more fled to Guinea, while Major Johnny Paul Koroma, who had been in prison for his alleged involvement in an attempted coup (which Koroma denied), became the leader of the land: chair of the newly established AFRC.[2] Once in power, "Koroma rang Foday Sankoh in Nigeria [where Sankoh was under arrest on a weapons charge], and Sankoh gave his blessing to the junta and ordered RUF fighters to come out of the bush and join the coupists" (Keen 2005: 208). Arriving in town soon afterward, the RUF "quickly established itself as the force behind the AFRC power, taking what amounted to full control over everything in the capital, including the lives and bodies of residents" (Gberie 2005: 102).

Gberie delivered fevered castigations for what followed. He stated, "Governance became little more than a chaotic orgy of rapine and terror and systematic intimidation; the beleaguered state effectively ceased to function in any meaningful sense" (102). In another passage, he called the new rulers a "street power taking over the state" that was propelled by "criminal impulses, wholly self-serving and predatory" (98). The junta gents indeed rampaged across the city. They burned down the National Treasury and attacked the Supreme Court building, including judges and magistrates (some of whom had sent many of the convicts to prison). Not for the last time, Sierra Leone had been turned upside down.

Before venturing any further, it is useful to meet the two central protagonists leading this new regime (calling it a "government" would be a stretch). Major Koroma was thirty-three when he assumed power. Gberie's open disgust for Koroma is palpable. He described Koroma as "a disarmingly taciturn and apparently naïve man with a well-shaven, anodyne face" who acted "with extraordinary recklessness and brutality" (2005: 106). Trained as an officer at Sandhurst in the United Kingdom, he had the sort of pedigree that might have pointed him in a different direction (Keen 2005: 208). But it didn't, and the decisions he made after becoming Sierra Leone's head of state were peculiar. Koroma seemed to give up power almost as soon as he had seized it, allowing the RUF to take charge of security for the AFRC junta rulers shortly after their arrival in Freetown. With this decision, he "virtually made himself hostage to the demented tactics of the RUF" (Gberie 2005: 106). As will be detailed, Koroma subsequently decided to ride out of Freetown with the RUF, again volunteering to be dominated by them. For many months, Koroma and his wife effectively became the hostages of Sam Bockarie (Keen 2005: 221, 222).

That decision becomes all the stranger and more unwise after learning about Bockarie himself. The man known as "Maskita" or "Mosquito" already was renowned (and deeply feared) for his brutality and treachery. Bockarie ruled over Kailahun and often served as Sankoh's deadly hatchet man, the RUF officer who carried out special orders for his leader. Eventually he became the RUF's second-in-command. Bockarie was the RUF's interim leader while Sankoh was abroad for parts of 1995 and 1996 (negotiating and then signing the initial peace accord in Abidjan) and again for two years (when the Nigerian government held Sankoh under house arrest from March 1997 until April 1999 for alleged arms trafficking) (Reno 2001: 220, 221). Sankoh "would not effectively lead the RUF again until 2000." His decision to promote a man "for his bravery and ruthlessness" to serve in his stead is telling (Marks 2013: 365). Mosquito was not a man known for high ideals. But he was exceptionally violent, and violent commanders seemed to thrive under his charge.

Once in Freetown, the spotlight began to shine more brightly on Bockarie, something he no doubt loved. With Sankoh in Nigeria, Bockarie became the "RUF commander on the ground" in Freetown. He also had developed "very strong links with Charles Taylor in Liberia" (Keen 2005: 194). In his formative years, the young Mosquito had dropped out of secondary school and worked as a diamond miner. Just like Strasser, Bockarie was a professional disco dancer as well, performing in diamond-mining areas as an entertainer.

He also was a women's hairdresser. Tragically for Sierra Leoneans, Bocka-rie during the war was a "self-styled general" who seemed to see violence as "something that would put him on the map" (234). In a way, it did: Mosquito claimed fame through infamy. Smillie considered him "narcissistic, dangerous and unbalanced." That seems about right for a man who "had become Foday Sankoh's most ruthless general, a man whose reputation for murder and may-hem had spread throughout the country and beyond" (2010: 107).

The marauding bands of AFRC and RUF members never ruled the nation of Sierra Leone because they had no idea how to govern. Doing so would have required restraint and forethought, characteristics neither group demon-strated or, it appeared, had much interest in. It is more accurate to say that these two military groups of Sierra Leoneans occupied their own country with a combination of violence, chaos, and lawlessness. Fofana notes that the rebels received unexpected and active support from "Rastas" in Freetown, who evidently decided, after their experience with reggae-loving Strasser and the NPRC, to support this new round of coup leaders. He surmised that "the total population" of Sierra Leonean Rastafarians in the capital was "believed to be in [the] thousands," and he stated that most of them "supported the [AFRC/RUF] junta and served as its foot-soldiers" (Fofana 1998b).[3] The situ-ation got worse for Sierra Leoneans when Charles Taylor extended his sup-port to the AFRC/RUF junta as the official president of Liberia, a role he as-sumed less than two months after the junta's rule began (July 1997). Libya and Burkina Faso also supported the junta (Keen 2005: 216).

In some ways, the AFRC and RUF were an odd pairing. To be sure, they shared a focus on collective mayhem, terror displays, and government take-over. However, they also were different kinds of operations, inhabited by, in some ways, different kinds of people. Some of the AFRC officers were pro-fessionally trained, Koroma among them. The army was reputed to con-tain a great many northerners, ethnic Temne in particular. AFRC fighters also tended to be older than their RUF counterparts, who were often chil-dren (girls as well as boys). There was a bit of a grey area here, because the AFRC snapped up children along the way, just as the RUF did. But for the most part, RUF members were younger and largely from poor, rural back-grounds. A civilian who left Freetown with his family right after the AFRC coup recalled seeing RUF troops on the road, heading into Freetown to join their new "junta" colleagues in the capital. His recollection of the RUF forces is telling: "The RUF were very dirty. Many were barefoot. The majority were under fifteen years old. We were surprised to see little boys." As will be dis-cussed in part 4, many RUF troops had received forced indoctrination as mil-itary training. As the RUF began in the south and east of the country and es-tablished many of their bases there, they had many ethnic Mende in their ranks. The two military groups thus had fairly separate cultures and ethnic compositions.

They also distrusted and were suspicious of each other, as illustrated by these takes from rival leaders. A former AFRC commander saw a clear difference between the two forces. "We AFRC are soldiers," he explained. "The RUF used guerrilla tactics because they are civilians. We used military tactics because we are soldiers." The view from an ex-RUF commander illustrated how the disregard was mutual. "When the two factions came together," he stated, "the terror tactics came out because some criminals joined the AFRC and the movement. They joined after spending a lifetime in Pademba Prison" in Freetown. In this commander's view, AFRC members were mere convicts who employed terror tactics while the RUF never did. It is a dodge and a complete distortion, since it obfuscates all of the terror the RUF practices created across the entire war period. It also denies the AFRC's military background (and, for its officers, professional training). The bitter AFRC–RUF rivalry only increased over time.

Koroma and Bockarie faced many problems. There were widespread citizen protests: with schools closed, the economy in dire straits and disorder everywhere, it is not surprising to note that the new rulers were extremely unpopular. The two groups also distrusted each other (with the RUF contingent far outnumbering the AFRC). They faced strong opposition from the Kamajors in much of the diamond area. Then again, some members of the army and the RUF also refused to stop mining. As Keen wisely notes, "Accessing diamond revenues was a challenge for any government in Freetown, as was controlling its own fighters" (2005: 211). Be careful what you wish for.

Finally, in February 1998, ECOMOG intervened militarily (with Kamajors in support). Fighting in Freetown was fierce, and ECOMOG employed considerable firepower. Freetown occupies a peninsula, and ECOMOG failed to block the junta fighters' only exit route. As doing this is an obvious military strategy, the decision appears intentional. Keen provides two theories to explain why. One was that blocking their departure would have caused still more deaths (of fighters and civilians, one imagines). Yet that is an odd argument, since of course unleashing these furious fighters on the remainder of the country (which is precisely what took place) was a far more deadly option.

In retrospect and to this observer, the second theorized reason for allowing the junta fighters to escape seems much more likely. A journalist offered it as a question: "Did ECOMOG intentionally open the door to the RUF, allowing fighting to continue and thus justifying the continuing presence of its troops in this diamond-rich country?" (de Torrente 1999: 8, quoted in Keen 2005: 2017). A UN official answered the question in a 1998 interview in Freetown. In the official's view, "ECOMOG allowed the AFRC/RUF convoy to escape into the forest. They could have been killed, but the ECOMOG guys allowed the AFRC/RUF to save face."

Why would the ECOMOG forces do that? The apparent motivation is exactly what the journalist intimated: diamonds. War enabled unregulated exploitation of Sierra Leone's rich diamond fields by every military outfit. Peace did the opposite.

The Diamond Underbelly

Sierra Leone has been one of the world's poorest countries for decades. Its ranking in the Human Development Index (HDI) has been at or very near the bottom since at least 1990, when it ranked 160th out of 160 countries in the United Nations Development Programme survey (UNDP 1991: 16). The UNDP describes the HDI as "a summary measure of average achievement in key dimensions of human development: a long and healthy life, being knowledgeable and have [sic] a decent standard of living" (2018a). A glance at the HDI data provides a sense of the dire situation that most Sierra Leoneans have experienced during their lifetimes. By 2018, Sierra Leone had managed to move a few rungs above the very bottom: 184th out of 189 countries. Life expectancy at birth for Sierra Leoneans was 52.2 years—the lowest age of all nations in the survey (2018b: 25). Yet within the context of Sierra Leone, 52.2 years constituted a dramatic improvement. In 2000 (using data from 1998), life expectancy at birth in Sierra Leone also was the world's lowest, but it was 14.3 years lower (a mere 37.9 years). In that year, and once again, Sierra Leone also had the lowest HDI rank in the world (UNDP 2000: 160).

The process of mining for diamonds makes it understandable why Sierra Leoneans would rage at the gross unfairness in their country, and why it just might drive a relative handful toward violence. To begin with, it is almost literally backbreaking work: much of it takes place in water, where men and boys (and very few women) stand for hours every day, searching nearly always in vain for a diamond. After a younger boy does the "bailing," pouring a pail of sand and gravel into a handheld grater (or "shaker"), the "washer" leans over his grater and stays bent for hours. Over and over again, he soaks the grit and pulls out sand by hand: first the larger stones, working down to the grains that remain, searching constantly for any sign of a diamond. Hands soaked by water easily get blistered and torn. Standing in rivers, marshes, and stagnant pools makes it easy for parasites to enter miners' bodies. Miners young and old (interviewed after the war) complained of headaches and pain in their necks from carrying huge bags of heavy sand down to the water's edge, and pain in their sides and backs from standing bent over their graters. Some boys spend their days diving for sand in rivers, hauling buckets from riverbeds to the surface. These workers, in particular, complain of continually feeling cold.[4]

A boy in charge of "bailing" sand and dirt to be sifted by the three washers behind him.
They worked under the broiling sun in a diamond mine called Mine 11, located just outside Koidu,
the capital of Kono District.

The litany of diseases and maladies to which diamond miners are exposed is long. A district medical officer located near diamond mines listed malaria, sexually transmitted diseases, hepatitis B, scabies, tuberculosis, hookworms, and roundworms as miner-related ailments. The district officer added that "schistosomiasis is very common with miners." A medical officer working for an international health NGO in a mining area cited malaria as "absolutely the number one issue" in the area, followed by pneumonia. The NGO officer also noted that severe malnutrition was very common and HIV and Lassa fever were present as well. A seventeen-year-old miner added still another affliction: black flies. "When they bite you," he related, "you can't see well. But it takes time for this to happen." The miner seemed to be describing onchocerciasis, or river blindness.

While tiny numbers of Sierra Leonean insiders make colossal profit from diamonds, the many tens of thousands of diamond miners (nearly all of whom have been male youth) mostly get impoverishment and a life spun from relentless hardship and just a bit of hope. Meanwhile, very little revenue from the gems has ever surfaced in the form of government services or support. In addition, "the mark-up between what a West African digger received and what a rough diamond fetched in Antwerp could be as much as five hundred to one thousand per cent." The extreme gap between the two left plenty of room for all kinds of middle men (starting in Sierra Leone) to enrich themselves from the truly hard labor of miners. Sierra Leone is stupefyingly poor in large part because its natural resources are vast and its inequality is profound. As Smillie sums up, "Sierra Leone's tragedy . . . is intimately linked to the diamond trade" (2010: 88, 96).

For some analysts, the power of diamonds overshadows all other rationales for Sierra Leone's civil war. Campbell characterizes the conflict as "the diamond war" that "was never more than an economic endeavor, a ten-year-long jewelry heist." He also argues that "the RUF's depravity served a military strategy: It induced tectonic population shifts away from the diamond areas" (2004: 13, 2, 72). Smillie agreed: amputating hands and feet (in addition to "horrific rape") was a "terror technique" that "had no rival in clearing the country's alluvial diamond fields, providing the RUF and [Charles] Taylor with a highly rewarding money machine" (2010: 96). Smillie and Campbell are on to something regarding RUF rationales for terror and depopulation. But their take is incomplete, since much of the war took place away from the diamond fields (rebel military strategy will be examined in more depth in upcoming chapters).

Although the origins of the diamond trade are detailed in chapter 5, it is necessary to connect it explicitly to the civil war and highlight Liberia's role. With that in mind, four characteristics of diamonds and the diamond trade are particularly important. One is universal: they are small and easy to smuggle, making them "the most portable form of wealth known to man" (Campbell 2004: xxiii). As Junger observes, "millions of dollars' worth can fit into a pack of cigarettes. Diamonds are so small, so valuable, and so easy to conceal that if taxes on them rise above a certain level, overall revenue falls because people simply start smuggling." Since dodging taxes on diamonds in Sierra Leone was routine and widespread, the focus often was on getting them out of the country. There were many ways to do this. They can be "heated and dropped into tins of lard," "sewn into the hems of skirts," "encased in wax and taken as suppositories," or perhaps "swallowed, hidden under the tongue, burrowed into the navel, or slipped into an open wound that is then allowed to heal." No such measures were necessary during Sierra Leone's war. The prime diamond smugglers were the RUF, and they simply transported diamonds either "over the maze of jungle paths that connect Sierra Leone to Liberia" or by small aircraft (Junger 2006).

The second characteristic about diamonds and Sierra Leone's civil war is that all of Sierra Leone's diamonds are alluvial. In diamond areas, they could be anywhere beneath your feet. This is a crucial characteristic of how diamond production arose and then propelled the war forward. Given the extraordinary value of such tiny stones, located in the dirt of one of the poorest

A bailer working with two washers in a Kono District diamond mine.

nations on the planet, a sense of the dynamics of power and poverty concerning diamonds in Sierra Leone is helpful.

The story begins in 1931 in the colonial era. The British territory "had been suffering from economic stagnation and depression for nearly a century because of its dire lack of resources" (excepting trade in slaves, which by that time the British had ceased). Prospectors discovered diamonds in the colony, after which "it became apparent that Sierra Leone would be an important source of high-value alluvial gem diamonds" (Smillie 2010: 32). The categorization of diamonds is important: gems are exponentially more valuable than industrial diamonds.

What took place next established diamonds as a force for both enrichment and unregulated activity. There were very substantial amounts of diamonds to be uncovered and sold. The focus was mainly in the areas of Kono (in the east of Sierra Leone) and Tongo Field (south of Kono). While the Sierra Leone Selection Trust (SLST) company received exclusive rights to diamond mining across a large swath of Sierra Leone, neither the company nor the colonial administration could stop what happened next. Ordinary Sierra Leoneans got in on the act, mining diamonds without the blessing of SLST or the colony and numbering an estimated 75,000 by 1956 (Smillie 2010: 98). The catalysts of this new trade were Lebanese immigrants who arrived in Sierra Leone (and many other parts of Africa) in the wake of the Ottoman Empire's collapse.

Lebanese traders already had set up shops in Kono by 1930, just before diamonds were discovered there. They thus were perfectly positioned to make use of this splendid opportunity. As a result, while SLST was operating in Kono and nearby areas, so were Lebanese traders, who "rapidly assumed the role of provocateurs and middle men, moving illicitly mined diamonds out of the [colony] in dozens of ways" (Smillie 2010: 97, 98). Over time, a system arose: the Lebanese traders purchased licenses to mine, which were too costly for ordinary Sierra Leoneans to afford. To do this, they struck deals with the paramount chief of the area, who granted them permission to mine in his chiefdom in exchange for hefty fees. The traders fronted diggers with equipment (water pumps and sieves), food, and very little pay. As sponsors, the Lebanese would buy the diamonds from the diggers (for a tiny fraction of their value) (Campbell 2004: 22). As noted, while the licenses may have been legally secured, smuggling the diamonds generally was far more profitable than legal exchange. Just like Momoh and others tried later on, SLST attempted to contain the unregulated trade by driving off miners (known as "strangers") with forced removal efforts called Operation Parasite and Operation Stranger Drive (Smillie 2010: 98). They were unsuccessful. By the 1950s, "it was estimated that 20 per cent of all stones reaching the world's diamond markets were smuggled from Sierra Leone" (80). Before the nation's independence, Sierra Leone already had become the diamond mother lode.

The third characteristic of diamonds and the diamond trade for Sierra Leone concerns how they were mined during the war: often (if not primarily) with forced labor. A decades-long veteran of the diamond mines in Kono, who was mining there during the war years, recalled that miners attempted to flee whenever rebels arrived because "the rebels captured people to force them to mine." The Truth and Reconciliation Commission (TRC) confirmed this: "The RUF used forced labour throughout the war for all kinds of work, including mining in the diamond pits. The workers were forcibly recruited in villages. The RUF fed them, but they did not receive any salary. They suffered mistreatment and torture, and they were forced to mine 'under gun point,' with armed men monitoring the washing of the gravel." It was not as if the RUF were the only military groups forcing people to mine. "There are also accounts of the Kamajors using forced labour to mine diamonds from 1997 onwards," the TRC related (2004b: 49). Most of the miners were boys over age fourteen only because "younger children were physically weaker and so [were] less productive" (51).[5] In Koidu, the capital of diamond-rich Kono District, rebel forces reportedly entered the town in 1998 with a novel approach. A Sierra Leonean researcher explained: "Rebels in 1998 forced people to dig up the floors in their houses. They viewed the earth under the houses as virgin territory. They got plenty diamonds there."[6]

The final characteristic of the diamond trade combines the easy portability of diamonds with the economy that emerged from alluvial mining. It is the well-established movement of diamonds out of the south and east of Sierra Leone to Liberia's capital city, Monrovia. Transporting diamonds out of one land to be sold in another is not unusual: a similar system existed for diamonds smuggled out of the Democratic Republic of the Congo (formerly known as Zaire) across the Congo River and into Brazzaville, the capital of the Republic of the Congo next door. Although Congo Brazzaville has "almost no diamonds at all" (even less than Liberia), it nonetheless exported many millions of dollars' worth of them to Belgium for many years ($454.6 million in 1997, at the height of war and instability next door) (Smillie 2010: 22). Countries that exported large amounts of diamonds while producing little or no diamonds themselves were, until fairly recently, not a big deal. That is because the entire diamond industry was almost completely unregulated. As Smillie explains, diamonds coming from Sierra Leone or Angola (among other conflict hot spots) "were laundered in half a dozen ways before they arrived in jewellery shops, but because nobody had ever asked questions before, most of those involved in the cover-up had taken no great pains to hide their trail. Antwerp [in Belgium], the centre of the world's diamond trade, had for years been importing hundreds of millions of dollars worth of diamonds from countries where none were mined. No questions were asked" (3).

The absence of regulation—all that mattered was the diamonds—facilitated what came to be known as conflict diamonds (or blood diamonds). In Smillie's view, "diamonds did not *cause* the war in Sierra Leone. Nor did they cause the wars in Angola and the Democratic Republic of the Congo. They did, however, pay for the rebel effort in these wars, making them significantly more horrific and long-lived than could ever have been the case without diamonds" (4, emphasis in original). Charles Taylor and Foday Sankoh exploited the absence of regulation on diamond sales of any kind, using those extracted from Sierra Leone to fuel the RUF's rebellion, make diamond mining a clear and obvious strategic wartime priority, and create fantastic wealth for Taylor, Sankoh, and other top leaders in the two countries (but Taylor well beyond all others). The civil war in Sierra Leone rightly became a featured example of how diamonds can fuel war.[7] As Gberie explains, diamonds "became the principal motivation for the RUF and its outside backers"—starting with Charles Taylor (2005: 7). Peters concurred: "Diamonds did not cause the war, but became a key factor in the war's continuation" (2011a: 119).

Smuggling diamonds into Liberia from Sierra Leone and selling them in Monrovia was an established tradition that started decades before the war took hold. Monrovia, in fact, was the most logical place to sell a diamond because Liberia's currency was fixed to the value of the U.S. dollar. This made it "the equivalent of hard currency." Sierra Leone's leone currency could not possibly compete (Campbell 2004: 22). Charles Taylor took over the diamond smuggling machinery in Liberia in the 1990s and made it hum. He had begun fueling his own war and enriching himself quite handsomely soon after his entrance into Liberia at the end of 1989. Between 1990 and 1992, Taylor averaged an estimated USD $100 million per year in trade for timber, rubber, and iron ore (Smillie 2010: 85). While in Liberia in 2005, I heard stories of how Taylor had reaped bountiful profits from timber companies operating in the once-virgin rain forest of eastern Liberia.

Diamond smuggling proved even more profitable than timber. The following description shares a sense of the gains that Taylor and Sankoh made through Sierra Leone's civil war:

> Sankoh's *modus operandi* in Sierra Leone, beginning in 1991, was essentially the same as Taylor's. . . . Throughout the 1990s, the RUF channeled millions of dollars worth of diamonds through Charles Taylor's laundering machinery, obtaining the funds it needed for its own war, and providing Taylor with a generous percentage to fund his own. Between 1994 and 1998, over 31 million carats, worth U.S.$1.96 billion—enough to pay off most of the Liberian national debt—were recorded at Belgian customs as Liberian. (Smillie 2010: 85, emphasis in original)

A second estimate put the portion of diamonds moving through Liberia from Sierra Leone at between USD $25 million and $125 million every year in the 1990s (88). Either way, it was more than enough to support two war efforts and leave a great deal for personal profit. It also set the stage for regular shipments of arms and munitions back into Sierra Leone for the RUF. The size of these shipments could be enormous. One shipment in 1999 featured a million rounds of ammunition, three thousand AKM rifles, twenty-five RPGs, and antiaircraft and antitank missiles. A shipment in 2000 included 10,500 Kalashnikovs, 120 sniper rifles, and 8 million rounds of ammunition (Chivers 2010: 369, 370). Campbell observed that "the precision and high degree of organization of the RUF's gunrunning operations is a powerful testament to the financial might of the diamonds they mine[d]." He added, "Almost none of it would be possible without the active participation of Liberia and its despotic leader, [former] President Taylor" (Campbell 2004: 64).

Charles Taylor's role in Sierra Leone's war largely took place in the shadows. But the war that emerged in large part was Taylor's making, from the way it started to the rebels' steadfast focus on diamond areas and the application of extreme brutality to serve their ends. The rebels usually were well armed too. Taylor, in the end, was the war's secret catalyst and orchestrator. A civil war in Sierra Leone most certainly could have happened without him. But the nature of the warfare that emerged reflected Taylor's handiwork. After the war, a village elder in Sierra Leone summed up what had taken place in the following way: "The war started in Liberia and infected us."

The Humanitarian Divide

In October 1998, I returned to Sierra Leone. A few days into my research trip, I received a short evening call from a UN official. Did I want to join a trip to Masingbi the next day? I had to make a decision immediately: a seat on the helicopter had just opened. If I didn't accept the offer, I'd lose it to someone else. I accepted the seat. I reported to tiny Hastings Airport on the other side of Freetown very early the next day. I strapped into my seat on one of the benches in the UN helicopter, with a bottle of water, my notebook, pens, and a camera in my day pack, and we set off.

Masingbi is due east from Freetown, 95 miles (152 kilometers) inland. It is a mere 45 miles (73 kilometers) by road to Koidu (the so-called highway is a rough, hard slog even in peacetime). The helicopter flew low over the forest. It swayed back and forth, presumably to make it harder for rebels to shoot at us. During this period, Masingbi was a kind of island territory: controlled by ECOMOG and Kamajor forces and surrounded by AFRC/RUF troops positioned in the nearby forests. The town had become a refuge for civilians who had fled fighting in Kono (Smith, Gambette, and Longley 2004: 237). Skirmishes between rebels in the forest and ECOMOG and Kamajor troops in the town regularly took place at night. UN officials had gone there to check on the humanitarian and security situation. I went to look, listen, and learn.

Landing in a helicopter must be the most dramatic way to enter or leave a place. It is loud and blows wind around furiously. It also is impossible to ignore. Our arrival lent the impression that everyone aboard was really important. Once we landed and separated ourselves from the blustery din, Nigerian military officers and armed Kamajor troops (many of them clearly children) escorted us from place to place.

The first stop was a reception hosted by the paramount chief (PC) for the area, and with representatives of humanitarian NGOs operating in his chiefdom. I was told that the chief was named Bai-Kurr (his full name, I later discovered, was PC Bai-Kurr Kanagbaro II).[8] He was dressed in stylish traditional clothing and immediately displayed a polished and smooth manner. He welcomed us warmly. The chief then opened his speech by praising ECOMOG. "ECOMOG is succeeding in making Sierra Leone a peaceful nation. In areas where there is no ECOMOG, there are atrocities." It was a telling indication of security during the war: the SLA had turned the tables on the state, becoming one of its most dangerous adversaries. Sierra Leoneans thus had to rely on outsiders to protect them. Perhaps with that reality in mind, the paramount chief added, "We are very grateful to Nigeria as a government [nearly all ECOMOG forces were Nigerian]. They are beginning to have the idea of a united continent." Then, addressing the many foreigners in the room, the paramount chief said, "We are very grateful to all of you who have left your homes and families to help us."

The ECOMOG commander spoke next. "The people in this area sleep comfortably," he remarked. He also stated that "security force relations with the Kamajors are very cordial." The Kamajors in Masingbi were a traveling contingent: they were up north, away from their Mende homeland. The suggestion of security and safety was at odds with a comment the paramount chief submitted a few minutes later. "It's a reality," he announced. "People are dying. People are starving." The gathered impression was that Masingbi was heavily guarded but lacked sufficient food and medicine for everyone living or sheltering there.

Next, the visitors toured the grounds. We did not stray far from the helicopter. We visited several primary school classrooms, where Sierra Leonean students demonstrated their acumen before us. Groups of energetic Kamajors kept close to us, their clothing adorned with charms. Most of them held AKs, and many appeared to be the same age as those inside the classrooms.

The final event of our short visit was a reception. The generous provision of sodas and snacks was awkward, given the desperate humanitarian situation for most people in Masingbi. But it did allow, at last, for some informal conversation. I spoke to the regional coordinator for the immediate area. Highlighting a now-familiar frustration, the government officer reported having a difficult time coordinating humanitarian services. The reason, he said, was that large international NGOs refused to be managed by his office. "They define their own areas and follow their own mandates," he stated. "They operate based on their own interests."

As our conversation wound down, I noticed that the Nigerian commander of the ECOMOG contingent was waiting patiently to speak with me. I was unsure why, as I held no formal position: I was merely a researcher, unattached to any agency in Sierra Leone. Perhaps my unaffiliated status was the reason. Regardless, the commander guided me to a relatively quiet corner of the noisy room, away from the crowd. Then he shared something that had happened to him the night before. During a skirmish with rebel fighters from the nearby forests, a rebel boy soldier had dropped his gun and walked straight at him. It was as if the boy had had a death wish: he seemed to be inviting the commander to put him out of his misery. With wide eyes, the commander asked, "How do you kill a child?" He did not, but the experience very clearly had unnerved him.

Although I wanted to find out more about this incident and the commander's take on island-like Masingbi, it was impossible. The UN security officer loudly gave the order: all the visitors had to return to the helicopter immediately. I was forced to exit my conversation with the commander swiftly as we were herded outside, where the helicopter already had started its engine. Hundreds of people had gathered to watch the takeoff in a field near the school. Once again, the helicopter's blades created a strong wind while the engine roared. Some of the young Kamajors briefly performed an informal dance with their guns. The scene was strange and theatrical, and suddenly, it was over. Masingbi was behind us as we returned to Freetown while it still was light, flying low over the dark green forest canopy. Together with the long day and sweltering heat, the back-and-forth movement of the helicopter made myself and some of the other passengers queasy.

Accepting the helicopter ride to Masingbi unintentionally landed me in hot water. The reason was that international agencies were riven with dissension and distrust, and they had divided into two adversarial groups. I had flown on the "UN helicopter," not the "ICRC helicopter" of the International Committee of the Red Cross (there actually was a third, run by the Sandline mercenary outfit, but it was tied to combat and lay outside of the dispute). The opportunity to venture up-country had come early in my return trip to Sierra Leone, and I had grabbed it. But in the eyes of those aligned with ICRC, who used ICRC's helicopter to venture up-country, my decision associated me with the UN position.

Before turning to the poisonous humanitarian divide, understanding the government context is useful. During my return visit to Sierra Leone, it was clear that the May 1997 coup by the AFRC had not changed the nature of governance all that much. Following the subsequent return of President Kabbah and his government to Freetown in February 1998, the status quo more or less resumed. The MNRRR of 1997 had morphed into the National Commission for Reconstruction, Resettlement, and Rehabilitation (NCRRR) of 1998. The newly invented government body seemed just as weak and overlooked as MNRRR had been. Moreover, relations between most international NGOs and the Sierra Leonean government remained frosty. Sierra Leonean government officials were, if anything, even more exasperated by their treatment by international entities, most particularly the large international NGOs (not UN agencies). In the view of one official, "The international NGOs go wherever they want [and] we can't coordinate them. This is a burning issue with us. Sometimes I find NGOs just putting up health centers or digging a well and that is it. Some NGOs send us monthly reports but don't say what money they have left. We don't know their future plans. But the problem of everything is that NGOs go to the people they choose in the government. The NGOs do what they want." Another government official said that things had gotten so bad that "'maybe we have to do like the Rwandans and Ethiopians' and expel some NGOs from the country" (Sommers 2000: 29–30). They never did. They also never criticized those who had empowered international NGOs (usually while simultaneously overlooking the Sierra Leonean government) in the first place: international donor agencies (101). A UN agency official summed up the situation simply. "The donors don't trust the government," he said.

Since Kabbah's return, international actors favored a handful of Sierra Leone government officials instead of just one. But the result of this practice was perhaps even more toxic:

> "The 'good' people [in the government] are earmarked as points of entry," said one [international] NGO official. "Then everybody goes to [them] with everything, and soon they can't do anything properly. It's a potential vicious cycle, and [soon] their [government] peers will call them a 'donor baby'— beholden to foreign interests [and] not a true patriot." By selecting which government officials to work with, international agencies sent a message to the Freetown authorities about power relations. They defended this in the name of expediency—they were trying to get things done fast to save lives. From the government's perspective, however, the message was different: international agencies, not the government, were calling the shots in their country. (Sommers 2000: 28)

Bitterness did not just flow between government officials and large international NGOs. As noted above, the humanitarian "community" was divided against itself. Problems began soon after the AFRC took power and ousted President Kabbah set up shop in Conakry, the capital of nearby Guinea.

Ahmed Tejan Kabbah was a man who entered Sierra Leone's presidency with abnormally low expectations. It would have been difficult *not* to be an improvement on the ruinous, violent, and predatory administrations of his predecessors (Stevens, Momoh, Strasser, and, eventually, Johnny Paul Koroma).[9] In contrast, Kabbah by most accounts was an affable, low-key, mild-mannered man (a journalist generously observed that he seemed "to lack dynamism" [Whiteman 2014]). The nation's first Muslim leader, Kabbah had an ethnic Mandingo for a father while his mother was a Mende from a prominent family. Although he trained as a lawyer, Kabbah eventually entered the United Nations Development Programme (UNDP), working in the bureaucracy for two decades before retiring in 1992. Kabbah thus may have been an unlikely choice for president of a country in the midst of an awful war except for one characteristic: he was a longtime member of the Sierra Leone People's Party (SLPP), by far the nation's largest opposition political party. More than anything else, that likely was his ticket to political success.

At the time of Momoh's overthrow by Strasser, Kandeh correctly had determined that the party of Stevens and Momoh (the APC) was "an unmitigated disaster" (2004a: 132). Kandeh also had surmised that Kabbah's first election as president in 1996 was merely because "people voted for the SLPP rather than for Kabbah; many SLPP die-hards in the south and east knew nothing about the man they were electing" (142). The democratically elected leader also inspired highly critical assessments. A UN official groused that UNDP, which was directly involved with the 1996 presidential election process, helped Kabbah win. "People believe that [Elizabeth] Lwanga [the head of UNDP in Sierra Leone at the time] put Kabbah in power," the official asserted. "UNDP facilitated the elections. Kabbah and she are old pals, at UNDP." While rumors based on mere association are unfair, Sierra Leone's rich legacy of nepotism gave it legs. Some Sierra Leoneans and foreigners I interviewed also judged Kabbah's swift exit from Freetown following the AFRC coup as a mark of cowardice (a common aside was that the president had been "on the first plane out" when Johnny Paul Koroma took over). That too may have been undeserved, since Kabbah presided over a nation whose military had just deposed him.

At the same time, Kabbah's instincts as a new leader were, to put it mildly, uninspiring. His first cabinet as president was expansive and included "politicians discredited by their complicity in past dictatorships" (Kandeh 2004b: 165). Corruption in his government also was "rampant." Emblematic of Kabbah's character and leanings, although Kabbah "was not directly implicated in specific acts of malfeasance" (no small accomplishment in Sierra Leone), "his policy on corruption was conceived in the spirit of amnesty and shaped by his pursuit of reconciliation" (169). In addition, some assessments of Kabbah's handling of peace negotiations near the end of the war were absolutely scathing. Although his reputation gradually improved after the war ended, particularly after he handed over power peacefully (and right back to the APC), Kabbah guided Sierra Leone with caution and compliance during the war years. Following Kabbah's death in 2014, one obituary concluded that "Kabbah undoubtedly has his place in history, but perhaps more as a victim of events than a shaper of them" (Whiteman 2014). Meek acquiescence to the agendas of powerful actors and institutions was a major characteristic of his style of governance. Kabbah seemed forever passive, an avoider of conflict, and an appeaser.

Except for what took place in Conakry. There, the president-in-exile (from late May 1997 to February 1998) was assertive and political. The RUF followed Kabbah's removal from office by pouring into Freetown. Their absence from some parts of rural Sierra Leone opened up spaces for humanitarian agencies to deliver food, medicine, and other assistance to up-country areas that the RUF previously had shut off. With expanded access suddenly available and many Sierra Leoneans seriously short of food, certain international NGOs sought to fill the void. But the change in wartime access unleashed toxic and lasting acrimony among international agencies and donors, as well as the Sierra Leonean government temporarily based in Conakry. This one time, Kabbah entered the fray and took a strong position.

After the coup in Freetown, Kabbah's government, together with UN agencies and many international NGOs, shifted their operations to Conakry. A sizable group of international NGOs (all based in western Europe), together with the ICRC, retained their headquarters inside Sierra Leone. A third group of international agencies tried to maintain operations on both sides of the border.

The group based in Conakry viewed relief operations inside Sierra Leone as far too dangerous to attempt. The group stationed inside Sierra Leone said just the opposite: "Their ability to deliver humanitarian assistance to areas outside the capital was better" than any time since 1993–1994 (Sommers 2000: 32). One official remarked, "We were never able to move as freely" as when the AFRC/RUF regime was in Freetown. This period also was when "the humanitarian needs were greatest." Mutual hostility ensued. Kabbah forcefully attacked those agencies retaining operational headquarters inside Sierra Leone, calling them "junta NGOs," an accusation designed to sting. A Humanitarian Exemptions Committee, formed in Conakry and constructed to review requests to exempt relief items from the international sanctions that had isolated the AFRC/RUF government, agreed to let a small number of deliveries (mostly food) cross into Sierra Leone. But at the border, the truck convoys loaded with humanitarian goods remained in Guinea. One UN official recalled how Kabbah had announced that "rice is a weapon of war." Following this logic, providing food assistance to people inside Sierra Leone effectively legitimated and propped up the AFRC/RUF government (32, 33). That was the argument, at least.

With strong support from ECOMOG, a clutch of high-level UN officials, and one particularly prominent diplomat (British high commissioner for Sierra Leone Peter Penfold), Kabbah got his way. According to the NGOs seeking to deliver the relief aid, ordinary Sierra Leoneans consequently suffered. The animosity separating these two groups seemed only to grow following the collective return of Kabbah's government and international agencies to Freetown once the ECOMOG and Kamajor assault in February 1998 had subsided. Two issues in particular were hotly contested. One concerned whether to embrace or maintain distance from Kabbah's government. "I believe that it is wrong to be neutral," a UNDP official explained. That is almost logical, another UN official stated, because "the host nation is a UN member." Naturally, the UN supports the government. "To remain neutral to [RUF and AFRC] cruelty is absurd," a third UN official asserted. Comparing a democratically elected government to the brutality of the rebels seemed to strike many who favored the government as an insult.

The perceptions of war in Sierra Leone that officials of ICRC and several European NGOs professed could not have been more different. An official with a European NGO summed up the collective view of their group in the following way: "Good and bad doesn't exist. They're all bad [in this war]. It depends on how you define atrocities. There's rape everywhere on both sides." With respect to attacking the RUF, another official wondered, "Since so many [RUF members] are children, are they really our enemies? What about killing children?" A third official expressed concern about reporting atrocities that they come across, since "If we report atrocities, it might limit our access to the population."

The robust accent on neutrality and impartiality in Sierra Leone's war stirred ICRC and the European NGOs to develop a separate code of conduct and insist that only those agreeing to their code could fly in the ICRC helicopter. The rationale for this decision was revealing. One official explained that since "the RUF has spies and relatives everywhere," using helicopters and vehicles aligned with the government means that "you don't have a chance of getting to the suffering in rebel-held territories."

The separate helicopters underscored the profound rift between the two groups. In the words of one veteran humanitarian official, the situation was "as divisive as it gets." The tension was so great that NGO officials aligned with ICRC almost did not meet with me, given my UN helicopter ride to Masingbi (in the end, they relented).[10]

A second dividing line emerged from divergent perceptions of security. It was apparent that those supporting the government intentionally wore rose-colored glasses. During interviews with United Nations Observer Mission in Sierra Leone (UNOMSIL) and ECOMOG officials in Freetown in October 1998, the gathered view was that RUF and AFRC forces were in retreat. Their collective efforts had turned the tide in the war. Meanwhile, ICRC and many European NGOs working in the field reported that insecurity was on the rise. The reversal in perspective was complete. In Conakry, ECOMOG, UNOMSIL, other UN agencies, and Kabbah's government in exile had focused on the coup leaders in Freetown and concluded that Sierra Leone was dangerous and insecure. Once back in Freetown, they promoted the opposite viewpoint: things were improving steadily. In both periods, ICRC and the European NGOs perceived precisely the reverse (Sommers 2000: 71, 74).

In retrospect, one can see weaknesses in the arguments of both sides. The agencies pushing to be seen as neutral were able to access up-country territory only when the RUF was not there. Indeed, the RUF gained notoriety in 1998 by again taking international officials as hostages as a matter of course (Keen 2005: 219). Negotiating humanitarian access with the RUF almost certainly was impossible. At the same time, those allied with Kabbah's government somehow did not know or appreciate that the RUF and AFRC were gaining strength and planning a new attack on Freetown. As soon as ECOMOG retook the capital in February 1998, Bockarie went to see Taylor in Monrovia and received a promise of support for his side. President Taylor, together with President Compaoré, consistently provided the rebels with support across 1998. Arms poured in via Bulgaria, Ukraine, Libya, and of course Burkina Faso and Liberia. Ukrainian and South African mercenaries now joined the rebel side, rearming and retraining AFRC and RUF fighters prior to their attack on Kono in October 1998 (220, 221).

The rebels actually had made steady gains across 1998. "Contrary to claims" by Kabbah's government "that the rebels were now on their last legs," the AFRC and RUF actually had "started to regroup and expand." They took over a succession of up-country towns. The distraction of diamonds once again undermined their adversaries. ECOMOG troops "were apparently too busy mining for diamonds to notice RUF movements" (Peters 2011a: 77). By the end of that year, the AFRC and RUF rebels began smuggling arms into Freetown in various ways, including inside caskets and baskets of cassava leaves (Keen 2005: 222). By December, rebel troops were again inside Freetown, having infiltrated the capital (Peters 2011a: 77).[11]

My two visits to Sierra Leone during the war took place right before major rebel assaults on Freetown (May 1997 and January 1999). In both cases, it was clear during interviews that Sierra Leonean government and international officials consistently underestimated the rebels, especially the RUF. Two Western government officials underscored this collective perspective by sharing the view of Sierra Leone from their respective headquarter offices. "Nobody puts their good people in Sierra Leone," a senior official had reminded one of her colleagues. "There is low interest in Sierra Leone" in her central office, the other official explained. Her supervisors had "the expectation that the Nigerians [ECOMOG] will solve this. They want to shift operations to [postwar] development"—as if the war already was over.

It wasn't, but to big donor nations, little Sierra Leone was an ignorable backwater. The rebel forces there were impossible to take seriously. Their numbers were small, and most of them were kids. They appeared wild and reckless. The junta leaders probably would have been considered little more than a pathetic laughingstock had they not been so brutal. Still, if the RUF did not seem in any way imposing or substantial, they nonetheless remained elusive and mysterious. As late as October 1998, seven years after the war had begun, a veteran UN humanitarian official would ask me, "Who are the RUF anyway?" Like so many of his colleagues, he simply did not know.

The arrogance of the RUF's opposition—Sierra Leone's government and its many international supporters, such as UNOMSIL and ECOMOG, as well as Western donor nations—opened the door for the RUF (and the AFRC) to dominate. The reality was that conventional forces, with all of their impressive matériel and training, were no match for child and youth soldiers and their brutally effective leaders inside the RUF and the AFRC. The pull of diamonds only helped their cause. That said, the rebels were very good at what they did. As Olonisakin observed,

> the best of armies have found it extremely difficult to overcome small guerrilla armies. Those who confidently predicted an ECOMOG victory over the AFRC/RUF forces blatantly ignored this fact. It was relatively easy for a conventional Nigerian force to dislodge the rebel and junta forces in the capital, Freetown, where the latter had no choice but to fight a conventional battle. However, once in the remote country area, the RUF and indeed the junta forces [that is, the AFRC] were able to utilise the familiar terrain of the countryside—remoteness and thick forests—to their advantage. Thus, even if ECOMOG troops were well armed and equipped, they were still likely to have found it severely difficult to dislodge the rebel forces. (Olonisakin 2004: 233–234)

The rebels took terrible advantage of being routinely belittled and underestimated as a military adversary. Of all their many talents and assets, the element of surprise was one they had gained by default.

CHAPTER 13

No Living Thing

From the Inside Out

Entering the world of the RUF begins by seeing Sierra Leone from the inside out. Maps make sense to foreigners and city dwellers. International borders represent separations between different sovereign nations. Maps reveal Sierra Leone's countryside mainly as roads, towns, villages, and farms, together with the occasional alluvial diamond mine. But what fills up most maps of the country appears to be negative space. Those spaces are where the RUF called home: that vast "other" Sierra Leone, the world of the rain forest, where the RUF lived and sometimes thrived during the war.

Peters details how a key turning point for the RUF was late in 1993, when NPRC forces RUF nearly routed them (detailed in chapter 9). This is when the RUF "changed its military tactics from a conventional type of guerrilla warfare (based on controlling territory) into a forest insurgency based on ambush tactics and pin-prick raids, intended to sow confusion and undermine enemy morale" (Peters 2011a: 97). Eventually the RUF set up ten camps in the rain forest, most of which "were located in inaccessible terrain, well away from roads." All of the camps either were "inside of tropical rain forest or thick (closed canopy) bush" (100). A plane or helicopter could fly overhead and never see the camp below. Seven of the camps were in the east and south of Sierra Leone, while three were located in the middle section of the country (68).

Peters notes that RUF "fighters used the narrow bush paths to launch quick hit-and-run attacks before disappearing into the forest" (66). One former RUF combatant described their preferred way of travel during the war: "We normally move at night through the bush. We use the bush paths at night. Then we sleep during the day. We carried food with us—that wasn't a problem." It is along these paths that RUF fighters would come across the people in their hiding places in the forests, as they shared the same forest spaces. Some former RUF members related in interviews that a person could traverse huge areas of Sierra Leone along forest paths (sometimes called highways), occasion-

On the edge of Kenema, the largest city in eastern Sierra Leone, stands the launching point for Kailahun District. Minibuses, and motorcycle and sedan taxis, load up with goods and passengers before embarking on the uncertain journey. This photo was taken during a rainy season in 2010. The rain reportedly had made the roadway into Kailahun a long, muddy, and difficult slog. Just beyond this staging area stands part of Sierra Leone's enveloping rain forest. The RUF occupied Kailahun for the entire wartime period.

ally moving along the edges of villages or crossing roads before reentering the forest again. The forest areas were well away from government or ECOMOG soldiers, who mainly used "heavy, and thus road-bound, equipment" (147). ECOMOG waited in settled areas until the RUF entered their environment, as in Masingbi (discussed in the previous chapter). The only group that managed to access the forest camps of the RUF were the Kamajors, who were able to travel within the forest and ultimately destroy many RUF camps by the end of the war (148–149).

The AFRC coup blew the roof off what had been an ugly but fairly contained up-country war that took place mainly in the vicinity of forests and diamond mines. Even when things got really bad in other parts of Sierra Leone, Freetown stayed mostly above the fray (with many government and international officials regularly denying wartime realities). Johnny Paul Koroma's junta government eventually changed all that. At the same time, the AFRC was lost, with no vision for what they wanted to do. As Hoffman notes, "The junta leaders blamed everyone for their marginalization, and once in power they created a paranoid regime that made few real efforts to govern. The regime's purpose was its own protection and enrichment" (2011: 96). Most of the RUF exited the forests, entered the capital city and joined the soldier-rebels. The RUF were led into town by Sam Bockarie, a man described as "a homicidal thug" whose "brutality verged on the psychotic" (Gberie 2005: 121). Under Bockarie's leadership, the RUF was distinctly apolitical. He displayed interest only in violent destruction, a thirst for diamonds and attention, and loyalty to Foday Sankoh and Charles Taylor.[1] The AFRC/RUF junta, in short, was less a government or movement than a nihilistic, terror-based upheaval with no apparent end in sight.

The Terror Rampage

The AFRC's 1997 entrance into the war theater catalyzed the practice of terror and atrocity in Sierra Leone. Even by the ghastly standards of Sierra Leone's conflict up to that point, the vicious war became even more ferocious once ECOMOG drove Bockarie's RUF troops and Koroma's AFRC soldiers out of Freetown (in February 1998). Every established military group involved—the RUF, the CDF and ECOMOG—became considerably more violent with the AFRC now in the mix. To appreciate how the AFRC moved the intensity of violence and predation up several notches in Sierra Leone's war, it is helpful to take a look at their leadership. The AFRC leader in Freetown, Johnny Paul Koroma, quickly became an afterthought. From the time the RUF and AFRC troops left Freetown, Koroma transformed into a semihostage to Bockarie's RUF and had virtually no role in what took place from then on. Replacing him at the top of the AFRC were a series of military commanders, all of whom developed reputations for exceptional ruthlessness and brutality toward civilians and opposing forces.

Although leaders such as Bombblast (Hassan Papa Bangura) and Gullit (Alex Tamba Brima) were feared and fearsome, the AFRC leader who played an increasingly decisive role in the rebel movement was Solomon Anthony James (known mainly as SAJ) Musa. A military officer, for a time he was the number two in the NPRC (before Strasser dismissed him in 1993 [Keen 2005: 111]). Following the attempted coup against the NPRC in December 1992, Musa is thought to have led the grisly torture and execution of the alleged plotters (TRC 2004a: 164). Musa again entered civilian government for the AFRC in 1997, becoming chief secretary of state under Koroma. Somewhat curiously (given the widespread focus on diamonds among AFRC and RUF members), he "accused government soldiers and RUF fighters of disobeying orders to desist from diamond mining in Kono" (Keen 2005: 211).

SAJ Musa inspired tremendous loyalty among his followers. Gberie considered him a "swashbuckling" military man who was "very popular with the rank and file soldiers" because he was brash and had a "seeming ability to represent their views to the officer corps" (2005: 123).[2] In addition, interviews with members of the Special Court in 2005 indicated that Musa was regarded as a formidable, if extraordinarily brutal, military tactician, and an inspirational leader of troops that were ferocious, pitiless, and, for a time, quite effective. His thirst for power was well known (TRC 2004a: 318–319). With SAJ

Musa in the lead, the AFRC commanders and their troops combined righteous anger with a personalized and thoroughly unbridled brand of terror, with their soldiers routinely amped up on drugs. It is not that the AFRC leaders invented anything new: veteran practitioners in Sierra Leone's war theater had already employed rapes, amputations, cannibalism, executions, burning people alive, disemboweling pregnant mothers, and much more to great effect. The difference seemed to be the boiling rage of their fighters: they were furious and fierce and drug addled. Naturally, they terrified civilians. And while the RUF generally took to the advanced style of roiling terror, it seemed to spook just about everyone else involved in warfare on the ground.

The change took place as soon as the AFRC and RUF exited Freetown. Inside the city, their retreat inspired claims that "the rebels were now on their last legs." The reality was just the opposite. Once outside Freetown, the rebel troops split up, with Musa heading north with AFRC troops and Bockarie returning to his forest hideaway in the east (Gberie 2005: 123). Together, the two sets of fighters initiated "Operation Pay Yourself," which featured "sustained waves of looting" (Keen 2005: 209). The troops looted anything they could find, from trucks, cars, and motorcycles to mattresses, cooking pots, and food. Although robbing ordinary citizens had been "standard practice" for the RUF since 1991, "the scale and intensity of 'Operation Pay Yourself' was unprecedented in Sierra Leone." The rebels also instituted this operation with "a heightened level of violence against civilians" (Smith, Gambette, and Longley 2004: 34). The title of this operation evidently drew from Charles Taylor's Liberia. Taylor was known not to pay his troops but instead implemented his well-known policy of allowing each of his soldiers to "pay yourself."

A month later (March 1998), the AFRC and RUF jointly launched "Operation No Living Thing," an initiative that peaked ten months later. For civilians, it was war at its worst: "This operation marked a specific period of military activity during which the scale and intensity of violence against civilians in Sierra Leone was elevated to new and unprecedented levels" (Smith, Gambette, and Longley 2004: 34). Bockarie kicked off the operation with a promise of revenge for being forced out of Freetown. He provided a statement to the BBC "in which he declared that he was going to kill everyone in the country 'to the last chicken'" (Gberie 2005: 121, 120). While the AFRC and RUF started this new phase of warfare, every major military actor contributed to the increased fury of violence and atrocity in Sierra Leone.

Three examples highlight the pivotal impact of the AFRC on warfare in Sierra Leone. Peters reports a variety of ways that RUF collaboration with the AFRC significantly changed the RUF. For example, "Clearly the collaboration with the AFRC—and subsequently the RUF's access to towns and the capital city—not only emptied the minds of the fighters and commanders of much ideological commitment generated in the bush, but also undermined the movement's organisational coherence" (Peters 2011a: 152). Little of the RUF's organization in forest hideaways seems to have traveled with them to Freetown. Instead, once the RUF soldiers left the isolated bush camps to join the AFRC in town, drug use and the performance of terror-based violence appears to have expanded and intensified. They also enjoyed newfound freedoms. In the city alongside the AFRC, you could take and drive any available vehicle. As one former RUF fighter said, "Imagine, if even your own parents never owned a car, and suddenly you have one" (151).

Peters reports questionable versions of the RUF's military comportment. Early in the war, one RUF fighter related that the RUF had a minimal cutting policy: mainly "fingers and/or thumbs." But later in the war, "amputations of the arms up to the elbow or shoulder became more common." He also provides commentary from two former RUF fighters, both of whom blame the AFRC—entirely—for all amputations (154). These comments are balderdash. The RUF, together with the SLA (sometimes operating as sobels), are reported to have initiated amputations against civilians in 1992 (TRC 2004e: 13; Smith, Gambette, and Longley 2004: 498). The practice expanded over time. It would be difficult to assess the proportion of amputations that the RUF performed, since civilians frequently had no idea who the "rebels" actually were. But blaming all amputations on the AFRC is an obvious dodge. There were plenty of amputees from the war period prior to the arrival of the AFRC, and plenty of reporting connecting the RUF (and the SLA) to the amputations.

A second example of AFRC influence involved the CDF. The largest group, the Kamajors, featured a secret initiation that took place in the bush. While initiates could not discuss details of the process with outsiders, a featured innovation could be discussed: the "bulletproofing immunizations," which they believed would protect them from gunshots (Hoffman 2011: 236, 240). However, after the arrival of the AFRC, a "shortened version of the initiation" emerged for new initiates who "required less vigorous screening, initiation, and restriction" (237). At the same time, after the AFRC coup, the Kamajors shifted their purpose from "defending rural communities to fighting to reinstate an elected government." Through this transformation, the Kamajors also "grew more predatory and more abusive toward the population it was ostensibly meant to defend" (100). Finally, what eventually arose among a part of the CDF was a "movement that powerfully identified as youth, and came to define themselves less in opposition to the deposed junta and the RUF [than] to a gerontocratic order from which they felt excluded." This inspired the following outcome:

> Many CDF fighters began to think of themselves more and more as part of a youth "rebel" movement that included the RUF and extended beyond the

borders of Sierra Leone. Gangsta icons from the United States like Tupac Shakur, reggae stars like Bob Marley and Peter Tosh, and a range of African guerrilla movements like UNITA in Angola and the Sudan People's Liberation Army were all discussed by CDF fighters as fellow travelers in a war that was as much against corrupt elders as it was against the RUF or the [AFRC] junta. . . . While most [CDF] combatants faulted the RUF for allowing their "revolution" to devolve into an undisciplined campaign of pillage, by the end of the war a significant number of CDF fighters referred to *themselves* as "rebels" and claimed to be in sympathy with the RUF's project of creating a different, youth-led future for Sierra Leone. (Hoffman 2011: 102–103, emphasis in original)

The AFRC's arrival seemed to transform their CDF opponents into fellow alienated male youth sharing the same heroes while opposing those dominating the status quo. And like others in the war theater, CDF principles and purposes became much harder to track. The war was atomizing down to the actions of smaller units, making it more complex and dangerous than before.

The growing influence of Tupac Shakur and Bob Marley over rebel operations underscores a third example of how the AFRC's junta catalyzed changes in warfare in Sierra Leone through the increased use of popular culture icons to support the actions of military groups. Here are two instances of this. The first came from residents of Makeni and featured the arrival of and occupation by Superman (the high-ranking RUF commander from Liberia, Dennis Mingo) and his troops in the city early in 1998.[3]

Once entering Makeni, Superman sought to empty the town of most of its residents. To do this, he ordered troops to play a cassette recording of Bob Marley's "Exodus" in every neighborhood. In the fervently religious song, Marley and the chorus speak of God's faithful followers (the people of Jah) who are on the move. It is a driving song, communicating urgency and inevitable redemption for the followers of Jah. The rebels' manipulation of this song hinged on their transformation of metaphorical references of movement toward God into a literal order of forced expulsion. The song mentions the word "movement" thirty-four times and employs "move" as an imperative verb nineteen times.[4] When civilians heard the song in their neighborhood, they were expected to drop everything they owned—all belongings had to be left behind—and either exit the city immediately or risk being shot by Superman's troops. By exploiting Marley's famous song in this way, Superman forced many of Makeni's residents to leave their homes. There were reports that the rebels employed "Exodus" in the same way to take other villages and towns. The leader of a youth organization following the war also recalled that "the rebels sang the song after they had taken a town" during the war.

The second instance featured Tupac Shakur. Despite indications of his influence over rebel forces as early as late 1991, published reports of Tupac shaping Sierra Leone's wartime scene appear to have begun to appear in 1998. The Sierra Leonean journalist Lansana Fofana reported on an AFRC/RUF attack on the northern town of Kukuna. The attack left thirteen dead, seven of whom bled to death following amputations by the rebels (Smith, Gambette, and Longley 2004: 155). The rebels amputated the limbs of some civilians for refusing to burn their houses down (Fofana 1998a). The AFRC/RUF fighters burned perhaps sixty homes, the town's health facilities, and much more (Smith, Gambette, and Longley 2004: 156). Fofana reported something else: the rebels wore Tupac T-shirts. One farmer reported seeing hundreds of young men and women wearing the T-shirt. The journalist notes that Bob Marley T-shirts were popular with rebel fighters in the war's early years. In those days, people wearing them "were detained or lynched in combat zones." But by 1998, the Tupac T-shirt had become part of the rebel's uniform. It was a shirt sold in cities across the country for about three U.S. dollars. In Kukuna following the attack, "anyone sporting the [Tupac] T-shirt is branded a rebel and thus subjected to interrogation or some form of punishment" (Fofana 1998a).

A more impactful illustration of Tupac's influence on rebel fighters surfaced with an AFRC contingent that named themselves in honor of Tupac (initially the West Side N****z or the West Side Junglers, later the West Side Boys). While it was true that many of the West Side Boys (WSB) had resided in barracks in the western part of Freetown and ultimately parked in the Okra Hills in western Sierra Leone, "the main reason for the 'West Side' name" was "the music of the American rapper Tupac Shakur" (Utas and Jörgel 2008: 492). Reno observes that AFRC and RUF fighters admired Tupac and his rival rapper, Biggie Smalls, as "men who began as enterprising and clever drug dealers, who like them had to live in the informal economy and depend on their wits and violence to survive" (2003: 60). For the WSB, the shift from eastern Sierra Leone in 1998 (in Kono) to the west "drew comparisons between Tupac's own move from the American East Coast to the West Coast" and was part of the "mythology of the group" (Utas and Jörgel 2008: 494). Their style and approach to warfare arose during their trip west, as well.

In their camp in Kono, the AFRC soldiers who eventually formed the WSB "just wanted to listen to Shakur music," one former WSB commander recalled, and "we began to plait our hair and behave like American boys" (Utas and Jörgel 2008: 493). Then, when ECOMOG drove the AFRC and RUF forces out of Kono in April 1998, "revenge was apparently the leaders' main motive for atrocities on the civil population," as well as destroying infrastructure. But in addition, "extreme violence transformed into [military] strategy," together with "building an aura of fear and ruthlessness around themselves." This strategy was "anything but random"—and it worked. Over time they shifted from attacking villages away from main roads to attacking military targets and collecting arms. "Within months, they went from a largely un-equipped, dispersed group . . . to a force that could, and in fact did, take Free-town" (494).

They still were yet to become the WSB. That took place after AFRC and RUF soldiers stationed in Makeni began to fight. RUF-affiliated groups drove them out of town. They traveled to the Okra Hills (near Freetown) and be-came the West Side Boys. From there, and "despite continuing world media emphasis on 'the RUF rebels,' it was actually these troops who formed the ma-jority of those attacking Freetown in January 1999" (Keen 2005: 222). When that incursion ultimately failed (as will be described shortly), "the WSB was to become a semi-sovereign body in Sierra Leonean politics over the next twenty months" (Utas and Jörgel 2008: 494). WSB members were known to write "2Pac" on the sides of their guns (Rogers 2011), in addition to wearing Tupac T-shirts and much more: vests, tattoos, turn-up trousers, bandannas, and some shaved heads. Together, the West Side Boys represented an extreme expression of what WSB and other former combatants would call "Tupac Sys-tem" (described in chapter 17).

The West Side Boys, and their specialized emulation of and identification with Tupac, were part of a larger tapestry of rebel warrior groups inventing new identities for themselves. Following the first retreat from Freetown in February 1998, the RUF and the AFRC divided into smaller groups that ram-paged across much of the country (during Operation Pay Yourself and the ini-tial stages of Operation No Living Thing). The military command structure was exceptionally decentralized: the ground forces generally featured per-sonalized alpha male (and occasionally alpha female) commanders and their cadre of troops (including SBUs), wives/sex slaves, and porters. Each group seemed to have particular, trademark ways of distinguishing themselves from other groups. Sometimes these groups operated in alignment with counter-part groups. Other times they fought each other. At all times, they preyed on ordinary civilians.

All of this was mystifying (and, of course, terrifying) to village and town folks across Sierra Leone. Yet the source of citizen bafflement seemed to have changed from the early civil war years (up until the AFRC coup in May 1997). In the first half of the war, it was hard to tell who was attacking you: an RUF contingent or army soldiers imitating rebels (the "sobel" phenomenon). Once the AFRC entered the scene, the uncertainty continued but its character was different. For many civilians, it was nearly impossible to detect which rebel group—the RUF or the AFRC—was on the attack; they were merely "rebels," or perhaps "junta rebels." The reason is that the second half of the war was marked by configurations of shifting alliances between commanders and their personalized militias. It may have been evident and clear whenever the two poles were in action: Bockarie's RUF troops or SAJ Musa's AFRC corps. But beyond that, confusion seemed to reign.

From the civilian perspective, it really didn't matter which affiliation a particular marauding warlord had. For example, very few civilians interviewed seemed to know whether the contingent of troops under the Liberian commander, Dennis "Superman" Mingo, was RUF or AFRC. In truth, Mingo was a top commander for the RUF.[5] But all that civilians on the ground knew was that Superman led "Superman Group," just as Adama Cut Hand led "Adama Cut Hand Group" (also, reportedly, an RUF affiliate). Most rebel groups had distinctive indicators of their identity, such as those having male fighters wearing a red bandanna (Rambo Group), red uniforms (8 & 9 Group), a knitted black mask (Superman Group), or shaving off half of their hair (Sofila Group). In contrast (as noted earlier), the "Cut Hand Group" was known to demonstrate their identity: amputations were their trademark.

Although, technically, each warlord—and truly, these were lords of war—might report either to Bockarie or Musa, the field commanders also were freelancers. Interviews with civilian survivors of their occupations fed an impression that the groups were devoid of any apparent purpose beyond predation and personal enrichment. The AFRC may have been the older and better-trained set of fighters. But for civilians, even that distinction appears to have been difficult to decipher, since AFRC groups abducted boys and girls, just as their RUF colleagues did.

Nowhere did this confusion between RUF and AFRC groups come to the fore more than in Makeni. It sits in the center of Sierra Leone, a major city in its own right and a kind of terminus between Freetown and the west, Kabala and the north, Koidu and diamond-rich Kono District in the east, and Bo and the south. Makeni thus was a prize for the taking. There was much for the rebels to fight over, and they did, plundering the city in February 1998, losing it to ECOMOG troops the following month, and then driving out ECOMOG by the end of that year. From this point, they would hold Makeni for well over two years (until April 2001), making it "the RUF/AFRC stronghold" during that time (Smith, Gambette, and Longley 2004: 127, 134, 128).

The long period of rebel occupation did not yield stability. A top religious leader in Makeni served two important roles for the rebels during this period. He was both a representative for civilian concerns and a mediator between rival rebel groups. The rebels seemed to rely on him, which probably preserved his position and his life. He asserted that the rebel leaders "feared men of God. They knew they were committing a lot of sins, so they prayed to God. They had a tremendous respect for me, and they'd listen to me." He also provided examples of his work. "When there was someone about to be executed, people [civilians] would report it to me and I'd go to the [rebel] high command." Sometimes, his intercession would succeed. He also regularly settled disputes between rebel groups over property that they had confiscated. In 1999, he mediated a settlement following a major fight between two sets of rebels. On one side, he recalled, were leaders with RUF ties (Superman and Gibril Massaquoi) alongside two top AFRC commanders (Gullit and Santigie Borbor Kanu, known as Five-Five).[6] On the other side were three long-time RUF heavies: Issa Hassan Sesay, Morris Kallon, and Augustine Gbao.[7] In this particular brawl, and in many others, Superman seems to have held off all comers.

In towns and villages near Makeni, the same instability and violence reigned. One group might occupy a village for a spell. Periodically, another rebel group would pass through. "Sometimes they quarreled among themselves," a town chief from the area recalled, "resulting in fighting and killing of each other." On other occasions, groups might break bread and negotiate an alliance. Either way, the traffic and movement could be high: one interview with former female members of rebel groups from Binkolo (near Makeni) revealed seven different units that each had spent time in their area.[8] Reflecting on her years-long experience of rebel occupation, a town councilor from Makeni simply said, "The rebel war made us to taste hell."

The Invasion

War and chaos unfurled across Sierra Leone in 1998. The entire nation appeared to be unsteady and vulnerable. It did not help matters that ECOMOG, the government's primary military force, seemed preoccupied with two things: mining as many diamonds as possible (during the months they held Kono) and playing things cautiously on the battlefront. The RUF-AFRC attack to retake Kono near the end of the year left ECOMOG troops "soundly defeated," as they were "apparently caught unawares as they mined diamonds" (Hoffman 2011: 47). Elsewhere, ECOMOG troops were risk averse, evidently "reluctant to leave main fortified positions, or support others in so doing, thereby handing RUF/AFRC forces immeasurable advantages" (Smith, Gambette, and Longley 2004: 34–35). By the end of the year, rebel forces simultaneously mined diamonds in the east and drove toward the capital in the west.

Although some analysts emphasize the role of the West Side Boys in the Freetown attack, an array of other rebel actors were heavily involved, as well. Some rebel units received considerable help (particularly the RUF), with Liberian president Charles Taylor in the lead. Mercenaries and Libyan military officers trained "rebel attack squads" from Sierra Leone inside Liberia in preparation for the Freetown assault. Taylor reportedly also sent two thousand of his former fighters into Freetown alongside the RUF (Keen 2005: 229). One analyst noted that "the attack bore the trademark tactical planning of South

African military strategists" (Howe 2001: 221, quoted in Hoffman 2011: 48). Another interpretation came from Col. Richard Iron of the British army, who assessed the AFRC in considerable detail. He came away impressed with SAJ Musa as a military commander, whom he believed transformed the AFRC into "the most effective military organisation in Sierra Leone" by the end of 1998. Iron surmised that Musa sought to attack Freetown by early January in part to "trump the RUF's planned attack which, if successful, would almost certainly solidify RUF dominance over the AFRC in any junta [government] that re-emerged" (Iron 2005: E-3, C-11). It is an indication of the separation and rivalry between the AFRC and the RUF. Significantly, Iron says that Musa "ordered that there was to be no looting or entering private houses" during the Freetown attack. That most certainly did not happen, in part because Musa was killed by shrapnel in an explosion just prior to the Freetown attack (D-1, D-2) and because most of the invaders very clearly had other ideas.

Right before the Freetown invasion, eerie, disconcerting events took place there. Near the end of December 1998, Joseph Hill and his Cuture reggae group gave a concert in the capital. It was their second of two Sierra Leone concerts, both of which took place during the war years (the first was in 1994, when the reggae-loving NPRC was in power) (Abdulai Mento Kamara 2019). Nuxoll observes that "Hill's concerts during wartime literally effected cease-fires, with rebel combatants laying down their arms for the duration of his visit so that they could attend his concerts" (2015: 10). Another report alleges that Hill told the RUF rebels his condition for coming to Freetown: the rebels would have to stop fighting first. Reportedly, "the rebels quickly obeyed him and lay down their guns." Chillingly, based on what was about to take place, the report adds that following the concert, the rebels "sent a message to the president saying 'You are lucky that Paa Joe Hill is in Freetown, else we will destroy Freetown within 24 hours'" (Savage 2016).

Meanwhile, Sierra Leone's government and its international supporters were stupendously out of touch. The dawn of 1999 brought indications that things were going extremely well in Sierra Leone. On January 3, just three days before Operation No Living Thing entered Freetown, Francis Okello, the UN special representative to the secretary-general (SRSG) for Sierra Leone, announced that "the situation is improving steadily" in the country (Sierra Leone Web 1999, quoted in Keen 2005: 225). Then, with their work thought to be completed—and on the very day that the rebel stampede began—"UNOMSIL completed its evacuation" from Sierra Leone (Keen 2005: 225).[9] Such contrived, self-serving actions left the government and its primary international supporters deeply unpopular with ordinary Freetown citizens, according to many I interviewed in Gambia in 2000 and afterward in Sierra Leone. It is easy to appreciate why.

With Gullit the AFRC's new commander and his AFRC troops (including the West Side Boys) out front, the rebel onslaught began on the sixth of January 1999, known to Sierra Leoneans simply as "January 6." Operation No Living Thing, which had begun ten months earlier, finally struck Freetown. Although its purpose may have been to retake political control of Sierra Leone, on the ground the rebels' aim "does not appear to have been the recapture of Freetown, but its destruction" (Hoffman 2011: 47).

What came next proved difficult to describe adequately. Some adopted an understated approach, such as Peters, who observed, "On 6 January 1999 a damaging battle for Freetown started" (2011a: 77). Others had trouble grasping what took place. Keen, for example, summed it up as "almost unimaginably brutal" (2005: 227) while Gberie called it "a regime of horror . . . so intense and bizarre that it almost defies description" (2005: 126). Still others seemed to deploy the most dramatic prose they could come up with. A shining example of this approach is Sebastian Junger:

> Teenage soldiers, out of their minds on drugs, rounded up entire neighborhoods and machine-gunned them or burned them alive in their houses. They tracked down anyone whom they deemed to be an enemy—journalists, Nigerians, doctors who treated wounded civilians—and tortured and killed them. They killed people who refused to give them money, or people who didn't give enough money, or people who looked at them wrong. They raped women and killed nuns and abducted priests and drugged children to turn them into fighters. They favored Tupac T-shirts and fancy haircuts and spoke Krio—the common language of Freetown—to one another because they didn't share a tribal language. . . . Realizing that they were going to lose the city, [the rebels] started rounding up people and detaining them until special amputation squads could arrive. The squads were made up of teenagers and even children, many of whom wore bandages where incisions had been made to pack cocaine under their skin. They did their work with rusty machetes and axes and seemed to choose their victims completely at random. "You, you, and you," they would say, picking people out of a line. There were stories of hands' being taken away in blood-soaked grain bags. There were stories of hands' being hung in trees. There were stories of hands' being eaten. (Junger 2006)

Terror that broke the bounds of what was conceivable seems to have been the collective purpose of the rebels' attack. One of the prime reported motivations for the attack was "the grievances of the disempowered." Also notable was the finding by the Truth and Reconciliation Commission that, in the postwar period, "AFRC soldiers continued to fail to comprehend the gravity of the abuses they had committed against the people of Sierra Leone" (TRC 2004a: 320). Taken together, these views likely powered the rebels' fury (for

RUF as well as AFRC combatants) while informing rationales for their actions. For the rebels, everything they did was justified.

Stepping back from the fray, one can make out a kind of depraved creativity in rebel acts—an exploration into the many ways that a human being might torture and traumatize another. It seemed to combine the array of terror techniques honed by the RUF over seven and a half years with the AFRC's knack for expansive, ruthless rage. Keen's take supports the view that the RUF sketched the terror canvas while the AFRC helped paint it in, as "many aspects of the violence echoed earlier RUF violence" (2005: 236). Given that some of the practitioners had been trained by mercenaries in Charles Taylor's Liberia, other influences surely contributed to the terror cocktail as well. Whatever the sources, "January 6" undoubtedly was the war's crescendo, the most significant example of terror warfare emerging from Sierra Leone's entire conflict.

Four factors set this stunning attack into context:

- First, the rebel invasion took place in two phases. The initial assault lasted five days, after which rebel forces controlled almost all of Freetown, including all of eastern Freetown, the downtown center, and 70 percent of the western half (Keen 2005: 226). The incoming force numbered approximately ten thousand people, including not just soldiers but "captive senior citizens, women, children and newborn babies" (TRC 2004a: 324). The second phase featured the rebels' (AFRC, RUF, Liberians, mercenaries) collective retreat. That took much longer, perhaps two and a half weeks (Gberie 2005: 131), before ECOMOG ousted them from the town a second time.

- Second, it is clear that ECOMOG forces lost it during the Freetown invasion, tumbling deeper into the abyss of violence alongside their rebel opponents (as well as the Kamajors). ECOMOG soldiers summarily executed some of the civilians who had fled to Freetown's National Stadium, for example (Smith, Gambette, and Longley 2004: 36).[10] There were a host of reasons for this: they often could not make out civilians from rebels (rebel spies regularly were mixed into civilian populations), morale was terrible, pay was low, and they "enjoyed a high degree of impunity" (Keen 2005: 244–246). The Nigerians in particular also had been suffering heavy losses, with more than one thousand killed and many thousands wounded during the ECOMOG engagement in Sierra Leone (Gberie 2005: 132).

- Third, the RUF (not the AFRC) sought and received credit for the attack, something they had become known for. The RUF always were eager "to take the credit for the sins of others," as it aligned with their tactic of using fear to advance their profile and reputation (Keen 2005: 222). I will explain shortly how this also enhanced their bargaining power in negotiations.

- Fourth, the rebels collectively saved the worst for last: the nastiest atrocities generally came as they retreated. Though it was true for the AFRC as much as for the RUF, Gberie observed that "the RUF always resorted to utterly repugnant acts of violence when it faced serious resistance or defeat" (2005: 135).[11]

While key terror war techniques will be examined in depth in part 5, some sense of the assessments of this intense battle are necessary here. Human Rights Watch (HRW) came out with a report following the Freetown assault that catalogued the terror atrocities committed by rebel troops. Significantly and strangely, there is no mention whatsoever of the leaders of the assault (the AFRC). Bockarie's boasting about the RUF seemed to work: all rebel atrocities were awarded to the RUF. For the RUF leaders, this was an achievement. The RUF were a small force dominated by children. They clearly knew that for terror warfare to succeed, lots of people need to be terrorized. Indeed, the RUF's success always rested on this: gathering a reputation for feverish, inhumane, extremely violent debauchery was necessary because it made civilians and opponents think that their troops were mightier than they really were.

HRW noted that there were specialized units for the performance of different kinds of atrocities (rape, execution, mutilation/amputation). Children were at the forefront of most of what took place, serving both as featured perpetrators and frequently targeted victims of rape, mutilation, and murder. Rebel soldiers moved within civilian groups fleeing the rebels, which allowed them to advance farther into the city and use civilians as human shields in street fights with ECOMOG. They looted civilians systematically. They tossed infants and other civilians into burning houses and shot those trying to escape. They attacked hospitals and clinics, and they converted the city's largest hospital into a rebel base, torturing, robbing, removing, and executing patients in the process. They used games to maximize terror, such as asking victims whether they preferred execution by gunshot, machete, or being burned alive. They mutilated hundreds of people and abducted thousands more during their retreat (mostly children and young women). They set entire city blocks on fire, leaving 5,788 homes and buildings destroyed and 51,000 people homeless (HRW 1999: I). The attack left more than five thousand people dead, more than a hundred people with amputated limbs, and thousands of women and girls raped (HRW 2003: 12). Some rebels were reported to have attempted to poison the city's water supply (Traub 2000: 62, cited in Keen 2005: 228).

Five aspects of the rebels' extravagant horror show are worthy of note. The first is the indication that the rebels "performed" the terror practices (a civilian reported that it was "a common word for atrocities against civilians"; quoted in Keen 2005: 238). It is a revealing choice of phrasing, as it separates terror acts from the persons who carry them out. The terror "performances" were often put on by groups of "performers" called such things as Burn House Unit, Cut Hands Commando, Blood Shed Squad, Kill Man No Blood (a unit that "beat people to death without shedding blood"), and Born Naked Squad (a group that "stripped their victims before killing them") (HRW 1999: IV).

Second is the finding that most of the rebels were heavily drugged while "performing" their atrocities. As HRW records, "Most victims and witnesses describe widespread usage by the rebels of drugs, marijuana, and alcohol and believe most of the atrocities were committed while under the influence of these substances." The report found that rebels gave themselves drugs via injection or by inserting brown or white powder into incisions on their faces (covering them with plaster or tape afterward). They also forced some abductees to consume food laced with drugs or gave them drug injections. This is a central element of many rebel indoctrinations, as well as a primary activity for rebels generally, as will be described later in this book (HRW 1999: IV). To be a rebel was to be high most of the time.

Third, being a rebel also meant living a highly sexualized life. A boy rebel was a specialized mauler of females; a girl rebel was a regular recipient of them. In the January 6 attack, sexual violence was a featured terror tactic ("individual and gang-rape, sexual assault with objects such as sticks and firewood, and sexual slavery" [HRW 1999: IV]). Rape often seemed to come first, before the burnings, amputations, and killings. A researcher into Sierra Leone's war related that the degree of rape undertaken by rebels was extraordinarily high. "From Cotton Tree to East End" (that is, from Freetown's downtown area across East Freetown), "maybe eight or nine women in ten were raped. The rebels would tell five women at a time to lie down, and then rape each one."

Here are examples of what the rebels did (or, using their lexicon, performed). A resident of East Freetown recalled in an interview what took place first when the rebels entered his neighborhood (in the earliest stages of the attack). The commander gathered girls and female youth and made them lay down in the street. With the entire neighborhood watching, the boy soldiers (and, most probably, the older male officers) systematically raped each female at least once. A male youth survivor also recalled that, from his experience, "The girl soldiers were the worst!" He then explained how female rebel soldiers would castrate boys and men in public. A woman survivor of the January 6 attack supported his take: "The rebels are human beings, but at the same time, they are not. They are too rough. [During the January 6 attack,] the rebels were not just boys. They had women and child rebels too. And the women [rebels] were worse than the men. They were too dangerous, and didn't have sympathy for young men." She added, "Some of these rebel women were pregnant" when they attacked male civilians.

Fourth is the need for terror war performances to have big audiences. There were a lot of witnesses to terror acts (such as the mass rape episode in East Freetown) for a reason. It is a key element of terror warfare: witnesses spread fear and help demoralize the opposition. The practitioners could have killed far more people than they did, but they did not. Traumatizing most people served their ends much more than mass slaughter.

Finally, much of what took place came with a soundtrack. From the very beginning of the attack, popular culture played a frontline role. For example, Keen records the recollection of a man held hostage by the West Side Boys during the attack. "Six ladies were executed" by members of the WSB. "After that, the commander put on Rasta religious music and took a lot of marijuana" (Keen 2005: 240). Interviews with refugee witnesses to the Freetown attack added a second use of music during the rebel assault: to support the rebels' practice of employing citizens as human shields. One woman recalled, "When the ECOMOG jets would fly overhead, the rebels would play Tupac [songs] and tell us to dance outside; 'to dance for peace.' And if we didn't, they would kill us all." At some point, the woman and her eldest child, together with her younger sister and her sister's son, all ran to the home of Freetown's Catholic leader, Archbishop Joseph Ganda. Apparently, they arrived after the RUF military police had abducted Ganda and other Catholic clergy and began moving them "from place to place" (HRW 1999). Thus in Ganda's home the sisters and their children found rebel soldiers who "told us to cook for them." In addition, "they would force us to dance and say we want peace before the ECOMOG fighters; to dance to Tupac's music or they would kill us." There also were accounts of rebels dancing to Tupac's music "during breaks in the action" (Sommers 2003b: 35).

The theatrical nature of the rebel invasion mixed direct references to popular culture icons with drugs. One reporter, for example, detailed what the rebels wore:

> Some wore the combat camouflage of Sierra Leone's disintegrated army. Some wore black jeans, knit polo shirts, Tupac Shakur T-shirts. A few had wrapped their hair in handkerchiefs patterned with the American flag. All of them wore red bandannas around their foreheads. Adhesive strips patched their faces, as if they had been scratched by angry cats. The strips masked incisions where the rebels had ingested cocaine, amphetamines or other drugs that wired their heads for battle. (Coll 2000)

The handkerchiefs and bandannas very likely reflected the direct influence of Tupac and Rambo, both of whom regularly wore similar headgear.

Yet the explicit Tupac references apparently emerged only in some parts of Freetown. The Tupac T-shirts evidently were worn only by certain groups of invading rebel troops. This was illustrated in interviews with civilians who lived in Freetown during the assault. Some related that they did not see any rebels wearing Tupac-related garb in their neighborhoods. For example, in one section of Freetown, a survivor recalled that, after the rebels had secured his part of the capital city, "they started celebrating":

> They were carrying some big tape recorders, which they had just looted. They danced and smoked djamba. They were dancing to reggae music, mostly songs by Bob Marley and Joe Hill. They shouted and sang "Freedom Time Again" ["Freedom Time," by Joseph Hill and Culture] and "Chase this Baldhead" ["Crazy Baldhead," by Bob Marley]. The rebels forced civilians to come out and celebrate with them. Even when I was praying in acute pain [the rebels had just amputated his right hand], they still expected me to come out and celebrate. One of them said, "This is the prize you have paid for; the freedom we are bringing to you. You are lucky. Others such as our commander SAJ Musa have died, and today they are not here to celebrate this big victory with us." These boys were indeed drunk with djamba and rum. They forced us to drink and smoke. They did not play any other music except Marley, Joe [Hill], and [Lucky] Dube.

The rebels he interacted with made no mention of Tupac or rap music. Instead, they demonstrated their affection for reggae musicians.[12]

Other Freetown residents detailed something entirely different: the invaders of their neighborhoods bore the unmistakable stamp of Tupac in many ways. One set of refugees (all of whom had fled Sierra Leone after the January 6 assault) detailed how the rebels arrived in their neighborhood in white vans and pickup trucks with the names of famous Tupac songs painted on the sides. They mentioned "All Eyez on Me," "Me against the World," "Hit 'Em Up," "California Love" and "Only God Can Judge Me." They also listed "Death Row," which was Tupac's record label near the end of his life, and "Missing in Action," which referred to a famous trio of mid-1980s wartime thriller movies starring Chuck Norris, an action hero and international contemporary of Sylvester Stallone and the Rambo war films.

Out burst the rebels: well armed, adorned in Tupac T-shirts, and exploding with drug-fueled rage. They very well could have been members of the West Side Boys militia. A male youth survivor supplied his take on the connection: "Tupac says he's against the world, and the rebels also say they're against the world." He added, "The West Side Boys are the Tupac group," a reference to the WSB's tight connection to Tupac Shakur's music and image. Two other refugees who survived the January 6 onslaught described similar rebel outfits.

A male youth of twenty-two related that the "rebel uniform" often consisted of a "red head cover or U.S. flag [bandanna]. Some wore Tupac T-shirts or combat pants." A twenty-seven-year-old young man similarly recalled, "The rebels had a uniform: a Tupac T-shirt, combat fatigue jacket and trousers, and an American flag handkerchief around their heads." The recollections roughly align with Coll's description given earlier: all wore Rambo- or Tupac-style bandannas, and many wore Tupac T-shirts.[13] Referring to the famous black Tupac T-shirt during the attack, a Sierra Leonean journalist summed up its significance: "That T-shirt gave them [the rebels] their cause."

"January 6" was a short-term occupation of Freetown. The rebels' plan was to overrun the city and take over the government. Although ultimately they failed, they also did not retreat immediately. They were in parts of the city for about three weeks. This provided citizens trapped by the rebels with a bird's-eye view of their behavior, tactics, and rationales. Many had time to appreciate what the rebels did and why they did it. A twenty-four-year-old female youth recalled, "When rebels came in, they burned houses in my neighborhood but didn't harm me." Like many others, she was with the rebels during their occupation. In interviews with Sierra Leonean refugees who had survived the assault, the following notable themes emerged:

- **Constant, heavy drug use.** There were persistent references to the rebels using drugs of all kinds. One refugee man, for example, explained that "most rebels have elastic bandages on them to stick drugs to their body. They cut their arms or head and put some drugs in the Band-Aid and stick it their skin." Interestingly, he also added, "During the AFRC-RUF occupation," many citizens also were heavily drugged: "Marijuana and alcohol in the population was very high. They needed [the drugs] to keep them tranquilized."

- **Enacting "motherfucker."** Sierra Leoneans who heard the curse word "motherfucker" invariably connected it to Tupac Shakur's songs. One refugee man, for instance, commented that "Tupac uses bad words. They are dangerous and very negative. Tupac says mother-fucker. I mean: to fuck your mother? The rebels take [such curse words] very literally and apply the lyrics." An indication of the "motherfucker" act surfaced in an interview with several refugee women. One initially stated, "The rebels have to use children." Then she provided her analysis:

  > The children can't think deeply, like big people [that is, adults]. So the rebels use drugs to control the children and tell them even to kill their mother. During "January 6," the small rebels were full of drugs. So

they could do anything. The bigger rebels could tell the small-small boys to rape their mothers. The rebels loved to watch that. That's why they love children: they do what they're told.

- **Exploiting girls in many ways.** "The rebels are the best spies," one refugee man explained. A refugee woman provided her take on how the rebel forces used girls. Spying was only one of their functions:

> During "January 6," the rebels were mostly interested in girls eight years and older. Why? Because they knew that they were virgins. So the rebels took them and raped them, taking them as wives and also using them against ECOMOG forces as human shields. ECOMOG soldiers also fell for the girls that the rebels had taken. They didn't know the girls were rebels. The girls were spies. They were very dangerous. [After being with the ECOMOG soldiers], they'd carry information back to the rebels. This helped the rebels attack ECOMOG.

The reference to abducted girls who became loyal rebel spies was corroborated in many other recollections of wartime experience. The belief that rebel girls were the superb "recces" seemed to be widely held.

- **Narrow escapes.** With rebels occupying much of Freetown, two recollections illustrate the danger, difficulty, bravery, and profound loss that successfully evading the rebels required. A twenty-eight-year-old mother recalled that

> I was in Freetown when the rebels arrived on Wednesday, January 6, 1999. I was seven months pregnant. I fled into a mosque, though I'm a Christian. Then I fled to a church, but the rebels burnt it. I kept running here and there. Then I took a canoe and paddled to Lungi [Airport, across the bay from Freetown] by myself. Then I took a boat, which I paid for by selling all my things. I lost track of my three other children and my husband.

An eighteen-year-old female student shared the following story:

> When the rebels came, my mother and my younger siblings ran away. My older brother and I stayed in the house [with their father]. But when the rebels started burning the house, my father said, "The tension is too much." The rebels saw us leaving and shot my father in the chest. The rebels caught me and my brother and held us for five days. After ECOMOG entered [our neighborhood] and fought the rebels, we escaped.

- **An appreciation of terror war tactics.** A woman refugee provided insight on rebel rationales. First, she described some of the acts they committed:

The young children used to suffer. The rebels would chop the hands they didn't want. They'd chop their hands because they were the leaders of tomorrow. They would ask whether you want long sleeve or short sleeve. If it's long sleeve, they would cut at the wrist. If it's short sleeve, they would cut you above the elbow.

Her reference to well-known amputations ("short sleeve" and "long sleeve") also contains the sort of deviant validation for atrocity that eventually became a kind of rebel hallmark. In this case, since potential "leaders of tomorrow" might rise up as their opponents, they had to be mutilated. Reflecting on the description, the woman shared the following analysis. "I learned this during the two Freetown attacks by the rebels [the first in May 1997, the second starting on January 6, 1999]: the rebels always explain what they do before they do it. They want to scare us, and they do."

This assessment sums up the rebels' collective brand of warfare. They mainly sought to terrorize civilians, not kill them. In this, they were exceptionally effective. More than any other set of events in Sierra Leone's war, the ferocious January 6 assault communicated the rebels' extreme approach to warfare.

One is left with the concept of the perverse universe as the underlying fuel and pedagogy for the rebels' performance of terror warfare. Three sets of analysis illustrate this. Looking at the entire war experience, Abdullah finds that, for the RUF, NPRC, and AFRC, "widespread looting was dubbed liberation," "the abduction of innocent children was considered a rescue operation," and "collective gang rape was seen as remuneration for combatants!" He concluded that "grotesque appropriation of what constitutes a revolutionary project produces grotesque results" (Abdullah 2002: 33–34). Gberie recorded a tragic event during the Freetown attack to disclose a deeper underlying meaning. A group of rebels entered a World Food Programme warehouse and found hundreds of new machetes (meant for farmers) instead of food. This inspired the rebels to "crudely and methodically cut off the hands of people, including those of hundreds of people who could have used them to grow food." With this realization, Gberie found that "the perversion was complete: the tragedy was brutally surreal" (2005: 129). Finally, Keen seems to have found "January 6" as the purest expression of the perverse universe that the rebels embraced:

The rebels were turning upside down a world perceived as corrupt and unjust. The rich and educated were to be humbled, many of the healthy crippled and the sane driven insane; but the sick or the crazy could sometimes incite sympathy, and the poor, the forgotten and the young (most of all, themselves) were now to be respected and applauded—often at gunpoint. Those who colluded (or appeared to collude) in this perverse world-view— whether from inside or outside a rebel group—stood some chance of surviving it. (Keen 2005: 241)

In the January 6 battering of Freetown and its residents, the rebels attacked the perverse universe by forcefully enacting perversion themselves. Reality— the way that society is structured, including those regaled and those denigrated—had to be attacked and ripped up in a way that was excruciating for witnesses. More than any other episode in Sierra Leone's war, the rebels' January 1999 attack on Freetown made terror cathartic for practitioners and absolutely devastating for survivors.

CHAPTER 14

The Dénouement

On to Lomé

If anyone wanted to write a handbook on how not to end a war, the case of Sierra Leone would be a good place to start. To begin with, there were three instances when the government side in the war took their foot off the gas and let the rebels off the hook. Each time, they had the rebels in significant retreat, and each time, the rebels rebounded with a vengeance. The first came late in 1993, when NPRC soldiers had the RUF on the brink of defeat—and then went diamond mining. The second took place soon after Strasser had hired Executive Outcomes (EO) in 1995 to lead the charge against the rebels. Once again, the RUF survived, and Kabbah even agreed to let EO exit Sierra Leone as part of the 1996 peace deal (just one example of the RUF's excellence in negotiating both the Abidjan and Lomé peace agreements). The third happened at the outskirts of Freetown in 1997, when ECOMOG forces had the AFRC and RUF forces cornered and then appeared to let them escape, evidently so they could go diamond mining too.

With so little motivation to extinguish the awful conflict, the end was a chaotic fiasco, with many turns in the road. The centerpiece was a peace accord in Lomé, Togo, that was dead in the water almost as soon as it was signed. It was presaged by heavy international pressure on the Kabbah government for a peace accord informed by denial of reality about the RUF. There was a second rebel march on Freetown, another planned coup, ceasefires ignored almost as soon as they had been agreed on, a botched RUF invasion of Guinea (spearheaded by Charles Taylor), the West Side Boys provoking the British military to enter the fray, atrocities committed by nearly every military actor, and an exceedingly underfunded and mismanaged disarmament, demobilization, and reintegration (DDR) program. Not least, Foday Sankoh and the RUF used the time between January 6 and the end of the war to suck as many diamonds out of the dirt in Kono and Tongo as they could manage (which was a lot).

The second retreat of the RUF and AFRC was even more vicious than the first. On vibrant display were the intensity and extremity of terror war tactics that RUF and AFRC soldiers employed. Their calculated focus was mainly on brutalizing people, not killing them: "As the rebels retreated east they laid waste to miles of Freetown's poor, densely populated neighborhoods and suburbs. The violence was extraordinarily cruel and personal. Victims were raped, dismembered, or burned alive while the rebels taunted them; family members were forced to watch, and even to perform atrocities; boy conscripts returned to their old neighborhoods to settle scores. Commanders with names like Captain 2 Hands and Betty Cut Hands organized special amputation squads in neighborhoods from which the rebels were retreating" (Packer 2003). At a place called Upgun Junction, a source from the Special Court of Sierra Leone reported that one of the top AFRC commanders, Santigie Borbor Kanu (known as Five-Five), performed the following: "Five-Five said it was time for amputating to begin in earnest. Then he publicly demonstrated the difference between long sleeve and short sleeve" by amputating the arms of civilians right on the roadway.

It was evident that Bockarie's insistence on taking credit for the fierce Freetown attack was paying dividends. The RUF was again on the rise, and everything, it seemed, was falling their way. The RUF-led rebels, who had retaken Kono in December 1998, "concentrated their actions on mining activities, strengthening their positions in the Northern Province and planning actions to take place on Guinean territory." Their strength in the north of the country "guaranteed a strong hand during peace negotiations" (Smith, Gambette, and Longley 2004: 37). Meanwhile, the AFRC, with Koroma still detained in Mosquito's Kailahun hideaway and SAJ Musa dead, were in disarray. Their central role in the January 6 assault had been forgotten. Without that recognition, and lacking the RUF's access to diamonds and support from Taylor and Compaoré, the AFRC leaders lost their leverage entirely.

The January 6 attack had promoted "a new mood of appeasement" nationally and internationally (Keen 2005: 248). Despite the rebels' retreat, it was Kabbah's government that was off balance. One can appreciate why: the government had a tiny army while the Nigerians of ECOMOG increasingly wanted out (223). Kabbah faced pressure to negotiate with the RUF from Nigeria, Ghana, Guinea, and Great Britain (250). The U.S. government also got heavily involved. Rev. Jesse Jackson, the "Special Envoy for the President and Secretary of State for the Promotion of Democracy in Africa," inexplicably compared the RUF to South Africa's African National Congress (Smillie 2009: 20) and Sankoh to "the revered Nelson Mandela" (Zack-Williams 2012: 28). He admonished Kabbah to break bread with the RUF, believing that "a power-sharing agreement would 'promote democracy.'" Members of the U.S. Congressional Black Caucus got involved as well, most prominently Rep. Donald Payne of New Jersey, who was "a personal friend" of Charles Taylor. Payne urged Sankoh to be released from prison without preconditions and to negotiate with him. In response to all of this, "Kabbah finally agreed to a cease-fire and released Foday Sankoh to join him for negotiations in Lomé" (Smillie 2009: 20, 21).

The Lomé negotiations made Foday Sankoh a star. He was "delighted at the international recognition surrounding Lomé" and even received a call from U.S. president Bill Clinton (Keen 2005: 252). What ensued were intense negotiations that yielded, on July 7, 1999, "a blanket amnesty for all RUF fighters" and four ministerial posts for the RUF. Foday Sankoh made out the best: vice president of the government and "head of a new commission to oversee the country's mineral resources, including the diamonds that he had been looting in order to finance his war effort" (Smillie 2009: 21). This was the pinnacle of Foday Sankoh's career. He now was famous, having secured international recognition and renown. "He clearly regarded himself as the freedom fighter Jesse Jackson had claimed he was," Gberie observed, adding that "the delusions of grandeur that had always underlined the warlord's brutal policies became starkly apparent." He proceeded to insult and upbraid global luminaries like U.S. secretary of state Madeline Albright (Gberie 2005: 163, 164). In Sankoh's mind, it appeared, he had arrived.

Denizens of Freetown celebrated on the day of the signing. A carnival atmosphere arose as people crowded into the streets, some of them beating drums. Among those reported to be "dancing with joy" across the city were amputees from the war (BBC News 1999). In addition, "some people carried radio-cassette machines aloft blaring out hopeful songs, including tunes by the late Jamaican reggae star Bob Marley" (Agence France Presse 1999).

But critics unloaded on the Lomé agreement. It "shocked the conscience of the world," Abraham assessed (2004: 213). Smillie contended that what had taken place "must go down in the annals of international diplomacy as one of the most cynical and disgraceful episodes of all time." He added, "The RUF had demonstrated that butchery paid off. Instead of being punished, they were rewarded, assisted in the process by the most powerful government on earth" (2009: 20, 21). Kandeh took Kabbah to task, contending that he "inherited a bad situation that got worse under his watch. . . . Kabbah's approach has been to pursue peace and reconciliation through appeasement" (2004b: 170). In contrast, Porter was empathetic, since "Sankoh and the RUF were in a strong position . . . [as they were] in control of some two-thirds of the country, and all of the diamond mines" (2003: 24). Olonisakin agreed: "the government had little option but to negotiate" (2008: 37). A Truth and Reconciliation Commission official concurred: "When you can't defeat the rebels, you have to have a compromise. The rebels demanded amnesty before handing over their weapons, and it was granted to them." All of this underscored the sudden fall of the AFRC, who weren't at the talks. Their high command had pushed for Johnny Paul Koroma's involvement in negotiations. But the RUF made sure he wasn't there (easy to do, since Bockarie still held him captive in Kailahun) (TRC 2004a: 342).

Within weeks of the signing of the Lomé agreement, Nigeria's president announced that Nigeria would pull out by the end of 1999. This shifted responsibility for defending Sierra Leone's government and protecting its citizens onto a new UN outfit, the United Nations Mission in Sierra Leone (UNAMSIL). It was not an observer mission (like its predecessor, UNOMSIL) and could deploy armed troops in the field. However, UNAMSIL relied on two assumptions that proved wildly inaccurate: "that the RUF would abide by the terms of the Lomé Agreement, and that the UN force could cope with challenges after ECOMOG's withdrawal" (Olonisakin 2008: 43, 41, 61). The RUF never took Lomé seriously, the agreement inflamed the AFRC, and the government's military backers were weak. Zack-Williams argued that Lomé undercut peace-building efforts. Since the accord "was more than the RUF could have expected to win on the battlefield," it "emboldened the [RUF] leadership to further illusions of grandeur and recalcitrant behavior" (Zack-Williams 2012: 28). Achieving real peace in Sierra Leone still was a long way off.

In the midst of such dread and insecurity in 1999, Joseph Hill reached out to Sierra Leoneans with a song called "War in Sierra Leone." He made reference to his late December 1998 concert in Freetown, but then seemed to struggle with who to blame for Sierra Leone's violence, including the notorious "long sleeve" and "short sleeve" amputations. Like so many others, Joseph Hill accounted for the war's horror without grasping the reasons why it had taken place.[1] That sentiment also informed an earlier song about Sierra Leone by Bob Marley's son, Ziggy. Called "Diamond City," it also does not explain why war descended on Sierra Leoneans. Instead, it highlights tragedy, the exploitation of diamond miners, and a region-wide need for revolution.[2]

It proved hard to end Sierra Leone's war for a number of reasons. One, of course, was diamonds. The head of the government's new mining commission (now Vice President Foday Sankoh) focused on pushing his RUF troops to extract and smuggle as many diamonds as possible out of the country. By the end of the war, the RUF "would virtually strip the mines [in Kono] of alluvial diamonds" (Patel 2002: 38, cited in Keen 2005: 269). A second factor slowing the road to peace was the hampered and hapless DDR program. Sankoh and other RUF leaders resisted having any combatants join the DDR process, as it would undermine their stature and influence (Keen 2005: 254). When Sankoh finally had a chance to boost his super-youthful cadres, he didn't.

It also had taken a long time to set up the DDR centers. Conditions for those that opened were underwhelming (Keen 2005: 257). "The idea that ex-combatants were being prepared for a future life beyond the war was largely a fiction," Keen concluded (258). Problems kept increasing, including the virtual exclusion of females associated with military groups. One study found that an estimated 48,216 child soldiers fought in Sierra Leone, 12,056 of whom (25 percent) were girl soldiers (McKay and Mazurana 2004: 92). The researchers also found that the CDF groups had significant numbers of girls who were initiated as soldiers, despite claims from CDF leaders that they were male-only organizations (95, 97). Yet only 8 percent of DDR participants were female. A mere 4.2 percent of girl child soldiers (506) managed to access the DDR process (99).

Events in May 2000 collectively created a turning point. Charles Taylor assumed the unlikely role of international peacemaker by negotiating the release of the last of the five hundred UNAMSIL peacekeepers whom the RUF had taken hostage earlier in the month. During this period, a major study surfaced that revealed Taylor's involvement in diamond sales and gunrunning. This ultimately led to sanctions on Liberian diamond exports (Olonisakin 2008: 76, 77, 78).[3] British forces arrived in Sierra Leone in May 2000 and were on hand when yet another RUF effort to conquer Freetown took place.

The War Is Over

The plan had been hatched in advance. Sankoh evidently was unsatisfied with merely being vice president and in charge of the nation's mining. It seemed he still sought to be president. Having returned to Freetown on the very day that AFRC leader Johnny Paul Koroma did (October 3, 1999) (Utas and Jörgel 2008: 501), Sankoh and his newly christened Revolutionary United Front Party (RUFP) settled in at a residence called Spur Road Lodge. Remarkably, President Kabbah's government decided that this was the time to award Koroma with the unlikely role of chair of the Commission for the Consolidation of Peace. With this, the AFRC was brought back to the government side. The move was shrewd but risky: as there did not seem to be limits on any of the state's security forces (including the CDF), bringing the AFRC straight into the mix was potentially explosive.

Koroma wasted no time in recruiting top leaders of the West Side Boys (and other AFRC officers) as his security detail (TRC 2004a: 366, 365). Having jumped to the government side, the West Side Boys, together with Kamajors, national army (SLA) troops, and the same violent police unit that Siaka Stevens had formed decades earlier to protect his interests (the SSD), formed an "ad-hoc state security force" that "effectively took the law into its own hands." After Koroma awarded them the unlikely title of Peace Task Force, the ad-hoc group went on a rampage, killing, looting, intimidating, and torturing with impunity (389, 448).

The West Side Boys in particular held Freetown "under siege for days with repeated looting raids and violence." But they also had read the RUF tea leaves, exposing considerable military acumen alongside the routine brutality that had become their calling card. They effectively snuffed out a coup attempt by arresting and holding many RUFP commanders (roughly, one supposes) on May 7 and 8, while also forcing back a sizable RUF troop contingent marching toward Freetown to join Sankoh from up-country (Utas and Jörgel 2008: 502, 503). The ensuing battle at Masiaka, where the SLA, Kamajors, and some of the West Side Boys defeated the RUF, "sent [the RUF] into a military decline from which it would never recover" (TRC 2004a: 460).

Back in Freetown, the Peace Task Force attacked Sankoh's Spur Road Lodge on May 8. It was a grisly affair, with Kamajors and West Side Boys reportedly leading the wanton slaughter of civilians, including children. Sankoh himself snuck out the back door with a few senior RUF officers, allegedly (and surprisingly) assisted by UNAMSIL officers. He surfaced again on May 17, got injured, and finally was arrested. The jig, at last, was up. Sankoh died in custody in July 2003 (TRC 2004a: 441, 430, 446–448), just as his trial for crimes such as mass murder and rape was ramping up. One of Foday Sankoh's final statements to the court was "I'm a god. I am the inner god. I am the leader of Sierra Leone" (Farah 2003).

Meanwhile, the West Side Boys reunited in their Okra Hills hideout and soon found themselves in a fix. Partly because they had scooped up and integrated former prisoners into their ranks (Keen 2005: 233), they were not seen as army regulars. This made it difficult for them to access DDR activities. In August 2000, they made their move, taking eleven British soldiers as hostages. On September 7, 150 British commandos attacked the West Side Boys in a firefight that left at least twenty-five dead (one of whom was British) (Keen 2005: 284, 285). The WSB released the remaining hostages and then dissolved. Several hundred of them gained access to DDR programming as Johnny Paul Koroma "declared that the AFRC was a thing of the past" (Olonisakin 2008: 100).

The war nonetheless pressed on, meandering into 2001, with the RUF weakening further and UNAMSIL strengthening (with the RUF's hostage taking serving as UNAMSIL's wakeup call; Keen 2005: 272). The RUF-Taylor diamond trade fell under heavy stress. Nevertheless, Taylor pressed the RUF to invade Guinea, even as the RUF "had reportedly not wanted to take part." Their incursion left the RUF "badly beaten" by Guinean and CDF forces (269). Taylor's role as "a mentor to Sankoh and a godfather figure to the RUF" (Olonisakin 2008: 71) had passed. His demise in Liberia also was drawing closer: the arrival of U.S. Marines in Monrovia ultimately forced President Taylor's hand, driving him into exile in August 2003 (Simmons 2003).

Back in Sierra Leone, the RUF and their longtime CDF rivals gradually ran out of gas. After more than a decade of war, the country was left phenomenally poor, with much of its infrastructure in ruins and thousands of homes destroyed, an excessively weak government, the mere trace of a national security force, masses of former combatants lacking support and drifting into cities, huge numbers of displaced civilians returning to their homes (or heading into urban areas), and large numbers of rape survivors and amputees. Strangely and without a hint of irony, on January 18, 2002, President Kabbah declared, "The war is over. Go and enjoy yourselves" (*PBS NewsHour* 2002).

This concludes the final chapter of the story of Sierra Leone's wretched war. One aim was to provide an accessible narrative of this complex and chaotic conflict, including a sense of the war zone experience. Another was to set the stage for what comes next in this book: a deeper examination of terror warfare, and how the widespread power and popularity of popular culture over war practitioners and witnesses fueled the horror while expanding the meanings and uses of pop culture icons.

PART 4

Becoming a Warrior

PREPARATIONS FOR TERROR

CHAPTER 15

John Rambo and War

Strong Minds and Hard Hearts

The salient characteristic of military training and tactics during Sierra Leone's civil war was widespread and heavy drug use. As two researchers have observed, "The rebels of the RUF, the soldiers in the army, and the militiamen of the Kamajoi [Kamajors] all used alcohol and drugs in one form or another" (Bøås and Hatløy 2005: 49).

Evidence about intense drug use, arising in interviews with former rebel fighters and commanders and those who witnessed and survived rebel attacks, is particularly overwhelming. New rebel recruits routinely were forced to take drugs, often starting soon after their capture. Commanders also mixed drugs into the food and water of their troops. Smoking marijuana, and consuming meals and drinks infused with marijuana, was both routine and widely practiced. Many other drugs also entered the lives and bodies of child and youth fighters, including cocaine and amphetamines. Some former rebels reported being high on drugs for virtually their entire tenure as members of the RUF or AFRC. Some even reported that their drug use was so heavy that sometimes they would forget who they were and what they had done.

Persistent and heavy drug use makes a young person pliant, facilitates brainwashing, and enables horrific acts of war. It was a ruthless and highly effective strategy, and it was practiced widely. The cynical manipulation of popular culture icons by military leaders in Sierra Leone's war theater supported this effort, none more so than the work of Bob Marley. Given the widespread adulation of Marley, together with his connection to revolutionary principles, using djamba-smoking and listening to reggae music to promote "conscious" thinking, and a lifestyle centered on youth pride and resistance in Sierra Leone, it is difficult to imagine youth-dominated warfare that did *not* feature Marley and his reggae colleagues. Over time, other global pop culture musicians entered the wartime mix, Tupac Shakur most prominently. Following the war, researchers observed that, for male youth in Sierra Leone, "the djamba [marijuana] that they smoke connects them to the world of Bob Mar-

ley and reggae music, and increasingly also to the heroes of American gangster rap such as Tupac Shakur and 50-Cent" (Bøås and Hatløy 2005: 48).

Interviews with former members of military groups in Sierra Leone highlighted two particular outcomes from heavy drug use. One was that it gave a
person a "strong mind," an unshakable conviction in what you did and why
you were doing it. The second was that it made a person "hard-hearted," a
performer of cruel tasks without hesitation or remorse.

The next two parts of this book roughly follow this division. The two chapters featured first (in part 4) jointly address how rebels and Kamajors turned
ordinary boys and male youth into warriors with strong minds. It opens with
an examination of John Rambo as a model fighter, and how the first three
Rambo films directly and explicitly influenced military training practices. The
next chapter examines the initiation practices of the rebels and Kamajors. Although drugs—especially marijuana—routinely played a major role in rebel
initiations, Kamajors reportedly turned to djamba and other drugs only after their initiations had ended. The following set of chapters (part 5) examine the hard-hearted dimensions of warrior practices for rebel units. It opens
(in chapter 17) with an examination of the exploitation of Tupac Shakur's music and reputation to inform terror tactics. Then chapter 18 probes the terror
practices of rebels in depth, with one exception: sexual violence.

Sierra Leone's war was extraordinarily male dominated. Girl and female
youth experiences of initiations and terror tactics were singular and profoundly disturbing. They are featured in the first of two chapters on gender
and war dynamics in part 6 (chapter 19). The last chapter on the war (chapter 20) features final reflections on what male youth on the ground said they
were fighting for, why terror practices were so pervasive, and how emasculation figured in all of this. It concludes with musings about the intentional distortions of Bob Marley's music and teachings by rebel leaders.

Eight Military Attributes

There comes a time in every Rambo movie when John Rambo puts on his
bandanna.[1] The bandanna is nothing more than a very long, rough-cut (or
torn) strip of cloth. Rambo ties it to his forehead and lets the ends fall onto
his shoulder or back. Once it's on, Rambo becomes the epic warrior that children and youth in Sierra Leone and counterparts across the world have venerated. During the 1980s and 1990s, the Rambo Trilogy films (all produced in
the 1980s) comprised what may have been the most influential war films in
the world, particularly in war zones. The most spectacular of the three films,
Rambo III, attained a couple of attention-grabbing firsts. Upon its 1988 release, the movie was thought to be one of the most expensive films in history (Pond 1988). By 1990, it also was considered the most violent movie ever

made, with 123 deaths and 245 acts of violence (1990 Guinness Book of World Records, cited in *Los Angeles Times* 1990).

In Sierra Leone, the large number of rebel commanders who assumed a Rambo nickname underscored the reverence for Rambo as the model of a fearsome warrior. There was both Rambo "the AFRC Brigade commander" (Special Court for Sierra Leone 2012: 252n1598) and "an RUF commander called Rambo" (269; also listed as the nickname for Boston Flomo [869]). There also were many more commanders known as some sort of Rambo, including Nasty Rambo (Richards 1996: 59); Rambo Red Goat and SLA Rambo (nicknames for Idrissa Kamara; Special Court for Sierra Leone 2012: 733); Rambo SLA (who also may have been Idrissa Kamara, 477n3103); Chief Security Officer Rambo (968) and the shortened name of CSO Rambo (nicknames for Moses Kabia, 243); "one RUF commander called CO Rambo" (336); RUF Rambo (alleged to be "a Liberian Mandingo by tribe and the RUF Deputy Operations Commander, Kono," also called "Premo," 244n1544); an AFRC officer known as Colonel Rambo (385); someone called "Rambo of the RUF" (484), who might also be "Rambo from the RUF" (1048); and Junior Rambo (also known as CO Isaac, 1011).[2]

A former RUF commander related that during the war, "people were taking nicknames." The widespread tendency extended into the postwar era (particularly among male youth and men), and to a degree I have not observed elsewhere. Yet while postwar nicknames frequently are playful, wartime nicknames trended toward the aspirational. The Rambo nickname was a prominent example: it proved popular among RUF commanders, the ex-commander explained, because "they wanted to be perfect like Rambo." The Rambo nickname also has been cited "as a *nom de guerre* for combatants on all sides of the war" in Sierra Leone (Hoffman 2005: 343, emphasis in original).[3]

The plethora of Rambos in the ranks invited surreal exchanges about the workings of rebel activities. Take, for example, this exchange between a prosecutor and a witness during the trial of Charles Taylor:

> PROS: Yesterday you testified about a communication between Gullit and RUF Rambo. You testified that RUF Rambo said "the SLA Rambo whom we referred to as 'Red Goat' who was with them." In your testimony so far you've referred to Moses Kabia who was SLA Rambo.
>
> WIT: No, this Red Goat was Idrissa Kamara.
>
> PROS: When you said that Rambo Red Goat was alongside them, with whom?
>
> WIT: He was with Superman. (Witte 2008)

It may be tempting to enjoy a degree of amusement from descriptions depicting, for example, the assertion that "Mosquito told Rambo to arrest Superman" (Sattler 2008). But such actions, and the people who drove them, were in no way childlike or comical. They were deadly serious. The military men chose nicknames not for fun but for the purpose of magnifying impressions of power and influence emanating from their respective holders. Their audience, for the most part, consisted of children and youth, together with terrified adults. Assuming Rambo or other nicknames was shrewd, and it worked.

But Rambo was much more than the gold standard for a truly formidable fighter. Many of the themes in the Rambo Trilogy attest to other important qualities. For one thing, he is stunningly resilient. In each film, he is injured. In two, he repairs himself and endures tremendous pain in the process. In the first movie (*First Blood*), Rambo uses the needle he carries in the handle of his huge knife to stitch up a gash on his arm. In the third (*Rambo III*), he pours gunpowder into a gunshot wound in his abdomen and ignites it (evidently to sterilize the wound and staunch the bleeding). In the second Rambo film (*Rambo: First Blood Part II*), there are three images that evoke crucifixion. Rambo finds an American prisoner of war tied up, arms apart, on bamboo. Once captured, Rambo himself is tied up with his arms over his head and kept in a cesspool of leeches and pig excrement. After one of his captors spits on him, he looks back serenely: this is a man habituated to pain and humiliation. Rambo then demonstrates this quality while tied up, standing with arms splayed apart and shackled to the metal frame of a coil mattress, and electrocuted repeatedly. His surprised Soviet torturer, Lieutenant Colonel Podovsky, is astounded by Rambo's stoic response. Apart from one bellow, Rambo endures excruciating agony in near-complete silence.

While the Christlike imagery accentuates Rambo's mind-boggling capacity to suffer (usually without words) and endure, there are other times when his humanity comes to the surface. The most dramatic example of this arrives at the end of *First Blood*, when he finally is cornered. It is perhaps the only time when Rambo distrusts his ability to escape multitudes of heavily armed attackers (nearly all of whom, just like those confronting James Bond in every one of his films, demonstrate a curious inability to aim their guns with even moderate accuracy). Rambo is completely surrounded. Colonel Trautman (Rambo's father figure and former commander) tells it like it is. Rambo's personal war invited this response. It cannot continue. Either Rambo surrenders or he dies. There are no other alternatives.

Rambo's response is fierce. After being virtually silent for most of the film, he explodes verbally. He cannot stop what he does, he says. He had tried the win the war in Vietnam, he shouts, but his superiors held him back. Then, after his heroic struggles on the war's front lines, he was forced to face the intense hatred of antiwar protestors, beginning as soon as he landed in the

United States. Then he breaks down and cries. John Rambo, the decorated Green Beret and seemingly invincible fighter, is traumatized. Early in the film, memory of Rambo tied up (as if on a crucifix) and brutally tortured initiates a desperate, violent response. Near the film's end, Rambo tells a story from Vietnam. While on leave from the front, one of his friends and fighting colleagues is blown up by a booby-trapped shoeshine box, loses his legs, and dies. Rambo remains haunted by his inability to save his friend's life.

It is a compelling moment because it captures Rambo's underlying vulnerability. Larger than life in so many ways, ultimately Rambo is someone with whom you can identify: he is astounding yet recognizable. In this sense, Rambo's elemental magnetism is remarkably similar to that of Tupac Shakur. Both communicate their susceptibility to recognizable human weaknesses (trauma and occasional anxiety for Rambo; fear and a range of other emotions for Tupac) with a mix of dynamism, courage, and focused expression (Rambo largely through action; Tupac through poetic, visceral lyrics). Although both are, in their way, awe inspiring, they also convey human frailty.

John Rambo and Tupac Shakur also are deeply alienated from mainstream American society and government institutions. They particularly distrust and are suspicious of the authorities who have attacked and punished them. For Tupac, it mainly involved run-ins with the law (including imprisonment), accusations of misconduct and much worse from law enforcement personnel, and a family heritage of resistance as radical Black Panther Party members. For Rambo, police and military forces unfairly arrest and repeatedly try to kill him in the first movie. In the second, government bureaucrats abandon him and the long-forgotten American prisoners of war he discovers (and ultimately rescues).

An important dimension of the Rambo character is his near-constant refusal to defend himself verbally. In *First Blood*, Sheriff Will Teasle picks him up and treats him as a vagrant and unwanted drifter. After Teasle informs him that he can go to a restaurant in another town, Rambo asks why he can't dine in Teasle's town. The reason is simple: Teasle won't allow it. It's not about legality: it's personal. Rambo responds by asking why Teasle is picking on him. After all, Rambo hasn't done anything to anyone there. Teasle tells Rambo to leave and never come back. When Rambo openly refuses, Teasle arrests him.

Then Rambo clams up. He won't give his name to police officers and won't let them fingerprint him. Rambo subsequently has opportunities to explain himself but, with two exceptions, refuses. After one police officer dies while trying to kill him, Rambo tells the others that he didn't cause it. He asks to end the conflict, repeatedly claiming his innocence. How do Teasle and his policemen respond? By spraying machine gun fire at Rambo. Later, while on the run, Rambo states his case by radio to Colonel Trautman, who has been brought in to negotiate with his former military specialist. Rambo insists that he was merely fighting back. Teasle and his men started it, not him.

Rambo films have little dialogue. While the main character clearly is a man of action and few words, the words he chooses to express are, in general, unusually meaningful. This dimension of the Rambo Trilogy films almost certainly facilitated the hero's appeal to youngsters in Sierra Leone and many other corners of the globe. An illuminating passage takes place in the second film. On a pirate riverboat, Rambo has a short chat with Co Bao, who briefly is his associate and love interest (she is shot and killed right after they kiss for the first and only time). When Co Bao askes Rambo why he's come back to Vietnam, Rambo explains that he's considered "expendable."

This passage reveals three important themes. First, the dialogue between Rambo and Co Bao is simple and easy to comprehend. The one challenging word in the dialogue—expendable—then is defined (it also later allows Co Bao to tell Rambo that, in her view, he's not expendable). The mainly basic English employed in the Rambo Trilogy movies undoubtedly made it easier for Sierra Leonean children and youth to grasp the dialogue regardless of their education level. Another reason supported their ability to grasp Rambo's words: the fact that the country's "universal lingua franca" is "an English-based creole known as Krio." As a result, virtually all Sierra Leoneans ("as much as 95 per cent of the population of Sierra Leone") are able to comprehend at least some English (Oyètádé and Luke 2008: 122). This allowed even very young Sierra Leonean children to appreciate some or all of Rambo's words, in addition to lyrics in songs by Bob Marley and many more English speakers in Sierra Leone's popular culture universe.

The second key theme is Rambo's acceptance that the U.S. government and much of the military establishment consider him unimportant, if not superfluous. The theme returns in *Rambo III* (1988) near the movie's beginning, when Rambo tells Robert Griggs, a U.S. embassy official, that he wants help entering Afghanistan (where Colonel Trautman has been taken hostage). Griggs insists that if Rambo is reported as captured, the U.S. government will refute all allegations of its involvement or even Rambo's existence. What is Rambo's response? He's accustomed to this sort of treatment. Rambo's perspective—that he is used to being overlooked by the powers that be—supports a sentiment resonating from the works of Bob Marley and Tupac Shakur as well. The world is perverse: Rambo acts according to honorable, moral principles. The government institutions and officials that ignore or condemn him are the ones who are immoral and in the wrong. It is a scenario that resonates with the context in Sierra Leone, where youth voices rarely are heard in a world dominated by powerful authorities, many of whom are corrupt.

A third theme arises from the fact that Rambo, at his core, is a principled ascetic. His practices do not have an explicit religious basis (even when he is found working for a Buddhist monastery at the outset of *Rambo III*). Yet his life is austere and upright. He maintains a simple life, and he operates in times of war and peace according to elemental values. In *First Blood*, Rambo only fights after he is forced to do so. In *First Blood Part II*, he accepts a mission (proposed by Colonel Trautman) to save the lives of American prisoners of war. In *Rambo III*, Rambo enters the war zone in Afghanistan to save Trautman's life. In his brief relationship with Co Bao, Rambo (save for a momentary slip) demonstrates his asceticism. One can sense a connection between the two. Yet throughout their engagement, Rambo is chivalrous: considerate, respectful, and courteous to Co Bao, and most definitely a team player during violent encounters with various enemies. Except for one fleeting kiss, he also is sexually distant. Rambo, in the end, operates as a kind of spirit-warrior: a fighter guided by enlightened, ethical codes and driven to right wrongs.

The Rambo Trilogy expresses eight military attributes that were highly relevant to Sierra Leone's civil war context:

1. **Forest expertise.** The first two movies demonstrate Rambo's knowledge and skill at fighting and succeeding in dense, jungle-like forests, often using the element of surprise. He is at home in the forest while his opponents clearly are not.

2. **Guerrilla techniques.** In every movie, Rambo fights against conventional government forces (first American, then Vietnamese [with some Soviet officers], then exclusively Soviet). While the multitude of regular soldiers he repeatedly faces are directed by superiors, Rambo mainly engages them as a self-sufficient war unit.

3. **Reliance on low technology weapons.** Rambo's primary weapon is an enormous hunting knife. He uses it to cut barbed wire, kill animals (primarily for food) and sometimes his opponents, and fashion booby traps from available materials. In the second and third movies, he also relies on a bow. Most of the arrows he shoots, it must be said, are impressive: they explode on contact, like small, silent missiles. Although he uses machine guns and mortars (and flies helicopters with exceptional skill), his philosophy is not modern. It is illustrated in an illuminating exchange with Marshall Murdock, the devious government bureaucrat who betrays him in *Rambo: First Blood Part II*. After Murdock boasts about the sophisticated weaponry he has at his disposal, Rambo bluntly replies that a person's mind is even more effective. They agree to disagree about whether technology or personal guile work better.

4. **Acting alone or leading small groups.** Rambo works as a military force of one or the leader of one or two associates (excepting the grand climax of *Rambo III*).

5. **Relentless drive and focus.** Rambo never seems to tire, hesitate, or lose his singular will to succeed militarily. His capacity to rise above pain and hardship is absolutely remarkable. John Rambo is unsinkable, selfless, and stupendously brave.

6. **The appropriateness of violence.** The Rambo Trilogy films present the case that the protagonist responds to injustice with violence only when he has no other choice. In *First Blood*, the authorities violently attack him, largely without justification. In *First Blood Part II*, Murdock abandons him and a prisoner of war during a gunfight with Vietnamese soldiers. In *Rambo III*, Rambo engages Soviet commandos for a singular purpose: to rescue Colonel Trautman.

7. **The utility of child soldiers.** In *Rambo III*, Hamid, an orphaned Afghan boy and veteran fighter, wants to join Rambo on a wildly dangerous mission to rescue Colonel Trautman, who is held in a heavily defended Soviet fortress inside Afghanistan. Although Rambo tries to discourage the child, once Hamid appears on the battle scene, he stays. The boy is loyal, brave, and skilled, joining Rambo in an exceptionally (if not impossibly) dangerous skirmish deep inside the Soviet fortress. Eventually it becomes apparent that Rambo is Hamid's role model and father figure. This impression is confirmed in the film's final scene, when Rambo gives Hamid his good luck charm and says he must leave. Hamid is heartbroken, while Rambo, yet again, seems haunted by his own sad and sensationally violent past. *Rambo III*—the dramatization of a child without parents in a war zone attaching himself to Rambo, whom he reveres and for whom he fights valiantly— provides a visceral and immediate military training example for child soldiering.

8. **Absolute trust in and loyalty to one's military commander.** A critical component of Rambo's character is his relationship with Colonel Trautman. In *First Blood*, Trautman had trained and commanded Rambo in Vietnam. It allows him to assert that he created Rambo as a warrior, not God. Later in the film, Colonel Trautman explains that he is, essentially, Rambo's family.

The close bond is mutually felt. At the start of *Rambo: First Blood Part II*, the ever-suspicious Rambo tells Colonel Trautman that he trusts him and no one else. The entire third film is fueled by Rambo's deep loyalty to Colonel Trautman. Mousa, the loyal and brave Afghan fighter who becomes Rambo's closest companion in the film, asks

Rambo why he aims to enter a heavily armed fortress to rescue the imprisoned Trautman. He is incredulous because the degree of risk is so high. But Rambo provides an unadorned, no-nonsense reply: he seeks to rescue Colonel Trautman because he would do the same for Rambo. The connection between soldier and commander could not be stronger. If employing "Rambo System" means embodying all of these attributes as military virtues, it is the tight relationship between soldier and commander that is perhaps the most useful to military officers seeking to train abducted young people: the commander as the only family the child and youth soldiers have, the father figure. Rambo films directly support this.

The Application

The RUF's reliance on Rambo films started even before the war began. In Liberia, after Taylor's NPFL soldiers corralled Sierra Leoneans in the country and brought them to Sankoh (more on that in the next chapter), Sankoh chose and trained his corps of revolutionaries (called vanguards) for the brand-new RUF. During this process of, essentially, creating the RUF, "Rambo videos were an essential part of the schooling for Sankoh's top men" (Voeten 2002: 208). Then, from the start of the war in 1991, "the RUF used the Rambo film *First Blood* (1982) as a training video of sorts." Two years later, the NPRC's Sierra Leone Army "screened Rambo movies to prepare its combatants for offensives" against the RUF. The films featuring Rambo "offered practical instruction in guerrilla warfare and inspiration to young combatants." In the early years of the war, "Rambo was an official icon of the RUF" (Prestholdt 2019: 119–120). Commentary from former commanders and combatants suggests that Rambo's influence extended across the entire war period, particularly with the RUF and (once they entered the scene in 1997) the AFRC. One of the reported ways in which rebel units used the Rambo films during the war was as a tool for in-service training. A former RUF combatant explained: "Rambo Part I and II, Commando and Missing in Action: these are all war films. Watching these films, the rebels learned many things, like war tactics, how to operate guns, how to identify parts of a gun. During the war, they watched these films." Other references to watching Rambo and other war films pointed toward a shared end. The films were not just popular; they demonstrated vital and relevant military skills and tactics, serving as useful reminders for appropriate warfare.

The Rambo films were, by far, the most influential and significant to the rebels (and, indeed, to Sierra Leonean youth). Interview data with former rebel commanders, combatants, and captives, in addition to civilians witnessing rebel activities firsthand, revealed two main ways that the RUF (and

AFRC) manipulated Rambo's aura, messages, techniques, and films for their purposes. The first was "Rambo Tactics," which featured direct reference to specific military training and combat techniques. The second was "Rambo groups," which were field units led by commanders called Rambo that enacted local interpretations of essential Rambo traits.

A former top RUF commander explained, "In the early stages of the war, there was intensive training to be like Rambo." That concept underscores the fundamental purpose of Rambo for all military groups across the entire war: to employ Rambo as a model for soldiering and to diagnose, practice, and enact his tactics in order to become Rambo-like in battle. The ex-RUF commander further explained that during RUF trainings, "Rambo and Commando films were watched. It wasn't a curriculum or a principle. They taught Rambo Tactics and martial arts." He added that *Commando* (starring Arnold Schwarzenegger) held a specialized purpose: it "was more for city attacks. Commando [tactics] were like being a one-man army. You applied this to target the city." The Rambo films, in contrast, were "more for guerrilla life, especially *Rambo III*. [In that film,] Rambo was aided by someone who knows the area like civilians, or captured army personnel." The ex-RUF commander also explained that when they had a generator, "we formally used" the Rambo and Commando movies (as well as war films starring Chuck Norris) for training sessions. However, "during the 1993–1995 period" when the RUF changed strategies and became a forest-based organization, "we didn't have the generator; we only explained these things [from the movies] to others."

Later in the war, an ex-combatant explained, solar power became more available (as it became a featured good to loot). "Generators have too much noise" but solar units were quiet, so they were used "in camp, in the bush. They used solar [power] to watch all films." He also explained the logic of how watching these films helped you hone your skills as a soldier: "You see, the football player watches football films to learn how to dribble; how to play football. So in the war, you use war films to learn how to attack and withdraw. When you attack, you remember how to attack from the Rambo films and the army-type of war films. You know how to withdraw from your enemy, as well. Because after you attack, you need to withdraw. It's in the Rambo films." The attack-and-withdraw approach described here is indicative of a military outfit that, quite often, neither held onto territory nor engaged with opposition fighting forces. Frequently, the RUF would come to a village or town to loot, commit atrocities, burn houses, abduct some civilians, and then take the loot and new abductees back to their base. In trainings, a second former top RUF commander explained, "They'd show you how to maneuver, how to attack. They trained us to attack like a commando, like Rambo First Blood, Sylvester Stallone." The fact that most training locations, over the course of the war, lacked the ability to show films was not important because "we all saw the *Rambo: First Blood* movie before the war." Of all the films the RUF drew from to train combatants, the first Rambo film appeared to be the most important, since virtually every soldier had watched it prior to the war. For this reason, "we used it to teach Rambo Tactics."

What kinds of "Rambo Tactics" were taught in an RUF military training course? There were two dimensions. One had to do with specific actions that Rambo taught them. These examples illustrate the diversity of ways the RUF used Rambo films for instruction. One researcher with deep knowledge of the RUF explained that trainers would show a part of a Rambo film "showing Rambo crossing on a rope bridge. Then in the afternoon, they would go and use the rope bridge [at the training site] like Rambo." Another Rambo Tactic was employing maneuvers that frightened the opposition: "Rambo was quite an experienced war tactician. He used terror tactics. For example, there's a fifty-gallon power drum. You put a power saw in it—it makes so much noise that you have no choice but to run away." A former RUF fighter described his training in Rambo Tactics as follows: "They were teaching us how to change position, moving from one place to another in an attack. For example, if you want to move from one end of the street to the other, from one house to another, you would need to stand still and watch for enemies, and then try to escape." All of these tactics stressed what a fighter could do on his own. Proactive, strategic action was a glowing Rambo trait. Through his films and example, RUF fighters learned that they could succeed by combining self-confidence and ingenuity.

The second set of Rambo Tactics concerned developing a kind of "Rambo state of mind." The application of this theme in the lives of RUF fighters appears to have been pervasive. A captive porter for the RUF related, for example, that when his captors could relax a bit, "when there was no threat of an enemy attack, they watched Rambo films. They confessed that the Rambo films inspired them to fight with endurance," just like Rambo. Then he explained exactly what this meant: "Rambo's tactics of jungle fighting helped the rebels go to places where they never would have gone but were able to find their way out and succeed in whatever they wanted to do." A veteran researcher explained that RUF trainers would use Rambo "to harden the initiates." They would tell them, "If Rambo has done it, you can do it." But what they taught was more than just endurance. The trainers would urge their trainees to become Rambo-like: "To be Rambo, you are like a mortar: you can go through anything. If you use Rambo Tactics, you are sure to succeed. You can use common sense to terrorize your opponents. You don't need too many bullets." The researcher also found that the process of forcing young trainees to emulate Rambo, in every way, in the field, started early. The initial phase of an RUF training, he explained, was brainwashing via peer competition: "Peer dynamics can really influence you. If James is ten years old and he can do it, then you can do it. If he has access to so many women, then I have access to women." Following the forceful orientation on domination—in war zones and over females—the trainers employed Rambo films in specialized ways: "After the brainwashing, [the trainers] would show Rambo films that showed rebels attacking. They would freeze on specific areas of the films and say, 'If only you have the will, you can do what Rambo does.'"

"Doing what Rambo does" was a widely shared goal for rebel combatants and perhaps the central component of "Rambo System." But a "system" seemed to always include some degree of attire connecting a boy or male youth to their idol (in my research, mention of this kind of Sierra Leonean "system" correlated exclusively with young males). During the war, enacting Marley System usually included a Bob Marley T-shirt, perhaps also with dreadlocks and maybe even faded jeans (alongside devotion to reggae music and marijuana). Some mix of a Tupac T-shirt, tattoos, a shaved head, a vest, turn-up trousers, and a bandanna all were part of Tupac System (together with strong drugs and a fondness for rap music). Rambo System seemed to feature wearing a bandanna (often either red or featuring the American flag) accompanied by a particular state of mind and set of military techniques.

Embodying Rambo System and "doing what Rambo does" nonetheless was a far cry from assuming Rambo's much-venerated name. That was a big deal: being called Rambo in rebel circles (or, indeed, on the SLA side) had to be earned and proven in combat. A person had to embody the locally defined idea of Rambo himself. Here is an example of how a boy of twelve gained the name of Young Rambo:

> I attacked the villages, killed people. I was the best, and especially with these drugs they used to give us or to directly inject in the brain.... After a lot of involvement in different attacks and missions in which I played a leading role, I was made a commando at [t]he age of 12 years. I had six girls that were my wives.... As a commando, I had well over 10 adults, 10 boys who were my age group, "elders" or adults; I was free to command, as I wanted.... I was feared by most of my colleague commandos because of my bravery and attacking skills. That was why my colleagues called me young Rambo. (TRC 2004A: 561)

The gathered document and interview data suggested that only a particular kind of leader could be called Rambo. Those known as Rambo were exceptionally fierce and violent field commanders who led by example, generated waves of civilian fear in their wake, and took a lot of drugs. The local interpretation of "being Rambo" thus only slightly dovetailed with the Rambo character in the three films. To begin with, John Rambo was White; only one rebel known as Rambo approximated that. One RUF commander recalled the Rambo he knew during the war: "Rambo was a small boy, a strong fighter.

He was the real Rambo. He was with us at this time [that is, at the beginning of the war]. He was about twenty-six years old, with a fair complex-
ion."[4] Quite unlike this particular Rambo, or Young Rambo or others with the
Rambo nickname during the war, the Rambo movie character either fought
on his own or, for most of *Rambo III*, with one or two colleagues (including a
child soldier). His lifestyle was spartan, austere, and removed. He did not take
drugs. Beyond one momentary dalliance, he displayed no interest in women
or sexual relations. All of this was quite unlike the Rambo commanders of Sierra Leone. They all seemed to take large quantities of drugs (as did those under their command).[5] They did not work alone. Their groups included abducted women. Like Rambo, they were all known to be absolutely fearless
(undoubtedly aided by drugs). Most if not all reportedly wore bandannas
(sometimes entire Rambo Groups sported red ones). Some wore matching
cloth tied around their wrists or biceps. Even here, there was variance: one civilian recalled that some members of the Rambo Group operating in his area
"did not wear clothes."

Unrelenting ferocity seems to have been the central shared characteristic
of rebel leaders called Rambo. People had to be afraid of you. You had to stand
out by demonstrating a high degree of brutality and ruthlessness. As detailed
during field interviews, Rambo Groups were ornery and threatening, and
known to quarrel. An ex-combatant, for example, noted that "wherever they
went, they always created terror, even with other rebel groups." Civilians also
took notice. Everyone seemed to be very afraid of Rambo Groups, and with
good reason. A town councilor from Makeni explained her experience with
two separate Rambo Groups. What did they have in common? "One thing we
knew about these groups is the fact that they were very tough. Tough in the
sense that they were well-armed and better than any other group." A former
rebel wife shared a similar recollection: "This was a strong group among the
RUF. It was well disciplined and did not include little boys in their group."[6]
A former RUF soldier recalled meeting one particular Rambo Group twice
during his military days. "This group was the most dangerous," he stated.
"They were fully armed and the most combat-ready of all time." After regis-
tering his appreciation of their might, a male elder ultimately did not remember one Rambo Group quite so fondly: "The Rambo Group thought that what
Rambo did as an actor was a reality. So they were not afraid to use their guns
against civilians and kill them indiscriminately. We are not sure whether God
will ever forgive these rebels."

In Makeni near the end of the war, the commander of one especially in-
temperate Rambo Group met his demise. A chief in Makeni explained that
this particular outfit was one of "the most difficult [rebel] groups to control."
He added, "Some people said that [the Rambo Group] was as brave as Rambo
the actor." At the same time, its members "did not respect or recognize the au-

thority of [RUF General] Issa [Sesay], only Foday Sankoh." Reportedly, they also did not recognize the many ceasefires that surfaced in the latter stages of the war.[7] Ultimately, while battling other rebels, this particular Rambo met his demise and was killed by either Superman or General Issa Sesay (the recollections conflict). News of Rambo's death shook many RUF members. "Other rebel commanders felt it when he was killed," one RUF fighter recalled. A former RUF wife remembered that "when Rambo was killed, many people felt it so much."[8] That included members of his group, as this description (which names Superman as Rambo's killer) suggests: "Superman and Rambo had a confrontation on the highway, and Rambo was murdered. This incensed his cadres, who went on a rampage" (Bolten 2012: 132).

During an interview in Freetown following the war's end, a former RUF combatant insisted on listing the many reasons why he admired Rambo: "He's a nice man. He acts well. He acts with so many Blacks. He's nice to Blacks. He's a good-looking man. He's famous. He's very interesting. He's a fighter." It underscored the enduring fascination that Rambo and the example he provided ultimately had inspired.

CHAPTER 16

Indoctrinations

Frames of Reference

This chapter reviews how Sierra Leoneans were inducted into a form of warfare driven by terror. The focus is on the two largest military groups: the RUF and the Kamajors, with some reference to the AFRC. For the RUF and Kamajors, the training systems they established diminished significantly over time. For the AFRC, their training of new recruits appears to have been slight throughout their wartime years. The analysis is unavoidably gendered: what boys and girls endured largely tell different stories. This chapter concentrates on initiations for males. Female initiations into the RUF are detailed in chapter 19.

Charles Taylor and Foday Sankoh laid the foundation for terror warfare in Sierra Leone before the war began. They started by rounding up adult Sierra Leoneans (nearly all of them men) residing inside Liberia. The training these Sierra Leoneans received was seasoned with Rambo film clips. But in its essence, it was uncommonly brutal. The captured and coarsened adults ultimately formed the RUF's vanguard, which in March 1991 entered Sierra Leone and commenced their peculiar yet devastating rebellion.

This section will draw on the rich literature on military training during Sierra Leone's civil war. The depth of information about structured training, particularly by the RUF, is remarkable. There is much less about the training practices of other military units, and still less about the informal initiation practices that increasingly pervaded the war theater. For the rebels in particular, the Rambo films served to instruct and inspire trainees in particular practices and attitudes. But something else surfaced as the war bore forward: the rise of Bob Marley's music and the intensive, forced use of marijuana as important rebel training practices.

The story of terror and terror warfare as an ingrained military approach in Sierra Leone starts in Liberia. Once again, the hand of Taylor played a sculpting role. He shared an agreement with Sankoh, made in Libya after they met in 1988, "to mutually support each other in their respective plans" to take over Liberia (by Taylor) and Sierra Leone (by Sankoh). The two also shared an abiding hatred of Joseph Momoh and his APC government in Freetown. For Taylor, that was due largely to his experience after he had ventured to Freetown in 1989 to ask Momoh for his blessing to allow Taylor's NPFL to launch attacks into Liberia from eastern Sierra Leone.[1]

Momoh not only denied this request but imprisoned Taylor and his aides. Then he allowed ECOMOG to use Lungi International Airport to bomb Taylor's forces (TRC 2004a: 96, 97). By mid-1990, with his war well underway and Sankoh in tow, Taylor ordered the arrest of civilians from ECOMOG member states (including Sierra Leoneans) in response to their air raids against his troops. On November 1, Taylor issued a vow of revenge against Sierra Leone's government via his favored mouthpiece: BBC radio (99, 98). The doomed Momoh had played his cards badly once more. His acts helped birth the RUF and spur the hard-hearted violence that followed.

Sankoh made his move in 1990. With Taylor's blessing and support, Foday Sankoh visited some of the detained Sierra Leoneans, with the aim of choosing vanguards to help lead his upstart rebellion. Exactly what he chose to do and emphasize, as a burgeoning revolutionary, is deeply revealing of his nature and vision. From the jump, Foday Sankoh made brutality and manipulation his calling cards. First, he laid bare what would happen if those he chose did not bend to his will: "Several groups of soon-to-be 'vanguards' were exposed first to a show of mercilessness, whereby innocent fellow detainees among their number were severely beaten, molested or executed in front of them. Conspicuously, though, the Sierra Leoneans were always spared such a fate when Sankoh was present" (TRC 2004a: 102). Next, he coerced obedience: "Sankoh's favoured means of recruitment depended on convincing people that their lives lay squarely in his hands and that if they refused to join him, they would be responsible for their own fate—effectively, he blackmailed them into becoming members of the RUF" (103).

Finally, he led the training of his kidnapped revolutionaries, which included the RUF's first cull of child soldiers (107).[2] Many of his trainers were NPFL commanders. Some of the techniques were drawn from training experiences in Libya (107, 108). The training itself was intentionally ferocious. It set a precedent that reverberated across the conflict just over the horizon: "The training left the vanguards unprepared to wage revolutionary warfare . . . [while] the exposure of the vanguards to extreme violence during training seemed to have had an enduring effect on each of them personally, creating a propensity to subject others to acts of personal violation and compulsion. This assertion is borne out by the fact that some of the vanguards went on to exercise their own reigns of terror over conscripts in the Sierra Leone conflict" (109). Foday Sankoh's first training of handpicked forces thus featured a characteristic that informed much of what took place during the war: violence undertaken with unusual viciousness.

The RUF were the catalysts and most persistent practitioners of terror warfare in Sierra Leone. In the early war years, the RUF's severe military training played an important role in shaping the terror warfare that ultimately spread across the country. Since their training process proved so influential, key aspects will be detailed in this section. But first, three comments on context are necessary. To begin with, terror war practitioners did not necessarily need to be trained. Some received low levels of military training, others none at all. However, the terror techniques that the RUF set in motion via abductions, initiations, and predatory violence spread like a virus to other military groups.

Second, the terror war approach featured, emphatically and throughout, males. The gendered quality of terror warfare in Sierra Leone relied on a binding patrimonial framework for all fighting groups (in addition to civilian society). Your commander was your patriarch, the caretaker and ruthless controller of his supporters. In addition, the war featured fierce domination of males over females—within wartime groups and during attacks. Rape and other forms of sexual domination were completely commonplace.

Finally, a trio of historical antecedents to terror war initiation and performance have been proposed. As many of the details have been covered earlier in this book, they will be reviewed only briefly here:

- **Legacy of slavery.** Shaw argues that slavery in Sierra Leone directly impacted the nature of warfare centuries later. In a vivid reflection of prior eras, during Sierra Leone's civil war "most captured boys have been made into fighters and diamond diggers, [while] those captured girls have become the modern equivalent of slave wives" (Shaw 2002: 200). The entire landscape of the war "recapitulated in modern form some of the worst excesses of precolonial and colonial slavery, which transformed Sierra Leonean men, women, children, and youth into forced laborers, sexual slaves, and slave soldiers" (Rosen 2005: 59). Cannibalism and views of women as "submerged, unfathomable, and hidden in Darkness" are two historic concerns that surface powerfully during Sierra Leone's war (Shaw 2002: 169). Rosen adds that the RUF's kidnapping of young people, tattooing them "with the mark of the RUF," the performance of "gruesome rites" featuring children publicly murdering members of their family or community of origin, collectively demonstrate "the trademark violence of a slave regime" (2005: 59).

- **Poro power.** In Sierra Leone, traditional initiations into adulthood constitute a kind of structured training that is demanding, terrifying, and transformative by definition: the initiates enter as children and exit as adults. *Poro* is the most common name for the powerful and secret manhood initiation rite that takes place (in different forms) across Sierra Leone.[3] Poro initiates are credited with armed resistance against British colonists. Rosen notes that "the sacred power exercised by the Poro often involved terror and violence." During the war, the RUF drew from Poro rituals, insisting that initiates become "sworn to secrecy" and receive loyalty oaths (Rosen 2005: 68, 72). RUF practices such as the intentional application of fear, pain and deprivation, "strict obedience to authority," and still more are mirrored in Poro traditions (Denov 2010: 115–116). A Mende elder and leading politician characterized the Poro institution as

> the most formidable force in society. The Poro can sanction your killing. I'm banned from talking about it. I can't talk—I will be killed [if I do]. If a high-ranking initiate in Poro tells you to do something, you obey.

Cannibalism reportedly is connected to secret society initiations. Some have related that in Bondo or Sande ceremonies (the female counterpart of Poro), initiates share a soup made from the genital cuttings of their group. The Civil Defense Forces, including the Kamajors, drew directly from Poro traditions, as well (Rosen 2005: 72).

• **Dangerous male youth.** Rosen joins many others in his depiction of twentieth-century male youth in Freetown as "alienated and hostile toward traditional and governmental authority" and "apolitical, antisocial, and violent." Organized urban violence eventually featured Rarray Boys, the name for wayward and dangerous youth that has never left Sierra Leone (Rosen 2005: 65, 69). As president, Siaka Stevens created a violent youth wing for his APC political party and sent them to terrorize real and imagined opponents. Some of their actions mirror atrocities undertaken during the war: burning houses, shooting children, parading and beating people in public, hacking people to death with cutlasses. Stevens's APC Youth became his very own paramilitary, and their violence became "the training ground for warfare." The fabulous enrichment of the few, while leaving a wasteland of unemployment and limited options in their wake, ultimately created a nation "filled with unwanted youth" (78, 79, 80). Those youth also are contained by a traditional system featuring *fityai*, which refers to behavior thought to be disrespectful (and disgraceful). Judging behavior as fityai allows leaders to silence dissent and perhaps even detain, ruin, or drive out the dissenters. Powerlessness was the prewar norm,[4] and the RUF in particular sought to upend traditional constraints on young people with humiliating, vengeful violence against elders and other representatives of the male hegemony. Shocking public demonstrations by youth against respected men suddenly positioned underneath them underscores the significance of the perverse universe idea in RUF thinking, and its utility as an instrument of terror warfare.

Military training seeks to transform civilians into soldiers. There is nothing unusual about demanding training regimes. The U.S. Marines, for example, proudly boast about the grueling nature of their twelve-week program: "Recruit training must remain demanding, formal, and challenging in order to achieve the desired end state: making a basic Marine. These basic Marines must be instilled with the discipline to obey orders, respect authority, and uphold our warrior ethos" (Marines, n.d.). The full-length RUF training regimen lasted about as long as preparations to become a marine. Yet the RUF version featured much younger people and was purposefully and intensely cruel. The trainers, in fact, seemed to employ just about everything they could imagine to induce hardship, suffering, and obedience.

Four aspects of their formal training process highlight the seminal role of RUF initiations in promoting and spreading terror-based warfare across Sierra Leone:

1. A Focus on Young People

The RUF came to feature children in their forces only after failing to retain adult recruits. Abducting children became essential because the conditions for RUF forces were awful, they were unpaid, the death toll was high, and the war itself featured "senselessness and brutality" (Denov 2010: 63). It clearly did not take them long to subscribe to the view that children make great soldiers.

There are many reasons for this, with the main ones outlined by Wessells. In most of the world, young people seem to be everywhere; children "typically compose half or more of the population," making them "as cheap as they are convenient." Children also are "controllable through terror and brutality," they "accept the most dangerous assignments," they often are "more receptive to new ideologies and systems of thought than adults," and they constitute, in the eyes of commanders, "unformed raw material to be molded as they wish." In sum, child soldiers are "pliable, exploitable, effective, and expendable" (Wessells 2006: 34–37). They also make just about the best spies imaginable. In Sierra Leone, children are seen as "liminal and unformed" and thus "more capable than adults of inhuman behavior" (Shepler 2010c: 313). The RUF seemed to know all of this quite well. Their SBUs, in particular, became vital instruments of the movement's terror.

Even by the drastic standards of military operations featuring child soldiers, RUF child soldiers were unusually young. One former SBU combatant for the RUF claimed that the youngest boys recruited were three years old, and that members of his unit were between ages five and ten. In one study of child soldiers in Guinea, Liberia, and Sierra Leone, the youngest age of children at the time of recruitment was five years old—in Sierra Leone. The other two were much older (nine years old for Liberia, fifteen for Guinea). The average age of child soldiers also was younger: 12.3 years for Sierra Leone, 14.6 for Liberia, and 16.3 for Guinea (Wille 2005: 186). A second study estimated that half of all RUF forces were child soldiers (22,500), and a third of that number were girl soldiers (McKay and Mazurana 2004: 92).

2. Traumatic Entry

At the very least, an armed force needs troops who obey and don't desert. The RUF employed drastic measures to achieve these essentials. Stories of capture in the interview data are uniformly chilling. A top RUF commander explained the situation simply. "Most of the people in the RUF were abducted to join forcibly. No objections were allowed." A former combatant detailed that he was hiding with his family in the bush, outside of their home village. Eventually, the rebels informed them that if they did not return to the village, they all would be deemed enemies and executed. Back in the village, he explained that "the rebels started maltreating us, especially we the boys. We learned later that it was a strategy to encourage us to join them. The punishment was so severe that many of us decided to join." Beah recalls witnessing rebels selecting boys from a group. Then one of the rebels announced, "We are going to initiate all of you by killing these [captured civilian] people in front of you. We have to do this to show you blood and make you strong. You'll never see any of these people again, unless you believe in life after death" (Beah 2007: 34).

The purpose of other abductions was to force new captures to commit atrocities so appalling that they might never return home, and thus they would not try to escape. A prominent example, a leader of the Truth and Reconciliation Committee explained, was boys who "were forced to rape their mothers," the so-called motherfucker act.[5] Denov explained the rationale for and impact of forced incest and other intimate atrocities: "Extreme violence against one's family or community was highly effective in alienating children from their communities and, in the process, ensuring undivided allegiance to the RUF" (2010: 104).

Another example of the forced shift from abductee to rebel comes from the capture of a boy named John, as shared by Chris Coulter. Rebels raped his mother and his aunt in front of him, and later gang raped them, killing his aunt's son, as well. Witnessing all of this created immense shame within John, particularly since he was powerless to protect his mother; trying to do so would have meant his death. In the end, he found his mother's body, with her feet cut off and her vagina mutilated by his captors. The intense trauma created a need for revenge—not against the rebels but against civilians. John suddenly sought to join the rebels, he explained, "because I had planned to do [to others] what was done to my mother." Coulter comments that John's response illuminates how "shame played an important part in people's responses to the sexual violation of female relatives during the war" (Coulter 2009: 144, 145).[6]

A second former combatant explained his own shame-driven response to the trauma induced by rebel attack. He was a former government soldier, not a child, and he had a daughter. Rebels attacked his village at night. Abruptly awakened by gunfire, he instinctively "ran into the nearby bush, leaving my five-year-old child behind." The RUF burned down all the houses in his village, including his house, with the man's daughter trapped inside. "I felt so bad because I heard her screaming, 'Papa, come and take me.'" The trauma and guilt of this event "caused me not to run away nor fear the rebels. I was ready to die, as my daughter had died."

The attackers' response reflects the unforgiving environment that all rebel soldiers endured. "The rebels said that I was lucky because it was only a child who was killed. They told me instances where some of them were asked to kill their parents" when they first were captured. The rebel fighters standing before him, who had just incinerated the man's young daughter, thus were able to sympathize with him. "Though I resisted, they persuaded me to be recruited." Since he was an army veteran, "I was enlisted with the rank of a captain. So I had my group of twenty gallant fighters and five in the Small Boys Unit." In his new role, "I punished civilians who didn't want to obey the authority of the RUF." Both this story and John's above appear to demonstrate traumatic transmission. In this process, after trauma is initiated, the initiators "push the initiated to transmit [trauma] by duplication, as a psychological way to cope with the traumatic image" (TRC 2004a: 557). Under pressure and duress, victims of cruelty respond by instigating cruelty against others.

3. Strategic Cruelty and Absolute Obedience

There is a school of thought about the RUF that they were principled revolutionaries who emphasized discipline and integrity during and after their trainings. Even if some of their means were brutal, their ends were at least somewhat honorable. What two former top RUF officials called their "ideology" during interviews in fact were a set of rules to regulate behavior. They detailed exacting prohibitions on rape, theft, and drug use. Another rule, one of the officials explained, was that "civilians must be treated nicely." Still another was that "you cannot kill any enemy that surrenders." A second high-level former RUF official reviewed the RUF's eight codes of conduct with me, as well as eleven general principles to guide battle.[7] A third former high-level official insisted that the RUF never amputated anyone before 1997 (when the AFRC joined the RUF as rebels). "But sometimes," the official continued, "during heavy artillery fire, people's arms or hands were hurt." In other words, what might *look* like an amputation in reality was an injury caused by bullets or mortars. In this version of events, things that went wrong (such as extreme atrocities) were RUF aberrations or "malpractices" (Peters 2011a: 139), frequently caused or initiated by others. One account, derived from former RUF members (combatants, commanders, and military police), blamed excesses in RUF wartime behavior on, in succession, mercenaries from Liberia and Burkina Faso, civilians siding with the CDF, and the AFRC (142). A former high-level RUF commander blamed the AFRC for all terror tactics undertaken by rebels because "some criminals joined the AFRC and the movement." In short, the RUF has been badly misunderstood and has received undeservedly bad press.

This is not the broad picture of RUF actions and motives that emerged from interviews with former combatants and commanders. Nor, indeed, is it often reflected in publications concerning these issues. The gathered record strongly suggests that distortions in the above account are significant. Across the many years of Sierra Leone's war, the RUF amputated, stole, raped, took drugs, executed civilians and enemy soldiers, and much more. They committed these acts with and without Liberians, the AFRC, or others by their side. The take on the war detailed in this book thus far, and which subsequently will be described, reflects evidence and observations that broadly align with this gathered perspective.

Yet no one seems to challenge the assertion that the RUF employed uncommonly strict and harsh military codes. Just hesitating to carry out a command, regardless of what it was, might result in flogging or death. In response, "Anything you can do to save your life, you do it," a former RUF fighter explained. A former SBU member for the RUF shared four examples of just how seriously the RUF viewed mistakes and misbehavior:

> If you try to eat without the command [from your commanding officer], he'll kill you.
>
> If you're on duty as a guard and you're found sleeping, you'll be killed.
>
> If you are found with money or diamonds, surely you'll be killed.
>
> If ten soldiers committed crimes in a day, you will all be killed.

This demand for absolute and unquestioned obedience began during RUF training. And since the recruits had been forced to join, "training and indoctrination had to be designed in such a way as to promote violence among those disinclined to do it, and to bind them to the rebel group" (Mitton 2015: 231).

Trainers employed a series of measures to attain this goal. In addition to learning military basics, such as how to "parade" (marching in line, turning on command); handle, shoot, and clean a gun; and endure long runs or swims, trainees faced a number of daunting challenges. One centered on surviving methods to winnow out the weakest. A twenty-three-year-old male diamond miner working outside of Koidu, in Sierra Leone's Kono District, related the following about his tenure with the RUF:

> I was captured in 1996 [at age fourteen]. The first thing we did at the train-ing base was to shave our heads. Then every morning, we jogged, singing some songs, like "The shaved head, mine is better than yours."
>
> In the morning, we would get one spoon of bulgur wheat. We did exer-cises like crawling. We were given sticks that we used as guns. We some-times divided into two groups: one group pretended to be an enemy group, and we'd attack each other. If you were captured and did not take the right command from your commander, you'd receive a dozen lashes with a big rubber strip. I was beaten in this way. Blood ruined my nose. I was beaten all over my body.
>
> After these exercises, we were exposed to real guns. We were taken to the gun store. You are trained to learn how to fix your magazine and how to handle your gun in battle. Then we were distributed to different commanders.
>
> There were 125 of us who trained together, including maybe twenty-two girls. Thirty of us died during the training.

The death of some trainees reportedly was by intention. "If someone dies during the training," a former male RUF combatant related, "the training com-mander is promoted." One way to gain such a promotion was to force train-ees to cross a body of water (such as a river). "Those who could not swim drowned," the former fighter recalled. "We lost many boys this way."

There were other severe trials, as well. One former SBU member recalled how he would receive no food until the evening, when he was given "a single spoon of cooked banana." They also had to jump over a ditch filled with bro-ken bottles. Those who fell into the ditch were cut up by the glass. In another challenge, boys and girls had to cross via monkey bars (above their heads, moving their hands forward, one bar at a time). Falling meant landing on barbed wire underneath. Still another exercise demanded that trainees walk on a piece of wood, high above the ground. The wood had nails sticking up-ward. "This would cause a lot of damage to your feet," a former trainee re-called. Trainers beat anyone who fell off. Yet another challenge was for boys only. Two former RUF combatants separately mentioned a "woman training instructor" named Monica (probably Monica Pearson, one of the original RUF recruits in Liberia). "Monica sometimes would appear before us, to see if we could be a real fighter who won't be attracted to women," one recounted. If any of the boys started to get an erection after she appeared, "you'll be punished." One former combatant mentioned "a separate group that was trained to amputate people," to which he did not belong.

Then came the final stage. A former RUF fighter described his last training ordeal: "The trainers would make a circle enclosed with concrete bricks. Fifteen trainees would be in there, and you'd have the trainers in there as well. The trainers beat the trainees while they went around the circle. Other rebels also would come to beat you with canes as you went around in a circle. This would last for thirty minutes. I don't know why they did that to us." All of these challenges were part of an overall push to transform young people into obedient, loyal fighters. "The rebels turned law and morality on their heads," one analyst explained. "What was illegal became, in practice, 'legal' (since it was not punished); and what was immoral became not only justifiable but even heroic" (Keen 2005: 76). Isolation from the rest of the world helped make the brainwashing/transformation process stick. "Within the context of a closed RUF 'community,'" a second analyst explained, "traditional family structures were replaced by militarized ones." In the process, "rigid military hierarchies were imposed and new values of detachment, cruelty, terror, group solidarity and cohesion were propagated" (Denov 2010: 103). The irony that informed their self-isolation seemed to be lost on the RUF membership. Through the RUF's lens, the "outside world represented death and suffering— mainly inflicted by RUF cadres themselves, in what was to become a self- fulfilling prophesy" (Peters 2011a: 89). The more they tortured and slayed civilians, the more separate and insulated they became.

The driving purpose of all of this was to make brutalization a way of life. As one analyst explained,

> brutalization provided an ongoing motive for the RUF to perpetrate atrocities, regardless of other strategies. The nature of the RUF world was such that combatants were immersed in a society in which violence was a fact of day-to-day life, whether performed in attacks or simply as shaping interpersonal interactions. To a great extent, this led to the routinization of violence, and accordingly, habituation to its performance. It also meant the RUF world was an exceptionally terrifying society to inhabit for many, where lack of brutality or displays of emotional weakness could be violently punished. (Mitton 2015: 237)

This process began with the way in which the RUF trained their new initiates, which was led by dominant adults. Like the rest of Sierra Leone, RUF society was patrimonial in its essence, as "the RUF drew upon and . . . reproduced (to the extreme) the prevailing and often violent patterns of patriarchal hegemony." Commanders transformed into patrons while their young forces became servile clients (nearly all of the commanders were men). They provided everything the cadres required to live and fight. In return, their youthful membership became "wholly dependent on their hostage-takers." Boys in particular often developed close ties to their commanders, who would "inflict severe distress" as well as "provide them with relief and succour." The young members became complaint, and "the use of solidarity and cohesion, role allocation, and rewards and promotion further promoted and cemented the realities of patronage and deference" (Denov 2010: 118, 115). The RUF's forced socialization thus reimagined the Sierra Leone context, drawing on certain traditions (like patrimonialism) to invent a walled-off new world featuring depravity and submission.

A remarkable example of obedience and servility was the RUF's large and respected reconnaissance corps, or "recces." Missions were undertaken either by RUF combatants in disguise or civilians "pretending to be on innocent searches for food, sex or protection from the soldiers whilst actually gathering information" (TRC 2004a: 189n181). Some civilians reportedly were coerced into working as RUF spies: if they did not gather relevant information behind enemy lines and report back to RUF officers, their family members would be killed. During the war, ECOMOG, SLA, and CDF forces would become concerned about RUF spies in their midst, and for good reason. There were a lot of them, and they were good. In one survey of former child soldiers from Sierra Leone, more than half had worked as spies. Their job was to "locate 'enemy' positions and to familiarize themselves with the layout and particularities of towns and villages prior to attacks" (Wille 2005: 203). RUF girls cultivated relationships with government or ECOMOG soldiers to secure sensitive information. They were found to be "the best spies," one analyst related, because "they could sleep with commanders on another side and then come back with all the goods, all the information." One former recce said that the RUF had a specialized training on reconnaissance, lasting two to three days. Many related during interviews that the RUF's intelligence capabilities were exceptionally high.

4. Instruments of Social Cohesion

The RUF employed many techniques to bind the new trainees to their society. It appears to have been a two-part process, first breaking down prior affiliations and then replacing them with a new wartime RUF identity. The change began with language. Coulter highlights a critically important RUF policy: Krio was the only allowed language. It was the nation's lingua franca, and RUF cadres hailed from many different ethnic groups. RUF members heard speaking their mother tongues could be killed. RUF leaders evidently feared that their captors (females in particular) could plan secretly either to kill them or to escape (Coulter 2009: 117).

Then there was the bodywork, which frequently amounted to crudely carving or branding the letters "RUF" onto a person's skin (Peters 2011a: 89–90). Denov considers this activity as "reinforcing group solidarity and ensuring attachment to the rebels" as well as reaffirming "the RUF's ferocity as a fighting force" (2010: 106, 107). The TRC reported that tattooing was part of a "closing ceremony" in which the initiation ordeal ends, RUF membership begins, and a new identity is created "that depicts values of ideal manhood" (2004a: 559). Peters emphasizes that those who tried and failed to escape were tattooed (2011a: 90). The effort pointed to deep insecurity among RUF leaders: even after forcing new captives to perform atrocities against family and community members (to prevent defections), they still feared attrition from their ranks. The emphasis on boys and male youth is yet another indication of the absolutely relentless focus on males and masculinity by wartime factions.

Identity transformation also included male initiates assuming new names. The new war names were "markers of the death of a former civilian identity . . . and the birth of a new rebel identity, shameless and fearless" (Mitton 2015: 143). The names might emphasize bravery or describe a personality, or they were names given by others. Regardless of their origin, many were intentionally terrifying. Here are some samples: High Firing, Necka (for "a man who frequently raped or had sex with any woman, young or old"), Nylon (a gent who "drops melted plastic in people's eyes"), and Mami Curse ("someone who insults mothers") (Coulter 2009: 118). There also were "several Rambos" (noted earlier) as well as "Van Damme, Chuck Norris and James Bond" (Keen 2005: 74). Keen notes that "violent heroes appear to have been important as part of a consumer culture which had a powerful attraction for young people, often disillusioned with traditional leaders and culture" (74).

That much is certain. However, there also were strong indications that the RUF's purposes were far more intentional than that. In fact, the second part of the process that RUF leaders employed to bind new initiates to them featured a second notable irony. On one hand, the RUF's social setup relied on thunderously patrimonial relations between alpha male commanders and their highly dependent minions. On the other, the RUF emphasized upending the perverse universe of the past, in which powerful older men dominated youth. As noted in Chapter 8, the RUF reportedly had a "simple populist revolutionary agenda, principally focused on land, education, health, and an end to corruption" (Peters 2011a: 126). But the boiled-down version was more rudimentary. An RUF leader who helped formulate the group's vision and purpose explained, "As for us in the RUF, the definition of our revolution was drastic fundamental changes, from the negative aspect to the positive aspect.

Life and property have always been taken away. Those who are fighting, they'll take what you have. Life and property are always the food of war. Money is the gun."

The nihilistic essence of the RUF's ethos burns through in this version of RUF aims: to implement radical change via looting and killing.[8] One apparent focus of all the looting and killing was to eradicate precedents and traditions that had bound youth to elders and tradition, something Coulter called the RUF's "reversal of the order of things" (2009: 118). An analyst of the RUF's ideas and practices explained this dimension: "The RUF desecrated Poro and Bondo sites. They tried to destroy those secret traditions and replace them with the Western culture. They targeted all the chiefs, the security, court officials—all had to be killed or humiliated in public. They wanted to destroy the whole social infrastructure, so that all that those young boys knew [were] these Western figures. The RUF goal was to undermine the social structure and create a new world." The RUF's extreme means tilted toward this unusual end: a youth-focused world, informed by certain aspects of Western culture. Notwithstanding this accent, youth superseding the RUF leadership was never in the cards. Foday Sankoh, Mosquito, and other RUF elders wielded immense power and control over their membership. There were no indications that they would ever give that up, Sankoh in particular. A former RUF officer who worked closely with him across the war years concluded that Sankoh had much in common with Charles Taylor and Prince Johnson (Taylor's formidable civil war rival in Liberia). All three "only believe in themselves," he stated. "They don't listen to others. Whatever they want to do, they do. They are all autocratic dictators."

Yet within the RUF world, references to the "West" highlighted those whom male youth and the RUF leaders jointly admired, Bob Marley and other leading reggae musicians in particular. This reverence is illuminated by new initiates growing dreadlocks, which was considered "a symbol of identification" with the RUF (TRC 2004a: 560). Groups of preteen and teenaged soldier boys with dreads: that alone would have made quite an impression on civilians during RUF attacks. Music also played a big role. Reggae songs were among those RUF trainers played for their initiates. They also "used statements made in reggae songs to convey codes of conduct and to clarify issues during ideology training in camp" (Nuxoll 2015: 8).[9]

The RUF's Rasta flavoring stayed with combatants, many of whom "turn[ed] to reggae for advice and motivation and in order to cope with and justify their involvement in the movement." They also "took on aspects of the Rastafarian lifestyle" by "adopting Rasta rhetoric," smoking marijuana, and wearing dreadlocks (Nuxoll 2015: 8, 12). Marijuana and many other drugs, in fact, constituted the final (and perhaps the most potent) ingredient in the RUF's process of transforming new initiates into active members. As one analyst observed, "The apparent abundance of alcohol and hallucinatory drugs deliberately and unquestionably contributed to the creation of efficient and aggressive soldiers" (Denov 2010: 100). An analyst in Sierra Leone characterized their fundamental significance for the RUF (and the AFRC) more succinctly: "They couldn't fight without drugs."

Other Rebel Initiations for Males

There were many ways to become a rebel. Relatively few received the sort of extensive, intensive formal training detailed in the previous section. Most were informal and gender-specific: what boys and male youth were put through differed significantly from the experiences of girls and female youth. Reflecting these differences, discussion of informal rebel trainings is split into two parts: this section discusses those for males while chapter 19 looks at those for girls.

The rebels' flexible approach to training and initiating their members seemed to be a well-known characteristic of their respective organizations (the RUF in particular, as well as the AFRC). As the director of an ex-combatant program in Sierra Leone commented, "The RUF had basic training guidelines. But there were variations: certain issues were common while others were not." In fact, the basic training guidelines were spare. A longtime ex-RUF veteran explained his military training experience with the rebels. He first indicated that, in the early part of the war, the top trainers were from Burkina Faso. But what the Burkinabé trainers provided, he related, was basic: "The children were trained how to take the machine gun apart, clean it, oil it, and then 'cup lock' [put] it together." He added that, in general, "Some [abductees] are never trained, others are trained." As for himself, "I was never trained. As soon as you know how to fire a gun, crawl on the ground and how to withdraw [from battle], that is your guerrilla training. That is all."

The dual RUF patterns of training some new members intensely while providing limited (or no) training to others evidently emerged from the highest levels of the organization. The story of a former RUF soldier during the war's early stages sheds light on this. He was from the town of Daru, home of the Moa Barracks, a large national military outpost positioned strategically along the Moa River and between the towns of Kenema and Kailahun. He described his capture as follows: "When the rebels attacked Daru, they gathered all of us and a large number of youth, including me. We were singled out. They took out some of us [from among the captured male youth] and killed them. Then they asked us, 'Which do you prefer, to die or join us and join the revolution?' So we all agreed to join." His captors took the twenty-five male youth to a training site called Burkina, "a camp in Kailahun in thick forest." The RUF trained them for two weeks. During that time, he explained energetically, "We smoked djamba properly!" In addition, "some [marijuana] ashes were given to us as a charm" to wear. The trainers also made incisions into the trainees' arms "and put djamba into our blood. It makes you very strong and brave." The strong emphasis on marijuana, quite often alongside the music and ideas of Bob Marley and other reggae musicians, proved to be a common dimension of rebel trainings and rebel life.

Following the two-week training session, the twenty-five trainees were assigned "the first test case." This meant that they would enter the war's front lines. The ex-RUF fighter described a rapid succession of battles, including an engagement with government soldiers in which his RUF contingent captured a village but took heavy losses in the process. Then his contingent "retreated to Zogoda Camp," which was not only a prime RUF encampment but also Foday Sankoh's main location for extended periods in the early war years. Together with a top commander, Sankoh decided to promote the new RUF member to the rank of commander. Why did the two RUF leaders make this surprising decision? The ex-combatant explained: "When I was captured, there were twenty-five [of us]. But after two months [two weeks training, six weeks fighting], I was the only survivor. So they made me a commander." After abducting twenty-five male youth at one time—quite a haul for the RUF— only one had managed to survive eight weeks as a rebel.

Rebel captives who did not become soldiers generally received no training or initiation of any kind. A supporter (or patron of miners) from Kono, for example, related the basics of his experience of rebel occupation of the diamond mine where he worked. He opened with an understated summation of his experience: "We weren't treated well. Sometimes when we would extract our gravel and wash it [that is, searching for diamonds while rinsing gravel in water], the rebels would chase us away and do the washing [themselves]. When they suspected a civilian [miner] of finding a diamond, and if you were lucky, they'd take the diamond and only beat you. Most of the time, they'd take the diamond and kill you." A former porter for the RUF (abducted at age nineteen) ultimately developed a less threatening relationship with his rebel captors. His first task was to haul a fifty-kilo bag of rice to a village ten kilometers away. Although he struggled with his load and was beaten many times along the way, he finally made it. Had he failed, he explained, the rebels would have killed him. But the porter wore dreadlocks. Because of this, "I became a friend to these rebels. In fact, they regretted their action [that is, beating and threatening to kill him]. They later considered me as Marley's son."

One of those interviewed detailed a nonfighting role known loosely as G5. This position evidently had its roots in RUF-controlled areas called liberated zones. These locations appear only to have existed near remote base camps and only when they were not under attack.[10] Certain discrete areas were in RUF hands for years (Peters 2011a: 106). In these places, the RUF developed a limited degree of a system and structure, including a "rough-and-ready land-reform agenda" that featured "driving out the elders" who formerly controlled the land (109). While G5 duties in so-called liberated zones were multifaceted and featured a hierarchy of RUF actors (131–132), the experience of a former G5 member in northern Sierra Leone was entirely different. There, the rebels played no role. Instead, certain captured civilians became G5 representatives who "served as [go-betweens] for the civilians and the rebels," he explained. It was difficult work. Essentially, his job entailed taking food, money, and palm wine from local civilians and handing it all over to rebel soldiers. However, if the supplies were insufficient or deemed inadequate, the G5 received the blame. He recalled one episode where the rebels forced him (at gunpoint) to drink all the palm wine he had collected for the rebels (20 liters) simply because they disliked it. The rebels also forced their G5 to smoke marijuana ("my first experience of smoking") immediately after his capture. Subsequently, he said, "I was forced to smoke djamba [by the rebels], and most of the time they played Marley's music."

Repeated references to Bob Marley and smoking marijuana in the interview data—in formal as well as informal initiations—strongly suggested that they were persistent and widespread rebel practices. Over and over again, when interviews with former male combatants for rebel troops turned to their entrance into rebel life, most mainly spoke of three things: smoking marijuana, listening to Bob Marley's music, and learning how to shoot a gun. The following recollection reflects this trend. When the rebels captured one youth during a raid near Makeni, he was taken to their commander, a man named Jossie. Jossie told him that he would be a fine rebel fighter, and that if he tried to escape, Jossie's troops would burn down his home village (where he had been captured). Then the ex-combatant explained what happened next:

> My first experience was that I was forced to smoke marijuana. When they first gave me the marijuana to smoke, one of [the RUF soldiers] said, "We are all Rastamen, so you too should be one!" A few of them were smoking [marijuana] and all of them were shouting and singing Marley's "Rastaman Live Up!" song.[11] I was so confused, I didn't say a single word. Then one of [the rebel soldiers] said, "This is your first weapon, learn how to handle it and use it well." The rice I ate that day also had marijuana in it. While I was eating and smoking, the small boys [SBUs] celebrated that I finally had become a member of the RUF. They called out and shouted, "Gallant soldier!" After I finished smoking and eating, I was helpless and went into a deep sleep.

The next day, the new abductee learned how to use his new gun. "It took me just one day to learn how to fire" his gun, he recalled. Then soldiers told him,

"The rest you will learn on the battlefield." With that, the boy's sudden initiation—consisting of capture, threat of punishment should he attempt to escape, forced marijuana use, receiving a gun and some time to learn how it worked, and the use of Bob Marley's music to encourage him to become a RUF "Rastaman" soldier—was done.

Of all the elements that surfaced in descriptions of such ad hoc male initiations into rebel soldiering, marijuana was the most important. In many cases, being forced to smoke djamba was the main initiation element. Sudden, heavy use, while also being pressured to assume soldiering duties, fueled the transformation of boys into fighters. The following recounting of capture and initiation from a former AFRC member reflects this. He was fourteen in 1999, when a military unit led by Gullit (the top AFRC commander who had led the January 6 assault on Freetown) captured him. The ex-fighter remembered the dual terrors he faced. Just before his abduction, he had witnessed the public torture of a rebel whom ECOMOG soldiers had captured. "If one day in the future I am caught by them, will I be treated like this rebel?" he asked himself. That memory alone subdued his urge to attempt escape. At the same time, "I felt really bad when [the rebels] took me along." But then Gullit's soldiers started the new captive's initiation. "The one thing that helped me to recover quickly from this situation was when I was forced to smoke djamba and was exposed to drinking rum." It worked. "Since the day I started smoking djamba," he explained, "I became brave and I started behaving like a rebel. I now had a mind to do anything I was told to do." For the boy's first three months in the AFRC, he carried "a stick and a cutlass as my weapons." Then, "after three months, I was given a gun and I was taught how to fire it. That was all." His military training was complete.

A second former AFRC fighter was out looking for food in 1997 (at age sixteen) when, on returning to his village, he discovered that "the rebels were beating [his] parents." When the rebel soldiers then turned to start beating his grandmother, "I came out of hiding and gave myself up, in place of my grandmother." His commander, called CC5, was "one of those released [from prison] during the Johnny Paul [Koroma, the AFRC leader] coup." The ex-fighter remembered him as "a mild commander" with a fondness for marijuana. However, the second-in-command, known as Abu Bastard Pikin [Child], "smoked djamba and took cocaine" and "killed innocent people rampantly." The youth was not trained, evidently because he had been captured by the RUF four years earlier and thus already knew soldiering. On the day of his first capture in 1993, he explained that "we smoked [marijuana] and went to attack." That was it. The marijuana clearly had made a significant impact on the twelve-year-old boy. As he returned with his group from his initial attack as an RUF soldier, "I stepped on a corpse as if I was stepping on dry leaves." The reason was that djamba had strongly influenced his state of mind. "When we smoked [djamba]," he related, "the one thing that will go away is sympathy [for others]. Even if they [had] asked me to kill my mother, I was ready to do it."

The transformative combination of forced marijuana use and forced entry into military life on a young boy's attitude and nature is underscored in the following story of capture and initiation by a former SBU commander for the RUF. When he was ten, after Makeni had fallen to the rebels in 1998, the boy's entire village emptied, shifting to the rain forest and creating a hiding place (a kind of soquoihun) there. His family built a shelter made of "sticks and palm leaves" and lived there for a spell. However, after seven years of warfare, the rebels were long accustomed to this sort of civilian maneuver. Discovering empty villages, they simply "went into the bush and farms to search for people, forcing them to come back to town." In the unlikely event that anyone would resist, "they would be considered enemies and would be killed." The boy's family went back, clearly terrified. "Coming back to town with this kind of threat was a difficult thing to do altogether," the ex-SBU recounted.

While the family was returning to their former home under rebel escort, a snap decision changed the boy's life: "The rebels thought I should be one of them." Using the matter-of-fact language that rebel captors always seemed to employ, one of them told the young boy, "You come here. You seem to be very smart. Stand here while we deal with this matter." His mother's immediate protest forced this exchange:

> When my mother asked where they were taking me, one of the rebels replied that my mother should not ask them that kind of question. "Don't you know that this boy is government [property] and that he is going to fight for you? Do not ask this question or else you will have to pay the price [that is, death]." My mother pleaded that I should not be taken, but they never listened. They spoke to me fine and promised that they will take care of me. I cried bitterly and waved to my parents. I was taken away.

Crying bitterly may have made his initiation considerably easier. The youngster met the commander, Captain Musa, who put him under the care of his wife. This temporary mother figure effectively became his first military trainer. "During my stay with this woman," the ex-SBU explained, "I was shown a gun and was told that this will be my weapon if I prove to be a good boy." He also was "encouraged not to be worried about anything because I was safe." Captain Musa's wife "sometimes encouraged me to be brave."

After two months with "my commander's wife," the young boy (now eleven) entered the fray, instantly becoming an SBU. This is when he was "formally introduced to the use of the gun." Over three days, he learned how to use and fire the one he had been given. This constituted his military training, he related. At the end of the three days, he was told, "This is what you need to learn. The rest you will have to learn when you go into battle. With this gun, you will either die or live." While he confessed to having difficulty knowing what Captain Musa "was telling me," the gist of what he needed to know was clear: "If I fight hard, I will survive. Otherwise I will be killed on the battlefield."

The former SBU fighter then reflected on the nature of his time with his commander's wife. His description is telling: "Remember when I told you that I cried bitterly when [the rebel soldiers] were taking me away? After one month [with Captain Musa's wife], I felt comfortable. I was given fine food to eat. She took great care of me, as if she was my mother." The seductive initiation that Captain Musa's wife performed also included being "introduced to smoking djamba." The powerful influence of marijuana on a child's mind proved catalytic: "When I started smoking, I began to feel differently. I started behaving in a different way, quarrelling with friends and threatening to beat them up. *I was not afraid of anything.* I started having the confidence to stay with the group, since there was no fear in me any longer. When finally I was put in charge of one SBU [i.e., he was the leader of an attack unit], I started smoking heavily, since I now was able to 'djamba' for myself. *When I smoke, I feel like a man.*" The italicized passages underscore how marijuana use connected the young boy to fearlessness and aggressive, manlike power. But one other factor cemented djamba and empowerment with rebel life: the music of Bob Marley. "My boss [Captain Musa] had no other [cassette] tape except that of Marley. Day and night, we danced to Marley's music. When we listened to those tapes, we would dance and smoke djamba. We also drank boiled djamba. We felt good and happy as we listened to these songs. Bob Marley was popular for two main reasons: his songs and the djamba. To me, these were the two main reasons why Marley was so popular. Since I joined the RUF, I have never stopped listening to Marley's music."

As will be explored further in this chapter and in chapter 18, field interviews, supported by a handful of published sources, indicated that many rebel commanders employed the marijuana-Marley combination to induce belonging for boys and male youth who became rebel fighters (the trend also surfaced in many Kamajor units). The frivolity that commanders routinely propagated steered his soldiers' thoughts away from traumatic memory and toward drug-induced delight. Marijuana was the centerpiece: keeping the underlings high ensured their compliance and seemed to keep everything in place. Marley's music (and occasionally that of other musicians, such as Joseph Hill and Tupac Shakur) often was used to foster an atmosphere of connection among the soldiers. Many commanders clearly wanted the young boys and male youth under their control to see each other as fellow Rastafarian fighters. Sometimes, a purpose was thrown in: they were fighting for a version of revolutionary, youth-led change about which Marley purported to sing. Forcing near-constant marijuana use and cultivating a vague sense that the soldiers were Marley-like freedom fighters appear to have been common practices among rebel commanders.

Most of this was a ruse. While many ex-rebel fighters depicted their former commanders as lovers of Marley, the combination of Marley with forced marijuana use (and, quite often, many other drugs) stimulated a version of Bob Marley and Rastafarianism that the originators definitely never intended: the promotion of terror warfare. The violence and reverie that perpetual drug use created, often mixed with near-constant music and hazy, manipulated interpretations of Bob Marley's messages, were powerful and emphatically masculine in nature. Tupac Shakur's music, for those rebel units who also played his cassettes (not all of them did), only accentuated the aura of masculine power that every rebel commander seemed to encourage.

The Kamajor Initiations

There were more Civil Defense Forces than rebel soldiers in Sierra Leone's war. One estimate put the rebels at 55,000 (45,000 RUF, 10,000 AFRC) and the CDF at 68,865 (nearly 10 percent more; McKay and Mazurana 2004: 92). The ethnic Mende Kamajors were the largest contingent of the CDF and, for much of the war, the rebels' primary adversary.

Kamajor initiation rites didn't last as long as formal RUF training processes. However, they were significant in their own way. Given their focus on traditional ideas (and magic), and the number and importance of the Kamajors in the war, a brief review of their initiation is useful.

The Kamajors had to get into the war fast. By 1995, the RUF had cultivated a myth of invincibility in its fighting against NPRC government troops and the Tamaboro CDF militias from the north. To prepare for their entrance, Kamajor initiations drew from Poro manhood ceremonies as well as "traditional magic, mysticism and Islam" (Muana 1997: 84, 87). They also drew from older traditions: "Kamajor" hails from the Mende word "*kamajoi*," which signifies a traditional hunter who "hunts at night and often alone." The domain in which they operate is "expressly male" and in opposition to the "excessive and unpredictable power of women."

In a theme that also surfaces with reference to the legacy of the slave trade and the extreme sexual violence that took place during Sierra Leone's war, the tradition's characterization of feminine power is key. Femininity is neither complementary nor a yin-yang counterpart to masculinity. On the contrary, gender relations in Sierra Leonean cultures tend to be volatile and unstable. From the tradition's origins, Kamajors (or *kamajoisia*) helped combat the perceived might of women. They viewed feminine power as "volatile and chaotic, like the forest itself." The secrets of the Kamajors thus never should fall into the hands of females, "not because women lack power but because their

power lacks control." In Mende society (and, indeed, among many other ethnic groups in Sierra Leone), women are nothing less than direct and intimate
threats to men. During the war, the step from males perceiving femininity as
menacing to male domination of females was short. Chapter 19 addresses perceptions of feminine power and the exceptionally brutal treatment of females
during the war.

The reimagined, modern-war Kamajors were antistate as well as anti-RUF
(Hoffman 2011: 63, 64, 79). On the political side, Kamajor membership flowed
straight through the traditional patrimonial system. In the early stages, chiefs
and elders decided who would become a Kamajor. In one way, that was quite
sensible: local chiefs and other male leaders were expected to vet members,
to ensure that they had not been former RUF or SLA soldiers (after Strasser's
NPRC came in) and had no criminal records (Wlodarczyk 2009: 100). It also
prevented "misfits"—yet another term for those male youth that mainstream
society deemed "bad"—from entering (Alie 2005: 57). Kamajors recruits were
connected to "chiefdom councils, town elders, and the local elites," not the national government or army, or the ruling party (Hoffman 2011: 75). Their ties
were local and sprung from the traditional patrimony.

Magic and mandates mixed during Kamajor initiations. One analyst stated
that their purpose "was to render initiates fit to serve at the war front, through
the granting of special powers such as the ability to be 'bullet-proof' and being
able to smell enemies" (Alie 2005: 57). They also had to follow many rules (just
like the RUF, they had a code of conduct), such as not looting villages, not
committing rape, and not having contact with women when in battle dress.
While their main role was to defend communities against "those who posed
the greatest threat," the outwardly ethical bent of the Kamajors also called
for respecting the international laws of war: during initiations, leaders would
read aloud excerpts from military manuals, guidelines on human rights from
Amnesty International, and other documents (Ferme and Hoffman 2004: 81,
82). This aspect is interesting as well as somewhat curious, given the prominent tendency for some Kamajors to practice cannibalism. The group's ethical conduct eroded as their well-earned reputation for committing atrocities
expanded.

The fact that we know quite a bit about Kamajor initiation rites contrasts significantly from the much earlier Poro and Bondo (or Sande) secret
initiations, which have retained a far higher degree of mystery over time.
Wlodarczyk, for example, learned that Kamajor initiates were cut with razors
and beaten repeatedly, and probably engaged in cannibalism during initiations (2009: 105, 106). Rubbing human blood onto new initiates, in addition,
"was done to give them a strong and fearless heart." Certain herbs and amulets promised to make initiates impervious to bullets and cutlasses (McKay
and Mazurana 2004: 96). One initiate shared many gruesome details to the

Special Court of Sierra Leone after the war, including some also found in RUF initiations: singing, tattooing/cutting, canings, and whippings (cited in Wlodarczyk 2009: 104–105n40).[12] Should an initiate seek the power to become invisible or practice shape-shifting, additional "ceremonies, spiritual stages, and taboos" were required (McKay and Mazurana 2004: 96).

The emergence of Aliu Kundorwai as the Kamajors' high priest during the war was, in the diplomatic words of one analyst, "perhaps not fortuitous." That was an understatement. Kundorwai (known simply as Doctor "to his adherents") ended up conducting "more initiations than all the other high priests put together" (Alie 2005: 57). In retrospect, that may not have been the best idea. Kundorwai evidently realized fairly swiftly that his new position could be lucrative. He started by initiating the first thirty-seven Kamajor members in 1995, using techniques that he either invented or developed with some initiator colleagues (Wlodarczyk 2009: 97). Later in the war, he charged much higher prices for his initiations, made their duration shorter, and promised that his updated techniques would bestow advantages well beyond those emerging from the original initiation process. Some of the newer initiates were called the Avondos (meaning "sweat," which, the high priest claimed, would help bulletproof the initiate). The Avondos in particular undercut the Kamajors' once-hallowed reputation, with the new initiates deemed "untrained thugs who used their semilegitimate security position to prey on the local population" (Hoffman 2011: 237). Kundorwai's sacking in 2000 was national news.

Interviews with former Kamajor members reflect the descent of discipline and organization in their militia over time. One former member described his initiation, which contrasted sharply from earlier versions: "They built a settlement and gave us something to drink: not alcohol [which was forbidden]. They'd write Koranic recitations with ink and wash it into a pail. Then everyone would drink the ink and water. Then they would cut you on your arms and give you tattoos. They would bleed you, and put medicine there [into the cut]. Then you are a member. The training lasted one week." The ex-Kamajor added that his superiors "talked about Tupac. They'd tell you to wear Tupac dressing [his T-shirt] but don't smoke. They [also] said you can wear Bob Marley style [dreadlocks and Bob Marley T-shirts] but don't smoke." An ex-Kamajor commander said that his "initiation only took five hours. [Then] they told you that you are in a society world and gave you tattoos." A second commander's initiation "lasted one day or just a few hours." Collectively, the three former Kamajor members presented a rather confusing picture. On one hand, they said that if a Kamajor broke sacrosanct Kamajor tenets (such as by touching a woman while wearing the Kamajor uniform, stealing from a civilian, smoking marijuana, or drinking alcohol), the charms and magic emerging from the initiation process wouldn't work. Accordingly, if a Kamajor was hit by a bullet, it only proved that he had broken the sacred rules prior to receiving the bullet wound. Every interviewed ex-Kamajor contended that Kamajor magic was never faulty.

On the other hand, the three men said that taking drugs while serving as Kamajors was not uncommon. "In the later part of the war," one commander recalled, "Kamajors used cannabis or djamba." He also insisted that "we would lynch some Kamajoh for taking drugs because the intoxication prevents you from protection [being protected]." These comments suggested that taking djamba may have been seen as different from taking other drugs. The gathered evidence indicated that marijuana use was ubiquitous among Sierra Leonean fighters during the war. Djamba was smoked, mixed into meals, and downed in water. For most local military units, its use was routine. Most other drugs were set into incisions (and covered with a "plaster") or taken orally, while alcohol was a special beverage. Some Kamajors reported using a mixture of drugs. For example, one ex-commander stated that he took cocaine and a lot of marijuana. "Before fighting," he explained, "I would smoke two or three packs of marijuana until my eyes became so red and I became hard-hearted." Sometimes he also "took a [Kamajor-approved] charm that also made you so hard-hearted." In fact, he said, "Most Kamajors took some [sort of] drug to become so hard-hearted." Just as with many rebels, becoming "hard-hearted" via drug use was an essential battle preparation.

The decline of discipline and purpose for the Kamajors set them up for critique. McKay and Mazurana found that the Kamajors (as well as the Gbethis, another CDF group) had women and girls active in their ranks "throughout the war" as "initiators, commanders, spiritual leaders, frontline fighters, medics, herbalists, spies and cooks." They also found that some girls were "fully initiated." Former female Kamajor and Gbethi members further reported that CDF groups practiced human sacrifice and cannibalism. The fact that female ex-Kamajors had such trouble being accepted on return to their communities following the war's end may have been due, at least in part, to the fact that, according to tradition, girls were not supposed have been members in the first place (McKay and Mazurana 2004: 96, 97). Indeed, not one former Kamajor combatant (all males) whom I interviewed for this book allowed that some females also were members, although one admitted that "there were women and children in Kamajor bush camps."

No analyst or set of analysts was nearly as critical of the Kamajors and their initiations as the Truth and Reconciliation Commission. In their view, Kamajor initiations were a sham and an outrage. "The traditions of peacetime secret societies through the ages [such as Poro and Sande] were done a terrible disservice by the cruel and aggressive interpretation they were given" by the wartime founders of the Kamajor militia. In the view of the TRC, the traditions that Kundorwai and his initiator cronies created "were perverted." Acts of cannibalism "came as a rude shock to some of the elders and chiefs." The initiation ceremony itself "was a cleverly manipulated process that duped the mass of the membership into believing that they were the chosen ones blessed by gods and ancestors to liberate their people." The initiators became "extremely powerful," and Kundorwai himself was accused as being driven by "raw greed." Initiators faked their magic, doctoring bullet cartridges so they wouldn't pierce the initiates' skin. This left the Kamajor initiates "convinced" of their "own immortality." Accordingly, the Kamajors' famed fearlessness was largely due to "misplaced gusto. . . . As a direct result of their initiation ceremonies, they did not think they could be killed by bullets." The final assessment of the TRC was scathing and encompassing: The high priest and all other Kamajor initiators "were responsible both directly and indirectly for the commission of human rights violations on an alarming scale." The TRC thus "condemns this perversion of the sacred and long-standing tradition of initiation and rites of passage" (TRC 2004a: 272, 274, 275, 276, 277).

What separated the Kamajors from the RUF? They certainly knew each other well, and both were familiar with and reliant on their knowledge of forests. Yet Kamajor practices were consciously connected to the hunter and Poro traditions of the past and much more directly linked to traditional magic. In direct contrast, the RUF "saw itself as the antithesis of tradition, ushering in a new order, different from what had gone before them" (Wlodarczyk 2009: 122). In addition, the Kamajors were well known for practicing cannibalism while the RUF were best known (in terms of atrocity specialization) for amputation. The Kamajors may have been less fearful during assaults than their rebel adversaries (if only due to the advertising of their initiators).

Ultimately, two major differences separated the RUF from the Kamajors and other CDF groups. One is that very few Kamajors were forced to join, while the RUF abducted the overwhelming majority of their members. Second, and not least, Kamajor members were optimistic. Their charms and potions to boost their confidence and reduce their pain, together with their "promised powers" of immunity and invisibility, "allowed the fighters to approach combat with greater buoyancy." Confidence in their magical powers enabled them "to maintain a degree of optimism that would perhaps have been lost on an outsider." The amulets and charms they wore and the special instruments they used (such as "controllers" that believers contended would drive bullets away from their holders) "sent a signal of magical prowess to the enemy" (Wlodarczyk 2009: 99, 128, 129). In Sierra Leone, where a great many people believe deeply in the power of magic and secret ceremonies, all of this created a sizable military advantage and helped make the Kamajors and other CDF units daunting rebel adversaries.

Regardless of how Kamajors, RUF, AFRC, and other military outfits were trained, they all followed the rebels' lead and employed terror techniques during the war. An examination of those techniques follows in part 5, where adaptations of the work of Tupac and Marley played big roles.

Marijuana Warfare

THE PERFORMANCE OF TERROR

CHAPTER 17

Tupac Shakur and War

Eight Military Attributes

The two chapters in part 5 focus on the mechanics of terror warfare as they were practiced mainly (but certainly not exclusively) by rebel groups in Sierra Leone. It will draw from interview data primarily with former combatants and officers with the main rebel groups (the RUF and the AFRC) as well as, to a lesser extent, interviews with former Kamajor members. There also will be considerable reference to the findings and analyses in relevant literature on warfare in Sierra Leone. Excessive drug use, the perpetration of various atrocities, decentralized military structures, and a pronounced focus on male youth all played central roles (in addition to the harsh, vindictive treatment of females and the conspicuous fixation on sexual violence, which are both examined in chapter 19). So did popular culture figures, who sometimes served to catalyze the rebels' terror war practices.

With this in mind, we begin our discussion by turning to Tupac Shakur's work and influence as a global icon and over Sierra Leonean male youth, both generally and specifically during the war years. Tupac's sway over rebel male youth and the practice of terror warfare grew over the course of the war. For some rebel fighters, using "Tupac Tactics" became a method for inspiring the use of extreme terror tactics.

In characteristic fashion, Tupac Shakur's famous "Hit 'Em Up," his blistering anthem of masculine fury, begins with a confession of vulnerability. He's friendless, he curses. Tupac's unforgettable song opens with his ever-present calling card: unvarnished honesty, together with the adjective form of the English-language curse word he employed the most in his music (motherfucker).

Then Tupac switches gears. Raising his voice and speaking with consuming anger, Tupac shouts that he had sex with his overweight adversary's woman, using three curse words that he regularly applied (fuck, bitch, and motherfucker) for effect. The recording is only a few seconds in and the hypnotic music and muscular rapping haven't even started yet. But already, the threatening tone, the messages of justified revenge and sexual aggression, and the aim to mow down adversaries by humiliating and emasculating them (the explicit intention to kill them arises soon afterward) are all underway. "Hit 'Em Up" is not only intensely threatening; it's also intensely personal.

Before diving deeper into this song, it is necessary to reflect on events that inspired it and contributed directly to Tupac's legendary status. In a compressed amount of time, a number of powerful events took place in the young life of Tupac Shakur. At the age of twenty-three, already a renowned global figure and controversial rap musician (as well as a budding movie star), Tupac was charged with sexual abuse. During his trial in New York a year later, Tupac agreed to contribute to a rap song for an artist named Lil Shawn (who was "an associate of Biggie Smalls," the talented musician named Christopher Wallace and also known as the Notorious B.I.G. [McQuillar and Johnson 2010: 154, 150]).

As all Tupac fans know, Biggie rests at the center of "Hit 'Em Up." He was a leading figure in the infamous rivalry involving "East Side" rap musicians (based in the eastern United States, Brooklyn in particular) and their "West Side" counterparts (based in the western United States, notably Los Angeles, with Tupac the featured member). Up to this point, Tupac had served as a kind of mentor, friend, and supporter to Biggie. Upon Tupac's arrival at the Quad recording studio (to contribute to a new song by rapper Lil Shawn), three men in the lobby shot Tupac five times. Bleeding profusely, Tupac somehow managed to take the elevator upstairs, where Biggie and other prominent East Side figures (notably Sean "Puffy" Combs, the founder of Bad Boy Records, the New York–based label of Biggie and many other rappers) were located (McQuillar and Johnson 2010: 151, 152).[1] After recovering in the hospital, Tupac was found guilty of first-degree sexual abuse on December 1, 1994, and sentenced to prison in February 1995 (James 1995). Just before his sentencing, Tupac reportedly told the judge:

> You know Your Honor throughout this entire court case you haven't looked me or my attorney in the eye once. It is obvious that you're not here in search of justice so therefore there is no point in me asking for a lighter sentence. I don't care what you do because you're not respecting us. This is not a court of law as far as I'm concerned. No justice is being served here and you can't look me in the eye. So I say do what you want to do. Give me whatever time you want because I'm not in your hands. I'm in God's hands. (McQuillar and Johnson 2010: 154)

The statement eventually became part of Tupac's legend, promoting his reputation for fearlessness, pride, dignity, and faith in God, as well for speaking out against injustice.

While in maximum security prison, Tupac's third album, *Me against the World*, was released. He "remains the first and only musician to have the number one album in the [United States] while doing time in jail" (McQuillar and Johnson 2010: 163). Tupac's ability to write and produce songs was remarkable: one former colleague recalled how he might write three or four songs on one day and six to seven songs on another (Dyson 2001: 11). His work ethic remained intact in prison, where he wrote many new rap songs. He also received information from unnamed "informants" that "Biggie and Puffy had at the very least known about the ambush" at the Quad recording studio "and did not warn him" in advance (allegations that Biggie and Puffy strenuously contested). Tupac also had "received word that there was a possible jail contract out" to murder him (McQuillar and Johnson 2010: 181, 182). Following this intense mix of tumult, suffering, and notoriety, "the man who walked out of prison" in October 1995 was out to prove "that he could rise once more to the pinnacle of rap music success and [get] even with Biggie, the former friend who, he felt, had betrayed him" (186).

Neither took long. By February 1996, Tupac's fourth album, *All Eyez on Me* (the first two-CD album by a rap musician), was released and became a massive success. Then "Hit 'Em Up," the song that sent shockwaves through the rap world because it "basically declared war on the East Coast" rappers (210, 225), was released in June. Less than a year after Tupac Shakur had left prison (and three months after "Hit 'Em Up" came out), he was shot again, this time in Las Vegas, where he had gone to watch a Mike Tyson fight. Mysteriously, the people who fired the shots were never identified. It has been assessed as "a professional hit" (McQuillar and Johnson 2010: 245). While rumors persist that Tupac remains alive, it was reported widely that Tupac died from gunshot wounds on September 13, 1996. Less than six months later, on March 9, 1997, Biggie Smalls was murdered in Los Angeles (Lynskey 2011). Linked in death as in life, Biggie also was killed in an unsolved drive-by shooting.

During interviews with male African youth, including former child soldiers, I regularly would be asked if I knew whether Tupac really was dead. Many contended that Tupac must have survived the 1996 shooting: how could a dead man release a long string of new songs after his passing? This fact alone proved to them that Tupac had never died. More than two decades since Tupac's alleged demise, claims that he remains alive continue (Reslen 2018).

While the starting point of "Hit 'Em Up" is Tupac's alleged affair with Biggie's estranged wife, Faith Evans, it is Tupac's direct and explicit references to violent revenge that are central to its worldwide and enduring appeal. Much in the song is actively rebellious. Near the start of the song, and returning again in the final section, young women unapologetically repeat a single phrase referring to theft. The statement arrives as declarative philosophy: this is what

Tupac and his Outlawz rap group do (the Outlawz members Hussain Fatal, Yaki Kadafi, and E.D.I. Mean each contribute incendiary passages to the song). The women don't sing the words as much as state them: crime is a mere refrain in this completely unapologetic song. The world is upside down, the song suggests, so why not steal? As his listeners already know, Tupac's oeuvre is full of details about the unjust system that traps him in a world of inequity, violence, and bigotry. Unlike John Rambo, Tupac spoke out boldly about his place in the world, accepting the controversy and misunderstandings that his analysis invited.

Tupac and the Outlawz present themselves as rebels as well as musicians. The refrain of "Hit 'Em Up" reflects their insurrectionist legal code. Reach for your pistols and notify the police as soon as you see Tupac, they instruct. You tried but failed to kill him. Now Tupac is coming to secure his vengeance, inevitably and without fear. The song's climax is fevered, relentless, and spellbinding. Tupac predicts that Biggie, Puffy, and all of their East Side colleagues will receive his vengeance. It may not seem right to kill others, but that's the way it is. The aggression mounts as he unleashes a torrent of alarming threats. He wants his enemies to suffer before they die. He will eliminate all of their children. The scorching song ends with a declarative statement about being killers, which is repeated several times. "Hit 'Em Up" transcends context: the direct expressions of targeted rage have the power to reach listeners virtually anywhere, as long as listeners know just a bit of English. The song is, essentially, a personal declaration of war. It is difficult to imagine another song as terrifying as this.[2]

Repeatedly, Tupac seems to search for curse words that can express his fury appropriately. He comes up short. He employs the same English language swear word for mother-son incest (motherfucker) twenty times in "Hit 'Em Up," fourteen of which are applied near the song's end, when Tupac's rage peaks. Set into context, "motherfucker" can serve up contrasting meanings. On one hand, it signals condemnation: "a despicable or very unpleasant person or thing." Yet the very same curse word can register a positive impression: "a person or thing of a specified kind, especially one that is formidable, remarkable, or impressive in some way" (Lexico, n.d.). In addition to "motherfucker," Tupac employs other methods to emasculate his adversaries. In an early passage, Tupac uses "bitch" twice to denigrate his enemies. Bitch refers to a female dog or "a malicious, spiteful, or overbearing woman—sometimes used as a generalized term of abuse" (Merriam-Webster, n.d.). In this case, Tupac appears to use "bitch" to humiliate the men who are his adversaries, probably to communicate the following: "a man who willingly or unwillingly submits to the will and control of a dominant partner in a sexual relationship, especially with another man, as in prison bitch" (Dictionary.com, n.d.). Then, near the end of the song, Tupac asks whether one of his adversaries has sickle cell anemia. It is a reference to sickle cell disease, which "is an inherited blood disorder that affects approximately 8 percent of African-Americans" (American Society of Hematology, n.d.). Tupac's biting reference aims to further humiliate his opponents by accusing them of elemental weakness.

The inflammatory, intentionally provocative nature of "Hit 'Em Up" naturally attracted considerable attention. "When the song dropped, it was too hot to touch," one analyst observed (Williams 2016). For Tupac, "the song that basically declared war on the East Coast" dramatically increased concerns over his personal security (McQuillar and Johnson 2010: 225). Eventually he wore a bulletproof vest, "on even short walks to the store" (Joseph 2006: 58). The song also inspired intense criticism. It "spits vengeful and mean-spirited lyrics," one scholar contended (Stanford 2011: 18). It constituted "a full-out, bloody, lyrical assault," one biographer stated (Joseph 2006: 54). The authors of another biography blasted the song, considering it "not a battle record. It was not a song. It shouldn't even be called music. It was simply rage unhinged" (McQuillar and Johnson 2010: 223).

But was it? Tupac Shakur had a knack for connecting with young people around the world, and "Hit 'Em Up" is expertly constructed to express rage and inspire fear and awe. The song's accent on violent revenge, in fact, may have resonated across the world in part because that feeling is so common. Homer's *Iliad*, written in perhaps 750 BC, opens with a request: "Goddess, sing me the anger, of Achilles" (in Kline 2009).[3] The "wrath" of Achilles rests at the center of the famous poem. One analyst observed:

> Achilles does not fit modern sensibilities. He is a killer, arguably a rapist, certainly a pillager. He is sulky, high-strung and oh boy, is he temperamental. He can be pitiless—actively enjoying the iron in his heart—and he can be murderously cruel. Yet there is still something fundamental about him to which we can all relate, even if it is also something particularly hard to rationalise and explain. He is faster, sharper, bigger, brighter and more important than other men. He is more beautiful. He rides on deeper emotional currents (when Achilles is upset, he is *seriously* upset). He is semi-divine and wholly precious. . . .
>
> Achilles in short, is a hero and taps into a need that most of us have to worship and admire. (Jordison 2016, emphasis in original)

Tupac Shakur's enduring popularity has much in common with Achilles: both are flawed, mercurial, yet deeply admired heroic figures.

The powerful responses that Tupac Shakur inspired divide into three camps. Two are situated largely within the United States. There have been "authors who emphasize[d] Tupac's intellectual gifts, humanitarian impulse, and outspoken critique of racism and injustice. These writers seek to contextualize Tupac's pejorative behavior by calling attention to his experiences as a son of the Black Power movement and growing up as a disadvantaged young Black male." In contrast, "Tupac's critics" have stressed "his impetuous and reckless behavior, accentuate his confrontations with the criminal justice system, and condemn his angry lyrics" (Stanford 2011: 4). Finally, there is an enormous third group. This group neither features judgements of Tupac's contradictory life and artistry nor is contained within a U.S. context.

To appreciate this huge third audience, consider that "Hit 'Em Up" has been categorized as nothing more than a "diss" song (a slang term for "to treat with disrespect or contempt" [Merriam-Webster, n.d.]), albeit "the most savage diss track ever" (Williams 2016). But reading the song merely as a diss requires the listener to view Tupac's words about murder and war as metaphorical. From this perspective, his alarming threats are symbolic and meant only to humiliate, as if Tupac didn't really mean what he said. However, that take runs counter to Tupac's reputation for incisive honesty: he was known and admired for fearlessly telling it like it was and never holding back. A literal reading of "Hit 'Em Up" suggests that nothing in the song requires interpretation. Taking Tupac at his word has had traction in war zones. American soldiers, for example, have used "Hit 'Em Up" as a wartime soundtrack. In Iraq, it was among the top songs that troops used to prepare them to, in the words of one soldier, "go kill or do whatever you have to do" (Serpick 2006).[4]

From the third perspective, Tupac neither is deserving of condemnation nor in need of contextualization. To be sure, Tupac sometimes behaved rashly or recklessly, occasionally got into trouble, and was prone to angry outbursts. But this is not "bad" or "pejorative behavior" as much as a handful of dimensions of a young person's impulses and life experience. The same Tupac who blasted forth with threats and furor in "Hit 'Em Up" at other times poetically expressed political activism and empathy for others, in addition to detailing a life where poor, young Black Americans are trapped in a denigrating and life-threatening existence. The complex of emotions and ideas that Tupac communicated led one analyst to conclude that "young people in many parts of the world have grafted their own experiences of alienation, of physical and psychological trauma, onto Tupac's iconography. The hyper-masculinity and glamour that Tupac exuded has led many young men to embrace him as a model of manhood, while interpretations of his narratives as reflections of universal frustration, suffering, and grievance insured a wide appeal. This helps to explain why Tupac has been seen as alternatively fashionable, inspirational, and prophetic" (Prestholdt 2009: 201).

According to Lock, songs by Tupac are examples of "cultural products," which she defines as "a form of text, which is read, interpreted, adapted and appropriated by different audiences in their own way." Audiences interpret cultural products on their own terms, creating "their own meaning, depending on a multitude of factors including cultural background, gender, knowledge and personal experience, position in the social hierarchy and so on" (Lock 2007: 2). It is in this way that the varied works of Tupac Shakur, just like the music and images of Bob Marley, the Rambo Trilogy films, and other cultural products in the global stratosphere, are received and interpreted.[5]

Tupac's influence on the practice of war in Sierra Leone connects to the experiences of male youth in Sierra Leone. As detailed earlier, the tradition of powerful leaders exploiting male youth extends back to the slave era. Since that time, male youth have served as slaves, war boys, and thugs in the service of others. They have been castigated as lumpens, hoodlums, gangsters, criminals, bandits, misfits, vagrants, and still more. Many have faced punishing life and work conditions and find it difficult if not impossible to marry and gain recognition as adults (Richards 2006a: 203–204). Add to this the severe government constraints on expression by Sierra Leonean musicians, together with a widespread facility across Sierra Leone with some degree of English (due to the use of Krio as the nation's lingua franca), and the result is a mass of widely denigrated and detested young people with limited options and a particular fondness for the rebellious music of reggae and rap musicians, particularly Marley and Tupac.

The most extensive consideration of Tupac Shakur's influence in Sierra Leone is by Jeremy Prestholdt. He notes that "Tupac's narration of violence has gained particular relevance in times of war." He then cites a succession of war zones where "combatants in many locales have drawn on Tupac imagery." An "Aboriginal uprising" on the island of Guadalcanal "claimed Tupac as a guiding figure for their movement." Rebel militia and government troops both used Tupac T-shirts as uniforms in the Democratic Republic of the Congo. The same trend persisted among "multiple rebel groups" in northern Côte d'Ivoire. In Sierra Leone, he found that Tupac, in addition to Bob Marley and Rambo, "were critical frames of reference" for youth in part because "they represented qualities to which young combatants aspired" (Prestholdt 2009: 202, 203).[6] Unlike John Rambo, Tupac offered Sierra Leonean combatants "a symbolic package" that was "more complex." That complexity was grounded in Tupac's apparent ability to empathize with young Sierra Leonean combatants while setting an example for fearlessness. Tupac "not only appeared to understand and sympathize with combatants, but he could articulate their anxieties while representing the kind of invincibility and bravery to which most combatants aspired." In addition, "Tupac offered an idealized image of black masculinity. He embodied much of what young Sierra Leoneans dreamed of: strength, intelligence, and wealth" (208).

Another element of Tupac's appeal stemmed from the fact that Tupac's "justifications of violence were more compelling" than action film characters like Rambo. "In image and word," Prestholdt asserts, "Tupac offered a compelling anchor for the frustrations and aspirations of young combatants who suffered horrible violence and, in turn, exercised extreme cruelty" (208, 214). Some military units used Tupac's image and word to help transform them into unusually vicious killers. This would include the West Side Boys, who collectively employed the "images and ideals of the American rap artist Tupac Shakur . . . to create a group mythology and common solidarity in a 'me against the world' fashion" (Utas and Jörgel 2008: 493, 498).

Tucker states that "rebel soldiers [in Sierra Leone] wore Tupac T-shirts, painted murals of him, added his slogans to their vehicles and loudly played his music as they rolled into battle" (Tucker 2013: 13). The reality of Tupac's influence was more precise. Field research uncovered eight attributes that military forces drew from Tupac's music and reputation:

1. **Personalized inspiration for male ground troops.** Marley's influence flowed from the top of rebel and military command down to foot soldiers. Tupac's did not: he appears to have been used mainly at lower levels of command, and then with troops on the ground. Unlike Rambo, Tupac's influence linked to attitude and look more than specific military tactics.

2. **Bravery and fearlessness.** The center of "Tupac System" in war was to curse and dress like him, and be as proud, courageous, and unafraid as him. Tupac System encouraged followers to dominate with violence. Fighters following Tupac System sought to embody the thug aura that Tupac detailed in his "All Eyez on Me" song: living a life of dominance and defiance, using drugs, and always attracting attention.[7]

3. **A distinctive military style.** Following or "becoming" like Tupac started by looking like him: going from ragtag to stylish by wearing a Tupac T-shirt, creating a "turn-up" (rolling up the trousers to the knee for one leg only), and wearing tattoos and a bandanna like Tupac.

4. **A soundtrack for battle.** Before, during, and after military attacks, music and drugs powered the mindset for violence. Beginning early in the civil war, patterns emerged of RUF rebel soldiers attacking towns to secure much more than food or children. They also sought batteries for their cassette decks, cassette tapes of popular music, and T-shirts, especially those featuring Tupac or Bob Marley. During Operation No Living Thing, playing tapes of Tupac or Marley after taking over Freetown neighborhoods was common.

5. **A spectacularly violent masculinity.** References to violence, or having no alternative to using violence, is a consistent theme running across many of Tupac's songs. The sexualized, supermasculine side of Tupac (including the frightening "Hit 'Em Up") is present only in some songs. This is a characteristic that soldiers in Sierra Leone emphasized. Tupac's masculine aggression (in some songs) probably explains why most female youth did not warm to Tupac's work during the war years.

6. **Using drugs to fuel battle ferocity.** References to drug use occur in many of Tupac's songs. He and his colleagues take drugs and like drugs. In Sierra Leone, Bob Marley was connected explicitly to heavy marijuana use while Tupac was linked to cocaine use *and* extreme violence.

7. **Justified violence and criminality.** Living life as a thug, taking money and becoming millionaires, using violence: some of Tupac's songs expressed justifications for lawbreaking and violence. But much more than that, they seem to have been interpreted in ways that the artist did not intend.

   A shining example of this is "Only God Can Judge Me." Many in Sierra Leone evidently understood this song as a justification for any act that fighters committed, hence the writing of "Only God Can Judge" on the side of some rebel vehicles entering Freetown during Operation No Living Thing. Yet the song's lyrics tell a different story. In one passage, Tupac talks about Black males caught up in dangerous lives. Due to stress and fear, they carry guns, even while knowing that it could get them killed. The police simply do not understand what it's like to be a Black male.[8] The theme of entrapment, so common in many of Tupac's songs, seems to have been overlooked in this particular song in Sierra Leone. What persisted instead was the idea that only God has the ability to judge the actions of combatants, including those of superviolent fighters.

8. **Acceptance (no matter who you are or what you did).** One of the most important features of Tupac's music is his repeated emphasis on forgiveness and acceptance. It is featured, for example, at the end of perhaps his most famous song about alienation and entrapment, "Me against the World." Here, Tupac raps directly to the listener. Life is difficult, but don't give up. Things will get better. Even when things look dire, retain your pride and self-confidence. Deal with difficulty. The hard times will pass.[9] Such encouragement was a component of other songs as well, including "Keep Ya Head Up."[10] They are examples of Tupac, a talented and stylish Black American male youth, connecting to Sierra Leoneans as an admirable, authentic, and honest friend from a faraway land.

The Application

While Bob Marley was popular across Sierra Leone, including with many adults, Tupac was divisive, controversial, and provocative. One word illuminated his unique renown: *fuck*. Together with the mother-son incest curse word, "motherfucker," "fuck" seemed to get everyone's attention in Sierra Leone. "Tupac used words that were not considered Sierra Leonean," a Freetown journalist explained, "like 'fucking bitch.'" Following the war, a government official summed up the alarm and threat that young people registered when they used the "fuck" word: "Everyone has become lawless. Some male and female youth can say, 'You just fuck off.' They lack those tender utterances. If you say this, you will find yourself useless. *Fityai* is the order of the day. There is so much *fityai*. This is a lawless thing."

Tupac Shakur was the ultimate "fityai boy." In many of his songs that were popular in Sierra Leone, Tupac was relentlessly confrontational, and he used inflammatory words routinely. His messages and style pushed back hard against the conformist ways that Sierra Leonean elders expected for a young person to dress, comport themselves, and socially engage. "Tupac," said a middle-aged man who directed an NGO working with ex-combatants, "is the kind of musician who inspires youth to commit violence in the society." He had a particular distaste for Tupac's many tattoos because, in Sierra Leone, "this is interpreted as a sign of violence: if one can be so wicked against oneself, one can do even worse [things] against others." Tupac inspired revulsion (and sometimes fear) among many adults as readily as he inspired emulation among many male youth. Traditional culture in Sierra Leone positioned young people as servile juniors in the patrimonial hierarchy. Tupac's work rebelled against all of that. It came across as youth centered and radical, making it easy to see why he was a hero to youth and a threat to elders simultaneously.

Although the entire RUF organization embraced Bob Marley, from Foday Sankoh down to their many field units, feelings about Tupac were complicated. The following commentary from a top RUF official illustrates the organization's conflicted view of Tupac and his powerful influence over their young male fighters. The official began by exuding a view shared by many older Sierra Leoneans: "Tupac is a rude boy. I don't have much time to study his behavior. Of course, some loved him and sang his songs, like 'motherfucker.' All these kinds of things. But Tupac culture doesn't fit [mainstream Sierra Leonean] culture. He has no shirt on his body, he's cursing, he does things to women [that is, sexual violence]." But then his assessment of Tupac shifted. Tupac's influence also served useful wartime purposes for the RUF: "For the young ones [in the RUF], yes of course, Tupac had some justifications. 'All Eyez on Me' meant that everyone was blaming the RUF for atrocities. 'Only God Can Judge' [referred to] all types of crimes in this country. It refers to the RUF, whether true or false, because the RUF started the rebellion in this country." In the view of this official, two of Tupac's most popular and influential songs promoted an interpretation of atrocity and criminal behavior that seemed to justify and help the RUF push back against harsh critiques. As will be described, the official's RUF-centric take on the meaning of Tupac's songs was not shared by male youth who venerated Tupac and employed what came to be known as Tupac Tactics. For them, Tupac's influence centered more directly on youth rebellion. As a male youth who became a refugee following the January 6 Freetown assault noted, "Tupac says he's against the world, and the rebels also say they're against the world."

As examined in chapter 13, Tupac's power to unsettle Sierra Leoneans during the war was on full display in the January 6 invasion of Freetown in early 1999. "When the rebels came into the city," a Freetown resident remembered, "many of the rebels were wearing the 'All Eyez on Me' T-shirt. They said that they were freedom fighters and against ECOMOG. They rode jeeps with the doors removed, so they could jump out of the car. They were crying out '*Wi de na ya!*' [We are here!]." In the wake of January 6, he explained that people in Freetown "considered Tupac as a bad influence on youth, with his drugs, gangsterism, and his tattoos. He was the head of a gang."

Analysis of field interviews revealed three prominent indicators of Tupac's widespread influence in the war theater. The first was the common notion that anyone wearing a Tupac T-shirt was a rebel. This was particularly the case in the latter war years (1998–2001). Indeed, nearly everyone seemed to share the idea that black Tupac T-shirts were rebel uniforms. Many rebels wore them during attacks. Some also had tattoos. ECOMOG troops, in response, were known to consider anyone wearing a Tupac T-shirt, or a tattoo, as a rebel. As one youth recalled from the later war years, "If you wore any tattoo on your arms or a Tupac T-shirt, you could be killed [by ECOMOG troops] straight away." Others corroborated this claim. Rebel units, in turn, considered every Tupac T-shirt "government property" (that is, theirs). "They'd wear the Tupac T-shirt and take the Tupac T-shirt from any civilian," a second male youth remembered. "Those who resisted were beaten." This policy reportedly began in 1992, in Koidu. The victim of a gang rape underscored the meaning of the T-shirt during the war. She presumed all five rapists were rebels "because they were wearing Tupac [Shakur] T-shirts" (Physicians for Human Rights 2002: 75).

A second significant indicator of Tupac's influence was cocaine. While marijuana use among RUF and AFRC troops was pervasive (and reported to be common among their CDF and national army adversaries, as well as some ECOMOG fighters), followers of Tupac favored cocaine. "Tupac is a great man," an ex-rebel combatant explained in 2010. "Some people believe he died but Tupac is still alive. He took cocaine. Today [in Sierra Leone], many youth take cocaine." Cocaine, smoked or applied via a "plaster" (inserted into an incision, such as at the temple), became an additional key component of Tupac System during the war. In addition to following the Tupac dress code—wearing the Tupac T-shirt and perhaps also having tattoos, a shaved head, vest, and bandanna, and wearing trousers in the "turn-up" style—authentic Tupac followers in rebel forces evidently also were high on cocaine (as well as other hard drugs) regularly. The emphasis on hard drug use served specific purposes for Tupac-oriented fighters. A former RUF fighter explained the significance of the drugs: "Those using Tupac Tactics were the frontline fighters using light weapons like AK-47 and G3 [a German-made machine gun]. Some used drugs like plaster, some even injected drugs. They'd say, 'We need to deaden ourselves before fighting.'" Tupac-influenced fighters also smoked marijuana, but it could be spiked to make the impact stronger. An ex-combatant explained the process. "You open a bullet and pour the gunpowder into a spoon," he explained. Next, "you scratch it on fire—it blazes. You scrape [the remains] out of the spoon, blend it with marijuana, and smoke it."

A third indicator of Tupac's influence during the war years was his ability to inspire fearlessness. This orientation played a central role in Tupac Tactics. A former commander for the West Side Boys saluted Tupac and explained his sway over WSB fighters: "We love Tupac because he's not afraid of anything. He loves violence. He loves to be angry. If he wants something, he takes it. He's not afraid to die for taking something. We love him." The veneration of a particular image of Tupac Shakur—the one that emerges from songs such as "Hit 'Em Up" and "All Eyez on Me"—promotes Tupac's aggression, righteousness, and disregard for his own safety. In Sierra Leone, this was Tupac imagined as the perfect gangster—an entirely different sort of warrior than those specializing in Rambo Tactics. In the RUF, Rambo and his forest-based techniques were mainstream. Tupac Tactics, in contrast, seemed to be merely tolerated. Still, surrounded by warfare, adapting Tupac's aura of menace for the battlefield could be inspirational. Heavy drug use, supported by Tupac System dress and style, prepared Tupac-guided warriors to employ Tupac Tactics. It was a mindset more than a set of specific techniques, and it wasn't for everyone. Descriptions from practitioners of Tupac Tactics—one from the early war years, the second from the later war years—shed light on what they were and how they worked.

A former RUF practitioner of Tupac Tactics from the early 1990s first set the scene. Although Bob Marley was everywhere, he had been around a while. Then came Tupac. He was a sensation, completely new to Sierra Leoneans. So was rap music. During these years (1991–1993), the ex-RUF combatant explained how Tupac "was very popular among the youth in Sierra Leone. Everybody knew him. Most of them, the youth, they got so excited about Tupac songs. And at that time, Sierra Leone was in the heat of war. So that's how they got to use Tupac for war." This was the period when some field units divided into Bob Marley and Tupac Groups, reflecting the dual popularity of Marley and Tupac with young Sierra Leoneans. It also was when Tupac Tactics emerged. The ex-fighter first warned that "Tupac is not a training." Instead, "If you are rude, indeed, you already conquered the Tupac. If you're afraid, you can't join the Tupac Group, the gang group. Either you don't fight or you join the Bob Marley Group. At times, the Tupac Group would say, 'Let's attack,' and the Bob Marley Group would say, 'Let's wait.' Tupac Tactics is not training, it's just rudeness." To explain how it worked, the ex-fighter said that rebel youth were highly motivated to attack towns where Bob Marley and Tupac T-shirts were available. Tupac T-shirts attracted the most attention. "The rebels came into the towns to get the new Tupac T-shirts," he explained, particularly those still wrapped in plastic. "Any time they would launch an attack on a town, they would loot the shops." They also looted Tupac music cassettes and batteries for their music players. In fact, "as soon as they [would] attack, the music [was] going on. Boys and girls enter playing the stereo tape of Tupac [on a portable player] as the attack is going on." With Tupac's music blaring, "the rebels [would] begin to abuse the civilians, using Tupac as their model. They wanted to abuse them, kill them, using Tupac language." They also looted the pharmacies.

"This," the former RUF soldier explained, "is Tupac Tactics. They knew if you do that, you will succeed." These tactics actually began in advance of attacks, when commanders would give their young soldiers marijuana, crack cocaine, heroin (via injection), and a series of pills (one called Top-Up, another called 5-Day Special, and valium) that were ground into powder and inhaled. "When you inhale [the drugs]," he recalled, "you even feel you can eat human beings like a chicken in front of you." During attacks, it was important to remember that "Tupac doesn't fear anyone." If the fighters are that fearless and "if they take the Tupac life, they will succeed because they know it's a thug life. They won't fear anybody and they won't spare anybody." After describing another attack, the ex-RUF soldier explained his take on why it was so successful: "We are more wicked than [other fighting groups] because we wear the Tupac T-shirt. We work like the Tupac, we gang, we have no soul, we have no fear. We kill everyone. Because of the hard drugs in our blood." Tupac Tactics combined heavy drug use, bravery, brutality, a Tupac soundtrack, and love of the defiant thug life he rapped about.

In this early example of Tupac Tactics, one can see the manipulations of commanders in the background: dividing their young fighters into Bob Marley and Tupac Groups, directing their soldiers' love of Marley and Tupac toward terror-based warfare, and filling them up with drugs prior to attacks to ensure a frightening impact. The impact differed with the West Side Boys in the later war years, since WSB commanders loved Tupac just as much as their followers. The WSB's strong collective identification with Tupac fed the ambitions of the outfit. The following, taken from an interview with five former WSB officers, reveals why and how the WSB applied Tupac Tactics in battle.

One ex-commander noted that some of the WSB leaders "went from school to the army" together. This aligns with analysis from Utas and Jörgel, who note that many WSB leaders came from military families and grew up together in Freetown's Wilberforce Barracks (2008: 492). While at school, "we started to imitate Tupac. We studied some of his ideology and skills from his music." Like many other Sierra Leonean male youth, they had no interest in other rap musicians, only Tupac Shakur. As one WSB officer explained, "We loved Tupac because he was a very hardcore N——, and we were behaving like Tupac. We always loved this guy, Tupac. We never loved any other rapper thugs, only Tupac. He didn't trust nobody unless it's himself. Too much self-belief: that is Tupac. If you want to be like Tupac, you must have self-belief. No fear: no fear, no war." The officer then shared the WSB's favorite songs of Tupac: two consistent favorites in Sierra Leone ("Hit 'Em Up" and "All Eyez on Me") was well as "Death around the Corner", "Me against the World", "Me and My Girlfriend" (a song about Tupac's gun), Trouble Song (probably "Troublesome '96"), and I'm Still Under Grave (probably "Cradle to the Grave"). Nearly all of them draw from the darker side of Tupac's body of work.

Tupac Tactics began in advance of attacks. One ex-officer explained how they used his music and language to get them in the mood for battle: "Whenever we prepared to fight, we listened to Shakur music to motivate us. We listened to Shakur's music to strengthen us and forget our problems. We said things to motivate us, like 'Hit them up, kill all the motherfuckin' souls, no compromise, kill all the fuckin' souls!'" This orientation, mixed with heavy drug use, prepared the WSB for battle. Their mental preparation focused on being as fearless and brave as Tupac. In describing one attack on an ECOMOG contingent, a former officer explained how WSB leaders inspired their forces with direct references to Tupac: "We attacked them; we had no fear of them. Our slogans were: 'We see death around the corner [a famous Tupac tune],' 'No die, no rest,' [and] 'Move fast, die young.' These were our slogans of Tupac. We used them to motivate our troops."

Once in battle, the merging of Tupac and terror—trying not to be terrified while creating terror in others—seemed to take over. The words "fuck" and "motherfucker" played big roles too. A WSB officer explained the orientation that the West Side Boys maintained during attacks: "Tupac didn't care to die [about dying]. Shoot anybody who tries to infiltrate him. Fuck everyone down that love him. Like you, motherfucker, you gotta fucking asshole. Fuck Mama, Fuck Biggie [a reference to 'Hit 'Em Up']! Tupac says what he's going to do, and then he does it." Recalling the WSB attacks on ECOMOG troops, he said, "When we attack them, we use the Tupac slang," such as "Till we die before it's over!" and "You motherfucker, fuck them! All on their side should die!" The officer explained, "We say this while firing the machine gun. We like these words when we're killing them. It's enjoyable when you're calling your enemy and you say, 'You motherfucker, you fuckin' N——! We kill you!'" Then, to demonstrate Tupac Tactics during battle, the five former West Side Boys commanders all jumped up and enacted what they did. All held imaginary machine guns. While firing them, they loudly shouted a mix of phrases, including "Die motherfucker, die!" and "Kill all you motherfuckers!" Their re-enactment filled the room, continuing for several minutes. Afterward, we all took a moment to settle down again.

The WSB also described Tupac Tactics as a means to trick their enemies. Again, the example used was ECOMOG.[11] The highest-ranking officer at the meeting (a former colonel and battalion commander) described the ruse. "We planned a tactic as if we'll surrender" to ECOMOG. During this period, the officers and their soldiers had not yet broken away to become the West Side Boys. They were still formally part of a sizable AFRC contingent led by SAJ Musa. The ex-officer said that those in front tied white cloths around their foreheads and to the muzzles of their guns, and held the guns over their heads. With this, "ECOMOG allowed us to come into Kabala, their headquarters." He stated that "ECOMOG [soldiers] were dancing, saying, 'Oh God, this war is over!'" Once inside the city, SAJ Musa gave the order in the following fashion: "What are you waiting for? Shoot and kill these guys. These are bad guys who came to kill you." At that, the AFRC soldiers in front lowered their guns and began shooting ECOMOG officers and soldiers. The former colonel considered the hoax as a component of Tupac Tactics. To explain how this connected to Tupac Shakur, he simply said, "We imitate everything about Tupac."

Tupac created space for male youth in Sierra Leone. He exemplified defiant liberation from social confinement and emasculation. No one could keep Tupac down. Yet during the war, love of Tupac revealed the high degree of fear that combatants experienced. Persistent reverence for Tupac's courage, following Tupac System and employing Tupac Tactics—including prodigious amounts of cursing, especially "fuck," which empowered users while unnerving battle adversaries and civilians generally—*still* were not enough. The warriors required (or were force-fed) lots and lots of drugs too. Being as stylishly audacious as Tupac may have been the goal. But a fighter couldn't even approach Tupac Shakur's gallantry without drugs.

CHAPTER 18

Drastic Measures

They Want to Scare Us (and They Do)

It is not clear how many people perished in Sierra Leone's civil war. For a long time, the most common estimate was 50,000.[1] Other estimates ranged between 10,000–30,000 and 70,000–75,000.[2] Whatever number is closest to reality, obviously it is a large number of deaths, particularly when the nation's population amounted to less than 5 million citizens during the war.[3] The contrast with Burundi's civil war is instructive. The twin civil wars largely were concurrent and lasted for about the same length of time: Sierra Leone's began in 1991 and expired in 2002 (about eleven years) while Burundi's conflict started in 1993 and ended in 2003 (about ten years).[4] Both African nations are small and have ranked as among the world's poorest for decades.

Yet the nature of warfare was remarkably different. The estimated number of deaths from Burundi's civil war is 300,000, four to thirty times as many as the number of those killed in Sierra Leone. The war broke into two phases of combat. The first was intense: massive slaughter at the outset (starting immediately after the assassination of the first-ever Hutu president, Melchior Ndadaye, on October 21, 1993). There were three kinds of killings: ethnic Hutu civilians (some closely associated with the slain president's party, some not) killing ethnic Tutsi civilians; national army soldiers (virtually all Tutsi) massacring Hutu civilians; and Tutsi civilians (with some help from Rwandan Tutsi refugees) killing Hutu civilians (Reyntjens 1993: 581, cited in Bundervoet 2009: 361). While the ethnic proportions of those who died is unclear, total numbers have been developed. Between October 21 and December 31, there were an estimated 116,059 casualties. That number includes more than a hundred thousand who were killed in the final week of October (UNFPA 2002, cited in Bundervoet 2009: 361). Atrocities of many kinds took place during the late October massacres. A United Nations commission also concluded that genocide was committed against Tutsi civilians during this brief period.[5]

The second phase of Burundi's civil war was less intense but still deadly.

After the initial week or so of the conflict, the remaining ten years left approximately two hundred thousand dead. The Tutsi-dominated national military rounded up Hutu civilians and deposited them in "regroupment camps" that, for some periods of the war, held hundreds of thousands of people. Additionally, the nation's armed forces "indiscriminately attacked civilians, burned their homes, and engaged in extensive rape and beating," and killed hundreds. The national military, in addition, killed many civilians, including those "selectively murdered" because the government viewed them as having the potential to ignite opposition to their rule ("particularly Hutu with wealth or education"). Government troops even attacked "Those suffering from chronic malnutrition," as malnourishment was considered a telltale sign of having lived in Hutu rebel-controlled areas (HRW 1998a: 1). In addition, national soldiers "engaged in rape, arbitrary arrest, looting, and destruction of property."

Similarly, the Hutu rebel groups killed Tutsi civilians and Hutu suspected of collaborating with the Tutsi-led government. Yet the armed insurgents "killed far fewer" people than the national army. Reportedly, that was only because they were "less well armed" and had fewer civilians to target: Tutsi comprise a small ethnic minority in Burundi and the national army protected many Tutsi civilians from attack. The insurgents nonetheless killed many, destroyed property, committed rape and injury to civilians, and even held some civilians as forced laborers (2).

Burundi's war featured high levels of civilian slaughter, particularly at the outset. The national army was formidable, well equipped, reasonably well trained, and far larger in size.[6] The fighting was ruthlessly ethnic in nature. Sierra Leone's war, in contrast, was quite different. The SLA was pathetically weak: poorly armed, trained, provisioned, and led. The ethnic dimension was present to some degree, but not in the foreground. Wartime killings were not genocidal. Perhaps more than anything else, war in Sierra Leone was fought on different terms, and in different ways. The primary purpose was to terrorize, not annihilate.

Terror war practices in Sierra Leone aimed to deliver messages, express rage, demonstrate power, send civilians fleeing (particularly from diamond-rich areas, except those needed to mine), radically upend traditional norms (such as respect for elders), and dehumanize people. A common RUF tactic was to let civilians know in advance that they would be attacking soon, so that some villagers would start to panic and flee. Such an approach is antithetical to war practices in Burundi, where adversaries sought to eliminate the ethnic opposition, not scare them away. But in Sierra Leone, rebel groups in particular mainly sought to terrorize and torment. While the war was indeed deadly and many thousands perished, terror warfare exerted its power over those who remained alive.

The Terror Performers

Sierra Leone's war did not look like warfare in classic films. To begin with, "there were very few battles between the combat groups. Most of the 'battles' were direct attacks on the civilian population" (TRC 2004a: 564). It was a tough place to be an ordinary citizen, as just about every military outfit viewed at least some civilians as favoring their foes or being secret members of an enemy group. Traditional norms of all kinds were under assault too, most particularly by the RUF, who decimated sacred initiation sites and humiliated elders of all kinds. Male attackers of every stripe pounced on a near-endless succession of females (another rebel specialty, addressed in the next chapter). Soldiers wore black T-shirts with the faces of famous pop culture icons on the front, often with bandannas and perhaps with an element or two from an ordinary military uniform mixed in. Relatively few male attackers wore women's clothes or entered villages and neighborhoods naked. Some attackers were girls. Some males wore dreadlocks, others had shaved heads and tattoos. Rebel groups were fond of bringing their soundtrack with them, playing Bob Marley, Tupac Shakur, or other musicians on portable stereos while making their assault. Having reached their target, rebel groups in particular stole, burned, cut, raped, disemboweled, demeaned, tortured, and abducted ordinary people. For part of the war, some of those looking like rebels were part-time sobel imposters. In other cases, attackers ate parts of people or drank human blood (or both). And while they killed some people, the fighters terrorized the strong majority of civilians but left them alive. Just about every single attacker was high as a kite on drugs. Not least, many of the soldiers were not just youthful. The most brutal aggressors often were the youngest children.

What took place when opposing forces clashed? In most cases, the RUF lost. Cohen calculates that the RUF were involved in 75 percent of all attacks (or ambushes) and actual battles over the course of the war.[7] This makes sense, since for the first six years of the war (until the AFRC came onto the scene), the RUF comprised the only official enemy force. The RUF lost nearly two out every three military encounters (63.9 percent). By Cohen's estimate, that amounted to 186 defeats (or, in RUF parlance, "withdraws") out of 291 battles, an average of well over one defeat per month across the course of the war (2013b: 474).[8]

All of these military encounters featured a style of warfare common in Africa. The sort of combat envisioned as a "battle" in the West is "virtually non-existent" in African contexts, where there generally are few "pitched battles between clearly defined forces engaging each other directly and with lethal intent." The primary style of warfare in Sierra Leone was the ambush, where the opponent is not destroyed but forced to retreat, hopefully leaving their weapons behind. In such an environment, "the main aim of firing weapons is not to kill as many of the enemy as possible but rather to display the superior power of one's own force and induce the enemy to flee." AK-47 machine guns, RPG-7s (Soviet-made grenade launchers), and mortars were fired. They were all noisy but "less useful when engaging fighters in the forest if the aim is to actually hit them." AKs routinely were fired "from the hip or held high in the air, dispersing bullets in all directions but straight ahead." This "emphasis on display over accurate targeting" supported the notion that military success connected to "effectively outperforming the enemy in terms of the display of power" (Wlodarczyk 2009: 119, 127, 128). War as theater, in short.

Accordingly, the T-shirts, dreadlocks, shaved heads, tattoos, bandannas, vests, and other elements of rebel outfits, as well as the charms, amulets, and ritually prepared protective clothing of the Kamajors and other CDF forces (such as the *ronko* vest), promoted the idea of performance against enemies and before civilians. The riot of bullets, mortars, and grenades flying in virtually all directions also cultivated a common secondary result: civilians getting hit by bullets during "crossfire" by enemy forces (to say they were hit by a stray bullet would be inaccurate because aiming a gun was a casual affair). In such an environment, the magical power of amulets and charms designed to deflect bullets held sway: a fighter wearing them could walk through a battle/ ambush, come out unscathed, and automatically prove their power. Alternatively, British forces could enter the scene and "provide a shock to the system of war that was in play." In a conflict where civilians were the main targets and pitched battles were rare, Sierra Leonean fighters were no match for forces trained to shoot straight and kill armed adversaries—many, if necessary. Even a small number of British troops could eviscerate military units such as the West Side Boys. The mercenary group Executive Outcomes was similarly effective in 1995–1996, largely because they also sought to kill their armed foes in battle. Neither group demonstrated Sierra Leone–style warfare.

The success of an ambush depends on three factors: "superior knowledge of the terrain, good intelligence and the successful execution of surprise" (Wlodarczyk 2009: 141, 142, 121). AFRC troops were experts in ambushes, as were CDF forces such as the Kamajors. The RUF trained for ambushes (and learned to "withdraw" from those that failed). In Sierra Leone, the targets mostly were ordinary civilians. Many interviews with former rebel, AFRC, and Kamajor combatants included discussions of ambush techniques, such as studying the village, town, or city in advance from afar as well as planting recce spies to gather intelligence in the target communities. Commanders then took the gathered data and devised ambush plans. Attacks usually began late at night or just before dawn. For rebels, a preferred attack time frame was just before or during festive holidays, when many people would be sleeping off big celebrations. It was a Charles Taylor specialty.

Examining what took place next—after a military unit entered a village, town, or urban neighborhood composed of ordinary civilians—revealed several tendencies. From the outset of the war in 1991, rebel forces abducted many people, converting selected civilians into forced laborers. In addition, "almost without exception, sexual violence against women accompanied the arrival of RUF/NPFL forces in a locality." Rebels also began burning homes and targeting "government and traditional authorities" (Smith, Gambette, and Longley 2004: 21). All of these acts created panic, mass displacement, and hunger. The first hand or arm amputation reportedly took place in Kono in November 1992. It appears to have been an act of improvisation and was not yet a specific rebel strategy. Ominously, the first reported victim, Tamba Ngauja, had both of his hands cut off by an RUF soldier after two civilians nearby had been beheaded (TRC 2004e: 13, 14). As the war moved ahead, certain atrocities became commonplace: looting and burning houses (including burning residents alive), sexual violence, torturing civilians in various ways (including amputations), abduction, forced labor, and killing people. Punishments meted out against civilians by SLA or CDF forces could be just as fierce. All of this illustrates how drastically the nature of warfare has changed over time. As Physicians for Human Rights (PHR) has noted, "In World War I, approximately 5% of casualties were civilians, whereas in the 1990s it is estimated that 80% of war casualties were civilians, many of whom are women and children" (2002: 35).

An investigation of 40,242 separate human rights violations, extracted from the statements delivered to the Sierra Leone Truth and Reconciliation Commission (TRC) by 7,706 victims and perpetrators in Sierra Leone's war, found that forced displacement and abduction were the most common violations. Mostly males were killed while mostly females were raped (TRC 2004d: 9, 13). The TRC also revealed these conspicuous group tendencies:

- The RUF "carried out the majority of violations and abuses" during the war. They also were the "pioneers" of forced recruitment, including of children, and bear "overwhelming responsibility for the widespread use of drugs by its members."

- The AFRC registered the second-highest number of human rights abuses and violations. They also "demonstrated a 'specialisation' in the practice of amputations" near the end of the war (1998–1999).

- The Kamajors were "responsible for almost all the CDF violations reported after 1996," which were significant (TRC 2004c: 11). This suggests that all the other CDF units maintained significantly higher levels of discipline within their ranks. In terms of being a terror actor, the Kamajors stood out. While the RUF and Kamajors both practiced cannibalism (TRC 2004a: 497), the Kamajors alone practiced forced cannibalism (that is, compelling others to eat humans or drink human blood).

- Every single Sierra Leonean armed group (RUF, AFRC and the West Side Boys, the CDF and the SLA) perpetrated sexual violence against females (TRC 2004c: 11, 15).

The main focus of Sierra Leone's combatants was perpetrating terror tactics against civilians. The remainder of this chapter unpacks the key elements of this approach to warfare, particularly among rebel units.

Smoking Properly: The Marijuana-Marley Through Line

In a survey of more than one thousand former combatants in Sierra Leone's war, most respondents reported that they received food from their faction but not drugs (with the exception of the West Side Boys, most of whom reported that they had received both) (Humphreys and Weinstein 2004: 27). The two issues—food and drugs—have complicated histories in Sierra Leone's war. The search for food often was a near-constant concern for rebel forces. This partly was a function of terror warfare: their forces routinely employed terror tactics to drive away those civilians whom they did not capture. Over time, pushing farmers from their fields and merchants from their goods reduced the availability of food to eat. Most rebel groups thus faced regular food shortages. Their leaders supplied them with food when it was available (usually after soldiers had secured it and carried it to their commanders), an issue that will be among those addressed in the next section.

The survey's response that the majority of combatants—RUF, AFRC, SLA, and CDF (including Kamajors)—reported that they did not receive drugs from their factions is curious, since evidence to the contrary is overwhelming. Even the finding that around 75 percent of ex-WSB fighters said that they received drugs does not account for the quarter of their membership who said they did not. A sampling from researchers of the war points to the preponderance of drugs among fighting groups.[9] "The drug culture was central to the social practices of both soldiers and rebels in the war front," Yusuf Bangura reports (2004: 30). The TRC found that "a number of researchers who have investigated the conflict have concluded that the only way to explain the [human rights] violations that occurred must relate to the widespread use of drugs by the combatants." The TRC added their own assessment: "hard drugs were widely used in the conflict" (2004a: 562). In another survey of former combatants, "interviewees report smoking marijuana, being prepared for battle with injections of amphetamines, [and] taking crack cocaine or a cocktail of local substances including gunpowder" (Peters and Richards 1998: 186).

With this in mind, what might explain why most ex-fighters in the survey said they did not take any drugs during Sierra Leone's war? One possible reason is "a concern with truth telling." Many respondents may have wished to hide their wartime drug use. A second possibility is memory loss (Humphreys and Weinstein 2004: 16). This was an issue for a small number of former combatants whom I interviewed, who confessed to not remembering many details of what had gone on during their time as combatants. However, their reported cause was heavy (and frequently forced) drug use. A third possibility is intimated in the following comment from a study on the West Side Boys: "Locally grown marijuana was so frequently used that it was not even viewed as a drug proper" (Utas and Jörgel 2008: 499). This finding points to a different kind of reality: just like former WSB members, survey respondents for the Humphreys and Weinstein survey may not have considered marijuana a drug. Through this lens, the survey results suddenly become understandable. According to this third option, just over a third of former RUF and AFRC members used drugs in addition to marijuana, as well as a quarter of ex-SLA troops, a sliver of ex-CDF members, and three quarters of ex-WSBs.

Marijuana is a crop in Sierra Leone. It is not indigenous but arrived in the late 1960s and early 1970s. Almost immediately, Sierra Leoneans found that their climate—"warm, humid, with plentiful sun and rain—was ideal for cultivating marijuana." There were additional benefits. Marijuana is more profitable than other crops and grows year-round. Cultivating and selling djamba in Sierra Leone is illegal. If apprehended, farmers may have to pay a sizable bribe to policemen. But many obviously consider growing and marketing well worth the risk: sales from a mere 200-square-meter plot, harvested twice a year, could allow farmers to "afford school fees [for their children] and live in relative comfort." No other crop promises to yield anything close to this level of profit. According to djamba farmers, this partly is due to its popularity abroad: only Jamaican djamba "has a higher level of THC than the marijuana cultivated in Sierra Leone."[10]

   While this claim is unproven, it was apparent from interviews that marijuana grown in Sierra Leone is unusually potent, powerfully affecting children and youth in particular. Farmers also consider djamba "a recreational drug," a cure for colds, malaria, and asthma, and "good for their sexual stamina." To them, it thus is entirely unlike "alcohol or other kinds of drugs" (such as heroin, cocaine, and tranquilizers), which "could be both dangerous to their individual health and have harmful consequences for their families" (Bøås and Hatløy 2005: 41, 42, 43). The idea that djamba rests in a category entirely separate from other drugs is a view shared by many former combatants interviewed for this book.

   Before the war, ethnic Temne in the north were thought to be the nation's main djamba farmers. The conflict years changed all that. Combatants across the country required regular and very sizable quantities of marijuana.[11] Just one year into the war, marijuana use among SLA soldiers already was considered "endemic." One Kamajor awaiting the January 6 onslaught by rebel forces with his colleagues related that they were given nothing more than food and djamba in preparation. Indeed, their leader (Hinga Norman) said that Kamajors should "be smoking this thing [djamba] so that we could be reaching our goal" (TRC 2004a: 162, 328). ECOMOG soldiers were drug users too (TRC 2004b: 304).

Yet the rebel groups' focus on djamba was comprehensive and fanatical. They grew it, confiscated it, smoked it, drank water boiled with it (called djamba tea), ate rice mixed with it, and sometimes (reportedly) cooked and ate "djamba leaf" or "jamba plasas" (TRC 2004b: 304), variations of traditional green-leaf sauces favored in Sierra Leone (served over rice), similar to those made with the leaves of cassava or potato plants. "Djamba was their staple food," a former rebel wife explained. "We ladies [rebel wives] would grow and harvest it for them [male rebels]. When any woman attempted to hide from watering the djamba farm, you will be beaten until you shit." A chief who engaged with rebels when they occupied Makeni remembered that "Djamba was considered as the most valuable government property [that is, rebel property]. When a civilian was caught with djamba without handing it over to the rebels, if he is lucky, he will be beaten, or else declared as an enemy. Enemies were treated by killing [that is, rebels killed those considered enemies]." A regular target of the "food finding missions" that rebel soldiers undertook was not just rice and vegetables. They sought djamba too. Indeed, as a former rebel combatant's wife recalled, "Marijuana was the most important item in a food finding mission. It is called 'Grandpapa chop,' like grandfather's food."

One critical attribute separates marijuana from all other drugs (and all other crops): its direct connection to reggae musicians, Bob Marley in particular. This too is rooted in history. As detailed in chapter 6, the music of Bob Marley and other reggae stars entered downtrodden youth worlds in Freetown in the 1970s and instantly became influential. The popularity of Marley and his fellow reggae musicians (Peter Tosh and Bunny Wailer, among others) expanded across all of Sierra Leone by the 1980s. Marley grew to exceptional prominence. So did marijuana smoking, wearing dreadlocks, and the practice of becoming "conscious," which incorporates smoking djamba and listening to reggae music to promote critical analysis of current realities. A veteran Sierra Leonean journalist defined "conscious music" as "music that will make you learn new things; to prepare for the challenges ahead, especially 'Get up, stand up, don't give up the fight,'" a direct reference to Marley's most famous and influential song across Sierra Leone. By the 1980s, he recalled, many youth who were "opposed to the one-party system of Siaka Stevens" believed that "the only way to change the system was by armed struggle." And during "all this time, they're listening to Bob Marley and smoking ganga [marijuana]."

Connections between Rasta followers of reggae music and smoking marijuana have been noted as a phenomenon that reached across all of West Africa. In the 1990s, a researcher found that "a substantial number [of West African Rastas] are or have in the past been involved in either peddling or smuggling" marijuana, which was illegal across the region. Direct connections between marijuana and Marley, "the foremost apostle of reggae on the African continent" (Savishinsky 1994: 28, 22), flourished within combatant societies during Sierra Leone's war. During the war years, Joseph Hill and Culture (known as "Joe Hills" in Sierra Leone), and to some extent the South African singer Lucky Dube, had surpassed other reggae musicians except for Bob Marley, who has persisted, by far, as the dominant reggae and Rastafarian figure in Sierra Leone across the decades. As already noted, during the war, Marley became a prophet-like guide to Foday Sankoh and the RUF. He was influential over Valentine Strasser and the NPRC, as well.

All of these factors—the high potency of marijuana grown in Sierra Leone, its easy availability and powerful impact on children and youth, its direct connection to Bob Marley and other reggae heroes, and the practice of developing political awareness and personal courage by listening to reggae music while smoking marijuana—drew from established practices and made djamba an omnipresent and dynamic force in Sierra Leone's war theater. Still another was critical to marijuana and Marley's influence: imitation. Sierra Leonean boys and male youth carefully copied the look and behavior of their idols, in the "system" fashion noted earlier (such as Marley System, Tupac System, and Rambo System). An older admirer of Marley, and a former civilian in rebel-held territory, surmised that "youth believed that Marley's source of inspiration in his music was the marijuana he smoked." In her view, "djamba was the silent weapon of the rebel war. It killed more [people] than the gun."

The linkage between djamba and Marley was a persistent theme in field interviews. It is here where the exploitation of Bob Marley's music, messages, and heavy marijuana use is pronounced. In the war zone, commanders converted Marley from a beacon of peace and resistance against injustice into a seductive force for violent warfare. As a porter for the RUF recalled,

> The rebels liked Marley, smoked marijuana, and took cocaine. I am not sure whether Marley took cocaine. Marijuana was real chop [food] for the rebels. To them, Marley was the King of Reggae and the Father of Marijuana. Bob Marley gave them the inspiration to fight on until they succeed. His songs were inspiring to what they did. But what created terror was the marijuana they smoked. Without smoking marijuana, they would have done less atroc-

ities during the war. But when these [rebel] boys smoke, then you will know
that there is a place called Hell.

Young combatants modeling a deeply perverted vision of Marley was a product of commander-cultivated rebel societies. The concentration on marijuana
and Bob Marley (and other reggae stars) could inspire unusual outcomes,
such as, for at least one rebel field unit, a unique application for Bibles. As a
former rebel wife explained, "The rebels believed that marijuana was good for
them, not only to carry out atrocities, but [also] because it was approved by
the wisest King of Reggae, Bob Marley. What surprised me most was the fact
that they wrapped their djamba in Bible papers. They believed that if you did
so, you will have double wisdom: from the djamba, and from the Bible. Wherever they saw a Bible, they would take it not to read but to wrap djamba [to
smoke]."

The interview data also revealed how many commanders orchestrated
djamba- and Marley-centered reverie in camp. If that seemed fun to those involved, the activities also directly informed their terror practices. "The rebels believed that djamba gave Marley wisdom to compose and sing his songs,"
a former rebel combatant explained. "When they smoked, they became creative in doing evil. It was like they would do whatever came into their minds."
SBUs in particular would become "wild and uncontrollable," a former rebel
wife remembered. "All the bad things that happened during the war was a result of the marijuana the rebels smoked, and the cocaine [they took]. They
were so grateful to Marley because he taught them how to smoke" djamba.
Said one civilian forced to live with rebels during the war, "Marley gave the
rebels the means by which they can fight hard. The marijuana smoking helped
them to do what they did. When they smoked marijuana, they could slaughter a person with joy."

Given the fevered and often violent responses that near-constant djamba
smoking, together with djamba-laced food and water, induced among young
rebels, it is somewhat surprising that anyone would conclude that additional
drugs were necessary. After all, marijuana-loaded rebel environments, goaded
by manipulated interpretations of music by Marley, other reggae musicians,
and sometimes Tupac Shakur, created a world where fighters could instigate
extreme violence before dancing and celebrating in djamba-addled merriment
afterward. However, notwithstanding its power, djamba by itself was deemed
insufficient. Many commanders and combatants during the war sought and
received regular amounts of other drugs, as well (with many becoming drug
addicts in the process). Commanders routinely forced their young fighters (as
well as porters, captive wives, and others under their control) to take other
drugs, in addition to djamba and (often) a variety of local alcoholic beverages.

The TRC aptly concluded that this practice—labeled "forced drugging"—infected and inflamed Sierra Leone's war: "Most members of the armed factions have admitted that they took a variety of dependence-inducing substances by habit. The Commission also received testimony of how children were forced into taking drugs, particularly before the onset of a battle or an attack. Testimony confirms that almost all of the commanders in most of the armed factions ensured that children were continuously drugged in order to keep control of them. . . . Children carried out the most atrocious violations while under the influence of these drugs" (TRC 2004b: 280). The focus on young fighters, across all of the armed factions, mixed with the need for them to carry out precisely what their superiors had ordered them to do. Two analysts of the war concluded, "It is this blind obedience, usually bolstered by psychotropic drugs, that the military organizations manipulated to get children to commit an array of violent, destructive and atrocious acts" (Abdullah and Rashid 2004: 243).

A fantastic array of drugs swirled across war fronts and into the bloodstreams and brains of virtually every combatant or faction member on the scene: cocaine, brown-brown (heroin), amphetamines and barbiturates known as blue boat or blue-blue, valium, gunpowder, and still more. The drugs arrived over the border from Guinea and Liberia via barter trade (a former rebel wife related that rebels also traded surplus marijuana for other goods at borders). Nigerian soldiers working for ECOMOG are said to have smuggled drugs (especially cocaine) into Sierra Leone's war theater (TRC 2004b: 303), something that researchers in Sierra Leone also asserted. Before sending youngsters into attacks, commanders routinely would fill them up with combinations of drugs. Pills were ground into powder and mixed with water to drink. Gunpowder was burnt and smoked with marijuana or mixed with food. Some drugs were injected. Perhaps the most common and visible application was "plaster," where incisions were made (often at the temple, allowing the drugs to enter the brain in seconds), cocaine and other drugs were pressed into the cut, and a bandage kept it all in place. Young members frequently didn't know what they had been given.

Merely calling these children and youth "high" or "drunk" would be a vast understatement. Forced drugging thrust them into a world of stupor-induced oblivion. Within this world, fear and terror intermingled: an array of former fighters attested to drugs dissolving their fears while inducing their performance of terror practices, the details of which they may not remember afterward. The young female and male fighters thus were ferocious, brave, and unknowing, transforming "into brutes who viewed and treated the civilian population, to use the words of one RUF witness, 'as chickens' or 'ants'" (TRC

2004a: 564). Several former rebel fighters used the chicken metaphor to describe their inability to appreciate what they were doing to civilians during attacks. It was as if they were not really there and civilians were not really people. Some related that they were so drugged that they could not remember many details about their life during the war.

The data about the forced drugging phenomenon was substantial. Nearly everyone who was interviewed shared compelling dimensions of drugs and warfare from personal experience. Here are three examples:

- A former rebel captive wife:

  "The rebels took drugs like rice. Then, before an attack, [rebel fighters] would drink [alcohol] and play music: Rasta music and Tupac music. Then they prayed to God—the Christian and Muslim gods. They say, "God, as we go into battle, help us conquer and kill them and win the battle." Then they fired in the air and then they moved, and the SBUs, they led. They would see people like animals, so they wouldn't be afraid to kill whomever came before them as an enemy."

- A former Kamajor combatant:

  "Here's the reason why you use drugs: if you have drugs you don't want to know who you kill. It made you too arrogant and wicked."

- A former SBU for the RUF:

  "After they [the RUF] capture you, the more you do drugs, the more you liked the game, the more you liked fighting. I was high all the time. I didn't know good from bad; I was just doing it. [Now] I don't remember a lot of things. I was too small."

During discussions of drugs and warfare, many returned to the resonant combination of marijuana and Bob Marley. Here are three examples:

- A 1992 rebel attack, related by a surviving citizen:

  "When the rebels entered, they were carrying tape recorders on their heads [that is, Walkmans with headphones]. They played Bob Marley. They'd use huge stereos and have civilians carry them. After they took over Kono, they were playing Bob Marley music while wearing Tupac T-shirts and tattoos. Some also had shaved heads like Tupac. Shooting guns in the air and dancing."

- A civilian survivor of the January 6 attack on Freetown in 1999:

  "Djamba is the main substance that helped the rebels to be brave [enough] to carry out the atrocities they committed. They killed people without knowing it. They cut people's limbs without knowing it.

They burned houses without knowing it. All of this was the work of djamba. They imitated what Bob Marley did, and to me they did it better than Marley himself. What they did as a result of their smoking was beyond human understanding. As they smoked, they danced and hailed Marley as the King of Reggae."

• A former rebel wife:

"It is difficult to talk about djamba without talking about Marley. If this is the case, then we had the experience of Marley. There was too much djamba-smoking among the rebels. Djamba was what gave the rebels the mind to do most of the things they did during the war, like raping, killing, and burning houses."

Finally, some interviewees drew from personal observation to conclude that drugs caused terror warfare. For example, one former rebel captive explained, "When a rebel who is sober relates with you, then you will know that it was drugs that helped them to do what they did." A former rebel wife insisted, "For sure, djamba has to do with Marley, who is the great hero for djamba smokers. No matter what people will say or think, one thing that is true is the fact that these rebels were terrible when they smoked. When they did, they were not able to distinguish between an enemy and their mothers or bush wives." Sitting alongside a second ex–rebel wife, she ended by stating authoritatively: "We are telling you the reality: we have suffered in their hands."

Getting up and standing up for your rights (à la Marley), and in ways that only God could judge (following Tupac), formed a loose philosophy that, in the midst of war, made sense to many. Commanders led the way in exploiting the popularity of idolized musicians by mixing distortions of their messages with forced drugging. The drugs pulverized the minds of its youthful recipients, dominated their wartime lives, and allowed their superiors to regularly set them up as fearless, ruthless terror specialists. A look at the commanders, and what troops did during their drug-powered attacks, comes next.

Burnings, Beheadings, and the Orchestrators

Terror warfare in Sierra Leone largely took place after the successful ambushes of ordinary men, women, and children were complete. As Human Rights Watch noted, "This is a war being waged through attacks on the civilian population" (1999b: 12). Many disturbing practices have been discussed in this book already. What follows here is a set of prominent themes about terror war practices that arose from analysis mainly of interview data but also published documents about the subject. The exception is sexual abuse and violence (including rape), which will be examined in the next chapter.

To set the scene, it again is useful to recall that all members of an ambush were drugged, quite often to a very high level—a state of mind characterized as being "hard-hearted." In a great many cases, the ambushes did not appear to be particularly dangerous or challenging, as normally they positioned armed soldiers against unarmed civilians. As a former SBU for the RUF recalled, "If you point a gun at someone, they'll give you anything they have." In addition, a former RUF and a Kamajor commander both agreed that, during ambushes and other military operations, their respective groups operated under *Boff Case*. The Kamajor commander then provided two definitions for this phrase: "Whatever I do, nothing happens to me," and "I'm above the law." The freedom to plunder and wreak havoc appeared to be quite high. For example, during Operation Pay Yourself, the countrywide AFRC-RUF offensive in 1998, an AFRC soldier recalled that his officers "used to say [to their soldiers], 'Gentlemen, go there and capture the area and pay yourself.' Then we [would] pay ourselves"—that is, take whatever they wanted for themselves (including captives) and raping females.

Former rebel combatants in particular also described an environment where they were often afraid and uncertain of what they might encounter, creating a mixture of fear and brutality following ambushes. Here are four prominent themes that emerged from analysis:

1. The Commanders

Marks describes stages of brutality and commander control within the RUF during the war. In the earliest stage, RUF commanders would violently repress any challenges to their authority, while NPFL fighters from Liberia were extra brutal to civilians. Ordinary RUF fighters copied their behavior (Marks 2013: 362). Styles were set: commanders demanded obedience over underlings who committed extreme acts of violence in the field. Sankoh began to leave Sierra Leone beginning in 1995 (to negotiate the first peace accord, followed by extended detention in Nigeria), which coincided with the rise of Kamajors and other CDF groups as adversaries and the emergence of Mosquito as the interim RUF leader. All of this inspired a "personalisation of power" by RUF commanders (as well as AFRC commanders, once they became rebels in 1997). Eventually, it also fueled infighting between RUF and AFRC leaders (366). Commander-led rebel groups increasingly became mostly autonomous, with each operating as separate, superviolent patrimonial societies, combining a dictatorial Big Man (or Big Woman, in a few cases) with abject subjects.[12] Overwhelmingly, the frame of reference for war among former rebels who were interviewed was the commander-led band to which they had belonged.

The worlds of the *bra* (meaning big brother, and shorthand for commander) catalyzed and guided terror warfare.[13] Everyone had to obey the *bra*. One former RUF member, for example, described a dynamic where SBUs, who would be killed "for committing minor crimes like stealing," responded in the field by killing people "at the command of their bosses." A second former RUF fighter remembered witnessing a moment when Mosquito, who "was very angry, started shooting some fighters because the Kamajors had defeated them." The *bra* created drug-induced worlds, controlled every aspect of the lives of his minions, and oversaw terror war practices in the field. Disobeying one's commander was inconceivable. This environment operated equally within AFRC groups (TRC 2004b: 178).

Two factors dominated virtually all rebel group societies. The first was high value placed on the practice of terror. From Sankoh on down, the RUF rewarded "hard" and fearless leaders. This trend created "a particularly violent leadership cadre" (Marks 2013: 370). The same dynamic applied within field units, where commanders praised and promoted the most ferocious fighters. The second factor was that field units were violent patriarchal societies where the Big Man (or, very occasionally, the Big Woman) and other officers (and sometimes their wives) formed family-like bonds with young underlings. Youngsters were isolated from the rest of the world and reliant on their superiors. RUF compounds have been described as centered around the commander and his wives, with "lower-ranking commanders, fighters and captives arranged into 'family units'" (McKay and Mazurana 2004: 93).

Commander-led field units drove Sierra Leone's war. A remarkable shared feature was that virtually every military unit on the ground was similarly organized. Interviews with former AFRC and Kamajor fighters and commanders revealed setups largely analogous to counterpart RUF field units. Abdullah and Rashid describe social environments featuring surrogate parents for rebel and national army (SLA) units alike. In both, discipline over young members equated with "manipulating these young minds to serve a variety of purposes" and demanding "unflinching obedience." They make it clear that this sort of leader maneuvering worked much better with younger combatants than older ones (Abdullah and Rashid 2004: 243).

At the same time, interviews with former female members of rebel groups suggested that some of them never developed any fondness for or loyalty to the group or their commander. After all, they essentially were slaves and were treated that way. But for many of the boys (particularly the younger ones), it was different: they often felt strong bonds with other members. Rebel group societies thus simultaneously were terror units and, for male members, reasonably cohesive. Similar social dynamics operated inside national army units and CDF groups.

2. Mutual Terror

Rebels who were trained received instructions and practice on how to ambush civilian settlements (villages, towns, and urban neighborhoods). But such trainings evidently never covered what to do next. The oversight showed. AFRC and RUF fighters were wary, distrustful, and sometimes afraid of civilians they had captured. Who were they, and whom did they support? On the other side, CDF, ECOMOG, and SLA soldiers seemed constantly concerned about rebel recces (spies) in their midst. Relations between armed units and civilians never were good, and things rarely seemed to go well. It is always important to recall that most if not all ambushers were heavily drugged. Communicating, much less negotiating, with such a person was not easy.

To provide a sense of what it was like to experience a rebel ambush, here is the recollection of a high court judge in Koidu: "The war just blew our minds. Something went wrong with people here. The fear . . . the fear that goes through you. You can't describe it. When we were running away, rebels killed all blind and angry people and said, 'We'll take you out of your misery.'" Recalling a rebel attack on his village, an elderly man remembered how afraid civilians were—and how confused and insecure the rebels were: "People were so afraid. When [the rebels] asked civilians to come out [of their homes], they threated to kill those who refused to come out. If you were too afraid and panicked, they called you a sabotager [saboteur]; [they said] that you were not supporting them. It was very difficult to understand the rebels because you didn't know what they wanted." The elder added that rebels would kill those who complained or "pretended to be tired" from carrying heavy loads for them. Interestingly, he also recalled that the young rebels called "old people useless and corrupt elements" and allowed some of them go free. This was a far softer response than others have noted. Keen, for example, states, "In the war, youths in particular often sought revenge against a system of chiefs and elders that excluded and exploited them."[14] It was a function of a grander wartime theme: "the imposition of extreme humiliation and shame on the victims" (Keen 2005: 67, 59).

Many efforts to humiliate and shame were extraordinary. For example, one analyst explained during an interview that rebel fighters might force people in a village to "buy limbs" they had just cut from another civilian. "If you refused [to buy the limb], you'd be identified as an enemy" and dealt with accordingly. Forcing chiefs and other respected male elders to commit degrading acts in public, torturing them, watching rebel boys rape their wives and daughters before them, and perhaps executing them—sometimes while forcing ordinary civilians to clap, dance, or laugh—was a particular set of acts that rebels undertook. The acts became particularly powerful when undertaken before community witnesses. This imposed the idea that youth now held absolute dominion over elders. Demonstrations of forced applause for atrocities performed in public also was a way for rebels to demand respect from civilians (Keen 2005: 73).

One of the most confusing elements of a rebel ambush was the common rebel contention that their ambush was an act of rescue. As a former longtime rebel combatant described, "The [RUF] commanders told people [in one village], 'Go back to the bush and tell them [other villagers] to come back. Don't fear. They should come back. We have come to rescue the village, the civilians.' But they were afraid." This fed a belief that seemed to inflame all invading military groups: civilians did not support them, and in fact some secretly supported (and spied for) the opposition. A conversation with a former RUF commander shed light on this concern. "You don't know if the civilians are with the enemy," he explained. "So you can't go peacefully, because all of you could be killed. So what you do is attack them." At least some civilians were traitors, in other words, and they had to be dealt with. An ambush thus swiftly could transform into assaults of many kinds.

One frequent initial act was killing men. A refugee woman recalled from RUF attacks in Kono that "men were targets. If they [the rebels] found one, they would torture or kill him. Torture: tying [a man] flat, naked, under the sun." Another woman explained that in her soquoihun, "The [rebel] fighters were looking for men much more than women. Men hid [because] they were hunted the most." She added, "We were afraid! Oh yes, even if a lizard ran past, you'd be so afraid." A male civilian survivor of a rebel attack (who worked with ex-combatants after the war) explained the rebels' rationale for killing men: "When the rebels attacked a village, they tried to create as much fear as possible to get the obedience of the population. So if you kill off some of the men, then women and children will obey." In his view, the rebels sought to "show their ruthlessness by getting a father to kill some of his children or a child to kill his parents." If the rebels forced civilians to perform such acts, then they would "change the status quo psychologically" and gain the civilian obedience they had sought. Such efforts were widespread.

Fear of civilians, particularly the suspicion that civilians harbored traitors, helped drive other military groups to conduct terror practices too. There were many stories during interviews of ECOMOG soldiers torturing or killing suspected rebel spies. Kamajors deservedly garnered a reputation for the "grotesque nature of [their] killings, at times including disembowelment followed by consumption of vital organs, such as the heart." These acts were "intended to transfer the strength of the enemy to those involved in the consumption." The targets of these killings and cannibal practices were those whom the Kamajors "believed to be members of the AFRC/RUF and their civilian supporters" (HRW 1998b: 24).[15] Like amputation for the rebels, cannibalism was the Kamajors' featured terror specialty.

3. Burn for Burn and the Food Imperative

In some cases, the rebel repertoire of terror acts performed on civilians seemed to be sheer freelancing, invented on the fly. Others, such as publicly degrading elders by the RUF or cannibalism by Kamajors, were regular practices. Another common rebel practice was burning civilian houses. An analyst for the Special Court identified a common sequence for rebel atrocities in villages they had ambushed. It started with "burning houses and making civilians stand around and listen to those burning and screaming." Then the rebels would "have everybody watch some [get] beheaded, some raped and killed, and some [receive] amputations." The analyst first concluded that the "hideous smorgasbord done to civilians" ultimately had "no military objective." But then she provided one: "It became a tool of fear. The abnormal became normal." Keen reflected on this and concluded that "prolonged exposure to this perverse universe must have profoundly messed with the rebels' sense of what was right and wrong and shameful, particularly since so many were children" (2005: 76).

On the other hand, over time such practices became normalized. Tradition intentionally was turned on its head, replaced by new and radical norms. "If an elder died in a village, they would take the corpse away," a veteran analyst in Sierra Leone explained. "It was taboo for a child to see a corpse. But with the RUF, they would show dead bodies in public, and kill in public. So it became normal." In addition, the frame of reference for rebel groups emerged from enforced seclusion in violent, commander-dominated worlds. A Kamajor commander shared an illuminating contrast between the two sets of groups. "In the war, most of the time, Kamajors were in the towns and rebels were in the bush. They were isolated while the Kamajors had contacts."

An NGO official who worked with ex-combatants explained a rebel tactic called "burn for burn." He considered it "selective" or "strategic" burning, where the rebels burned only some homes in a village. One function of this practice was to ensure that young rebels would not escape. "If a rebel was sent back to burn his own village, then he can't return home," he explained. In this way, it served a purpose similar to drugging and sending boys back home to rape their mothers (the "motherfucker" act).

The focus on burning villages was long lasting. Beginning in 1994, one set of analysts noted that "RUF strategy involved emptying the countryside. Many villages were burned." Once CDF units were in the field (starting in 1996), they sought to "re-populate the countryside" and stop the rebels from moving about freely (Richards, Bah, and Vincent 2004: 22). Yet the rebel fascination with burning down houses and other buildings extended across the entire war. Outside diamond-rich Koidu, in Kono District, one resident related how the RUF burned his village twice: in 1992 and again in 1995. "I don't know why they burned the village," he reflected. A former rebel wife shared a similar experience: rebel groups burned her family house on two separate occasions. After the second time (in 1998), a rebel group abducted her. Most dramatically, AFRC and RUF units burned large swaths of Freetown during their forced retreat early in 1999.

Burning houses and other buildings served some useful terror war purposes. It certainly propagated fear and sent many fleeing. Beyond people burned alive inside homes (or thrown into fires), the burnings generally were part of terror practices that kept most civilians alive. As a survivor of one rebel ambush recalled, "They burned houses but spared the lives of people."

But house burning also helped create a significant problem. The rebels may have been able to loot family belongings before burning down a home. The main focus was food stocks. In some cases, civilians were "kept" to farm. But in most of the country, securing regular supplies of food was a problem. In some AFRC or RUF groups, commanders sent out groups called Food Finding Units (FFUs) in search of food every day. This could include moving through rain forests in search of civilians in soquoihun hiding places. Yet such people often were barely alive themselves and had little food. So FFUs would continue their search for food and other goods to loot and, perhaps, females to rape and people to capture. There were many stories of rebels showing up when girls and women were cooking meals. It appeared that FFU members would eat what they could and take the rest back to their camps. Some rebel groups evidently experienced substantial food shortages. For example, one former RUF fighter recalled that as a member, "I ate food that I had never eaten before," including dogs and snails. Some of those interviewed reported that becoming a rebel allowed them to secure food for themselves and hopefully sneak food to their families in soquoihun hiding places. This only underscores an endemic rebel challenge: their practices created food scarcity.

4. The Cuttings

Sierra Leone's war was infamous for the frequency of one awful atrocity: amputation. As the TRC noted, "the scale of amputations in Sierra Leone was far greater than that of amputations in other African countries" (2004e: 14). The Sierra Leone War Crimes Documentation Survey estimated that there were 6,173 amputations during the war (Guberek et al. 2006: 5). But precise numbers proved impossible to calculate, in part because many of those amputated died soon afterward.

In 1997 a man displays the prosthetic arm and hand he wears following the "short sleeve" amputation he received from armed combatants.

Amputation is a particularly intimate atrocity. Three styles became especially infamous. Rebels were known to offer victims the option either of "long sleeve" (amputation at the wrist) or "short sleeve" (amputation at the elbow), as detailed in Chapter 13. A third amputation option was the "One Love" mutilation, explained here by a former RUF soldier: "'One Love' meant cutting all fingers and leaving the thumb. The army started it, saying, 'Go tell your friends about One Love.' Then we [the RUF] did it too." One Love referred directly to two things: Bob Marley's famous song and the symbolic appropriation of the song—via a thumb's-up hand signal—by the NPRC following their 1992 coup. The RUF changed the meaning of the One Love mutilation. As the ex-RUF combatant explained, "The RUF was against the elections [of March 1996, won by Ahmed Tejan Kabbah, who became president]. So whenever they caught civilians or any [government] fighters, they were dead meat. 'One Love' cutting by Foday Sankoh was to oppose the Kabbah election of 1996. Foday wanted peace before elections, but Kabbah said elections before peace."[16] Kabbah became president before he and Sankoh signed the first peace accord in November 1996.

Although amputations by rebel and other forces took place across virtually the entire wartime period (starting in 1992), Carey identified three main phases. The initial phase (September 1995–October 1996) featured amputations as messages for "the government and/or the international community," such as the RUF's opposition to the elections (Carey 2006: 112).[17] Carey's second major phase of amputation (March–August 1998) took place following the rebels' first retreat from Freetown in February 1998. The messages behind these amputations were vague, meant to either deliver various messages or threaten a new attack. "On the surface, this conversation was directly aimed at President Kabbah and his allies," Carey explains (115). The third major amputation phase took place during the second Freetown assault by the rebels (January 1999) (117).

People who recently had become amputees delivered vivid messages to others. An analyst researching this issue for the Special Court for Sierra Leone provided three examples of the messages they communicated. "Many amputees said that they were told to 'Go tell Pa Kabbah; he will give you a new hand." Another was to pin a letter onto the amputated person and send them to ECOMOG or the SLA to warn them that "the rebels were on their way." A third allegedly was undertaken by a West Side Boys commander named Junior Lion, who "used to amputate hands, make a necklace out of them, put it around the neck of a girl, and send her to a village to tell the residents, 'We're coming.'" In the view of a veteran analyst, another possible message was that the rebels "were determined to achieve their goal and you'll be the next victim if you do not obey" them. A former RUF commander focused on amputations as a means for dealing with spies: "When we capture a person we're not satisfied with, I'd tell the SBUs to amputate the civilian—the amputee would go off and tell our enemies that we're here and ready for them. We especially amputated people we suspected were recces. The commanding officer would tell us what to cut: a hand, or fingers or toes. Cutting off fingers meant: tell people that we are on alert for them. Every group did this: the Kamajors did it too. Everyone who was suspected as a recce was amputated."

Beyond targeted messages to specific groups, Peters suggested that amputations, as a specific act of terror, ultimately communicated to a much wider audience: "The purpose of terrorism is demoralisation, so the specific forms were atrocities that 'spoke' to important local social and cultural concerns. One set of such concerns focuses on the integrity of the body. . . . Mutilating living individuals sent a signal to warn an entire society." To illustrate this point, he added the following comment from a former RUF fighter: "the commander can decide to make the area 'fearful' by amputating some people" (Peters 2011a: 149). The ex-combatant's comment suggests that amputations were effective in frightening civilians. He also seems nonchalant about the atrocity. For the RUF, amputations were merely one of many possible terror war options. The same could be said for other amputation specialists during the war, the AFRC and SLA in particular.

Implied in all of this discussion is that amputations were horrific physical punishments that did not kill people. This is suggested by Carey's comment that "amputation destroyed a part of the humanness of the individual" (2006: 116). It also is inferred by the following definition of amputation by the TRC: "the removal of one or more hands, feet, arms or legs" (2004a: 472). But some amputations killed people. For example, it often was not possible for victims to last long if their one of their legs was cut off.

Another important form of cutting was beheading. While the act is not properly considered an amputation, Sierra Leoneans often did not make that distinction. Such killings appeared to be fairly common. An ex-commander for the RUF explained, "When you take a town where you have serious enemies and you're fortunate to capture one of the strong enemies that you fought against—any senior fighter—you would behead him." In some cases, heads would be delivered to enemy forces by civilians. Rebel or Kamajor forces also might put a head atop a tall stick to announce their presence in a particular location.

However military groups performed beheadings and used the heads, beheadings struck lasting terror in civilians. A woman shared her recollections eight years after one took place: "Even now when I think of it, I start shivering. After I first saw the rebels parade a head on a stick, I could only drink water for a week. My father saw his friend beheaded. He was so terrified that he ran away and smashed his kneecap. When he reached his house, he was so afraid that he hid under a bed for days. We would pull him out only to feed him."

One girl of eighteen shared a remarkable story that had taken place when she was eight: "While we were in the soquoihun, the rebels arrived again. They started shooting at random. Then I was captured. After they arrested me, they said, 'Let's cut off her head.' That's when they made the mark on my throat." It turned out that the rebels' attempt at beheading her had failed. But then, in succession, they succeeded in cutting off the heads of her mother, younger brother, and twin sister. "I was the only one that survived," she related, and then she described what took place next: "They [the rebels] noticed that after cutting my neck, I was still alive. So they took me to Kono while I was bleeding and bleeding. When I would eat or drink, it would come out of my neck. I was like that until I reached Kono. It took four days." The rebels had captured some nurses in Kono who helped the girl recover from her wound. The rebels then allowed her to return to Tongo, where she had grown up.

In Sierra Leone's war, amputated limbs and the heads of dead people became portable expressions of terror warfare. They registered horror in civilians and announced their might to rival warrior groups. Sometimes they had political meanings. But the subtext of all amputations and beheadings was the same: they demonstrated that fighting forces were capable of just about anything.

The Boy Conquerors

If field commanders were the war's primary terror orchestrators, then Small Boys Units (SBUs) stood out as the featured practitioners. There were limited numbers of Small Girls Units (SGUs) as well. However, it was the boy child fighters in SBUs that consistently surfaced as prominent, particularly within rebel forces.

SBUs and SGUs drew from the Taylor-made import model from Liberia. SBUs in particular were near-perfect instruments for the terror warfare. As little people, they consumed minimal amounts of food and were compact vessels for the marijuana and other drugs they took. It was easier for them to get very high and stay there. As young children, they were obedient, impressionable, and eager to please—a combination that made them easy for their commanders to manipulate. As youngsters, they served the dual role of being effective yet replaceable in a population loaded with very young people. SBUs embodied a world turned completely upside down, with the youngest rebels in the lead, especially hostile to older civilians and being the fiercest of them all. And as boys, they embodied the male rage that rebels conveyed—even if SBUs were too young to fully appreciate what that rage was all about.

SBUs were so central to RUF intentions and terror practices that it is impossible to imagine the RUF without them. SBUs were feared, including by many other members of their groups (especially the girls). Descriptions of rebel dynamics indicate that they were the extremists within already-extreme rebel groups. While plenty of youth in their teens and twenties also populated the rebel ranks, few or no military outfits in recent times featured a younger corps of foot soldiers than the RUF. In the awful logic that informed child-based militaries, SBUs served as a cost-effective and exceptionally efficient means for promoting terror. In Sierra Leone, the boy soldier—drugged, unquenchably malicious, and seemingly unreachable—was the RUF brand.

Mazurana and Carlson state that boys between ages six and fifteen were in SBUs for the RUF. The range may have been wider. One former RUF wife said SBUs in her rebel group contained boys up to age seventeen. According to one former SBU, the youngest was age three. A second ex-RUF combatant described how SBUs were "small-small boys," some of whom "were dragging their guns on the ground because they were too heavy to hold." Mazurana and Carlson highlighted three main activities for SBUs: "scouting to prepare attacks and food raids" (recce spy activity), raiding for food, and being "dispatched to execute some of the most violent killings and mutilations." They added that SGUs performed similar activities (2004: 14). SGUs were far fewer in number, however, and some girls were members of boy-dominated SBUs. Girls usually performed a larger proportion of recce surveillance work than boys.

Child soldiers were part of every Sierra Leonean military faction during the war. This was partly an outcome of the difficulties all factions faced in securing older males as fighters: "The high death toll, the wretched conditions of service, the meagre salary which forced some soldiers to augment their pay through looting or mining, the summary executions, and above all, the senselessness of the war, discouraged responsible adults from enlisting on either side" (Abdullah and Rashid 2004: 242). While the RUF started the trend, by 1998 nearly one in four members of all fighting forces were "children and the under-aged." The benefits of using children as soldiers were compelling to military leaders. You didn't have to pay them, they had little clout or leverage, and they were obedient. Child soldiers were, in short, "expendable commodities to be captured or recruited" (242, 243, 252). And through their work during attacks and occupations, SBUs and SGUs shook social norms and values to their core, viciously enacting the supremacy of youngsters over elders.

Commentary from former members of fighting forces attests to the brutal effectiveness of children as terror war agents. "The SBUs were the most notorious killers," an ex–rebel wife stated. "They were gallant soldiers who were always ready to fight," another ex–rebel wife explained. "They always tied a piece of cloth round their head," the salute to Rambo and Tupac noted earlier. "Sometimes we did amputate," a former SBU recalled, "but mostly, we flogged people." He added, "The girls [in his SBU contingent] were more vicious" than the boys, and that, "When you're fighting, you always did what your commander told you." SBUs performed amputations when their commander ordered them. Responding to orders—all orders, no matter what they were—was an SBU trait that many highlighted during interviews. An ex-member of another rebel unit remembered that "SBUs were very smart, and did most of the killing at the command of their bosses [that is, their commanders]." A former head of an SBU explained that "sometimes, when people committed crimes [within the field unit], my group was responsible for carrying out the appropriate punishment." He explained, "I disciplined people no matter their age or how the person was [that is, regardless of rank or stature]. Once the command had been passed, my responsibility was to carry out my duty as instructed."

In some field units, the SBUs led ambushes on villages and towns. In others, the SBUs came in right after their older colleagues had secured a location. As a former RUF fighter recalled, "When we'd attack an area and capture the place, we'd deploy the SBUs there. While they are there, the SBUs were at liberty to do anything [required] to hold the town." Obedience was a characteristic of SBUs that regularly surfaced during interviews. "The SBUs would do anything [you ordered them to do] until you told them to stop," the ex-RUF fighter continued. "If you say, 'Burn the houses,' they will do it. If you say, 'Kill everyone,' they will do it. Often, we would tell them to stop, that they had done enough." Then he added, "One of their professional works was doing amputations." A second prominent activity was rape. "Why did SBUs rape women the age of their mothers?" an ex-RUF commander asked. Then he supplied his answer. "That was part of the war: to show that they were wicked and capable of anything. They could do anything." There were indications that the SBUs did not turn off their aggression when they were inside their rebel community. For example, a former rebel wife explained how "the little boys [within her rebel field unit] were the most wicked because when they asked us to have sex with them, they would hunt you and put you down [that is, rape you]." She added, "The SBUs didn't have wives but they could force anyone to have sex" with them. These very young boys appeared to exert violent authority over girls and women during ambushes and occupations, and in camp.

It is important to recall that commanders controlled and guided the behavior of SBUs (and SGUs), as well as everyone one else in their field units. SBUs raped girls and women within their groups only if their commander allowed it. During ambushes and occupations, SBUs followed commands to the letter. And, of course, commanders kept the children heavily drugged. Child soldier work was exceedingly dangerous, and many lost their lives on the front lines (as well as while serving as recces). Commanders and their officers have been found to treat child soldiers generally with "extreme cruelty," which drove children on the front lines to equate survival with "being even more brutal" than their commanders. All of this led many to become "hardened and immune to the savagery they were inflicting on others." Within the RUF, calling an SBU a "ruthless fighter," "wild boy," or "hard boy" were high compliments (TRC 2004b: 282, 295, 294).

Wessells identifies five psychological processes that child soldiers undergo. The first is "the will to survive," which can drive them to become proactive killers. Second is obedience, which "enables killing by shifting responsibility to the person who issued the orders," such as their commander. The third is "the normalization of violence. The more children see people being killed, the more they become desensitized and numbed to it." Related to this is a fourth process: "satisfaction derived from killing." Reflecting John's motivation for joining the rebels in chapter 16, Wessells explains that "killing provides satisfaction for children who seek revenge for what the enemy did to them or their families." Torturing, humiliating, and raping people also appear to meet this desire for payback. The fifth psychological process is ideology. Nearly all ideologies were crude and simplistic in Sierra Leone's war: to drive out foreigners, upend or destroy the social status quo, enact vengeance, or (drawing from Marley's famous song) fight for your rights. But as long as child soldiers saw their fighting as just, then they would "take pride in their ability to kill enemies" (Wessells 2006: 79–81).

In all of this, it is essential to view child soldiers as children who (for the most part) demonstrate their resilience by "adapting and making the best of perilous circumstances" manufactured by adults (84). One method for adapting to child soldiering in Sierra Leone arose in field interviews: SBUs abducting an adult woman (who could be elderly) to become their surrogate mother (called a Mommy Queen or Sugar Mommy).

The rebels' terror architecture—featuring malicious, dominant field commanders, young fighters fueled with drugs and intentionally distorted messages from pop culture heroes, a burning policy that emptied areas of people (and reliable food supplies), diverse terror practices that sunk people to their knees in horror, and small boys usually in the lead—worked effectively and efficiently in Sierra Leone for more than a decade. The style of warfare leaned toward terrorizing ordinary people: the primary rebel group, the RUF, was ineffective in winning military encounters and focused on attacking and assaulting civilians. Over the course of the war, the rebels sucked most of the diamonds out of the ground and crudely broadcast their anger and might.

Rebel leaders also led an exceptionally male-dominated brand of warfare. The treatment of females by virtually every military unit during the war was not just cruel but vengeful too, particularly among rebel outfits. Situated within the larger war, the obsessive focus on females by male militants drew from male emasculation and other sources, as well as the particular dynamics of the RUF's ethos and organization. These issues are addressed in the next chapter, which is followed by final reflections on male youth, terror warfare, and the cynical wartime manipulations of Bob Marley's music in Sierra Leone.

PART 6

Gender and War Dynamics

CHAPTER 19

The War on Girls

Gender and Slavery

For centuries, the Atlantic slave trade fundamentally destabilized Sierra Leonean societies. Local wars between raiders and the raided arose. European
traders raised the conflict stakes by arming both sides. Those captured during
these engagements increased the supply of slaves for the international market.

Two gendered outcomes from this era have directly informed Sierra Leonean worlds ever since. The war boys that fueled the conflicts were male
youth whom chiefs and other elite men deployed as hired mercenaries and
bodyguards. Subsequently, paramount chiefs and other patriarchs used male
youth to intimidate and attack civilians to suit their needs. The male youth
they corralled and deployed typically were struggling mightily, unable to
marry or gain recognition as adult men. And the more these youth did the
bidding of powerful men, the more unpopular they became.

The second outcome emerged from the Portuguese and British slavers'
particular interest in capturing and exporting men. It created conspicuous
gender imbalances that had to be addressed on the ground. As an immediate,
practical response, polygamous marriages increased, with wealthy, elite men
taking larger numbers of wives. However, the multitude of women in slave-
era societies also cultivated the perception of feminine power as feral, chaotic, and threatening to the social order. This fueled a basic domestic tension:
although all women had to be married (and controlled via marriage), women
simultaneously posed an intimate danger to husbands, their households, and
societies.[1]

The two chapters in part 6 probe the unsettling gender dynamics that arose
during the slave era and helped shape Sierra Leone's war. The next chapter
highlights the views of male youth on the social margins regarding what the
war was about and the manipulation of Marley's messages, as well as the significance of male youth emasculation.

This chapter looks at the way that military units and male combatants
dealt with females within the war theater. Often expressed as sexual terror, it

flowed from a deep reservoir of gendered uncertainty and volatility in Sierra Leonean worlds, and it wreaked extensive damage.

The Rebel Roles for Females

A postwar research study briefly reviewed what the authors considered the two main military roles of girls and female youth in the RUF. One was "female fighters," the proportion of which "may have been larger than 5%." The second was bush wives and laborers, some of whom "were married to commanders." While the study mentioned "large numbers of young women seized and abused" by the RUF, they characterized fighting and married life as largely separate roles for young females (Richards et al. 2003: 18, 19). A second study found something different. It uncovered an array of overlapping roles that females played (for both the RUF and the AFRC). More than two in five (44 percent) received basic military training, informally delivered by "their commanders or captor 'husbands.'" The majority of all females worked part-time as cooks, porters, or informal nurses. Nearly half (44 percent) farmed, and nearly a quarter (22 percent) worked as spies. Still others worked in diamond mines ("for their commanders or captor husbands"). All of those who said that their main role was being a fighter "were forced to be captive 'wives,'" as well (Mazurana and Carlson 2004: 12). Such arrangements were commonly called bush or, even more appropriately, AK-47 marriages (Denov 2010: 110).

The undercurrent of captivity emerging in these studies was a prominent theme in field interviews with former members of rebel units. The enslavement of females started with the entrance of girls and female youth into rebel units. It never let up. This is reflected in this description of one activity that a former SBU member performed for his RUF commander: "When we'd capture girls, we'd hand them to the commander, who would decide which one to take. Sometimes the girls were used to cook for us. If an SBU was interested in having one, he'd ask the commander for his permission, and he'll allow you to take any." In just three sentences, the former SBU outlined rebel society dynamics by highlighting two important wartime themes. The first is the absolute power and patrimonial authority of commanders over everyone beneath them. The second is the notion of young females serving as the property of men and boys. The main role that females played in their lives amounted to sexual slavery.

Coulter spotlights the unusual intensity of sexual violence in Sierra Leone: "Historically and in the present, in Africa and elsewhere, rape and sexual abuse seem commonplace in war; still, the level of rape during the Sierra Leonean war was remarkable. At certain times during the war, and in certain areas, sexual violence appeared endemic" (2009: 152). Wartime rape and sexual violence will be addressed in the next section. How females entered rebel

A former rebel captive, following the war.

worlds is featured here. In this particular war, females played two roles simultaneously. They were active yet subservient contributors to the society, and sometimes the military activities, of rebel units. At the same time, and regardless of whether they were members of fighting forces or ordinary civilians, young females collectively comprised the playing field on which profound sexual terror took place. The captive "wife" of a male rebel might be "sexed" (a common descriptor employed by former female members of rebel units) by her "husband" and perhaps others, frequently and across several sessions, in a single day. When the male fighters went off to look for food, to "jaja" (loot), or just to attack civilians wherever they found them, the male youth and boys would rape still more females. Former female members of rebel outfits generally put this evidently unquenchable thirst for sex and rape down to drugs: virtually everyone in a rebel camp was high on drugs most or all of the time, the males in particular. Many of those interviewed about this issue insisted that the aggression of the males in their midst lessened significantly when the spell of drugs tailed off. Perhaps, but drugs alone cannot fully explain the obsessive nature of sexual predation that informed the behavior of males caught up in war.

The two general trends that former female members of rebel units described during interviews were the violent style of capture and the casual nature of initiation. Similar stories and themes emerged from different locations and time periods. Following attacks on Zimmi (a prominent diamond mining area in the south) soon after the war began in 1991, a former RUF member said that her family tried to escape to Kenema on foot. "Then they [the RUF rebels] captured me," she recalled. She was nine years old. "They raped me and took me along. I was with them from 1992 to 1995." In what was to become a common practice, smoking marijuana was a central part of her initiation into rebel life. "Initially," she related, "every day they gave me djamba to smoke and asked me to fetch water. And every one of them [that is, male rebels] could have sex with me at any time." Many female former rebel members said marijuana was used to soften their resistance to sexual advances. She eventually was "assigned to one person. He was a man. I don't know how old [he was]." In her particular rebel group, "none of the girls fought."

Years later, near the end of 1998, rebel forces attacked the town of Binkolo, located just northeast of the main northern city of Makeni. The rebels arrived at night, a second former female rebel member (age seventeen at the time of the attack) explained, and "burned houses but spared the lives of people." She and her family ran into the nearby forest, hiding there for two weeks before residing in a nearby village. Eventually, the rebels attacked again. When that took place, "they took all of our property and one of the rebels took me away as his bush wife. I was still too young to become a wife, but with the threat of being killed, I accepted. Automatically I became a rebel wife, joining other wives. Sex with a rebel husband was not pleasurable, especially when he was drunk."[2] Her "initiation" included smoking marijuana. At first, she refused. The men responded by mixing it with her rice. "Unknowingly, I ate it. After that, they told me, 'You have eaten djamba.' I started feeling drunk."

One former rebel member described the domestic dynamics within her military unit. "Each [male] rebel had three to four girls, or five," she explained. "The girls stayed permanently with each rebel." They never left the camp: in her words, "we cooked for them." None received any training. The nature of sleeping arrangements reflected the rebels' concern that the girls might try to escape. In one room, there might be "four girls and one rebel husband." The girls "were not allowed to move by themselves: to go to the bathroom, a junior officer must be with you." Inside their bedrooms, there was "no good place to sleep, we had mosquito bites, and we slept on the ground, often wet ground." They also had "fear of attack from other groups." Moving between rebel groups evidently made no difference in a girl's life. When one rebel group attacked another (in the latter war period, it was common), "girls would use it as an opportunity to escape." It was hard to do. She provided an example of a much more likely fate: "If Superman Group attacks 8 & 9 Group, they'll capture girls and force them to carry their loads [of loot], and you'll never be released. When you arrive in the next camp, you'll become a wife there." The captive life of females points to a larger theme that will be examined later in part 6: that the war was not, in any way, about girls, female youth, or women. Its purpose overwhelmingly featured males, who largely fought and mainly (if not exclusively) hoped to benefit from it.

During field interviews, military training for rebel girls and female youth (when it did take place) was informal. Here is a story from a former female member of the rebels. In 1998, when she was thirteen and visiting her aunt during the Christmas holidays, the rebels attacked her aunt's village (on December 28). They fled to the bush, together with the girl's cousin (aged about five). Her aunt asked the two of them to carry food one kilometer, to the home of another relative. During their walk, a group of rebels apprehended them. "They told the little child [her cousin] to go and tell my family that I have become a rebel soldier wife." One of the rebels informed her, "You have nothing to do now, sister. Either you go with us or you die: choose one." It was January 4, 1999. The rebels took her to their camp "and handed me over to Captain Assault, who later became my husband." He was twenty years her senior. "It was Captain Assault who forced me to have sex with him." That was "when I had my first experience of sex." The pain from the early rapes lasted for a week. She also was introduced immediately to "smoking djamba and drinking strong drink. That made me to live a wild life." Since she was the wife of a captain, she was "required to have a gun, although I did not fire a single shot throughout the one year I was with him." She was one of five of Captain Assault's wives, and the only one who was literate. Captain Assault was not.

Another story reflects four themes contained in the story above: capture, captivity, sexual violence, and the barest of military training. At age seventeen, SBUs "stormed into my father's house and I was taken away." They took her to their commander, who immediately took her as one of his wives. "I was forced to have sex with him," which was her first experience of intercourse. She was given a gun, "though I was not trained how to use it. The gun was a 'morale booster.'" She failed to escape several times. Each time her rebel captors caught her, they threatened to kill her. Though she accompanied male fighters on some food finding missions, she spent most of her time "as a housewife doing domestic work." "My sexual experience was bitter," she recalled, "especially in the first month, and when my husband was drunk."

One initiation story was unique. Rebels captured a girl of fifteen and took her to their leader, a woman named Colonel Sarah. The girl was supposed to become a rebel wife. However, Colonel Sarah "took me as a personal attendant. She gave me a gun. She really took care of me. I was not maltreated. I was taking care of her children." The problem was that Colonel Sarah's husband "proposed love" to the girl, who realized that "if Colonel Sarah knows [finds out] about this, she will kill me." During an attack by another group of rebels, she managed to escape. The story illuminates how small numbers of females had a degree of ease and even influence in rebel units. Some so-called wives of commanders, for example, gave orders when their husband was away, had their own bodyguards, and received large amounts of loot from successful raids by the group's fighters. Of course, if the commander-husband of the captive-wife tired of her and selected another wife to favor, she was out, and could be sent to the front lines as a fighter (McKay and Mazurana 2004: 93–94). The power a commander's wife wielded was always tenuous.

Captive girls with no special profile might serve many roles in a rebel unit: cooking (that role was certain), washing clothes and dishes, fetching water and firewood, caring for younger children. Young captive boys would join them in this work. They both also would carry very heavy loads. This was not an insignificant task, since rebel life was unstable and often required move-ment. Collectively, these roles proved vital to the functioning of rebel units. In the RUF, providing sexual services to men and boys was simply one of the many duties that women and girls carried out (Denov 2010: 108, 109).

Of course, some girls did fight too. They did not embody "a submissive feminine ideal" by any stretch. Some Sierra Leoneans attested to the idea that "women had been even tougher than the men"—crueler and deadlier. This may have been because females had to establish themselves "by becoming more violent than their male counterparts" (Coulter 2009: 136, 137). They also gained little, if anything, by entering into combat. The differences with women fighters in other parts of Africa are stark. To begin with, "in Sierra Le-one few female fighters had not experienced sexualized violence by the very force that recruited them." This simply did not take place in some other war-time contexts, such as Mozambique. Female combatants in Mozambique also "were ideologically empowered and motivated." Again, not so for their coun-terparts in Sierra Leone. Women fighting in liberation movements in Eritrea and Rhodesia/Zimbabwe, moreover, "were said to be motivated by a sense of freedom and camaraderie." Yet again, this was simply not the case for female fighters in Sierra Leone. Instead, "the violence they committed was not eman-cipatory and in most cases was not perceived as meaningful in any ideolog-ical sense." They also were not "motivated by any promises of improved sta-tus for women in postwar society." Not only did their combat experience draw a huge blank in terms of purpose. They also walked along the edge of a razor during combat. A female fighter who hesitated to kill would be punished ("of-ten through rape"). And if she was captured by an enemy group, she almost certainly would "be raped before being killed" (138, 139).

With few exceptions, the experience of females in rebel units in Sierra Leone were slave-like and centered on sex. Yet one didn't have to be captured to be treated with aggression. All of the experiences detailed in this section are tied to male rebels who bothered to abduct girls. Sometimes they didn't try. Even then, many raped before they moved along. One girl who had fled with her family into the forest at age six and survived in a soquoihun shed light on this other reality. "I was vaginated [raped] three times by the rebels. Three times, by different groups. They all left me there."

Military organizations and their commanders brutalized and manipulated male combatants. At the same time, the male combatants' severe and highly sexualized treatment of females was a big part of what they did. And what many did to females usually began right after they encountered one.

Sexual Vengeance: The Persistent Obsession

Male rape in war zones is a perfect crime and a compelling act of terror warfare. Or so it would seem. Raping a man humiliates and emasculates the victim, the combination of which often leads them never to report, much less even mention to others, the horrific crime perpetrated against them. Many girls and women also never report crimes of rape and other forms of sexual violence. However, female rape remains the norm while male rape is not. The latter act thus can leave a particularly silent trail of destruction. In the view of one analyst, the "lack of attention to sexual abuse of men during conflict is particularly troubling given the widespread reach of the problem." The analyst then provided a sampling of conflict zones where male rape has been reported: Chile, Greece, Croatia, Sri Lanka, El Salvador, Iran, Kuwait, the former Soviet Union, the Democratic Republic of the Congo, and the former Yugoslavia (Stemple 2008: 612).

In sharp contrast, documented research about Sierra Leone's war, and nothing discovered in analysis of more than three thousand pages of field interview notes for this book, surfaced mention of male rape.[3] Cohen finds (via survey data) that "women participated in one in four of the reported incidents of gang rape," although "neither single women nor groups of women were reported as perpetrators of rape" (2013a: 399, 400).[4] Given the intensity of sexual violence that characterized every single year of that conflict, the low reported levels of male rape is unusual and peculiar. The overwhelming focus on males raping females instead suggests that something deeper than just rape as an appalling act of war was going on. What took place had much to do with females and femininity, and what they represented to males and their masculinity inside Sierra Leone.

This section thus will attempt to answer two questions:

- First, why was sexual violence against females so prevalent in Sierra Leone?
- Second, why did the RUF commit the most rapes?

Before discussing the tunnel vision on females by male combatants during the war, it is first necessary to address the reporting of sexual abuse by men. Analysis of sexual violations detailed by the TRC found that "a substantial proportion of males reported sexual abuse, especially the group aged 65 and above." The analysts hypothesized that "elderly community leaders were the targets of violations such as killings and sexual abuse, and that perpetrators targeted this subpopulation as a means of intimidating the broader community" (Guberek et al. 2006: 21–22). The nature of sexual abuse that men reported differed significantly from the experiences and reporting by females. HRW considered some of the sexual acts involving men as psychological torture. One example of this was "making [civilians] clap or sing in praise while watching family and friends being killed, raped or mutilated." HRW also labeled other rebel acts as violations of cultural norms, such as forcing sons to rape sisters, making fathers rape or dance naked before their daughters, or rebels raping old women and breastfeeding mothers. Many such acts were performed in public, and some of them involved female as well as male combatants. Rebels also raped females in mosques, churches, and sacred initiation sites.

Although violations involving men conformed to the concept of sexual abuse, men usually were witnesses, not targets. This was a prominent purpose of rebel actions. Rebel groups employed sexual violence in part to "force the civilian population into submission." By seeking "complete domination by doing whatever they wanted with women," they "violated not only the victim but also her family or the wider society" (HRW 2003: 33, 36, 35). In patrimonial, Big Man Sierra Leone, where venerating male elders is an elemental value, all of these acts deliberately humiliated and degraded elite male authority. They announced that formerly emasculated young males were Sierra Leone's new overlords.

Combatants publicly performing many sexual acts in public, and forcing male civilians to perpetrate others, generally conformed with strategic rape theory, where rape (and, more broadly, sexual and gender-based violence) acts as a means for subjugating populations, instilling fear, curtailing movement and economic activity, stigmatizing women, and undermining community and family structures (Kelly 2010: 3).[5] However, many of the rebels' violent sexual acts neither took place in public nor communicated a broader purpose. Rates of sexual violence were ferocious: PHR estimated that between 215,000 and 257,000 women and girls in Sierra Leone were victims of sexual violence during the war (2002: 3–4). That figure does not account for the many cases of extensive violations against individual women and girls. Nor does it detail the diversity of violations that took place, such as gang rape, shoving various objects into the victim's anus or vagina (including burning firewood and boiling oil; HRW 2003: 33, 34), or detention in "rape camps" (TRC 2004b: 131). Other examples of severe sexual abuse and violence surfaced in field interviews, such as rebels ramming the belly of a newly captured pregnant girl against a wall until she miscarried (presumably to make her more attractive to her captor) and keeping females in caves to await visits from their "husbands." In all of this and still more, many male combatants and their male commanders fixated on displays of sexual power and sexual terror involving girls and (to a lesser extent) women.

Where did this prodigious thirst for masculine sexual dominance and violence come from? Many theories and explanations have been provided. The most prominent in field interviews was drugs. Coulter found in her field research (mainly with female ex-rebels) that her informants "often talked of drugs being the reason bush husbands wanted to have sex so often" (2009: 107). Field interviews for this book revealed a widely held view that drug use also made many male rebels more violent, including with their rebel wives. Here are three examples. "When they smoke" djamba, an ex–rebel wife reflected, the male rebels in her group "would lose all sense of feeling and act like animals in the bush." A second former rebel wife recalled that when her "rebel husband smoked, he became violent and ready to kill. He attempted to kill me on two occasions." Concerning their sexual relations, she said, "It is needless to talk about his attitude toward sex. He was so rough, especially when he was drunk [that is, high on drugs]. Even when I am tired after having sex with him three or four times per night, he would always ask for more. When I complained, he would beat me, alleging that I am satisfying other boys when he was away. When he went away, I was happy, but when he was around, I was worried."[6] The reference to other boys is telling. As indicated in the discussion about SBUs in the previous chapter, raping girl "wives" when their rebel husband was away appears to have been common. Meanwhile, of course, many of the rebel boys and male youth who were away (perhaps performing an ambush, a "jaja" looting spree, or a food finding mission) may have raped other females during their various attacks. Something similar evidently took place among at least some Kamajor field units. Regarding sexual violence involving women, a veteran former Kamajor commander explained that "Kamajors weren't doing it effectively." They were prohibited from touching a woman while in uniform, he stated. However, Kamajors "could of course attack women if they were on drugs." Given how frequently combatants in all military units were on drugs during the war, it may have been quite often.[7]

There was limited commentary on a second apparent cause of violent sexual acts: porn. As discussed earlier, there was a strong tendency for impressionable young males to imitate their heroes, such as Bob Marley, Tupac Shakur, or John Rambo. Several of those interviewed made reference to the powerful influence of films (in video form). A former male combatant recalled the popularity of films about Marley, Tupac, and the rapper 50 Cent. "Youth learn more negative aspects from these artists," he said. He added that the films that held particular appeal were "sex and love films." A former rebel wife explained this phenomenon: "When boys watch films and see how artists engage in sex, and [how] musicians sing about sex, [then] youth want to try what they see in the films and hear in the songs." Coulter identified indications of the influence of porn on sexual behavior during the war. She observed that "much has been written about the influence of action films such as *Rambo* and *First Blood* [that is, the first two Rambo films] on the formation of a rebel culture" (2009: 128; italics in original). Yet "nothing has been mentioned about whether or to what extent pornography circulated during the war."

Coulter speculated that pornographic films were "distributed and consumed by combatants during the war." In addition, the kind of sexual abuse that women experienced during Sierra Leone's war "was a type that was unprecedented in rural Sierra Leone and has to be located in a global warscape where pornography often plays an important role." Coulter described certain sexual acts that a female informant shared with her—specifically, fellatio and having sex with more than one man at a time—as being "unheard of" in Sierra Leone, and even "unthinkable." Other sorts of acts, such as being stripped and raped in public, and raped in the daytime, were clear violations of sexual taboos (128, 127, 129). While she admits that her findings are suggestive,[8] it is plausible (and perhaps probable) that pornographic films from abroad influenced the nature of sexual violence in Sierra Leone significantly. Following the war, members of a Child Welfare Committee for one chiefdom recorded virtually the same phenomenon. "The [boy] children practice from the [pornographic] films," one member explained. "They get the theory from the films and then do the practical."

A third potential cause concerns whether superiors in the various military outfits ordered rape, an issue that is debated. According to the TRC, "victims reported to the Commission that RUF commanders had given orders to their troops to carry out acts of sexual violence" (2004b: 172). In contrast, Cohen reported that her field interviews with former combatants "revealed little evidence that combatants were ordered to rape" (2013a: 408). My own interviews suggested variance on this issue. There were relatively few reports of commanders or other superiors ordering subordinates to rape. However, there was a great deal of evidence, from female and male members of military groups, as well as commanders, that rape and other forms of sexual violence were condoned. Boys, male youth, and men not only were able to "do whatever they wanted with women," as noted earlier by HRW, but rape was a strategy for promoting rebel terror. In addition, it appeared that rebel commanders rarely were called to order male underlings to rape. Subordinates already were raping proactively.

These conditions did not apply merely to rebel units. The TRC found that in CDF units, rape and other forms of sexual violence "appear to have been condoned, particularly if the women were labelled 'rebel collaborators' or 'rebels', or if they had family members who were associated with the RUF, the SLA or the AFRC." In addition, "the CDF, particularly in the latter period of the conflict, pursued the deliberate strategy of abducting civilian women and girls believed to be in any way connected to the RUF or who had collaborated with them, and detained them in a cruel and inhuman way, with the intention of deliberately violating them, either by raping them or using them as sexual slaves" (TRC 2004b: 177). The targeting of females to be raped and/or enslaved may have been narrower for CDF troops than for RUF or AFRC units. But as long as the females had some perceived connection to the rebels, then CDF behavior was much the same as that of their rebel counterparts toward females. Official CDF prohibitions on sexual deviance failed to have lasting impact in the field. When it came to females, the behavior of male combatants during the war was consistent.

A fourth possible cause of pervasive sexual violence toward females in wartime relates to marriage. MacKenzie described three types of marriage in Sierra Leone: customary, religious (taking place in churches or mosques), and those legally registered with the government. The last form provides legal protection for inheritance to widows (the first two do not). At the same time, even after the war, sexual assault taking place within a marriage was "still not widely viewed as a criminal offense in Sierra Leone" (MacKenzie 2012: 105). Coulter highlighted the traditional belief that all women must get married and outlined two additional kinds of marriage. One was wife stealing, which pertains to already-married women who marry another man, forcing the new husband to pay compensation (called "damages") to the first husband. The other was love marriage, which concerns a man and an unmarried woman who choose to marry (the man can already be married and decide to take another wife). A common cause of divorce is a husband who fails to provide for his wife (Coulter 2009: 74, 80–81, 85).

These marriage options stood as mighty challenges for the sort of poor and marginalized boys and male youth who got caught up in Sierra Leone's war. In rural villages, farming depends on physical labor (due to the "near-total absence of animals or machines"). There has been a major labor shortage in rural areas since diamond mining became an option for young males decades ago. In villages, community leaders have tried to keep male youth around by forcing them into marriages requiring young grooms to contribute labor as a form of bridewealth. Even if they were unmarried, young males could fall victim to the "incalculable arbitrariness" of customary justice. Countless male youth thus have lit out, many heading to the diamond mines where, despite onerous work and awful pay and living conditions, they at least could "experience some social freedom." The other main option was Freetown, where life on the edges of society, perhaps in the outcast Rarray Boy/lumpen/thug category, probably awaited them (Peters 2011a: 55, 57, 58, 59).

Sierra Leone's war provided poor male combatants with unparalleled access to females. Keen observed that "the possibility of 'getting whatever girls they wanted' was sometimes seen as a part of the attraction of being a rebel" (2005: 68). To be sure, some boys and male youth took advantage of their opportunity to marry, albeit in the informal bush variety. Some former rebel wives declared their love for their former rebel husbands after the war (Coulter 2009: 208). The feelings could be mutual (MacKenzie 2012: 111). That said, young love had little chance in the war theater. For example, RUF camps have been described as places where "violence was an integral feature of daily interaction" and an "aura of terror" ensured group "cohesion and obedience" (Denov and Maclure 2009: 61, 62). Boy and male youth combatants may have delighted in the opportunity to access girls and sex so easily. Yet prewar marriage frustrations by themselves do not explain the high intensity of sexual violence during the war.

A fifth potential cause, perhaps combined with the others, just might. It digs deeper, into the cultural psyche of Sierra Leoneans and what femininity represents. To begin with, some male civilian survivors, as well as male ex-combatants and commanders, made clear that the most fearsome fighters were females. Much of that fear surfaced from how female fighters contorted traditional images of womanhood and femininity. Adama Cut Hand clearly terrified (and awed) other rebels, as well as civilians. During interviews, she was described as a vicious leader in battle (reportedly switching from commanding a band of SGUs to SBUs after finding that the girls were insufficiently savage) and able to smoke more djamba than male commanders. A male youth who became a refugee recalled that, among the rebels, "the women were more bad than the men. They were too dangerous. They didn't have sympathy for young men. And some of the rebel women were pregnant." A violent female attacker is frightening. A pregnant one is even scarier, as it unseats traditional imagery and ideas about motherhood. One particular atrocity seemed especially unsettling. "The women commanders were fearsome because they liked to castrate men and boys," a former male RUF combatant explained. Just to be sure I had heard this, he added, "That's true." Adama's legend and both of these images—pregnant women fighters and women fighters castrating men and boys—directly confront the "hegemonic model of femininity" that highlights "being a wife and a mother."

Earlier in this book, analysts of Sierra Leone detailed the deep and historic cultural belief that feminine power is unruly and destructive—and men must control it. Indeed, the traditional idea is that women must be "domesticated." In the rural area where Coulter conducted her fieldwork, she found "a notion of women as being by nature raw, wild, and dangerous, [and] not at all inherently peaceful." Accordingly, some of the older women she interviewed informed her that "the purpose of female circumcision [also known as female genital mutilation, or FGM] was to calm and control women's wildness." An exceptionally violent woman rebel leader, and pregnant and castrating female warriors, appear to vividly demonstrate the potency of femininity and their ability to dominate, terrify, and intimidate males. Coulter speculates that this helps account for "comments about female combatants as more wicked and brutal than men" (2009: 74, 216, 241, 142). It may illuminate still more: applying violent masculine force to tame uninhibited femininity is culturally ingrained, the analysts collectively suggest. Faced with the "destructive and uncontrolled femininity" that "life in the bush" among rebel forces had unleashed, with females assuming roles as bush wives and female fighters, male combatants and commanders appear to have responded with sexualized vengeance to punish and domesticate females simultaneously (241). This constitutes one of the five proposed reasons for the expanse of sexual violence during Sierra Leone's war. Given all that took place, one cause, by itself, seems highly unlikely.

The question of why the RUF committed the largest proportion of wartime rapes remains. There likely was more than one reason. A high level RUF commander conceded that "it happened but it was not approved by RUF command." In fact, RUF laws prohibited rape. Those found guilty of the offense faced execution (Marks 2013: 369).

Why did the exact reverse take place? One reason was that the law usually was ignored. Indeed, "execution for rape would have eliminated some of the fiercest fighters upon whom the RUF relied for strength in battle," such as Mosquito and Superman. Second, Marks reports Sankoh's contention that "the best way to prevent the rape of civilians was by RUF fighters having wives." This was problematic in part because abducted girls and women usually were raped during their abduction. RUF marriages also have been called "institutionalized rape," a frame of reference that does not include those abducted females deposited in rape camps or used as sex slaves. They were females not taken as wives who were exploited by many male rebels. In addition, RUF commanders almost certainly appreciated "the strategic military benefits of rape, as a form of particularly transgressive violence that cows victims and their communities without killing the population" (Marks 2013: 371, 364, 370, 375, 373).

All of this illustrates how the RUF neither enforced their own laws effectively nor enacted a policy that differentiated between marriage and sexual violence. Given high levels of violence that characterized RUF society generally, the organizational efforts clearly made little headway. It should be noted that RUF groups largely were forest based and developed their own logics and habits, including the routine raping of many females whom male RUF members encountered (excepting commanders' wives and perhaps a few others). What seemed like rape to outsiders may not have been considered rape to male members socialized into these isolated communities.

The rape-oriented RUF societies evidently also fueled a popular shared practice in the field: gang rape. Cohen keyed her analysis to the fact that nearly all RUF fighters had been abducted, asserting that "when fighters are forcibly recruited, rape serves to socialize recruits into a coherent force." She found "abundant detail" to support this conclusion (2013b: 474, 475–476). The young male perpetrators described gang rape as fun and a shared entertainment. As one former male RUF member explained, during gang rapes "the entire unit watches. Everyone laughs and is jubilating" (Cohen 2013a: 404). Another observation speaks to masculine competition. In one recounting, the victim remembered hearing one of the perpetrators saying to a hesitating colleague, "Boh, if you not oh man, tell we" (Brother, if you are not a man, tell us) (Coulter 2009: 129). It is safe to conclude that RUF males raped a lot.

Although "wartime rape is probably as old as war itself" (Kelly 2010: 3), it neither is automatic nor preordained. Wood identifies rebel forces with strong ideologies, training regimens, laws, and enforcement methods that virtually removed rape from their repertoire of violence. El Salvador's civil war, for example, featured government forces raping "suspected insurgent supporters (including men)" and an exceptionally disciplined rebel group (the Frente Farabundo Martí para Liberación Nacional, or FMLN) that employed a "highly selective use of violence" and did not rape (Wood 2009: 152). Not a single military unit in Sierra Leone exhibited anything close to this trend. The lone exception would be signs of successful early enforcement of prohibitions on sexual violence by CDF units. But that standard deteriorated rapidly over time: when warfare expanded across Sierra Leone in 1998–1999, the Kamajors in particular raped almost as rampantly as any of their rebel rivals.

Sexual violence during Sierra Leone's war was out of hand in time and in space, extending across the entire wartime era and eventually reaching virtually the entire country. It appeared to open the door for males to "do whatever they wanted" to females, cultivating perverse sexual enrichment, broadcasting vindictive humiliations, enslaving females as personal property, accruing wives and concubines on a whim, bonding as boys, and relentlessly perpetrating merciless and ruthless sexual acts that attempted to undo endemic emasculation. If rape truly is "primarily a problem associated with degraded masculinities" (Bourke 2007: 436), then Sierra Leone's long history of debasing male youth while pulverizing females and femininity set the stage for brutal excess. An inchoate and uncontrolled wartime environment generated highly sexualized vengeance everywhere.

With all of this in mind, it is deeply sad to note Coulter's observation that "not much is written about women's contributions and position in the country [of Sierra Leone] in general or in the context of war" (2009: 55). Despite considerable examination of sexual violence during Sierra Leone's war by a small selection of analysts, there are many more studies of the war where sexual violence arises only in the background. Given the centrality of sexual violence in the practice of warfare in Sierra Leone, that is absolutely confounding.

CHAPTER 20

Through Male Youth Eyes

What Were They Fighting For?

This closing chapter about Sierra Leone's war features the views of former male youth combatants and commanders. It begins by revisiting the purpose of the war from their perspective, followed by reflections on the terror practices they carried out. Two themes surface prominently. One concerns the inescapable dominance of emasculation in male youth lives. The second is how male youth enmeshed in the war continually returned to Bob Marley's music and ethos for guidance and support. Indeed, it was Marley—not wartime leaders—who reminded fighters and commanders of what they sought to achieve via their violent struggle. Ultimately, Marley played a unifying role: regardless of their unit's position in the war, male youth interpreted Marley's message as equally relevant to all of them. The chapter ends with a last look at the disturbing distortions of Marley's messages by the RUF leadership.

What were the rebels fighting for? The answer should not have been as mysterious as it was. After all, the RUF issued a manifesto of sorts in 1995, in their *Footpaths to Democracy* (Revolutionary United Front, n.d.; see chapter 9). Yet the manifesto never came up in any of the interviews with former rebel combatants, commanders, or even top ex-RUF officials. No one seemed to have read it, or had it read to them. On the other hand, the view that nothing existed in terms of rebel goals or objectives also was not entirely the case. Rosen contends that the RUF's wartime effort "was not separatist, reformist, radical, or even a warlord insurgency." The group started a war that was "virtually without ideology" (2005: 61). This section will sidestep the clamorous debate over whether or not an overarching rebel creed, detailed belief system, or guiding ideology ever emerged. Instead, it will explore elemental purpose. What did former members of fighting squads, and their commanders, recount about the end point of their efforts? What did they hear from colleagues and superiors about what the war was all about, and what did they conclude themselves? Did they seek anything from their fighting beyond survival or escape? Was there a greater good to fight for and believe in?

For some, there was. However, before exploring those beliefs, two points require mention. First, RUF members did not necessarily accept the messages they received. Force had much to do with this: nearly all RUF soldiers, porters, wives, sex slaves, spies, civilian G5 members, and even field commanders and top officials had been abducted. During initiations and in the midst of war itself, they were told certain things that some privately questioned, including a former high-ranking RUF official. RUF members "weren't happy," he explained, "but you couldn't say that or you'd be killed." He added, "Some people were there to collect stolen property," reflecting the argument of some analysts that the RUF was nothing more than a criminal enterprise. "So everybody was there, but everybody was not happy."

He also suspected that Foday Sankoh had sold out his followers. "When Foday was arrested in Nigeria" in 1997, he recounted, "Foday told everyone to give the diamonds to [Charles] Taylor, and then Taylor would give the money to [second-in-command] Bockarie," more commonly known as Mosquito. "That was Foday's order. We had no say in the matter." Strikingly, he added, "Even Foday couldn't tell us if he got money from the diamonds. But I'm sure that boy [Taylor] would have given Foday money." The story of the RUF's diamond wealth suggests that not even Foday's close advisers (excepting Mosquito) ultimately would benefit personally from the RUF's efforts. Some of the proceeds apparently came back to the RUF from Taylor, sometimes in the form of arms and ammunition. Yet the top official's comments communicate reciprocal doubt: about the commitment of RUF followers to their leaders, and the commitment of the highest RUF leaders to their followers.

Questioning the sincerity of RUF leaders also surfaced in the recollections of a former RUF foot soldier. During his RUF training session, he and his fellow trainees received the following message: "In this country, we Sierra Leoneans are suffering. We have diamonds and minerals, but the Big Men in the country don't care about the youth. They only care about their children, who they send abroad for schooling and job opportunities. If we fight and succeed in overthrowing the government, we the young fighters will be rewarded by receiving good government jobs in the RUF government." The young boy was about to become an SBU member. Within the RUF's coercive environment, he explained, "I had no option but to believe what they told me. Because when I was captured, I had two options: to believe and fight along with them or not to believe and be killed." There was no indication that the threats ever turned him into an RUF believer.

Second, in terms of intent, the AFRC is a separate case. A civilian leader and mediator (chosen for the role by rebel commanders) in rebel-held Makeni in 1999 developed a take of the views of AFRC and RUF leaders about what they wanted from war. The AFRC had little to say. "All they were fighting for was being reinstated into the army." Given the simplicity of their goal, and keeping in mind that wrecking a nation to rejoin the nation's army seems an inefficient means of achieving their specific end, there was more to what they sought than that. Boiling rage seemed to be a particular AFRC specialty. Their intentions were blunt and emotional: aggressive revenge against past wrongs, tethered to a determination to take over the country. And certainly, the AFRC was not a reflective bunch. The coup that initiated their rebellion in May 1997 did not lead to an informed style of rule. Together with the RUF, they governed chaotically and violently. When they entered Freetown a second time (unforgettably, in January 1999), they again had no governing plan, just fury and terror. In the end, vengeance seemed to be the AFRC's underlying purpose.

About the underlying RUF purpose, there is a great deal more to detail. Based on what their leaders explained to him, the civilian leader whom rebel leaders forcibly retained in Makeni summed up RUF intentions:

> According to the RUF, they wanted to get rid of all people age thirty-five years old and above—those who were corrupt and responsible for the hardship in the country. So they thought that all junior boys who were illiterate would support them, because the RUF were a bunch of illiterates. They told the boys that in Freetown, they'd take over the government. They would force educated young men to be secretaries while the RUF commanders would be ministers of the government and Foday would be president. And as soon as that happened, they [the junior boys who had joined] would have free transportation and free education because the country is rich. This was the RUF's idea: to kill everyone in the country over thirty-five years old because they were the source of the country's corruption. All RUF [members] will tell you that.

As will be noted shortly, the leader's mention of "junior boys" and not junior girls expressed the RUF's gender-specific notion of revolution. It was for males. As also will be discussed, this general idea of society as a perverse universe, and the need to upend the elder-dominated status quo, also resonated in the messages of revered popular culture icons.

Other ideas in the Makeni leader's recollections aligned with the recounting of others, such as the country being rich, the government being corrupt, and the radical plan to put male youth on top. "The aims of the revolution," a second former high-ranking RUF official explained, "were free education. The school is free. Community members and ex-combatants can go [to school] for free. The farming is with a seed bank. So it's free." A "supporter" of miners (forced to mine diamonds for the RUF) said that RUF commanders "would come and tell us their ideology. They were fighting to overthrow the corrupt government. They said they would kill all the older people then [following the overthrow]." A former male combatant said that during his training period, his trainers "explained about the RUF. They said, the people suffer. The rich people don't care about the poor. The APC [the ruling party of Stevens and Momoh] doesn't care about the youth. That's why we were fighting: for the youth to take over the government, so that we too can enjoy our lives. We should not allow the minerals of the country to go in vain. They [the RUF] would deal with the Big Men in the government severely." Reflecting on all of this, the ex-fighter added, "They told me more, but I wasn't always listening because I was worried about what would happen to me." Regarding whether he believed what his RUF leaders had told him, he said, "Whether it's a true ideology or not, you just had to abide. I was forced to join them. Some believed in the RUF ideology, some didn't. I did not."

During interviews, two former captive RUF wives made clear that the war was all about "the rebels," who exclusively were boys, male youth, and men. As one explained, "I was an ex-combatant wife [that is, the ex-wife of an RUF combatant]. I didn't even know where the rebels' ideas came from. I was not taught their ideas." A second ex-wife recalled her RUF captors discussing liberation from foreign forces. While they attacked Nigerian troops in Makeni, the RUF fighters used to sing a song that meant "This land is ours and we must own it." By singing this song, she explained, "the rebels were sending the message to the Nigerian soldiers that Sierra Leone belongs to them and the foreigners must pack and go." As for females who became RUF fighters, their motives were complex. However, Coulter's research did not unpack any ideology: "There seem to have been a number of reasons why women became [RUF] fighters. Survival and control was an issue for some; for many others it was fear, anger, and even resignation; but there were some who mentioned the prestige and resources involved in being a fighter as their prime motivator. Many were constantly drugged and in hindsight could not recall having had any motivation whatsoever" (2009: 148). Coulter adds that, in field interviews with former rebels (nearly all of whom were female), she found that, when asked "why they thought the rebels were fighting or what they thought the war was about," most replied that "they did not know" (147). The absence of female connection to the RUF's broader intents (such as they were) was a prominent theme in Coulter's field research, as well as in mine. Indeed, there was no indication, from any of the major wartime players, that the war was being fought for females of any kind. Sierra Leone's war was exclusively for and about boys, male youth, and men.

Some boys and male youth developed their own boiled-down version of wartime purpose. Before providing details about this, it first is necessary to ap-

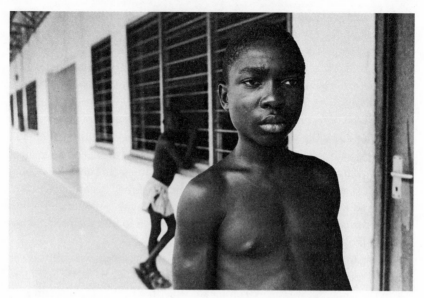

An ex-combatant, in 1997.

preciate the following wartime phenomena. As Sierra Leone's war dragged on, fighters began to switch sides. One analyst found that "fighters moved with relative ease between fighting factions depending on the balance of power in a given area" (Wlodarczyk 2009: 102).[1] According to the Truth and Reconciliation Commission, the breadth of this trend was singular: "The Commission identified an astonishing 'factional fluidity' among the different militias and armed groups that prosecuted the war. Both overtly and covertly, both gradually and suddenly, fighters switched sides or established new 'units' on a scale unprecedented in any other conflict of which the Commission is aware. These 'chameleon tendencies' spanned across all factions without exception; they say much about the character of the general 'breed' of combatant who participated in the Sierra Leone conflict" (TRC 2004a: 550). The apparently unique sort of fighter so perturbed commission members that they seemed to throw up their collective hands in despair over the young male Sierra Leoneans who participated in the war. "In the end," their report intoned, "it is difficult to answer the question, why the combatants fought the war. If they claimed any overriding agenda, the fluidity in their membership and their transient loyalties make it difficult to perceive, much less understand their agenda" (552).

Ironically, had the commission focused on the motives of female members of fighting forces, their conclusion may have resonated more strongly. As noted above, it did not appear that many girls or female youth caught up in war shared any purpose beyond immediate ones (such as survival and escape). Yet the commission's focus on the mystifying chameleon-culprits who wreaked havoc across the country points toward poor male youth. Indeed, the underlying idea of a separate, disloyal, mercenary, inchoate, unlikable, and thoroughly exasperating male youth "breed" seeps through. Here, near the end of their exhaustive examination of the war, the commission seems no closer to understanding the motivations of the gents who were its chief exemplars. Their take aligns with a theme that has surfaced many times in this book: something is wrong with those thugs, non-male youth profess, and no one else bore any responsibility for their deviance. What made those very bad boys tick remained a mystery.

When the commission issued their conclusion about male fighters, the analysis pared the fighters themselves away from the ideas and sway of military leaders. Given the many influences that surrounded wartime participants and the hierarchy in which they existed, that is difficult to do. Yet during interviews, many ex-combatants who explained their reasons for fighting raised similar themes. Speaking about her former combatant husband, one ex-RUF wife identified certain issues that many others also raised:

> I told my [rebel] husband that I loved Marley's songs more than any other musician. He loved Joseph Hills' songs too. In good times, when we lay down in our bed and we played music, though he was illiterate he was able to explain the message of Marley's songs. When I asked how he was able to learn and understand the meaning of these songs, even though he could not read and write English, he told me that when he was recruited as a rebel in 1993, they were taught the meaning of these [Marley's] songs as part of their training. They were advised to play these songs and meditate on them, because these were the songs that helped them [the RUF rebels] to know what they were fighting for and how they should not give up at all.

She also described the setting for all of this meditation about Marley: "It was normal to play Marley's songs and smoke djamba."

For many rebels, Marley's messages formed the crux of military purpose and motive. This was not coincidence: Foday Sankoh routinely referred to Marley's songs in speeches to his followers. Marley (as well as Rambo) surfaced in the RUF's full-on trainings/initiations. Trainers often encouraged male trainees to wear dreadlocks and speak like a Rasta. Thinking about Marley while smoking djamba, in addition, was thought to be essential to becoming "conscious" of underlying forces afflicting male youth lives. It was a pursuit that Sierra Leonean youth began to practice in the 1970s. RUF members and their leaders continued it in the 1990s, exploiting a tradition and the messianic presence of Bob Marley, who already was spectacularly popular throughout the land. Valentine Strasser and his NPRC government only underscored the significance of Marley to Sierra Leoneans and why the war was fought.

The extreme manipulation of Marley's songs to communicate core RUF ideas appeared to be widespread. "The songs of Marley had meanings," a former RUF combatant explained, "and the meaning of these songs helped us to understand the reason why we should continue to fight and get our rights." The ex-rebel fighter's direct reference to the refrain in "Get Up, Stand Up"— urging people to stand up for themselves and fight for their rights—was the most cited and significant passage from any song in Marley's sizable body of work.

The RUF used Marley's call to validate violent struggle. "As young boys," the ex-fighter continued, "when we listened to Marley's songs, our boss [his field commander] explained to us the meaning of these songs and told us the reasons why we were fighting." Among the reasons his commander shared with them was, "Our leaders are not treating us fine. They have taken what belongs to the nation and kept it for their personal use." As a result, "if we do not stand up and fight, we will continue to suffer." Another male ex-RUF fighter recalled virtually the same thing from his commander: "He told us that if we do not stand up and fight, then young people and the next generation will continue to suffer in our homeland. I began to understand more deeply the messages of Bob Marley's songs, such as 'Stand up for your Right' [a common reference to 'Get Up, Stand Up']. The RUF ideology is not too different from the messages in Marley's songs."

In many recollections of purpose, Bob Marley was the central source and promoter of RUF thought. "Get Up, Stand Up" spotlighted a particularly powerful message for profoundly alienated young people and a populace viewing those in power as swindlers. A succession of ex-RUF male fighters described how the RUF transformed Marley into their champion. "Reggae music helped us as RUF fighters to stand up for our rights," related one former combatant. "Marley preached about equality and what to do when equality does not work. The RUF ideology teaches us that we must take back what belongs to us." By manipulating Marley's message and merging it with RUF extremism, the critical implication of this interpretation is clear: it justifies extreme violence. As one ex-RUF combatant explained, "The RUF admired the messages of Marley's songs and believed the messages of these songs, and acted upon them. The RUF believed in the need to fight for their right[s], and this they did fearlessly."

The RUF's exploitation of Marley was impossible to miss. "In good times, when Marley's songs were being played, some of the senior officers would impress upon us the meaning and message of the songs," an ex-RUF combatant recalled. Then came a self-serving exaggeration: "They would tell us how Marley was a freedom fighter who inspired many African leaders to rise up and fight for their rights, like Robert Mugabe of Zimbabwe. Today, Zimbabwe is free because a group of people stood up and fought for their rights. So why can't we do the same thing? If we are to liberate Sierra Leone, we must fight to the end!" However distorted (Marley never was a soldier), the pitch proved convincing. "As young people," the former fighter explained, "we were convinced that we should fight to free our minds and get back our rights."

Bob Marley's immense popularity and sway over young Sierra Leoneans naturally moved across battle lines. Most if not all fighting units during the war listened to and venerated Bob Marley. No matter what side you fought on, or what group you fought for, "Get Up, Stand Up" was almost certain to inform your thinking. He was that ubiquitous and that loved. For many male fighters, so was Tupac Shakur and, particularly in the later war years, Joseph Hill and Culture (mainly referred to as "Joe Hills"). Young people jumping from one fighting force to the next must have enhanced the commonality of the music they listened to, and the ideas they drew from songs they deemed important, together with heavy marijuana use (and many other drugs).

An example of how shared core ideas and practices moved across battle lines emerged from the following interview with two former commanders: one who fought for the RUF, the other for the RUF's unsinkable adversary, the Kamajors. When I asked them what they had been fighting for during the war, the ex-RUF officer answered first. "My main purpose for joining the rebels was to help organize the country in a better way; to bring it back to normalcy, just as it was in the colonial days." Nostalgia for British rule was a theme that some Sierra Leoneans raised (usually adult men). It captures the revulsion that many citizens felt about governance in the postcolonial era. The former Kamajor commander entered the discussion. "I was fighting for freedom of movement and developmental freedom, mainly for the youth in the country," he explained. "Like the Bob Marley song, 'Get Up, Stand Up.'" Then he provided an example of his motivation to join the war: "If there's a quarrel between you and a Lebanese man, and you go to court, he can even slap you there, just because he has money. He'll go 'Scot free.' And you, the poor, innocent man, he [the judge] will lock you up. And this was the reason why I was seriously fighting." The story of powerlessness, disrespect, and injustice resonated with his new friend, the ex-RUF commander. "That's the exact same for me," he said. "I agree completely."

More than any other figure, Bob Marley—his music and the marijuana that accompanied listening to it—personalized Sierra Leone's war. For the boys and male youth who fought it, Marley provided pure meaning and purpose. Experts may debate whether Sierra Leone's awful war was a criminal, religious, or political project. However, through male youth eyes, the optics change entirely. Revenge, redemption, respect, and freedom were intimate values and aims that surfaced during interviews. They emerged from interpretations of what became the portable anthem for male combatants across the wartime landscape: Marley's "Get Up, Stand Up."

Why Terror?

TERROR IN CONTEXT

Interviews with experts, practitioners, and donors in the fields of international development and countering (or preventing) violent extremism collectively revealed how, in practice, "gender" equates with adult women (and sometimes girls) while "youth" points toward male youth (Sommers 2015: 15, 157; Sommers 2019a: 17). Interviews with government officials across Africa have revealed that their perspectives generally reflect the exact same tendencies. The two constricted definitions are that prevalent, and in both, female youth virtually evaporate. Through the youth = male youth lens, they either reside deep in the background or are excised out of the youth category entirely. Within the gender = women landscape, female youth transform into young women and play a junior role to their older adult women superiors. In the accepted mainstream worlds of youth and gender, female youth vacillate between insignificant and invisible.

The narrowing of youth and gender concepts promotes harmful distortions and outcomes. Framing youth exclusively as masculine facilitates destructive stereotyping. In the hands of many, "youth" are inherently dangerous, irrational, destabilizing, and violent characters, with the poorest and the most marginalized among them often converting into the worst that maleness can represent.[2] And just as a male youth cannot be called a man, a female youth is not a woman. In much of the world, womanhood and manhood signify arrival as socially accepted adults. Being a youth does not.[3] In addition, interpreting gender as female (and mainly as older women) invites unbalanced analyses of and approaches to gender challenges. It also runs the risk of

- Undercutting examinations of and responses to disempowered girls and female youth;
- Subordinating vital female youth/young women's issues to those of their adult women seniors;
- Diminishing gendered concerns involving boys, male youth, and men;
- Envisioning masculinity only as a negative force;
- Overshadowing the importance of other gendered identities (such as lesbian, gay, bisexual, transgender, queer, or questioning, often known as LGBTQ); and
- Dodging the towering significance of emasculation on females, males, societies, politics, and governance.

The exclusionary nature of youth and gender concepts makes it difficult to grasp and address the challenges that female and male youth, and adult women and men, each face, and much harder to deploy both concepts at once.

These trends are reflected in analyses of Sierra Leone and its destructive war. "Youth" implicitly refers exclusively to male youth in most studies. The youth = male youth lens minimizes the centrality of female youth to the practice of warfare. Meanwhile, the gender = women scope typically features older adult women and separates gendered concerns from boys, male youth, and men. Emasculation can result in public humiliation and too often funnels toward self-destruction and many forms of violence.

Male youth emasculation plays a sculpting role in Sierra Leone's history. From the time of precolonial slavery, the labor of male youth was in demand and ripe for exploitation. Chiefs and other Big Men lorded over a patrimonial social system that entrapped the poor and young. For female youth, their future almost certainly ended in marriages where their power, actions, and voice were contained and protection from violence scarcely existed. They also would have had their clitoris removed during a secret initiation ceremony. Elite men sought many wives in part to trick unmarried male youth into adultery, securing their labor via the woman damage (adultery) repayment. Paying off a bride price was another way to extract male youth labor.

Many male youth turned to education because it promised "recognition within a meritocracy" and a "route to global recognition and success." The aspiration illustrates the urge for Sierra Leonean youth to seek answers well beyond their social norms and national borders. But the education option fell apart after primary and secondary education withered in the 1980s. Marriage was a trap and rising via education was a dream. Peters records the result: former male combatants who not only resented the absence of educational opportunity for them but also expressed "a seething resentment at a class system through which the schooling of the children of landowners and chiefs is paid for by the sweated labour of young [male] commoners expended in earning the right to reproduce" in marriage (2011a: 52, 53, 51). Diamond mining and urban survival were escape options, but they too were dead ends. Worse, male youth were under attack. The Stevens-created ISU and SSD headlined the state forces waiting in the wings to strike. Devious politicians sought desperate male youth to do violent deeds on their behalf. Chiefs condemned those stepping out of line as *fityai* boys. And elders, intellectuals, politicians, and still other elites called them names, such as vagrants, hoodlums, outlaws—and thugs. Emasculation and alienation encircled most male youth lives, while traditional society's need for males to control feminine power made FGM and marriage almost inevitable for female youth. For male as well as female youth, there was no way out.

When the war came, Marley, Tupac, and Rambo were low-hanging fruit for military leaders. Many young males already identified profoundly with their righteous outsider-heroes. Male CDF combatants considered themselves rebels, just like their "People's Army" rebel counterparts (in the AFRC, WSB, and RUF) (Hoffman 2006: 9). The universe that Marley and Tupac preached about and Rambo fought against was structurally contradictory: society labeled youth as wrong and bad when the opposite was the case. Mainstream forces were unjust and resistance was the antidote. The boys in Sierra Leone needed to advocate for their rights, precisely what rebels discussed at night while becoming "conscious" with marijuana and the music of Marley, Tupac, and Joseph Hill (and, on rare occasions, also watching a Rambo film). It seemingly would have been impossible for Foday Sankoh, Valentine Strasser, and other wartime leaders and field commanders *not* to incorporate Marley, Tupac, and Rambo into their military efforts. Keen described what came next: rebels who actively and consciously created a "perverse universe" by reversing accepted morals and norms, humiliating elders, and normalizing aberrant behavior (2005: 76). CDF violence on the other side was not much different.

The terror that exploded across Sierra Leone largely emerged from RUF, AFRC, WSB, CDF, and SLA leaders and commanders who goaded and exploited their youthful troops, saturated them with drugs, and manipulated pop culture icons toward devious ends. Underneath these actions lay something deeper: *structural violence.*

The concept fits Sierra Leone's female and male youth like a glove. It "draws our attention to unequal life chances, usually caused by great inequality, injustice, discrimination, and exclusion in needlessly limiting people's physical, social, and psychological well-being." Such endemic and long-standing conditions provoke "frustration, anger, ignorance, despair, and cynicism, all of which greatly increase the potential for acute violence." In these and other passages, Uvin explained how structural violence in Rwanda helped activate genocide (1998: 105, 107). Much of what he described applies equally to young Sierra Leoneans, where the result was not extermination but many forms of terror.

TERROR IN PRACTICE

The rebels' civilian-centered terror tactics cooked up a buffet of complementary interpretations. As has been suggested in this book, there was something for just about everyone. Evidence of base violence and criminality was always there. Rebel leaders drugged and pushed their male underlings to commit atrocities by the bushel, loot liberally, and sexually punish females fanatically. Using terror to coerce displacement from areas with diamond mines always was present, as well. The rebels also cut off arms, hands, fingers, and heads, sometimes to make crude political gestures.

The RUF created an underlying political philosophy and to a very limited degree implemented it, particularly during the war's early stages. But the RUF lacked cohesion, discipline, or, after a while, collective spirit. Many of the RUF and AFRC commanders were little more than me-first exploiters. Superman, Adama Cut Hand, Mosquito, and Gullit, to name four prominent examples, set examples for nihilism, not revolution. By the time rebel violence had ramped up across the nation in 1998–1999, the rebels' political project vacillated between vague and nonexistent. Rebel efforts to pervert the existing universe resembled real-time vengeance much more than a striving for lasting, substantive change. On the other hand, the personalized, youth-centered ideologies of John Rambo, Tupac Shakur, and especially Bob Marley were in play on the ground virtually everywhere and across the war's entire time frame, starting when Foday Sankoh adopted and broadcast Marley's doctrine as the war began. Over time, drugs, terror, sexual aggression, and adulation for Bob Marley framed the male warrior lifestyle. In camps, the philosophy of standing up for your rights seemed ever-present. Social life promoted a twisted camaraderie in extremism, with brutality pervading camp life and military attacks.

In military terms, terror warfare was a practical cover for obvious weaknesses. The RUF may have been good at terrorizing civilians and extracting diamonds. But they were far less capable at fighting adversaries. Their most refined military specialty was resilience: they proved hard to snuff out. The AFRC, in contrast, were multitaskers. They sometimes could beat ECOMOG and the Kamajors (especially when SAJ Musa was alive) as well as inflict mighty terrors on ordinary people. But their forces were much smaller. The West Side Boys militia was smaller still (once they separated from the rest of the AFRC). For them, terror as the central military strategy was absolutely necessary. Utas and Jörgel explain that the WSB "systematically used extreme violence, acts of madness and perceived anarchy, in order to instil fear and respect in the enemy." Their main aim was "making the bush insecure."

Terror made the WSB appear mightier than they were. It began with becoming "fearful yourself." One commander explained the process: "You pull [off] your clothes, wear hot pants and people will know that it is bush he comes from—he is different from those in town. So when you stand up and open fire the people will be afraid" (Utas and Jörgel 2008: 506). According to Utas and Jörgel, the West Side Boys cultivated their reputation for spectacle—"known for wearing bizarre clothing—women's wigs and flip-flops are favourites—and being almost perpetually drunk" (BBC News 2000)—to cultivate the hoped-for result: making the area insecure. Their underlying purpose was to radiate strength while avoiding direct confrontation. The WSB had to do this because "they could not stand up against any of the other military actors on Sierra Leonean soil" (Utas and Jörgel 2008: 506). They also required lots of drugs to pull this off.

The WSB's military approach aligns with those employed by other AFRC units, as well as the RUF. Even though terror as a military strategy arose from weakness, the rebels honed their awful craft well. Abdullah and Rashid, in fact, argue that the RUF's heavy reliance on children and drugs set them apart. After comparing the RUF to Taylor's NPFL and the RENAMO rebels of Mozambique, they concluded that "the terror in Mozambique and Liberia were reproduced ten fold in the Sierra Leone context" (Abdullah and Rashid 2004: 252).

Some of those interviewed shared their analysis of why the rebels had featured terror in their work. A former leading RUF official described two main purposes for attacks. One was "to use terror to displace people from Kono and Tongo Field [two diamond-rich areas]; to force civilians out of there so the rebels could get rich from the diamonds." A second was more basic: "to frighten the enemy; to send a signal to them. You wiped out civilians and cleared people out to get more territory, for the world to know that the RUF was there." He regretted the tactics that the RUF had used. "It was a bad thing, that civilians should be wiped out," he said. "Beating people, forcing them out, just to get diamonds: I never approved of that. It was a bad thing [and] it wasn't what the movement was about." The ex-official's reflections revealed the contrast between organizational intent and follow-through.

A central reported motivation for rebel attacks on ordinary civilians was uncertainty about who the civilians were and what side they were on. This left rebel fighters insecure, so they attacked. "One of the RUF terror tactics was to instill fear," an ex-Kamajor commander remembered, "so you don't come closer to them. They didn't want people to resist them. [They wanted] to chase people away, so they could take their food and mine" for diamonds. A former RUF commander underscored the RUF's fear of civilians. "You don't know if the civilians are with the enemy." As a result, "you can't go peacefully because you could be killed. So what you do is to attack them [the civilians], drive the enemy away, and take food from the civilians." Examples of civilians taking revenge remained strong in the memories of some ex-rebels, such as one former male RUF fighter, who explained that "during the retreat [from Freetown in January 1999], the civilians tried to burn us. They put a tire around a rebel soldier and the [rebel] collaborators, poured in gasoline, and set [them] on fire." The rebels retaliated with amputations. Some civilians provided a similar frame of analysis, such as this explanation from a civilian survivor and director of an NGO for ex-combatants: "When rebels attacked a village, they tried to create as much fear as possible to get the obedience of the population. If you kill off some of the men, then the women and children will obey. Women will want to safeguard their children. Men don't want to be killed. You show your ruthlessness by getting a father to kill some of his children or [get] a child to kill his parents. So you change the status quo psychologically."

A smaller subset of interviewees spotlighted ethnicity as a motivation for terror warfare. While reporting on the issue was limited, the intensity of the commentary was not. The descriptions always situated the northern Temne against the Mende of the south and east. These two groups dominate Sierra Leone demographically and politically. The APC of Stevens is largely Temne, while the SLPP of Kabbah is mainly Mende. Despite this, it would have been difficult for ethnicity to surface as a prominent factor in the war. Mende Kamajors had to coordinate their efforts with CDF counterparts comprising Temne and other groups. The AFRC was largely Temne (or purported to be), while the RUF was ethnically mixed. Sankoh himself was a Temne based in Mende-dominated areas during the war. All of this did not prevent ethnic rivalry from being a motivator for terror practices. But it likely was localized in nature, subject to certain fighting groups confronting particular adversaries or civilians.

Rebel manipulations of two emotions round out this brief review. The first is shame. In traditional societies, acts that shame individuals simultaneously shame their families and communities (McKay and Mazurana 2004: 44). During Sierra Leone's war, publicly shaming elders and raping females were persistent trends. The starting point for at least some male perpetrators with the RUF, in turn, was shamelessness. These combatants were "not ready to be judged by a society they themselves deemed violent and corrupt" (Keen 2005: 75). RUF commanders made violence a "moral good" for their fighters and reluctance to commit violence "transgressive and shameful." The leaders' portrayal of the civilian world as "rotten and ruined" also cultivated a second emotion: feelings of disgust among subordinates. This revulsion converted extreme RUF violence against civilians into "punitive and purging" acts (Mitton 2015: 137, 193, 199). The concept of cleansing civilians by torturing and killing them is reminiscent of *génocidaire* philosophies that arose in Bosnia, Cambodia, Germany, Rwanda, and elsewhere.

In the end, what can one make of this form of warfare? It relied on three basic elements: manipulating young people, centering attacks on civilians, and normalizing extreme violence. The rebels drew from a bounty of available material to make it happen:

- A greedy, violent, and unpopular state;
- An impoverished and aggrieved population;
- The historic emasculation, entrapment, and alienation of male youth;
- The historic drive to control females and feminine power;
- A pantheon of adored pop culture icons who could be exploited to rationalize rebellion and make it all seem youth centered; and
- Seemingly endless quantities of diamonds, drugs, and children.

None of these ready-made factors automatically led to terror warfare. But easy access to all of them certainly bequeathed a matchless opportunity to a collection of angry insurgents and Charles Taylor, their wily benefactor in Liberia.

Bob Marley and War: Reflections

Reggae music and rude boys emerged in 1960s Jamaica. Politicians used some of the rude boys as mercenaries to suit their political purposes. Those considered *cultural* rude boys had a political orientation, disdaining standards defined by Whites and the unequal benefits they received. A blending of youth, music, and Rasta religion paralleled the rise of the rude boys and presented "a posture of contempt for the status quo" while demanding social change (Edmunds 2003: 109).

The three leaders of the Wailers music group—Bob Marley, Peter Tosh, and Bunny Wailer—shared these sentiments. Their home was Trench Town, "a most notorious ghetto in Jamaica." Edmonds stated that outside observers often have viewed the reggae music that grew from this time and place as "protest music," particularly its "militant call to 'Get up, stand up. Stand up for your rights.'" But reggae music, he insisted, was much more than that. In fact, "the issues facing the poor of African descent, interpreted from a Rastafarian perspective and expressed in Rastafarian terms, constitute the dominant element in reggae lyrics" (109, 110).

The West African nation of Sierra Leone in the 1970s had its own sweltering ghettos, rude boys, and political ferment. It also had Siaka Stevens, who hired some of the cornered, fed-up male youth to do his dirty work. The country was fertile ground for the alternatively searing and uplifting messages in Bob Marley's music. Marley and his reggae music colleagues from Jamaica captured male youth imaginations, especially in Freetown. Over time, Marley's popularity expanded across the country and generations of Sierra Leoneans. When the war began, Marley became a big part of the RUF's "deliberate strategy to instrumentalize, misappropriate, and recontextualize music as [a] weapon" and "an accomplice of violence." Their exploitative efforts "contributed considerably to the incitement of fear and terror" across the land. The RUF shrewdly manipulated the works of Marley and other influential musicians, including Tupac Shakur, Joseph Hill and Culture, and even "Bubu music [a traditional Sierra Leonean music form] and traditional drums" to serve their ends (Nuxoll 2015: 16).

Marley's featured role in RUF manipulations inspired a diversity of reactions from Sierra Leoneans after the war. A man working with refugee returnees contended that "Marley didn't always mean a violent revolution. The RUF interpreted Marley's [political] theory. Marley created awareness about your rights and your suffering. But then the RUF interpreted Marley to brainwash the youth." He reserved particular scorn for Tupac, whom he believed had "radicalized the revolution that Bob Marley came to preach" and made the RUF even more extreme. "The ruthlessness of Tupac's method of doing things was contrary to Bob Marley's approach. The rebels who admired Tupac were the ones who became gangsters," he concluded. His assessment reflects the simultaneous appreciation of Marley and loathing of Tupac that many adult Sierra Leoneans share.

A former abducted wife of an RUF combatant did not focus on Tupac and was no fan of Marley or Joseph Hill. From what she had observed, the two reggae superstars made the wartime situation much worse. "The message of their songs gave the rebels the zeal to fight," she insisted, "especially when they knew what they were fighting for: to gain their rights and control power." In her view, Marley and Hill had spurred marijuana-fueled violence. After contemplating this, she said, "I wish Marley and Joe Hill were alive. I would have asked them why they [had] promoted such a wicked thing."

Musings from ardent and longtime fans of Bob Marley reflected their personal connection to the man and his music. Two sets of comments signaled broad regret about Marley's misuse. Neither blamed the RUF specifically. What mattered most was Marley's call to Africans everywhere. One of the devout followers of Marley had begun wearing dreadlocks before he was abducted into the RUF. He shared his take on what had occurred:

> Marley's message was completely misunderstood. Instead of bringing peace in Africa, it has brought fighting and killing. Instead of fighting against the colonial powers [a theme in Marley's music], Africans now fight each other.
>
> This is sad. Marley smoked marijuana but never took [up] arms to fight anybody. In as much as I agreed that Marley contributed to youth resistance to the government, that was not what he intended Africans to do.

Similar sentiments emanate from the reflections of a journalist and fellow Marley devotee: "When Bob Marley said, 'Don't give up the fight,' many people saw this as a call to take up arms. That is a misinterpretation of his message. Marley believed it was more favorable to use our intelligence, our sense of patriotism in Africa, to turn things around. Even if you're in a difficult situation, you don't forget the message of peace, love, and nonviolence to pass on your message."

RUF leaders disregarded Marley's preaching about nonviolence and amplified his calls for revolution. They went to war to extract vengeance and diamonds and take power by any means necessary. Marley, Tupac, Rambo, drugs, kids, diamonds, and more became terror war tools to power their cause. This does not mean that leaders of the RUF or other wartime military groups did not admire Bob Marley and believe in some of his ideas. Many did. But they deployed Marley, the works of other musicians, and war films featuring Rambo and others merely to suit their purposes.

Ultimately, the war produced titanic damage for fighters on all sides, captive members of military groups, and the country at large. A sense of where all of this left Sierra Leone's youth, particularly some of those featured in the warfare, will close this story of a country and its unforgettable conflict in part 7.

Postwar Worlds

CHAPTER 21

Alienation and Rights

Frustration and Forgetting

In 2010, at the end of my field research trip to Kenema, I boarded an early morning bus headed for Freetown. Just after the bus driver started our trip, there was a sudden explosion of voices from the front of the bus. I thought there was a fight between at least two men. But the bus driver kept driving as if nothing were happening.

It wasn't a fight. Instead, it was shared exasperation about politics in Sierra Leone. Two men loudly cursed the country's two main parties: Stevens's Temne-dominated APC from the north, and Kabbah's Mende-dominated SLPP from the south and east. Kenema was SLPP country, but the eight or so adults in the front of the bus showed no favoritism. "We should stop politics and develop this country," one of the angriest men bellowed at the top of his voice. Then he warned that "the war can come again!" "Yes!" called out three other adults in front, a mix of women and men. A woman called out, "I don't like any party. They just care for themselves." The bus driver chimed in, "You go into office with no money and you get nothing." "Big Men only go for themselves," the woman added, "leaving small people behind."

The man beside me tried to put it all in context. "When the British ruled the country," he explained, "there were so many good roads. Now, there is no development. Instead, there is nepotism, corruption, and politics." The abrupt flare-up soon died down and the rest of the bus trip was uneventful. I discovered that the man sitting next to me was a town planner for the city of Freetown, heading back to the capital after visiting relatives. It was an opportunity to ask about the actual population of postwar Freetown, as available estimates seemed very low. What is the working figure for the city's population that his office used for their work? I asked. The town planner had no idea. Our conversation shifted to genial topics.

The emotional upsurge at the outset of the bus journey was not a singular event. From time to time, I noticed how people would erupt with frustration about the status quo. What would seem like a public dressing-down of another person instead was merely an accepted way to blow off steam. Once, a woman delivering fruit to my hotel set down her wares and began yelling at the receptionist about corruption. Such outbursts did not attract much attention from others. Something had happened to her earlier that day. Once a person cooled down, those nearby would quietly console them or add their own stories. They were signs of how the awful war had failed to unseat those in power or the way they wielded it. Styles of governance and politics were much the same. Politicians and chiefs ruled, largely as before, in the Big Man, patrimonial, leader-followers style, and evidently with impunity. On top of that, the need to pay bribes to pass through checkpoints, escape from police encounters, and secure virtually any government service became daily servings of salt in the wound.

Development too seemed to be foundering. In 2013, a doctor in the town of Koidu, capital of Kono District, filled with diamond miners wading daily into bilharzia-filled waters to do their work, shared a sense of the local medical situation. "Most of the boys here are miners," he said, while "most commercial sex workers are [girls] under eighteen" years of age. "Right now, I'm the only doctor in the district," he said. "I'm the surgeon, pediatrician, and everything else." He excused himself to go to "the theater," where he would conduct a surgery without electricity or suction. "The conditions are very difficult," he understated. "But the best healer is God."

After all the loss, destruction, and misery, had nothing in Sierra Leone changed? A great deal, it turned out, was indeed new. Never have I been in a nation where the subject of youth had a higher profile than early postwar Sierra Leone. Prewar controls over political critique and moderate expression also were long gone. The first radio station I tuned to, at the outset of my first postwar research trip to the country in 2005, played hip-hop songs mentioning "fuck" and "motherfucker" (among other curse words) repeatedly. There was soaring urban population growth, with Freetown and Bo leading the way, and Kenema and Makeni not far behind. Marijuana was easily available and used almost everywhere. Diamond mining continued, but alongside the mining of gold and other minerals, and now including women and very young child miners. Waves of community reconciliation and youth-focused programs flowed across the land.

Something else was taking place too: the method of "forgetting" to manage the trauma of war. In 2005 a judge outlined the approach. "The war was a Pandora's box," he related. "That's why it should be left alone. There were atrocities, and it took atrocious means to stop them." The judge did not consider the law a means to settle things. Instead, he wanted everyone to move on. "I think it would have been better to forgive and forget and move ahead" instead of allowing the Special Court for Sierra Leone—an international body with international support—to prosecute some of the war's kingpins, he added. Many shared his general sentiment on forgetting. Listening to "the music of Tupac and Bob [Marley] can make you dance and forget your trauma," a former male youth combatant explained. A former rebel wife explained that her favorite Nigerian pop song "is beautiful and gives me courage. It makes me dance and forget about my worries." "Some women smoke djamba," a twenty-eight-year-old single mother explained to me. "It's not just for men. When I smoke it, I forget my problems for a while." "Considering what I did during the war," a second ex–rebel wife reflected, "it is sad to say that I have regretted [what I did] greatly. But let us forget about it totally." "Sometimes it is difficult to talk about what we went through," a male elder related, "especially now that I am forgetting the past. All I could say in one word was that we suffered so much."

Shaw found that Sierra Leoneans' response to deeply upsetting memories of the war "did not mean the erasure of personal memories, but their containment in a form that would enable them to recover their lives." Shaw considered this process directed forgetting, and her research indicated that Sierra Leoneans regularly practiced it as a means of processing personal memories of the war. Yet a war is difficult to forget or move beyond while living inside a house the rebels had burned down. The "art of forgetting" relies on "the ability to build a future." That is the key. As Shaw observed, "the purpose of directed forgetting, following a violent past, is to be able to reconstruct one's life, and is undermined by the absence of material resources to do so" (2007: 194, 196, 197). In this way, practical postwar reconstruction that reaches individuals in authentic and empowering ways has the potential to heal the psychic wounds of war at the same time. An elderly woman referred to directed forgetting and the required response that Shaw detailed. "When you recall what happened" during the war, she explained, "you feel tormented and it will aggravate you." She thus tried not to dwell on her wartime experiences. However, that proved difficult to do because "until you repair the houses wrecked during the war, we can't stop being reminded of the war. And we want to move on."

Sierra Leone during the time of my field research reflected in the three chapters of part 7 (2005 and 2010 primarily, 2009 and 2013 secondarily) generally did not suggest that appropriate efforts to help people reconstruct their lives had been put forth. That would have been a tall task for any postwar nation, particularly one as collapsed by war as Sierra Leone, and one that also had been in dire straits prior to war's emergence. But Sierra Leone's government hardly moved with alacrity. Shaw, for example, noted that the TRC's final report called for a sizable reparations program, urgently implemented. Its primary focus was "the rehabilitation of the victims [of human rights violations during the war] through the distribution of service packages and symbolic measures which acknowledge the past and the harm done to victims and gives victims the opportunity to move on" (TRC 2004c: 232). The government's response was weak tea, with its evasive written response amounting to "a stalling maneuver" highlighting limited resources and an absence of specific next steps. "The implications of this [government] unresponsiveness for the process of social repair and restorative justice are serious," Shaw warned (2007: 206, 206n67). Most Sierra Leoneans no doubt would have agreed.

The chapters in part 7 examine Sierra Leone in the aftermath of war, drawing largely from interviews with Sierra Leoneans. What was the view from the ground? Where did it leave ordinary Sierra Leoneans? How were the war's young participants managing? Former female and male members of military groups share the spotlight, including those considered Rarrays following their return to civilian life. Rarray Boys and Girls are among the many names with which down-and-out youth are burdened. The twin terms are significant because they cast male and female youth as outsized, reckless children. The first two chapters in this section feature examinations of issues, people, and forces found to impact youth. The third chapter focuses on the influence of Rambo, Tupac, and Marley in the postwar era. The frame of reference for all three chapters is the decade or so following the war (from 2002 to 2013). It thus ends just before the 2014 arrival of the Ebola pandemic and a new context and set of circumstances for Sierra Leone.

The Outliers

Evidence from field interviews and other research suggests that Sierra Leone entered the postwar era with large numbers of ex-combatant youth addicted to (or heavily reliant on) drugs and alcohol (e.g., Bøås and Hatløy 2005). The lion's share appeared to be male youth, although female youth (as well as some boys) resorted to drug and alcohol use too. These were not surprising outcomes, given how the war played out and the expansive influence of marijuana across the land afterward. In the postwar era, drugs were featured elements in many male youth's lives.

Those who engaged with drugs and alcohol visibly and emphatically resisted tradition. It was one way to project the attainment of manhood as a distant possibility. Many of those who turned to drug and alcohol use also displayed a particular fondness for marijuana and Bob Marley. Indeed, Marley's ability to transcend context, shifting with ease into postwar male youth lives following sustained prewar popularity and being a featured wartime presence, is an important theme in part 7. A second is marriage for female youth. It was a regular theme in interviews with most female youth about their current and future horizons.

That was not the case with male youth, which is a third postwar theme. Most seemed unable even to envision a realistic path toward manhood. How is manhood even possible without the prospect of a viable and stable income?

What if few male youth have the ability to marry a female youth? One shared option was to demonstrate adulthood by becoming a parent, a useful (and common) mode of gaining a modicum of recognition as adults, especially for female youth. For male youth, parenthood was fleeting recognition of adult success, as a small proportion had any ability to support a family. Without such prospects, remaining with the new mother and child was a social impossibility. The situation underscored how masculinity and manhood are unstable moving targets for male youth and men, and how femininity and womanhood tie deeply to subordination and fertility.

This section features assessments of what "Rarray Boy" and "Rarray Girl" meant to different people, including those inescapably ensnared by the Rarray identity. The next section reviews how adults and young people define being a youth and an adult, as well as takes on how female and male youth viewed prospects for their attainment of, respectively, womanhood and manhood. It also reviews the arrival and impact on the ground of new laws collectively known as "human rights." The interview data for the two sections feature the views of young people and adults in up-country Sierra Leone. Taken together, they frame and inform the descriptions of postwar lives that follow in the next two chapters.

Being a Rarray meant different things to different people. For many adults, it signaled the failure of young people to accept social responsibilities and expectations. "Rarray Boys are youth who do not care about becoming men in the future," a town chief declared. "They go about enjoying themselves with women and in their social activities. They run away from responsibilities." Rarray Girls deserved a similar level of contempt, as "they are the same as Rarray Boys. They enjoy living the carefree life: the prostitute." A senior teacher chimed in with a broad condemnation of the Rarrays. "They are the unserious people in society," he declared. "They enjoy living a useless life." Then he went further: "These people are not productive in society, killing and finding it extremely difficult to earn their living. Mostly [Rarray Boys earn their living] through gambling and stealing. Girls become prostitutes."

Rarray Boys equated with the thugs of yore. The boys bore the stereotype of being a kind of lost generation of "idle, dangerous youth" (Finn and Oldfield 2015: 44). Their Rarray Girl counterparts were unmarried female youth. Together, they bucked tradition. Accordingly, while all working definitions of Rarrays drew from the same underlying characterization—Rarray Boys were drug-using thieves while Rarray Girls marketed sexual availability—their unpopularity hinged on a deeper social tension. Rarrays resisted the guidance and accepted norms prescribed by elders and established tradition. Their lifestyle announced to all that they were not on the road to adulthood and may never desire such recognition. By pointedly resisting the elder set and living lives of pronounced disrepute, they embodied permanent social resistance—a postwar rebel lifestyle, perhaps. As the veteran teacher despaired, "Sometimes when we look at the situation, we adults begin to ask, 'Where is the future of Sierra Leone?'"

Like Rambo, Rarrays did not negotiate a truce with mainstream overlords. Like Tupac, their lifestyle openly defied social expectation. The Rarrays' collective stance invoked electric responses to questions about Rarray Boys and Girls from non-Rarray youth interviewees, as well. For many striving for recognized adulthood, their Rarray-resistor counterparts constituted an affront, perhaps because Rarrays cared so little for all they were working toward. Two ambitious female youth described how Rarray Girls were, in their view, unwomanly. "They are not ashamed of quarreling with men who do not want to pay for sex," one remarked. Rarray Girls "cannot make it [to gain recognition as women] because they use the money they earn to buy expensive dresses and body cream in order to make them more attractive." Two former male youth rebels condemned Rarrays as comprehensively as their elders might. "They dress recklessly"—a common criticism of Rarray Boys and Girls—"and do not cooperate with authorities," said one. The other complained of the "short and transparent skirts" that Rarray Girls wore, and the shared affinity of Rarrays for "smoking djamba, drinking rum, and spending most of their time in bars and ghettos." Together, the two male youth prescribed the same two remedies for Rarrays that many adults also mentioned: religious counseling for the boys and marriage for the girls. One problem with these outcasts was that there were so many of them. A Rarray in postwar Sierra Leone was unexceptional. In addition, Rarrays lived in the moment, not for the future. "They do not want to own things," a male youth renting bikes in Makeni remarked. "They live a free life: these are the Rarray Boys and Girls."

No critiques of Rarrays contained expressions of interest in knowing what they thought about anything. Instead, non-Rarrays treated them as bad people who created unsettling problems. The attitude is not unlike the broad castigations of many analysts of Sierra Leone's prewar and wartime periods against wayward male youth deemed thugs, lumpens, vagrants, and so on. There's something wrong with those Rarrays, all of these assessments implied. Following the war, many who were interviewed contended that Rarrays needed to subordinate themselves to tradition and strive to become respectable. Even after its horrid war, Sierra Leoneans generally did not take kindly to rebellion of any kind. Rarrays seemed to deserve no compassion, empathy, or wiggle room that would allow either for their resistance to conformity or the state they were in (many of those interviewed seemed reliant on drugs and had lost one or both parents during the war). The war seemed to have created

Boys and male youth on the outskirts of Kenema following the war.

more Rarrays than ever before, yet traditional Sierra Leonean society refused to deal with them.

Three sets of male youth discussed what it was like to be categorized as a Rarray Boy. All of them were from poor backgrounds. Many were orphans. All but one was a former combatant. One set of four male youth (one was thirty-nine years old but said he still was not recognized as a man) decried society's labeling of them as Rarrays. "After the war, up to now, Rarrays are marginalized," a thirty-year-old former combatant stated in Kenema in 2010. "We sleep in the markets on the tables," he added. They paid to sleep there. The place where they slept created the perception that they were Rarrays. The male youth defined Rarray as "someone in the street who has no definite address and no definite job." But he and his three colleagues could not be Rarrays, he insisted, "because we wash cars in the river." Despite having an occupation, it did not appear that many people agreed with them.

Two pairs of male youth also challenged mainstream society's rendering of them as degenerates. "Rarray Boys and Girls are the common names that adults use to call people whom they think are not serious and have no plan in life," explained a twenty-six-year-old former combatant. Adults also contend that the Rarrays "live useless lives and can be rebellious," he added. As a condemned Rarray Boy, he reflected on his lack of options. "I think society needs to recognize us as useful members of society, regardless of who we are," he stressed. "If they think that becoming an adult man means bearing the responsibility of feeding other mouths and having a wife, then I will remain where I am forever." Then he referred to himself in his chosen social category: "Thank God I am happy being a Youthman." The term refers to a state of being for male youth who are unable to meet the traditional demands of manhood. As they age, they become too old to be youth yet are not viewed as men.[1] The ex-fighter's colleague, a twenty-nine-year-old former rebel fighter, was more upbeat about their shared situation. "Those who call themselves adults today were once called Rarray Boys or Girls," he insisted. "Let the adults leave us alone. One day, we will be like them." His compassion for Rarray Girls was notable. "For Rarray Girls, the emphasis is on marriage [to gain recognition as a woman], regardless of the kind of marriage, whether it is good or bad." For a female, entering marriage means surrendering one's rights, since they "will undergo any kind of suffering, just in the name of marriage."

The rebellious dimension of the Rarray Boy moniker was a prominent point of discussion for two male youth (one an ex-RUF fighter) who bonded as Rastafarians. "They call us Rarray Boys because we do not accept what they want us to do," the ex-fighter (age twenty-nine) explained. "We are not living in the same world. They have nothing to do with our world. They should leave us alone." Their focus, his twenty-four-year-old friend explained, was living for the moment. "For now, we are trying to live our life as young people," he said. "When we grow up, then we will forget about everything and live like adults." Then he proposed a question: "If we do not enjoy now, when shall we enjoy?"

A key issue arose in interviews with all three sets of male youth deemed Rarrays by others. How did they manage to deal with their social separation and condemnation? Their separate answers shared the same primary source of inspiration and guidance: Bob Marley. "Many great men are living the life we are living," explained the youngest of the two Rastafarians. "Some of them are rich men while others come from rich families. What is wrong if we lead the same life? Bob Marley was the King of Reggae. He lived the same life [as we are] and he died a hero." He also mentioned Joseph Hill, Tupac, and his fellow rapper, 50 Cent. "We always love to listen to their music. It makes us forget about our problems. We are sure we will make it one day." Two other former rebel fighters focused on Marley's influence over their lives. "Bob Marley is shaping our life," one stated. "He is helping us to be conscious of our rights."

The reference to developing an inner consciousness (or awareness), along the lines of Marley's call to advocate for your rights in "Get Up, Stand Up," proved an enduring influence over many young Sierra Leoneans, especially males. "We the youth, we are people of no nonsense," he continued. "Come on May 11, we will go out and celebrate Marley's Day. He is the King of Reggae." The third set of youth brought up how memories of war haunt them. "Many youth died during the war," a twenty-seven-year-old former fighter explained. "Some had their feet cut off, others had their hands cut off. Some peoples' houses were burned down. Some lost their parents and caregivers. And after the war, the worries caused by this made people to go mad." After stating this, his colleague, an ex-fighter of thirty-one, added, "Plenty people went mad." In response to shared hardship and social condemnation, the four ex-combatants and their colleagues emphasized how they are all "conscious youth," a direct reference to the practice of smoking marijuana and listening to Marley and other reggae artists to gain awareness of social situations and their rights.

But Bob Marley, defiance, and collective efforts to generate self-confidence seemed to get these male youth only so far. Life remained hard and the future was uncertain. "If you do not have support," one of the Rastafarians explained, "you will not be able to become an adult. Look at me: there is nobody to support me." His friend faced similar circumstances. "I wish I had somebody to take care of me," he said. "This is the big difference. Although adults say that we are not serious, I am sure that if they took care of us fully, we could change to become better people." He and his friend shared the same problem: they could not become adult men "because we don't have the foundation to support ourselves."

Female youth known as Rarray Girls tended to have a way to support themselves: commercial sex, and sometimes informal payments from boyfriends. One described the latter arrangement as follows: "Our boyfriends give us money. This is the reason why we have multiple boys: if I go to one of these boys at the end of the day, I will get something to eat."[2] Four female youth operating in these fields shared their views on being labeled as Rarrays. Two were former rebel wives, while the other two started laboring as commercial sex workers (CSWs) during the war. One learned the trade with ECOMOG soldiers, who were her first paying customers. For all of them, commercial sex was the most lucrative available work. "Rarray Girls is what they call us," one of the ex–rebel wives said, "girls who do not have permanent boyfriends." It didn't seem to bother her. "Whatever name they call us," she related, "we don't mind." The two ex–rebel wives had no time for Rarray Boys, whom one of them deemed "mostly former rebels who continue to live the life they lived during the war." None of the female youth expressed interest in marriage. For one ex–rebel wife, marriage "is for the old people." She added, "This is not the time when girls should depend on one man." To her, the reason was obvious: "These are unserious men." Another stated, "We do not want to become married because this would restrict our business." And yet, the two who had not been rebel wives expressed considerable regret over their future limitations. "People consider us as failures in life," said one. "But we do not have the opportunity to become adults in society or play adult roles." As they were situated well beyond the social mainstream, her colleague was fatalistic about the future. "If we should die in this life, it is fine, because this is what God has destined for us."

Separations

Youth known as Rarrays seemingly had stepped off the treadmill toward adulthood, at least for a while. But what exactly was the proper way to achieve manhood or womanhood? With the war over and impoverishment common-place, the road ahead was unclear. Shepler's analysis of how Sierra Leoneans defined youth and adult categories sheds light on the social ambiguity that young people inhabited in the postwar era. All apprentices and secondary school students are youth regardless of age. Youth are "generally understood to be male" and not Big Men (or females). Writing in 2014, she noted that "with life expectancy hovering around forty, one can easily live one's whole life as a 'youth'" (Shepler 2014: 27–29).

Interviews with Sierra Leoneans during the postwar era reflected this ab-sence of clarity over youth and adult definitions. A discussion in a village near Makeni with about forty people (youth and adults) fell into a broad debate over the youth question. A male youth said, "Only males are youth." A female youth retorted that a female youth is "one who hasn't given birth yet." An el-derly man insisted that "when someone has money, he's no longer a youth—he's a Big Man. Even if he's twenty-two, he's not a youth [if he has money]." A second male youth agreed: "With money, you can become a Big Man. They can respect and even fear you, and they will call you *Pa*. If you're poor, you're a youth." A *Pa* is a Big Man with considerable influence over others. "If I'm an elder without much money," a second elderly man explained, "and my younger brother has money, what do I do? I have to respect him and call him *Pa*." This ingrained interpretation of social relations undergirds the pervasive, superpatrimonial, Big Man–little followers setup across the land.

The debate continued. "Yes, a girl can be a youth," a female youth insisted, as long as she "hasn't given birth to a baby." It is difficult for married females ever to attend youth group meetings regardless of their age because it would cause "marital problems" with their husbands, she added. Even so, what about girls who are married off, via prior arrangement between the girl's parents and a male suitor, when they are a year old? Such a person, it appeared, would never become a youth: they would shift instantly from girlhood to woman-hood whenever marriage to the much older man took place.

Many adults who were interviewed detailed how the war had altered a young person's pursuit of adulthood. Traditionally, all boys and girls went through initiation ceremonies (generally called Poro for boys and Bondo (or Sande) for girls). Young people would enter into Poro or Bondo at around age eighteen (after they had been deemed mature). Among the purposes of the initiations was introducing the youth to sexual intercourse. A male elder ex-plained other purposes. Male youth "were trained in male roles and responsi-bilities in society" such as "skills in farming, setting traps for animals, and the use of herbs." Meanwhile, female youth "were trained to become responsible housewives." Male and female youth who completed their initiations were expected to marry soon afterward and become parents. A newly married young man, in addition, also must be able "to farm and take care of his family," as a senior man from a village in central Sierra Leone related.

There was broad agreement that the attainment of manhood and womanhood was up for grabs following the war, particularly for males. Initiations cost money, and families without funds could not send their children to them. Orphan youth may have no chance to go, even if they had sought to enter an initiation. Male and female initiates also reportedly could be as young as five years old. Traditional initiation ceremonies thus became one of the reasons why Sierra Leoneans were having children at ever-younger ages. Other reasons that surfaced were the precedent of forced marriages for young girls during the war period and a widely cited interest among many girls and female youth to bear children and thereby enter a kind of entry-level womanhood as unmarried mothers (formal marriage promised to upgrade her status to a full adult). Indeed, many female and male youth insisted that demonstrating fertility by becoming a mother *increased* a young mother's chances of getting married.

On the other hand, male youth who became fathers seemed to enter into a youth-adult netherworld. Does a poor male youth who fathers a child automatically become a man? Some would say yes. If so, then he would become a fairly insubstantial one, since most were unable to perform the essential everyday requirement of supporting a wife and children. While the new setup created much consternation and worry among adults, their frustrations only seemed to expand when adults tried to structure a young person's life. Curiously and significantly, this concern centered around the issue of human rights. Many adults viewed the expansion of new laws and regulations protecting the rights of Sierra Leonean individuals as undercutting traditional parental authority.

Before turning to postwar changes related to rights, some context is required. Trends involving youth that had begun before the war were expanding. In rural areas, most male ex-combatant youth did not seek a life in farming because they considered "the idea of involving oneself in agriculture and rural life unattractive" (Peters 2007: 48). They also continued to be repelled by the exploitative practices and absence of voice in the chiefdoms (Paintin 2008: 231). Local chiefs and elders thus had difficulty rounding up male youth to engage in community work, such as the "collective brushing on community-owned land" (Peters 2005: 289).[3] Drawing from fieldwork at the end of Sierra Leone's war period, researchers found that traditional deference toward chiefs and elders, from women as well as youth, had "collapsed" (Archibald and Richards 2002: 345). In addition, male youth viewed urban neighborhoods and diamond mines as "places of refuge for the culturally modernized" (Fanthorpe and Maconachie 2010: 253). Many were vacating rural areas, with Freetown the prominent destination (Peeters et al. 2009: 13). The capital city had ballooned from about a half million before the war to four times that size afterward (Shepler 2010d: 19). By 2010, an estimated six in ten youth in Sierra Leone were unemployed (New Humanitarian 2010).

Still other changes were underfoot. The year 2007 became a watershed for human rights laws in Sierra Leone when the Child Rights Act came into being amid considerable excitement. In a country with long-standing child labor, child marriage, and other child exploitation practices, nothing close to the new law had ever existed. Following Parliament's approval of the Child Rights Act on June 7, UNICEF breathlessly announced that it "represents a unique opportunity for making a number of national laws and policies more aligned with international standards, which is unprecedented in the history of Sierra Leone" (UNICEF Press Centre 2007). However, while the law may have been unparalleled, implementation barely got off the ground. Three years on, a review of Sierra Leone's protection system expressed "significant concern" that the Child Rights Act "relies too heavily upon voluntary mechanisms" to prevent and mediate family crises while the legal response system relies too much on law enforcement and the courts (Thompstone 2010: 1–2).

This approach contrasted with how parents raise children in Sierra Leone, how communities protect children (or not), child labor traditions, and the long-established practice of going to the chief with cases of child abuse, neglect, or exploitation (2).[4] Moreover, civil society and international community officials expressed concern that the bill itself was incomplete by intention. In a meeting in 2010, they asserted that "several integral aspects" relevant to the bill were left out because the Ministry for Social Welfare, Gender, and Children's Affairs "turned blind eyes to them." Ministry officials admitted to "some lapses" and promised to work to ensure that the government would "maintain international standards that enliven the plight of children" (Kanu 2010).

The events underscored how laws only matter if they are implemented. Two district-level officials stressed just how difficult implementing the Child Rights Act would be. "It's a very good law," a district council official explained. "But the problem is how to implement it. I don't know how to do it." A social development officer shared her approach to implementation: encouraging parents "not to flog their children." She predicted that implementation of the Act will take time because "in Sierra Leone, we don't respect the rights of the child. Parents treat children like slaves, and children also will rebel. We tell parents that slavery is over. They should treat their children with dignity."

A similar trend arose following the passage of three bills called the Gender

Acts of 2007. They emerged in a land where protections for girls and women were exceptionally limited. During the period of their passage, nine in ten girls and female youth had undergone female genital mutilation (usually during Bondo initiation rites) (Smet 2009: 152),[5] the subordination of women and girls to fathers, brothers and husbands was longstanding (Maclure and Denov 2008: 616), and there were consistently high rates of violence against women (Amnesty International 2006: 8). The three new bills collectively addressed domestic violence, customary marriage and divorce. They outlawed the tradition of forcing widows to marry a member of her dead husband's family and allowed "men and women to inherit equally" (Denney and Ibrahim 2012: 6). The equal inheritance provision evolved into the "50/50" marker that, in practice, was thought to apply to the everyday practice of marriage (detailed shortly). The bills were the product of two forces: growing pressure from international actors (NGOs and UN agencies) and local NGOs, and an interest by the main political parties to deliver something to women voters before parliamentary elections. Spurred by support from the UNDP, the government fast-tracked a poorly coordinated lawmaking process to pass the three gender acts just before the 2007 elections (Zureick 2008). The haste showed. Reflecting on the challenges of implementation, Hawa Kamara shared the following observation: "In order for the [three Gender] Acts to be meaningful, individuals must be able to claim their rights in both formal and informal courts. Currently, the formal court system is inaccessible to a large proportion of the population due to high costs, distance, complexity, delay in proceedings etc. In the informal courts (local court), used by a greater percentage of the population, these laws are hardly recognized, let alone implemented" (2016).[6]

The laws protecting children and women had an explosive impact on the lives of many Sierra Leoneans. Although regular enforcement of the new laws seemed fairly rare, an awareness of new rights for the formerly disempowered very clearly was in the air. During interviews, adult men and women viewed the changes, and the concept of human rights generally, as invasive and threatening. This was illustrated during an interview with a set of village elders in 2010. The conversation turned to a training they had received from, in the view of one elder, "overseas countries." At the training, members of the village were taught two new rights, he recalled. The first concerned individual choice: "Let us observe the right of everybody." The second emphasized personal freedom: "You know what you want and what you don't want." The immediate and lasting results of the two new teachings, in the elders' collective view, were disastrous for the village. Collective group work fell apart, they related, because young people now were free to disobey their orders. As one elder explained, "The way these human rights have been interpreted has made it difficult for everybody to be under control and take advice from the elderly and parents. Because now, everybody knows that everybody is free to do what they want." The oldest of the elders (he was ninety) then chimed in. "Because when you say anything, the youth will reply by saying, 'It is our human rights.'" Another elder added, "That's why even in school, teachers don't punish and beat children. So, all the children are wild. They say, 'It's our human rights.'" He insisted that these changes actually began during the war, when young people "took one step away from obedience." The wave of entirely new human rights arrived after war's end, and these new rights "crowned it all." Now young people "have the green light: you do this, it's your right. You do that, it's your right. They only speak of their rights, not their responsibility: it's only about women's rights, youth rights, children's rights."

The new rights certainly attempted to undercut patrimonial control. On the ground, they had made a dent. All of the men cited above were patriarchs in their respective villages, expected to provide for and dominate their followers. Now they were impoverished and confronted huge challenges receiving the sort of reverence (and, no doubt, fear) that had been their provenance before the war. They also were not paying attention to new ideas in the air. The notion of young people standing up for their rights, as Bob Marley had instructed, had begun to echo across Sierra Leone long before the war ever started. After the war, many adults in rural areas who were interviewed expected young people to return with them to a world that no longer existed. Regardless of what war had disrupted and how young people viewed themselves in the twenty-first century, they still envisaged young people acting in ways they viewed as timeless. Many adults in villages and towns, elders in particular, found it difficult to change while young people continued to exit villages and small towns.

As a result, the theme of human rights threatening custom and tradition echoed across interviews with adult men and women. "After the war, youth asked to be paid to do the [communal] work," said a pastor living in Makeni. "They never asked for money before the war." "The youth seem to have no interest in working for elders anymore," a village elder lamented. If male youth refuse to do communal work, he said, "then we will take them to court. The court will tell the youth how to behave." If youth still resist, "then they can go somewhere else." National trends suggested that this was precisely what many youth were doing. The elder's laments continued. Before the war, fathers could flog their sons. "But now they cannot." An elder man in another village focused on the impact of the revolutionary human rights following the war: "Maybe we can say that the concept of human rights is responsible. Sometimes when we want to take tough measures against children, they talk about their human rights. When we force them to farm after school, they will talk about human rights. How can human rights help you to learn to become a man or a woman?" Adult women also expressed bewilderment over the changes that "human rights" had played over their children. A Mammy (or Mommy) Queen (a prominent position for women in chiefdoms) worried about "the kind of useless adults we have in society today." "You cannot force your children to do anything these days," a mother sadly stated. "If you force them, they'll report you to the police and you'll be apprehended. The police will come, grab your hand and ask, 'Why did you beat your child?'"

Many female youth, as well as adult men and women, were concerned about the arrival of "50/50." They viewed the new idea of marriage relations as invasive and destabilizing. The 50/50 term appeared to have arrived with trainings on the new rights laws by a well-known women's organization based in Freetown called the 50/50 Group of Sierra Leone.[7] Interviews around Kenema in 2010 suggested that the trainings had impacted males as much as females. A sixteen-year-old female youth shared her take on the impact of 50/50:

> The only reason I know for why many men don't want to marry is [that] they're afraid of responsibility because of the hardship in the country. There's a program known as the 50/50 Group for women's empowerment. It's become the mouthpiece for men. Men say, "The White people came to Sierra Leone and said, 'Human rights [and] equal rights for men and women.'" So, in any relationship, the man will tell you [the woman] to contribute 50 percent of what the household needs. If you are unable, then you are out. That's why life is so hard.

She then explained her situation. The man in her life recently had told her that "he'd give me 1,500 leones a day. He told me to get another 1,500 [every day]." However, "I can't find that money. Now he has left me." A female youth of seventeen shared her analysis of how 50/50 had affected struggling male youth and married men: "[Let's say] a woman stays with you [the man in her life] for five to ten years. If we're in a house together, we share things 50/50. But if she leaves and goes to the police, she will get 50 percent of everything." If the man in this relationship "doesn't have money, he will find it very difficult to be a man, very difficult to have a life. The elders will call him a dropout, a failure in life, a thief." In the view of many female youth interviewed, 50/50 was driving men away from relationships.

Although "human rights" was a new concept for many Sierra Leoneans, the laws were part of a broader social movement. The war seemed to have broken tradition and the claims of adults over youngsters. A male elder sagely summed up the situation: "Adults are not in tune with youth behavior, and they are opposed by youth because both are living in different worlds. The adult world is outdated." A male ex-combatant shared similar views. "Before the war, when we enjoyed peace, youth lived with their parents who supported and guided them to adulthood," he said. "Youth were supported in terms of education. Parents arranged marriages for their children." But after the war, the ground had shifted radically, away from those norms, customs, and shared expectations. "Today," he elaborated, "many youth desire to live independently. So, they lack the opportunity of parental counseling." In the postwar world, "most youth choose their own way of life."

Research in Sierra Leone after the war underscored the growing separation between generations. Most people's lives were fundamentally unstable. Parents generally were unable to support their children while many young people had set out on their own. The mix of widespread poverty, unsettled social conditions and incoming international standards for rights and entitlements proved to be a lot to handle for just about everyone, even if some of the alterations (namely, empowerment and protection for women and children) were much needed and late to arrive. Lives were simultaneously hard and new, and change seemed to be everywhere.

Except that conservative forces were on the rise at the same time. Paramount chiefs received a helping hand from some of the same actors supporting the new rights regime for women and children: the West. Their intent was to put the top chiefs and their entourages back where they had been before the war (even if women and youth gained more representation this time around, and even as lower-level authorities faced big challenges on the ground). Helped by new British funding (and support from other donors), the setup that began during the British colonial regime—powerful chiefdoms operating in parallel to the national government—was rebuilt. Taken together, the foreign-supported reforms seemed to push Sierra Leone in opposite directions concurrently: toward elemental gender and generational transformation while boosting paramount chiefs. The next chapter looks at the big chiefs' still-formidable influence in this sea of uncertainty.

CHAPTER 22

The Power of the *Pa*

Dominance and Progress

During field interviews, Rwandans and Burundians identified two kinds of people in their respective societies: those with power and those affected by power. References to those with power as "high people" and everyone else as "very low people" or even "ignorant people" were common (Sommers 1998: 4; Sommers 2006: 85). In development contexts, it was customary for the empowered and entitled class to refer to "the population" (*abanyagihugu*), a term that distanced those in control from the seemingly amorphous mass of fellow citizens toiling on farms or in urban neighborhoods. Such people were not to be understood as much as sensitized, a term implying subtle coercion toward preestablished notions of progress and development (Sommers 2012: 83; Sommers 2013: 25). Elites did not engage with nonelites as much as direct or drive them in particular directions.

Sierra Leonean society also featured a pronounced line of separation between the powerful and the powerless. As in Central Africa, ordinary citizens who were interviewed did not refer to a middle class. It did not seem to exist. Yet relations between the empowered and the disempowered differed. Instead of elites enlightening and pressurizing their social underlings from afar, Sierra Leone's patrimonial landscape connected Big Men to personalized collections of followers who relied on their supporter. Those living outside of these relationships were vulnerable outliers (such as Rarray Boys and Girls) positioned on society's margins. Followers conformed to their Big Man's norms and inclinations, never challenging his authority, expecting his protection, and hoping for his assistance.

All of this became clear in the tussle over the nation's 149 paramount chiefs—rural Sierra Leone's ultimate Big Men—and their respective chieftaincy administrations. The outcome (favorable to the chiefs) reflects how postwar countries regularly reconstruct the powerful institutions and practices that were central causes of warfare. Concerning Sierra Leone, sixteen years after war's end, two analysts observed that, while Sierra Leone "enjoyed relatively peaceful elections in 2007 and 2012 and one of the fastest economic growth rates in sub-Saharan Africa, largely based on a revival of its mineral extractive industry led by international corporate investment," it nonetheless was "experiencing only a thin type of negative peace in which many of the causes of grievance and conflict remain unaddressed" (Higgins and Novelli 2018: 38).[1] Regarding the chiefs, one analyst considered it "surprising that the institution of the chieftaincy was so easily restored when its performance had been one of the grievances that led young men to join the RUF."

A deeper look at the context and actions illuminates how the outcome was never in doubt. For one thing, many of the chiefs were proactive, incorporating youth and women into their government activities during the war years (Vincent 2012: 21). Much more important, the chiefdom institution has proven to be exceptionally resilient over time. During the colonial era, the British created local councils "as a counterweight to chiefs' power." It didn't work. The chiefs moved swiftly to dominate the councils, and soon after independence, they were abolished. Nonetheless, in 2004—only two years after the war had ended—the World Bank sponsored a government reform package that recreated the councils as democratically elected institutions responsible for development issues (health, education, agriculture) (Reed and Robinson 2013: 8).

The United Kingdom's Department of International Development also entered the local government fray with their Paramount Chief Restoration Programme (Hennings 2019: 28). The subtext of their efforts was "reforming the chieftaincy in order to support local councils, guided by a belief in the popularity and indispensability of chiefs." Yet not even such qualified support to the chiefs proved sufficient: chieftaincy reform was "said to be led largely by 'foreigners,'" thus having questionable legitimacy (Broadbent 2012: 38, 36). The paramount chiefs seemed to want it all, and to a large extent, that is what they, and the bevy of section chiefs, chiefdom speakers, tribal authorities, and so on underneath each of them, all received. While struggles between elders and the younger generation played out on the ground, those with higher positions and more power ended up sitting pretty. All they had needed was to make "a few adjustments" to the postwar context (Hennings 2019: 28).

As a result, despite fulsome wartime attacks on the chieftaincy institution and paramount chiefs with particularly notorious reputations,[2] nothing particularly substantive changed. The conclusions of those researching the issue bear this out. "Chieftaincy remains the most important system of authority across rural Sierra Leone," said one expert (Ryann Elizabeth Manning 2009: 19). "Rural people appear to be locked into relationships of dependence with traditional elites," commented a set of researchers (Acemoglu, Reed, and Robinson 2014: 363).[3] Councilors and local courts, the two formal government offices at the chiefdom level, certainly exist. However, in comparison to the extensive chiefdom apparatus, they are puny and simply cannot compete with informal, chiefly government.[4]

Goaded by the conflicting interventions of influential international actors, postwar Sierra Leone pulled in opposing directions: toward both modern standards for rights and protections and familiar, old-style, traditional institutions. Since the two didn't mix well, one side had to win. Encouragingly, one researcher found that the push for reform had many backers: "According to many ordinary Sierra Leoneans, if there is one positive effect of the war in Sierra Leone, it is that 'our eyes are open now' and 'nobody can fool us anymore.' They realize that corruption, nepotism, the socioeconomic exclusion of youths, and the marginalization of ordinary people in general, are causes that led to the war. People see the need for change" (Peters 2011b: 148). None of these backers, however, were powerful.

Meanwhile, the authority and influence of paramount chiefs and their chiefdoms rebounded following the war. Writing in 2012, Broadbent found that the international community's "support to the chieftaincy has never faltered and the current arrangements continue to play into the hands of chiefs" (37). The playing field between ordinary citizens and powerful actors in Sierra Leone remained tilted, as ever, toward the authorities. This left youth with the following choice: opt out or give in. If they refused to obey big leaders, they would be forced to either buckle under chiefly power or exit the area. One could become a Rarray renegade or migrate to a town, city, or mine. The only other option was servility. The authorities would allow some exchanges, insisted many of those interviewed. But doing so risked crossing the arbitrary line of those in power. It was dangerous.

This returns us to notions of *fityai*. As noted earlier, in the view of chiefs, elders, and others in charge, *fityai* implies disrespect. It also legitimates whatever comes next: public humiliation and, quite often, detention without charge. The common description of arrest was putting the *fityai* person into a *tait kɔna* or *tait ples* (meaning, respectively, "tight corner" and "tight place"). For many youth and others who dared challenge those in power, *fityai* essentially meant speaking truth to power—and suffering the consequences for doing so.

Let us quickly review views from the top. "The key thing is the manner of expression to the authority," one paramount chief explained. "Once it is said in a respectable way, we will listen and understand." On the other hand, "if you say something in a disrespectable manner, we will shun you, definitely." The chief administrator of one district council, who reported to have had many challenging exchanges with chiefs, broadened the context of *fityai*. He argued that the 2007 laws concerning children's and women's rights "have made *fityai* worse." In his view, children and women are "taking their rights violently." Yet there was a second important context. "If there's a corrupt official," he elaborated, "he will take a youth coming to him [and raising the corruption issue] as a *fityai* boy." An interview with secondary students expanded on the latter use of *fityai*. Although it means "treating an elderly person with disrespect," one student explained, "telling the elders the truth is disrespectful." "Saying the truth," a second student added, is only allowed with members of your peer group. Young people "have no right to say the truth to an elderly person." They labeled the act of verbal truth-telling "blowing your mind." Since "you can only blow your mind with friends, nothing changes."

Officials from separate district councils elaborated on how *fityai* operates across society. One official suspected a corrupt transaction involving a paramount chief. Despite his position in government (in theory, a district official sits above all chiefs), the official could not investigate what had happened: "When you assert your rights, that is a kind of *fityai*. If I challenge the paramount chief, he can call me a *Bobo*. He's powerful, he's a king. I'm just the head of the district council. I don't have money, so I'm a *Bobo*. He can call the national government to remove me from the area." The official translated the Krio term *Bobo* as "those without authority: you don't have money or power. You are a *Bobo* regardless of your age." A *Pa*, on the other hand, was one of "those in authority"—in this case, a paramount chief (and always a dominant male power broker). A second district council shared similar views. Should the official inquire about the enforcement of laws that are being broken, the official explained that "this is where *fityai* comes in: when lower-level government officials attempt to challenge some of these issues, like law enforcement. Asking [about these issues] is your right, but it can be interpreted as being disrespectful to elders and leaders. So, when we even speak about such things, they say we're challenging the government. For me, they won't put me in detention. They will just ignore me." However, in the official's view, the immunity of chiefs and other authorities from being challenged (much less investigated) via *fityai* meant that "it appears that there are no laws" in the land. "They are not enforced. They are just on paper."

Field research uncovered one village that challenged their paramount chief and ended up marginalized and labeled as a "*fityai* community." In an interview with members of a child welfare community from another village, one of the members explained that no suspicions of corruption by their superiors ever could be expressed. "Do you want to *fityai* the chief?" one asked. "Ah, you can't do that." A national government official privately related that *fityai* behavior that challenges authority or calls out corrupt practices "is too dangerous for radio." If station managers even attempt it, "they will be stopped."

The gathered understanding of *fityai* suggested that the mere threat of severe censure for raising questionable behavior bequeathed authorities with an almost unassailable power. Laws, Sierra Leoneans kept suggesting, meant little in their land. The power of the *Pa*, in all his mighty masculine forms, was what really mattered.

Big Men, Youth, and Development

While chiefs and other patriarchs were ascendant following Sierra Leone's war, young people were in a tailspin. Two responses to the daunting challenges that female youth faced following the war surfaced during interviews with unmarried mothers working as sex workers and in outdoor hair salons in Kenema in 2010. The first was a broadly shared interest in gaining access to a training program. The aim was to learn a trade that would provide reliable income. Second, most were interested in marriage, even if the chances were slim. As one young female sex worker (FSW) explained, "Many girls pray to God to get married, but the boys have no money for marriage." An inexpensive drug manufactured in India, called Hungry Heptin and nicknamed Super Appetite, was thought to increase a female youth's marriage prospects. A twenty-year-old hairdresser explained that Super Appetite "allows me to sleep without feeling discouraged." In addition to helping a person relax and sleep, it also was thought to increase one's appetite. Many contended that, if a person used it long enough, Super Appetite would give a woman a larger behind. As a second hairdresser explained, "Once you have a peace of mind, you will develop big buttocks" by taking Super Appetite regularly. A more fulsome derrière promised to make it easier to attract a man (hopefully one deemed suitable and who would become your husband). A pharmacist in Kenema confirmed this take. "Super Appetite makes you sleepy and gives you more appetite to eat," he explained. "It is supposed to give you bigger buttocks," as well.[5]

In postwar Sierra Leone, almost half (47 percent) of the nation's children lived with one or no parents. Nearly two in three secondary school-age children (63 percent) were not in secondary school. Almost nine in ten girls and women ages fifteen to forty-nine (88 percent) "had some form of female genital mutilation [FGM]" (Statistics Sierra Leone and UNICEF-Sierra Leone 2011: 127, 93, 109). As many as one in ten females in the land worked as a commercial sex worker. The proportions climbed in mining areas, ranging from one in eight females to nearly one in three of all residents.[6] The number of female sex workers in Sierra Leone was perhaps twice the number of artisanal miners nationally. The latter was a common boy and male youth profession that also signaled elemental desperation.[7] It also often recreated relations between boys, male youth, and men established during the war, with former soldiers mining and former commanders operating as their supervisors.[8]

The fabled Big Diamond, the dream and lofty goal of all diamond miners, as depicted by a muralist. The image occupies a wall outside of a diamond trader's office, in Kenema. The traders seek to entice miners to bring their diamonds to them.

Interviews in Koidu sketched the postwar diamond mining situation well. Male youth continued to migrate from villages and towns to mine in the area. Local primary and secondary school students mined part-time. Together with the full-timers, the hoped-for result was finding "Big Diamond." Those working in Mine 11 looked to the "Mountain of Hope" for riches. It was a huge hill of sand astride the mine. The sand had been dumped there after a mining company had sifted it for diamonds decades earlier. Day after day, the miners searched for diamonds that the machines may have missed. "The Mountain of Hope is the place everyone comes to try his luck," a twenty-six-year-old miner explained. "When the time comes, God will help you." Rarely, if ever, did they find much of anything. The grinding toil under the baking sun, and dim prospects for success, bore down on many miners. Two assessments of diamond mining in the area characterized the context of their efforts. The head of an organization advocating for miners' rights observed that "people still mine even though the diamonds have gone." After describing a range of parasites that typically infect diamond miners, an official with an NGO working on mining issues explained that, as Sierra Leoneans, "we just accept these conditions. It's natural. It's like your fingers: they are not all equal. The things that you cannot avoid, you just endure."[9]

Three derogatory names framed the hopes and limitations of young people in postwar Sierra Leone. Two referred equally to female and male youth. One was the Rarray title, a way of delineating society's unwanted (and despised) misfits. The other was "dropout." This name referred to those who sought to complete secondary school but never did. It was a particularly painful name to be called, as it announced that a young person had tried but failed to gain a toehold on stability, and perhaps success. Avoiding connection to this damning name was the aim of a collection of male youth mining for gold in southern Sierra Leone. A twenty-year-old who had been forced to leave secondary school explained the pain this name caused. "When they call us dropouts," he said, "I feel offended. I feel so bad." Another male youth miner defined a dropout as "someone who doesn't have anything and doesn't know anything." People who are "well off can call a person a dropout." So can female partners. "They also call me dropout," a third gold miner related. "When they call me that, I will cool down my temper and find another way. I will try hard to get money to further my education."

The third disparaging label applied only to male youth and men and regularly surfaced during interviews in the diamond mines: Area Moba (pronounced "area moBAH"). An Area Moba was a complete and utter disappointment, a failed or lost man.[10] Since it was so hard to find a diamond of any kind, ending up as an Area Moba seemed to haunt many of the miners. "If you stay in the mines," an adult miner warned, "you'll become an Area Moba. If you're thirty-five or forty years old and you're still not profiting, they will call you Area Moba." For the many migrants to the mines, failing to uncover diamond wealth usually meant that you couldn't leave. "We want to go home without money," a sixteen-year-old miner explained, "but it would be disgraceful. That's why we stay here." Reflecting on the power of the name, a miner of forty-three said, "Too many become an Area Moba. I'm one. I came here [to become a miner] at age six. I'm still here. I have been here all my life and I have nothing. Some men have women at home, and they can't take care of them. And so, when there's a quarrel, the woman will say, 'Just leave me, you're an Area Moba.' If she calls you that, you don't feel good. When some men get old [as miners], they're too ashamed to go back home [to their original area] because they have no money. An Area Moba can never go home." One group of five adolescent boys (none of whom knew their exact age) who mined sand from the Mountain of Hope together said that their shared aim was to become the opposite of an Area Moba: a *Bomba*. One of them defined Bomba as "a man who has everything. Like a White man."[11]

Perhaps the most poignant reflection on mining and the Area Moba title came from the self-proclaimed imam of Mine 11. "In my sermons, I talk about mining," he related. "I tell [the young miners] it's good to find something to do. I say, 'Pay attention to mining, and if you find diamond, use the money to please God.'" If you pray five times a day and go to the nearby mosque once a day, "You have a better chance to get diamond." Alas, the imam had not been so fortunate. "I'm seventy-eight years old," he stated. He had begun mining thirty-three years earlier. "I got a small diamond three or four years ago," he recalled. "It was the last time I found one." Looking back on his life, he shared a sad reflection. "I have children, and I come to work among children and youth. So, I consider myself an Area Moba."

Dread haunted many urban male youth too. A veteran researcher in Freetown related that many male youth in town had "an outright fear that you don't know what will happen." The threat came from the urban equivalent of chiefs: the police. "The police are arresting people left and right," the researcher related in 2005. "People are so afraid of the state, especially youth who see themselves as disconnected from the system." This included a lot of ex-combatant male youth. The researcher contrasted the plight of poor youth in rural and urban Sierra Leone. In villages, "there are fewer police but much stronger traditional law." There, life is predictable: "You know what the chief will do." But in Freetown, "it's just completely random." A male youth "can be kidnapped by the police, who can throw you into Pademba Prison," the infamous penitentiary where Foday Sankoh had been incarcerated in the 1970s. To get out, the researcher related, "You have to have a Big Man, or somebody who knows a Big Man, or somehow find the money to pay the police [the required bribe]. Otherwise, you're stuck." One way for a male youth to protect himself in town is "to have an illegal connection to the police or others in power." If you can sell them "stolen things or marijuana, then you have a connection to a powerful person who can protect you against trouble." The power of patrimonialism to shape lives reached right across Sierra Leone.

Development efforts promised to address postwar youth challenges in rural and urban Sierra Leone. The results were mixed. One survey of the DDR initiative for former combatants gave it a passing grade. Although "many combatants voiced dissatisfaction with the DDR program," ultimately "the DDR programs received very positive overall reviews from ex-combatants" (Humphreys and Weinstein 2004: 3). This finding must be taken with at least two grains of salt. First, the program gained unfortunate renown for excessive discrimination against ex-combatant females. "At every stage, DDR processes need to take into account girls' and women's distinctive needs and risks," Wessells warned (2006: 167). In Sierra Leone, a mere 8 percent of all DDR participants were females, mostly women. Very small numbers of former girl child soldiers gained access (McKay and Mazurana 2004: 99). Second, even those former combatants who participated in DDR found much that still was needed, including additional assistance to find jobs, sustained training, help to start businesses, and a higher rate of financial allowances (Humphreys and Weinstein 2004: 3).

A second large and rapid response for youth, including ex-combatants, also had questionable lasting impact. The ambitious Youth Reintegration Training and Education for Peace (YRTEP) began before the war had ended and eventually included over forty thousand ex-combatants and other youth as participants in communities across Sierra Leone. Participants and other village members lauded the swiftness of YRTEP: it boosted morale, eased the entrance of former members of military units back into village life, and "inspired an impressive degree of community activism." On the other hand, gender balance and inclusion among participants was not a prominent feature. In addition, the program's success raised expectations for sustained engagement and impact. That didn't happen: there was no coordinated follow-up once the program expired (it lasted from six months to a year). This turned out to be a source of significant frustration in the communities where it had taken place. Indeed, evaluators highlighted "an attitude that end-of-program issues did not require the same level of attention as the start-up and implementation phases" (Hansen et al. 2002: x, 27, 30).

Sierra Leone after the war featured a national economy "unable to absorb the already large numbers of unemployed and semi-skilled youth" (Paintin 2008: 230). Job creation became a central priority. International development agencies funded the major efforts, not the government. Nothing is free, however. Programming to spur job creation was part of a recipe for postwar recovery mandated by the powerful international actors. The foreign players sought to restructure Sierra Leone's economy and improve the government's legitimacy partly "to improve its ability to service debt" owed to international lenders. In the view of one analyst, the extensive, internationally led "statebuilding project" (sometimes called liberal peace building or liberal peace) nonetheless left Sierra Leone with "a weak government with minimal capacity to deliver anything at all" and an approach that "play[ed] into the hands of local elites," all while leaving "the challenge of giving people a stake in government" unresolved.

In short, despite considerable expense and effort, a lot had not changed all that much. The country needed "not simply development" but "a sense of a unified nation, shared entitlement, and good leadership." That seemed a very long way off. One analyst concluded her assessment by stating that "no meaningful change has come for the governed" in Sierra Leone (Cubitt 2013: 109–112). Another analyst declared: "Macroeconomic and structural reforms imposed by the World Bank/International Monetary Fund (IMF) and attendant stringent conditionalities, exacerbated economic instabilities instead of stabilizing the economy and restoring growth. Poverty has remained endemic and widespread, and threatens the human security of Sierra Leoneans" (Pemunta 2012: 203). Yet another assessment acidly concluded that Sierra Leone's postwar, internationally sanctioned brand of "trickle-down peace" ended up favoring "international actors over those who survived the conflict" (Castañeda 2009: 249).

While these international actors were distinctly powerful, some of their policies invited pushback. In Sierra Leone's agricultural sector, there was a standoff over what constituted development for Sierra Leone's farmers. As Bolten reported in the postwar era, "Aid organizations want to re-create the pre-war 'normal' of small-scale subsistence agriculture." The farmers themselves did not, viewing the push to return to prewar miseries "as an imposition of the highly impoverished form of farming—backbreaking, lacking in dignity, inadequately small-scale and unable to bring profit." Returning to the past was scarcely even possible, given the "years of government inattention to food security and a draining of labor to the diamond fields and schoolhouses." What the outsiders viewed as "normal" was precisely what Sierra Leonean farmers viewed as "backward" (Bolten 2009: 71). Postwar reconstruction implies a return to the prewar era. Sierra Leone underscored the very good reasons why this vision is unpopular with so many wartime survivors.

All of these assessments may have been somewhat unfair. Sierra Leone at the dawn of peace was in ruins. In subsequent years, it achieved stability and some economic growth, as well as democratic elections and much more. The successful 2007 election, by itself, has been deemed "an extraordinary achievement" and a "happy outcome" (Gberie 2009: 7). The 2012 work of three analysts concluded that, rather than dismissing the country as "a basket case," Sierra Leone's accomplishments arrived when "few observers would have thought this last decade of peace and prosperity was possible" (Casey, Glennerster, and Miguel 2012: 17, 18).

But Sierra Leone's mighty achievements came at a price. When Transparency International released its Global Corruption Barometer in 2013, Sierra Leone topped the list with the highest bribery rate in the world. Among Sierra Leoneans, 84 percent surveyed admitted to paying a bribe over the prior year (Transparency International 2013: 33–34). That level outdistanced the other 106 countries in the survey, most of them by a country mile. While Liberia was in second place (at 75 percent), followed by Yemen and Kenya (74 and 70 percent, respectively), the global bribery rate stood at 27 percent, less than a third of Sierra Leone's proportion. An international agency official related that, predictably, "the government went ballistic" after learning that Sierra Leone had gained unfortunate notoriety as "the most corrupt nation on earth" (McCarthy 2013).

The survey results broadcast the way in which things *really* worked for ordinary citizens. In some respects, things simply had reverted to the prewar days, and some trends, such as endemic corruption and heavy constraints on peaceful dissent, have remained constant ever since (Freedom House 2021). The big changes lauded internationally and by the national government following the close of the war indeed were noteworthy. But frequently, they were hard to make out on the ground. Youth as well as officials engaged in youth programming who were interviewed for this book certainly contended that this was the case. A look at youth programs, and youth employment programs (YEPs) in particular, reveals a discouraging sameness for ordinary young people.

Interviews with youth pointed to their strong interest in youth programs, especially YEPs. They were in high demand among female youth despite emphatic gender stereotyping that seemed to influence the vocational offerings of every YEP. After overlooking females almost entirely in DDR, agencies providing YEP offerings steadfastly stuck to traditional gender norms. Male youth in programs often learned trades like carpentry, construction, and sometimes auto mechanics. Making soap and learning *gara* tie-dying, to name two ever-present examples, provided female youth with trades promising no more than minimal economic gain. Yet these realities did not dim interest in the programs. Just gaining access mattered a great deal, and in this, youth views were uniformly pessimistic. Only "youth who know politicians" gain access to those programs, a twenty-seven-year-old former Kamajor commander told me. "You have to know a minister or a mayor to get into a jobs program or get a job," a second Kamajor commander stated. During the DDR process, "we learned construction, but we're not professionals. So we can't get jobs." A youth employment program "is for big people," said a fifteen-year-old female sex worker. "This country operates on who knows you," a twenty-nine-year-old former Kamajor fighter said to me. "We are praying for a chance" in a youth employment program, a female youth told me. Her thoughts turned to getting married. "I can't wait for a youth program," she said. Then she asked, "What if it doesn't come?" "The one that has the opportunity" to decide on who gets into a youth program "will not consider me, since I don't have anything," a twenty-eight-year-old female youth told me. She was referring to payment of a bribe or kickback that would be required to gain access. A man of thirty-one who washed cars in a stream explained that, for himself and his fellow car washers, "We are [all] poor and we're not connected." It was as if "we live in another country."

In essence, they did. Subsequent exchanges with officials involved in youth programs left a strong impression that what youth had told me about getting into programs was not cynical at all. They merely were stating the facts. It was *Pa*-centered development. Chiefs and other politicians dominated the programs—just as they always had, evidently. As one veteran politician asked, "How do politicians compensate those who helped them during campaigns?" Then he supplied the answer: "That's what the youth programs are for." "When you have youth projects," a Sierra Leonean official working for an international agency related, "most of the beneficiaries are selected by the National Youth Council or village chiefs, relatives of chiefs, or political leaders." Recalling the selection of "beneficiaries" (the name implies that everyone in a program automatically benefits) for one initiative, he said that "there were quite a large number of favored youth. The selection was very political." The head of a Sierra Leonean NGO working with youth explained his take on how it all worked in 2010. "The politicians use youth employment programs for politics," he said. Then he shared a recent example. The minister of youth "had a YEP," he recalled. It was for 250 youth in Kenema. There were fifty spots reserved for the minister, fifty for the local APC (ruling party) regional chairman, and a hundred for the APC party office in town. He was informed that "there were only fifty openings for all organizations dealing with youth." That was it.

The NGO official was upset about the obvious and explicit use of programs as patronage. But other people involved in these programs were not. Privileged access was simply part of the system. During one interview with Sierra Leonean officials working for an international development agency implementing a nationwide YEP, the officials explained how chiefs and other local politicians chose most of the participants. "Beneficiaries in almost all areas [of the country] are selected by local authorities," one official matter-of-factly related. "You can't work in their area without their involvement." To drive home his point, he added, "It's their area." Challenging chiefly entitlement, however slight, was out of the question, even if it left "youth feeling neglected." One can imagine how that might have felt, since one of the other officials explained that "chiefs picked people who weren't youth." Often, they were far too old to be youth, including "very old women." A deflated international official working for a UN agency intimated that no one seemed to have answers to the massive challenge that Sierra Leone's youth presented. "If you ask youth what they want, they will [say that they] want a training [program] and access to money." Then the official added, "The UN agencies meet on youth issues, but there are no answers." At the same time, at least some international agencies appeared to be going with the flow, effectively bequeathing to chiefs and other Big Men control over participant (or beneficiary) lists. "There's a huge tension between youth and the elders here," one of the Sierra Leonean officials remarked. It was easy to appreciate why.

In an interview with another group of experienced Sierra Leonean development officials (also in 2010), we discussed the backgrounds of those who had gained national recognition as youth leaders. All of them were male elites who regularly were chosen to attend big meetings sponsored by international NGOs or UN agencies. Together, we came up with the names of ten of these well-known youth. Nearly all of the male youth on this list had a close relative serving in a high-ranking government position, the officials explained. I shared this list with other Sierra Leoneans with knowledge of prominent youth leaders. They corroborated the names and their connections. One of the officials at the meeting also shared his take on the perspective of Sierra

Leone's anointed youth leaders: "They push the government's views," he explained. They probably didn't have much of a choice.

Predictably, the blanket of blatant nepotism and control by power brokers over youth leaders and youth programs summoned regular frustration. The view from female youth in one village was particularly revealing. Drawing from firsthand experience, one of the youth explained that the process for starting a program normally began with an NGO visiting their village to "ask them about their problems and their experience during the war." When the program subsequently commenced, those who were interviewed naturally would "want to be considered." But instead "the NGOs will look for the chief and youth leader and young boy chief [a son of the chief] and the Mommy Queen." Together, "these four will plan and implement the program for the NGO. And they'll make sure their children and family members" gain access to the program.

A second female youth continued. "The only time they need the girls is when there's a visitor," she said. The chief "will force us to go and talk to the visitor," she explained. "And sometimes, he'll tell us what to say." Refusing the chief's orders was unthinkable, she insisted, as "you'll be in the bad book of the chief. So, when you have any problem and you go to him, you'll be dealt with seriously." The female youth also were told to dance for seven White men who visited the village. "They were the sponsors of the program," one explained. "The White people were so impressed." But the dancers were not members of the youth program, they said.

Were these stories of youth program access orchestrated by powerful Sierra Leoneans and passively compliant international agency officials consistent across all programs and all parts of the country? The data shared here cannot claim or confirm any such assertions. However, the strength of interest in youth programs (especially YEPs) by youth who were interviewed, and the passion with which virtually everyone commenting on the subject shared their views, converted this issue into a prominent set of field research findings.

The burning issue on this subject was access: the few who got in and the throngs who did not. Since so many sought to participate and so few succeeded, determinations of restricted entrée communicated a grander picture of power and Big Men excluding most young lives. Most female and male youth were on the outside, and there seemed to be no hope of altering that dynamic. Many young people not only lacked important connections to the powerful. They also were on their own, or they networked only with others just like them: the masses of young people struggling to stay afloat and perhaps get ahead. In these surroundings, many turned toward old and new friends in popular culture for support, guidance, and acceptance. The next chapter examines this issue, with an eye to uncovering how Rambo, Tupac, and Marley fared in the years after Sierra Leone's war had ceased.

CHAPTER 23

Filling a Void

The Fundamentals on the Ground

Postwar Sierra Leone is a democracy. While national elections still seem like staged duels between titanic rivals (as ever, the APC and SLPP), their quality and credibility were scarcely imaginable under Stevens or Momoh. For example, international observers of the 2018 presidential elections—where former NPRC honcho and coup leader Julius Maada Bio emerged as the SLPP's victorious candidate—showered praise on the National Election Commission "for effectively fulfilling its duties despite budget constraints, logistical challenges, and pressure from the [APC] government." Very significantly, the 2018 presidential elections "marked the second peaceful transfer of power between rival parties since the end of the civil war in 2002" (Freedom House 2021).

At the same time, many of the fundamentals on the ground had not changed all that much. *Pa*-centered social and political life remained dominant and suffocating. During campaign seasons, opposition parties routinely face "police violence and restrictions on assembly." Corruption "remains a pervasive problem at every [government] level," bribery rates "remain high among ordinary citizens seeking basic services," the nation's "courts are prone to executive interference, particularly in corruption cases," and "parents often must pay bribes to register their children in primary and secondary school." Sierra Leone's police force is "poorly paid and minimally trained," while its members "are rarely held accountable for physical abuse and extrajudicial killings, which remain frequent." Although there is a wide variety of independent newspapers and radio and television stations, journalists still must watch their step because "public officials have previously employed libel and sedition laws to target journalists, particularly those reporting on elections and high-level corruption." Freedom of expression exists to some degree, although it "may be affected" by the *fityai*-like "threat of violence from powerful interests." Moreover, the nation's civic groups "are constrained by onerous regulations," and gender-based violence and female genital mutilation persist as additional "long-standing concerns" (Freedom House 2021).

A small selection of Sierra Leone's implacable everyday challenges inevitably also surfaced in the process of conducting field research in the country. One day, out in Mine 11 in Koidu, two men slowly walked near the miners working in the river water. All of the miners stopped to watch them. I walked over to inquire. They were representatives of the local paramount chief.

They viewed mining as a blessing. In the view of one of the representatives, the work stopped boys and male youth from getting involved in crime. He also volunteered his analysis for "why the area is so poor and the facilities and roads are so run down." "It's the head [that is, their paramount chief] who is getting the money," he said. At the outset of an interview with two former RUF combatants in one of their homes (a rented room in Freetown), they informed me that they both sold marijuana as a side job. They explained it as a protection strategy. The police regularly swept through and plundered their neighborhood, said one. But since the police ran the marijuana trade, they did not loot the rented rooms they each lived in. A female sex worker informed me that she could not go to the police when customers beat her, refused to pay for services rendered, or robbed her. She could not afford the tip that police required to investigate. Instead, she brought up the incidents with policemen who were her occasional customers.

A succession of daily visits to one village revealed an array of other dispiriting everyday challenges. I had hired two motorcycle taxis to drop off me and my translator and research colleague in the morning and pick us up again midafternoon. At the outset of every morning ride, we had to pass a police checkpoint. Each time, I waved, smiled, and said hello to the same policeman who let the rope down and let us pass. By the third or fourth day, the policeman returned my greetings with a scowl. By the end of the week, he pulled my driver aside. The driver shared the policeman's message later. Unable to charge the driver a small bribe (his "morale booster") for passing his checkpoint in my presence, and presuming that the drivers were receiving lofty fees for transporting the White man and his colleague around, the policeman would extract his revenge. Both of our hired drivers would expect to pay a total of the given rate for each day they had passed with me and my colleague, plus a penalty—in short, a lot of money in one payment.

A steady stream of dispiriting episodes, separation between generations, a pervasive sense that most youth were excluded from access to opportunity, and the presence of many young people pitched out on their own collectively set the stage for an exploration into the role of Rambo, Tupac, and Marley in youth lives after the war. Did they still matter to young people? If so, had their appeal changed in the new era of postwar peace? Most important: did the three pop culture heroes of the recent past aid them in any way?

Fading Rambo

Rambo faded early. During interviews, many Sierra Leoneans had much to say about the Rambo films and their influence during the war. But not in the present. Very occasionally, I spied a poster of a Rambo film outside a video parlor in a town I was visiting up-country. But the only prominent sign of Rambo came on Easter Sunday in Sierra Leone in 2005. I was returning to Freetown from up-country with my research team. After entering the city by car, I saw posters of Rambo movies outside a succession of video parlors along Bai Bureh Road. I discussed this with my colleagues and followed up with others as well. Evidently, watching Rambo films on Easter (after attending church) had become something of a tradition for some Sierra Leoneans. But for the most part, Rambo had become a wartime relic. By my visit in 2010, I did not notice or hear about any screenings of Rambo films. In retrospect, the three films had had an extremely good run in Sierra Leone (about a quarter century). John Rambo was a formidable prewar and wartime presence in Sierra Leone. But his heyday had passed.

What had not expired was the fascination of young Sierra Leoneans with international videos. Once again, the issue of imitation regularly surfaced: of female and male youth studying videos carefully and incorporating what they had learned into their lives. As will be noted shortly, local musicians and young listeners were influenced by internationally famous musicians, as well. And just like youth across the world, many adored and avidly followed football clubs in the English Premier League and elsewhere in Europe. Adults uniformly berated young people for their conspicuous talent for precise observation and emulation of such international offerings. A senior judge, for example, was not impressed. "There's a copycat tendency" among Sierra Leone's youth, he lamented. "There are no values, and no value system except money." In the prewar days, an elderly man stated, "when young women dressed, you would see the decency in women." After the war, "when they see the [international] artists dressing with a short skirt and transparent dresses, they too want to dress like them. Go to the university or other higher institutions and what you will see will make your heart bleed."

The dual expressions of despair over young people were indications of a sea change well underway, where many young Sierra Leoneans sought to break away from tradition and the heavy weight of its expectations and judgments, while many adults clung to norms and customs that, to them, were timeless and sacrosanct. The new forms of expression arriving from beyond Sierra Leone's borders provided different ideas for a young person's lifestyle and general approach—a frame of reference for modern living. Most adults offered nothing of the kind. None of this was new: fascination for and emulation of Rastafarian ways, arriving from faraway Jamaica, began many decades earlier, for example. Nonetheless, the changes seemed sudden to many adults, and sometimes extreme (even to some youth).

Sierra Leone after the war appeared to be playing two symphonies simultaneously: one where chiefs and other Big Men reclaimed their prewar thrones, and another where young people celebrated difference, experimentation, and global connection. Elite adults did not trumpet their heavy reliance on international benefactors to rehabilitate the patrimonial playing field and return Big Men to the top of the heap. In dramatic contrast, young people avidly celebrated the international influences on their lives. In the world of ideas, Sierra Leone had become a joust.

Tupac's Example

Jousting, of course, was a Tupac specialty: "Hit 'Em Up" was but one demonstration of this particular area of his expertise. He was an original who, in the words of fellow rapper 50 Cent, "didn't sound like anyone who came before him" (2011). His popularity in Sierra Leone endured well after the war's demise. One researcher named Beyoncé "the single most popular artist among Freetown's young women" and described Tupac as "venerated by most young men" (Stasik 2016: 224). He was especially prominent and on the minds of male youth during my 2005 field visit. "In Freetown music clubs, when they play Tupac, everybody knows all the words," a devout Tupac fan told me. "Everybody! Everybody dances like him, they wave their arms like him, hold their fingers like him. They sing his music word for word. It's unbelievable!" He added, "All [Sierra Leonean] rappers use their hands just like Tupac." The pastor of a church in Makeni related that male youth in his choir "do Tupac dance moves to gospel music." Church leaders "tried to discourage this, but the youth persisted and refused. And the movements became part of the youth gospel singing program." The pastor was no fan of Tupac, yet his reflection on Tupac's influence in his church was revealing. "I learned that the youth don't want to be violent anymore," he explained. "It's the injustice parts of Tupac that they like now."

The evolving influence of Tupac on his ardent male youth corps was notable. With the war over, many related how they fashioned Tupac's example to suit a postwar lifestyle. Tuning out the abrasive elements of Tupac was not difficult. He set an example for others, and that mattered. This is reflected in the following assessment of Tupac's influence by a male twenty-eight-year-old youth in Freetown:

> I love Tupac. We still love him [in Sierra Leone]. I heard that his father was not there and his mother was in jail. Imagine you are from nowhere and you become a pioneer in the society. We admire a person like that so much.

> There are so many sufferers here. I used to hear about people who suc-
> ceeded, like Tupac. I'm from nowhere, but someday I can make it. Tupac is
> an example for us.

Other male youth identified especially with Tupac's complex relationship
with mainstream society, as someone who confronted the status quo while
trying to make it. It seemed to mirror their own challenges. For people who
routinely described themselves as sufferers, strugglers, and disgruntled, and
often depicted their daily efforts as a process of straining, Tupac resonated.
"Tupac, he's a man," a former male youth combatant told me. "He gathered
the youth and told them to take their steps, the true steps." What were those
steps? Those of an outlaw: "to go for drugs, for clubs [and] go buy and drink
wine." Inferred in his description was the need to believe in oneself. That was
because following Tupac's true steps would "let [youth] live a life that the various communities around them will be ashamed of." His colleague, another
former combatant, related the need to share Tupac's open defiance against
the appraisals of others. Even though others "class you as bad boys," the reality was that "Tupac's message helps [male youth] to be civilized." Because
of Tupac's influence, "some wash daily, others dress fine." In his view, Tupac
"makes them [become] used to civilization, go to clubs and learn to drive."

Adapting Tupac's example as a guide for life as a social outsider was a perspective that resonated with many others, as well. The leader of a Sierra Leonean NGO working with youth watched Tupac's video "clips" (that is, his
music videos) and concluded that "he's more of a gangster." In his view, after
a while, unemployed male youth "begin to walk like Tupac, dress like Tupac.
That's what gets them to behave like outcasts." "Tupac is a living heritage,"
a veteran researcher explained in 2005. "People are still listening to Tupac."
His outlaw status related to how many viewed themselves in Freetown. "Most
[male] youth see themselves as outlaws from society," said the researcher. "For
some, it's imagined marginalization. For others, it's more real." Either way,
"their own definition of youth is to be in opposition to the system, the people
in power."

Tupac's influence over male youth in Sierra Leone has been aptly recorded
earlier in this book. One last exchange involving male youth and Tupac's influence, on a Freetown street in 2005, again sheds light on their studied analysis of Tupac and what his followers adapted from his renowned life to their
own. The exchange began when one male youth asked the others, "Is it a sin
to like Tupac?" A second said no, and then proceeded to tell an elaborate version of Tupac's entire life, starting before he was born and weaving in Tupac's
parents, other rappers (including "Snoop Doggy" and Notorious B.I.G.), selling drugs, going to prison, having sex with B.I.G.'s wife, and much more. "He
was the King of Thug!" he exclaimed. "Tupac no die" [that is, Tupac is not

Tupac's "All Eyes on Me" trademark, on the back of a minibus on a Sierra Leonean roadway in 2013.

dead], said another. An older man listening to the dramatic story joined in. Tupac could not be alive because "we know about bullets, because of the Sierra Leonean war," he said. "If you're shot [from] very close, you can't live. We know the cartridge." The popular debate over whether Tupac was dead or alive continued for a while. Then the storyteller pulled the conversation back to Tupac's legacy: "White people don't see the reality or the essence, the consciousness of this music. Most of his music, like 'Me against the World,' he's not talking about 'me against the world' in a negative way. He's talking about how a man must lead his life against the world in a positive way. Pac was just like a pastor: he says the reality but did not do it. You live by the gun, you die by the gun: that is the reality of the outlaw life. White people don't understand."

The impassioned statement calls up much of what Tupac inspired within many male youth in Sierra Leone. For his followers, Tupac's music inspired an awareness of underlying realities, along the lines of the practiced consciousness that Marley's followers enact. His identity as a Black man was important: he was misunderstood by White people while living a life that mixed pride with alienation. That stance helped guide many male youth outsiders in Sierra Leone in the face of condemnation by insiders. For this fan, Tupac's complicated final message seemed to move in two directions at once: toward being ready to kill and die as an outlaw while inspiring followers not to go there.

Tupac's power to fascinate and exemplify a dignified outcast lifestyle seemed to keep him on the minds of at least some male youth across a great many years. But over time, other rappers, and other musicians generally, surpassed (or perhaps succeeded) Tupac. It seemed to be a natural progression. Akon, the Senegalese American rapper, became "immensely popular" in the country starting in 2006—the equivalent of the Beatles or Michael Jackson, according to one analyst (Tucker 2013: 16). There also were new forces on the scene who had much to say about emerging challenges in Sierra Leone. One was Emmerson Bockarie, the "artist best known for his attacks on 'big men.'" An early song was called "Borbor Beleh" (meaning "Belly Boy," signifying a corrupt, corpulent man). It came out in 2002, the same year the war had ended, and it did not hold back. Emmerson confronts elders in the song, asking them whether they still can "eat" whatever they like. Then he proclaims that their era has ended because youth are prepared to "stand up strong" to them. Among youth in Sierra Leone, Emmerson "is beloved as the first of the youth artists to stand up to politicians and for his *fityai*" (Shepler 2010a: 637). He was daring in the extreme, and he was getting away with it.

Emmerson's stature as "Sierra Leone's number one revolutionary artist" eventually involved his work in national politics. After the APC had won the 2007 elections, he was among those receiving credit for "helping to usher in a new era of democracy." Two years later, Emmerson had had enough. Feeling that the APC government "was not acting as they had promised," he came out with "Yesterday (Better Pass Tiday)" (Yesterday is better than today). It was hugely popular. During my 2010 fieldwork, I noticed how the song's title had become a common descriptor of one's situation. The war may be over, but things are getting worse. Soon after the song's release, a second Sierra Leonean rapper, Innocent, produced "Una Gi Dem Chance," essentially a plea for giving the APC a chance "to prove its worth." Youth I spoke to about Innocent's response song panned it as unconvincing and a pale replica of Emmerson's captivating tune. Over time, "it started to become clear that Innocent was a tool of the APC" (Tucker 2013: 34).

Emmerson's famous *fityai* songs were difficult to envision ever taking place in the prewar era. One can much more easily picture someone as young and daring as Emmerson being picked up and placed in a *tait kɔna* for quite a while. That alone indicated hard-won progress for ordinary Sierra Leoneans. Notably, an analyst of Sierra Leonean music said in 2010 that Sierra Leonean musicians (including Emmerson and Innocent) hid direct mention of the war era. Instead, singers would refer to the war as the "years of darkness." It was an indicator of the directed forgetting approach to memories of wartime loss that many Sierra Leoneans practiced. The terrible war should not be mentioned in songs.

Marley on Top

In Sierra Leone, someone who revered Marley was a follower, and all followers smoked marijuana. The two seemed inseparable in people's minds. You could like Marley without smoking djamba, of course. Many did; while some adults professed not to be familiar with Tupac and his work, everyone knew Marley. Most seemed to agree with his precepts too. He stood for integrity, standing up against inequality and always defending, if not asserting, your rights. In this way, Marley held a unique place in Sierra Leonean culture, a figure above the fray of Big Men, self-censorship, gross inequality, and poverty, and one who seemed to give many people hope for something better.

For many youth (most especially male youth), Marley stood at the top of a kind of pantheon of pop culture heroes. While those positioned below him might rise and fade, Bob Marley, known across Sierra Leone as the "King of Reggae," held steady. Marley maintained an irresistible attraction for young Sierra Leoneans for two reasons. Unquestionably, he was a phenomenal artist. His worldwide and seemingly endless renown draws from artistry of a very high order. For Sierra Leoneans, his clarity of purpose and integrity seemed to stand out most. He was a seer of the future, and he somehow knew what they were going through. He was mystical. Tupac's and Rambo's claims on Sierra Leonean imaginations also were powerful: Tupac was impossibly daring and Rambo was absurdly brave. Both were skillful and unsinkable too. Tupac in fact was still more. He was articulate, he had immense style, he was honest, and he knew he would die young. He also was Black and a fellow sufferer. Just like his fans in Sierra Leone, and well beyond. Many other remarkable international pop culture heroes have passed through the pages of this book: Chuck Norris and Arnold Schwarzenegger, the much-beloved Joseph Hill ("Joe Hills"), Michael Jackson, Akon, 50 Cent, Burning Spear, and Peter Tosh. Many others undoubtedly were not mentioned. Research for this book clearly positioned Rambo, Tupac, and Marley emphatically at the top, but Bob Marley most of all.

The second reason for Marley's significance to young Sierra Leoneans was because he filled a void for profoundly alienated youth. They needed inspiration and he provided it. Marley rose to importance in the 1970s, a time when peaceful dissent was a frightening option, and when few to no inspirational figures were allowed to emerge domestically. In Freetown, Marley and other reggae stars found an eager following. Marijuana, which had arrived a decade earlier, conveniently was available too. Marley and many others from the pop culture world eventually spread across Sierra Leone. Their subsequent role in the war was as unavoidable as it was commonsensical. Tupac was the fearless, "blow your mind" *fityai* boy, and Rambo knew just how to fight in the forest.

A man sports a Bob Marley shirt, featuring the title of Marley's famous "One Love" song. In the early war years, Strasser's NPRC government promoted Marley's "One Love," which could be silently signaled via a thumbs-up hand sign.

Marley was even more: he *was* resistance and revolution, and the prophet of hope too.

After the war, Marley's ability to inspire pushback against censure and validate a person's struggle for their rights regularly surfaced during interviews with youth, including one on the outskirts of Kenema in 2010. Two former male combatants shifted our wide-ranging conversation back to Marley. "Bob Marley is like a messiah to us because he talks to us—about our rights, our freedom," one stated. His colleague continued: "The reason why some people see Bob Marley as a threat is this: there are certain hidden things in society which the rich people and the politicians don't want to be known. Those are issues that Bob Marley transformed into music, making them open to everyone." Another male youth entered the discussion. He used the example of how youth groups are formed to clarify why young people turn to Marley (as well as Tupac): "When they come to set up a youth group, they won't consider you, because they say you are a dropout. When they do that to us, we feel bad. Like Marley says: he told the truth for the poor people. Not only Bob Marley—we also listen to Tupac, just to encourage our lives. We need their music when we feel bad." Two female youth chose their moment to contribute. "Yes, we also listen to their music when we feel bad," said one, on behalf of female youth.

Then her friend, a female youth of twenty-nine, spoke: "Like Bob Marley says: don't give up."

No wonder there was a war. Sierra Leone after the conflict exposed how most of its young people still had very little room to maneuver. Many of Sierra Leone's old ways had retrenched. It was a land where nepotism and corruption again reigned, nearly half of all children had only one or no parents, one in ten females worked "on the track" as sex workers, nine in ten girls and women had had their genitals mutilated, many tens of thousands of boys, male youth, and even men searched for diamonds with scant hope of success, and much, much more. Speaking out risked censure and detention, and special words expressed traditional society's utter condemnation of young people who pushed back or publicly failed. Emasculation for males and suppression for females seemed difficult if not impossible for most to avoid.

In such an environment, are young people working for the police in the marijuana trade or sometimes selling sex to policemen really lawbreaking Rarrays? Can development aid intended for young people succeed if it runs through the power brokers? The dignity, patience, and thoughtfulness of Sierra Leone's youth that surfaced in interviews was as routine as it was, given the context, thoroughly remarkable. More than anything else, Sierra Leone's prodigious postwar stability is due to the fortitude, peacefulness, and perseverance of its young people.

PART 8

The Lessons of Disconnection

CHAPTER 24

Young People and War

The Instructive Story of Sierra Leone

On the surface, Sierra Leone's awful war seems unremarkable—a mere member of the broad band of civil conflicts that emerged in the 1990s. The collapse of the Soviet Union, Kaldor's influential depiction of a new kind of warfare (1999), and the sheer expanse of combat served to overshadow the particular specifics that inform all violent conflicts. Sierra Leone is tiny, and it mainly attracted attention for its seemingly bizarre and "primitive" dimensions. But that's about it. As seems to have happened so often in Sierra Leone's history, the country slipped into the background, lost in the shuffle amid a plethora of deadly conflicts, and swept aside when other contexts attracted attention, such as Rwanda's genocide and Yugoslavia's implosion.

For the most part, Sierra Leone mainly garnered international notice during its war years via a racist distortion. The amputation of civilian limbs by an outwardly exotic rebel group reinforced the vision of Black Africa as a forlorn basket case. Kaplan expanded on the general take on Sierra Leone as a disregarded location:

> Sierra Leone is a microcosm of what is occurring, albeit in a more tempered and gradual manner, throughout West Africa and much of the underdeveloped world: the withering away of central governments, the rise of tribal and regional domains, the unchecked spread of disease, and the growing pervasiveness of war. West Africa is reverting to the Africa of the Victorian atlas. It consists now of a series of coastal trading posts, such as Freetown and Conakry, and an interior that, owing to violence, volatility, and disease, is again becoming, as Graham Greene once observed, "blank" and "unexplored." . . . Sierra Leone is widely regarded as beyond salvage. (Kaplan 2000)

Then came *Blood Diamond* (2006). The vivid depiction of virtually every Sierra Leonean male youth as irrational and violent reasserted Sierra Leone as a disturbing, dangerous, and very sad backwater.

Fortunately, researchers did not stay away. While their main audience was academic (and thus quite limited), there now exists a canon of available research on Sierra Leone's extraordinary war. Much of it is useful, some of it is superb, and virtually all of it is intriguing (I have drawn extensively from this abundant resource for this book). Yet even this body of work has not changed Sierra Leone's reputation all that much. The message still seems to be: it's OK to overlook this benighted little West African state.

One purpose of this book is to help change that dynamic. The story of Sierra Leone has so much to tell us: about youth alienation, the enveloping power of global icons, the application of terror and drugs for wartime purpose, and still more. History grounds this effort. For decades at least, the source of much control and domination over young people was patriarchal authority. The British colonials' most influential legacy was their establishment and empowerment of paramount chiefs. The British raised up and recognized certain chiefs above all others, giving them key roles in their system. Ultimately, they created a set of local rulers whom they could not control, particularly when vast wealth from diamond mining entered the scene. This laid the groundwork for a second tradition emerging from the colonial era: the fake state. As Sierra Leone moved from a colonial property to an independent nation, local patriarchs built and dominated power structures while national leaders undermined their own governments, instead emphasizing personalized, Big Man–follower control over vast networks of people and resources. Many of these trends—weakening the formal state, exploiting male youth, and expanding patrimonial authority above all else—came together under the lodestone himself, Siaka Stevens, whose many actions and impacts form a central story line in this book.

Two men had sculpting influences over the degradation and destruction that followed in their wake: Stevens and Charles Taylor. Stevens's style of rule laid out the path to rebellion and war by undermining his own government (and the national military) while legitimizing and empowering his personalized brand of wealth extraction and violent repression. Unlike Stevens, Taylor didn't require a state in order to extract wealth and dominate with violence. Taylorland, in fact, had more heft and impact, in almost all ways, than Liberia's government and its paltry institutions, which he assumed as its democratically elected president in 1997. Taylor also desired far more than diamonds from Sierra Leone. It started with a thirst for revenge (a tale dating back to Momoh and ECOMOG). But more than anything else, Charles Taylor sought regional domination—perhaps an empire. Foday Sankoh was his minion, although Sankoh, his RUF underlings, and his AFRC counterparts had plenty of room to freelance too. The terror warfare that emerged was a collaborative invention. But it bore the stamp and approval of Taylor. In a sense,

Stevens and his style of rule incited exceedingly violent warfare while Taylor kicked everything into gear and then guided it along the way. Their complementary roles expand the notion of the Big Man into tiers: Stevens over paramount chiefs (among others) before the war and Taylor over Sankoh, Bockarie, and many of the local warlords operating in Sierra Leone's war theater.

The story of Sierra Leone, including its experience of war, contains lessons of global import. Aspects of the story of Sierra Leone's youth, for example, have much to contribute to our understanding of youth alienation. There are further lessons to be drawn from the historic influence of the Atlantic slave trade on male youth emasculation and female suppression, the practice of terror warfare, the exploitation of youth and young children for wartime purposes, the impact of drugs in war theaters, gender concerns emerging in war zones, the nature of governance, the dynamics of resource exploitation, and the remarkable power of local interpretations of popular culture figures on both warfare and young people.

The first three chapters of part 8 detail lessons emerging from the tale of alienated young people, terror-infused warfare, and popular culture icons with influence and applications reaching far beyond, undoubtedly, anything the artists themselves (and, in the case of Rambo, their creators) could have anticipated. Although Sierra Leone's war finally expired over two decades ago, global approaches to the perspectives and priorities of huge youth populations remain grossly inadequate, fake states persist (in some quarters), popular culture and drugs still play big roles in young lives and (sometimes) in war zones, and terror is an established component of the international security landscape. We can learn a great deal from Sierra Leone, in short, because much of what happened there was so extreme and, in a certain way, so innovative.

This chapter focuses on issues concerning young people. The next boils down youth interpretations of Bob Marley, John Rambo, and Tupac Shakur, and considers how their takes reflect nuanced understandings of underlying meanings. Chapter 26 considers powerful forces that impact the lives and ideas of citizens, states, and international institutions. The book's final chapter sets out recommendations for reforming the policies and practices of development and diplomacy, with particular reference to youth, governance, and security challenges.

Harvesting Children

Why do children play vital roles in some war zones? One story from South Sudan sheds light on their potential to transform the practice of warfare and children themselves. One morning in the autumn of 2003, I hopped aboard a tiny UN plane that would take me from northern Bahr el Ghazal in what was then southern Sudan (now the nation of South Sudan) to our destination just before sunset: the northwestern tip of Kenya, Lokichoggio. It was a long trip, with many stops on dirt runways en route. One stop required our pilot to shoo a boy and his cattle off the runway by nearly landing before rising, circling around, and trying to land, over and again. As the young boy smiled broadly and waved to us in the plane, a man finally ran onto the runway and herded the cattle and the boy onto the nearby grass.

Another of our stops was the town of Rumbek. Its secondary school was famous for two reasons: it was the entire region's first (founded in 1948), and some of the ethnic Dinka students who met at school ultimately became top leaders of the Sudan People's Liberation Army (SPLA; Sommers 2005: 57). Rumbek was the only stop where the plane's passengers could exit and stretch for a spell as workers manually refueled the plane (the entire region had no electricity). During our stop, I met and chatted with a handful of officials from UN agencies. What they told me illuminated the challenges that international institutions face when they tackle issues concerning children and war.

UNICEF was tasked to provide DDR support to former soldiers under the age of eighteen (that is, child soldiers). It was a difficult task, and in the end, the results were mixed.[1] Officials related that they had had trouble hiring local staff (their initial attempt attracted teachers from Rumbek's historic secondary school, as their pay was higher than a teacher's salary). But another reported challenge concerned the notion of childhood. UNICEF had expected to provide protection and support for children. But one official related the following story. An adolescent boy of fifteen or sixteen refused to accept UNICEF's assistance. He wanted money. When it was explained that, as he was a child, he would not be receiving cash, he was offended. In no way was he a child, he insisted. To prove his point, he asked the official, "Do you want to meet my wife? Do you want to meet my children? *I'm a man!*"

As the South Sudan example illustrates most tellingly, defining a child as an age range is artificial and abstract. In the case of UNICEF (and the United Nations Convention on the Rights of the Child), a child is every human being under the age of eighteen (UNICEF, n.d.). In South Sudan, this young fellow had jumped from childhood straight into adulthood. He had no time to be a youth. His age was irrelevant: he was a soldier (perhaps an officer), a husband, and a father. The international agency approach suggests that children are vulnerable and should be protected and cared for. Problems necessarily arise when the abstraction—childhood—must become reality. In war contexts, the fit can be awkward.

Childhood nonetheless is viewed widely as a precious and delicate commodity. In the United States, such values have inspired extravagant outcomes. There are, for example, terms such as helicopter parenting ("the practice of hovering anxiously near one's children") and snowplow parenting ("clearing any obstacles in their child's path to success, so they don't have to encounter failure, frustration or lost opportunities") (Miller and Bromwich 2019) that characterize an unusually protective approach to raising a youngster.

Contrast this to the approach of commanders of child soldiers. For such adults, children are not particularly precious, since they are abundant and easily replaceable in today's unusually youthful world. But they *are* exceptionally and uniquely useful: in a war zone, there's almost nothing they cannot do. This is particularly the case for girls, who often are considered the best spies and generally supply sexual services far more often than boys. With proper brutal training, a dose of brainwashing and heartless treatment, woven together by a fatherlike figure in the form of one's commander (and, in the case of the RUF, a grandfatherly Foday Sankoh), child members of military outfits tend to be compliant and resilient. They also require limited amounts of food and general upkeep. If they convert deep trauma into a death wish (courageous to the point of fatalistically seeking death in battle), then they likely will be extraordinarily brave and able to strike fear in the hearts of civilians. If they become too traumatized to perform required tasks, they can be removed (killed, abandoned, or driven away) with ease. Either way, they are useful and unique cogs of terror warfare.

The brutality that such children experience can be difficult to contemplate. One of the bush kids who drew pictures in Sahn Malen asked me, "Do you want to see my prison?" I said that I did. He turned over his piece of paper to reveal a drawing in yellow of a semicircular structure composed of saplings bent into bars. After the RUF captured him, he told me, that is where he had lived. He was eleven years old.

Commanders routinely unlock the potential of young people that civilian adults can scarcely conceive. Conducting surveillance behind enemy lines is difficult and unusually dangerous work. An exposed spy likely will face interrogation, torture, and death. In Sierra Leone, children performed this "recce" work for rebel groups with consummate skill. Guiding fellow child soldiers into battle or attacking unarmed civilians also requires leadership skills and a degree of bravery and brutality that becomes inspirational. In these and similar cases, the commanders of children see potential that peacetime adults cannot. Then they exploit it. As Stokes and Chkhaidze observe, "In the well-developed cult [such as the RUF and other military outfits with many child soldiers], unethical and unrelenting leadership . . . engages in manipulative control, abusive power, and willingness to intimidate irresponsibly in order to demand dedicated compliance" (2017: 204). Some commanders also reward their child soldiers' valor and obedience with commendation afterward, thereby cultivating loyalty in return. Quite a bag of tricks.

Child soldiers seem able to perform almost any task that is asked of them.

Some child fighters, domestics, "wives," porters, spies, and so on are so talented, resilient, efficient, and versatile that it is useful to reflect on the term invented in Sierra Leone for such people: *smɔl smɔl yut* (very small youth). Children who become soldiers (often, but not always, against their will) frequently are treated like little adults. While such young people are severely exploited and probably traumatized in the process, there is a side to the experience that, in some cases at least, is empowering. It is a level of potential that officials of agencies, much less snowplow or helicopter parents, are unlikely to envision. Rarely are the exceptional skills or achievements of child soldiers recognized in peacetime. Hiding who they are and what they did is all too common.

Child soldiering has stretched conventional expectations of what a very young person can accomplish. Yet the lesson of the military men and women who exploit children is right before us: children can (and often do) accomplish immeasurably more than adults anticipate. A gender dimension also is part of the DDR challenge: why do postwar societies tend to shun girls abducted and abused by rebel groups and accept boys who had been child soldiers? This is the trend that Shepler found in postwar Sierra Leone (2010b: 96). Such social rejection invites a second question. Given the exclusion and marginalization that many young people experience (in Sierra Leone and elsewhere), how can someone be "reintegrated" into a society following a war (the "R" in DDR) if they had not been an integral part of society beforehand? For excluded young people, "reintegration" (not "integration") points to a comfortable and imagined reality that never existed. It is a reassuring ruse.

In a war where child soldiers were unusually prominent, the RUF had the youngest soldiers of them all (Humphreys and Weinstein 2004: 20). Following the war, they also were the least likely to return home (a mere 34 percent did so). These trends are supported by a third: those combatants who were abducted were less likely to return to their former homes (39). Taken together, the profile of most RUF combatants differs from the usual in substantial ways. Failing to address this allows former combatants to fall through the cracks. Freetown, for example, seems to be loaded with former combatants who have never received program support. This is particularly the case for former female members of military groups. McKay and Mazurana found that only 6 percent of girls who were in the RUF participated in DDR programming. That appallingly low number actually is substantially larger than all of the other fighting forces (2 percent for the AFRC and SLA, and a miniscule 0.4 percent of girls who were with Civil Defense Forces, including the Kamajors (McKay and Mazurana 2004: 100).[2]

Reintegration presupposes prewar social integration. Many former child and youth combatants never experienced it. "DDR" should convert to "DDI" to reflect the commonplace need for first-time integration.

Youth under Attack

What is it like to be alienated? Alienation is an emotional positioning arising from a profound and what can seem like inescapable social separation. Even as it is vital to the emotional architecture of exclusion, it remains a largely overlooked concern. The expanding emphasis on quantitative data by governments and international agencies facilitates the separation between what it is like to be young and separate from the antiseptic fashion in which youth issues, challenges, or problems routinely are addressed.

Youth currently are more often represented by numbers than narratives. Insiders tend to rely on statistics to make policy decisions that impact outsiders. Nearly always, they make them without input from or appreciation of lives lived on the outside, such as youth condemned as thugs, lumpens, prostitutes, vagrants, and all of the other terms regularly employed to castigate many if not most of those in Sierra Leone. Policies that are informed by two-dimensional quantitative data sets about young people, and not balanced with the sort of nuance that quality, qualitative research can provide, invite distorted outcomes. Crucial underlying realities lie in their stories, which provide detail about uncountable concerns and forces. It is in this way that alienation routinely is unknown, underappreciated, or set aside.[3]

Alienation rests at the center of the dystopian difficulties that characterize and contain many young people. Bob Marley repeatedly warns listeners to be on guard for the false claims that others sell and the wily manipulations that they propose. Tupac's life and a significant proportion of his oeuvre was driven by alienation. Rambo's character, social situation, and drive arise from life as a loner who threatens institutions and bureaucrats merely through his presence. Such views and deeds radiate to the countless cadres of profoundly alienated youth in our world. That includes Sierra Leone: the towering significance of youth alienation is one of the fundamental findings arising from research and analysis for this book. It also cements youth connections to Marley, Tupac, and Rambo, all of whom communicate to and uphold multitudes of young people existing outside of mainstream society.

Reflecting on the depth and significance of alienation as a powerful emotional element in youth lives is instructive. One source defines it as "the feeling that you have no connection with the people around you" (*Cambridge Dictionary*, n.d.). Another states that the word "describes the feeling that you're not part of a group" (Vocabulary.com, n.d.). Alienating someone causes them "to become indifferent or hostile," explains a third. An alienated person is "withdrawn, or isolated from the objective world" (Dictionary.com, n.d.). Synonyms of alienation include disaffection and estrangement, while words related to alienation include envenoming, animosity, bitterness, fury, outrage,

A female and male youth "harvest" sand at a riverside.

and wrath (Merriam-Webster, n.d.). In Sierra Leonean jargon, this is the state of being disgruntled.

Alienation can incite blowback. For example, some youth "may turn to violent underworlds that offer alternative sources of status, recognition and social cohesion" if they "feel alienated from political processes and believe they cannot influence key decisions that affect their lives" (McLean Hilker and Fraser 2009, cited in Simpson 2018: 32). Yet it is the patience and endurance of most youth, even in the face of forces that actively marginalize them, that is most striking. The overwhelming majority of youth are peaceful, no matter what (Simpson 2018: 35; Sommers 2015: 24).

Education systems are regular promoters of systemic youth exclusion, including in Sierra Leone. As Lopes Cardozo et al. note, "The differential capacity of elites to access education at all levels underlines how in many conflict-affected societies, formal education systems continue to create social divisions and reproduce the hierarchies and inequalities that have been drivers of conflict and youth alienation" (2016: 55). This exemplifies how states and their national and international partners effectively stimulate environments that overlook injustices and sanction insider advantages. Reassuring postwar tonics like peace education or citizenship training for victimized young people will prove inadequate if elite promoters of societal instability maintain stratagems that favor their flocks.

The situation of youth in Sierra Leone strongly suggests that alienation is a product of this sort of endemic exclusion. The nature of their exclusion has many dimensions. It was systemic, as elites limited access to quality education, adulthood, and reputable work. Life for many young Sierra Leoneans also was antagonistic: options much beyond diamond mining, sand harvesting, quarry work, or prostitution were difficult to imagine. Social humiliation was part of life. *Fityai* is a means to maintain the status quo by condemning and controlling people who challenge it. The road ahead emerges from lessons drawn from Sierra Leone: reverse policies and practices that deny nonelite youth access to essential opportunities, keep them under the thumb of patriarchs, and foster their denigration.

War Boys and Captive Girls

How do gender norms control youth? To a significant degree, that which held gender norms in place, and instituted the punishing conditions that most Sierra Leone's male and female youth endured for generations, was due to absolute patriarchal dominance and (with a big boost from British colonials) the patrimonial political system it birthed. Beginning with the era of the Atlantic slave trade, powerful Sierra Leonean men exploited male youth to serve as "war boy" mercenaries either to terrorize people or become personal guards for chiefs. Mobilizing male youth to intimidate, threaten, and (sometimes) employ violence continued through the colonial and independence eras. The discovery of diamonds vastly accelerated the patrimonial power of some patriarchs (such as paramount chiefs with diamond mines in their chiefdoms). At the same time, many male youth found it difficult to marry, gain recognition as men, stay in school, or stay out of the mines.

The result was enforced emasculation, described as a male-focused "crisis of youth." Male youth lacked promising options and, it appeared, even hope. Some of them enacted the threat and violence that Big Men sought. These trapped male youth nonetheless attracted sustained condemnation from many. Yet the unsavory behavior of so-called thugs, lumpens, and misfits connected to centuries-long traditions that spotlighted their abuse, control, and manipulation by superpowerful patriarchs.

A key thread in Sierra Leone's story is how violence begat more violence. As with male youth, the female youth experience in Sierra Leone has featured social control and degradation. Profound female youth difficulties also took shape during the slave era. As men exited via international slavery and women were enslaved in the domestic market, male acts to contain and control feminine power emerged. These proved long-standing: the male need to assert authority over females ultimately extended from the time of slavery to the civil war period and beyond. Females were under extreme attack during the conflict years, when obsessive sexual violence became a wartime main-stay. Rebel groups took many females as sex slaves, and even those away from war theaters often had their lives subjugated. For example, since many refugee parents believed that unsupervised girls may become pregnant and end up as sex workers, they kept them out of school. Beyond such approaches to child protection, it was the thoroughly alarming exploitation of females by boys and men during the war that underscored the vulnerability of girls and female youth and, in too many cases, contained them in near-complete invisibility—life as chattel, in effect, and lives that too often took place in the shadows.

Gender—of males and masculinity, and females and femininity—is never a minor dimension of warfare. It is difficult to understand Sierra Leone's war without appreciating three seminal gender dimensions of prewar and war-time Sierra Leone:

(1) The dominance of patriarchal overlords and their patrimonial systems;
(2) The emasculation of male youth; and
(3) The subordination of females.

While the first two dimensions generally have received attention, the third, for the most part, has not. Just how girls and female youth have played subsid-iary roles in many (and perhaps most) written accounts of Sierra Leone's war is mysterious, given their emphatic and disturbing centrality. There is a vast gender deficit. It is unfortunate.

The pressure and violence against female youth has subsided only some-what in the postwar era. This is suggested in a recent ranking of 167 countries regarding their performance in the Women's Peace and Security Index. Sierra Leone ranked fifteenth from the bottom. Of all nations in the index, 91.6 per-cent had a higher ranking. According to the data, more than one in four Sierra Leonean women (28.7 percent) experienced partner violence over a twelve-month period, while less than half (48.1 percent) felt safe walking alone at night (GIWPS and PRIO 2019: 62, 65).

Alas, the tale of disenfranchised male youth in Sierra Leone has been detailed to a far greater degree than the corollary story of disempowered female youth. It remains remarkable that discussions of "youth" in Sierra Leone generally promote the impression that, mainly or exclusively, they are males. Tragically, it is a profound and unfortunate truth that emasculated males are easy targets for public humiliation while female youth are easily ignorable.

We Are the Gods for Today

Why is generational separation so acute in Sierra Leone? Reflections from adults and youth in chapter 21 underscore their distanced relationship, and an apparent future where recognized adulthood is as rare as adult mentorship of youth. Prior research on male elders' heavy control over access to marriage and recognized adulthood (Richards 2006a) seems to have become a concrete reality. There is no turning back, it seems. For many in Sierra Leone (and, indeed, many other nations), traditional pathways to manhood and womanhood seem to have become historical artifacts. In nearly all ways now, youth are on their own.

The war catapulted this reality onto Sierra Leoneans. The RUF in particular upended tradition during the conflict years, and the curse "We are the Gods for today" signifies revolutionary change. In his memoir, Ishmael Beah describes an example of the RUF's angry, incoherent, youngster-oriented approach. In a village where he and five of his friends had fled from an RUF attack, the boys joined a group of others—boys, girls, and adults—who also had survived. Two young male RUF rebels met them there. Though Beah does not estimate their ages, he records that "the youngest rebel" humiliated a man who was weak and "probably in his sixties." The young rebel pushed the elder down, pointed a gun at his head, and forced the man to stand up. Then the older rebel measured his bayonet against the old man's neck and concluded that "it looks like a perfect fit." The old man was terrified with fear, while the older rebel is described as having "fierce red eyes"—an apparent indication that he was high on some drug (Beah 2007: 32, 33).

The flagrant degradation of an elder by two boys stirs Beah to set what he saw into context: "Before the war a young man wouldn't have dared to talk to anyone older in such a rude manner. We grew up in a culture that demanded good behavior from everyone and especially from the young. Young people were required to respect their elders and everyone in the community" (33). The humiliation of the elderly man continued. The older rebel accused the old man of fleeing his village "because you are against our cause as freedom fighters" and proceeded to fake an execution, shooting his gun near the man's head. The old man, of course, panicked, thinking he had been shot, then realized he was unscathed. The rebels "were very amused at the old man's reaction," Beah states (33).

The contrast between the RUF's "We are the Gods for today" approach and Tupac's use of "motherfucker" reflects the extremity of exploitation of children and youth in Sierra Leone. Tupac repeatedly returns to this reference of mother-son incest as his most prominent word to accentuate anger, threat, emasculation, disdain, condemnation, indignation, and much more in his songs. The diversity of applications for this one curse word is remarkable: Tupac even refers to himself as one. In "Breathin'," Tupac describes the outcome of his dangerous, kill-or-be-killed life: he's the only "motherfucker" left.[4] After a while, Tupac's use of "motherfucker" becomes commonplace, thus losing some of its ability to startle listeners. To accentuate its meaning, Tupac sometimes slows down his rapping to stress the first and third syllables in "motherfucker." But in the end, it is merely a single curse word. It was the best Tupac could draw on, from his language, dialect, and idiom, to express an array of emotions.

The use of curse words and phrases emerging from Sierra Leone's wartime context transcended Tupac and his American rap contemporaries in at least two ways. First, the RUF reportedly enacted the American "motherfucker" curse by forcing heavily drugged boys under their control to rape their mothers and become *authentic* motherfuckers. Second, the vision that emerged from some of the cursing was downright revolutionary. "We are the Gods for today" signals a new way of life and style of society, where the children are in charge and everyday life is completely upended. The enactment of a new and perverse reality—young people as obscenely violent dictators—left indelible memories.

The ground truth emerging from this wartime experience is that young Sierra Leoneans cannot be disregarded, much less castigated. Times must change. Young people need respect and space to register their views. The patriarchal denigration of youth may be an expiring option.

CHAPTER 25

No Contradiction

Pop Culture and Alienation

Why are pop culture icons so important to alienated youth? In this book, popular culture functions not just as a reassuring salve. The world that the works of Bob Marley, Tupac Shakur, and John Rambo collectively detail configures life as perversely and cruelly structured, where those in the right are blamed while the powerful exploit them. The work of all three confirm a person's separateness—it is all too real—as well as validate their indignation, explain why they live on the outside, and provide a rationale and pedagogy for responding to their subjugation and manipulation. Marley and, especially, Tupac and Rambo have experienced, understood, and responded to their aggressive castigation as "bad" people. Through their described and demonstrated instructions, suspicious and seemingly powerless young people across the world can analyze their situation and extract information on how to respond and, just perhaps, bust out. Nihilism never plays a part: their shared response to the world's punishing injustices is to demonstrate active, fearless, and righteous resistance, living through Marley's dictum to push proactively for yourself and your rights.

All of their ideas resonate globally, and with persistent relevance. While the combination of Marley, Tupac, and Rambo came together in a most particular fashion in Sierra Leone, the influence of all three international superstars has resonated across the world, right up to the present. Tupac Shakur has been deified as a saint in the hip-hop world (Ralph, Beliso–De Jesús, and Palmié 2017). Sylvester Stallone keeps the Rambo brand alive with sequels to the original Rambo Trilogy films.[1] And Bob Marley's music and commanding influence persist, seemingly without end. Regard for Marley and Tupac in particular seems to have cultivated their status as the lions of entire musical genres (reggae and rap, respectively).

Other pop culture icons have been influential, of course. In Sierra Leone during the war years, reggae stars like Peter Tosh and Joseph Hill, and action movies starring Chuck Norris and Arnold Schwarzenegger, also were

contributors to the cause. Elsewhere, 50 Cent's music, particularly the hit album and movie called *Get Rich or Die Tryin'*,[2] have been exceptionally significant, perhaps nowhere more than South Sudan, where the song's title became
a maxim and theme song for Juba's many "N***a" gangs (Martin and Mosel
2011; Sommers and Schwartz 2011). Like Sierra Leone's militia group the West
Side Boys, which was named after Tupac's affiliation with "West Side" rappers
in the United States, one of the most feared N***a gangs of Juba was G-Unit,
evidently named after a 50 Cent–led music group of the same name (a second
gang is called Westlife, an apparent homage to Tupac) (Lazareva 2018).[3]

The precise combination of Marley, Tupac, and Rambo in Sierra Leone is
instructive because it brings together and highlights the extraordinary power
of global artists over alienated young people enduring exceptionally difficult
circumstances. Indeed, this book would not have become a reality were it not
for the remarkable ability of young Sierra Leoneans to integrate and apply the
ideas and instructions of these three pop icons into their lives and times—and
for the actions of military commanders to exploit and manipulate the locally
interpreted messages emanating from the enormously persuasive trio.

The work of the "Big Three" did not emerge simultaneously in Sierra Leone. They arrived on the Sierra Leonean scene in different decades. Over
time, young people in Sierra Leone identified the complementary compo-
nents of their messages and wove them together. Across the nation, the ubiq-
uity of Krio, a creole language drawing directly from English, boosted the
ability of Sierra Leoneans to grasp many international popular culture icons
and products significantly. The language made songs and movies in English
accessible to virtually every Sierra Leonean. While messages from other artists were incorporated as well, field and documentary research make clear
that Marley, Tupac, and Rambo were, unquestionably and by far, the three
pop culture icons with the most influence on youth lives and war practices in
Sierra Leone. Again and again, youth turned to Bob Marley for inspiration,
Tupac Shakur for friendship, and John Rambo for instruction. A brief review
of their influence and significance follows, in chronological order.

Bob Marley: The Dignified Ideologue

The Rastafarian superstar, Bob Marley, and his many reggae music colleagues
from Jamaica, entered Sierra Leone's youth world in the 1970s. They arrived
following the advent of marijuana as a crop in Sierra Leone in the 1960s, and
just as Stevens's henchmen, the Special Security Division (SSD) and the Internal Security Unit (ISU), had begun throttling male youth perceived as resistant and uncouth. Marley's music, messages, religion, and lifestyle all resonated deeply with young people, in Sierra Leone and elsewhere.

As noted throughout this book, Bob Marley promoted resistance and pride among poor and disregarded people, and Africans in particular: he sang about the plight of Africa and Africans often. His work was both mystical and spellbinding. It promoted a spiritual consciousness that would enable listeners to analyze repression and move toward rebellion and revolutionary change. The combination of unmistakably clear, captivating lyrics, an unflinching way of singing, analysis of a world ordered by injustice, the promotion of profound self-belief, a captivating connection to a religion with African roots, and a conviction that the oppressive status quo must be overthrown all emerged from Marley's powerful music.

Being a listener of Marley quite often meant being a follower as well, particularly for those enduring situations of discrimination and subjugation. Sierra Leone most certainly was among those contexts where connection to young listeners (most of them male) seemed almost natural. Bob Marley found extremely fertile ground in Sierra Leone. Ultimately, the connection between reggae music, Rastafarian religion, and heavy marijuana use to become "conscious" connected Marley and marijuana to rebellion during the war and self-belief afterward.

The Marley-marijuana connection delivered an incomparable lever to military commanders seeking to influence and control young members of their groups. Keeping them high all the time (an RUF and AFRC specialty) made children and youth easier to manipulate and manage. At the same time, Marley was a powerful ideological inspiration for Foday Sankoh and the RUF in particular, but also for Valentine Strasser and his NPRC colleagues and many other groups engaged in warfare as well. The simultaneous (if temporary) position of Marley and his reggae musician cohorts as venerated theorizers for the RUF and the NPRC underscores just how pervasive their impact really was during the war years. Marley's influence never waned following the war either; like marijuana smoke wafting across a room, he seemed to be almost everywhere.

John Rambo: The Principled Warrior

Many years ago, a fellow researcher related the story of a girl running from her village in Sierra Leone after rebels had attacked. To figure out what to do next, she asked herself, "What would Rambo do?" The story underscores the magnetic influence of Rambo over young Sierra Leoneans. He was more than a model warrior (although unquestionably, he was that too). Some young people spoke of Rambo as a kind of distant friend. The ability to identify with John Rambo, the character whose first three movies so many young Sierra Leoneans had set to memory, is a remarkable feature of the Rambo Trilogy movies.

John Rambo entered Sierra Leone in the 1980s. To many who recalled that time to me (as well as in descriptions from Paul Richards), Rambo penetrated the worlds of children in dramatic fashion. Members of villages or workers in diamond mines would watch a Rambo film in the open air at night, via a generator-fueled projector. The vivid experiences cultivated powerful memories. All three films resonated, but particularly the first one (*First Blood*). An entire generation of Sierra Leoneans identified with Rambo as misunderstood and mistreated: a single man who was punished for fighting against a predatory, unjust system. That this justified his rebellion proved powerful during the war era. In addition, there were his distinctive "Rambo Tactics," which informed military training methods and curricula. That many of Rambo's maneuvers in the first two movies had taken place in forests proved especially helpful, since rain forest covers much of Sierra Leone.

More than Marley or Tupac, Rambo appealed to female as well as male youth. His significance as an independent, brave, and highly skilled bush warrior who fought honorably, selflessly, and for admirable principles proved a powerful combination. Consistently and across all three films, John Rambo was chivalrous, noble, self-reliant, brave, and disciplined. Tortured in crucifix positions in the first and second films, Rambo becomes a father figure to a child soldier in *Rambo III*. And at the end of all three films, Rambo is alone: arrested in the first film and heading off by himself in the other two, with no clear destination. Rambo's films and character captivated young Sierra Leoneans as he set an example for how to fight effectively and live honorably against nefarious, callous institutions.

Tupac Shakur: The Impassioned Partner

Tupac Shakur's music, style of dress, and image arrived in Sierra Leone in the early 1990s like a thunderclap. His impact on male youth was almost instantaneous and proved to be magnetic for male youth in specific ways. His songs were highly personal; Tupac seemed to know what marginalized youth everywhere were going through. Whereas Marley sometimes played the role of wise philosopher and Rambo largely kept to himself, Tupac's connection was visceral and immediate. Sometimes he was reflective, other times he was inflamed. But always, he was honest, direct, and authentic. His sense of purpose influenced boys and male youth in Sierra Leone. Tupac voiced a fierce belief in asserting oneself and responding proudly and strongly to injustice. It inspired his followers.

Neither Marley nor Rambo was as connected to terror tactics as Tupac. Some military commanders locked in on the rapper's justifications for violent rage (in some of his songs). They exploited Tupac's popularity by emphasizing the focused fury that informs only a portion of Tupac's work. "Tupac Tactics" seemed designed to inspire young adherents to become enraged fighters, cursing often (relying especially on some form of the word "fuck") and attacking fearlessly while heavily drugged.

The Tupac that emerged in the postwar years differed significantly. Male youth fans of Tupac referred to the pride and self-belief that he radiated, his ever-present rebelliousness, and the fact that he also was a young Black man fighting for dignity and respect. If Marley often played the role of venerated truth teller who explained and justified resistance, while Rambo embodied the characteristics of a virtuous, expert warrior, connections to Tupac were more complicated. On one hand, Tupac could inspire acts of vicious, intimate violence. On the other, Tupac was an inspirational friend. As one observer noted, "Tupac Shakur was a mercurial artist who ripped through the pop world like a twister. Even his biggest fans didn't know from track to track which Shakur would blow toward them next: Tupac the healer . . . or Tupac the destroyer" (Coker 1996).

That twister touched down in Sierra Leone and stayed for quite a while. Tupac's defiant pride in being called a thug, announced by the "Thug Life" tattoo looping across his abdomen, validated the lives and value of all of those young male youth condemned as thugs, Rarrays, vagrants, and much more across the decades. Whereas Marley and Rambo both demonstrated a more classic brand of heroism, Tupac was the antihero of the underclass.

A lasting theme arising from the influence of Bob Marley, John Rambo, and Tupac Shakur over Sierra Leone and its youth was the absence of contradictory messages that their many followers in Sierra Leone received from them. In a world that routinely applies a moral lens to human actions, judging them as "right" or "wrong," "good" or "bad," youth views of these three did not change when violent conflict turned toward peace in Sierra Leone. It was logical to turn to the same three pop culture mentors for instruction and guidance in wartime or peacetime. All that was needed was adapting their lessons to context. The meaning and utility of "Get Up, Stand Up" could transform from a war cry into a reminder for individuals to insist on respect. While the Rambo movies provided specific instruction for fighters engaged in violent conflict, values such as honor and friendship arising in all of the Rambo movies could guide young people in postwar contexts too. Similarly, followers of Tupac could turn away from his songs about violence to those about self-worth and resilience after the war subsided. Doing this was neither confusing nor inconsistent. One merely drew from different aspects of the work of pop culture idols.

CHAPTER 26

Patterns of Pretend

The Fake State

Much too often, current approaches to states, alienated youth, and terror groups are incompatible with underlying realities. Because of this, patterns of pretend—the tendency to presume that governments are functional, development initiatives are suitable, quantitative data sets are accurate, systemic exclusion and state repression can be sidestepped, and so on—surface implicitly. Findings and analysis arising in this book drive the consideration of issues highlighted in this chapter.

How should we deal with states that are weak by intention? The case of Siaka Stevens's presidency in Sierra Leone highlights what takes place when a government is inept on purpose. Earlier in the book, analysts of Sierra Leone labeled his government a façade or wafer-thin, or one of many shadow states in the region. Sierra Leone under Stevens also developed an almost-perfect form of neocolonialism: his government delivered minimal services to ordinary people while extracting as much wealth as possible for himself and his cronies.

Such a state required heavy repression to make things run. He made sure of that too. Life was cheap in Stevens's Sierra Leone, and in that way, he embodied Mbembe's concept of necropolitics, defined as the subjugation of life "to the power of death" (Mbembe 2019: 92). Stevens was hardly the only national leader to concoct and implement a form of government that featured an intentionally dysfunctional state backed up by necropolitical threat. One does not have to look far to find other practitioners. Taylor, of course, comes to mind, as he was a benefactor of what Reno considers "the sanctity of African states" even when his government too was a "façade" (Reno 2011: 21, 20). Right up to the present, in Africa and elsewhere, there are many practitioners of fake states that deliver little or no services to citizens while personally profiting, hugely and blatantly, and administering state repression to ordinary citizens as a matter of course.

What is notable about this mode of governance is its broad acceptability. The international order of states remains trapped by Westphalian precedent. All nations, regardless of magnitude or legitimacy, receive equal votes in the General Assembly in the United Nations. That began following "the establishment of the United Nations in 1945," which ushered "in a world order based on a system of sovereign states extending to every continent" (Ellis 2011: 130). States are absolute realities, the current international order insists, and the lines that divide them are pristine. Anderson asserted that such claims of indisputable authenticity are examples of "imagined communities" of shared nationality (1991). However they are categorized or labeled, the international system effectively awarded unquestioned legitimacy to President Stevens in Sierra Leone, just as it does to other despots reigning over country fiefdoms today. While important exceptions most certainly are noteworthy, including the international repudiation (with some exceptions) of the AFRC-RUF regime in Sierra Leone in 1997–98, depraved standards of national governance regularly receive international recognition.

Examples of such governments unfortunately are numerous. In a single corner of the world (East and Central Africa), the Enough Project states that four countries—Central African Republic, Democratic Republic of the Congo, South Sudan, and Sudan—"each have systems of violent kleptocracy." These four national kleptocracies all "are perpetuated or orchestrated by powerful political, military, and business leaders within these countries. Networks of international facilitators who enable kleptocratic activities extend from the conflict zones in East and Central Africa into the world's legitimate international finance, trade, and transportation systems. These systems, in turn, fund and equip warring parties and launder the spoils of war" (Adeba and Enough Project 2019: 7). These are all wartime contexts. But even for some countries without warfare, it often is not a pretty picture. Chayes has provided fascinating (and complex) diagrams of different systems of state corruption. In addition to war-torn Afghanistan, she examines Egypt, Tunisia, Nigeria, and Uzbekistan. Each state has a different system for patronage and the extraction of state resources into private pockets. Chayes observes that Afghans were not taxed while revenue streams exiting the system arise from sources such as "donor $ [international donor funding], contracts, natural resources, land, extortion, bank fraud, arrest as kidnapping, customs, etc." (2015: 213). Only two of those governments (Egypt and Uzbekistan) deliver even a modicum of public services.

Instead of using states as the starting point, Burgis follows how Africa's vast natural resources are exploited and who benefits from their exploitation. In his analysis, he doesn't really find states in play at all. Instead, in Africa today, there is "a looting machine" composed of "new empires controlled not by nations but by alliances of unaccountable African rulers governing through shadow states, middle-men who connect them to the global resource economy, and multinational companies from the West and the East that cloak their corruption in corporate secrecy." In conclusion, Burgis gives a warning: "As long as we go on choosing to avert our gaze, the looting machine will endure" (2015: 244). If we do not look away, we will see how many actors (and consumers) are complicit in an arrangement where Africa's mighty natural wealth is stolen.

There is yet another place to begin. Rather than looking at states or resource trails, it is possible to focus on political actors and their highly personalized and patrimonial networks. One concept is that of the Big Man, or the phenomenon known as "Bigmanity." Utas argues that "Bigmanity is a response to a lack of formal structures." That probably is subject to debate, since a Big Man like Stevens had an evident distaste for strong formal government structures. He weakened most of them on purpose (with the exception of those from which he benefited, such as the much-feared SSD and ISU units that did his bidding). In addition, it certainly is apparent that paramount chiefs are Big Men. Yet their status allegedly came from structural endowments emanating both from royalty and the national government (from there, they freelanced). Regardless, Utas notably observes that "Big Men networks may or may not involve the façades of the state. . . . The fewer functioning checks and balances there are, the more room there is for the Big Man to manoeuvre" (2012b: 8). A Big Man can operate behind a weak, façade-like government (like Stevens) or outside of it (like Taylor, when he ruled Taylorland).

The notion of states as façades also surfaces in de Waal's description of the political marketplace and those who dominate it. Yet in his conception of governance, dominant political leaders in "poorly institutionalized countries" (2015: 20) do not fill a government void. For all practical purposes, effectively they replace it. De Waal's option is intentionally personalized, as his analysis of power and how it operates does not feature state (or nonstate) institutions. Through his lens, it all comes down to the machinations of exceptionally powerful (and talented) men. He employs a business lens on politics because, he contends, that is what skilled individual politicians do. At the center of his analysis are men who wield power with "cash and coercion." "Those brute realities" are de Waal's "main concern" (33).

Taking a step back, it is interesting to note just how little the issue of gender—concerning forceful, hegemonic maleness—enters discussions of power in any of these analyses. De Waal, for example, reserves one paragraph for the subject. That is much more than most, and while he does say that "the gendered nature of the business of power should be evident on every page" of his book (34), his accounting does not constitute gender analysis. The general implication arising in de Waal and elsewhere seems as obvious and straightforward as blue sky or green grass: men dominate politics, as if it were a law of nature.

That much seems evident. However, such depictions do not explain how others will react. De Waal infers that men who rule political marketplaces are almost destined to succeed. Nothing seems to stop them. This appears to leave weak nations and nearly all of their citizens in a sorry state, and there seems to be no way out. He ends his book on the subject with the following dispiriting observation: "The final paradox of real politics in the Horn of Africa is that it is simultaneously an impersonal and dehumanizing system, and one that operates, visibly and inescapably, through the actions of men who use their power to get their way over others. Poor and powerless women and men understand this quite well, and respond as best they can to preserve humanity at the margins. The point of departure for challenging this cruel reality is to be honest to their experience and insight" (217–218). The "cruel reality" to which de Waal refers could apply to contexts far beyond the Horn of Africa. In fact, it is this state of affairs, in impersonal and dehumanizing systems across the world, that can inspire powerlessness among the poor and other citizens.

Perhaps that is not the only possible outcome. One lesson emerging from Sierra Leone's war is the underlying political message in the work of Marley, Tupac, and Rambo. It starts with perceptions of the everyday. Some international actors may prod nation-states that have international recognition but appalling reputations. Others may not. Either way, corporations, financial institutions, and others often team up with leaders to exploit a country's resources. While all of this may seem unfair, over time it also may seem unexceptional. It's just the way it is. Many countries where leaders wield governance and ignore the acute social and economic inequality they have propagated may indeed receive acceptance (and support) in today's Westphalian world. Realistically (and cynically), what can be accomplished in weak states?

To those viewing the local, national, and international overlords of injustice from below, the everyday may not be acceptable. Indeed, their actions can transform the idea of a perverse universe into vivid reality. Those analyzing the work of Marley, Rambo, Tupac, and other pop culture rebels while enduring inequality, injustice, and state violence may come to believe that they have the chance to challenge rulers of political markets and turn international actors into bystanders. For if one draws from what their heroes sing and enact, then conditions that many see as unseemly and at the same time everyday are, in reality, unjust and intolerable.

In such contexts, the messages of Marley, Rambo, Tupac, and other pop culture rebels become rousing calls to upend the dystopian order of things.

In the eyes of ordinary people, leader-exploiters and their international legitimizers may transform into Marley's Baldheads, Murdock's backers in *Rambo: First Blood Part II*, and the adversaries of Tupac's alter ego, Makaveli. In the messages of many such pop culture heroes, resistance and sometimes even violence to overthrow impersonal and dehumanizing systems are justified. The worrying dimension of the Westphalian world, in short, is that it can set the stage for impassioned opposition to the everyday and, just perhaps, an explosive, vengeful rebellion. In so many contexts, the status quo is the problem.

Aiming Low?

Does the international development aid system support a status quo that works against most youth? Given analysis provided in the previous section, the short answer would seem to be yes. Yet in general, the stated purposes of international aid appear to support youth in development and conflict-affected contexts. This section will probe this question.[1] It begins with an analysis of five major themes about the orientation and rationales that inform international development (sometimes simply called aid). The first two feature findings arising earlier in this book. This section will end with reflections on where development aid sits today, with respect to the challenges that poverty, systemic inequality, and bad governance present, and how excluded, alienated youth view all of this.

The first major theme concerns misunderstanding or overlooking local and national contexts. Earlier passages in this book indicate that many international agency officials did not seem to understand or appreciate how the government of Sierra Leone really operated. A story recounted in chapter 6 featured one international agency official working in prewar Sierra Leone who grew so disgusted with corruption among government officials that the official concluded enhancing their capacity was simply not possible. The official's limited appreciation of context appears to have influenced that conclusion. Sierra Leone experts such as Paul Richards and William Reno are among those who have emphasized that statehood and state institutions in Sierra Leone merely have been façades (Richards 1996: 60; Reno 2003: 45–46). Training or mentoring to enhance a government official's capacity to operate within a system that outsiders did not comprehend may have seemed irrelevant, particularly if the training and mentoring were built on inaccurate assumptions about how government institutions in Sierra Leone truly operated. No wonder the efforts failed.

Examples from chapters 11 and 12 detailed how many international humanitarian agencies (donor and implementing agencies alike) sought to work around or ignore the government. In both cases, the foreigners' take on Sierra Leone's government was quite similar. In one revealing comment, the director of a major NGO stated the situation with clarity: "The government complains that NGOs have taken over their role." That would be a natural government complaint if it were true. With regard to the humanitarian work taking place in the country, it probably was. Openly relying on one government official for access and permission only undermined government credibility still further. Yet these were the methods used to address the problem of an exceedingly weak government bureaucracy. The reasoning seemed to be as follows: a government that operates poorly must not hinder the urgent humanitarian work that must be done. International donors openly supported this arrangement (although, in all of my field interviews, government officials never criticized the powerful donor agencies for doing so).

Was this the appropriate way to deal with a weak government during a humanitarian crisis (as well as a war)? In the short term, it may have been. But it also left bitterness with government officials, and it enfeebled the government even further. At the same time, devising a longer-term, strategic approach to a significant governance challenge was not on the minds of the international humanitarians. The government was an impediment, not a project. Governance did not change.

The question of which youth gain access to development work constitutes a second theme. Following the war, there were signs of strategic co-optation of international development work featuring youth by government officials in Sierra Leone. During my trips to Sierra Leone in 2005 and 2010, I noted how "youth" was a persistent catchphrase in government and international development circles. Yet the impact of the pronounced focus seemed to benefit very few young people, as detailed in chapter 22. Access to programs available to small proportions of young people mattered most, and Big Men controlled that access. More than anything else, the programs demonstrated the power of nepotism, and how programs can exacerbate social inequalities.

The tradition-bound orientation of much of international development is a third major theme. In most respects, international development is an unlikely location for reforming systems that exclude or exploit people. That is partly because the general setup targets much smaller concerns. The starting point is international development's formulaic setup. Work usually revolves around projects (single initiatives or endeavors) and programs (larger efforts that may [or may not] feature a set of linked projects). Initiatives tend to be targeted and focused on highly specific activities, such as providing water pumps in a rural area or delivering training for a specific skill set. Funding for this work frequently comes from multilateral sources (such as the World Bank or the European Union), agencies of wealthy donor nations, or private funders (foundations and companies). There is regular discussion about effective donor coordination and "scaling up" initiatives (that is, dramatically enlarging them). Neither happen often.

A significant portion of a typical international agency project or program budget covers substantial outlays that merely set the stage for the delivery of featured materials and/or services for an initiative. These include overhead for the agency or agencies undertaking the endeavor, salaries and a range of benefits for personnel (workers from overseas tend to cost many times more than local counterparts because their salaries generally are much higher and they also may receive costly benefits such as funding for housing, schooling for their children, and health insurance), equipment to implement the initiative (such as office rent, security, and vehicles), and much more. Development projects and programs thus tend to be expensive. They also mostly operate within areas of activity known as sectors (such as agriculture, health, or education). The two nicknames for sectors—stovepipe and silo—underscore their narrow and confining orientation. Crosscutting themes aim to broaden access to initiatives taking place within sectors. Gender (which almost always refers to women and girls) is a common theme. Youth (which refers mainly to male youth) is less common. Taking a step back, these are curious conceptions, given the enormity of their hugely overlapping populations.[2] However, given development's strong orientation toward sectors, crosscutting themes are featured inclusion methods. Getting more women or youth into sector-based activities often is all that inclusion means in much of the development world. It illustrates how development largely operates within its preestablished take on reality.

A fourth major theme is the need to demonstrate efficient forward progress. This is a very big deal in international development, and it is here where the pressure on development actors to be conservative and risk averse is particularly prominent. Andrew Natsios, a former USAID administrator, details an array of factors that drive development work toward a singular kind of result (2010). All work is subject to regulatory constraints, and donor agency auditors are powerful. The need for development practitioners (NGOs and UN agencies) to focus on compliance with donor-specified regulations results in an emphasis on short-term work, and a de-emphasis on longer term and harder-to-measure efforts like policy reform and institution building. A contributing factor is the outsized influence of development economists, who run the numbers, establish cost-benefit strategies, and establish development priorities. The general emphasis on countable results prioritizes activities that produce quantifiable outputs, like the number of children vaccinated, people trained, wells dug, and schools built. Interviews with donor and practitioner officials found that pressure to demonstrate success in youth programs allowed elite (and often mostly male) youth to gain access to their programs (since they are most likely to deliver positive results). Some also related how reliance on local leaders allows those leaders to identify youth participants whom they favor, just as paramount chiefs reportedly do in Sierra Leone (Sommers 2015: 163–168). Such actions effectively (if unintentionally) demonstrate nepotism and promote inequality.[3]

Operating in what she calls "Peaceland" (consisting of "a community of expatriates who devote their lives to working in conflict zones"), Séverine Autesserre finds similar trends (2014: 2). Among them are a "notorious lack of coordination" among international actors, an orientation toward "technical, short-term, and top-down solutions to complex social, political, and economic problems," strong favoritism for solutions that produce "quantifiable results," and "enormous pressure to demonstrate results quickly" (249). Through this process, local people and local knowledge are subordinated. Expatriate professionals "too often lack an adequate grasp of the contexts in which they work," have a hard time building trust and networks with local people, and consequently rely on "dominant narratives" that "routinely paint oversimplified and, at times, biased pictures of local conditions." All of this can "shape responses that are often ineffective and may potentially aggravate the very problems the interveners are trying to solve" (250).

There is a decidedly authoritarian bent to all of this. Many expatriates "who question the dominant modes of operation end up either forced to fit into the mold or so frustrated that they change careers and leave Peaceland" (251). This appears to be a by-product of the nature of most development work. As Ben Ramalingam observes, "Aid tends to try and solve simple problems through narrow, prescribed interventions." In addition, "Aid agencies persist in treating the world in a certain way, so their *available* solution becomes *the solution*" (2013: 38, 39, italics in original). This sort of environment creates an unlikely arena for cultivating open discussions of new ideas and questions. In the international peace-building world, Autesserre identified a generic formula. "Foreign peacebuilders run the show," she observed. "They interact with political and military leaders, rely on external expertise and resources, and use the same kind of solutions all over the world." This inherently inflexible, "top-down, outsider-led way of working remains the status quo" (2021: 5).

Such rigid constraints on development work are sculpted by the pervasive hustle for upbeat success. Some development activities are notable and also reflect the general orientation on numbers and demonstrable attainment. The Millennium Development Goals (MDGs), followed by the even more ambitious Sustainable Development Goals (SDGs), constitute a unique worldwide attempt to eradicate extreme hunger, get every child into primary school, promote gender equality, empower women, reduce child mortality, expand investment in development work, and much more. Large public and private investments have supported both UN-led efforts. The efforts advertise reliance on quantitative data to "measure what we treasure" because "what gets measured gets done" (United Nations 2015a: 10). The MDGs and SDGs also have pressured governments to provide basic services and some rights (increased women's representation, for example).

Some of the results thus far are impressive. If one looks at the goal of universal primary education, for example, "the primary school net enrolment rate in the developing regions has reached an estimated 91 percent in 2015, up from 83 per cent in 2000" (United Nations 2015a: 4). It is a remarkable global achievement. Yet there is a potential downside as well. The effort has proven less effective at assessing how children got into school (state coercion was one factor),[4] the quality of education received, and the nature of what students learn in school. In addition, some of the most basic elements of a formal education, such as teacher training and school infrastructure, persist as major weaknesses in many developing countries (United Nations Economic and Social Council 2019: 11). Still other objectives are daunting in the extreme, such as SDG Goal 10, which calls for a reduction of inequality within and among countries. Four years since the launch of the SDGs, "Income inequality continues to rise in many parts of the world" (16).

My interviews with development professionals surfaced strong pressure for donor and implementer alike to produce numeric evidence of positive achievements. Signs of such pressure also are evident in widespread suspicions about the veracity of evaluations of development initiatives (Sommers 2015: 159–161, 168–175). In their examination of research evaluations in the health sector, Storeng et al. provide reasons for such doubts. The authors assert that "perverse incentives exist across the global health and development sectors to use simplistic indicators of success and bad or fudged data. Donor agencies exacerbate the problem by distorting research findings to exaggerate their own successes." The "collective drive to demonstrate success" is influenced by many actions, among them "interference in the research and evaluation process" by donor officials whose programs the evaluators are investigating and "subtle acts of self-censorship and data embellishment" by evaluators themselves (2019: 1).

Storeng et al. also find that "research that threatens the position of powerful elites—such as research into high-level corruption—is lacking" (1). This ability for elites to influence and control international development work constitutes a fifth major theme in development practice. It is taking place as the economic might of the super-rich escalates. Staggering and still-rising inequality magnifies the plight of the world's poor and further separates them from global plutocrats. Oxfam reported that "wealth is becoming even more concentrated." In 2018, their analysis found that the twenty-six richest people in the world owned as much wealth as "the 3.8 billion people who make up the poorest half of humanity" (Lawson et al. 2019: 12). This state of affairs sets the stage for a phenomenon that Anand Giridharadas (2018) calls "Market-World." MarketWorld rebrands self-preservation among the world's elite, and protection of the status quo from which they benefit so immensely, as selfless generosity.

To enhance their status and preserve their position, rich and powerful people have co-opted magnanimous giving. "MarketWorld is an ascendant power elite," Giridharadas explains, "that is defined by the concurrent drives to do well and do good, and to change the world while also profiting from the status quo." Its membership consists of "enlightened businessmen and their collaborators in the worlds of charity, academia, media, government, and think tanks." They have their own "thinkers" (called "thought leaders"). Collectively, they have produced "a culture and state of mind." In MarketWorld, "generosity is a substitute for and a means of avoiding the necessity of a more just and equitable system and a fairer distribution of power." He cites one analyst of MarketWorld (Bruno Giussani) who noted that "ideas framed as being about 'poverty' are more acceptable than ideas framed as being about 'inequality'" (Giridharadas 2018: 30, 164, 122). Poverty, the analyst explained, is something that a charity can address. In contrast, addressing inequality equates with system change, which effectively involves examining (or challenging) the privilege of the giver. That is to be avoided, since "inequality is about how you make the money that you're giving back in the first place" (122–123). Since systemic inequality cuts much too close to the bone, focusing instead on poverty is deemed the safer bet.[5]

It is safe to say that the apparent motivation for those engaged in international development generally derives from a simple (and simplistic) contention: that "aid is an expression of global compassion" (Ramalingam 2013: 7). This notion facilitates the idea that contributions that make the lives of others better is a good thing. The pursuit of such good works increasingly has turned philanthropists and their charities into major and sometimes dominant players in the integrated world of global giving and development work. Some of the world's wealthiest people, such as Bill and Melinda Gates and their Gates Foundation, wield enormous power in development circles. That influence is only growing, given the trend toward mixing public and private resources in development efforts. It also is evident that challenges posed by poverty often are addressed with seemingly technical and apolitical inputs. There are sensible reasons for such an approach, since institutions and their money would be unlikely to access poor people in many nations if their work had a political agenda. But Giridharadas is arguing that the work of the private funders of development in reality is both political and conservative, since their efforts effectively preserve and protect the systems and structures from which they benefit so grandly. In the end, one might reasonably conclude that most of the work of mainstream international development is not (and never was) revolutionary or systems-changing. Development helps poor people in many ways. But it rarely rocks the boat.

Given the five themes outlined just above, it remains unclear whether the international development status quo can address large and complex issues such as systemic exclusion, gross corruption, and intentionally fake states. Duncan Green confidently posits a way ahead. He first states, "The best kind of aid strengthens responsive state structures." In contrast, "bad aid . . . props up repressive governments and weakens their accountability to their citizens." Therein lies a paradox: "Aid tends to work best in countries that need it least." Yet there are ways to operate in unsavory environments. For example, regarding hugely corrupt governments and their leaders, he states that donor governments can punish "corporations that pay bribes" and close "tax havens where ill-gotten gains can be safely hidden" (2012: 300, 302).

Others are not so sure, because development aid so often focuses on efforts blessed by autocrats. William Easterly delivers a body blow to mainstream development practice. He attacks what he sees as the cultivated unreality of good works, declaring that "morally neutral approaches to poverty do not exist." His starting point is what he considers "a technocratic illusion: the belief that poverty is a purely technical problem." The prevailing development approach, he argues, proceeds from the contention that "poverty results from a shortage of expertise" while the reality is that "poverty is really about a shortage of rights" (Easterly 2013: 6, 7). Easterly states that this mistaken belief system informs and guides the work of the World Bank and "the Gates Foundation, the United Nations, and U.S. and UK aid agencies." He finds that mainstream international development is dominated by the idea of "authoritarian development," where "well-intentioned autocrats" are "advised by technical experts" from the West (6). However, "the autocrats have offered a false bargain to meet material needs while we overlook their suppression of rights" (339). Growth connects to rights and both thrive in democratic environments. "Unrestrained power will always turn out to be the enemy of development," he concludes. Accordingly, Easterly argues that even "an incremental change in freedom will yield a positive change in the well-being of the world's poor" (339, 351, 344).

Jessica Trisko Darden's analysis of foreign aid from the U.S. government finds that it "contributes to state violence and government repression in countries receiving American aid" (2020: 2). The concept of foreign aid (or foreign assistance) is inclusive of international development as well as much more. It also encompasses direct assistance to governments in service to security (military aid), economies (economic aid), and more specific aid, such as the provision of food (food aid). In Darden's analysis, foreign aid in general "can build up a state's coercive capacity—its military and security services—which can then, under certain conditions, be used to repress, torture, and even kill its citizens." It also "enables recipient governments to divert precious resources toward security sector spending or other means of maintaining power, such as patronage networks" (110).[6] Darden's research comes to the following conclusion: there is "a status quo where states remain the dominant actors and where foreign assistance feeds the ability of insecure governments to remain in power by any means necessary" (115). This take aligns with Helen C. Epstein's analysis of Uganda. Epstein argues that the "genius" of Uganda's longtime ruler, Yoweri Museveni, has been to "capitalize on Western ambivalence about Africa's capacity for democracy and self-determination." Although Museveni has meddled in and fueled conflicts across the region, Epstein asserts that he effectively received "America and Europe's blessing" to use "generous foreign aid to turn Uganda into a military dictatorship dressed up to look like a democracy" (2017: 22).

What, then, should be done? Darden cautions against the policy that many donors employed during Sierra Leone's civil war: funding international NGOs instead of the government. That is because "foreign-funded NGOs tend to be more accountable to donors than beneficiaries and are more focused on service delivery than social change" (2020: 114). Instead, she calls for "a radical rethinking" of the purposes of foreign aid "and a renewed focus on its true beneficiaries." She urges an emphasis on both the successes and failures of food aid and democracy promotion programs, for example, and asserts that "human rights abuses should be a focal point, not a talking point, in U.S. foreign assistance policy" (118, 119). To do this in the international peace-building field, Autesserre proposes a simple and practical way ahead: international donors must contribute as hands-off "model interveners: by letting local activists decide when and how to use the money, rather than imposing their ideas, priorities, and solutions" (2021: 169).

Like Easterly's, Darden's recommended way forward is activist: development (and, more broadly, all foreign aid) should lead with and be informed by a human rights agenda. They collectively present much international development and foreign aid work as Machiavellian benevolence: if indicators of human advancement are apparent (electricity becomes available to more citizens, poverty and mortality rates go down, literacy rates go up, and so on), then violent, corrupt governance and disturbing political contexts can go largely unheeded. Together with Epstein, Easterly and Darden assert that bolstering such governments is shortsighted, misguided, and ultimately counterproductive. Political context, they all insist, really matters.

International development is risk averse and market savvy. It specializes in targeted technical inputs that promise to yield predictable, countable, and upbeat outputs. Authentic critical reflection within the development world tends to be cautious and constrained. The pressure-packed setup frequently sidesteps inescapable realities, including that all contexts are political, quantitative data provides narrow understandings of context, and many initiatives are limited in their reach and impact over the longer term. Since regularity and certainty are so important to development today, efforts can flounder in situations where ambiguity is ripe (such as in conflict and postconflict environments), and in nations where state violence and corruption thrive and government institutions either are ineffective or devious. Sadly and ironically, this is precisely where strategic and even daring efforts are required. Every so often, sufficient resolve and contextual expertise allow for promising efforts to move ahead. Yet development agendas—the need for demonstrable success or the sheen of success—usually are uneasy fits for those locations where calculated, reform-oriented investments are needed most.

There unquestionably is useful and productive work taking place in the field of international development. There also are encouraging global-level developments, such as the groundbreaking UN Security Council Resolution (UNSCR) 2250 on Youth, Peace, and Security, which effectively transforms youth into partners in peace building, in part by "affirming the important role youth can play in the prevention and resolution of conflicts" (United Nations 2015b). At the same time, important endeavors such as UNSCR 2250 underscore just how much work must be done to achieve sustainable changes in society and governance. It is not a question of taking small initiatives and "scaling them up" to a grand size because most of the main problems are systemic.

Occasionally, systemic issues are addressed, often due to extreme pressure to act. One example of this partly emerged from Sierra Leone's war. Largely in response to sustained lobbying from activist NGOs, the Kimberly Process created a formula for preventing the sale of diamonds to fund wars (Smillie 2010). That is some degree of progress. Yet such progress against outright theft by government and nongovernment leaders remains ad hoc and generally does not address issues like systemic exclusion, rampant disregard for citizens, intentionally weak government institutions, far-reaching corruption schemes, and state violence. The landmark study emerging from UNSCR 2250 recommends that "the systems that reinforce exclusion must be transformed to address the structural barriers limiting meaningful youth inclusion and participation in peace and security" (Simpson 2018: 117). The jury is still out.

All of this leads to a final point: as also noted near the end of the previous section, youth are watching how foreign agencies and actors respond to them and their governments. Since international development agencies usually work alongside governments (or with their blessing), and marginalized youth generally are unpopular with government leaders (the feeling tends to be mutual), then ordinary people may view international agencies as lining up behind their repressors—even when this is unintentional, or when it seems, in terms of practicality, unavoidable.

Yet the problem nonetheless persists, it is profound, and in the broader and longer-term scheme of things, the approach of international agencies and foreign governments ultimately may prove to be unstrategic. That is partly because young people who are alienated and harassed by repressive states and unbending societies view their situation quite differently from entitled members of the status quo. Like Sierra Leone's Rarray youth, they know they are not just separate from the rest but despised and distrusted too. The easily available messages of pop culture rebels may help them fashion a lens for interpreting what they see. When they do, a particularly perverse universe may appear. Through this lens, international governments and institutions easily can be interpreted as supporters of Baldheads, Murdock, and other agents of state violence and theft that must be resisted, if not taken down. In the end, alienation is a truly pressing development and diplomatic challenge.

Terror and Governance in West Africa

Does terror warfare work? Practitioners of terror tactics do extreme things to cultivate powerful emotional responses in people and institutions (including governments). They are savvy opportunists, often basing their operations in forgotten areas with forgotten people. Their ruthlessness is strategic: they perform grisly, horrific, dramatic acts to catalyze widely felt and dramatic outcomes. Their purposes are elemental: to undercut the social, cultural, religious, and political worlds that civilians inhabit. They seek to explode what it means to be human and promote profound fear and vulnerability in psyches and the most basic principles of humanity. They push the idea that no one is safe and everyone—*everyone*—is a potential target. They do that which is normally unthinkable. It is that elemental.

Nordstrom's theory of terror warfare usefully expands the realm of terrorism from those seen globally as terrorist outfits, such as ISIS, to include civil war insurgents normally seen merely as rebels (like Renamo, the AFRC and the RUF). As noted in chapter 2, Sierra Leone's terror war practitioners shared certain practices with some of their terrorist counterparts, such as the enslavement of women and the use of drugs to expand their fighters' capacity to terrorize. In addition, it appeared that the RUF employed terror partly because its ability to confront military units successfully was so deficient. As a military group, they were weak. They lost the strong majority of their encounters with rival troops. Three times, their limited abilities in military encounters were so great that they approached the brink of annihilation: NPRC government forces had them on the run at the end of 1993; government forces and Kamajors, led by Executive Outcomes mercenaries, forced a sustained RUF retreat in 1995; and ECOMOG forces had RUF and AFRC forces trapped during the rebels' desperate retreat from Freetown in February 1998. Each time, the rebels escaped, and each time the reasons were suspicious. The NPRC appeared distracted, at least in part, by their pursuit of diamonds. During negotiations for the first peace treaty in 1996, the RUF somehow got their government counterparts to agree to move Executive Outcomes out of Sierra Leone. And the evident decision of ECOMOG to allow their rebel adversaries to escape Freetown fueled a popular theory that ECOMOG did this to prolong the war, thus facilitating their ability to mine still more diamonds. Whether these theories are true, it nonetheless is apparent that the RUF's elemental weakness in fighting military groups helps explain why they focused so fiercely on attacking civilians.

That was their area of expertise. Terror warfare, and the RUF in particular, broaden the definition of an effective military force. In conventional warfare, the RUF could not consistently beat anyone. On the other hand, the RUF (together with the AFRC) were supreme terror specialists. Their expertise lay in driving many civilians away while abducting and enslaving others. In addition to providing regular access to some of the world's most lucrative diamond mines, their acts of terror routinely garnered them attention—from nearby villages and mines as well as towns and cities, in addition to the national government and, on occasion, an international audience.

That mattered. They were a spectacle, with young girls and boys among the perpetrators and the performance of atrocities that previously seemed unimaginable, especially during the period between the rebels' first exit from Freetown in February 1998 and the second Freetown invasion in January 1999. Boosted by the militarily formidable AFRC corps, they frequently seemed unstoppable. All of this awarded the rebels a considerable negotiation advantage at Lomé in mid-1999. Mere months after the RUF and their AFRC cohorts capped their Operation No Living Thing by undertaking a stupendous demonstration of terror warfare in the capital city, the Sierra Leonean government and the international powers on hand bequeathed the RUF complete amnesty and a near-complete hold over diamonds (the AFRC did far less well, mostly due to rivalry issues with the RUF).

Terror warfare, in the immediate term, most certainly worked for the top RUF leaders. It never did for their troops; the RUF leaders' wholesale disregard for their own fighters was remarkable (AFRC leaders seemed slightly more interested in the fate of their fighters). But the spoils and benefits of terror warfare for the top leaders didn't last. Foday Sankoh, Mosquito, and Charles Taylor always seemed to thirst for much more. In Sankoh's case, he wanted nothing short of ruling Sierra Leone. When that failed, in a pathetic close to his time in the limelight, the jig was up. In any case, the Special Court for Sierra Leone was determined to erase Lomé's amnesty for the rebels and bring the curtain down on the rebel leadership, and even some of their main adversaries. For the most part, they did.

Nordstrom's field research detailed how ordinary Mozambicans did not give in to terror. Instead, they found ways to resist it, and in the process they unwound war and violence as an option. Their quietly heroic acts in the face of violence laid the foundation for viable peace accords. Sierra Leone's context differed. The two peace accords (Abidjan in 1996 and Lomé in 1999) largely were ignored by the parties in conflict. War and terror continued after both. Connections between resistance to warfare by ordinary Sierra Leoneans and the formal peace processes, laden as they were with international involvement, did not seem to exist. Some of the most heroic Sierra Leoneans were those silently surviving in soquoihun hiding places. It took extraordinary bravery to carry on amid constant hardship and vulnerability to rebel forces. But such tactics took place in extreme isolation. Few knew they were even there.

As long as there was a war, terror warfare produced major successes for their respective practitioners in Mozambique and Sierra Leone. The RUF and their eventual allies, the AFRC, were the master practitioners of terror warfare in Sierra Leone. Sierra Leonean Army "sobels" also were specialists, together with CDF units. Once the wars in both nations had ended, terror warfare's impact withered. In the case of the RUF, its transition into a political party was dead on arrival.

Sierra Leone and Mozambique demonstrate how terror makes waves, generates impact, and is difficult to extinguish. A brief look at its effectiveness in West Africa, in the years following the demise of the RUF and AFRC, sheds light on the potency of its practices. While direct connections between Sierra Leone's rebels and terror groups in the Sahel are hard to make out, there are many similarities in their practices and approach. In addition, the groups collectively known as violent extremists, operating in countries such as Mauritania, Mali, Burkina Faso, Nigeria, Niger, and Chad, very effectively exploit the same root cause of instability in all the countries where they are present: appalling governance.

The Sahelian states of West Africa are among the poorest in the world.[7] Just like in Sierra Leone, corrupt governments that either cannot or are uninterested in elemental protection and service provision set the stage for destabilizing violence: "Across the Sahel, armed groups have been able to entrench themselves first and foremost in those areas which have been neglected by weakened and corrupt central authorities, often by positioning themselves as providers of security, justice and basic services. In this way, it is crucial to view corruption not just as the consequence of conflict, but more often as its root cause and therefore a critical element for any attempt at resolution to address" (Steadman 2020). Violent extremism has increased both in intensity and geographic reach. In three short years (from 2016 to 2019), the number of people killed in terrorist attacks in Burkina Faso, Mali, and Niger went up 500 percent (Moody 2020) while displacement due to terrorist violence shot up 1,000 percent (UN News 2020). The Sahel is engulfed in a deep crisis, as groups affiliated with ISIS and Al-Qaeda dominate the landscape (Counter Extremism Project, n.d.).[8]

There is another essential element in this drama: Libya. An irony of Mu'ammar Gaddhafi's career was how his strident desire to overthrow established governments (directed by his World Revolutionary Headquarters, guided by his Green Book) mostly was realized following his violent death in Libya in 2011.[9] That is because it led to two destabilizing outcomes. First, once the dictator was gone, his personalized state practically evaporated, leaving an immense security vacuum "filled with heavily armed militias and groups that lacked any sense of professionalism, discipline or cohesion." This allowed Libya to become "a hot bed for extremist Jihadist groups" (Eljarh 2016: 6). Almost immediately, violent extremist groups based in southern Libya began to move operations southward, into the Sahelian states.

Second, Gaddhafi had bought massive quantities of arms and munitions and hired mercenaries to help him fight against insurgents. Once he was dead, the warehouses overloaded with weaponry were left unguarded. Before returning to their homes in northern Mali, ethnic Tuareg mercenaries stopped by the warehouses, loaded their pickup trucks to the brim with arms and munitions, and headed southwest. Their arrival back in Mali soon precipitated the fall of the democratically elected government in May 2012. An alliance of Islamic jihadists entered Mali's new power vacuum, joining Tuareg separatists in establishing a quasi state in the northeast of the country (Patrick 2013). They moved out from there. Destabilization, displacement, and many deaths across the Sahel, and then southward into coastal West Africa, have followed.

One ethnic group has proven particularly ripe for exploitation during West Africa's jihadist surge: the Fulani. An estimated forty million strong, the Fulani are dispersed across fifteen West African nations (including Sierra Leone).[10] They are mainly Muslim and largely live and work as pastoralists in countries governed by people from farming groups. In West Africa and many other regions, pastoralists and farmers conflict over grazing, land, and water rights (Sangare 2019: 3, 4, 5). The human population of Sahelian states includes the two countries with the youngest median ages in the world: Niger (15.4 years) and Mali (15.8 years). The other countries in the Sahel approach that level (Central Intelligence Agency, n.d.). The Sahel also is being devastated by climate change, which further intensifies herder-farmer conflicts (Sangare 2019: 7). Social and political marginalization of the Fulani is widespread. Finally, the

Fulani, who led empires in prior centuries, today divide into nobles (including their own chiefs) and slave descendants called Rimaibé (Bekoe et al. 2020: 29). While the two share the same culture and language, "there is still a clear divide." A comment from a Fulani representative in Burkina Faso recalls Sierra Leone: "Everybody knows their place," said the official (International Crisis Group 2017).

As terrorist groups gained ground and influence inside its country, Burkina Faso's government repeatedly displayed a knack for making things much worse for itself. Taylor shares two well-known dimensions of awful governance and violent extremism. The first concerns location: "A state's inability to secure its territory" allows "violent extremists the physical geography to operate freely and with little restraint." Hiding underneath a rain forest canopy (a rebel specialty in Sierra Leone) thus is not required. Vast, arid, and largely ungoverned spaces in Sahelian West Africa provide plenty of effective cover, as governments are largely or completely absent there (Taylor 2019: 66). These ungoverned spaces easily traverse borders. Similar to remote locations like Kailahun District, where the RUF was based for the entire war, many other parts of West Africa also feature porous national borders, which "have facilitated transnational terrorism" (Strategic Comments 2019).

The second dimension concerns how "government corruption and blatant disregard for people" cultivates grievances among citizens, particularly among those especially overlooked or marginalized. This approach to governance is a gift to violent extremist groups, who "fill the void with local security, albeit usually with brutality, and basic social services, which increase the public's support, or at least acquiescence, of them." The service provision also awards them "local legitimacy" (Taylor 2019: 66).

The dual dimensions apply to the northern spaces of Burkina Faso and its government's astonishingly self-destructive behavior. The north is where many of that nation's Fulani cattle herders reside. They "have long been stigmatized and discriminated against" (Turse 2020). This has made it easier for militants to do two things at once: recruit Fulani "while still attacking Fulani villages." Violent and unjust governance is the main motivation. Tabital Andal Association of Koranic Masters of the Sahel conducted workshops with Muslim religious scholars, citizens in affected communities, and security force officials from Mali and Niger, as well as Burkina Faso. Their inquiries found that 80 percent of those who have joined terrorist groups did so "because their father or mother or brother was killed by the armed forces." In the wake of these killings, "there has been no justice" (Turse 2020). This finding aligns with many other studies on why people join violent extremist organizations. A report by the UN Special Rapporteur on the Promotion and Protection of Human Rights and Fundamental Freedoms while Countering Terrorism, for example, detailed that "study after study reveals that the experience or perception of abuse and violations by government authorities are determining factors that contribute to the level of vulnerability to violent extremism, or violence thereto" (Special Rapporteur on the Promotion and Protection of Human Rights and Fundamental Freedoms while Countering Terrorism 2020: 8). Interviews with former recruits of an array of violent extremist groups in Africa revealed that "a striking 71 percent" of respondents "pointed to 'government action,' including 'killing a family member or friend' or 'arrest of a family member or friend,' as the incident that prompted them to join" (UNDP 2017: 5).

A journalist visiting Burkina Faso's destabilized north reported that the national military's motive for attacking Fulani citizens of their nation is simple, unstrategic retaliation. After terrorist insurgents "have killed and mutilated soldiers," the army responds by attacking "villages suspected of harboring or supporting jihadists." The military has "no proof that the villagers they kill are collaborators." Often the jihadists "exchange their short pants for army combat uniforms," and sometimes military soldiers wear "turbans and sandals for attacks," say surviving villagers. The result is a level of confusion reminiscent of that caused by Sierra Leone's sobels during their war, except that in Burkina Faso, the civilians are clear on who is responsible: soldiers. The Burkina Faso government then made the situation even worse by the inclusion of ethnic vigilante groups, the most noteworthy of which is the Koglweogo. The group is largely ethnic Mossi, a mainly Christian group from the south.

Vigilante groups in Burkina Faso originally "sprang up to fight crime." However, with armed terrorist groups based in territory populated by Muslim Fulani citizens, many of the vigilantes "now serve as military informants and accompany soldiers on operations." Similar to the Kamajors and other CDF groups in Sierra Leone, the vigilantes also carry "handmade hunting guns and long knives." A new law passed in January 2020 allows some of the vigilantes to become trained and armed government supporters (Maclean 2020). Indeed, all that is required to join the new volunteer force is to be a citizen over age eighteen, have no political affiliation, and be "loyal and patriotic" (Bekoe et al. 2020: 32). The law seems to have rewarded at least some of the soldiers and vigilantes with a sense of impunity. A vigilante leader, for example, detailed how soldiers killed and left bodies along roadsides. "He was incredulous at the suggestion that people suspected of collaborating with terrorists should be arrested and prosecuted, rather than summarily killed" (Maclean 2020).

Additional similarities between the violent extremist groups operating in Burkina Faso and Sierra Leone's rebels also are present. One is how terrorist groups in eastern Burkina Faso support their efforts partly through the mining and selling of gold (ISSAfrica 2020). The approach recalls the rebels' strong focus on mining diamonds. Like Sierra Leone's Siaka Stevens, Burkina

Faso's government also combines undercutting basic service provision with excessive state violence.

Such challenges are as well known as they are long-standing. A high-level UN official states the general situation bluntly: "The failure of policymakers to take into account the decades of knowledge and data on local political grievances, underlying drivers of conflict, long-term structural instability and political tensions over resource allocation is unforgivable, given the stakes involved" (Special Rapporteur on the Promotion and Protection of Human Rights and Fundamental Freedoms while Countering Terrorism 2020: 8). The absence of appropriate changes in governance practices creates openings for practitioners of terror warfare and terrorism to draw from the same source for validation and legitimacy: predatory, inequitable, violent governance. It also has been established, over and over again, that security responses to rebel and violent extremist groups, by themselves, generally are ineffective. Indeed, in the longer term, violent assaults against extremist groups run the risk of expanding extremist violence, not crushing it (OECD/SWAC 2020: 16). Not even four coups in West Africa in the space of seventeen months (the last in Burkina Faso in January 2022), spurred largely by failed government responses to violent extremist threats, have changed this dynamic (Ochieng 2022).

Everyone knows better. Moderate development policies or state force, or a mix of the two, are common. Neither address foundational change. Without this essential work, insurgents will keep rising up. The next chapter lays out an alternate option.

CHAPTER 27

Toward Foundational Change

Questioning the Status Quo

The inherent logic that informs international development and diplomacy is shortsighted. Risk aversion makes repressive yet stable governments attractive. System deficits that violent extremist organizations exploit—such as pronounced exclusion, injustice, state repression, and feeble service provision—seem too daunting to address. State managers redirect sizable government assets and revenues to personal gain, sometimes with the understated support of international creditors and firms. Yet addressing such actions appears too big to tackle. The status quo has become a safe harbor amid seas of inequality and instability.

This is precisely the world that pop icons like Bob Marley, Tupac Shakur, and John Rambo challenge. Malign governments and power brokers separate themselves from citizens, while Marley, Tupac, Rambo, and other global heroes inspire legions of followers to analyze and oppose those in control. There are essential lessons to be drawn from the young and disconnected, and from Sierra Leone's experience with alienation, terror, and rapacious governance.

To position the guidance for foundational change featured in this chapter, here are three questions to consider:

- First, *what is it that all youth share*? A central finding of a seminal study of youth and youth groups globally was exclusion. Young people everywhere were found to experience "political, social, cultural and economic disempowerment." For them, going along with the general state of things or accepting some degree of moral compromise is not an option. What they seek is authentic change (Simpson 2018: 63). Their collective stance directly confronts the development-diplomacy status quo.

- Second, *in the face of this direct call for change, how do governments respond*? Two researchers examined the general orientation of governments of countries with youth-dominated populations. Virtually all of Africa's nations—and many more on other continents—reside easily within this so-called youth bulge category. They found that "governments facing a youth bulge are more repressive than other states" (Nordås and Davenport 2013: 926). Unyielding states, not young people, drive contentious youth-state relations.

• Third, *what do heightened levels of state repression yield*? States that repress their own citizens are unpopular. Yet while youth and other citizens seek substantial improvement in the quality and caliber of governance, many states routinely respond with still more repression. This inadvertently opens the door for adversaries and opportunists to exploit gaping governmental deficiencies. As noted in the previous chapter, this is precisely what has taken place (OECD/SWAC 2020). "The assumption that military domination of insurgent groups must precede governance-focused efforts" is the prevailing approach, and it is faulty. An expanding chorus of studies clearly reveal that "the problem is not the absence of state authority, but rather the presence of states that are corrupt, repressive, and unaccountable to the people" (Minter and Schmidt 2021).

A Framework for Reform

The aim here is to draw from the findings and analysis featured in this book to broaden the scope of strategic policy and action, addressing the diplomatic and security dimensions of international engagement, in addition to development concerns.[1] The focus is on the many states that are troubled by internal and/or external instability. States that rely on repression and surveillance for their stability are a big part of this mix. Regional and global forces and influences are always presumed. The proposed reform framework is as follows:

1. **Draw from ideas about the upside-down world.** Gross unfairness perverts the everyday. When such perversions are backed with epic levels of state violence, surveillance, and throttled dissent, explosions become much more likely.

   Appreciating the logic of repressive, unpopular governments, and the views of private sector and elite civil society members, is necessary. However, even the little that members of these groups may know about ordinary lives likely is distorted. Accordingly, an essential and instructive information source for grasping country context are the views and voices of the excluded. In addition to direct exchanges, finding out what excluded people are watching, reading, and listening to—and how they are interpreting the information—should inform policy formulation.

Alienated female and male youth and others on the margins likely are decoding the works of international pop culture icons in incisive, meaningful ways. If they are allowed to do so, trendy local artists almost certainly will be communicating issues of significant importance to their followers, as well. Whatever is hugely popular, in short, should be probed and discussed with viewer-listeners on the ground, and used as central guides for policy and program reforms.

2. **Learn from insurgent and violent extremist groups.** Government actors that suck money from systems and starve essential services only make countries more inviting for predatory groups seeking to exploit opportunity.

Seeing states as adversaries is an instructive perspective. The absence of state institutions that reliably and equitably provide schools, clinics, roads, electricity, justice, and basic protections, combined with the enforcement of inequality via state-authorized violence, converts governments into, effectively, occupying forces. This is particularly the case for excluded youth or marginalized ethnic groups under attack by their own governments. When this dynamic arises, the stage is set for insurgent and violent extremist groups to have a field day.

3. **Rework the counterproductive "youth = male youth" and "gender = women" definitions.** The starting point is to change how we think about the foundational gender identities (male and female) and youth. The intrinsic overlap between the two—everyone has a gender identity and many are youth—make them naturally complementary, not adversarial. However, as conceived and practiced, "gender" and "youth" frequently conflict with each other, with female youth playing minor roles in both categories. As detailed earlier, Sierra Leone features the enforced emasculation of male youth, the unremitting degradation of female youth, and patriarchal dominion over both. Understanding these dynamics requires an understanding of gender and youth identities, norms, and lives—and how they interconnect.

The concepts and application of gender and youth should mutually support and correspond. Reaching this objective likely will be difficult, given the current perverse territorial divide, where separate conceptions, policies, and programs demonstrate exclusion, not inclusion. This undercuts the potential impact of both. In response, every reasonable effort should be made to integrate the youth and gender fields and combat the too-common transformation of gender into women and youth into male youth.

4. **Prioritize gender in security analyses of violent conflict and extremism.** Pigeonholing or ghettoizing gender is counterproductive. When

examining or working in contexts impacted by war and/or violent extremism, boxing in gender as a minor or women-specific issue, while excluding masculinity from the mix, undercuts understanding and effectiveness. Failure to change this dynamic runs the risk of handing an advantage to violent extremist competitors, who routinely demonstrate gender expertise in their recruitment of female and male youth (Sommers 2019a).

5. **Mainstream the towering significance of governance.** Governance is the big lift, and it will take gumption to change the status quo. It's also imperative: corrupt, repressive governments and their leaders unmoor states from their citizens, invite invasive state intelligence as well as police and security force violence, and unintentionally open the door to violent nonstate adversaries such as violent extremist groups.

It is essential to see governments for what they are, not what they should be. Here are four general steps to follow:

- Accurately gauge the situation on the ground (including in the shadows);
- Identify viable priorities to ensure decisive impact;
- Develop a coordinated diplomatic, security, and development strategy; and
- Strive to implement it.

As indicated just below, this all-purpose guidance must incorporate contextual specifics.

6. **Customize the strategic response to government dysfunction, predation, and violence.** Sustained effort is required to change the course of self-destructive governments. To be effective, Minter and Schmidt wisely note that "there is no general formula for improving governance and reducing violence. Any proposal for change must consider the details of each case rather than only general advice" (2021). Answering these ten sets of questions promises to address this challenge:

i. How does the government *actually* function, nationally and locally?

ii. What are the areas of authentic expertise and weakness of the government?

iii. In what ways is the state under real or potential threat?

iv. How do advocates and adversaries (such as armed and nonviolent political opponents, civil society actors, private sector interests, regional powers, and insurgent and violent extremist groups) manipulate state weaknesses and tendencies? What are the local, national, regional, and global dimensions of state behavior and action?

v. Who enacts, facilitates, and benefits (locally, nationally, regionally, globally) from illicit dimensions of governance? What does this web look like and who is in it?

vi. What are the underlying purposes of governance for key government actors?

vii. How do key government officials perceive various international actors who engage with them? The latter group should include international diplomatic, development, and security personalities and entities, regional governments and organizations, and private sector outfits and individuals seeking licit or illicit profit.

viii. What are the main ways that female and male youth and other citizens are being systemically excluded and attacked by their government and others in power (such as elder councils and business leaders)? How do the systematically excluded and attacked respond?

ix. What factors or forces drive youth alienation?

x. What role does gender play in all of this?

While trust-based, qualitative research methods are strongly recommended (detailed in Sommers 2019b), quantitative research approaches and data also are required. A mixed-methods approach promises to compile a much more complete picture of illicit, exclusive, and violent governance and its many impacts.

No strategy can do everything. However, quality research and analysis, as outlined here, promises to identify opportunities that balance necessity with feasibility. To sustain impact, the strategy for enhancing government provision, protection, and inclusion should incorporate vigorous responses to those global, regional, and local actors who enable and facilitate systems of corruption (creditors, money launderers, illicit dealers, and so on). It also should draw a bead on restructuring (or removing) specific policies and practices that promote systemic exclusion and state terror.

The collective aim of this guidance is to inspire movement toward more informed, proactive, and productive engagement both with predatory, violent states and the youthful masses whose alienation and separation position them as outliers in their own societies. It promises to guide local, national, and international action toward a far more hopeful future.

NOTES

Preface

1. I compiled this description from interviews with witnesses and passages in Junger (2006) and Keen (2005).

2. The Mende spelling is an approximation (written Mende employs a different alphabet). Speaking with Mende-English translation experts revealed another way of spelling hiding place: *sorkwaehun*. Two other spellings are *sorkoihun* and *sorquehun* (Smith, Gambette, and Longley 2004: 398n1108). There is a related Mende word that means "corner," or "in the corner," in English. Two spellings of that word that I received are *sorkwihun* and *soquihun*. Pronunciation between the two words is subtle: "so-kway-hun" for hiding place and "so-kwee-hun" for corner/in the corner.

Chapter 1. The Innovator

1. Private interview.

2. Taylor awarded himself the praise name Ghankay because it meant "strong" or "stubborn" in Liberia's Gola language and would emphasize "his indigenous roots" (Ellis 2006: 92). He gave himself the ceremonial title of Dahkpannah (meaning "chief"; also spelled Dankpannah), he said, because it came with becoming president of Liberia (Special Court for Sierra Leone 2009: 29289). The roots of his claim of being a "doctor" are more obscure.

3. This approximation does not include estimates that more than USD $1 billion passed through Taylor's personal bank accounts when he was Liberia's president from 1997 to 2003 (Simons 2008: 4).

4. Taylor was adept at getting what he wanted. Innes reports that "Taylor was aggressive in his pursuit of international media attention, regularly calling the BBC and demanding to be interviewed. . . . He maintained contact with the BBC's popular *Focus on Africa* program when his whereabouts were in doubt and rumours abounded, dissimulating on his location and the disposition of NPFL forces to the show's host, Robin White" (2003: 5–6, emphasis in original).

5. Private interview.

Chapter 2. The Perverse Universe

1. Nordstrom also refers to it as dirty-war (2004: 69), or dirty warfare. I will refer exclusively to the main title she uses for her theory: terror warfare.

2. Publications about the Mozambican rebel group/political party feature two spellings: either Renamo or the all-caps RENAMO. As the former was found to be more common, it is featured in all citations and references in this book. Similarly, the ruling party and chief Renamo adversary will be spelled Frelimo in this book, not FRELIMO.

3. Mitton's analysis found that "the RENAMO rebel group of Mozambique . . . conducted a similar systemic brutalization of its forced captives [like the RUF], and there are many parallels from the RUF in regards to the forms of violence it produced" (2015: 276).

4. Taylor's NPFL, in contrast, was far less interested in such matters.

5. The "lumpen" term also is used by many scholars of Sierra Leone. It first was made famous by Karl Marx and Friedrich Engels. "Lumpen" literally means "ragged" or "scoundrel" (Bussard 1987: 675).

6. Private interview.

7. No widely accepted name for the Islamic State in Iraq and Syria (ISIS) exists. Among the other labels employed for the declared caliphate are State of the Islamic Caliphate (SIC), Islamic State of Iraq and the Levant (ISIL), or its Arabic equivalent (al-Dawla al-Islamiya fil 'Iraq wal-Sham (abbreviated as Da'ish but frequently spelled Daesh). Although "Da'ish is the name that has widely stuck among Arabs," members of ISIS/SIC/ISIL "call it simply the State, al-Dawla, for short, and threaten with lashes those who use Da'ish" (M.R. 2014).

Chapter 3. Popular Culture in War and Peace

1. The distinction appears to have confused Stallone as well. In an interview, he remarked, "I've got to do what audiences expect me to do. Let's face it, there was a bond between me and Rocky and Rambo. Over the years, it became difficult to tell the fictional and real characters apart" (Weinraub 1993: 3).

2. Greenburg (2015, 2016, 2017, 2019); Greenburg and Robehmed (2018); Pomerantz (2012, 2013, 2014).

3. Notably, it is the first three films, on which Rambo's worldwide fame is based, that remain the highest-grossing films, as well.

4. "Burnin' and Lootin'" by Bob Marley. On *Burnin'*, Bob Marley and the Wailers, 1973, produced by Chris Blackwell and the Wailers, Island Records and Tuff Gong.

5. Writing in 2008, LeVine considered Abeer to be "not the only Palestinian Israeli female rapper" but also "without a doubt the most talented. Her voice sounds as if it's been through a life of pain and joy far longer than her twenty-three years should have given her." Abeer's home, he reported, "is festooned with pictures of her idol, Tupac" (2008: 124).

6. All quotations in this section are from Abeer (Sabreena da Witch) speaking at Can Hip Hop Beat Conflict?, United States Institute of Peace, April 18, 2008, http://www.usip.org/events/can-hip-hop-beat-conflict. Abeer's words were transcribed from http://www.usip.org/files/hip_hop.mp3.

7. "Them Belly Full (But We Hungry)," Bob Marley and the Wailers, written by Carlton Barrett and Leon Cogil, produced by Chris Blackwell and the Wailers, on *Natty Dread*, 1974. Lyrics accessed on March 9, 2021, from https://genius.com/Bob-marley-and-the-wailers-them-belly-full-but-we-hungry-lyrics.

8. "Me against the World," Tupac Shakur, featuring Dramacydal, written by Tupac Shakur, Minnie Riperton, Richard Rudolph, Leon Ware, Burt Bacharach, and Hal David, produced by Soulshock and Karlin, on *Me against The World*, 1995. Lyrics accessed on March 9, 2021, from https://www.azlyrics.com/lyrics/2pac/meagainstthe world.html.

9. I will not discuss the two subsequent Rambo films in this book. The fourth

film is simply called *Rambo* (2008) while the fifth is titled *Rambo: Last Blood* (2019). All five films star Sylvester Stallone as John Rambo. *Rambo* and *Rambo: Last Blood* emerged long after Sierra Leone's civil war had ended. Neither has had the worldwide impact of the Rambo Trilogy films.

10. Jewett states his take on this succinctly: "The paranoid notion that degenerate elected officials refused to win the Vietnam war is carried forward in this film" (1987).

11. Cosentino and Richards have highlighted similarities between Rambo and Musa Wo, the Mende trickster god whom Carey defines as "an individual capable of destroying order and bringing about total chaos" (2006: 106). The analysis is fascinating but speculative. It is not clear from the data of either researcher whether soldiers or other Mende youth made a conscious connection between Rambo and the traditional deity (Cosentino 2005: 11–14; Richards 1996: 59). Yet the possibility is stirring and reminiscent of field research with Burundian refugees in 1998, where children associated government soldiers with the Igihume, a shape-shifting folk figure in Burundian culture (Sommers and McClintock 2003: 36).

Chapter 4. Trust and Understatement

1. Field research undertaken in 2005 and 2010 was approved by the Charles River Campus Institutional Review Board of Boston University.

2. Four of the six commander/officials were RUF, one was AFRC, one was Kamajor; three field officers were Kamajor, four were AFRC, one was RUF, and one was Sierra Leone Army (an "SLA," that is, a national soldier who did not join the AFRC rebellion).

3. Here are the stats for the noncombatant groups: paramount and town chiefs (3), town councilors (2), high court judges (2), a commissioner of the Truth and Reconciliation Commission (1), a high-ranking former police official (1), officials of the Special Court for Sierra Leone (5), officials of Sierra Leonean and international nongovernment organizations (NGOs) (15 and 11, respectively), security and intelligence experts for the United Nations (3), veteran researchers of Sierra Leone (3), professional rap musicians (2), nightclub DJs (2), a pharmacist (1), a longtime supporter of miners (1), local civilian leaders who negotiated either with the RUF or the AFRC (3), several meetings with village elders and village women's groups, NGOs created to assist excombatant female youth (2), dozens of Sierra Leonean civilians with firsthand experiences of the war and dozens of noncombatant youth in and around Freetown, Kenema, Koidu, and Makeni.

4. I wrote over eleven hundred pages of field interview notes in 2005 and 2010, while my research associate wrote over three hundred pages in 2009 and 2010. The total number of pages of handwritten field interview notes (for 2005, 2009, and 2010) was 1,443. These figures do not include the well over fifteen hundred additional pages of my field interview notes (recorded mainly in Sierra Leone, as well as Guinea and Gambia, in 1997, 1998, 2000, and 2013) from which I also have drawn interview data for this book.

Chapter 5. The Trampled Land

1. It was a curious arrangement. Freetown began as "a settlement for freed slaves from Britain and the New World." It was founded by the British Crown Colony in 1787 before becoming "a Crown Colony ruled by a British governor" in 1808. Mean-

while, "the British made the Atlantic slave trade illegal for all British subjects" in 1806, promoting trade in "products such as timber, camwood, palm oil, palm kernels, and groundnuts." However, since the trade depended on slaves to produce and transport such goods, "the British allowed internal slavery to continue in the hinterland for more than a century" (Shaw 2002: 37, 38).

2. Although Reno does not call the chiefs empowered by the British paramount chiefs, his regular reference to "chiefs" appears to equate with paramount chiefs.

Chapter 6. Rebellion Rising

1. Nuxoll's findings also point to the significance of "conscious music" in the prewar era as well: "Music was an integral part of creative youth initiatives challenging hegemonic structures, and reggae in particular fuelled the mobilization of students to engage in university politics and public protest. The engagement with 'conscious' music, as roots reggae is often described, also contributed to the development of a more revolutionary and radical political stance among disaffected youth" (2015: 7).

Chapter 7. Terror and Purpose

1. Gberie states that the armed forces for the entire nation numbered three thousand at the start of the war (2005: 60). Keen notes that half of that number were reservists, "a significant proportion" of the army was serving as peacekeepers in Liberia at the time of the RUF's entrance into Sierra Leone, and many in the army were armed with colonial-era muskets while many of the RUF had AK-47 machine guns (2005: 83, 84). The "largely ceremonial role" of the national army was the intent of Siaka Stevens, who was suspicious of a strong national army (83)—a tendency, as we will see, that a subsequent president, Ahmed Tejan Kabbah, tragically shared.

2. Sierra Leone's Truth and Reconciliation Commission report broadly shares this assessment: "Partly because of the miscreant activities of the NPFL and partly because of the acts committed by inexperienced or dishonest RUF fighters, the RUF contrived to alienate the civilian population from the very earliest throes of its revolutionary incursion" (TRC 2004a: 132).

3. After the video was captured by government forces, copies were eventually sold in Freetown with the title, "The History of the RUF" (Gberie 2005: 61).

4. Richards draws on a sample of over 420 interviews for a chapter in his book on videos and violence (1996: 106). A second chapter draws from 421 interviews on forest produce and "attitudes to the forest and forest conservation" (139–140). A third chapter drew on prior research in a dozen Sierra Leonean villages on "demographics, household organization, kinship, and occupations" (129). Data sources for chapters on the RUF are less apparent.

5. A source from the Special Court of Sierra Leone looked into this question and concluded that "Sankoh was illiterate" (private interview, 2005). A second source, a veteran Sierra Leonean researcher, took a slightly different view. Sankoh "was literate," the researcher insisted. "But he could barely read and write."

6. Private interview.

Chapter 8. Bob Marley and Foday Sankoh

1. "Get Up, Stand Up," Bob Marley and the Wailers, written by Bob Marley and Peter Tosh, produced by Bob Marley and the Wailers and Chris Blackwell, on *Burnin'*,

1973. Lyrics accessed on March 9, 2021, from https://www.azlyrics.com/lyrics/bob marley/getupstandup.html.

2. "Crazy Baldhead," Bob Marley and the Wailers, written by Rita Marley and Vincent Ford, produced by Bob Marley and the Wailers, on *Rastaman Vibration*, 1976. Lyrics accessed on March 9, 2021, from https://www.lyrics.com/lyric/3179874 /Bob+Marley/Crazy+Baldhead.

3. "Could You Be Loved," Bob Marley & the Wailers, Written by Bob Marley, Produced by Chris Blackwell and Bob Marley, Album: *Uprising*, 1980. Lyrics accessed on March 9, 2021, from https://www.azlyrics.com/lyrics/bobmarley/couldyoubeloved .html.

4. "Natural Mystic," Bob Marley and the Wailers, written by Bob Marley, produced by Bob Marley and the Wailers, on Exodus, 1977. Lyrics accessed on March 9, 2021, from http://www.songlyrics.com/bob-marley/natural-mystic-lyrics/.

5. "War," by Bob Marley and the Wailers, written by Carlton Barrett and Allen Cole, produced by Bob Marley and the Wailers, on *Rastaman Vibration*, 1976. Lyrics from Nuxoll (2015, 9).

Chapter 9. Both Sides Now

1. The purchasing power of USD $500 million in 1985 would equal $1,390,187,665.18 U.S. dollars in 2022 (November 3 data). Estimate provided by Inflation Tool: https://www.inflationtool.com/us-dollar/1985-to-present-value?amount =500000000&year2=2022&frequency=yearly.

2. Events following the entrance of Foday Sankoh and the RUF into Kailahun District on March 23, 1991, are detailed in chapter 7.

3. The subaltern term appears to originally have referred to "a British commissioned army officer below the rank of captain." Eventually it came to refer to "someone with a low ranking in a social, political, or other hierarchy," "someone who has been marginalized or oppressed," or "someone who has no political or economic power, such as a poor person living under a dictatorship" (Vocabulary.com, n.d.).

4. "One Love/People Get Ready," by Bob Marley and the Wailers, written by Bob Marley and Curtis Mayfield, produced by Bob Marley and the Wailers, on Exodus, 1977. Lyrics accessed on March 9, 2021, from https://www.azlyrics.com/lyrics/bob marley/onelovepeoplegetready.html.

5. Private interview with a veteran researcher on Sierra Leone.

6. Opala explained that "disadvantaged youths have long had a fascination with Bai Bureh, the [ethnic] Temne chief who waged the 'Hut Tax War' of 1898, the most important revolt against British rule in the colonial era." He also described Madam Yoko as "a famous pre-colonial chief" and Sengbe Pieh as "the young [ethnic] Mende man from Sierra Leone who led the famous slave revolt aboard the ship *Amistad*, in 1839" (Opala 1994: 199, 200, 202).

7. Peters notes that the document reportedly was written in 1995 (2011a: 127).

8. Hoffman lists the "ethnically coded titles" of the main CDF forces as follows: the Kuranko *Tamaboro*, the Temne *Gbethis* and *Kapras*, the Kono *Donsos*, and the Mende *Kamajors*. The Kamajors (sometimes called Kamajoisia or Kamajohs) were far and away the largest of the CDF forces (Hoffman 2007: 642).

Chapter 10. Groups and T-Shirts

1. The "RUF" incision, carved into a member's shoulder or torso, was not a tattoo but a kind of involuntary branding: an intentional, raised indicator of forced RUF membership. The purpose was to ensure that abductees would never try to escape. The incision marked them as RUF property. It will be considered in chapter 16.

2. Wlodarczyk also noted this phenomenon during the war. In her view, particular decisions on dress by military groups signified "emblems of power." For the RUF, there "tended to be a mixture of accessories associated with popular culture personae." She found Rambo to be the favorite, "but hip-hop and gangsta rap personalities also featured in their repertoire." She did not mention Marley or other reggae stars in the mix. Sometimes, she noted that rebels also wore "the masks of secret society traditions." The Kamajors, in contrast, sported "more exclusively traditional" garb, such as "amulets, charms, and specially prepared protective clothing" (2009: 120).

3. In the article, Fofana also points to a deep distaste for Tupac's work and life: "The late rap star preached violence, rape and female-bashing, and was reportedly a 'gang-banger,' who engaged in gun shootings and other forms of violent exploits, on the streets of California in the United States" (1998a). His take of Marley is the precise opposite, as suggested in the opening of the earlier article: "Bob Marley would turn in his grave. The reggae legend, who preached black unity, has become a target in Sierra Leone's civil war" (1995).

4. What appeared to be the most popular version of the Tupac T-shirt arose later in the war. It is described as having "a black background, showing Tupac (spelled '2Pac') looking alert, with U.S. dollar signs ringing the collar and his most popular slogan, 'All Eyez on Me,' across the bottom" (Sommers 2003b: 35).

5. Although he said it took place in 1991, it must have been in 1992, after Tupac's initial 1991 album came out.

6. A source from the Special Court of Sierra Leone characterized this RUF specialty group as follows: "A group of SBUs [Small Boys Units], they were small, drugged and trained to amputate. [They operated] in the north, in Kailahun and in Kono."

7. A veteran researcher of Sierra Leone's war related that the Yarmotor Group would "bayonet you and pull out your heart." The Truth and Reconciliation Commission report provides additional detail: "A group within the Kamajors, called the 'yarmotor' is reputed to be a cult of warriors in traditional Sierra Leonean society. Witnesses claim that this group carried out most of the cannibalism violations" (TRC 2004a: 497). The group's name also has been spelled Yamorto (Wlodarczyk 2009: 118).

8. Black December also was the name for a CDF-led operation in late 1997, which aimed "to shut down the major roadways, preventing the AFRC [then in power, alongside the RUF] from moving logistic supplies out of Freetown and isolating its upcountry units" (Hoffman 2011: 45–46).

Chapter 11. When the War Came to Us

1. Will Scully tells the tale of his mighty defense of the Mammy Yoko against rebel forces in his book, *Once a Pilgrim: The True Story of One Man's Courage under Rebel*

Fire (1998). After "over 1,000 men, women and children, mostly Americans with 200 British and a few other expatriates, had been whisked out of the chaos of Freetown to safety on the USS *Kearsarge*," Scully remained at the hotel. In his words, "Now the locals saw the expats and the rich leaving, like the proverbial rats, these being the very people who had urged Sierra Leone towards the democratic institutions which had so dramatically failed, while all the time behind them the violence in the town washed ever closer to the enclave of the Mammy Yoko" (86–87).

2. The average exchange rate for 1997 was 981.9 leones per U.S. dollar (Rwegasira 2009: 54).

Chapter 12. Diamonds, Humanitarians, and the Rebel Takeover

1. Kabbah evidently had "moved the economy from a negative growth rate of minus 6.4 percent to a positive rate of 6 percent in just one year" (Gberie 2005: 100).

2. The brief description of events was drawn largely from Keen (2005: 208–209).

3. Rastas received a customized kind of citizen backlash the following year. A few weeks after ECOMOG troops had forced the AFRC and RUF troops out of Freetown, Fofana reports that "an irate lynch mob rampaged through Freetown forcing Rastafarians to cut off their dreadlocks, as punishment for alleged collaboration with the ousted military junta" (1998b).

4. Campbell found similar conditions in the mines: "It's hard to imagine a job more difficult or demanding [than diamond mining in Sierra Leone]. The workday starts at sunrise and ends at sunset. There are no lunch breaks and no days off. For their efforts at recovering diamonds from the soil, the diggers each receive two cups of rice and the equivalent of 50 cents a day. Bonuses based on the value of their personal production are dependent almost entirely on the trustworthiness of the miner they work for" (2004: 6–7).

5. It should be noted that Peters contests many of the arguments put forward by others in this section. He appears skeptical that Taylor had a direct connection to Sankoh and the RUF in the diamond trade, for example. In addition, he contends that if you "set aside the worst cases of extremely exploitative practices," the practices applied to civilians in the diamond mines "would not have been significantly more exploitative than those in place before and after the war" (Peters 2011a: 117).

6. A diamond mine supporter in Koidu added, "When the rebels settled here in 1998, they forced people to mine inside their houses."

7. In characteristically dramatic terms, Campbell notes that the "conflict diamonds" term emerged after reporting about the conflict zone origins of some diamonds starting in 1999. Once the information began to surface, "it gradually became known that some stones carried the blood of innocent victims, killed or mutilated by rebel groups in Africa who used the profits of diamond sales to continue their campaigns of brutality and inhumanity" (2004: xxiv).

8. Later I found out that the eloquent, elegant paramount chief subsequently had attracted considerable attention on the national stage, having served for many years as a minister of Parliament. Some of it was not positive. In 2005, for example, the *Standard Times (Freetown)* reported that the paramount chief had "abandoned his chiefdom in search of diamonds in the Kono district," at least according to "reports" (Saidu Kamara 2005). A second Sierra Leonean newspaper (*Concord Times*) related that the paramount chief was a "21st century tyrant and oppressor who is ready to

stampede anyone who dares to oppose his alleged misrule." One source of the story was "a section chief [serving under Bai-Kurr Kanagbaro II] who begged for anonymity [and] described the traditional ruler as a nightmare and one who employs dictatorial means to control his subjects." In addition to alleging forced labor, the section chief "claimed that whoever challenges the chief's authority would be beaten and detained in a secret detention centre, as they would be treated inhumanely" (Saffa 2015).

9. Bio is not included in this list. Despite suggestions of collusion (described in chapter 9), his tenure in 1996 was transitional and short.

10. The UN Observer Mission in Sierra Leone (UNOMSIL), made up of perhaps seventy military observers and logistical support, started in Sierra Leone on July 13, 1998 (Smith, Gambette, and Longley 2004: 35).

11. A recollection of this infiltration is shared by an elderly man who lived on the eastern side of Freetown: "It was between ten and twelve p.m. [midnight] on January fifth [the night before the rebel assault began] that I saw a heavy crowd moving from the East End of Freetown, that is, Calaba Town. This was a fearful scene. I was wanting to know what was happening or where the crowd was coming from and going. Nobody spoke to me. People were just moving without talking to anybody. There was only one person who said, 'Wait, you will know tomorrow.' I never suspected these [people] were rebels."

Chapter 13. No Living Thing

1. Bøås fixed Bockarie (or Maskita) into chilling context. Bockarie "took things to extremes, yet there is a clear line of continuity between the behavior of previous Sierra Leonean 'big men' and Maskita's actions. Every institution or aspect of society was there for the taking, to be milked dry. What had started out as a social revolt (we do not know if Bockarie ever shared RUF's initial ideology) ended up as a perverted version of the state the movement initially rebelled against. This is not unique to Bockarie and the RUF but seems to be a common pattern among current armed insurgencies all over Africa" (Bøås 2007: 51).

2. Iron considered him "an iconic figure who was revered and respected by his men" (2005: D-2).

3. Reports gathered from Makeni residents suggest that Superman and his troops arrived in February on the highway from the east (Magburaka) as part of the "Operation Pay Yourself" rebel effort in February–March 1998 (Smith, Gambette, and Longley 2004: 134). Dennis Mingo reportedly received his Superman nickname "because he allegedly threw his victims off high places" (Voice of America 2009). He dominated Makeni for three years before slipping out of town in February 2001 (*Concord Times* [Freetown] 2001).

4. "Exodus," by Bob Marley and the Wailers, written by Bob Marley, produced by Bob Marley and the Wailers, on *Exodus*, 1977. Lyrics accessed on March 9, 2021, from https://www.azlyrics.com/lyrics/bobmarley/exodus.html.

5. Mingo indeed was a founding RUF member. While Taylor and Sankoh were recruiting Sierra Leoneans (mostly through force) for the still-new RUF "vanguards," Taylor also wanted some Liberians from his NPFL to be part of the RUF. "It was through this channel that a former NPFL fighter named Dennis Mingo (alias 'Superman') became part of the vanguards," Sierra Leone's Truth and Reconciliation Com-

mission report states. "Mingo was identified by most RUF members as a Liberian of the Gbandi ethnic group; yet one of his parents was Sierra Leonean and he thus spoke Mende and Krio with ease. He was transferred to the RUF under Foday Sankoh in 1990, mostly on account of his prowess as a front-line fighter and mastery of Sierra Leonean languages" (TRC 2004a: 106).

6. A source from the Special Court linked the two in another way. After analyzing their military exploits, the source concluded that "Gullit and Five-Five were brilliant soldiers. If they'd been in any other army, they'd have had brilliant careers."

7. This trio was linked after the war as well: on February 25, 2008, the Special Court for Sierra Leone "found Sesay and Kallon guilty on 16 of 18 counts, and Gbao guilty on 14 counts" against them. Ultimately, "Sesay was sentenced to a total of 52 years in prison, Kallon to 40 years and Gbao to 25 years" (Special Court for Sierra Leone and the Residual Special Court for Sierra Leone, n.d.).

8. They were as follows: Superman Group, Rambo Group, Issa [Sesay] Group, 8 & 9 Group, Sofila Group, Mosquito Group (led by a commander who shared the "Mosquito" nickname with Sam Bockarie), and Adama Cut Hand Group.

9. Porter considers the stunning absence of knowledge about the advancing invasion of Freetown, by many thousands of troops from the AFRC, the RUF, and Liberia. One of the main apparent causes was denial by the SRSG and UNOMSIL. One UN official related that Okello "'equated support to the Government with ignoring the reality of what was going on in the country'"(Porter 2003: 23). An account of this denial of reality by UNOMSIL, ECOMOG, and Kabbah's government, and the debate over security of which it was a part, is detailed in Sommers (2000).

10. Human Rights Watch reported "over 180 summary executions of rebel prisoners and their suspected collaborators, mostly by ECOMOG forces but also by members of the Civil Defense Forces (CDF), and the Special Security Division (SSD) of the Sierra Leonean Police" (HRW 1999: V).

11. Keen found precisely the same pattern: the rebels "were at their most dangerous in defeat, responding to their own military humiliation with an escalation in abuses against civilians" (2005: 246).

12. The head of the Sierra Leone office of an international NGO described something similar. "After Jan. 6 [1999], they [the rebels] played Joe Hills, Burning Spear, and Bob Marley. I heard Joe Hills and Bob Marley, especially in the East end of Freetown."

13. They also align with the reporting from a source at the Special Court for Sierra Leone. "From Freetown witnesses," the source related in 2005, "most said [the rebels] were wearing Tupac T-shirts and bandannas with U.S. flag colors (like Rambo)."

Chapter 14. The Dénouement

1. Joseph Hill, 1999, "War in Sierra Leone" by Culture, on *Payday*, produced by Clive Hunt and Joseph Hill. Lyrics accessed on April 26, 2019, from https://www.jah-lyrics.com/song/culture-war-in-sierra-leone.

2. Ziggy Marley and the Melody Makers, 1997, "Diamond City," on *Fallen Is Babylon* by David Ziggy Marley, produced by Steve Thompson, Michael Barbiero, Jonathan Quarmby, and Kevin Bacon. Diamond City lyrics © S.I.A.E. Direzione Generale, Ishti Music.

3. The January 2000 study was *The Heart of the Matter: Sierra Leone, Diamonds,*

and Human Security, by Ian Smillie, Lansana Gberie, and Ralph Hazleton (Ottawa: Partnership Africa Canada), https://cryptome.org/kimberly/kimberly-016.pdf.

Chapter 15. John Rambo and War

1. The discussion here refers exclusively to the first three Rambo pictures—*First Blood, Rambo: First Blood Part II*, and *Rambo III*—which were made in 1982, 1985 and 1988, respectively.

2. There was also an RUF commander, Emmanuel Williams, who assumed the name of Sylvester Stallone's other movie icon. He was known both as Rocky and CO Rocky (Special Court for Sierra Leone 2012: 252, 869). In addition, "An RUF base in Northern Province, near Mabang, Tonkolili District, was also under the command of a man nicknamed First Blood," the key phrase in the title of the first two Rambo films (Prestholdt 2019: 259n64).

3. Physicians for Human Rights lists a succession of noms de guerre that surfaced in their research in Sierra Leone, including Blood, Pepper, Nasty, Bullet, Cut Hand, Poison, God Father, Rebel Baby, Dry Gin, Rambo, Commando Around the World, Gold Teeth, and Body Naked (2002: 75).

4. This appears to be "Boston Flomoh (alias 'Rambo')," also known as RUF Rambo. This particular Rambo was considered among the most senior of RUF commanders (TRC 2004c: 49).

5. One ex-RUF fighter described a leader named Rambo as wearing "an American flag [bandanna] on his forehead and a plaster on his jaw," the latter usually marking an incision where hard drugs are inserted into the bloodstream.

6. The absence of an SBU unit, by itself, was unusual.

7. As a former RUF wife explained, "This group hardly obeyed the commands of their leaders. When they went into a ceasefire, they [still] would do their own thing."

8. The particular Rambo referenced here evidently was "Colonel Boston Flamoh or Flomoh (alias 'Rambo' [also known as RUF Rambo]): killed by RUF comrades in Makeni" (United Nations Panel of Experts 2000: 70).

Chapter 16. Indoctrinations

1. Taylor ended up starting his war at the very end of 1989, from Côte d'Ivoire, on Liberia's eastern border.

2. Some of those whom Sankoh chose and trained in Liberia stayed with him across the entire war period, including Jonathan Kposowa, who became the RUF's chief administrative officer (adjutant general) in Liberia and retained that position throughout, and one of his first five child soldiers, Sheriff Parker (known as Base Marine). During the war, Base Marine rose to become an SBU commander before serving as a brigade commander (TRC 2004a: 125, 194, 357).

3. Ferme and Hoffman define the Poro secret society as "the bush training-school that imparts to young Mende men the expectations of manhood, including the moral conduct of war and the relationship of a man to his community" (2004: 81). While Poro and Bondo or Sande (the main names for the female secret society counterpart) often are used to refer to male and female secret societies generally across Sierra Leone, the frame of reference here is ethnic Mende, whose traditional home is in the south and east of Sierra Leone.

4. Mitton summed up the situation as follows: "Certainly for the future RUF conscripts, a sense of powerlessness underpinned day-to-day living" (2015: 131).

5. The incest-based rapes were not just with mothers. As Baldi and MacKenzie note, "In order to sever young soldiers' ties with their families, and to demonstrate their loyalty to the armed group, some boys and young men were forced to rape their sisters, mothers, and even grandmothers" (2007: 81).

6. Mitton explains that "by systematically creating shame and simultaneously presenting itself as the only means to eliminate it, the [RUF] rebel group was able to bring captives to locate their sense of self-worth in its brutalizing social world" (2015: 134).

7. Peters spells out both sets, in complete form (2011a: 128).

8. Adding to the official's view of a drastic, rather confusing, and controlling version of fundamental change, he added, "There's no money anywhere. We need to be realistic. We need to move to [the] development stage. Until the ground is settled and people come back and take care of their properties and houses, then you'll be allowed to buy."

9. Reggae was only one of many kinds of songs employed during training. Another one was "Commandos are brave, Commandos are intelligent, You don't fuck with us, Commandos hardly die" (Denov 2010: 101).

10. Peters claims that from the signing of the Lomé accord in July 1999 and January 2002, "the RUF was the de facto government of a significant part of Sierra Leone" (2011a: 106). This assertion was not found to be substantiated by other published sources, nor did indications of this surface in my field interview data.

11. "Rastaman Live Up!", Bob Marley and the Wailers, written by Bob Marley, produced by Bob Marley and the Wailers, executive producer Rita Marley, on *Confrontation*, 1983. Lyrics accessed on August 8, 2020, from https://genius.com/Bob
-marley-and-the-wailers-rastaman-live-up-lyrics.

12. The testimony is from SC-SL Witness TF2-021, November 2, 2004.

Chapter 17. Tupac Shakur and War

1. As McQuillar and Johnson explain, "By the end of ['Hit 'Em Up'], Tupac had threatened Biggie, Puffy, Lil Kim, and everyone else associated with Bad Boy Records" (2010: 223). The hugely successful Combs, a rap musician, producer, and entrepreneur, has accumulated a variety of names over the years: from Puff Daddy (or Puffy) to P. Diddy (or just Diddy) to, more recently, Love or Brother Love (Boal, n.d.).

2. "Hit 'Em Up," Tupac Shakur, featuring Outlawz, written by Tupac Shakur and Outlawz, produced by Johnny "J," released in 1996. Lyrics accessed on March 9, 2021, from https://genius.com/2pac-hit-em-up-lyrics.

3. A recent estimate of the date of *The Iliad* is "762 B.C., give or take 50 years" (Shurkin 2013).

4. Davey predicted in 2005 that, for American soldiers who were fighting there, "rap may become the defining pulse for the war in Iraq. It has emerged as a rare realm where soldiers and marines, hardly known for talking about their feelings, are voicing the full range of their emotions and reactions to war. They rap about their resentment of the military hierarchy. But they also rap about their pride, their invincibility, their fallen brothers, their disdain for the enemy and their determination to

succeed." One U.S. soldier declared that he "might be part of the Tupac generation" (Davey 2005).

5. The need to scrub up Tupac Shakur's captivating legacy persists. Following his death, Lynskey states that Tupac "became the rapper as icon, scrutinised by academics and revered worldwide as a latter-day Bob Marley, with many of his troubling contradictions washed away" (2011).

6. Prestholdt includes the action movie actor Chuck Norris with the trio. Field research for this book did not find the movies of Chuck Norris to be nearly as significant as those of Sylvester Stallone's Rambo character.

7. "All Eyez on Me," Tupac Shakur, featuring Big Syke, written by Johnny Jackson, J. P. Pennington, and Tupac Shakur, produced by Johnny "J," Tupac Shakur, and Suge Knight, on *All Eyez on Me*, 1996. Lyrics accessed on March 9, 2021, from https://genius.com/2pac-all-eyez-on-me-lyrics.

8. "Only God Can Judge Me," by Tupac Shakur, featuring Rappin' 4-Tay, written by Doug Rasheed and Tupac Shakur, produced by Harold Scrap Frettie, Doug Rasheed, Tupac Shakur, and Suge Knight, on *All Eyez on Me*, 1996. Lyrics accessed on March 9, 2021, from https://genius.com/2pac-only-god-can-judge-me-lyrics.

9. "Me against the World," Tupac Shakur, featuring Dramacydal, written by Tupac Shakur, Minnie Riperton, Richard Rudolph, Leon Ware, Burt Bacharach, and Hal David, produced by Soulshock and Karlin, on *Me against the World*, 1995. Lyrics accessed on March 9, 2021, from https://www.azlyrics.com/lyrics/2pac/meagainsttheworld.html.

10. "Keep Ya Head Up," Tupac Shakur, featuring Dave Hollister, written by Tupac Shakur, Daryl Anderson, Stan Vincent, and Roger Troutman, produced by DJ Daryl, on *Strictly 4 My N.I.G.G.A.Z . . .* , 1993.

11. The attack he discussed appears to have been the AFRC and RUF assault on Kabala in northern Sierra Leone on either July 27 or 28, 1998. Rebel forces occupied the town for about a week before withdrawing (Smith, Gambette, and Longley 2004: 177).

Chapter 18. Drastic Measures

1. See, for example, Reuters 2008.

2. Reported in Guberek et al. (2006: 3–4); Zack-Williams (2012: 13).

3. The 2004 census, undertaken after the war had ended, listed the nation's population at 4,976,871 (Sesay et al. 2006: ix).

4. There are two subsequent dates when the civil war was thought to end. One was in 2005, when a democratically elected government, led by the primary rebel group, the Conseil National pour la Défense de la Démocratie–Forces pour la Défense de la Démocratie (CNDD–FDD), assumed power. A second was 2009, when "the off-again-on-again civil war in Burundi . . . officially came to an end" as "the last of its rebel groups formally became a political party" (Kron 2009). But for the most part, the war was thought to expire when CNDD–FDD agreed to a peace deal in 2003 (Samii 2013: 222).

5. The commission decreed that "a legal determination that the crime of genocide had been committed in Burundi was made only in respect of the 1993 massacres of Tutsis" (United Nations 2005: 8).

6. In 1998, in the latter stages of the war, Burundi's national army was estimated

to have over forty thousand troops (Human Rights Watch 1998: 3). The postwar DDR process in Sierra Leone surfaced an estimated fourteen thousand members of Sierra Leone's national army, the SLA (McKay and Mazurana 2004: 92).

7. The working assumption here is that what Cohen termed an "attack" more or less equated with what Wlodarczyk or members of military groups considered an ambush.

8. The calculation is based on 130 months of war: from March 1991 through 2001 (even though not much warfare was taking place in that final year).

9. Many other corroborating assessments have been made elsewhere in this book.

10. "Delta9-Tetrahydrocannabinol, or THC for short, is the active substance found in marijuana. It is responsible for its psychoactive effects. THC binds to cannabinoid receptors found in certain areas of the brain associated with cognition, memory, pleasure, coordination and time perception, producing a euphoric high in the process" (Puiu 2017).

11. The TRC noted that "marijuana was grown and harvested on different farms all over the country by the different fighting forces. Cultivation of marijuana in some cases supplanted crops that could have provided a source of food for a largely starving population. It was easy to grow and became readily available and cheap throughout the conflict period" (2004b: 303).

12. The relatively few female rebel commanders almost always left an impression. As the TRC observed, "Female commanders were often given appellations that characterised the forms of behaviour for which they were notorious: Adama 'Cut Hand'; Lieutenant 'Cause Trouble'; Kumba 'Blood'; Lady 'Jungle Law'; and Hawa 'Two Barrel', for example. Killing, maiming, looting, burning and amputations were among the violations attributed to females in the TRC database" (2004b: 187). Adama Cut Hand was, by far, the most famous female commander among the rebel groups.

13. The TRC found that "during the conflict, the declarations and suggestions of a *bra* carried all the more persuasive weight because they were backed up by threats of summary punishment for non-conformists" (2004a: 551). Peters and Richards also highlight the *bra* phenomenon (1998: 186).

14. Notably, when Keen refers to "youths," his descriptions make clear that he is referring exclusively to male youth. It is a prominent trend in analysis of terror in Sierra Leone: to imply male-infused rationales for violence while, in most instances, not delineating the gendered context.

15. Wlodarczyk's findings support this analysis. She explained that "Kamajor fighters on several occasions dismembered enemy victims and ingested parts of their bodies—particularly the heart and liver. The symbolism of the practice—or the tradition echoed—is the acquisition of power through ingestion." She added that Kamajor acts of cannibalism "also took place on the battlefield without the seclusion of a camp or the benefit of condiments" (Wlodarczyk 2009: 117, 118).

16. A former RUF combatant explained, "The RUF said [to civilians], 'When you have your arms, you can vote. Without them, you can't vote.' This was after Kabbah was elected. They'd tell civilians, 'Go to your president and tell him to give you another arm. Then you can vote.'"

17. A second alleged message connected amputating the hands of farmers to the RUF: "The RUF effectively showed that farming and food production would be al-

lowed to take place when and where the RUF decided" (Carey 2006: 113). This claim is speculative but worthy of note.

Chapter 19. The War on Girls

1. Some of this analysis draws from the works of Mariane Ferme (2001), Rosalind Shaw (2002), and Susan Shepler (2014) in chapter 5 and Danny Hoffman (2011) in chapter 16.

2. In the West, marijuana makes you high and alcohol gets you drunk. But in Sierra Leone, one word—drunk—is applied to both outcomes.

3. One of the very few sources to mention male rape was the 2003 report by Human Rights Watch, which did not document any crimes of sexual violence against males during its research in Sierra Leone. However, it noted that, according to a Sierra Leonean NGO (Forum for African Women Educationalists, or FAWE), "boys and men were also raped by male rebels." Human Rights Watch concluded that sexual violence against males was "apparently committed on a much smaller scale than sexual violence committed against women and girls" during Sierra Leone's war (42). One research team found that 5 percent of their sample of former male child soldiers in Sierra Leone reported sexual abuse. Although the team also suspected that "rape was underreported by males," the frequency of sexual violence (including rape) of males during the war appears to be low (Betancourt et al. 2011: 26). It proved difficult to find corroboration for the low frequency of male rape reported in this study.

4. Cohen also shares a statement from a former male RUF combatant that slightly challenges the survey data. The ex-fighter reported that women both held down female civilian victims during gang rapes and raped the same victims with sticks or bottles (Cohen 2013a: 404).

5. It also can serve to help bond perpetrators to each other, an issue surfacing later in this section. In some cases (though not for Sierra Leone), rape during war can be a tool to "deliberately pollute the bloodline of the victimized population" (Kelly 2010: 3).

6. Coulter also records how drug use increased the sex drive of male rebels during the war (see, for example, 2009: 130).

7. Corroborating evidence is shared later in this section.

8. For example, Human Rights Watch records the unusual act of a rebel husband forcing his captive wife to "take his penis in [her] mouth" but does not comment about its potential significance (2003: 44).

Chapter 20. Through Male Youth Eyes

1. The phenomenon included children: a survey revealed that more than two in five former child combatants "changed factions at some point during the war" (Aning and McIntyre 2005: 74). Aning and McIntyre's analysis "suggests a state of chaos in which children could find themselves recruited during attacks on their communities, then counter-recruited during retaliation by an opposing party" (76).

2. Weber lists a sequence of prior research publications that link correlations between youth bulge demographics and a higher risk of civil unrest or war, higher rates of violent crime, decreased political stability, volatile inter-state relations, and diminishing chances for liberal democracy (2019: 81). His implied reference point is male youth. Other researchers have raised questions about the context and significance of

such claims. This general trend, which has been called the "youth bulge and instability thesis," "is challenged by context rather than defined by it" (Sommers 2015: 22; see also Urdal and Hoelscher 2009; Sommers 2011, 2017, 2019a).

3. See, for example, Eguavoen (2010), Honwana (2012), and Singerman (2013).

Chapter 21. Alienation and Rights

1. "Youthman" also is the title of a popular 2008 song depicting lives of hardship by the Sierra Leonean musician Steady Bongo (cited in Sommers 2015: 13, 202n8; Honwana 2012: 24).

2. Coulter also found the same "girlfriend business" phenomenon, with postwar female youth having "one or two lovers who would give them money, clothes, and food" (2009: 246).

3. "Brushing" is the grueling, strenuous process of clearing out weeds and often rapid jungle growth from farmland by hand. Traditionally, male youth performed this work.

4. As Thompstone observed, "In the majority of cases of [child] abuse, neglect or exploitation, it appears that communities are more likely to turn to local mediation structures to resolve child protection incidents." These structures were based on "the traditional role of the Chief as mediator within communities" (2010: 2).

5. The most commonly practiced form of female genital mutilation is Type II, also known as "radical circumcision" (McFerson 2011: 135).

6. Quite often, enforcement of laws relating to the protection of children and women fell to the Family Support Unit (FSU) of the national police. Founded in 2001, FSUs are tasked with addressing all domestic, sexual, and gender-based violence across the nation with limited institutional reach, capacity, and reliable support (Ibrahim 2012: 45–46).

7. As noted in a study on violence against women in Sierra Leone, "People now refer to 'that 50/50 thing' as shorthand for increased women's representation in public life (this is almost certainly the result of advocacy efforts by the 50/50 Group, which has received significant donor support in Sierra Leone)" (Denny and Ibrahim 2012: 7).

Chapter 22. The Power of the *Pa*

1. Citing an array of sources, Higgins and Novelli list six separate causes of grievance and conflict in postwar Sierra Leone: (1) "a 'trickle down' process of wealth redistribution"; (2) "the failure of the statebuilding mission of international peace operations, oriented more to meeting international goals of global security than to enabling the Sierra Leone state to meet the 'everyday' needs and aspirations of its people for improved social services"; (3) "specific drivers of grievance, especially amongst the population's youth constituency," including "lack of job opportunities for youth" and "the co-option of youth into political violence by political elites during election times and the continuation of patronage politics"; (4) "resentment in some parts of the country, in particular Kono, at the operation of international mining companies, and a perception that the country's resource wealth is being exploited by global business with little tangible benefits to local populations"; (5) "widespread resentment amongst local mining affected communities at the perceived collusion of elites, local and national, in this process, who are perceived to

be monopolizing wealth accruing from such business activity"; and (6) "continuing widespread distrust and dissatisfaction between the state and its citizens" (Higgins and Novelli 2018: 38).

2. Richards catalogs many instances of outrages and abuses of chiefly power mentioned by youth (fourteen in Sierra Leone and three more in Liberia) (2005b: 577–579).

3. Here are two more examples. "For the poor, securing political leaders that remain downwardly accountable is an absolute priority," said another expert, adding, "Many continue to find chiefs preferable to elected politicians and bureaucrats" (Fanthorpe 2005: 45). Still another expert commented, "Even though grievances against some of the chiefs had led some young people to join the RUF, the institutions of chieftaincy were still quite popular and were easily and universally re-established after the war" (Vincent 2012: 18).

4. Manning's chart convincingly illustrates the web of chiefdom positions below the paramount chief and alongside the formal government representatives (2009: 4).

5. A package of Hungry Heptin lists cyproheptadine (4 mg, also listed as cyproheptadine hydrochloride [Anhydrous]) as the active ingredient. Also known as Periactin in the United States, it appears to be used there mainly with young children. It is "an antihistamine (similar to benadryl), which frequently has the side effects of increase in hunger." In addition, "the biggest side effects you see are sleepiness, and irritability" (Brackett 2015).

6. Of the entire population of Sierra Leone, 4 to 5 percent (180,000–300,000 citizens) were female sex workers (FSWs). Assuming half of all Sierra Leoneans are female, then the ratio of FSWs (or female CSWs) is 1:10. In mining areas, 12 percent of girls and women worked as FSWs (UNAIDS 2013: 7). The proportions can go much higher. In the Baumahun mining area as many as 30 percent of all residents might have been female sex workers (26).

7. In 2008, there were an estimated 120,000 artisanal miners in the country (mining zircon and gold, as well as diamonds) (Bermúdez-Lugo 2010: 35.1). A second source asserted that the actual number was "much larger" (Cartier and Bürge 2011: 1081). The mining population included "children as young as 3 years old" (Campbell 2012). A UN official stated that "watchers" at diamond mining sites (watchers guard the gravel when miners are away) "are as young as five years old."

8. The TRC found that "many child miners in Kono are former child combatants and 18% of the mine supporters interviewed were former commanders employing their former child combatants. This continuity means that the patterns of abuse against children during the conflict are still in place. Many child ex-combatants are still displaced from their families and thus have to rely on their former commanders to provide their subsistence" (2004b: 52).

9. A survey of children and youth working as diamond miners in Kono District (where Koidu is located) after the war found that one in four miners between ages fourteen and seventeen were orphans. Beyond the option of diamond mining, "there are few other economic opportunities available for such youths, making the diamond mining area a magnet for these children." School was not an option, since finding sufficient funds "is next to impossible for most orphans." The researchers concluded that "very few of the children and youth involved in diamond mining would like to continue with their current activities. All of them dream about another life, and for

most that life includes education as an integral component" (Bøås and Hatløy 2006: 77, 78).

10. A second name with the same meaning, Hardup Man, was less common.

11. In Freetown, a young man with sudden wealth became a Baron.

Chapter 24. Young People and War

1. Apparently referring to this initiative, Liah noted that "in Bhar el Ghazel in 2001 and 2003, most of the children released from the fighting forces had been kept in a compound in Rumbek town without reunification and proper reintegration. They had only been given reinsertion packages as morale boosters before they were taken home. Back in their communities, they had difficulties adjusting to the daily life in the villages" (2011: 5).

2. The proportions also were significantly lower than women's access to DDR programming. For example, among RUF fighting forces, nine times more women than girls entered DDR programs (McKay and Mazurana 2004: 99).

3. Research on this issue is detailed in chapter 4 of Sommers (2015).

4. *Breathin'*, Tupac Shakur, featuring Outlawz, written by Tupac Shakur, Johnny "J," E.D.I. Mean, Napoleon (Outlawz), Young Noble, and Kastro. produced by Johnny "J," on *Until the End of Time*, 2001. Lyrics accessed on March 9, 2021, from https://genius.com/2pac-breathin-lyrics.

Chapter 25. No Contradiction

1. Twenty years after the release of *Rambo III*, the fourth Rambo film, called simply *Rambo*, was released (2008). Eleven years later, a fifth film, called *Rambo: Last Blood*, was released.

2. 50 Cent's debut album was *Get Rich or Die Tryin'* (Shady Records/Aftermath Records/Interscope Records, 2003). It was a smash hit. A movie with the same title was released in 2005 (Paramount Pictures).

3. 50 Cent has attracted considerable attention in South Sudan in recent years. A song by the South Sudanese rap musician Emmanuel Jal was called "50 Cent" (2008). Jal commented, "When I wrote my song 50 Cent, I wanted to tell him that he is a role model to young people so he needs to come up with a different style, he needs to tell children it is not cool to be a gangster and kill. Otherwise he is creating a genocidal society" (Nikkhah 2009). More recently, 50 Cent himself traveled to South Sudan (in 2016 and 2017) to initiate a variety of projects for the South Sudanese and tour the country as a donor to the United Nations' World Food Program (Kuria 2017).

Chapter 26. Patterns of Pretend

1. I addressed this broad issue in detail in *The Outcast Majority* (Sommers 2015). A review of key points concerning youth and development also are found in Sommers (2017). What follows is an updated and more focused examination.

2. Many of these issues are reviewed in part 2 of chapter 4 in Sommers (2015). The underlying meanings of youth and gender for practitioners also is discussed in chapter 1 (also in Sommers 2015) and in Sommers (2019a).

3. The findings here draw directly from the discussion in Sommers (2015: 139–140).

4. The following reflects the strong push that some governments employed in

their effort to secure universal primary education in their countries. One mother in Burundi shared the following about coercive state practices that pressure parents to send their young children to primary school: "The authorities tell us, 'Don't think that those children are yours. Your children belong to the state. Yes, you gave birth to them. So in some way, they are your children. But now that they are old enough to attend school, they don't belong to you anymore. You must send them to school'" (Sommers 2013: 21).

5. It has been established that inequality and poverty are linked, and that "higher income inequality is associated with higher rates of poverty." Moreover, "increases in income inequality are associated with increases in poverty" (McKnight 2019: 1).

6. There have been other indications that foreign aid can inspire governments to reduce investments in particular sectors. For example, research has found that "in sub-Saharan Africa, where many governments receive significant health aid directly from developed countries, international organizations and global health initiatives, aid appears in part to be replacing domestic public health spending instead of supplementing it fully. For every health aid dollar spent, governments moved from 43 cents to $1.14 from their health budget to other priorities" (Morton 2010). This information is drawn from Lu et al. (2010).

7. Out of 189 nations, UNDP's 2019 Human Development Index ranking listed Niger as having the lowest level of human development (189th), closely followed by Chad (187th), Mali (184th), and Burkina Faso (182nd). Two other Sahelian states fared slightly better: Mauritania (at 161st) and oil-rich Nigeria (159th). Sierra Leone slots in at 181st (UNDP 2019: 302–303).

8. Moody notes, "While there are numerous . . . militant groups operating in the Sahel, the two primary perpetrators of attacks over the past few years have been the Islamic State (IS)–affiliated Islamic State in the Greater Sahara (ISGS) and the Al Qaeda–affiliated Jama'at Nasr al-Islam wal Muslimin (JNIM)" (2020).

9. Asser (2011) highlights a second irony, featuring the dictator's *Green Book*, which held so much influence on Sierra Leonean revolutionaries exposed to it. To Asser, it was little more than "a series of fatuous diatribes." He also found it "bitterly ironic that a text whose professed objective is to break the shackles imposed by the vested interests dominating political systems was used instead to subjugate an entire population" under Gaddhafi's rule in Libya.

10. Other names for the Fulani are Fula, Fulbe, Peul, and Fallata.

Chapter 27. Toward Foundational Change

1. The guidance in this chapter complements the detailed framework provided at the end of *The Outcast Majority* (Sommers 2015). That framework features sixteen elements for reforming institutional action, with particular focus on excluded youth, and a six-step process for reforming development work at the country level.

REFERENCES

Abdullah, Ibrahim. 1998. "Bush Path to Destruction: The Origin and Character of the Revolutionary United Front/Sierra Leone." *Journal of Modern African Studies* 36(2): 203–235.

———. 2002. "Youth Culture and Rebellion: Understanding Sierra Leone's Wasted Decade." *Critical Arts: South-North Cultural and Media Studies* 16(2): 19–37.

———. 2004. "Bush Path to Destruction: The Origin and Character of the Revolutionary United Front (RUF/SL)." In *Between Democracy and Terror: The Sierra Leone Civil War*, Ibrahim Abdullah, ed. Dakar: Council for the Development of Social Science Research in Africa.

———. 2013. "History and Memory in Contemporary Sierra Leone: Reinscribing Fragments from an Atlantic Past." In *Paradoxes of History and Memory in Post-Colonial Sierra Leone*, Sylvia Ojukutu-Macauley and Ismail Rashid, eds. Lanham, Md.: Lexington Books.

Abdullah, Ibrahim, and Patrick Muana. 1998. "The Revolutionary United Front of Sierra Leone: A Revolt of the Lumpenproletariat." In *African Guerillas*, Christopher Clapham, ed. Bloomington: Indiana University Press.

Abdullah, Ibrahim, and Ismail Rashid. 2004. "'Smallest Victims, Youngest Killers': Juvenile Combatants in Sierra Leone's Civil War." In *Between Democracy and Terror: The Sierra Leone Civil War*, Ibrahim Abdullah, ed. Dakar: Council for the Development of Social Science Research in Africa.

Abraham, Arthur. 2004. "The Elusive Quest for Peace: From Abidjan to Lomé." In *Between Democracy and Terror: The Sierra Leone Civil War*, Ibrahim Abdullah, ed. Dakar: Council for the Development of Social Science Research in Africa.

Acemoglu, Daron, Tristan Reed, and James A. Robinson. 2014. "Chiefs: Economic Development and Elite Control of Civil Society in Sierra Leone." *Journal of Political Economy* 122(2): 319–368.

Adeba, Brian, and the Enough Project Team. 2019. *A Hijacked State: Violent Kleptocracy in South Sudan*. Washington, D.C.: Enough Project. https://enoughproject.org/wp-content/uploads/AHijackedState_Enough_February2019-web.pdf.

Africa Confidential. 1999. "West Africa According to Mr. Taylor." *Africa Confidential* 40(2): 2.

Agence France Presse (English). 1999. "Sierra Leone Peace Agreement Signed." *Agence Press France* (July 7, Lomé).

Ahearn, Laura M. 2010. "Agency and Language." In *Society and Language Use*, Jürgen Jaspers, Jan-Ola Östman, and Jef Verschueren, eds. Handbook of Pragmatics Highlights, vol. 7. Amsterdam: John Benjamins.

Alexiou, Joseph. 2011. "Explained! Why No One Knows How the Hell to Spell Qaddafi/Gadhafi/Gaddafi/Qadhafi." *Business Insider* (February 23). http://www.business insider.com/qaddafi-gaddafi-kadafi-qadaffi-libya-spelling-2011-2.

Alie, Joe A. D. 1990. *A New History of Sierra Leone*. London: Macmillan.

———. 2005. "The Kamajor Militia in Sierra Leone: Liberators or Nihilists?" In *Civil Militia: Africa's Intractable Security Menace?*, David K. Francis, ed. Aldershot, U.K.: Ashgate.

———. 2006. "Background to the Conflict (1961–1991): What Went Wrong and Why?" In *Bound to Cooperate: Conflict, Peace, and People in Sierra Leone*, Anatole Ayissi and Robin Edward Poulton, eds. Geneva: United Nations Institute for Disarmament Research.

American Society of Hematology. n.d. "Sickle Cell Disease." Accessed October 26, 2018, at http://www.hematology.org/Patients/Anemia/Sickle-Cell.aspx.

Amnesty International. 2000. *Sierra Leone: Childhood, a Casualty of Conflict*. Amnesty International (August 30), no. AFR 51/069/2000. https://www.amnesty.org/download/Documents/132000/afr510692000en.pdf.

———. 2006. *Sierra Leone: Women Face Human Rights Abuses in the Informal Legal Sector*. Amnesty International (May 17), No. AFR 51/002/2006. https://www.amnesty.org/download/Documents/68000/afr510022006en.pdf.

Anderson, Benedict. 1991. *Imagined Communities: Reflections on the Origin and Spread of Nationalism*. 1983; rev. ed. London: Verso.

Aning, Emmanuel Kwesi, and Angela McIntyre. 2005. "From Youth Rebellion to Child Abduction: The Anatomy of Recruitment in Sierra Leone." In *Invisible Stakeholders: Children and War in Africa*, Angela McIntyre, ed. Pretoria: Institute for Security Studies.

Appiah-Nyamekye Sanny, Josephine, Carolyn Logan, and E. Gyimah-Boadi. 2019. *In Search of Opportunity: Young and Educated Africans Most Likely to Consider Moving Abroad*. Afrobarometer Dispatch no. 288 (March 26). http://afrobarometer.org/sites/default/files/publications/Dispatches/ab_r7_dispatchno288_looking_for_opportunity_africans_views_on_emigration1.pdf.

Archibald, Steven, and Paul Richards. 2002. "Converts to Human Rights? Popular Debate about War and Justice in Rural Central Sierra Leone." *Africa* 72(3): 339–367.

Asser, Martin. 2011. "The Muammar Gaddafi Story." BBC News (October 21). https://www.bbc.com/news/world-africa-12688033.

Attwood, Charlotte. 2017. "Is Ex-Warlord Charles Taylor Pulling Liberia's Election Strings from Prison?" BBC News (October 6). https://www.bbc.com/news/uk-41509896.

Autesserre, Séverine. 2014. *Peaceland: Conflict Resolution and the Everyday Politics of International Intervention*. New York: Cambridge University Press.

———. 2021. *The Frontlines of Peace: An Insider's Guide to Changing the World*. Oxford: Oxford University Press.

Baldi, Giulia, and Megan MacKenzie. 2007. "Silent Identities: Children Born of War in Sierra Leone." In *Born of War: Protecting Children of Sexual Violence Survivors in Conflict Zones*, R. Charli Carpenter, ed. Bloomfield, Conn.: Kumarian.

Bangura, Joseph. 2009. "Understanding Sierra Leone in Colonial West Africa: A Synoptic Socio-Political History." *History Compass* 7(3): 583–603.

Bangura, Yusuf. 1997. "Reflections on the Sierra Leone Peace Accord." *African Journal of International Affairs* 1(1): 57–78.

———. 2004. "The Political and Cultural Dynamics of the Sierra Leone War: A Critique of Paul Richards." In *Between Democracy and Terror: The Sierra Leone Civil*

War, Ibrahim Abdullah, ed. Dakar: Council for the Development of Social Science Research in Africa.

Barker, Gary, and Christine Ricardo. 2006. "Young Men and the Construction of Masculinity in Sub-Saharan Africa: Implications for HIV/AIDS, Conflict, and Violence." In *The Other Half of Gender: Men's Issues in Development*, Ian Bannon and Maria C. Correia, eds. Washington, D.C.: World Bank.

Bassey, Celestine Oyom. 2003. "The Nature and Character of Civil Wars in West Africa in the 1990s." In *Civil Wars, Child Soldiers and Post Conflict Peace-Building in West Africa*, Amadu Sesay, ed. Ibadan: College Press & Publishers Limited.

Bazzi, Mohamad. 2011. "Essay: What Did Qaddafi's Green Book Really Say?" Sunday Book Review, *New York Times* (May 27). http://www.nytimes.com/2011/05/29 /books/review/what-did-qaddafis-green-book-really-say.html?pagewanted=all &_r=1&.

BBC News. 1999. "World: Africa: Joy at Sierra Leone Peace." BBC News (July 7). http://news.bbc.co.uk/2/hi/africa/388631.stm.

———. 2000. "Who Are the West Side Boys?" BBC News (August 31). http://news .bbc.co.uk/2/hi/africa/901209.stm.

Beah, Ishmael. 2007. *A Long Way Gone: Memoirs of a Boy Soldier*. New York: Farrar, Straus & Giroux.

Bekoe, Dorina A., Stephanie M. Burchard, Sarah A. Daly, and Austin C. Swift. 2020. *Interpreting Group Tactics and the Role of the Government's Response in the Crisis in Cabo Delgado: Lessons for Combatting Violent Extremism in Africa*. Alexandria, Va.: Institute for Defense Analyses. https://www.ida.org/research-and -publications/publications/all/i/in/interpreting-group-tactics-and-the-role-of -the-governments-response-in-the-crisis-in-cabo-delgado.

Bermúdez-Lugo, Omayra. 2010. *2008 Minerals Yearbook: Sierra Leone*. U.S. Department of the Interior and U.S Geological Survey. https://s3-us-west-2.amazonaws .com/prd-wret/assets/palladium/production/mineral-pubs/country/2008/myb3 -2008-sl.pdf.

Betancourt, Theresa S., Ivelina I. Borisova, Marie de la Soudière, and John Williamson. 2011. "Sierra Leone's Child Soldiers: War Exposures and Mental Health Problems by Gender." *Journal of Adolescent Health* 49(1): 21–28.

Boal, Amy. n.d. "All The Names Sean Combs Has Used Over the Years." Ranker. Accessed September 30, 2018, at https://www.ranker.com/list/sean-combs-names /amylindorff.

Bøås, Morten. 2007. "Marginalized Youth." In *African Guerrillas: Raging against the Machine*, Morten Bøås and Kevin C. Dunn, eds. Boulder, Colo.: Lynne Rienner.

Bøås, Morten, and Anne Hatløy. 2005. *Alcohol and Drug Consumption in Post War Sierra Leonean Exploration*. Oslo: Fafo (Report 496). https://www.fafo.no/media /com_netsukii/496.pdf.

———. 2006. *"Living in a Material World": Children and Youth in Alluvial Diamond Mining in Kono District, Sierra Leone*. Oslo: Fafo (Report 515).

Bolten, Catherine. 2009. "The Agricultural Impasse: Creating 'Normal' Post-War Development in Northern Sierra Leone." *Journal of Political Ecology* (16): 70–86.

———. 2012. *I Did It to Save My Life: Love and Survival in Sierra Leone*. Berkeley: University of California Press.

Bourke, Joanna. 2007. *Rape: Sex, Violence, History.* [Emeryville, Calif.]: Shoemaker & Hoard.

Brackett, Krisi. 2015. "Cyproheptadine (or Periactin) to Boost Appetite." Pediatric Feeding News (May 16). http://pediatricfeedingnews.com/cyproheptidine-or -periactin-to-boost-appetite/.

Broadbent, Emma. 2012. *Research-Based Evidence in Africa Policy Debates: Case Study 4: Chieftaincy Reform in Sierra Leone.* Overseas Development Institute (June). https://www.odi.org/sites/odi.org.uk/files/odi-assets/publications -opinion-files/9120.pdf.

Bundervoet, Tom. 2009. "Livestock, Land and Political Power: The 1993 Killings in Burundi." *Journal of Peace Research* 46(3): 357–376.

Burgis, Tom. 2015. *The Looting Machine: Warlords, Oligarchs, Corporations, Smugglers, and the Theft of Africa's Wealth.* New York: Public Affairs.

Bussard, Robert L. 1987. "The 'Dangerous Class' of Marx and Engels: The Rise of the Idea of the Lumpenproletariat." *History of European Ideas* 8(6): 675–692.

Cain, Kenneth L. 1999. "The Rape of Dinah: Human Rights, Civil War in Liberia, and Evil Triumphant." *Human Rights Quarterly* 21(2): 265–307.

Cambridge English Dictionary. n.d. "Alienation." Accessed July 18, 2019, at https:// dictionary.cambridge.org/dictionary/english/alienation.

Campbell, Greg. 2004. *Blood Diamonds: Tracing the Deadly Path of the World's Most Precious Stones.* New York: Basic Books.

———. 2012. "The Rock-Mining Children of Sierra Leone Have Not Found Peace." *Atlantic* (May 31). https://www.theatlantic.com/international/archive/2012/05/the -rock-mining-children-of-sierra-leone-have-not-found-peace/257899/.

Carey, Martha. 2006. "'Survival Is Political': History, Violence, and the Contemporary Power Struggle in Sierra Leone." In *States of Violence: Politics, Youth, and Memory in Contemporary Africa*, Edna G. Bay and Donald L. Donham, eds. Charlottesville: University of Virginia Press.

Cartier, Laurent E., and Michael Bürge. 2011. "Agriculture and Artisanal Gold Mining in Sierra Leone: Alternatives or Complements?" *Journal of International Development* 23: 1080–1099.

Carvajal, Doreen. 2010. "Accused of War Crimes, and Living with Perks." *International Herald Tribune*, June 4: 1, 3.

Casey, Katherine, Rachel Glennerster, and Edward Miguel. 2012. *Healing the Wounds: Learning from Sierra Leone's Post-War Institutional Reforms.* Cambridge, Mass.: National Bureau of Economic Research. NBER Working Paper No. 18368. https:// www.nber.org/papers/w18368.

Castañeda, Carla. 2009. "How Liberal Peacebuilding May Be Failing Sierra Leone." *Review of African Political Economy* 36(120): 235–251.

Castells, Manuel. 2021. "From Cities to Networks: Power Rules." *Journal of Classical Sociology* 21(3–4): 260–262.

Central Intelligence Agency. n.d. "Country Comparison: Median Age." *World Factbook.* Accessed December 14, 2020, at https://www.cia.gov/library/publications /the-world-factbook/rankorder/2177rank.html.

Chayes, Sarah. 2015. *Thieves of State: Why Corruption Threatens Global Security.* New York: W. W. Norton.

Chipika, Stephen. 2012. *Review of the Sierra Leone National Youth Policy* (First Draft,

November 20). Freetown: Integrated Projects Administration Unit/Youth Employment Support Project, Ministry of Finance and Economic Development, in collaboration with the Ministry of Youth Employment and Sports, National Youth Commission, and the World Bank. http://www.nationalyouthcommission.sl/pdf %20files/Sierra%20Leone%20National%20Youth%20Policy%20First%20Draft%20 20%20November%202012.pdf.

Chivers, C. J. 2010. *The Gun.* New York: Simon & Schuster.

Christensen, Maya Mynster. 2012. "Big Man Business in the Borderland of Sierra Leone." In *African Conflicts and Informal Power: Big Men and Networks,* Mats Utas, ed. London: Zed Books. Published in association with the Nordic Africa Institute, Uppsala.

Cohen, Dara Kay. 2013a. "Female Combatants and the Perpetration of Violence: Wartime Rape in the Sierra Leone Civil War." *World Politics* 65(3) (July): 383–415.

———. 2013b. "Explaining Rape during Civil War: Cross-National Evidence (1980–2009)." *American Political Science Review* 107(3) (August): 461–477.

Coker, Cheo Hodari. 1996. "Makaveli: The 2 Sides of Tupac." *Los Angeles Times* (November 3). https://www.latimes.com/archives/la-xpm-1996-11-03-ca-60628 story.html.

Coll, Steve. 2000. "The Other War." *Washington Post* (January 9). https://www .washingtonpost.com/wp-srv/WPcap/2000-01/09/097r-010900-idx.html.

Concord Times (Freetown). 2001. "Sierra Leone: Superman Disappears from Makeni" (February 28). https://allafrica.com/stories/200102280360.html.

Conrad, Joseph. 1902. "Heart of Darkness." In *Youth: A Narrative, and Two Other Stories.* Edinburgh: William Blackwood & Sons.

Conteh-Morgan, Earl, and Mac Dixon-Fyle. 1999. *Sierra Leone at the End of the Twentieth Century: History, Politics, and Society.* New York: Peter Lang.

Cosentino, Donald. 2005. "Muso Wo: Precognition of Civil Violence in Mende Oral Narrative Tradition." In *Representations about Violence: Art about the Sierra Leone Civil War,* Patrick K. Muana and Chris Corcoran, eds. Madison, Wisc.: 21st Century African Youth Movement.

Coulter, Chris. 2009. *Bush Wives and Girl Soldiers: Women's Lives through War and Peace in Sierra Leone.* Ithaca, N.Y.: Cornell University Press.

Counter Extremism Project. n.d. "Côte d'Ivoire: Extremism and Counter-Extremism." Accessed December 14, 2020, at https://www.counterextremism.com/countries /cote-d-ivoire.

Cubitt, Christine. 2013. "Responsible Reconstruction after War: Meeting Local Needs for Building Peace." *Review of International Studies* 39(1): 91–112.

Darden, Jessica Trisko. 2020. *Aiding and Abetting: U.S. Foreign Assistance and State Violence.* Stanford, Calif.: Stanford University Press.

Davey, Monica. 2005. "Fighting Words." *New York Times* (February 20). https://www .nytimes.com/2005/02/20/arts/music/fighting-words.html.

Denney, Lisa, and Aisha Fofana Ibrahim. 2012. *Violence against Women in Sierra Leone: How Women Seek Redress.* Politics and Governance Programme (December). London: Overseas Development Institute. https://www.odi.org/sites/odi.org.uk /files/odi-assets/publications-opinion-files/8175.pdf.

Denov, Myriam. 2010. *Child Soldiers: Sierra Leone's Revolutionary United Front.* Cambridge: Cambridge University Press.

Denov, Myriam, and Richard Maclure. 2009. "Girls and Small Arms in Sierra Leone: Victimization, Participation and Resistance." In *Sexed Pistols: The Gendered Impacts of Small Arms and Light Weapons,* Vanessa Farr, Henri Myrttinen, and Albrecht Schnabel, eds. Tokyo: United Nations University Press.

de Torrente, Nicolas. 1999. "Rebels Bounce Back." *World Today* (February).

de Waal, Alex. 2009. "Mission without End? Peacekeeping in the African Political Marketplace." *International Affairs* 85(1): 99–113.

———. 2015. *The Real Politics of the Horn of Africa: Money, War and the Business of Power.* Cambridge: Polity Press.

Dictionary.com. n.d. "Alienation." Accessed July 18, 2019, at https://www.dictionary.com/browse/alienation.

———. n.d. "Bitch." Accessed October 26, 2018, at https://www.dictionary.com/browse/bitch.

Dimitriadis, Gregory. 2001. *Performing Identity/Performing Culture: Hip Hop as Text, Pedagogy, and Lived Practice.* New York: Peter Lang.

Doyle, Mark. 2009. "Charles Taylor—Preacher, Warlord, President." BBC News. http://news.bbc.co.uk/2/hi/2963086.stm.

Dumbuya, Peter A. 2008. *Reinventing the Colonial State: Constitutionalism, One-Party Rule, and Civil War in Sierra Leone.* Lincoln, Nebr.: iUniverse.

Dyson, Michael Eric. 2001. *Holler If You Hear Me: Searching for Tupac Shakur.* New York: Basic Books.

———. 2020. "Foreword: 2Pac's Legacy from the Hip-Hop Platform." *Sociology of Sport Journal* 37: 165.

Easterly, William. 2013. *The Tyranny of Experts: Economists, Dictators, and the Forgotten Rights of the Poor.* New York: Basic Books.

Edmonds, Ennis Barrington. 2003. *Rastafari: From Outcasts to Culture Bearers.* Oxford: Oxford University Press.

Eguavoen, Irit. 2010. "Lawbreakers and Livelihood Makers: Youth-Specific Poverty and Ambiguous Livelihood Strategies in Africa." *Vulnerable Children and Youth Studies* 5(3): 268–273.

Eljarh, Mohamed. 2016. *Security Challenges and Issues in the Sahelo-Saharan Region: The Libya Perspective.* Dialogues: Sécuritaires dans l'espace sahélo-saharien. Bamako: Friedrich-Ebert-Stiftung. https://www.fes-pscc.org/fileadmin/user_upload/documents/publications/New_Country_Study_Chad.pdf.

Ellis, Stephen. 2006. *The Mask of Anarchy: The Destruction of Liberia and the Religious Dimension of an African War.* 2nd ed. New York: New York University Press.

———. 2011. *Season of Rains: Africa in the World.* Chicago: University of Chicago Press.

Epstein, Helen C. 2017. *Another Fine Mess: America, Uganda, and the War on Terror.* New York: Columbia Global Reports.

Escritt, Thomas. 2013. "Liberia's Charles Taylor Loses Appeal against War Crimes Conviction." Reuters (U.S. Edition) (September 26). http://www.reuters.com/article/2013/09/26/us-warcrimes-taylor-appeal-idUSBRE98P0DP20130926.

Fanthorpe, Richard. 2005. "On the Limits of Liberal Peace: Chiefs and Democratic Decentralization in Post-War Sierra Leone." *African Affairs* 105(418): 27–49.

Fanthorpe, Richard, and Roy Maconachie. 2010. "Beyond the 'Crisis of Youth'?

Mining, Farming, and Civil Society in Post-War Sierra Leone." *African Affairs* 109(435): 251–272.

Farah, Douglas. 2003. "Foday Sankoh Dies." *Washington Post* (July 31). https://www.washingtonpost.com/archive/local/2003/07/31/foday-sankoh-dies/6e4d2d41d756-412e-92f3-f802f9b6a91a/?utm_term=.ac0afa5af278.

Farr, Jason. 2005. "Point: The Westphalia Legacy and the Modern Nation-State." *International Social Science Review* 80(3/4): 156–159.

Fellman, Gordon. 1998. *Rambo and the Dalai Lama: The Compulsion to Win and Its Threat to Human Survival.* Albany: State University of New York Press.

Ferme, Mariane C. 2001. *The Underneath of Things: Violence, History, and the Everyday in Sierra Leone.* Berkeley: University of California Press.

Ferme, Mariane C., and Danny Hoffman. 2004. "Hunter Militias and the International Human Rights Discourse in Sierra Leone and Beyond." *Africa Today* 50(4): 73–95.

Fiedler, Leslie A. 1990. "Mythicizing the Unspeakable." *Journal of American Folklore* 103(410): 390–399.

50 Cent. 2011. "Tupac Shakur." In "100 Greatest Artists" (No. 86), *Rolling Stone.* https://www.rollingstone.com/music/music-lists/100-greatest-artists-147446/nine-inch-nails-6-81385/.

Finn, Brandon, and Sophie Oldfield. 2015. "Straining: Young Men Working through Waithood in Freetown, Sierra Leone." *Africa Spectrum* 50(3): 29–48.

Finnegan, William. 1992. *A Complicated War: The Harrowing of Mozambique.* Berkeley: University of California Press.

Fofana, Lansana. 1995. "Sierra Leone-Politics: Bob Marley Joins the War." Inter Press Service News Agency (June 6). http://www.ipsnews.net/1995/06/sierra-leone-politics-bob-marley-joins-the-war/.

———. 1998a. "Sierra Leone: Rap Star's T-shirt a Major Factor in Conflict." Inter Press Service News Agency (October 1). http://www.ipsnews.net/1998/10/sierra-leone-rap-stars-t-shirt-a-major-factor-in-conflict/.

———. 1998b. "Music-Sierra Leone: Taming Rastafarians." Inter Press Service News Agency (October 6). http://www.ipsnews.net/1998/10/music-sierra-leone-taming-rastafarians/.

Fortna, Virginia Page. 2015. "Do Terrorists Win? Rebels' Use of Terrorism and Civil War Outcomes." *International Organization* 69(3): 519–556.

Freedom House. 2021. "Freedom in the World 2021: Sierra Leone." https://freedomhouse.org/country/sierra-leone/freedom-world/2021.

Freemantle, Simon. 2011. *Africa Macro: Insight and Strategy: The Five Trends Powering Africa's Enduring Allure: Trend 1: A Larger, Younger and More Affluent Population.* http://www.standardbank.com/Resources/Downloads/Africa%20Macro_5%20trends%20powering%20Africa%27s%20allure%20%28trend%201-Demographics%29.pdf.

Fyfe, Christopher. 1962. *A History of Sierra Leone.* London: Oxford University Press.

Gaddhafi, Mu'ammar. 1976. *The Green Book. Part One: The Solution of the Problem of Democracy: "The Authority of the People."* London: Martin Brian & O'Keeffe.

Gberie, Lansana. 2005. *A Dirty War in West Africa: The RUF and the Destruction of Sierra Leone.* Bloomington: Indiana University Press.

———. 2009. "Rescuing a Fragile State: The Case of Sierra Leone." In *Rescuing a Frag-*

ile State: Sierra Leone 2002–2008, Lansana Gberie, ed. Waterloo, Ont.: LCMSDS Press of Wilfrid Laurier University.

Georgetown Institute for Women, Peace and Security (GIWPS) and Peace Research Institute Oslo (PRIO). 2019. *Women, Peace and Security Index 2019/20: Tracking Sustainable Peace through Inclusion, Justice, and Security for Women.* Washington, D.C.: GIWPS and PRIO.

Gersony, Robert. 1988. *Summary of Mozambican Refugee Accounts of Principally Conflict-Related Experience in Mozambique.* Bureau for Refugee Programs, Department of State.

Gettleman, Jeffrey. 2007. "Rape Epidemic Raises Trauma of Congo War." *New York Times* (October 7). www.nytimes.com/2007/10/07/world/africa/07congo.html.

Gilroy, Paul. 2005. "Could You Be Loved? Bob Marley, Anti-Politics and Universal Sufferation." *Critical Quarterly* 47 (1–2): 226–245.

Giridharadas, Anand. 2018. *Winners Take All: The Elite Charade of Changing the World.* New York: Alfred A. Knopf.

Goldman, Lea, and David M. Ewalt, eds. 2007. "Special Report: Top-Earning Dead Celebrities." *Forbes* (October 29). http://www.forbes.com/2007/10/29/dead -celebrity-earning-biz-media-deadcelebs07_cz_lg_1029celeb_land.html.

Goldman, Lea, and Jake Paine. 2007a. "Celebrities: Top-Earning Dead Celebrities." *Forbes* (October 29). http://www.forbes.com/2007/10/26/top-dead-celebrity-biz -media-deadcelebs07-cz_lg_1029celeb.html.

———. 2007b. "In Pictures: Top-Earning Dead Celebrities: Bob Marley." *Forbes* (October 29). http://www.forbes.com/2007/10/26/top-dead-celebrity-biz-media -deadcelebs07-cz_lg_1029celeb_slide_13.html.

Gordon, Olu. 2006. "Sumanguru's War Cry: A Commentary." Patriotic Vanguard (June 11). http://thepatrioticvanguard.com/sumanguru-s-war-cry-a-commentary.

Green, Duncan. 2012. *From Poverty to Power: How Active Citizens and Effective States Can Change the World.* Bourton-on-Dunsmore, U.K.: Practical Action Publishing / Oxford: Oxfam GB.

Green, Elliott D. 2012. "Demographic Change and Conflict in Contemporary Africa." In *Political Demography: How Population Changes Are Reshaping International Security and National Politics*, Jack A. Goldstone, Eric P. Kaufmann, and Monica Duffy Toft, eds. Boulder, Colo.: Paradigm.

Greenburg, Zack O'Malley. 2015. "The 13 Top-Earning Dead Celebrities of 2015." *Forbes* (October 27). https://www.forbes.com/sites/zackomalleygreenburg/2015 /10/27/the-13-top-earning-dead-celebrities-of-2015/#159c921e59f7.

———. 2016. "Michael Jackson's Earnings: $825 Million in 2016." *Forbes* (October 14). https://www.forbes.com/sites/zackomalleygreenburg/2016/10/14/michael -jacksons-earnings-825-million-in-2016/#f32e2913d720 and https://www.forbes .com/pictures/57e4376b4bbe6f24d1f87cf/6-bob-marley-21-million/#6f2225de22b6.

———. 2017. "The Top-Earning Dead Celebrities of 2017." *Forbes* (October 30). https://www.forbes.com/sites/zackomalleygreenburg/2017/10/30/the-top-earning -dead-celebrities-of-2017/#6a23e98141f5.

———. 2019. "The Top-Earning Dead Celebrities of 2019." *Forbes* (October 30). https://www.forbes.com/sites/zackomalleygreenburg/2019/10/30/the-top-earning -dead-celebrities-of—2019/#7537d26d4e5e.

Greenburg, Zack O'Malley, and Natalie Robehmed. 2018. "The Highest-Paid Dead Celebrities of 2018." *Forbes* (October 31). https://www.forbes.com/sites /zackomalleygreenburg/2018/10/31/the-highest-paid-dead-celebrities-of-2018 /#1545b41b720c.

Grimes, Katie. 2014. "But Do the Lord Care? Tupac Shakur as Theologian of the Crucified People." *Political Theology* 15(4): 326–352.

Guberek, Tamy, Daniel Guzmán, Romesh Silva, Kristen Cibelli, Jana Asher, Scott Weikart, Patrick Ball, and Wendy M. Grossman. 2006. *Truth and Myth in Sierra Leone: An Empirical Analysis of the Conflict, 1991–2000.* Benetech Human Rights Data Analysis Group and the American Bar Association. https://hrdag.org/wp -content/uploads/2013/01/Benetech-Truth-Myth-Sierra-Leone-1991-2000.pdf.

Hagerman, Brent. 2012. "Everywhere Is War: Peace and Violence in the Life and Songs of Bob Marley." *Journal of Religion and Popular Culture* 24(3): 380–392.

Hansen, Art, Julie Nenon, Joy Wolf, and Marc Sommers. 2002. *Final Evaluation of the Office of Transition Initiatives' Program in Sierra Leone.* Washington, D.C.: Basic Education and Policy Support (BEPS) Activity, Creative Associates International. http://www.beps.net/publications/FINAL%20EVALUATION%20OF%20 OTI%20PROGRAM%20IN%20SIERRA%20LEONE.PDF.

Harris, David. 1999. "From 'Warlord' to 'Democratic' President: How Charles Taylor Won the 1997 Liberian Elections." *Journal of Modern African Studies* 37(3): 431–455.

Hennings, Anne. 2019. "From Bullets to Banners and Back Again? The Ambivalent Role of Ex-combatants in Contested Land Deals in Sierra Leone." *Africa Spectrum* 54(1): 22–43.

Higgins, Sean, and Mario Novelli. 2018. "The Potential and Pitfalls of Peace Education: A Cultural Political Economy Analysis of the Emerging Issues Teacher Education Curriculum in Sierra Leone." *Asian Journal of Peacebuilding* 6(1): 29–53.

Hodge, Daniel White. 2017. *Hip Hop's Hostile Gospel: A Post-Soul Theological Exploration.* Leiden, Netherlands: Brill.

Hoffman, Danny. 2005. "West-African Warscapes: Violent Events as Narrative Blocs: The Disarmament at Bo, Sierra Leone." *Anthropological Quarterly* 78(2): 328–353.

———. 2006. "Disagreement: Dissent Politics and the War in Sierra Leone." *Africa Today* 52(3): 3–22.

———. 2007. "The Meaning of a Militia: Understanding the Civil Defence Forces of Sierra Leone." *African Affairs* 106(425): 639–662.

———. 2011. *The War Machines: Young Men and Violence in Sierra Leone and Liberia.* Durham, N.C.: Duke University Press.

Honwana, Alcinda. 2006. *Child Soldiers in Africa.* Philadelphia: University of Pennsylvania Press.

———. 2012. *The Time of Youth: Work, Social Change, and Politics in Africa.* Sterling, Va.: Kumarian.

Howe, Herbert. 2001. *Ambiguous Order: Military Forces in African States.* Boulder, Colo.: Lynne Rienner.

Human Rights Watch (HRW). 1998a. *Proxy Targets: Civilians in the War in Burundi.* New York: Human Rights Watch. https://www.hrw.org/sites/default/files/reports /BURU983.PDF.

———. 1998b. *Sierra Leone: Sowing Terror: Atrocities against Civilians in Sierra Le-one.* Sierra Leone vol. 10, no. 3A. New York: Human Rights Watch. https://www .hrw.org/legacy/reports98/sierra/.

———. 1999. *Sierra Leone: Getting Away with Murder, Mutilation, Rape: New Tes-timony from Sierra Leone.* Sierra Leone vol. 11, no. 3A. New York: Human Rights Watch. https://www.hrw.org/legacy/reports/1999/sierra/.

———. 2003. *"We'll Kill You If You Cry": Sexual Violence in the Sierra Leone Conflict.* Sierra Leone vol. 15, no. 1A (January). New York: Human Rights Watch. https:// www.hrw.org/report/2003/01/16/well-kill-you-if-you-cry/sexual-violence-sierra -leone-conflict.

Hume, Cameron. 1994. *Ending Mozambique's War: The Role of Mediation and Good Offices.* Washington, D.C.: United States Institute of Peace Press.

Humphreys, Macartan, and Jeremy M. Weinstein. 2004. *What the Fighters Say: A Survey of Ex-Combatants in Sierra Leone, June–August 2003.* New York: Colum-bia University / Stanford, Calif.: Stanford University. In partnership with the Post-Conflict Reintegration Initiative for Development and Empowerment (PRIDE). Interim Report (July). http://www.columbia.edu/~mh2245/Report1_BW.pdf.

Huntington, Samuel P. 1996. *The Clash of Civilizations and the Remaking of the World Order.* New York: Simon & Schuster.

Ibrahim, Aisha Fofana. 2012. *The Integration of a Gender Perspective in the Sierra Le-one Police.* Geneva: Geneva Centre for the Democratic Control of Armed Forces (DCAF). https://www.dcaf.ch/sites/default/files/publications/documents/Final _web_version_15.01.13.pdf.

Innes, Michael A. 2003. "Scorched Ether: Radio Broadcasting in the Liberian Civil War." Paper presented to the Montreal Institute for Genocide and Human Rights Studies, Concordia University, Montreal, February 14, 2003.

Institute for Economics and Peace. 2022. *Global Terrorism Index 2022: Measuring the Impact of Terrorism.* Sydney: Institute for Economics and Peace (March). https:// reliefweb.int/report/world/global-terrorism-index-2022.

International Crisis Group. 2002. "Liberia: The Key to Ending Regional Instability." Africa Report no. 43, Freetown/Brussels.

———. 2017. *The Social Roots of Jihadist Violence in Burkina Faso's North.* Africa Re-port no. 254 (October 12). Translated from French. Brussels: International Crisis Group. ahttps://www.crisisgroup.org/africa/west-africa/burkina-faso/254-social -roots-jihadist-violence-burkina-fasos-north.

IRIN. 2007. "DRC: Behind the violence in South Kivu." www.irinnews.org/Report .aspx?ReportId=73567.

Iron, Colonel Richard. 2005. *Military Expert Witness Report on the Armed Forces Revolutionary Council.* Annex A of Prosecution Filing of Expert Report Pursuant to Rule 94(BIS), Prosecutor against Alex Tamba Brima, Brima Bazzy Kamara, and Santigie Borbor Kanu, Case No. SCSL—2004-16T, Special Court for Sierra Leone, Office of the Prosecutor, Freetown, Sierra Leone (August 5). http://www.rscsl.org /Documents/Decisions/AFRC/366/SCSL-04-16-T-368.pdf.

ISSAfrica. 2020. "ISS: Breaking Terrorism Supply Chains in West Africa." Defence Web (June 8). https://www.defenceweb.co.za/joint/diplomacy-a-peace/iss -breaking-terrorism-supply-chains-in-west-africa/.

Iwamoto, Derek. 2003. "Tupac Shakur: Understanding the Identity Formation of Hyper-Masculinity of a Popular Hip-Hop Artist." *Black Scholar* 33(2): 44–49.

Jackson, Michael. 2004. *In Sierra Leone.* Durham, N.C.: Duke University Press.

Jacobs, Steven. 2009. "Rebel Music from Trenchtown to Oaktown: The Lyrics of Bob Marley and Tupac Shakur as Counter-Hegemonic Culture." Master's thesis, University of Florida.

James, George. 1995. "Rapper Faces Prison Term for Sex Abuse." *New York Times* (February 8). https://www.nytimes.com/1995/02/08/nyregion/rapper-faces -prison-term-for-sex-abuse.html.

Jewett, Robert. 1987. "Zeal without Understanding: Reflections on Rambo and Oliver North." *Religion Online.* Originally published in *Christian Century* (September 9–16). https://www.religion-online.org/article/zeal-without-understanding -reflections-on-rambo-and-oliver-north/.

Johnson, Obediah. 2020. "Liberia: Charles Taylor Fears Losing Life in Prison Due to COVID-19; Request to Serve Remaining Term in a Safe Country Denied." *Front Page Africa* (September 10). https://frontpageafricaonline.com/news/liberia -charles-taylor-fears-losing-in-life-in-prison-due-to-covid-19-request-to-serve -remaining-term-in-a-safe-country-denied/.

Jordison, Sam. 2016. "Achilles Is Brutal, Vain, Pitiless—and a True Hero." *Guardian* (February 16). https://www.theguardian.com/books/booksblog/2016/feb/16 /achilles-homer-iliad-brutal-vain-pitiless-hero.

Joseph, Jamal. 2006. *Tupac Shakur: Legacy.* New York: Atria Books.

Junger, Sebastian. 2006. "The Terror of Sierra Leone." *Vanity Fair* (December 8). https://www.vanityfair.com/news/2000/08/junger200008.

Kaldor, Mary. 1999. *New and Old Wars: Organized Violence in a Global Era.* Stanford, Calif.: Stanford University Press.

Kalyvas, Stathis N. 2001. "'New' and 'Old' Civil Wars: A Valid Distinction?" *World Politics* 54(1): 99–118.

Kamara, Abdulai Mento. 2019. "Joseph Hill's Son to Stage Reggae Concert in Freetown, Sierra Leone." Sierra Express Media (February 1). http://sierraexpressmedia .com/?p=86799.

Kamara, Hawa. 2016. "Challenges Faced in the Implementation of the Gender Laws in Sierra Leone." Centre for Accountability and the Rule of Law (August 11). https://www.carl-sl.org/pres/challenges-faced-in-the-implementation-of-the -gender-laws-in-sierra-leone/.

Kamara, Saidu. 2005. "Sierra Leone: Paramount Chief Abandons Chiefdom in Search of Diamonds." *Standard Times* (Freetown) (April 6). https://allafrica.com/stories /200504060538.html.

Kandeh, Jimmy D. 1999. "Ransoming the State: Elite Origins of Subaltern Terror in Sierra Leone." *Review of African Political Economy* 26(81): 349–366.

———. 2004a. "In Search of Legitimacy: The 1996 Elections." In *Between Democracy and Terror: The Sierra Leone Civil War,* Ibrahim Abdullah, ed. Dakar: Council for the Development of Social Science Research in Africa.

———. 2004b. "Unmaking the Second Republic: Democracy on Trial." In *Between Democracy and Terror: The Sierra Leone Civil War,* Ibrahim Abdullah, ed. Dakar: Council for the Development of Social Science Research in Africa.

Kanu, Mohamed. 2010. "In Sierra Leone, Flaws in Child Rights Act May Delay Enactment by P'ment." *Awareness Times* (Freetown) October 25). http://www.awareness times.com/drwebsite/publish/article_200516606.html.

Kaplan, Robert D. 1994. "The Coming Anarchy: How Scarcity, Crime, Overpopulation, Tribalism, and Disease Are Rapidly Destroying the Social Fabric of Our Planet." *Atlantic Monthly* (February), 44–76.

———. 1996. *The Ends of the Earth: A Journey at the Dawn of the 21st Century*. New York: Random House.

———. 2000. "The Coming Anarchy: How Scarcity, Crime, Overpopulation, Tribalism, and Disease Are Destroying the Social Fabric of the Planet." In *The Coming Anarchy: Shattering the Dreams of the Post Cold War*. New York: Random House.

Keen, David. 2005. *Conflict and Collusion in Sierra Leone*. A project of the International Peace Academy with James Currey (Oxford) and Palgrave (New York).

Kellner, Douglass. 1995. *Media Culture: Cultural Studies, Identity and Politics between the Modern and the Postmodern*. London: Routledge.

Kelly, Jocelyn. 2010. *Rape in War: Motives of Militia in DRC*. United States Institute of Peace Special Report no. 243 (June).

Kline, A. S. (translation of Homer). 2009. "BkI:1–21 Invocation and Introduction." *Homer: The Iliad*. Poetry in Translation. https://www.poetryintranslation.com /PITBR/Greek/Iliad1.php.

Koroma, Abdul K. 1996. *Sierra Leone: The Agony of a Nation*. Freetown: Andromeda.

Kron, Josh. 2009. "Burundi: Official End to a Civil War." *New York Times* (April 22). https://www.nytimes.com/2009/04/23/world/africa/23briefs-burundi.html.

Kuria, Magdaline. 2017. "'I Want to Be More but as a Person,' 50Cent Visits South Sudan." KISS FM (June 15). https://kiss100.co.ke/155055-2/.

Lawson, Max, Man-Kwun Chan, Francesca Rhodes, Anam Parvez Butt, Anna Marriott, Ellen Ehmke, Didier Jacobs, Julie Seghers, Jaime Atienza, and Rebecca Gowland. 2019. *Public Good or Private Wealth?* Oxford: Oxfam GB (for Oxfam International). Oxfam Briefing Paper (January). https://www.oxfamamerica.org/static /media/files/bp-public-good-or-private-wealth-210119-en.pdf.

Lazareva, Inna. 2018. "Lack of Hope in South Sudan Camps Drives Youth into Gang Crime." Reuters (June 4). https://www.reuters.com/article/us-southsudan-youth -crime/lack-of-hope-in-south-sudan-camps-drives-youth-into-gang-crime -idUSKCN1JooIL.

Lee, Grace. 2003. "The Political Philosophy of Juche." *Stanford Journal of East Asian Affairs* 3(Summer): 105–112.

LeVine, Mark. 2008. *Heavy Metal Islam: Rock, Resistance, and the Struggle for the Soul of Islam*. New York: Crown.

Levithan, Josh. 2013. *Roman Siege Warfare*. Ann Arbor: University of Michigan Press.

Lexico. n.d. "Motherfucker." Accessed March 6, 2021, at https://www.lexico.com/en /definition/motherfucker.

Liah, Kim Jial. 2011. *Disarmament, Demobilization and Reintegration (DDR) in Post Conflict South Sudan: A Study of Challenges Facing Reintegration of Ex-Combatants (XCs) in Selected Areas of South Sudan*. Master's thesis, Faculty of Education and International Studies, Oslo University College. https://oda-hioa .archive.knowledgearc.net/bitstream/handle/10642/2753/Liah.pdf?sequence =2&isAllowed=y.

Little, Kenneth. 1967. *The Mende of Sierra Leone: A West African People in Transition*. Revised ed. London: Routledge & Kegan Paul.

Lock, Katrin. 2007. "Violence in Cultural Contexts: Film and Hip Hop Music: The Sound of Gangster Rap Echoing in the Purse of Reebok and in the Deep Forests of Sierra Leone." Conference paper presented at War as in Peace: Youth Violence—A Challenge for International Co-operation (November 14–16), Loccum, Germany.

Lopes Cardozo, T. A. Mieke, Sean Higgins, and Marielle L. J. Le Mat. 2016. *Youth Agency and Peacebuilding: An Analysis of the Role of Formal and Non-Formal Education: Synthesis Report on Findings from Myanmar, Pakistan, South Africa and Uganda*. Amsterdam: Research Consortium Education and Peacebuilding, University of Amsterdam. https://educationanddevelopment.files.wordpress.com /2016/06/youth-agency-synthesis-report-final16.pdf.

Los Angeles Times. 1990. "By the Numbers: 12 Movie Superlatives." April 9. http:// articles.latimes.com/1990-04-09/entertainment/ca-691_1_violent-movie.

Lu, Chunling, Matthew T. Schneider, Paul Gubbins, Katherine Leach-Kemon, Dean Jamison, and Christopher J. L. Murray. 2010. "Public Financing of Health in Developing Countries: A Cross-National Systematic Analysis." *Lancet* 375(9723): 1375–1387.

Lynskey, Dorian. 2011. "Tupac and Biggie Die as a Result of East/West Coast Beef." *Guardian* (June 12). https://www.theguardian.com/music/2011/jun/13/tupac -biggie-deaths.

MacKenzie, Megan H. 2012. *Female Soldiers in Sierra Leone: Sex, Security, and Post-Conflict Development*. New York: New York University Press.

Maclean, Ruth. 2020. "When the Soldiers Meant to Protect You Instead Come to Kill You." *New York Times* (June 22). https://www.nytimes.com/2020/06/22/world /africa/burkina-faso-terrorism.html.

Maclure, Richard, and Myriam Denov. 2009. "Reconstruction versus Transformation: Post-War Education and the Struggle for Gender Equity in Sierra Leone." *International Journal of Educational Development* 29(6): 612–620.

Magubane, Zine. 2006. "Globalization and Gangster Rap: Hip Hop in the Post-Apartheid City." In *The Vinyl Ain't Final: Hip Hop and the Globalization of Black Popular Culture*, Dipannita Basu and Sidney J. Lemelle, eds. London: Pluto.

Manning, Patrick. 1990. *Slavery and African Life: Occidental, Oriental, and African Slave Trades*. Cambridge: Cambridge University Press.

Manning, Ryann Elizabeth. 2009. *The Landscape of Local Authority in Sierra Leone: How "Traditional" and "Modern" Justice Systems Interact*. Justice and Development Working Paper Series, vol. 1, no. 1. Washington, D.C.: World Bank. https:// openknowledge.worldbank.org/bitstream/handle/10986/18099/490760WP0 REVIS10Box338942B01PUBLIC1.pdf?sequence=1&isAllowed=y.

Marines. n.d. "MCRD Parris Island: Eastern Recruiting Region: 'We Make Marines.'" https://www.mcrdpi.marines.mil/Recruit-Training/.

Marks, Zoe. 2013. "Sexual Violence Inside Rebellion: Policies and Perspectives of the Revolutionary United Front of Sierra Leone." *Civil Wars* 15(3): 359–379.

Martin, Ellen, and Irina Mosel. 2011. *City Limits: Urbanisation and Vulnerability in Sudan: Juba Case Study*. Humanitarian Policy Group, Overseas Development Institute (January). https://www.google.com/url?sa=t&rct=j&q=&esrc=s&source =web&cd=&ved=2ahUKEwj-j5CP2472AhUmWN8KHSi6DdkQFnoECAMQAQ

&url=https%3A%2F%2Fodi.org%2Fdocuments%2F517%2F6511.pdf&usg
=AOvVaw3Cy1Yu5gR_-1MtcJaUvqCF.

Mazurana, Dyan, and Khristopher Carlson, with Sanam Naraghi Anderlini. 2004. *From Combat to Community: Women and Girls of Sierra Leone.* Women Waging Peace and Hunt Alternatives Fund. https://www.peacewomen.org/assets /file/Resources/NGO/PartPPGIssueDisp_CombatToCommunty_WomenWage Peace_2004.pdf.

Mbembe, Achille. 2019. *Necropolitics.* Durham, N.C.: Duke University Press.

McCarthy, Niall. 2013. "Sierra Leone Is the Most Corrupt Nation on Earth." Statista (July 10). https://www.statista.com/chart/1259/sierra-leone-is-the-most-corrupt -nation-on-earth/.

McClancy, Kathleen. 2014. "The Rehabilitation of Rambo: Trauma, Victimization, and the Vietnam Veteran." *Journal of Popular Culture* 47(3): 503–519.

McFerson, Hazel M. (2011). "Women and Post-Conflict Society in Sierra Leone." *Journal of International Women's Studies* 12(4): 127–147.

McIndoe, Ross. 2020. "Bob Marley's 30 Most Memorable Quotes and Lyrics on Would Have Been the Singer's 75th Birthday." *iNews* (February 6). https://inews .co.uk/culture/music/bob-marley-quotes-lyrics-songs-75th-birthday-death -394991.

McKay, Susan, and Dyan Mazurana. 2004. *Where Are the Girls? Girls in Fighting Forces in Northern Uganda, Sierra Leone and Mozambique: Their Lives During and After War.* Montreal: Rights and Democracy, International Centre for Human Rights and Democratic Development.

McKnight, Abigail. 2019. *Understanding the Relationship between Poverty, Inequality and Growth: A Review of Existing Evidence.* CASEpapers (216). Centre for Analysis of Social Exclusion, London School of Economics and Political Science. http:// eprints.lse.ac.uk/103458/.

McLean Hilker, Lyndsay, and Erika Fraser. 2009. *Youth Exclusion, Violence, Conflict and Fragile States.* London: Social Development Direct (report prepared for the Department for International Development). https://gsdrc.org/document-library /youth-exclusion-violence-conflict-and-fragile-states/.

McQuillar, Tayannah Lee, and Fred L. Johnson III. 2010. *Tupac Shakur: The Life and Times of an American Icon.* Philadelphia: Da Capo.

Merriam-Webster. n.d. "Alienation." Accessed July 18, 2019, at https://www.merriam -webster.com/thesaurus/alienation.

——. n.d. "Definition of bitch (Entry 1 of 2)." Accessed October 26, 2018, at https:// www.merriam-webster.com/dictionary/bitch.

——. n.d. "Diss." Accessed October 31, 2018, at https://www.merriam-webster.com /dictionary/diss.

Messerschmidt, James W. 2019. "The Salience of 'Hegemonic Masculinity.'" *Men and Masculinities* 22(1): 85–91.

Miller, Claire Cain, and Jonah Engel Bromwich. 2019. "How Parents Are Robbing Their Children of Adulthood: Today's "Snowplow Parents" Keep Their Children's Futures Obstacle-Free—Even When It Means Crossing Ethical and Legal Boundaries." *New York Times* (March 16). https://www.nytimes.com/2019/03/16/style /snowplow-parenting-scandal.html.

Minter, William, and Elizabeth Schmidt. 2021. "The Failure of Counterterrorism in

Africa Is Revealed." Responsible Statecraft (April 8). https://responsiblestatecraft
.org/2021/04/08/in-africa-an-acknowledgement-that-counterterrorism-has
-failed/.

Mitton, Kieran. 2015. *Rebels in a Rotten State: Understanding Atrocity in the Sierra Leone Civil War*. New York: Oxford University Press.

Moody, Jessica. 2020. "The Sahel's Uphill Battle to Halt the Expansion of Islamist Extremism in 2020—Part I." Africa Portal (January 14). https://www.africaportal.org /features/sahels-uphill-battle-halt-expansion-islamist-extremism-2020/.

Moran, Mary H. 2006. *Liberia: The Violence of Democracy*. Philadelphia: University of Pennsylvania Press.

Morton, Carol Cruzan. 2010. "International Health Aid: Following the Money." *Harvard Medical School News and Research* (May 28). https://hms.harvard.edu/news /international-health-aid-following-money.

Moyer, Eileen. 2005. "Street-Corner Justice in the Name of Jah: Imperatives for Peace among Dar es Salaam Street Youth." *Africa Today* 51(3): 31–58.

M. R. 2014. "The Economist Explains: The Many Names of ISIS (Also Known as IS, ISIL, SIC and Da'ish)." *Economist*, September 28. http://www.economist.com /blogs/economist-explains/2014/09/economist-explains-19.

Muana, Patrick K. 1997. "The Kamajoi Militia: Civil War, Internal Displacement and the Politics of Counter Insurgency." *Africa Development* 22(3/4): 77–100.

Murphy, William P. 2003. "Military Patrimonialism and Child Soldier Clientalism in the Liberian and Sierra Leonean Civil Wars." *African Studies Review* 46(2): 61–87.

Myers, Holly, and Marc Sommers. 1999. *A Charade of Concern: The Abandonment of Colombia's Forcibly Displaced*. New York: Women's Commission for Refugee Women and Children.

Nair, Roshila. 1999. "Fatherhood, Peace and Justice." *Centre for Conflict Resolution* 8(3): 1–3.

Natsios, Andrew. 2010. *The Clash of the Counter-bureaucracy and Development*. Center for Global Development. https://www.cgdev.org/sites/default/files/1424271 _file_Natsios_Counterbureaucracy.pdf.

New Democrat. 2009. "Liberia: TRC's Economic Criminals" (July 6). http://allafrica .com/stories/printable/200907061643.html.

New Humanitarian. 2010. "Sierra Leone: A Ballooning Drug Problem." April 7. https://www.thenewhumanitarian.org/report/88727/sierra-leone-ballooning -drug-problem.

Nikkhah, Roya. 2009. "Emmanuel Jal: 'Music Is My Weapon of Choice.'" *Telegraph* (February 28). https://www.telegraph.co.uk/culture/music/4885017/Emmanuel -Jal-Music-is-my-weapon-of-choice.html.

Ninja, The. 1999. "Foday Sankoh Breaks His Silence." April 22.

Nordås, Ragnhild, and Christian Davenport. 2013. "Fight the Youth: Youth Bulges and State Repression." *American Journal of Political Science* 57(4): 926–940.

Nordstrom, Carolyn. 1997. *A Different Kind of War Story*. Philadelphia: University of Pennsylvania Press.

———. 1998. "Terror Warfare and the Medicine of Peace." *Medical Anthropology Quarterly* 12(1): 103–121.

———. 2004. *Shadows of War: Violence, Power, and International Profiteering in the Twenty-First Century*. Berkeley: University of California Press.

The Numbers. n.d. "Box Office History for Rambo Movies." Accessed March 25, 2020, at https://www.the-numbers.com/movies/franchise/Rambo#tab=summary.

Nunley, John W. 1987. *Moving with the Face of the Devil: Art and Politics in Urban West Africa*. Urbana: University of Illinois Press.

Nuxoll, Cornelia. 2015. "'We Listened to It Because of the Message': Juvenile RUF Combatants and the Role of Music in the Sierra Leone Civil War." *Music and Politics* 9(1): 1–25.

Ochieng, Beverly. 2022. "Burkina Faso Coup: Why Soldiers Have Overthrown President Kaboré." BBC News (January 25). https://www.bbc.com/news/world-africa -60112043.

Olonisakin, 'Funmi. 2004. "Nigeria, ECOMOG, and the Sierra Leone Crisis." In *Between Democracy and Terror: The Sierra Leone Civil War*, Ibrahim Abdullah, ed. Dakar: Council for the Development of Social Science Research in Africa.

———. 2008. *Peacekeeping in Sierra Leone: The Story of UNAMSIL*. Boulder, Colo.: Lynne Rienner.

Onishi, Norimitsu. 2001. "Guinea in Crisis as Area's Refugees Pour In." *New York Times* (February 24). http://www.nytimes.com/2001/02/24/world/guinea-in -crisis-as-area-s-refugees-pour-in.html.

Opala, Joseph A. 1994. "'Ecstatic Renovation!': Street Art Celebrating Sierra Leone's 1992 Revolution." *African Affairs* 93(371): 195–218.

Organisation for Economic Co-operation and Development / Sahel and West Africa Club (OECD/SWAC). 2020. *The Geography of Conflict in North and West Africa*. Paris: OECD Publishing, West African Studies. https://read.oecd-ilibrary.org /development/the-geography-of-conflict-in-north-and-west-africa_02181039-en.

Oyètádé, B. Akíntúndé, and Victor Fashole Luke. 2008. "Sierra Leone: Krio and the Quest for National Integration." In *Language and National Identity in Africa*, Andrew Simpson, ed. Oxford: Oxford University Press.

Packer, George. 2003. "The Children of Freetown." *New Yorker* (January 13). https:// www.newyorker.com/magazine/2003/01/13/the-children-of-freetown.

Paintin, Katie. 2008. "The Lost Generation." *Public Policy Research* (December 2007– February 2008): 229–233.

Patel, Ricken. 2002. *Sierra Leone's Uncivil War and the Unlimited Intervention That Ended It*. Case Study for the Carr Centre for Human Rights Policy, Harvard University.

Patrick, Stewart M. 2013. "Collateral Damage: How Libyan Weapons Fueled Mali's Violence." Blog post (January 29). The Internationalist and International Institutions and Global Governance Program, Council on Foreign Relations. https:// www.cfr.org/blog/collateral-damage-how-libyan-weapons-fueled-malis -violence.

PBS NewsHour. 2002. "Sierra Leone Leaders Declare War Over." January 18. https:// www.pbs.org/newshour/politics/africa-jan-june02-sierra_01-18.

Peeters, Pia, Wendy Cunningham, Gayatri Acharya, and Arvil Van Adams. 2009. *Youth Employment in Sierra Leone: Sustainable Livelihood Opportunities in a Post-Conflict Setting*. Washington, D.C.: World Bank.

Pemunta, Ngambouk Vitalis. 2012. "Neoliberal Peace and the Development Deficit in Post-Conflict Sierra Leone." *International Journal of Development Issues* 11(3): 192–207.

Peters, Krijn. 2005. "Reintegrating Young Ex-Combatants in Sierra Leone: Accommodating Indigenous and Wartime Value Systems." In *Vanguard or Vandals? Youth, Politics and Conflict in Africa*, Jon Abbink and Ineke van Kessel, eds. Leiden, Netherlands: Brill.

———. 2007. "Reintegration Support for Young Ex-Combatants: A Right or a Privilege?" *International Migration* 45(5): 35–59.

———. 2011a. *War and the Crisis of Youth in Sierra Leone*. Cambridge: Cambridge University Press.

———. 2011b. "The Crisis of Youth in Postwar Sierra Leone: Problem Solved?" *Africa Today* 58(2): 128–153.

Peters, Krijn, and Paul Richards. 1998. "'Why We Fight': Voices of Youth Combatants in Sierra Leone." *Africa* 68(2): 183–210.

———. 2011. "Rebellion and Agrarian Tensions in Sierra Leone." *Journal of Agrarian Change* 11(3): 377–395.

Phillips, Dom. 2001. "Death Becomes Him." *Guardian* (April 13). https://www.theguardian.com/books/2001/apr/14/books.guardianreview1.

Physicians for Human Rights (PHR). 2002. *War-Related Sexual Violence in Sierra Leone: A Population-Based Assessment*. Physicians for Human Rights, with the support of the United Nations Assistance Mission in Sierra Leone. https://phr.org/wp-content/uploads/2002/06/sierra-leone-sexual-violence-2002.pdf.

Pomerantz, Dorothy. 2012. "Elizabeth Taylor Tops 2012 List of the Top-Earning Dead Celebrities." *Forbes* (October 24). https://www.forbes.com/sites/dorothypomerantz/2012/10/24/elizabeth-taylor-is-the-new-queen-of-dead-celebrities/#6803e73f1597.

———. 2013. "Michael Jackson Leads Our List of the Top-Earning Dead Celebrities." *Forbes* (October 23). https://www.forbes.com/sites/dorothypomerantz/2013/10/23/michael-jackson-leads-our-list-of-the-top-earning-dead-celebrities/#2e57f13450a1.

———. 2014. "Michael Jackson Tops Forbes' List of Top-Earning Dead Celebrities with $140 Million Haul." *Forbes* (October 15). https://www.forbes.com/sites/dorothypomerantz/2014/10/15/michael-jackson-tops-forbes-list-of-top-earning-dead-celebrities/#7aadb2be7dd3.

Pomerantz, Dorothy, and Zack O'Malley Greenburg, eds. n.d. "Special Feature: The Top-Earning Dead Celebrities: Michael Jackson Once Again Biggest Earner in Afterlife." *Forbes*. Accessed May 19, 2014, at http://www.forbes.com/special-report/2013/dead-celebrities.html.

Pond, Steve. 1988. "'Rambo III' the Cost Célèbre." *Washington Post* (May 6). https://www.washingtonpost.com/archive/lifestyle/1988/05/06/rambo-iii-the-cost-celebre/d5539328-5943-4204-98ed-481f4a167e24/.

Porter, Toby. 2003. *The Interaction between Political and Humanitarian Action in Sierra Leone, 1995 to 2002*. Geneva: Centre for Humanitarian Dialogue.

Prestholdt, Jeremy. 2009. "The Afterlives of 2Pac: Imagery and Alienation in Sierra Leone and Beyond." *Journal of African Cultural Studies* 21(2): 197–218.

———. 2019. *Icons of Dissent: The Global Resonance of Che, Marley, Tupac, and Bin Laden*. New York: Oxford University Press.

Puiu, Tibi. 2017. "What Is THC: The Main Psychoactive Ingredient in Marijuana." ZME Science (July 31). https://www.zmescience.com/science/what-is-thc-433/.

Ralph, Michael, Aisha Beliso–De Jesús, and Stephan Palmié. 2017. "Saint Tupac." *Transforming Anthropology* 25(2): 90–102.

Ramalingam, Ben. 2013. *Aid on the Edge of Chaos: Rethinking International Cooperation in a Complex World*. Oxford: Oxford University Press.

Reed, Tristan, and James A. Robinson. 2013. "The Chiefdoms of Sierra Leone." Harvard University (July 15). https://scholar.harvard.edu/files/jrobinson/files/history.pdf.

Reeves, Marcus. 2008. *Somebody Scream! Rap Music's Rise to Prominence in the Aftershock of Black Power*. New York: Faber & Faber.

Reno, William. 1993. "Foreign Firms and the Financing of Charles Taylor's NPFL." *Liberian Studies Journal* 18(2): 175–188.

——— . 1995. *Corruption and State Politics in Sierra Leone*. Cambridge: Cambridge University Press.

——— . 1998. *Warlord Politics and African States*. Boulder, Colo.: Lynne Rienner.

——— . 2000. "Clandestine Economies, Violence and States in Africa." *Journal of International Affairs* 53(2): 433–459.

——— . 2001. "The Failure of Peacekeeping in Sierra Leone." *Current History* 100 (646): 219–225.

——— . 2003. "Political Networks in a Failing State: The Roots and Future of Violent Conflict in Sierra Leone." *Internationale Politik und Gesellschaft* 2: 44–66. http://www.fes.de/ipg/IPG2_2003/ARTRENO.HTM.

——— . 2004. "The Collapse of Sierra Leone and the Emergence of Multiple States-within-States." In *States-within-States: Incipient Political Entities in the Post–Cold War Era*, Paul Kingston and Ian S. Spear, eds. New York: Palgrave MacMillan.

——— . 2006. "The Political Economy of Order amidst Predation in Sierra Leone." In *States of Violence: Politics, Youth, and Memory in Contemporary Africa*, Edna G. Bay and Donald L. Donham, eds. Charlottesville: University of Virginia Press.

——— . 2011. *Warfare in Independent Africa*. New York: Cambridge University Press.

Reslen, Eileen. 2018. "Dissecting Every Conspiracy Theory That Tupac Is Still Alive: We Break Down the Claims, the Videos, and Photos of the Hip-Hop Legend." *Esquire* (October 4). https://www.esquire.com/entertainment/music/a23595101/tupac-is-still-alive-conspiracy-theories/.

Reuters. 2008. "Factbox: Sierra Leone's Civil War." January 8. https://www.reuters.com/article/us-warcrimes-taylor-war/factbox-sierra-leones-civil-war-idUSL066107120080108.

Revolutionary United Front. n.d. *Footpaths to Democracy: Toward a New Sierra Leone*. Accessed January 24, 2019, at https://fas.org/irp/world/para/docs/footpaths.htm.

Reynolds, Dean. 2010. "Essays: Representations of Youth and Political Consciousness in the Music of Bob Marley." *Review: Literature and Arts of the Americas* 43(2): 237–242.

Reyntjens, Filip, 1993. "The Proof of the Pudding Is in the Eating: The June 1993 Elections in Burundi." *Journal of Modern African Studies* 31(54): 563–583.

Richards, Paul. 1994. "Videos and Violence on the Periphery: Rambo and War in the Forests of the Sierra Leone–Liberia Border." *IDS Bulletin* 25(2): 88–93.

——— . 1995. "Rebellion in Liberia and Sierra Leone: A Crisis of Youth?" In *Conflict in Africa*, Oliver Furley, ed. London: Tauris.

———. 1996. *Fighting for the Rain Forest: War, Youth and Resources in Sierra Leone.* London, International African Institute with James Currey (Oxford) and Heinemann (Portsmouth, N.H.).

———. 1999. "Youth War in Sierra Leone: Pacifying a Monster?" Conference paper, Eleventh International Colloquium on Ethnic Construction and Political Violence, Cortona Centro S. Agostino (July 2–3).

———. 2003. *The Political Economy of Internal Conflict in Sierra Leone.* The Hague: Conflict Research Unit, Netherlands Institute of International Relations Clingendael (Working Paper 21, August). http://www.clingendael.nl/search?query=The %20Political%20Economy%20of%20Internal%20Conflict%20in%20Sierra%20 Leone.

———. 2005a. "Green Book Millenarians? The Sierra Leone War within the Perspective of an Anthropology of Religion." In *Religion and African Civil Wars*, Niels Kastfelt, ed. New York: Palgrave Macmillan.

———. 2005b. "To Fight or to Farm? Agrarian Dimensions of the Mano River Conflicts (Liberia and Sierra Leone)." *African Affairs* 104(417): 571–590.

———. 2006a. "Young Men and Gender in War and Post-War Reconstruction: Some Comparative Findings from Sierra Leone and Liberia." In *The Other Half of Gender: Men's Issues in Development*, Ian Bannon and Maria Correia, eds. Washington, D.C.: World Bank.

———. 2006b. "The Accidental Sect: How War Made Belief in Sierra Leone." *Review of African Political Economy* 33(110): 651–663.

———. 2009. "Dressed to Kill: Clothing as a Technology of the Body in the Civil War in Sierra Leone." *Journal of Material Culture* 14(4): 495–512.

Richards, Paul, Steven Archibald, Khadija Bah, and James Vincent. 2003. *Where Have All the Young People Gone? Transitioning Ex-Combatants towards Community Reconstruction after the War in Sierra Leone.* Unpublished report (final version, November 30).

Richards, Paul, Khadija Bah, and James Vincent. 2004. *Social Capital and Survival: Prospects for Community-Driven Development in Post-Conflict Sierra Leone.* Social Development Paper no. 12. Washington, D.C.: World Bank Group.

Rodney, Walter. 1970. *A History of the Upper Guinea Coast, 1545 to 1800.* London: Oxford University Press.

Rogers, Paul. 2011. "African Rebel Soldiers and Their Eerie Obsession with Tupac Shakur." *LA Weekly* (September 12). https://www.laweekly.com/african-rebel -soldiers-and-their-eerie-obsession-with-tupac-shakur/.

Rosen, David. 2005. *Armies of the Young: Child Soldiers in War and Terrorism.* New Brunswick, N.J.: Rutgers University Press.

Rwegasira, D. G. 2009. *Sierra Leone: Selected Issues and Statistical Appendix.* IMF Country Report No. 09/12 (January). Washington: International Monetary Fund. https://www.imf.org/external/pubs/ft/scr/2009/cr0912.pdf.

Saffa, Victoria. 2015. "Subjects Say Paramount Chief Is a Dictator, Nightmare." *Concord Times* (February 25). http://slconcordtimes.com/subjects-say-paramount -chief-is-a-dictator-nightmare/.

Samii, Cyrus. 2013. "Who Wants to Forgive and Forget? Transitional Justice Preferences in Postwar Burundi." *Journal of Peace Research* 50(2): 219–233.

Sangare, Boukary. 2019. *Fulani People and Jihadism in Sahel and West African Coun-*

tries. Fondation pour la recherche stratégique. Observatoire de Monde Arabo-Musulman et du Sahel (March). https://www.frstrategie.org/en/programs/observatoire-du-monde-arabo-musulman-et-du-sahel/fulani-people-and-jihadism-sahel-and-west-african-countries-2019.

Santacroce, Rita, Elisabetta Bosio, Valentina Scioneri, and Mara Mignone. 2018. "Viewpoint: The New Drugs and the Sea: The Phenomenon of Narco-Terrorism." *International Journal of Drug Policy* 51: 67–68.

Sattler, Erna. 2008. "2nd Session: Cross-Examination of Komba Sumana Continues." International Justice Monitor (October 7). https://www.ijmonitor.org/2008/10/2nd-session-cross-examination-of-komba-sumana-continues/.

Savage, Joel. 2016. "How Joseph Hill's Visit to Sierra Leone Halted the Rebels Activities during the War." *A Mixture of Periodicals* (March 6). https://joelsavage1.wordpress.com/2016/06/03/how-joseph-hills-visit-to-sierra-leone-halted-the-rebels-activities-during-the-war/ (no longer available).

Savishinsky, Neil J. 1994. "Rastafari in the Promised Land: The Spread of a Jamaican Socioreligious Movement among the Youth of West Africa." *African Studies Review* 37(3): 19–50.

Schafer, Jessica. 2004. "The Use of Patriarchal Imagery in the Civil War in Mozambique and Its Implications for the Reintegration of Child Soldiers." In *Children and Youth on the Front Line: Ethnography, Armed Conflict and Displacement,* Jo Boyden and Joanna de Berry, eds. New York: Berghahn.

Scully, Will. 1998. *Once a Pilgrim: The True Story of One Man's Courage under Rebel Fire.* London: Headline.

Sengupta, Somini. 2003. "Mortal Combat Rages, but 'Mortal Kombat' Rules." *New York Times* (June 10). https://www.nytimes.com/2003/06/10/world/bunia-journal-mortal-combat-rages-but-mortal-kombat-rules.html.

Serpick, Evan. 2006. "Iraq Music: Soundtrack to the War." *Rolling Stone* (August 24): 20, 22.

Sesay, Ibrahim Mohamed, Andrew A. Karama, and Jinnah J. Ngobeh. 2006. Republic of Sierra Leone: 2004 Population and Housing Census: Analytical Report on Population Distribution, Migration and Urbanisation in Sierra Leone. United Nations Population Fund (UNFPA), Statistics Sierra Leone, and European Union (EU). https://www.statistics.sl/images/StatisticsSL/Documents/Census/2004/2004_census_report_on_population_distribution_migration_and_urbanisation.pdf.

Shaw, Rosalind. 2002. *Memories of the Slave Trade: Ritual and the Historical Imagination in Sierra Leone.* Chicago: University of Chicago Press.

———. 2007. "Memory Frictions: Localizing the Truth and Reconciliation Commission in Sierra Leone." *International Journal of Transitional Justice* 1(2): 183–207.

Shepler, Susan. 2010a. "Youth Music and Politics in Post-War Sierra Leone." *Journal of Modern African Studies* 48(4): 627–642.

———. 2010b. "Post-war Trajectories for Girls Associated with the Fighting Forces in Sierra Leone." In *Gender, War, and Militarism: Feminist Perspectives,* edited by Laura Sjoberg and Sandra Via. Santa Barbara, Calif.: Praeger.

———. 2010c. "Are 'Child Soldiers' in Sierra Leone a New Phenomenon?" In *The Powerful Presence of the Past: Integration and Conflict along the Upper Guinea Coast,* Jacqueline Knörr and Wilson Trajano Filho, eds. Leiden, Netherlands: Brill.

———. 2010d. "Child Labour and Youth Enterprise: Post-War Urban Infrastructure and the 'Bearing Boys' of Freetown." *Anthropology Today* 26(6): 19–22.

———. 2011. "The Real and Symbolic Importance of Food in War: Hunger Pains and Big Men's Bellies in Sierra Leone." *Africa Today* 58(2): 43–56.

———. 2014. *Childhood Deployed: Remaking Child Soldiers in Sierra Leone*. New York: New York University Press.

Sheridan, Maureen. 1999. *The Stories behind Every Bob Marley Song, 1962–1981*. New York: Thunder's Mountain Press.

Shurkin, Joel N. 2013. "Mind: Geneticists Estimate Publication Date of *The Iliad*." *Scientific American* (February 27). https://www.scientificamerican.com/article /geneticists-estimate-publication-date-of-the-illiad/.

Siddle, D. J. 1968. "War-Towns in Sierra Leone: A Study in Social Change." *Africa* 38(1): 47–56.

Sierra Leone Web. 1999. "Sierra Leone News" (January). http://www.sierra-leone.org /Archives/slnews0199.html.

Simmons, Ann M. 2003. "Taylor Resigns as President of Liberia, Leaves the Country." *Baltimore Sun* (August 12). https://www.baltimoresun.com/news/bs-xpm-2003 -08-12-0308120316-story.html.

Simons, Marlise. 2008. "Gains Cited in Hunt for Liberia Ex-Warlord's Fortune." *New York Times International (*March 9): 4.

Simpson, Graeme. 2018. *The Missing Peace: Independent Progress Study on Youth, Peace and Security*. United Nations Population Fund (UNFPA) and the United Nations Peacebuilding Support Office (PBSO). Complete report version. https:// www.youth4peace.info/system/files/2018-10/youth-web-english.pdf.

Singer, Peter W. 2005. *Children at War*. New York: Pantheon.

Singerman, Diane. 2013. "Youth, Gender, and Dignity in the Egyptian Uprising." *Journal of Middle East Women's Studies* 9(3): 1–27.

Slim, Hugo. 2008. *Killing Civilians: Method, Madness, and Morality in War*. New York: Columbia University Press.

Smet, Stijn. 2009. "A Window of Opportunity—Improving Gender Relations in Post-Conflict Societies: The Sierra Leonean Experience." *Journal of Gender Studies* 18(2): 147–163.

Smillie, Ian. 2009. "Orphan of the Storm: Sierra Leone and 30 Years of Foreign Aid." In *Rescuing a Fragile State: Sierra Leone, 2002–2008*, Lansana Gberie, ed. Waterloo, Ont.: LCMSDS Press of Wilfrid Laurier University.

———. 2010. *Blood on the Stone: Greed, Corruption and War in the Global Diamond Trade*. London and New York: Anthem Press. Co-published with the International Development Research Centre (Ottawa).

Smith, L. Alison, Catherine Gambette, and Thomas Longley. 2004. *No Peace without Justice: Sierra Leone Conflict Mapping Program: Violations of International Humanitarian Law from 1991 to 2002*. Preliminary edition (March 10). Freetown: No Peace without Justice.

Smith, W. Alan. 2005. "Songs of Freedom: The Music of Bob Marley as Transformative Education." Presented at the annual meeting of the Religious Education Association, November 4. www.religiouseducation.net/member/05_rea_papers /wasmith_2005.pdf.

Sommers, Marc. 1997. *The Children's War: Towards Peace in Sierra Leone*. New York: Women's Commission for Refugee Women and Children.

———. 1998. *Reconciliation and Religion: Refugee Churches in Rwandan Camps*. Occasional paper. Uppsala: Life and Peace Institute.

———. 2000. *The Dynamics of Coordination*. Providence: Humanitarianism and War Project, Brown University.

———. 2003a. *War, Urbanization, and Africa's Youth at Risk: Understanding and Addressing Future Challenges*. Washington, D.C.: Basic Education and Policy Support (BEPS) Activity and Creative Associates International.

———. 2003b. "Youth, War, and Urban Africa: Challenges, Misunderstandings, and Opportunities." In *Youth in Developing World Cities*, Blair A. Ruble, Joseph S. Tulchin, Diana H. Varat, and Lisa M. Hanley, eds. Washington, D.C.: Woodrow Wilson International Center for Scholars.

———. 2005. *Islands of Education: Schooling, Civil War, and the Southern Sudanese (1983–2004)*. Paris: International Institute for Educational Planning.

———. 2006. "In the Shadow of Genocide: Rwanda's Youth Challenge." In *Troublemakers or Peacemakers? Youth and Post-Accord Peacebuilding*, Siobhán McEvoy-Levy, ed. South Bend: University of Notre Dame Press.

———. 2011. "Governance, Security and Culture: Assessing Africa's Youth Bulge." *International Journal of Conflict and Violence* 5(2): 292–303.

———. 2012. *Stuck: Rwandan Youth and the Struggle for Adulthood*. Studies in Security and International Affairs Series. Athens: University of Georgia Press, in association with the United States Institute of Peace.

———. 2013. *Adolescents and Violence: Lessons from Burundi*. Discussion Paper #2013.02, Institute of Development Policy and Management, University of Antwerp. https://www.uantwerpen.be/images/uantwerpen/container2143/files/Publications/DP/2013/02-Sommers.pdf.

———. 2015. *The Outcast Majority: War, Development, and Youth in Africa*. Athens: University of Georgia Press.

———. 2017. "The Outcast Majority and Postwar Development: Youth Exclusion and the Pressure for Success." In *The Fabric of Peace in Africa: Looking beyond the State*, Pamela Aall and Chester A. Crocker, eds. Waterloo, Ont.: Centre for International Governance Innovation.

———. 2019a. *Youth and the Field of Countering Violent Extremism*. Washington, D.C.: Promundo-U.S. https://promundoglobal.org/wp-content/uploads/2019/01/Youth_Violent_Extemism.pdf.

———. 2019b. *Trust-Based, Qualitative Field Methods: A Manual for Researchers of Violent Extremism*. Djibouti, Djibouti: Intergovernmental Authority on Development (IGAD) Center of Excellence for Preventing and Countering Violence. https://igad.int/documents/15-trust-based-qualitative-field-methods-a-manual-for-researchers-of-violent-extremism/file.

Sommers, Marc, and Elizabeth McClintock. 2003. "On Hidden Ground: One Coexistence Strategy in Central Africa." In *Imagine Coexistence: Restoring Humanity after Violent Ethnic Conflict*, Antonia Chayes and Martha Minow, eds. San Francisco: Jossey-Bass.

Sommers, Marc, and Stephanie Schwartz. 2011. *Dowry and Division: Youth and State*

Building in South Sudan. United States Institute of Peace Special Report no. 295 (November). https://www.usip.org/publications/2011/11/dowry-and-division -youth-and-state-building-south-sudan.

Special Court for Sierra Leone. 2007. "The Prosecutor against Charles Taylor: Case No. SCSL-03-01-PT: Public: Prosecution's Second Amended Indictment." Freetown (May 29, unpublished).

———. 2009. "Case No. SCSL-2003-01-T: The Prosecutor of the Special Court v. Charles Ghankay Taylor, Tuesday, 22 September 2009, 9:30 a.m., Trial, Trial Chamber II." www.rscsl.org/Documents/Transcripts/Taylor/22September 2009.pdf.

———. 2012. *Prosecutor vs. Charles Ghankay Taylor: Judgement.* Case No. SCSL-03-01-T-1283 (May 18). http://www.rscsl.org/Taylor_Trial_Chamber _Decisions.html.

———. 2015. "Judgement, 18 May 2012." In *The Law Reports of the Special Court for Sierra Leone,* vol. 3: *Prosecutor v. Charles Ghankay Taylor (The Taylor Case),* Charles Chernor Jalloh and Simon M. Meisenberg, eds. (book 2, part 4). Leiden, Netherlands: Brill.

Special Court for Sierra Leone and the Residual Special Court for Sierra Leone. n.d. "The RUF Trial: The Prosecutor vs. Issa Hassan Sesay, Morris Kallon, and Augustine Gbao." Accessed June 6, 2020, at http://www.rscsl.org/RUF.html.

Special Rapporteur on the Promotion and Protection of Human Rights and Fundamental Freedoms while Countering Terrorism. 2020. *Human Rights Impact of Policies and Practices Aimed at Preventing and Countering Violent Extremism: Report of the Special Rapporteur on the Promotion and Protection of Human Rights and Fundamental Freedoms while Countering Terrorism.* Geneva: United Nations Human Rights Council (February) (A/HRC/43/46). https://digitallibrary.un.org /record/3872336.

Stanford, Karin L. 2011. "Keepin' It Real in Hip Hop Politics: A Political Perspective of Tupac Shakur." *Journal of Black Studies* 42(1): 3–22.

Stanley, Henry M. 1890. *In Darkest Africa: or, the Quest, Rescue, and Retreat of Emin, Governor of Equatoria.* 2 vols. New York: Charles Scribner's Sons.

Stasik, Michael. 2012. *DISCOnnections: Popular Music Audiences in Freetown, Sierra Leone.* Leiden: African Studies Centre, Leiden University; Bamenda: Langaa Research and Publishing Common Initiative Group.

———. 2016. "Real Love versus Real Life: Youth, Music and Utopia in Freetown, Sierra Leone." *Africa* 86(2): 215–236.

Statistics Sierra Leone and UNICEF-Sierra Leone. 2011. *Sierra Leone Multiple Indicator Cluster Survey 2010: Final Report* (December).

Steadman, Matthew. 2020. "Crisis in the Sahel: Why Tackling Corruption in Defence and Security Is Essential to Securing Peace." Transparency International Defence and Security (February 19). https://ti-defence.org/sahel-conflict-boko-haram-mali -niger-burkina-faso-defence-corruption/.

Steed, Brian L. 2016. *ISIS: An Introduction and Guide to the Islamic State.* Santa Barbara, Calif.: ABC-CLIO.

Stemple, Lara. 2008. "Male Rape and Human Rights." *Hastings Law Journal* 60(3): 605–646.

Stevens, K-Roy. 1996. "Sierra Leone: The Man in Exile (II)." *West Africa* (October 28–November 3): 1676.

Stokes, Trevor F., and Nino Chkhaidze. 2017. "Terror and Violence Perpetrated by Children and upon Children." In *Terrorism, Political Violence, and Extremism: New Psychology to Understand, Face, and Defuse the Threat*, Chris E. Stout, ed. Santa Barbara, Calif.: Praeger.

Storeng, Katerini T., Seye Abimbola, Dina Balabanova, David McCoy, Valery Ridde, Veronique Filippi, Sidsel Roalkvam, Grace Akello, Melissa Parker, and Jennifer Palmer. 2019. "Action to Protect the Independence and Integrity of Global Health Research." *BMJ Global Health* 4(3): 1–5.

Strategic Comments. 2019. "Burkina Faso and Jihadism in West Africa." *Strategic Comments* 26(6) (August 19).

Sweeney, Frank. 1999. "'What Mean Expendable?': Myth, Ideology, and Meaning in First Blood and Rambo." *Journal of American Culture* 22(3): 63–69.

Taylor, William A. 2019. "Violent Extremism and Terrorism." In *Contemporary Security Issues in Africa*. Santa Barbara, Calif.: Praeger.

Thompstone, Guy. 2010. *Mapping and Analysis of the Child Protection System in Sierra Leone*. Final Report (April). Hong Kong: Child Frontiers, Ltd. https://resource centre.savethechildren.net/node/5096/pdf/5096.pdf.

Toop, David. 2000. *Rap Attack 3: African Rap to Global Hip Hop*. 3rd ed. London: Serpent's Tail.

Toynbee, Jason. 2007. *Bob Marley: Herald of a Postcolonial World?* Cambridge: Polity Press.

Transparency International. 2013. *Global Corruption Barometer 2013*. https://www .transparency.org/en/publications/global-corruption-barometer-2013.

Traub, James. 2000. "The Worst Place on Earth." *New York Review of Books* (June 29).

Truth and Reconciliation Commission (TRC). 2004a. *Witness to Truth: Report of the Sierra Leone Truth and Reconciliation Commission: Volume 3A*. Freetown: Sierra Leone Truth and Reconciliation Commission.

———. 2004b. *Witness to Truth: Report of the Sierra Leone Truth and Reconciliation Commission: Volume 3B*. Freetown: Sierra Leone Truth and Reconciliation Commission.

———. 2004c. *Witness to Truth: Report of the Sierra Leone Truth and Reconciliation Commission: Volume 2*. Freetown: Sierra Leone Truth and Reconciliation Commission.

———. 2004d. "Appendix 1: Statistical Appendix to the Report of the Truth and Reconciliation Commission of Sierra Leone." A Report by the Benetech Human Rights Data Analysis Group to the Truth and Reconciliation Commission by Richard Conibere, Jana Asher, Kristen Cibelli, Jana Dudukovich, Rafe Kaplan, and Patrick Ball (October 5). Part of *Witness to Truth: Report of the Sierra Leone Truth and Reconciliation Commission*. Freetown: Sierra Leone Truth and Reconciliation Commission.

———. 2004e. "Appendix 5: Amputations in the Sierra Leone Conflict." Part 1: Amputations in the Sierra Leone Conflict, written by Artemis Christodulou. Part of *Witness to Truth: Report of the Sierra Leone Truth and Reconciliation Commission*. Freetown: Sierra Leone Truth and Reconciliation Commission.

Tucker, Boima. 2013. *Musical Violence: Gangsta Rap and Politics in Sierra Leone*.

Current African Issues 52. Uppsala: Nordiska Afrikainstitutet. http://nai.diva
-portal.org/smash/get/diva2:618529/FULLTEXT01.pdf.

Turse, Nick. 2020. "U.S.-Funded Counterterrorism Efforts in West Africa Aren't
Helping." Vice World News (December 3). https://www.vice.com/en/article
/k7a7be/us-funded-counterterrorism-efforts-in-west-africa-arent-helping.

UNAIDS. 2013. *Population Size Estimation of Key Populations: August 2013.* UNAIDS,
in collaboration with the Government of Sierra Leone. http://www.nas.gov.sl
/images/stories/publications/Population%20Size%20Estimation%20Study%20
Report%20August%202013.pdf.

Ünal, Mustafa Coşar. 2016. "Terrorism versus Insurgency: A Conceptual Analysis."
Crime, Law and Social Change 66(1): 21–57.

UNICEF. n.d. "Convention on the Rights of the Child Text." Accessed March 26,
2020, at https://www.unicef.org/child-rights-convention/convention-text.

UNICEF Press Centre. 2007. "News Note: Sierra Leone Approves the National Child
Rights Bill." UNICEF (June 7). https://www.unicef.org/media/media_39951.html.

United Nations. 2005. Letter dated 11 March 2005 from the Secretary-General addressed to the President of the Security Council. United Nations Security
Council, S/2005/158 (March 11). https://www.un.org/ruleoflaw/files/Burundi
20S2005158.pdf.

———. 2015a. *The Millennium Development Goals Report 2015.* New York: United
Nations. https://www.un.org/millenniumgoals/2015_MDG_Report/pdf/MDG%20
2015%20rev%20(July%201).pdf.

———. 2015b. "Security Council, Unanimously Adopting Resolution 2250 (2015),
Urges Member States to Increase Representation of Youth in Decision-Making at
All Levels." United Nations Meetings Coverage and Press Releases (December 9).
https://www.un.org/press/en/2015/sc12149.doc.htm.

United Nations Development Programme (UNDP). 1991. *Human Development Report 1991.* New York: Oxford University Press (Published for the United Nations
Development Programme).

———. 2000. *Human Development Report 2000: Human Rights and Human Development.* New York: Oxford University Press (Published for the United Nations
Development Programme).

———. 2013. *Human Development Report 2013: The Rise of the South: Human Progress in a Diverse World.* New York: UNDP. http://hdr.undp.org/en/media/HDR
_2013_EN_complete.pdf.

———. 2017. *Journey to Extremism in Africa: Drivers, Incentives and the Tipping
Point for Recruitment.* New York: UNDP. https://journey-to-extremism.undp.org/.

———. 2018a. "Human Development Index (HDI)." In *United Nations Development Programme Human Development Reports: 2018 Statistical Update (English).*
http://hdr.undp.org/en/content/human-development-index-hdi.

———. 2018b. "Latest Human Development Index (HDI) Ranking." In *United Nations Development Programme Human Development Reports: 2018 Statistical Update (English).* http://hdr.undp.org/en/2018-update.

———. 2019. *Human Development Report 2019: Beyond Income, Beyond Averages,
Beyond Today: Inequalities in Human Development in the 21st Century.* New
York: United Nations Development Programme. http://hdr.undp.org/en/2019
-report/download.

United Nations Department of Economic and Social Affairs. 2020. *World Youth Report: Youth Social Entrepreneurship and the 2030 Agenda*. New York: United Nations. https://www.un.org/development/desa/youth/world-youth-report/wyr2020.html.

———. n.d. "Definition of Youth." Accessed March 12, 2022, at https://www.un.org/esa/socdev/documents/youth/fact-sheets/youth-definition.pdf.

United Nations Economic and Social Council. 2019. *Special Edition: Progress Towards the Sustainable Development Goals: Report of the Secretary-General* (May 8). https://undocs.org/E/2019/68.

United Nations Panel of Experts. 2000. Report of the Panel of Experts Appointed Pursuant to UN Security Council Resolution 1306 (2000), Paragraph 19 in Relation to Sierra Leone. United Nations Security Council (December). https://mondediplo.com/IMG/pdf/un-report.pdf.

United Nations Population Fund (UNFPA). 2002. *Situation démographique et sociale Burundi. Résultats de l'enquête sociodémographique et de santé de la reproduction*. Burundi: Département de la Population du Burundi.

UN News. 2020. "'Unprecedented Terrorist Violence' in West Africa, Sahel Region." January 8. https://news.un.org/en/story/2020/01/1054981.

UN Special Rapporteur on the Promotion and Protection of Human Rights and Fundamental Freedoms while Countering Terrorism. 2020. *Human Rights Impact of Policies and Practices Aimed at Preventing and Countering Violent Extremism: Report of the Special Rapporteur on the Promotion and Protection of Human Rights and Fundamental Freedoms while Countering Terrorism*. Human Rights Council, UN General Assembly, A/HRC/43/46 (February 21). https://daccess-ods.un.org/TMP/230936.240404844.html.

Urdal, Henrik, and Kristian Hoelscher. 2009. *Urban Youth Bulges and Social Disorder: An Empirical Study of Asian and Sub-Saharan African Cities*. Policy Research Working Paper No. 5110. Washington, D.C.: World Bank.

USAID. 2012. *USAID Youth in Development Policy: Realizing the Demographic Opportunity* (October.) https://www.usaid.gov/sites/default/files/documents/1870/Youth_in_Development_Policy_0.pdf.

Utas, Mats. 2005. "Agency of Victims: Young Women in the Liberian Civil War." In *Makers and Breakers: Children and Youth in Postcolonial Africa*, Alcinda Honwana and Filip de Boeck, eds. Trenton, N.J.: Africa World Press.

———. 2012a. *Urban Youth and Post-Conflict Africa: On Policy Priorities*. Policy Notes 2012/4. Uppsala: Nordiska Afrikainstitutet. https://www.files.ethz.ch/isn/153939/FULLTEXT02-4.pdf.

———. 2012b. "Introduction: Bigmanity and Network Governance in African Conflicts." In *African Conflicts and Informal Power: Big Men and Networks*, Mats Utas, ed. London: Zed Books. Published in association with the Nordic Africa Institute, Uppsala.

Utas, Mats, and Magnus Jörgel. 2008. "The West Side Boys: Military Navigation in the Sierra Leone Civil War." *Journal of Modern African Studies* 46(3): 487–511.

Uvin, Peter. 1998. *Aiding Violence: The Development Enterprise in Rwanda*. West Hartford, Conn.: Kumarian.

Vincent, James B. M. 2012. *A Village-Up View of Sierra Leone's Civil War and Re-*

construction: Multilayered and Networked Governance. IDS Research Report 75. Brighton, U.K.: Institute of Development Studies. https://opendocs.ids.ac.uk /opendocs/bitstream/handle/20.500.12413/4269/IDS%20Research%20report %2075.pdf?sequence=1&isAllowed=y.

Vocabulary.com. n.d. "Alienation." Accessed July 18, 2019, at https://www.vocabulary .com/dictionary/alienation.

———. n.d. "Subaltern." Accessed January 10, 2019, at https://www.vocabulary.com /dictionary/subaltern.

Voeten, Teun. 2002. *How De Body? One Man's Terrifying Journey through an African War.* Originally published 2000; translated from Dutch by Roz Vatter-Buck. New York: St. Martin's Press.

Voice of America News (VOA). 2009. "Former Sierra Leone Court Prosecutor Reflects on Guilty Verdicts" (November 2). https://www.voanews.com/a/a-13-2009-02-25 -voa42-68768642/410776.html.

Weber, Hannes. 2019. "Age Structure and Political Violence: A Re-Assessment of the 'Youth Bulge' Hypothesis." *International Interactions* 45(1): 80–112.

Wehrfritz, George. 1999. "The Tupac Uprising: Outlaws with a Cause." *Newsweek* (August 15). https://www.newsweek.com/tupac-uprising-outlaws-cause-165624.

Weinraub, Bernard. 1993. "On the Set with: Sylvester Stallone; All Right Already, No More Mr. Funny Guy." *New York Times* (June 9). http://www.nytimes.com/1993 /06/09/garden/on-the-set-with-sylvester-stallone-all-right-already-no-more-mr -funny-guy.html.

Weiss, Brad. 2009. *Street Dreams and Hip Hop Barbershops: Global Fantasy in Urban Tanzania.* Bloomington: Indiana University Press.

Wessells, Michael. 2006. *Child Soldiers: From Violence to Protection.* Cambridge, Mass.: Harvard University Press.

Whiteman, Kaye. 2014. "Ahmad Tejan Kabbah Obituary." *Guardian* (April 3). https:// www.theguardian.com/world/2014/apr/03/ahmad-tejan-kabbah.

Wille, Christina. 2005. "Children Associated with Fighting Forces (CAFF) and Small Arms in the Mano River Union (MRU)." In *Armed and Aimless: Armed Groups, Guns, and Human Security in the ECOWAS Region,* Nicolas Florquin and Eric G. Berman, eds. Geneva: Small Arms Survey.

Williams, Stereo. 2016. "Controversial: Tupac's 'Hit 'Em Up': The Most Savage Diss Track Ever Turns 20." *Daily Beast* (June 4). https://www.thedailybeast.com /tupacs-hit-em-up-the-most-savage-diss-track-ever-turns-20.

Witte, Eric. 2008. "Witness Describes Amputations, Burnings as Rebel Force Withdrew from Freetown." Trial/Charles Taylor, *International Justice Monitor* (April 23). https://www.ijmonitor.org/2008/04/1200-witness-describes-amputations -burnings-as-rebel-force-withdrew-from-freetown/.

Wlodarczyk, Nathalie. 2009. *Magic and Warfare: Appearance and Reality in Contemporary African Conflict and Beyond.* New York: Palgrave Macmillan.

Wood, Elisabeth Jean. 2009. "Armed Groups and Sexual Violence: When Is Wartime Rape Rare?" *Politics and Society* 37(1): 131–162.

Yoder, John Howard. 1995. "How Many Ways Are There to Think Morally about War?" *Journal of Law and Religion* 11(1): 83–107.

Zack-Williams, Tunde. 2012. "Multilateral Intervention in Sierra Leone's Civil War:

Some Structural Explanations." In *When the State Fails: Studies on Intervention in the Sierra Leone Civil War*, Tunde Zack-Williams, ed. London: Pluto, in cooperation with Nordic Africa Institute.

Zur, Ofer. 1987. "The Psychohistory of Warfare: The Co-Evolution of Culture, Psyche and Enemy." *Journal of Peace Research* 24(2): 125–134.

Zureick, Alyson. 2008. "Implementing the Gender Acts in Sierra Leone." Skoll Foundation Archives (January 29). https://archive.skoll.org/2008/01/29/implementing -the-gender-acts-in-sierra-leone/.

Discography

50 Cent. 2003. "Intro (Get Rich or Die Tryin')." By 50 Cent, Eminem, and Dr. Dre. Released on February 6. Track 1 on *Get Rich or Die Tryin'*. CD.

Hill, Joseph, and Culture. 1992. "Freedom Time." Track 5 on *Wings of a Dove*. CD.

——. 1999. "War in Sierra Leone." By Joseph Hill. Track 9 on *Payday*. CD.

Marley, Bob, and the Wailers. 1973. "Burnin' and Lootin." By Bob Marley. Released on April 1. Track 4 on *Burnin'*. CD.

——. 1973. "Get Up, Stand Up." By Bob Marley and Peter Tosh. Released on April 1. Track 1 on *Burnin'*. CD.

——. 1974a. "No Woman, No Cry." By Vincent Ford and Bob Marley. Released on October 25. Track 2 on *Natty Dread*. CD.

——. 1974b. "Them Belly Full (But We Hungry)." By Carlton Barrett and Leon Cogil. Released on October 25. Track 3 on *Natty Dread*. CD.

——. 1976a. "War." By Carlton "Carlie" Barrett and Allen "Skill" Cole. Released on April 30. Track 9 on *Rastaman Vibration*. CD.

——. 1976b. "Crazy Baldhead." By Rita Marley and Vincent Ford. Released on April 30. Track 6 on *Rastaman Vibration*. CD.

——. 1976c. "Who the Cap Fit." By Bob Marley. Released on April 30. Track 7 on *Rastaman Vibration*. CD.

——. 1977a. "Exodus." By Bob Marley. Released on June 3. Track 5 on *Exodus*. CD.

——. 1977b. "Natural Mystic." By Bob Marley. Released on June 3. Track 1 on *Exodus*. CD.

——. 1977c. "One Love/People Get Ready (Medley)." By Bob Marley and Curtis Mayfield. Released on June 3. Track 10 on *Exodus*. CD.

——. 1979. "So Much Trouble in the World." By Bob Marley. Released on October 2. Track 1 on *Survival*. CD.

——. 1980. "Could You Be Loved." By Bob Marley. Released on June 10. Track 8 on *Uprising*. CD.

——. 1983. "Rastaman Live Up!" By Bob Marley. Released on May 23. Track 10 on *Confrontation*. Tuff Gong amd Island Records. CD.

Marley, Ziggy, and the Melody Makers. 1997. "Diamond City." By David Ziggy Marley. Released on July 15. Track 12 on *Fallen Is Babylon*. CD.

Shakur, Tupac. 1991. 2*Pacalypse Now*. Released on November 12.

——. 1993. "Keep Ya Head Up." By Tupac Shakur, Daryl Anderson, Stan Vincent, and Roger Troutman. Released on October 28. Track 11 on *Strictly 4 My N.I.G.G.A.Z . . . .* CD.

——. 1994. "Cradle to the Grave." By Tupac Shakur, Mopreme Shakur, Macadoshis,

Big Syke, Rated R, and Pro-Jay. Released on September 26. Track 9 on *Thug Life: Volume 1*. CD.

————. 1995a. "Death around the Corner." By Tupac Shakur and Johnny J. Released on March 14. Track 14 on *Me Against the World*. CD.

————. 1995b. "Me against the World." By Tupac Shakur, Minnie Riperton, Richard Rudolph, Leon Ware, Burt Bacharach, and Hal David. Released on March 14. Track 3 on *Me against the World*. CD.

————. 1996a. "All Eyez on Me." By Johnny Jackson, J. P. Pennington, and Tupac Shakur. Released on February 13. Track 24 on *All Eyez on Me*. CD.

————. 1996b. "California Love (Remix)." By Tupac Shakur, Dr. Dre, Roger Troutman, Larry Troutman, Woody Cunningham, and Norman Durham. Released on February 13. Track 12 on *All Eyez on Me*. CD.

————. 1996c. "Only God Can Judge Me." By Doug Rasheed and Tupac Shakur. Released on February 13. Track 10 on *All Eyez on Me*. CD.

————. 1996d. "Hit 'Em Up." By Tupac Shakur and Outlawz. Released on June 4. CD.

————. 1996e. "Me and My Girlfriend." By Tupac Shakur, Darryl Harper, Ricky Rouse, and Hurt-M-Badd. Released on November 5. Track 10 on *The Don Killuminati: The 7 Day Theory*. CD.

————. 1998. "Troublesome '96." By Tupac Shakur. Released on November 24. Track 13 on *Greatest Hits*. CD.

————. 2001. "Breathin'." By Tupac Shakur, Johnny "J," E.D.I. Mean, Napoleon (Outlawz), Young Noble, and Kastro. Released on March 27. Track 7 on *Until the End of Time*. CD.

Filmography

Blood Diamond. 2006. Directed by Edward Zwick.

Braddock: Missing in Action III. 1988. Directed by Aaron Morris.

Commando. 1985. Directed by Mark L. Lester.

First Blood. 1982. Directed by Ted Kotcheff.

Get Rich or Die Tryin'. 2005. Directed by Jim Sheridan.

Missing in Action. 1984. Directed by Joseph Zito.

Missing in Action 2: The Beginning. 1985. Directed by Lance Hool.

Rambo: First Blood Part II. 1985. Directed by George P. Cosmatos.

Rambo III. 1988. Directed by Peter MacDonald.

Rambo. 2008. Directed by Sylvester Stallone.

Rambo: Last Blood. 2019. Directed by Adrian Grunberg.

INDEX

Page references to images are in italics.